BEHIND

THE SHORT STORY

From First to Final Draft

EDITED BY

RYAN G. VAN CLEAVE
Clemson University

TODD JAMES PIERCE
California Polytechnic State University

PEARSON
Longman

New York • San Francisco • Boston
London • Toronto • Sydney • Tokyo • Singapore • Madrid
Mexico City • Munich • Paris • Cape Town • Hong Kong • Montreal

Managing Editor: Erika Berg
Development Editor: Barbara Santoro
Executive Marketing Manager: Ann Stypuloski
Production Manager: Eric Jorgensen
Project Coordination, Text Design, and Electronic Page Makeup: Electronic Publishing
   Services Inc., NYC
Cover Designer/Manager: Wendy Ann Fredericks
Cover Art: Steve Satushek/Iconica/Getty Images, Inc.
Manufacturing Buyer: Lucy Hebard
Printer and Binder: Courier Corporation
Cover Printer: Courier Corporation

For permission to use copyrighted material, grateful acknowledgment is made to the
copyright holders on pages 401–402, which are hereby made part of this copyright page.

Library of Congress Cataloging-in-Publication Data
Behind the short story : from first to final draft / edited by Ryan G. Van Cleave, Todd James
Pierce.
    p. cm.
   Includes bibliographical references and index.
   ISBN 0-321-11724-7 (pbk.)
  1. College readers.   2. Short stories, American.   3. English language—Rhetoric.   4.
Fiction—Authorship.   5. Creative writing.   I. Van Cleave, Ryan G., 1972–   II. Pierce,
Todd James, 1965–
PE147.B3955 2006
808.3′1—dc22   2005027626

Please visit our website at www.ablongman.com

ISBN: 0-321-11724-7

12345678910—CRS—08 07 06 05

CONTENTS

PART THREE

On Revising   297

PREFACE TO THE INSTRUCTOR

A work of art is informed by a vision, but it's also a matter of structure: chapters, paragraphs, sentences. On that level the work succeeds or fails.
—Joyce Carol Oates

The challenges student writers face when deciding to write a short story are legion. Among them are focusing on the rewards of writing versus the writing process itself, not having a range of professional examples handy to serve as models, worrying that revision will actually make what they've already written worse, not knowing how to start when faced with a blank page. Perhaps John Gardner says it best in *The Art of Fiction*: "About all that is required is that the would-be writer understand clearly what it is that he wants to become and what he must do to become it." That, in essence, is the mission of this book. It offers twenty-seven different blueprints to become a successful writer, and no single one is better than another.

Behind the Short Story provides a solid foundation for writing successful short stories. Unlike traditional creative writing texts, this book offers students the opportunity to be mentored by twenty-seven successful short story writers and fiction instructors, each of whom discusses skills that lead to a deeper understanding of fiction's craft.

This book is much more than a compilation of exercises or essays; it allows students to work at their own pace through in-depth, teacher-assisted instruction or independent, self-initiated study and shift their focus from product to process. With the help of the materials in this book, an aspiring writer should be able to:

- Imagine and research potential story ideas
- Organize and structure prospective story material
- Handle the elements of a scene
- Use point of view effectively
- Develop organically three-dimensional characters
- Understand the role of description, imagery, and theme
- Recognize and apply strategies for revision
- Develop an idea through multiple drafts to a finished, polished story

What Was Asked of the Contributors

The contributors featured in this book were chosen not just because they are accomplished, award-winning writers of short fiction, but also because they are experienced *teachers* who have developed their own ways of explaining the sometimes mysterious process of fiction writing. It seemed particularly appropriate to ask these writers to begin a conversation with students about all of those issues that help make some writers successful and others less so. After all, the difference between a good writer and a great one often is an issue of understanding craft.

Most contributors focus primarily on a single topic, such as the role of first person narrators. They were also asked to speak from their own experiences and beliefs as makers of art and to discuss their own artistic values while answering such common student questions as:

- What is the value of prewriting?
- How do I develop believable characters?
- Where do compelling story ideas come from?
- How do I use plot to create a story readers will enjoy?
- What is the best point-of-view for my story?
- How do I craft realistic dialogue?
- How do I develop my own voice?
- How do I revise my story?

In effect, *Behind the Short Story: From First to Final Draft* invites readers behind the curtain, revealing the skills and techniques behind contemporary short fiction. This text shows that there aren't secrets so much as there are choices—some easy, some difficult—and a great deal of thought and passion that goes into the writing process. Taken together, the experiences of these twenty-seven writers show that a commitment to fiction and in particular the process of revision will get students past the early stages of story writing and into the habit of creating successful, effective stories.

Organization of the Text

This book is patterned after the habits and routines of professional writers who regularly write and publish short fiction. Though it seems upon first glance that each writer uses a varied and individualized writing process, all of the contributors do, in fact, share similar patterns that provide the rationale and flow of this text.

Part One: On Prewriting contains strategies for generating and organizing raw material. **Part Two: On Writing** focuses on the essential skills necessary for writing a first draft. **Part Three: On Revising** reinforces the multi-draft process by introducing revision and line editing.

Because insights can be gained by studying these stories in relation to their stylistic concerns and elements as well, **Appendix C** provides suggestions on how stories can be grouped according to the elements of fiction, such as characterization, point of view, and writing style. **Appendix A** chronicles each writer's own individual path to success, while **Appendix D** offers a glossary of key fiction terminology. **Appendix B** collects resources for fiction-writing in general as well as opportunities to become a more active member of the literary community.

Distinctive Features of the Text

- **Student-Oriented Stories.** Well-known and respected contemporary American short story writers choose one of their own stories and discuss what makes it effective. Because these writers have significant experience teaching short fiction, their selections were chosen with an eye towards providing a variety of stories as models. In short, these are highly "teachable" stories from which readers can learn, both inside and outside of classrooms and between formal programs of study.

- **Behind-the-Scenes Craft Advice.** Each writer offers the "behind-the-scenes scoop" on serious fiction issues such as voice, style, structure, revision, audience, and other topics. In addition, each writer offers advice to aspiring short story writers on how to develop and improve upon their craft in a clear, process-oriented style. This pragmatic approach engages students in the aesthetic views, personal ideas, and rarely shared practical advice from experts of the contemporary American short story.

- **Storytelling Exercises.** Following each commentary is a sequence of writing prompts (one technique exercise, one story-generative exercise, one revision exercise, and one field exercise). These prompts encourage students to reflect upon the advice offered in the commentary and then employ this advice directly into their own writing. The last exercise in each group of four exercises contains a research question that asks students to "go into the field," to examine the life of the writer in the wider culture, to experience advances in technology. This exercise calls into question the nature of fiction, and furthers their "conversation" with the twenty-seven contributors by seeking out more of their work.

- **Quotations.** Each section of the text includes inspiring quotations by a host of published writers beyond the twenty-seven contributors. These quotations amplify, further explain, and enrich the discussion of fiction writing begun in each commentary.

- **Extensive Appendices.** The text offers four appendices to help students further develop and strengthen their appreciation for and writing of fiction. Appendices include biographies on the writers featured in the text, suggestions for further reading, and an alternate table of contents grouped by the elements of fiction. The text also includes a glossary of definitions and examples of key terms mentioned or discussed throughout the commentaries.

Acknowledgments

The authors wish to thank their editor, Erika Berg, for her encouragement and patience during the writing of this book, as well as for her invaluable guidance and shaping of the final product. They are also indebted to many other people at Longman who helped make this project come together: Lauren Puccio, Barbara Santoro, Ruth Curry, Michele Cronin, Eric Jorgensen, and Christopher Myers.

A special thanks to the late Jerome Stern, whose teaching inspired many of the approaches and lessons in this book.

The authors are especially thankful to the many instructors and teachers of creative writing who tested out parts of this book in their classrooms and contributed valuable feedback. Also, a special thanks to the many instructors who have reviewed this book during its various stages of development and offered many helpful comments:

Craig Albin, *Southwest Missouri State University*
Ed Allen, *University of South Dakota*
Mary Baron, *University of North Florida*
Cathleen Calbert, *Rhode Island College*
Steve Cooper, *California State University, Long Beach*
Annie Dawid, *Lewis & Clark College*
Marcia Douglas, *University of Colorado, Boulder*
David Galef, *University of Mississippi*
Deborah Hall, *Florida State University*
Cheri Johnson, *University of Minnesota*
Persis Karim, *San Jose State University*
Brian Leung, *California State University, Northridge*
Wendell Mayo, *Bowling Green State University*
Sandee McGlaun, *North Georgia College and State University*
Alyce Miller, *University of Indiana, Bloomington*
Alyssa O'Brien, *Stanford University*
Michael Piafsky, *University of Missouri*
Elaine Anderson Phillips, *Tennessee State University, Nashville*
Micheal Raymond, *Stetson University*
Carl M. Schaffer, *University of Scranton*
Dennis Sjolie, *University of South Dakota*
Maya Sonenberg, *University of Washington*
Bill Stevenson, *Saddleback College*
Susan Swartwout, *Southeast Missouri State University*
John Tait, *University of North Texas*
Lou Ann Thompson, *Texas Women's University*
Mark Wallace, *George Washington University*
Lynna Williams, *Emory University*

Finally, and most importantly, they thank the many students who diligently worked through the exercises, writing activities, and research projects, and offered valuable suggestions at critical times in this endeavor. Without them this book would have been impossible.

The editors welcome suggestions, ideas, concerns, or comments via their web site, http://www.behindtheshortstory.com, which contains many resources and information beyond what is included in this text (including sample syllabi, writing prompts, and multiple drafts of student stories that change in response to critical feedback).

RYAN G. VAN CLEAVE
TODD JAMES PIERCE

Introduction to the Student

In the golden age of American magazines (1920s to 1940s), short stories evolved from tales of regional life and domestic intrigue into popular entertainment. It may come as a surprise to contemporary readers that American authors, such as F. Scott Fitzgerald, Jack London, and Eudora Welty, earned the majority of their income from the publication of short stories in magazines rather than from the publication of novels. The American reading public of the 1930s would've known Fitzgerald for his contributions to *The Saturday Evening Post* and *Look*, not for *The Great Gatsby*. Under the watchful gaze of such readers, the short story evolved into the form in which we best recognize it today—a short tale capable of being read in one sitting but, because of its honest exploration of the human spirit, imparts to the reader an experience that lasts a lifetime.

The twenty-seven contributors in this textbook include recent links in the great chain of American short story writers, a chain that began with Washington Irving and Edgar Allen Poe and continued through Mark Twain, Herman Melville, O. Henry, Ernest Hemingway, Shirley Jackson and Flannery O'Connor. There is no one way to write a short story—as you will soon discover through this book's commentaries and accompanying exercises. One contributor, Janice Eidus, approaches the coming-of-age tale through the transformation of a girlhood memory into fiction, while another contributor, Adam Johnson, creates imaginary characters to express his feelings of loss for a beloved real-life mentor. Though both authors present main characters forced to mature, their stories are nothing alike. They are as different as Poe's atmospheric tales of terror are from the terse, deceptively straightforward stories of Hemingway.

As a beginning writer of short stories, you will be asked to develop compelling characters and create meaningful plots. To help you better understand the craft and process of fiction writing, this book offers a rare multi-vocal approach, in which twenty-seven accomplished writers explain the craft of fiction, each from his own perspective, and describe, step by step, their particular process of writing a short story, from first to final draft.

Consider this book your invitation to join a community of practicing short story writers. The contributors in this book speak not only for themselves, but for the chorus of literary voices that influenced them. They speak for the heritage of Poe and Fitzgerald and for their own contribution to the form as it passes from their hands and into the hands of writers who will carry the tradition for the next generation.

Ryan G. Van Cleave
Todd James Pierce

PART
One

———∾———

On Prewriting

We do not write in order to be understood; we write
in order to understand.
—C. Day Lewis

Introduction

Whether you're a first-time writer of fiction or an old pro, the challenge is the same: the blank page before you. Established writers have been down this road before, but still, the task of facing an empty page or computer screen can be daunting. How does one produce compelling characters and scenes that will eventually blend into a finished story? How does one begin to separate those ideas fruitful for short stories from those that are less so? How does one translate the desire to be a writer into the act of writing?

In this section, **On Prewriting**, we discuss three approaches to generating material for stories: **Creating Raw Material, Discovering Stories Through Personal Experience,** and **Discovering Stories Through Observation and Research.** These three sections offer a number of different styles and ways to get your fiction under way. They will also show ways to develop ideas and explore them in writing before you begin the first full draft. The material in the subsequent sections will explain in much greater detail the process of writing full drafts and revising these stories.

Having written one or even twenty-one previous stories doesn't mean that you'll find the act of writing fiction easy. In fact, many otherwise talented writers give up under the stress of creating something out of nothing—a state of mind called writer's block.

The good news is that there are lots of ways to get started. Peter Meinke writes about the advantages of journaling, jotting down the bits and pieces of life that might otherwise pass you by. Steve Almond's commentary on "The Soul Molecule" shows how you can find ideas anywhere in your life, while Janice Eidus explains in detail how to transform actual life experiences into characters and scenes that will be successful in fiction. If you think that your own life is too boring to serve as the raw material for good short stories, then Julianna Baggott's commentary on how research plays a role in her story, "Dr. Ishida's Case," might be for you. Finally, Elizabeth Graver pulls back the curtain on the often-mysterious process of where stories come from.

Each commentary is followed by four writing suggestions: The first suggestion asks you to explore one fiction technique discussed in the preceeding commentary; the second provides an assignment designed to generate a full scene or an entire short story; the third asks you to work with revision; and the fourth invites you into the world of fiction and short stories outside the classroom. The writing suggestions in **On Prewriting** are intended to help you as you begin to work with fiction.

Taken together these stories, commentaries, and writing suggestions will better equip you to explore material that will lead to your own short stories. And for a new writer of fiction, this is where it all begins.

Getting Started: Essay and Writing Suggestions

Because getting those initial words on the page can be the most difficult challenge for many writers, we offer the following prompts to get you thinking and writing about ideas, situations, characters, and themes that might well lead to productive stories. Give each a good faith effort and see which type(s) of writing assignments appeal to you, then ask yourself why those speak more to you than do others. What does that say about you as a writer? Are these the same sort of issues that interest you as a reader? Do the prompts that appeal to you work toward your strengths?

The Memory Freewrite

Bring up a blank page on your word processor, and then turn the monitor screen off. Without paying attention to spelling, grammar, or punctuation, type, "I remember," and let your mind go. If you ever catch yourself stalling, start again with "I remember" and keep typing it until something comes to you. Give yourself a full ten minutes, and then turn on the monitor and reread your work, identifying the three strongest phrases. How was the experience of writing these three phrases different than that of writing other sentences?

Personal Details

Write a list of twenty details about an eccentric, charismatic, or interesting person you've met. Describe appearance, gestures, and attitudes. After you've finished your list, decide which three details best capture the personality behind the description. In your opinion, why do those details suggest this particular person's character? How many of these descriptions are concrete, offering specific images and sounds, as opposed to abstractions, which offer impressions and opinions without supporting details?

Showing, Not Telling

Find a snapshot in your family photo album—a photo to which you have a strong emotional connection. In two or three full paragraphs, write about the minutes leading up to the moment this photo was taken. Use only concrete descriptions, no words naming abstract feelings (such as happy, morose, bitter, gloomy). But find a way through specific language to suggest the emotion that, for you, underpins the experience.

Modified Memory

In a page, describe what you did the last time you went out with your friends, changing only one element, so that the events become slightly more dramatic than they were in real life. Would your fictional self challenge the local pool shark to a game, ask someone out of your league to dance, or happen across someone you haven't seen in years? How would this one change affect later events the same night?

Capture the Voice

Listen carefully to the voice of a distinctive character in a movie or TV show—such as Carrie Bradshaw (Sarah Jessica Parker) in *Sex and the City*, Detective Alonzo Harris (Denzel Washington) from *Training Day*, George Costanza (Jason Alexander) from *Seinfeld*, Lester Burnham (Kevin Spacey) from *American Beauty*, Erin Brockovitch (Julia Roberts) from *Erin Brockovitch*, or Ferris Bueller (Matthew Broderick) from *Ferris Bueller's Day Off*. In a page, narrate the events of your morning borrowing this character's voice. How does language suggest the personality behind it? What are the differences between your voice and the voice of this character? Be careful not to let your narration become a simple parody.

Behind the Music

Select a song that has strong personal meaning for you. Without mentioning the song's title or lyrics, describe the experience of listening to this song in a scene no longer than one page. How can a scene (through description, action, and gesture) convey the emotional experience of listening to music?

Characters and their Background

Consider the following five people: a twenty-nine year old Zen master who once spent three weeks in jail for shoplifting, an elderly man who never kept a job more than six months, a mother who secretly scribbles greeting card verses on napkins while caring for her children, a fast-food manager who constantly hits on employees, a banker who falls in love at least once a month.

For each person, answer the following:

- What single aspect of this character do friends find the most interesting?
- What is the one big regret each has?
- What secret have they never admitted to their parents?
- Which movie star/celebrity would he or she most want to date?

- What one national event (JFK's shooting, September 11th, the Million Man March, etc.) affected this person the most?
- What is his or her most meaningful childhood memory?
- What score would each earn on an IQ test?
- What would each want on a tombstone?

In a small group or as a full class, share your answers with other class members, paying particular attention to the ways that each detail suggests something important about the character's peronality.

Section 1

CREATING RAW MATERIAL

Peter Meinke

Unheard Music

From *The Gettysburg Review* and *New Stories of the South 2005*

James Vilag liked the idea of driving through unheard music, so at night he would leave the radio off as he made his rounds, his car nosing into endless waves of possibility, his shiny left shoe tapping like a metronome. He was most moved by the more emotional music he couldn't hear, pieces by Chopin and Tchaikovsky, Dvořák's *Slavic Dances* or Debussy's *En Blanc et Noir*. When he rolled down the window, he could feel them flow over him like tides in a harbor, filling the car with as much intensity as he could handle. *Largo, maestoso* . . . the idea that they were all "out there" at the same time made him breathe so heavily that the seat belt hurt his chest.

"That's just your imagination," Janice said. "And keep that seat belt on even if you think the whole goddamn London Symphony Orchestra is in the backseat."

"Seat belts lead to careless driving," he told her. "You wear your seat belt for twenty years and never have an accident, it's been a complete waste of time. To make it worthwhile you've got to have an accident or two."

"You're a loony tune," she said, "and I won't let you drive on your rounds unless your seat belt's on." So he would start each night safely buckled and later undo it as the music flooded in.

He was an insomniac and had volunteered to drive the late night crime watch in his neighborhood on a more or less regular basis. He didn't need much sleep anyway, and his job as editor of the in-house bulletin of St. Anthony's Hospital wasn't demanding. During the two months of his watch, there had been no burglaries, and everyone was giving him full credit, though he had never seen or even heard anything suspicious. He didn't tell them he did it partly for the unheard music and partly to avoid his dreams. He didn't care about burglaries; they seemed like petty crimes at most. People became too attached to *things*. James couldn't think of any *thing* he'd really mind losing.

His dreams had always been bad: for many years he dreamed he had killed someone, a stranger, at random, and would lie awake night after night grinding his teeth in agitation. There was a time in his life, before he met Janice, when what he did and what he dreamed became confused. When he was awake he thought he was dreaming. When he was asleep he'd dream of going to sleep and dreaming other dreams, often about dreaming, so the effect was like a hall of mirrors where the real self gets lost in a maze of distorted images.

One time during this period, he or his dream self was walking home from dinner in a strange part of town. The dinner itself had been upsetting: the waiter, insinuating and ambivalently sexed, had a pink face and a throaty feminine voice.

"Where have you been?" the waiter said. "You've never been here before."

"No, it's a little out of the way for me. I went to a concert and it got to be later than I thought." Why was he talking to this waiter? The concert had been a piano duet and the last piece, *Le Bal Martiniquais*, was still thrumming in his head. "I'd like the schnitzel, I think, and a glass of the white zinfandel."

"Oh my god, not the schnitzel!" The waiter arched perfectly clipped and rounded eyebrows. "Anything but the schnitzel. Our cook is Polish and hates anything German."

"Well, what do you recommend?"

"The duck with baked apple is pretty good tonight, or the chicken cacciatore."

"OK, the duck." He closed the menu and began tapping out a cigarette, but the waiter remained by the table. James asked, "Are you waiting for something?"

"The captain has asked that all cigarettes be distinguished," the waiter said and smiled. James wasn't sure he had heard him right and continued tapping, saying nothing.

"Not the zinfandel," said the waiter, still smiling. "Not with duck."

"Jesus, bring me anything."

"Yes, sir." When he bowed, the waiter's bald spot showed, seven long hairs pasted over it. "*Egri Bikaver*, Bull's Blood." He padded away with a slight penguin waddle.

The dinner was further marred by an Englishman, perhaps an Australian, at a nearby table who sat quietly with a bottle of Foster's Ale in front of him, reading a letter with foreign stamps on it. He would smile as he read and suddenly begin crying, then start all over again, reading and rereading the letter. At the time, James lived alone in a single room cluttered with books and records; watching the Englishman, he felt drowned in loneliness. Who would write *him* such a letter?

He ate as fast as he could, to get out of there. The duck, he had realized too late, was so expensive he could hardly taste it anyway, and the tip he left—all the money he had— was insufficient. This made him both embarrassed and angry with the waiter: the schnitzel was five dollars cheaper. Each table had its own loaf of bread, bread knife, and cutting board, and as if this were a way to get even, he slipped the serrated, wood-handled knife into his pocket. He thought of taking the breadboard, too, sliding it under his shirt, holding in his stomach, but it seemed like too much trouble, and he settled for the knife and the book of matches that—oddly, he thought—was white and blank. Had the Englishman noticed? James didn't care. He waited until the waiter went into the kitchen, then he tucked his last bills under the wine glass and hurried into the night.

It was raining lightly, and on his walk he slipped and stumbled over the uneven sidewalks. It never snowed in Florida, but the rain looked like snow under the street-lamps and like colored confetti in front of the bars and restaurants with their blinking neon signs. In places, his own reflection rose toward him like the cardboard mannequins on a bayonet field. He was tingling with an unfocused fear—stealing the knife had been an atypical and stupid thing to do—and he walked randomly in a westerly direction, heading toward the river rather than his own apartment. Mendelssohn's

Andante and Variations, from the evening's concert, surged in his ears as if someone had turned on a switch.

At some point he realized that he had begun following a well-dressed man in a pale overcoat whose black shoes reflected the light and made sharp tapping sounds as he walked. James felt the man was drawing him like a whirlpool, against his will, down into the darkest part of the city, where redbrick buildings crowded the sidewalk and swallowed what little light there was. The footsteps began to echo at his sides and behind him, and in his fear and accompanied by music, he walked faster and faster, and when he at last caught up with the man, he found the bread knife in his hand and stabbed him with all his might high in his back, and the man groaned and dropped like a side of beef at James's feet.

He felt nauseous, terrified. His first instinct was to run, but as he looked around he knew this was only a dream . . . he was almost certain it was a dream. *Just the same,* he thought, *dreams are real too, they don't come from nothing, this is a part of what I am.* And suppose he *wasn't* dreaming: here he stood, with blood on his shoes, a knife in his trembling hand and a dead man at his feet. It seemed best to do something, to act it out.

No one was around. The neighborhood looked dead, too, except for a few dingy lighted windows down the street. James bent over and grasped the man under his arms, dragging him to an open iron gate that led down to a darkened apartment below street level. As he pulled the body down the few steps, he backed into a garbage can, making such a clang that his heart nearly stopped. He froze there for a minute, standing on the bottom level, the man's feet still three steps up. For the first time James looked at his victim's face. He was a middle-aged man with thick graying hair, a healthy face frozen in a grotesque semblance of a smile like the mask of comedy. He looked familiar: the Englishman from the restaurant? James didn't think this was possible; he thought he, James, had left the restaurant first, but thinking back on it, he wasn't sure. Holding his breath, he tugged the man's wallet out of the tight back pocket.

There was a small amount of money, and he put that in his pocket without counting it and then looked at the driver's license: Jack Phillip Middleton, 77 Franklin Street. James wiped the wallet clean and forced it back into the man's pocket, an act that seemed as violent as the actual stabbing. He pulled the body behind the garbage cans and went up into the street. A young couple scurried through the shadows on the opposite sidewalk. James kept his face averted and headed for the river. He felt exhausted now, as if he had been walking under water for hours; he had to kick the air aside with every step. When he reached the river, he threw the knife as far as he could—*This is my message to the world*, he thought—and turned for home.

The next morning, after he woke up, that was the tricky time. First he checked his shoes: no blood. But he could have cleaned them last night; he was a careful man. He found two incriminating items: money in his wallet and the matches in his pocket. These could be explained, too—he often resupplied his wallet at night for the next day, keeping a small supply of cash in his desk drawer for that purpose; and a pack of matches was hardly evidence that he had killed someone.

No, the real question was whether he had dreamed it or not and which side of the dream he was on. He often had dreams that encompassed several days in a row, dreams in which he went to bed and woke up, that were indistinguishable from real life. He thought about this all the time as he drove his rounds at night. It was diabolical. It made it impossible to check on himself. So what if he read the newspaper from front to back and there was no mention of a body found near the river? He could be dreaming right now. He found it hard to take action. Editing someone else's words and—a few years later—driving in circles on his crime watch was about all he was capable of performing. And there was Janice now, helping him keep his balance: without her it was difficult to breathe.

"You're my ozone," he told her. "You're my safety margin."

"Ozone, shmozone," she said. "Buckle up." She had always been solid and quick, that's what he liked about her. He was so slow himself, everything seemed slippery to him. Earlier, when he had called her on the telephone to ask her to a movie, she had wanted to talk.

"Phones make me nervous," he said. "I don't think I've ever said anything intelligent over the phone."

"Why don't you read me a few pages of Henry James and break your record?" she'd asked. He wanted to be like her.

Sometimes he thought, *What if I actually saw a burglar?* Would he chase him and corner him? He could tell him, *I killed a man at random and I'll kill you too, if you don't give yourself up.* These scenarios were ludicrous, but as James enacted them in his mind, his hands turned cold on the steering wheel and he put his fingers on the even colder tire iron Janice insisted he keep on the seat beside him.

A while ago he had gone to a prominent psychiatrist, Dr. Walton Pharr, for help, but he proved impenetrably stupid. James often thought there was nothing wrong with the world that a little more intelligence couldn't solve. He felt surrounded by people strolling around with three pounds of suet in their skulls. He believed he would have been brilliant at college if his father had chosen to send him—he had won every spelling bee he had ever been in. If he had been born ten years later, when they began having national spelling bees, he might have been famous—picture in the papers, the works.

The psychiatrist had asked about his father. And his mother, and his childhood, and the army. What he couldn't seem to understand was that James already *knew* about these things. He knew he was marred from childhood—who wasn't? Dr. Pharr, who was fat and chain-smoked, obviously had problems with self-esteem himself; any idiot could see that. What James wanted to know was, simply, how to tell real life from dream life.

"Try pinching yourself," the psychiatrist suggested. He was really a dip.

"You can dream you're pinching yourself," James replied.

"Tell me about your dreams."

James described some of his dreams but was reluctant to tell him about the night at the weird café; that would be too much like a confession, and perhaps dangerous. He didn't trust Fatso farther than he could throw him. "I've been dreaming of an animal," he said. "I'm standing by a tree in a large backyard, maybe behind the house I grew up in, and this dark animal crawls up over a stone wall on the other side of the tree. At first I think it's relatively harmless, like a fat beaver or a porcupine, but as it gets nearer it elongates and gets bigger and turns into a wild boar. I've never seen a wild boar, but I know that's what it is. Its eyes are red, and it has ugly fangs or tusks.

"Anyway, nothing much happens, but I'm terribly frightened. We stare at each other. I pick up a heavy stone. Then, usually, he turns away and goes back over the wall. Sometimes he just disappears, and I have the feeling he may pop up on any side."

"Very interesting," said Dr. Pharr. "What do you think it means?"

"Maybe I'm eating too much pork." The psychiatrist brought out the worst in him. He knew Dr. Pharr wanted him to link the boar with his father, the apple tree—now he saw it was an apple tree—with his mother. But he could do that himself, he didn't have to pay seventy-five dollars an hour to find that out.

One time, during James's sophomore year in high school, his father burst into a house at 2 A.M. and struck him across the face in front of three of his friends. They had been playing chess and lost track of the time—James in particular would fall into the world of bishops and knights and all else would disappear. He was supposed to have been home at eleven.

"What the hell's wrong with you?" his father shouted, while the other boys froze in their chairs. "Your mother's worried sick!" And then he slapped him, the sound cracking like a gunshot in the silent room. *You would think*, James thought later, *a father would be proud of a son staying up all night to play chess.* He, James, would be proud if *his* son had done that, if he had a son. But he didn't say anything at the time. He was as tall as his father already, and he just stared at him for a minute, and they both knew this was the last time the older man would hit him. Then he followed his father out into the car.

He thought about all this, peering into the darkness for burglars, nosing the car slowly around corners, music rising and falling through the limp leaves of magnolias, jacarandas, and twisted live oaks. He had asked Dr. Pharr, "Tell me, how do I know I'm not dreaming *you?*"

"You'll know I'm real when you get my bill." That was the extent of the psychiatrist's sophistication.

Early on, James tried to solve the problem himself. For several days he carried around in his mind the vivid imprint of the Englishman's name and address: Jack Phillip Middleton, 77 Franklin Street. Finally, one evening after work, he gathered up the nerve to look it up, then impulsively called a cab and gave that address. Franklin Street was a middle-class city block with a few trees and attached houses, each with a front stoop and a little patch of grass behind an iron railing. Number 77 was in the middle of the block, and rain started pouring down as he stood, bareheaded, heart bouncing like a headless fish, staring at its unlighted windows that stared blankly back.

From the street he could barely make out a nameplate underneath the number, and he forced his leaden limbs to open the gate and go up the brick steps to the door; but even as he was reading the name and feeling the rain running down his face, he knew with anguish that he couldn't tell if he were wide awake or dreaming.

Meinke on Journaling

"Unheard Music" is the story of an insomniac who—when he gets a chance to sleep—has vivid and upsetting dreams. Because he's so strung out he's lost his grip on reality, and at any given point isn't sure whether he's asleep or dreaming. In the story, he dreams he's killed someone. Or did he really do it? He's not sure.

That's a thumbnail sketch of the story, but it didn't appear to me as a plot or even a straight narrative. I wrote it sentence by sentence, slowly, as various aspects of my own life popped into my head and transformed into the protagonist's character and experience.

Several years ago, after a few burglaries hit our quiet and somewhat spooky neighborhood (lots of overhanging live oak trees), I volunteered for our Crime Watch group. "Unheard Music" got its start one evening when I was taking my turn on watch. I was parked on a dark corner with my lights out, listening to NPR and some classical music station. Eventually, worried about the battery, I turned off the car radio and, being a writer, took out my little notebook and began making notes in the dark (hard to read my handwriting the next day). Very shortly I came upon the idea that the music I had been listening to was still out there, surrounding me, waiting to come in—and more or less wrote the first line of the story.

I wrote, "Jim Williams liked the idea of driving through unheard music, so at night he would leave the radio off as he made his rounds, his car nosing into endless waves of possibility." After a week or two, as the story began taking sinister turns, "Jim Williams" became "James Vilag"—a name I just made up, with little echoes of "villain" and "gulag" in it.

I of course wrote down other things—about the twisted oak trees, about suspicious characters who turned out to be my neighbors, etc.—but it was the unheard music that caught my imagination. I kept pushing it, and the rest dropped out of the story.

The experience of being on Crime Watch, now common for huge numbers of Americans, is a dreamlike one, far from our sunny "real" lives; and it leads to thoughts and dreams with violent content (suppose one actually confronted a criminal?). More, it brings up questions like "Am I really doing this, or am I dreaming it?" and "How am I different from the criminal?" At least it did for me, and therefore for Vilag, my protagonist. Like him, I'm a mild insomniac, and once I got the story started I stayed with it for many nights, to the great detraction of the neighborhood's safety. After I got it well started, I returned to writing in the morning, my usual habit.

As I moved the story along, I fused truth and fiction. For example, there *is* a St. Anthony's Hospital in our town, but whether it has an in-house bulletin I have no idea, and didn't check. But being its editor seemed like a good job for James Vilag.

I, too, have dreams, some few of them violent. I once dreamed I shot someone with a rifle (I was a soldier and trained on the M-1), but I knew it was a dream. Still, I also have had times when I knew I was dreaming, and times when I wasn't sure, when the line between dreams and reality was fuzzy. Sitting there in the dark car, I tried to follow that feeling as far as I could.

I'm not sure where the restaurant scene came from, but once Vilag entered the dining room, I remembered a very demonstrative waiter we once had whose conversation I had jotted down in my little notebook. The only line I took from him is "Our cook is Polish and hates anything German," but the slightly surreal tone came right from my memory of it.

The knife and breadboard are standard equipment in our local fish bistro, and not until I described it in the story did I realize that Vilag was going to kill someone, at least in his dream. Then I had to decide who, and how; and, slowly, the death of the stranger in the restaurant emerged. I couldn't just make him a complete nonentity, so I sketched in a few characteristics, including a crying scene my wife and I had once witnessed: a man sitting at a table, reading letters and crying.

One useful thing for a writer is to keep track of his or her dreams. I don't remember most of mine, but those I do, I write down in my notebook. The dream about a boar attack that Vilag describes to his psychiatrist came from there.

Writing is, among other things, a plunge into the subconscious and memory. One uncomfortable memory that came up during the writing of the story was of the time my father dragged me out of a friend's house: we were playing chess and forgot what time it was. In "Unheard Music" I made it a bit more dramatic, but the fact that I've remembered it all these years showed it was an indelible moment in my life.

I guess the moral of this is that intense stories can spring from very little material: a little everyday life, a scattering of dreams, and some close thinking about their relationship. Vilag is not me, but only I could have written him. And, my memory being what it is, even I couldn't have written him without the help of my little notebook, with its record of dreams, dinners, conversations, and semirepressed memories. Lastly, I couldn't have written him without having read the wonderful stories of Cheever, Chekhov, Oates, Updike, and all the others who have formed my ideas of what short stories should be like.

Writing Suggestions

1. Write a scene where a character is lurking in a suburban neighborhood at night. Let him or her be a catburglar, a drunken teenager trying to spy on a crush, a low-paid security patrol officer, a teenager who snuck out after curfew to drink beers, or a neighborhood watch member. Create a situation that sets up a conflict, one that results from this person encountering someone he or she would like to avoid. Draw out the suspense for a page or more. What is the easiest way to create tension in a night scene? How does your character's mind-set come into play? How can language contribute to the atmospheric tension? (Variation: Night scenes lend themselves to suspense. Challenge yourself to create an equally suspenseful scene set in the afternoon—at a ballpark, the beach, a mall, a suburban backyard.)

2. Keep a journal by your bed. Each morning, set your alarm so you can write for ten minutes before you begin the day. Focus on capturing your dreams using as much vivid detail as possible. In your dreams do you notice patterns, such as similar stories, similar settings, recurring images or people? After three weeks, take the most interesting dream moment and craft a story from it, using it as the first scene. Do your dreams offer possibilities that self-conscious story writing doesn't allow?

3. Begin a reading response journal that tracks your reactions to stories assigned for class. After reading each story, write one to two fully developed paragraphs in which you discuss sections of the story where you were most involved as a reader. How did the story engage your emotions, your curiosity? Did you respond to the story's writing style, to characters, to the progression of a plot, to a particular scene? As best you can, articulate the reasons why this aspect of the story interested you. After reading and responding to at least six stories, list three specific techniques—such as using an

unreliable narrator or using details to place readers fully in the scene—that you can attempt in your own stories to achieve a similar narrative intensity. These ideas might particularly help you with revision as your writing progresses.

4. Handwrite an actual pen-and-paper letter (it's more personal than typing) to a writer whose work you admire. Send it to that writer in care of the publisher for their latest book or at the university where they work. After giving a specific compliment on one aspect of their fiction (even better, a specific element of a specific story), ask a question. What's the best writing advice you ever received? How long does it take you to write a single story? What writer do you most admire? Most writers will take the time to respond to a brief, upbeat letter from a fan. Writing is a terribly solitary act and it's well worth the effort to spend a little time connecting with the community of fiction writers in general.

> *I can't explain inspiration. A writer is either compelled to write or not. And if I waited for inspiration I wouldn't really be a writer.*
> —Toni Morrison

Steve Almond

The Soul Molecule

From *Tin House* and *New Stories from the South 2003*

I was on my way to see Wilkes. We were going to have brunch. Wilkes was a minor friend from college. He played number one on the squash team. I'd challenged him once, during a round-robin, but he annihilated me with lobs. Afterwards, in the showers, he told me his secret.

"Vision," he said. "You have to see what's going to happen."

Now it was five years on and I still felt sort of indebted to him. This was idiotic but I couldn't unpersuade myself. I kept remembering those lobs, one after another, as elegant as parasols.

Wilkes was in the back of the restaurant, in a booth. We said our hellos and he picked up his menu and set it down again.

"We've known each other a long time, haven't we, Jim?"

"Sure," I said.

"Eight years now, coming up on eight."

"That sounds about right."

"You wouldn't think less of me if I told you something, would you?"

"Heck no," I said. Mostly, I was wondering how much breakfast would cost, and whether I'd have to pay.

"I've got a cartridge in my head," Wilkes said.

He had that drowsy pinch around the eyes you see in certain leading men. He was wearing a blue blazer with discreet buttons. He looked like the sort of guy from whom other guys would buy bonds. That was his business. He was in bonds.

"A cartridge has been placed in my head for surveillance purposes. This was done a number of years ago by a race of superior beings. I don't know if you know anything about abduction, Jim. Do you know anything about abduction?"

"Wait a second," I said.

"An abduction can take one of two forms. The first—you don't need to know the technical terms—the first is purely for research purposes. Cell harvesting, that kind of thing. The second involves implants, Jim, such as the one in my brain."

Wilkes was from Maryland, the Chesapeake Bay area. He spoke in these crisp, prepared sentences. I'd always thought he'd be a corporate lawyer, with an office in a glass tower and a secretary better looking than anyone I knew.

"You're telling me you've been abducted," I said.

Wilkes nodded. He picked up his fork and balanced it on his thumb. "The cartridges can be thought of as visual recorders, something like cameras. They allow the caretakers to monitor human activity without causing alarm."

"The caretakers," I said.

"They see whatever I see." Wilkes gazed at me for a long moment. It was eerie, like staring into the big black space where an audience might be. Finally, he looked up and half rose out of his seat. "Mom," he said. "Dad. Hey, there you are. You remember Jim."

"Why of course," said his mother. She was a Southern lady with one of those soft handshakes.

"Pleasure," Mr. Wilkes said. "Unexpected pleasure. No, no. Don't make a fuss. We'll just settle in. What are you up to, Jim? How're you bringing in the pesos?"

"Research," I said.

His face brightened. "Research, eh? The research game. What's that, biotech?"

"Yeah, sort of."

I'd never done any research. But I liked the way the word sounded. It sounded broad and scientific and beyond reproach.

"Your folks?" Mr. Wilkes said.

"You'll remember us to them, I hope," Mrs. Wilkes said.

I had no recollection of my parents having met the Wilkeses.

"What are you two birddogs up to?" Mr. Wilkes said. He was from Connecticut, but he sometimes enjoyed speaking like a Texan.

Wilkes was squeezed next to his dad and his voice was full of that miserable complicated family shit. "We were talking," he said. "I was telling Jim about the cartridge in my head."

Mr. Wilkes fixed him with a look and I thought for a second of that Goya painting, Saturn wolfing down his kids like chicken fingers. Mrs. Wilkes began fiddling with the salt and pepper, as if she might want to knit with them eventually.

"How about that?" Mr. Wilkes said. "What do you think of that, Jim?"

"Interesting," I said.

"*Interesting?* That the best you can do? Come on now. This is the old cartridge in the head. The old implant-a-roony."

I started to think, right then, about this one class I'd taken sophomore year, the Biology of Religion. The professor was a young guy who was doing research at the medical school. He told us the belief in a higher power was a function of biological desire, a glandular thing. The whole topic got him very worked up.

Mr. Wilkes said: "Do you know why they do it, Jim?"

"Sir?"

He turned to his son again. "Did you explain the integration phases to him? The hybrids? The grays? Anything?"

"He just got here," Wilkes said.

Mr. Wilkes was sitting across from me. He was one of these big Republicans you sometimes see. The gin blossoms, the blue blazer. His whole aura screamed *yacht*.

"They teach you any folklore in that fancy college of yours? Fairy, dybbuk, goblin, sprite. Ring a bell, Jim? These are the names the ancients used to describe our extraterrestrial caretakers. 'Their appearance was like burning coals of fire and like the appearance of lamps: it went up and down among the living creatures, and the fire was bright and out of the fire went forth lightning.' That's straight from the Book of Ezekiel. What's that sound like to you, son? Does that sound like God on his throne of glory?"

"No," I said. "I guess not."

"There's a reason Uncle Sam launched Project Blue Book," Mr. Wilkes said. "He was forced to, Jim. Without some kind of coherent response, there'd be no way to stem the panic. Let me ask you something. Do you know how many sightings have been reported to the Department of Defense in the past ten years? Guess. Two point five million. Abductions? Seven hundred thousand plus. They are among us, Jim."

Our waitress appeared.

"Do you serve Egg Beaters?" Mr. Wilkes said.

The waitress shook her head.

"Toast," Mrs. Wilkes said. "You can have some toast, dear."

"I don't want toast," Mr. Wilkes said.

Wilkes looked pretty much entirely miserable.

"What about egg whites?" Mr. Wilkes said. "Can you whip me up an omelet with egg whites?"

The waitress shifted her weight from one haunch to the other. She was quite beautiful, though a bit dragged down by circumstance. "An omelet with what?" she said.

"The white part of the egg. The part that isn't the yolk." Mr. Wilkes picked up his fork and began to simulate the act of scrambling eggs.

"I'm asking what you want *in* the omelet, sir."

"Oh. I see. Okay. How about mushroom, swiss, and bacon."

"*Bacon?*" said Mrs. Wilkes.

I didn't know what the hell to order.

The waitress left and Mr. Wilkes turned right back to me. He'd done some fundraising for the GOP and I could see now just how effective he might be in this capacity. "Mrs. Wilkes and I, we both have implants. It's no secret. Not uncommon for them to tag an entire family. Did Jonathon already explain this?"

"I didn't explain anything," Wilkes said. "You didn't give me a chance."

"Yes," Mrs. Wilkes said. "You must've dominated the conversation, Warren."

"Remember Briggs?" Wilkes said.

"Who?"

"Briggs. Ron Briggs. Played number four on the team. He's got an implant. He lives out in Sedona now."

"Do we know him?" Mrs. Wilkes said.

Mr. Wilkes waved his hand impatiently. "Now I'm not going to bore you with some long story about our abductions, Jim. How would that be? You show up for breakfast and you have to listen to *that*. What you need to understand is the role these beings play. If they wanted to destroy us, if that was their intent, hell, I wouldn't be talking to you right now. They're caretakers, Jim. An entire race of caretakers. I'm not trying to suggest that these implants are any bed of roses, mind you. You've got all the beta waves to contend with, the ringing. Val's got a hell of a scar."

Mrs. Wilkes blushed. She had an expensive hairstyle and skin that looked a bit irradiated. "He's going to think we're kooks," she said.

"Not at all," I said quietly.

"Hell, we *are* kooks," Mr. Wilkes said. "The whole damn species is kooks. Only a fool would deny it."

I waited for the silence to sort of subside and excused myself. I needed some cold water on my ears. I filled the sink and did a quick dunk and stared at the bathroom mirror—really *stared*—until my face got all big-eyed and desperate.

When I got back to the table, the food had arrived and the Wilkeses were eating in this extremely polite manner. I'd visited them once, on the way back from a squash match at Penn. All I could remember about their home was the carpets. They must have had about a thousand of them, beautiful and severe, the kind you didn't even want to step on. I couldn't imagine a kid growing up in that place.

My French toast was sitting there, with some strawberries, but I wasn't hungry.

Mrs. Wilkes frowned. "Is something wrong with your food, dear? We can order you something else."

"That was pretty funny," I said finally. "You guys had me really going. You must be quite the charade family."

The Wilkeses, all of them, looked at me. It was that look you get from any kind of true believer, this mountain of piety sort of wobbling on a pea of doubt.

I thought about my biology professor again. Toward the end of class, just before I dropped out in fact, he gave us a lecture about this one chemical that gets released by the pineal gland. He called it the soul molecule, because it triggered all kinds of mystical thoughts. Just a pinch was enough to have people talking to angels. It was the stuff that squirted out at death, when the spirit is said to rise from the body.

Mr. Wilkes was talking about the binary star system Zeta Reticuli and the Taos hum and the Oz effect. But you could tell he wasn't saying what he really wanted to. His face was red with the disappointed blood.

The waitress came and cleared the dishes.

Wilkes started to mention a few mutual friends, guys who made me think of loud cologne and urinals.

Mrs. Wilkes excused herself and returned a few minutes later with fresh makeup.

Mr. Wilkes laid down a fifty. It was one of his rituals and, like all our rituals, it gave him this little window of expansiveness.

"I don't know the exact game plan, Jim. Anyone tells you they do, head the other direction. But I do know that these beings, these grays, they are essentially good. Why else would they travel thirty-seven light years just to bail our sorry asses out? It's the mission that affects me," he said. "Mrs. Wilkes and Jonathon and I, all of us, we feel a part of something larger." He gazed at his wife and son and smiled with a tremendous vulnerability. "I know how it looks from the outside. But we don't know everything. We all make mistakes." He tried to say something else, but his big schmoozy baritone faltered.

Mrs. Wilkes put her hand on his.

"What the hell do I know?" Mr. Wilkes said.

"We all make mistakes," his wife said.

"I'm not perfect."

"Nobody's perfect, love."

There was a lot passing between them. Wilkes started to blush. His father seemed to want to touch his cheek. "They're just trying to save us from ourselves, so we don't ruin everything."

The waitress had come and gone and left change on the table. All around us people were charging through their mornings, toward God knows what.

The Wilkeses were sitting there, in their nice clothing, but I was seeing something else now, these whitish blobs at the centers of their bodies. It was their spirits I was seeing. I wasn't scared or anything. Everyone's a saint when it comes to the naked spirit. The other stuff just sort of grows over us, like weeds.

I thought about that crazy professor again. He'd called me to his office after Thanksgiving to tell me I was flunking. He was all torn up, as if he'd somehow betrayed me. He asked if I'd learned anything at all in his class. I said of course I had, I'd learned plenty of things, but when he pressed me to name one or two, I drew a blank. Just before I left, he came over to my side of the desk and put his hand on my shoulder and said, *We all need someone to watch over us, James.*

"Do you believe that?" Mr. Wilkes said.

I was pretty sure I'd never see the three of them again and it made me a little sad, a little reluctant to leave.

Wilkes was smoothing down his lapels. Mrs. Wilkes smiled with her gentle teeth and Mr. Wilkes began softly, invisibly, to weep. His spirit was like a little kerchief tucked into that big blue suit.

"I think we're going to be alright," I said. "That's the feeling I get." This was true. I was, in fact, having some kind of clairvoyant moment. Everything that was about to happen I could see, just before it did.

Outside, up in the sky, above even the murmuring satellites, an entire race of benevolent yayas was maybe peering down at me with glassy black eyes. I started waving. The waitress breezed by and blew me a kiss. Mr. Wilkes slid another fifty across the table and winked. The sun lanced through a bank of clouds and lit the passing traffic like tinsel. I waved like hell.

Almond on Generating Story Ideas

A couple of years ago I did a reading with a poet named Peter Richards. The thing I love most about poets—aside from the fact that they make even less money than fiction writers—is that they often tell stories to help explain their poems. Peter did this with his first poem. He told the audience that it was inspired by going to meet a friend of his who announced, quite casually, that he had a cartridge in his head, implanted by aliens. Then he read the poem. It was a lovely poem, spooky and evocative. But it didn't really tell the *story*: what it would be like to have a friend go *X-Files* on you.

So that's how I started writing "The Soul Molecule." It just grew out of a situation that struck me as dramatically interesting. I know this sounds sort of vague and hap-hazard, but most of my stories come from this basic template. I actually find that the less I worry about the Big Things (plot, characterization, point of view, and so on) the more I can focus on that central concern: *what happens next?* In this way, my writing is really a kind of improvisatory play. I try to stay as loose as possible, because if I start planning everything out, I wind up creating equations, rather than telling a story. My basic point here is that a sense of mystery isn't something to be feared: it can and should drive a story forward.

Which is not to say that I just fart around and hope my characters bump into our old friends, conflict, meaning, and epiphany. What I actually do is fart around *according to certain basic rules*:

1. Love your characters—all of them—at all times.

2. Force them into emotional danger.

3. Embrace the unexpected.

4. Forget style—just tell the truth.

5. You're not God (and will need to revise).

These bad boys are basically ingrained. That is: I don't have them taped to the edge of my computer screen to remind myself. They're simply the way I do business when I'm writing well. So, for example, when Wilkes tells the narrator about his alien abduc-tion, there's an immediate emotional danger. The narrator is embarrassed; his friend seems to have gone off his rocker. And Wilkes himself is taking a risk: what if the nar-rator thinks he's crazy?

But that story will only take us so far. The narrator and Wilkes aren't really great friends, so it's just a weird little event, an anecdote, if nothing else happens. I must have known this when I was writing the story, because suddenly Wilkes's parents showed up. Again: I didn't say to myself: *Hey, Steve, this is really just an anecdote, you need more dan-ger.* The possibility just popped into my head, because I was loose, riffing, eager to up the ante. So now the parents were in the scene.

The most obvious possibility, of course, was for them to react to their son's con-fession with distress—which is precisely why I went the other direction. I wanted to embrace the unexpected: that these wealthy, buttoned-up parents also had been abducted, and that they were even more adamant about the experience than their son.

Now things were getting interesting. The narrator (and, by proxy, the reader) was facing a very awkward meal. I was enjoying his efforts to cope with all this. Attractively, Mr. Wilkes turned to be something of a blowhard. He was pushy. He was a loudmouth. He was condescending to people. And it was clear that he made his son miserable. It would have been easy enough to play him as a fool right up until the end. But that would have violated the most important rule on my list: love all your characters. In fact, once I realized the dad was a buffoon, it became obvious to me that the story had to redeem him.

So how does that happen? Well, in this case, I just let him talk and talk. I wanted to hear what he had to say. Most characters, if you just let them talk, will lead you to the truth, because most human beings (including the ones dreamed up by other human beings) share a compulsion to confess.

The topic Mr. Wilkes returned to, over and over, was caretaking. Now I started to put some things together. Here was a father who had made mistakes in his own role as a caretaker, and he saw these aliens as a kind of larger, rescuing force. That's generally how it works with any kind of deistic belief system: we ascribe to God the qualities we wish to possess ourselves. As for the specifics—all this business about the cell harvesting and the Oz Effect—they came from a book I checked out of the library. A little research goes a long way in fiction.

The more I listened to Mr. Wilkes, the more I came to see his bluster as a defense, meant to keep at bay his feelings of guilt—the crushing sense of his own insufficiency as a caretaker. This emotional revelation is really the heart of the story. It's what I was writing towards: to see this guy laid bare and, in some sense, forgiven.

So that's how the first draft ended. The dad had this little breakdown and he was comforted by his wife and sort of implicitly forgiven by his son. But I knew something was missing, and that was the narrator's story, what he made of all this. I wanted him to be affected by the experience, not just diverted for an hour or so, but *transformed*.

I think here of the last line of the famous Frank O'Connor story, "Guests of the Nation": "And anything that ever happened me after I never felt the same about again." That's the definition of a successful short story: the hero, and the reader, should never see the world in quite the same way again.

So I started to develop the narrator's backstory. I wrote a whole bunch about him, lots of eloquent crapola, before I realized that I didn't need his whole life story, because he wasn't the main attraction in this story. He was more of a compassionate observer. I just needed those few crucial memories that would connect him to the Wilkses, to the universal need for nurturance.

This sense of connection was what set the stage for that moment of grace at the end. But I didn't discover the actual ending until the third or fourth draft. I was reading over the story and I kept fixing on this little piece of dialogue from early on: "*Vision,*" *Wilkes said.* "*You have to see what's going to happen.*"

Then it struck me—the narrator has a clairvoyant moment. And it's this semi-mystical experience that draws him toward the Wilkeses, even as he's about to leave them forever.

The careful reader will have discerned at this point that I've said nothing about rule number four, the one concerning style. The reason is this: I don't much believe in style. In fact, most young writers screw themselves royally when they make a conscious effort at style. They overdo the metaphors and adverbs and clever phrases. They call attention to themselves, relentlessly, rather than to the fictional world they're trying to create.

I'm not suggesting that writers should ignore the beauty and elegance of the language. But I am suggesting that such beauty and elegance must emerge *organically* from an effort to tell the truth. Style is a function of the truth. It is not some free-floating gloss you can dump on your work to make it shine. If you force your characters to face their darkest truths, the language of the story will naturally rise into the lyric register. It will have to do so, in order to express the depth of their feelings.

Let me say one final thing, about the generation of story ideas. In short: <u>follow your obsessions. Write about things that matter to you.</u> If your mind snags on a fragment of dialogue, or a disturbing image, or a creepy idea, that's usually an indication that you've found a good trigger.

And place nothing off-limits. Most people consider reality shows on TV like *The Bachelorette* to be piffle, mind candy for the intellectually numb, blah-blah-blah. But that doesn't mean that there isn't a brilliant short story to be written about it. In fact, I love writing stories that reveal the hidden depths of subjects that most people tend to dismiss—such as heavy metal or Michael Jackson or alien abduction.

In the end, there's no such thing as a mindless topic. As superficial as the world tries to be, people are constantly experiencing intense feeling states, of fear and loathing and hope and desire. Your highest calling as a writer is to key into those feelings states, to cast your characters (and yourself) into the deep rough of consciousness—and thereby to help your readers feel less alone with their own chaotic insides.

Enough with the platitudes. Get out there and do it.

Writing Suggestions

1. Poet Rainer Maria Rilke claimed that childhood is one of the inexhaustible sources for fiction. Write a two-page scene focusing on one important day from your childhood. Steve Almond would, of course, utilize the popular culture of his childhood to accurately portray his youth. Dredge up what you can remember and imagine the rest. Think about what triggers memories—family members, TV shows, toys, special days, specific songs, films. If the two pages come easily, consider finishing the story.

2. Steve Almond's story, in part, hinges on the way the soul molecule changes the narrator's outlook on life. According to the story, it triggers "all kinds of mystical thoughts." In effect, this theory forces the narrator to reevaluate his overall understanding of human existence. Write your own story in which the narrator changes not only because of the drama but also because of a new intellectual understanding of life. How can your story maintain the grittiness of real dramatic action while also exploring "mystical thoughts"? Such "mystical thoughts" often arise from issues encountered in philosophy, psychology, and religion, but can also be found in sociology, literature, film, and elsewhere.

3. Revision is often the hardest thing a writer has to do. Some writers compare cutting their own words out of a story with the idea of killing their children. Take a story or a scene you've already written and trim it by 50 percent (keep a copy of the original, however). Should you cut dialogue, exposition, action? Should you start at a different spot or perhaps stop earlier? What does this radical cutting do

for story flow? Unity? Meaning? Does this forced attention to language make you reevaluate the strength of each word? Do any words, sentences, or paragraphs seem less strong than you originally thought? What elements did Almond seem to trim from his story while still keeping the tension high? Does cutting your own work offer a type of liberation or loss?

4. While at the grocery store, thumb through celebrity gossip magazines near the checkout counter, such as *People* and *National Enquirer*. Find stories in which a celebrity has recently made a life-altering change—there's one in almost every issue—and then, in the article, find (or imagine) the dramatic situation that gave rise to such change. Replace the real-life person with a character of your own making and see if you have the blueprint for a story of your own.

So little of the [story's] construction is objectively conceived. It's
organic and instinctive and subconscious.
I can't tell you how I arrive at it. Though, with each book, I go
through a long time when I know what I want to do and I'm held
back and puzzled and appalled because I don't know before I begin
to write how I'm going to do it,
and I always fear that I can't do it.
—Nadine Gordimer

Section 2

~~~~~~

DISCOVERING STORIES THROUGH PERSONAL EXPERIENCE

Janice Eidus

Vito Loves Geraldine

From *The Village Voice Literary Supplement* and
The O. Henry Awards 1990

Vito Venecio was after me. He'd wanted to get into my pants ever since tenth grade. But even though we hung around with the same crowd back at Evander Childs High School, I never gave him the time of day. I, Geraldine Rizzoli, was the most popular girl in the crowd, I had my pick of the guys, you can ask anyone, Carmela or Pamela or Victoria, and they'll agree. And Vito was just a skinny little kid with a big greasy pompadour and a cowlick and acne and a big space between his front teeth. True, he could sing, and he and Vinny Feruge and Bobby Colucci and Richie DeSoto formed a doo-wop group and called themselves Vito and the Olinvilles, but lots of the boys formed doo-wop groups and stood around on street corners doo-wopping their hearts out. Besides, I wasn't letting any of them into my pants either.

Carmela and Pamela and Victoria and all the other girls in the crowd would say, "Geraldine Rizzoli, teach me how to tease my hair as high as yours and how to put my eyeliner on so straight and thick," but I never gave away my secrets. I just set my black hair on beer cans every night and in the morning I teased it and teased it with my comb until sometimes I imagined that if I kept going I could get it high enough to reach the stars, and then I would spray it with hairspray that smelled like red roses and then I'd stroke on my black eyeliner until it went way past my eyes.

The kids in my crowd were the type who cut classes, smoked in the bathroom, and cursed. Yeah, even the girls cursed, and we weren't the type who went to church on Sundays, which drove our mothers crazy. Vito was one of the worst of us all. He just about never read a book or went to class, and I think his mother got him to set foot in the church maybe once the whole time he was growing up. I swear, it was some sort of a holy miracle that he actually got his diploma.

Anyway, like I said, lots of the boys wanted me and I liked to make out with them and sometimes I agreed to go steady for a week or two with one of the really handsome ones, like Sally-Boy Reticliano, but I never let any get into my pants. Because in my own way I was a good Catholic girl. And all this time Vito was wild about me and I wouldn't even make out with him. But when Vito and the Olinvilles got themselves an agent and cut a record, *Teenage Heartbreak*, which Vito wrote, I started to see that Vito was different than I'd thought, different than the other boys. Because Vito had an artistic soul. Then, on graduation night, just a week after Vito and the Olinvilles recorded *Teenage Heartbreak*, I realized that, all these years, I'd been in love with him, too, and was just too proud to admit it because he was a couple of inches shorter than me, and he had that acne and the space between his teeth. There I was, ready for the prom, all dressed up in my bright red prom dress and my hair teased higher than ever, waiting for my date, but my date wasn't Vito, it was Sally-Boy Reticliano, and I wanted to jump out of my skin. About halfway through the prom, I couldn't take it any more and I said, "Sally-Boy, I'm sorry, but I've just got to go over and talk to Vito." Sally-Boy, who was even worse at school than Vito, grunted, and I could tell that it was a sad grunt. But there was nothing I could do. I loved Vito and that was that. I spotted him standing alone in a corner. He was wearing a tux and his hair was greased up into a pompadour that was almost as high as my hair. He watched me as I walked across the auditorium to him, and even in my spiked heels, I felt as though I was floating on air. He said, "Aay, Geraldine, how goes it?" and then he took me by the arm and we left the auditorium. It was like he knew all along that one day I would come to him. It was a gorgeous spring night, I could even see a few stars, and Vito put his arm around me, and he had to tiptoe a little bit to reach. We walked over to the Gun Hill Projects, and we found a deserted bench in the project's laundry room, and Vito said, "Aay, Geraldine Rizzoli, I've been crazy about you since tenth grade. I even wrote *Teenage Heartbreak* for you."

And I said, "Vito, I know, I guessed it, and I'm sorry I've been so dumb since tenth grade but your heart doesn't have to break any more. Tonight I'm yours."

And Vito and I made out on the bench for awhile but it didn't feel like just making out. I realized that Vito and I weren't kids anymore. It was like we had grown up all at once. So I said, "Vito, take me," and he said, "Aay, Geraldine Rizzoli, all right!" He had the keys to his older brother Danny's best friend Freddy's car, which was a beat up old wreck, but that night it looked like a Cadillac to me. It was parked back near the school, and we raced back along Gun Hill Road hoping that Sally-Boy and the others wouldn't see us. Even though Vito didn't have a license, he drove the car a few blocks away into the parking lot of the Immaculate Conception School. We climbed into the back seat and I lifted the skirt of my red prom dress and we made love for hours. We made sure I wouldn't get pregnant, because we wanted to do things just right. Like I said, I was a good Catholic girl, in my own way. Afterwards he walked me back to Olinville Ave. And he took out the car keys and carved "Vito Loves Geraldine" in a heart over the door of the elevator in my building, but he was careful to do it on another floor, not the floor I lived on, because we didn't want my parents to see. And then he said, "Aay, Geraldine Rizzoli, will you marry me?" and I said, "Yeah, Vito, I will." So then we went into the staircase of the building and he brushed off one of the steps for me and we sat down together and started talking seriously about our future and he said, "Aay, you know, Vinny and Bobby and Richie and me, it's a gas being Vito and the Olinvilles and singing those doo-wop numbers, but I'm no fool, I know we'll never be rich or famous. So I'll keep singing for a couple more years, and then I'll get into some other line of work and then we'll have kids, okay?" And I said sure, it was okay with me if he wanted to sing for a few years until we started our family. Then I told him that Mr. Pampino at the Evander Sweet Store had offered me a job behind the counter which meant that I could start saving money right away. "Aay, Geraldine, you're no fool," he said. He gave me the thumbs up sign and we kissed. Then he said, "Aay, Geraldine, let's do it again, right here in the staircase," and he started pulling off his tux, but I said I wasn't that kind of girl, so he just walked me to my door and we said good night. We agreed that we wouldn't announce our engagement until we each had a little savings account of our own. That way our parents couldn't say we were too young and irresponsible and try to stop the wedding, which my father, who was very hot-tempered, was likely to do.

The very next morning, Vito's agent called him and woke him up and said that *Teenage Heartbreak* was actually going to get played on the radio, on WMCA by The Good Guys, at eight o'clock that night. That afternoon, we were all hanging out with the crowd and Vito and Vinny and Bobby and Richie were going crazy and they were shouting, "Aay, everyone, WMCA, all right!" and stamping their feet and threatening to punch each other out and give each other noogies on the tops of their heads. Soon everyone on Olinville Ave. knew, and at eight o'clock it was like another holy miracle, everyone on the block had their windows open and we all blasted our radios so that even the angels in Heaven had to have heard Vito and the Olinvilles singing *Teenage Heartbreak* that night, which, like I said, was written especially for me, Geraldine Rizzoli. Vito invited me to listen with him and his mother and father and his older brother Danny in their apartment. We hadn't told them we were engaged, though. Vito just said, "Aay, ma, Geraldine Rizzoli here wants to listen to *Teenage Heartbreak* on WMCA with us, okay?" His mother looked at me and nodded, and I had a feeling that she guessed that Vito and I were in love and that in her own way she was saying, "Welcome, my future daughter-in-law, welcome." So we sat around the kitchen table with the radio set up like a centerpiece and his mother and I cried when it came on and his father and Danny kept swearing in Italian and Vito just kept combing his pompadour with this frozen grin on his face. When it was over, everyone on the block came pounding on the door shouting, "Aay, Vito, open up, you're a star!" and we opened the door and we had a big party and everyone danced the lindy and the cha cha all over the Venecios's apartment.

Three days later *Teenage Heartbreak* made it to number one on the charts, which was just unbelievable, like twenty thousand holy miracles combined, especially considering how the guidance counselor at Evander Childs used to predict that Vito would end up in prison. The disk jockeys kept saying things like "these four boys from the streets of the Bronx are a phenomenon, ladies and gentleman, a genuine phenomenon!" Vito's mother saw my mother at Mass and told her that she'd been visited by an angel in white when she was pregnant with Vito and the angel told her, "Mrs. Venecio, you will have a son and this son shall be a great man!"

A week later Vito and the Olinvilles got flown out to L.A. to appear in those beach party movies, and Vito didn't even call me to say goodbye. So I sat in my room and cried a lot, but after a couple of weeks, I decided to chin up and accept my fate, because, like Vito said, I was no fool. Yeah, it was true that I was a ruined woman, labeled forever as a tramp, me, Geraldine Rizzoli, who'd made out with so many of the boys at Evander Childs High School, but who'd always been so careful never to let any of them into my pants, here I'd gone and done it with Vito Venecio who'd turned out to be a two-faced liar, only interested in money and fame. Dumb, dumb, dumb, Geraldine, I thought. And I couldn't tell my parents because my father would have taken his life savings, I swear, and flown out to L.A. and killed Vito. And I couldn't even tell Pamela and Carmela and Victoria, because we'd pricked our fingers with sewing needles and made a pact sealed in blood that although we would make out with lots of boys, we would stay virgins until we got married. So whenever I got together with them and they talked about how unbelievable it was that skinny little Vito with the acne and the greasy pompadour had become so rich and famous, I would agree and try to act just like them, like I was just so proud that Vito and Vinny and Bobby and Richie were now millionaires. And after a month or so I started feeling pretty strong and I thought, ok, Vito, you bastard, you want to dump Geraldine Rizzoli, tough noogies to you, buddy. I was working at the Evander Sweet Store during the day and I'd begun making out with some of the guys in the crowd in the evenings again, even though my heart wasn't in it. But I figured that one day someone else's kisses might make me feel the way that Vito's kisses had made me feel, and I'd never know who it would be unless I tried it.

And then one night I was helping my mother with the supper dishes, which I did every single night since, like I said, in my own way, I was a good Catholic girl, when the phone rang and my mother said, "Geraldine, it's for you. It's Vito Venecio calling from Los Angeles," and she looked at me like she was suspicious about why Vito, who'd been trying to get into my pants all those years when he wasn't famous and I wouldn't give him the time of day, would still be calling me at home now that he was famous and could have his pick of girls. When she'd gone back into the kitchen, I picked up the phone but my hands were so wet and soapy that I could hardly hold onto the receiver. Vito said, "Aay, Geraldine Rizzoli," and his voice sounded like he was around the corner, but I knew he was really three thousand miles away surrounded by those silly looking bimbos from the beach party movies. "Aay, forgive me, Geraldine," he said, "I've been a creep, I know, I got carried away by all this money and fame crap but it's you I want, you and the old gang and my old life on Olinville Ave."

I didn't say anything, I was so angry and confused. And my hands were still so wet and soapy.

"Aay, Geraldine, will you wait for me?" Vito said, and he sounded like a little lost boy. "Please Geraldine, I'll be back, this ain't gonna last long, promise me, you'll wait for me as long as it takes."

"I don't know, Vito," I said, desperately trying to hold onto the phone, and now my hands were even wetter because I was crying and my tears were landing on them, "you could have called sooner."

"Aay, I know," he said, "this fame stuff, it's like a drug. But I'm coming home to you, Geraldine. Promise me you'll wait for me."

And he sounded so sad, and I took a deep breath, and I said, "I promise, Vito. I promise." And then the phone slipped from my grasp and hit the floor, and my mother yelled from the kitchen, "Geraldine, if you don't know how to talk on the phone without making a mess all over the floor, then don't talk on the phone!" I shouted, "I'm sorry, Ma!" but when I picked it up again, Vito was gone.

So the next day behind the counter at the Evander Sweet Store, I started making plans. I needed my independence. I knew I'd have to get an apartment so that when Vito came back, I'd be ready for him. But that night when I told my parents I was going to get my own apartment they raised holy hell. My mother was so furious she didn't even ask whether it had something to do with Vito's call. In fact, she never spoke to me about Vito after that, which makes me think that deep down she knew. The thing was, whether she knew or didn't know, seventeen-year-old Italian girls from the Bronx did not leave home until a wedding ring was around their finger, period. Even girls who cut classes and smoked and cursed. My parents sent me to talk to a priest at the Immaculate Conception Church, which was right next door to the Immaculate Conception School, the parking lot of which was where I gave myself to Vito in the back seat of his older brother Danny's best friend Freddy's car, and the priest said, "Geraldine Rizzoli, my child, your parents tell me that you wish to leave their home before you marry. Child, why do you wish to do such a thing, which reeks of the desire to commit sin?"

I shrugged and looked away, trying hard not to pop my chewing gum. I didn't want to seem too disrespectful, but that priest got nowhere with me. I was going to wait for Vito, and I needed to have my own apartment ready for him so the instant he got back we could start making love again and get married and start a family. And besides, even though the priest kept calling me a child, I'd been a woman ever since I let Vito into my pants. I ran my fingers through my hair trying to make the teased parts stand up even higher while the priest went on and on about Mary Magdalene. But I had my own spiritual mission which had nothing to do with the church, and finally I couldn't help it, a big gum bubble went pop real loudly in my mouth and the priest called me a hellion and said I was beyond his help. So I got up and left, pulling the pieces of gum off my lips.

The priest told my father that the only solution was to chain me up in my bedroom. But my mother and father, bless their hearts, may have been Catholic and Italian and hot tempered, but they were good people, so instead they got my father's best friend, Pop Giordano, who'd been like an uncle to me ever since I was in diapers, to rent me an apartment in the building he owned. And the building just happened to be on Olinville Ave, right next door to my parents' building. So they were happy enough. I insisted on a two bedroom right from the start so that Vito wouldn't feel cramped when he came back, not that I told them why I needed that much room. "A two bedroom," my mother kept repeating. "Suddenly my daughter is such a grown up she wants a two bedroom!"

So Pop gave me the biggest two bedroom in the building and I moved in, and Pop promised my father to let him know if I kept late hours, and my father said he'd kill me if I did, but I wasn't worried about that. My days of making out with the boys of Olinville Ave. were over. I would wait for Vito, and I would live like a nun until he returned to me.

My mother even ended up helping me decorate the apartment, and to make her happy I hung a velour painting of Jesus above the sofa in the living room. I didn't think Vito would mind too much since his mother had one in her living room too. I didn't intend to call Vito or write him to give him my new address. He'd be back soon enough and he'd figure out where I was.

And I began to wait. But a couple of weeks after I moved into the apartment I couldn't take not telling anyone. I felt like I'd scream or do something crazy if I didn't confide in someone. So I told Pop. Pop wore shiny black suits and black shirts with white ties and a big diamond ring on his pinky finger and he didn't have a steady job like my father who delivered hot dogs by truck to restaurants all over the Bronx, or like Vito's father who was a construction worker. I figured that if anyone knew the way the world worked, it was Pop. He promised he'd never tell, and he twirled his black mustache and said, "Geraldine Rizzoli, you're like my own daughter, like my flesh and blood, and I'm sorry you lost your cherry before you got married but if you want to wait for Vito, wait."

So I settled in to my new life and I waited. That was the period that Vito kept turning out hit songs and making beach party movies and I'd hear him interviewed on the radio and he never sounded like the Vito I knew. It sounded like someone else had written his words for him. He'd get all corny and sentimental about the Bronx, and about how his heart was still there, and he'd say all these sappy things about the fish market on the corner of Olinville Ave., but that was such crap, because Vito never shopped for food. His mother did all the shopping, Vito wouldn't be caught dead in the Olinville fish market, except maybe to mooch a cigarette off of Carmine Casella, who worked behind the counter. Vito didn't even like fish. And I felt sad and worried for him. He'd become a kind of doo-wop robot, he and the Olinvilles, mouthing other people's words. I noticed that he'd even stopped writing songs after *Teenage Heartbreak*. Sometimes I could hardly stand waiting for him. But on Olinville Ave., a promise was a promise. People had been found floating face down in the Bronx River for breaking smaller promises than that. Besides, I still loved Vito.

Pamela married Johnny Ciccarone, Carmela married Ricky Giampino, and Victoria married Sidney Goldberg, from the Special Progress Accelerated class, which was a big surprise, and they all got apartments in the neighborhood. But after a year or two they all moved away, either to neighborhoods where the Puerto Ricans and blacks weren't starting to move in, or to Yonkers or Mount Vernon, and they started to have babies and I'd visit them once or twice with gifts but it was like we didn't have much in common any more, and soon we all lost touch.

And Vito and the Olinvilles kept turning out hits, even though like I said, Vito never wrote another song after *Teenage Heartbreak*. In addition to the doo-wop numbers, Vito had begun letting loose on some slow, sexy ballads. I bought their forty fives and I bought their albums and every night after work I would call up the radio stations and request their songs, not that I needed to, since everyone else was requesting their songs, anyway, but it made me feel closer to Vito, I guess. And sometimes I'd look at Vito's photograph on the album covers or in the fan magazines and I'd see how his teeth and hair and skin were perfect, there was no gap between his front teeth like there used to be, no more acne, no more cowlick. And I kind of missed those things, because that night when I gave myself to Vito in the back seat of his older brother Danny's best friend Freddy's car, I'd loved feeling Vito's rough, sandpapery skin against mine and I'd loved letting my fingers play with his cowlick and letting my tongue rest for a minute in the gap between his front teeth.

So, for the next three, four years, I kind of lost count, Vito and the Olinvilles ruled the airwaves. And every day I worked at the Evander Sweet Store and every night I had dinner with my parents and my mother would ask whether I was ever going to get married and have babies and I'd say, "Come on, Ma, leave me alone, I'm a good Catholic girl, of course I'm gonna have babies one day," and my father would say, "Geraldine, if Pop ever tells me you're keeping late hours with any guys, I'll kill you," and I'd say, "Come on, Pa, I told you, I'm a good Catholic girl," and then I'd help my mother with the dishes and then I'd kiss them goodnight and I'd go visit Pop for a few minutes in his apartment on the ground floor of the building and there would always be those strange men coming and going from his apartment and then I'd go upstairs to my own apartment and I'd sit in front of my mirror and I'd tease my hair up high and I'd put on my makeup and I'd put on my red prom dress and I'd listen to Vito's songs and I'd dance the lindy and the cha cha. And then before I went to sleep, I'd read through all the fan mags and I'd cut out every article about him and I'd paste them into my scrapbook.

Then one day, I don't remember exactly when, a couple of more years, maybe three, maybe even four, all I remember is that Carmela and Pamela and Victoria had all sent me announcements that they were on their second kids, the fan mags started printing fewer and fewer articles about Vito. I'd sit on my bed, thumbing through, and where before, I'd find at least one in every single mag, now I'd have to go through five, six, seven magazines and then I'd just find some real small mention of him. And the radio stations were playing Vito and the Olinvilles less and less often and I had to call in and request them more often because nobody else was doing it, and their songs weren't going higher than numbers fifteen or twenty on the charts. But Vito's voice was as strong and beautiful as ever, and the Olinvilles could still do those doo-wops in the background, so at first I felt really dumb, dumb, dumb because I couldn't figure out what was going on.

But I, Geraldine Rizzoli, am no fool, and it hit me soon enough. It was really simple. The girls my age were all mothers raising kids, and they didn't have time to buy records and dance the lindy and the cha cha in front of their mirrors. And the boys, they were out all day working and at night they sat and drank beer and watched football on t.v. So a new generation of teenagers was buying records. And they were buying records by those British groups, the Beatles and the rest of them, and for those kids, I guess, an Italian boy from the Bronx with a pompadour wasn't very interesting. And even though I didn't look a day older than I had that night in the back seat of Vito's older brother Danny's best friend Freddy's car, and even though I could still fit perfectly into my red prom dress, I had to face facts, too. I wasn't a teenager any more.

So more time went by, again I lost count, but Pop's hair was beginning to turn grey and my father was beginning to have a hard time lifting those crates of hot dogs and my mother seemed to be getting shorter day by day, and Vito and the Olinvilles never got played on the radio at all, period. And I felt bad for Vito, but mostly I was relieved, since I was sure then that he would come home. I bought new furniture, Pop put in new windows. I found a hairspray that made my hair stay higher even longer.

But I was wrong. Vito didn't come home. Instead, according to the few fan mags that ran the story, his manager tried to make him into a clean cut type, the type who appeals to the older Las Vegas set. And Vito left the Olinvilles, which, the fan mags said, was like Vito had put a knife through their hearts. One mag said that Vinny had even punched Vito out. Anyway, it was a mistake on Vito's part not to have just come home right then. He made two albums and he sang all these silly love songs from the twenties and thirties, and he sounded really off-key and miserable. After that, whenever I called the disk jockeys they just laughed at me and wouldn't even play his records. I'd have to go through ten or fifteen fan mags to find even a small mention of Vito at all. So I felt even worse for him, but I definitely figured he had to come home then. Where else could he go? So I bought a new rug and Pop painted the wall. And I sat in front of my mirror at night and I teased my hair and I applied my makeup and I put on my red prom dress and I danced the lindy and the cha cha and I played Vito's albums and I'd still cut out the small article here and there and place it in my scrapbook. And I hadn't aged a day. No lines, no wrinkles, no flab, no grey hair. Vito was going to be pleased when he came home.

But I was wrong again. Vito didn't come home. He went and got married to someone else, a skinny flat-chested blonde model from somewhere like Iowa or Idaho. A couple of the fan mags ran little pieces, and they said she was the best thing that had ever happened to Vito. Because of his love for her he wasn't depressed any more about not having any more number one hits. "Aay," he was quoted, "love is worth more than all of the gold records in the world." At first I cried. I kicked the walls. I tore some of the articles from my scrapbook and ripped them to shreds. I smashed some of his albums to pieces. I was really really angry, because I knew that it was me, Geraldine Rizzoli, who was the best thing that had ever happened to him! That blonde model had probably been a real goody-goody when she was growing up, the type who didn't cut classes or smoke or tease her hair or make out with lots of guys. No passion in her skinny bones, I figured. And then I calmed down. Because Vito would still be back. This model, whose name was Muffin Potts, was no threat at all. Vito would be back, a little ashamed of himself, but he'd be back.

Soon after that, Vito's mother and father died. A couple of fan mags carried the story. They died in a plane crash on their way to visit Vito and Muffin Potts in Iowa or Idaho or wherever she was from. I didn't get invited to the funeral, which was in Palm Beach. Vito's parents had moved there only six months after *Teenage Heartbreak* became number one. Five big moving vans had parked on Olinville Ave., and Vito's mother stood there in a fur coat telling everybody about the angel who'd visited her when she was pregnant with Vito. And I'd gone up to her and kissed her and said, "Good bye, Mrs. Venecio, I'm going to miss you," and she said, "Good bye, Carmela," like she was trying to pretend that she didn't remember that I was Geraldine Rizzoli, her future daughter in law. The fan mags had a picture of Vito at the funeral in a three piece suit, and the articles said he cried on the shoulder of his older brother Danny, who was now a distributor of automobile parts. There were also a couple of photos of Muffin Potts looking very bored.

Then I started to read little rumors, small items, in a few of the magazines. First, that Vito's marriage was on the rocks. No surprise to me there. I was surprised that it lasted an hour. Second, that Vito was heavy into drugs and that his addiction was breaking Muffin's heart. Really hard drugs, the mags said. The very worst stuff. One of the mags said it was because of his mother's death and they called him a "Mama's Boy." One said he was heartbroken because of his break-up with the Olinvilles and because Vinny had punched him out. And one said he'd been doing drugs ever since Evander Childs High School, and they had the nerve to call the school a "zoo," which I resented. But I knew a few things. One, Vito was no Mama's Boy. Two, Vito and the Olinvilles still all loved each other. And, three, Vito had never touched drugs in school. And if it were true that he was drowning his sorrows in drugs and breaking Muffin Pott's heart, it was because he missed me and regretted like hell not coming home earlier!

Soon after that I read that Muffin had left him for good and had taken their child with her. Child? I stared at the print. Ashley, the article said. Their child's name was Ashley. There was no photo, and since Ashley was a name with zero personality, I wasn't sure whether Ashley was a girl or boy. I decided it was a girl, and I figured she looked just like her mother, with pale skin and a snub nose and milky-colored hair, and I wasn't even slightly jealous of that child or her mother because they were just mistakes. True, Vito kept acting dumb, dumb, dumb, and making some big fat mistakes, but I didn't love him any less. A promise was a promise. And I, Geraldine Rizzoli, knew enough to forgive him. Because the truth was that even I had once made a mistake. The way it happened was this. One day out of the blue, who should come into the Evander Sweet Store to buy some cigarettes but Petey Cioffi, who'd been one of the guys in our crowd in the old days. A couple of years after graduation he married some girl from the Grand Concourse and we all lost touch. But here he was in the old neighborhood, visiting some cousins and he needed some cigarettes. Anyway, when he walked in, he stopped dead in his tracks. I could tell he was a little drunk, and he said, "Aay, Geraldine Rizzoli, I can't believe my eyes, you're still here, and you're gorgeous, I'm growing old and fat, look at this belly, but not you, you're like a Princess or something." And it was so good to be spoken to like that, and I let him come home with me. We made out in my elevator, and I felt like a kid again. I couldn't pretend he was Vito, but I could pretend it was the old days, when Vito was still chasing me and trying to get into my pants. In the morning, Petey said goodbye, looked at me one last time, shook his head and said, "Geraldine Rizzoli, what a blast from the past!" and he slipped out of the building before Pop woke up. He probably caught holy hell from his wife and I swear I got my first and only grey hair the next morning. But my night with Petey Cioffi made it easier to forgive Vito, since I'd made my mistake too. And I kept waiting. The neighborhood changed around me. The Italians left, and more and more Puerto Ricans and blacks moved in, but I didn't mind. Because everyone has to live somewhere, I figured, and I had more important things on my mind than being prejudiced.

Then I pretty much stopped hearing about Vito altogether. And that was around when my father, bless his heart, had the heart attack on the hot dog truck and by the time they found him it was too late to save him, and my mother, bless her heart, followed soon after. I missed them so much, and every night I came home from work and I teased my hair at the mirror, I put on my makeup, I put on my red prom dress, I played Vito's songs, I danced the lindy and the cha cha, and I read through the fan mags looking for some mention of him, but there wasn't any. It was like he had vanished from the face of the earth. And then one day I came across a small item in the newspaper. It was about how Vito had just gotten arrested on Sunset Strip for possession of hard drugs, and how he was bailed out by Vinny of the Olinvilles, who was now a real estate salesman in Santa Monica. "I did it for old times sake," Vinny said, "for the crowd on Olinville Ave."

The next morning, Pop called me to his apartment. He had the beginnings of cataracts by then and he hardly ever looked at the newspaper anymore, but of course, he'd spotted the article about Vito. His face was red. He was furious. He shouted, "Geraldine Rizzoli, you're like my own daughter, my own flesh and blood, and I never wanted to have to say this to you, but," he waved the newspaper ferociously, which was impressive, since his hands shook, and he weighed all of ninety pounds at this point, although he still dressed in his shiny black suits and those strange men still came and went from his apartment, "the time has come for you to forget Vito. If he was here I'd beat the living hell out of him." He flung the paper across the room and sat in his chair breathing heavily.

I waited a minute before I spoke just to make sure he was going to be okay. When his color returned to normal, I said, "Never, Pop. I promised Vito I'd wait."

"You should marry Ralphie."

"Ralphie?" I asked. Ralphie Pampino, who was part of the old crowd, too, had inherited the Evander Sweet Store from his father when Ralphie Sr. died the year before. It turns out that Ralphie Jr., who'd never married, was in love with me, and had been for years. Poor Ralphie. He'd been the kind of guy who never got to make out a whole lot. I'd always thought he looked at me so funny because he was constipated or had sinuses or something. But Pop told me that years ago Ralphie had poured out his heart to him. Although Pop had promised Ralphie that he'd never betray his confidence, the time had come. It seemed that Ralphie had his own spiritual mission: he was waiting for me. I was touched. Ralphie was such a sweet guy. I promised myself to start being nicer to him. I asked Pop to tell him about me and Vito, and I kissed Pop on the nose and I went back upstairs to my apartment and I sat in front of my mirror and I teased my hair and I put on my make-up and I put on my red prom dress and I listened to Vito's songs and I danced the lindy and the cha cha.

The next day, Ralphie came over to me and said, "Geraldine Rizzoli, I had no idea that you and Vito . . . " and he got all choked up and couldn't finish. Finally, he swallowed and said, "Aay, Geraldine, I'm on your side. I really am. Vito's coming back!" and he gave me the thumbs up sign and he and I did the lindy together right there in the Evander Sweet Store and we sang *Teenage Heartbreak* at the top of our lungs and we didn't care if any customers came in and saw us.

But after that there wasn't any more news about Vito, period. Most everyone on the block who'd known Vito and the Olinvilles was gone, and I just kept waiting. Just around that time an oldies radio station, WAAY, started up and it was pretty weird at first to think that Vito and the Olinvilles and all the other groups I had spent my life listening to were considered "oldies" and I'd look at myself in the mirror and I'd think, "Geraldine Rizzoli, you're nobody's oldie, you've got the same skin and figure you had the night that you gave yourself to Vito." But after awhile I got used to the idea of the oldies and I listened to WAAY as often as I could. I played it every morning first thing when I woke up and then Ralphie and I listened to it together at the Evander Sweet Store, even though most of the kids who came in were carrying those big radio boxes turned to salsa or rap songs or punk and didn't seem to have any idea that there was already music on. Sometimes when nobody was in the store, Ralphie and I would just sing Vito's songs together. There was one d.j. on the station, Goldie George, who was on from nine in the morning until noon and he was a real fan of Vito and the Olinvilles. The other d.j.s had their favorites too. Doo Wop Dick liked the Five Satins, Surfer Sammy liked the Beach Boys, but Goldie George said he'd grown up in the Bronx just two subway stops away from Olinville Ave. and that he and his friends had all felt as close to Vito as if they'd lived on Olinville Ave. themselves, even though they'd never met Vito or Vinny or Bobby or Richie. I liked Goldie George, and I wished he'd been brave enough to have taken the subway the two stops over so that he could have hung around with us. He might have been fun to make out with. One day Goldie George played thirty minutes straight of Vito and the Olinvilles, with no commercial interruptions, and then some listener called in and said "Aay, whatever happened to Vito anyway, Goldie George, he was some sort of junkie, right?"

"Yeah," Goldie George said, "but I'm Vito's biggest fan, like you all know, because I grew up only two subway stops away from Olinville Ave. and I used to feel like I was a close buddy of Vito's even though I never met him, and I happen to know that he's quit doing drugs and that he's found peace and happiness through the Chinese practice of Tai Chi and he helps run a mission in Bakersfield, California."

"Aay," the caller said, "Goldie George, you tell Vito for me that Bobby MacNamara from Woodside says, 'Aay, Vito, keep it up, man!'"

"I will," Goldie George said, "I will. I'll tell him about you, Bobby, because, being so close to Vito in my soul when I was growing up, I happen to know that Vito still cares about his loyal fans. In fact, I know that one of the things that helped Vito to get through the hard times was knowing how much his loyal fans cared. And, aay, Bobby, what's your favorite radio station?"

"AAY!" Bobby shouted.

And then Goldie George played another uninterrupted thirty minutes of Vito and the Olinvilles. But I could hardly hear the music this time. I was sick to my stomach. What the hell was Vito doing in Bakersfield, California running a mission? I was glad he wasn't into drugs any more, but Bakersfield, California? A mission? And what the hell was Tai Chi? I was so pissed off. For the first time I wondered whether he'd forgotten my promise. I was ready to fly down to Bakersfield and tell him a thing or two, but I didn't. I went home, played my albums, danced, teased my hair, frowned at the one grey hair I'd gotten the night I was with Petey Cioffi, and I closed my eyes and leaned my head on my arms. Vito was coming back. He just wasn't ready yet.

About two weeks later I was behind the counter at the Evander Sweet Store and Ralphie was arranging some Chunkies into a pyramid when Goldie George said, "Guess what, everyone, all of us here at the station, but mostly Vito's biggest fan, me, Goldie George, have arranged for Vito to come back to his home town! This is Big Big Big Big News! I called him the other day and I said, 'Vito, I grew up two subway stops from you, and like you know, I'm your biggest fan, and you owe it to me and your other loyal fans from the Bronx and all the other boroughs to come back and visit and sing *Teenage Heartbreak* for us one more time,' and I swear Vito got choked up over the phone and he agreed to do it, even though he said that he usually doesn't sing any more because it interferes with his Tai Chi, but I said, 'Vito, we love you here at AAY, man, and wait'll you hear this, we're going to book Carnegie Hall for you, Vito, not your grandmother's attic, but Carnegie Hall!' How about that, everyone. And just so you all know, the Olinvilles are all doing their own things now, so it'll just be Vito alone, but hey, that's okay, that's great, Vito will sing the oldies and tickets go on sale next week!"

And I stood there frozen and Ralphie and I stared at each other across the counter, and I could see a look in his eyes that told me that he knew he'd finally lost me for good this time.

Because Vito was coming back. He may have told Goldie George that he was coming home to sing to his fans, but Ralphie and I both knew that it was really me, Geraldine Rizzoli, that he was finally ready to come back to. Vito worked in mysterious ways, and I figured that he finally felt free of the bad things, the drugs and that boring Muffin Potts and his own arrogance and excessive pride, and now he was pure enough to return to me. I wasn't wild about this Tai Chi stuff, whatever it was, but I could get used to it if it had helped Vito to get better so he could come home to me.

Ralphie sort of shook himself like he was coming out of some long sleep or trance. Then he came around the counter and put his arm around me in this brotherly way. "Geraldine Rizzoli," he said really softly, "my treat. A first row seat at Carnegie Hall."

But I wouldn't accept, even though it was such a beautiful thing for Ralphie to offer to do, considering how he'd felt about me all those years. I got teary-eyed. But I didn't need a ticket, not me, not Geraldine Rizzolli. Vito would find out where I lived and he'd come and pick me up and take me himself to Carnegie Hall. He'd probably come in a limo paid for by the station, I figured. Because the only way I was going to the concert was with Vito. I went home after work and I plucked the one grey hair from my scalp and then I teased my hair and I put on my makeup and I put on my red prom dress and I danced and sang.

All week Goldie George kept saying, "It's unbelievable, tickets were sold out within an hour! The calls don't stop coming, you all remember Vito, you all love him!"

On the night of the concert Pop came by. He had to use a walker to get around by then and he was nearly blind and lots of things were wrong. His liver, gall bladder, stomach, you name it. He weighed around seventy-five pounds. But he still wore his shiny black suits and the men kept coming in and out of his apartment. And he sat across from me on my sofa, beneath the velour painting of Jesus, and he said in a raspy voice, "Geraldine Rizzolli, I didn't ever want to have to say this, but you're like my own daughter, my own flesh and blood, and as long as Vito wasn't around, I figured, okay you can dance to his albums and tease your hair and wear the same clothes all the time and you're none the worse for it, but now that he's coming home I've got to tell you he won't be coming for you, Geraldine, if he cared a twit about you he would have flown you out to L.A. way back when and I'm sorry you let him into your pants and lost your cherry to him, but you're a middle-aged lady now and you're gonna get hurt real bad and I'm glad your mother and father, bless their souls, aren't around to see you suffer the way you're gonna suffer tonight, Geraldine, and I don't wanna see it either, what I want is for you to drive down to Maryland tonight real fast, right now, and marry Ralphie, before Vito breaks your heart so bad nothing will ever put it together again!"

I'd never seen Pop so riled up. I kissed him on the nose and I told him he was sweet, but that Vito was coming. And Pop left, shaking his head and walking slowly, moving the walker ahead of him, step by step, and after he left, I played my albums and I teased my hair and I applied my lipstick and I danced the lindy and the cha cha and I waited. I figured that everyone from the old crowd would be at the concert. They'd come in from the suburbs with their husbands and their wives and their children, and even, I had to face facts, in some cases, their grandchildren. And just then there was a knock on my door and I opened it and there he was. He'd put on some weight, but not much, and although he'd lost some hair he still had a pompadour and he was holding some flowers for me, and I noticed that they were red roses, which I knew he'd chosen to match my prom dress. And he said, "Aay, Geraldine Rizzoli, thanks for waiting." Then he looked at his watch. "All *right*, let's get a move on! Concert starts at nine." And I looked in the mirror one last time, sprayed on a little more hairspray and that was it. Vito took my arm just the way he took it the night I gave myself to him in the back seat of his older brother Danny's best friend Freddy's car, and we went downtown by limo to Carnegie Hall, which was a real treat because I didn't get to go into Manhattan very often. And Carnegie Hall was packed, standing room only, and the crowd was yelling, "Aay, Vito! Aay, Vito! Aay, Vito!" and Pamela and Carmela and Victoria were there, and all the Olinvilles came and they hugged Vito and said there were no hard feelings, and Vinny and Vito even gave each other noogies on the tops of their heads, and everyone said, "Geraldine Rizzoli, you haven't aged a day." Then Goldie George introduced Vito, and Vito just got right up there on the stage and he belted out those songs, and at the end of the concert, for his finale, he sang *Teenage Heartbreak* and he called me up on stage with him and he held my hand and looked into my eyes while he sang. I even sang along on a few of the verses and I danced the lindy and the cha cha right there on stage in front of all those people. The crowd went wild, stamping their feet and shouting for more, and Goldie George was crying, and after the concert Vito and I went back by limo to Olinville Ave. and Vito gave the limo driver a big tip and the driver said, "Aay, Vito, welcome home," and then he drove away.

And ever since then Vito has been here with me in the two bedroom apartment. He still does Tai Chi, but it's really no big thing, an hour or two in the morning at most. Pop died last year and Vito and I were with him at the end and his last words were, "You two kids, you're like my own son and daughter." Vito works in the Evander Sweet Store now instead of me because I've got to stay home to take care of Vito Jr. and Little Pop, who have a terrific godfather in Ralphie and a great uncle in Vito's older brother, Danny. And, if I'm allowed to do a little bragging, which seems only fair after all this time, Vito Jr. and Little Pop are very good kids. They go to church on Sundays and they're doing real well in school because they never cut classes or smoke in the bathroom or curse, and Vito and I are as proud as we can be.

Eidus on Transferring Personal Experience Into Fiction
Developing the Idea

It was Geraldine's voice that came to me first—early one morning about ten years ago. As I poured myself a cup of coffee, I heard the voice of Geraldine inside my head. I didn't know her name yet, but there she was, generously and earnestly offering me hairstyling tips based on her own regime: "I set my black hair with beer cans every night," she declared.

This sudden and unexpected "visitation" brought me back to my childhood in the Bronx. I remembered riding in an elevator with an older girl whom I'd seen a few times in the neighborhood. She looked down at me and asked, "Wanna know how I get my hair to look like this?" I stared at her brittle dome of hair, adorned by a red satin bow above her bangs. "I set it with beer cans every night," she said.

Of course, back then, I had no idea, as a Jewish girl growing up in the Bronx, I would grow up to be a writer, and that one day the words of that tough-cookie, teased-hair girl in the elevator would appear in a story of mine. Yet, here I was, sitting at the breakfast table, nursing a cup of coffee, hearing her voice in my head.

Within moments, I was writing down her words. As I wrote, I found myself weaving a lot of rock & roll into Geraldine's story. Rock & roll has always been important to me; as a little kid I loved the doo-wop music that my sister and brother, and the kids like Geraldine, all loved. To my great pleasure, Vito himself emerged from the rock & roll imagery—a wannabe doo-wop singer, loosely inspired by the pompadoured-and-leather-jacketed boys I'd seen singing their hearts out on street corners, all hoping to become the next Dion & The Belmonts. Once Vito appeared on the scene, "Vito Loves Geraldine" evolved into a humorous, romantic Bronx fairy tale/love story, replete with all the angst, tumult, lust, and glory every bona-fide love story should have.

Using Autobiography to Create Fiction

Fiction is enriched by that which is "real." Reality enables writers to ground their prose with authenticity and the logic of everyday life. Fiction that feels authentic and true does so because it *reflects* truth—not necessarily the truth of hair color or verbatim dialogue, but, rather, the greater truth of passion, ideas, and ideals.

Many incidents and characters in my fiction, while based upon things I remember, are transformed. Sometimes they're subtly transformed (a few new details to conceal the identity of an old friend), and other times they're radically transformed, as in Geraldine's case, since her inspiration is a girl with whom I spoke only briefly, although I so vividly recalled her thick black hair, the flowery, almost cloying, scent of her perfume, and her skin-tight, hot-pink, pedal-pusher pants.

I kept a very detailed diary from the time I was a small child until I finished graduate school. These diaries served me as a fiction writer in a number of ways: they helped me to become a disciplined writer; they forced me to analyze the psychological insights I had into myself and others; and finally they served to jog my memory about specific events in my life. Occasionally I found that pieces of my diary inspired the first line of a story.

Beginning to Write

Often, I compose first drafts in longhand, using my favorite pen. Sometimes I write while tipping back in a comfortable leather recliner. At other times, I write in a local café. In these early drafts, I make giant, illogical leaps. I give in to hokey dialogue, exaggerated action, ellipses and hyphens, notes for later scenes. I just need to get the ideas out on the page—good details, bad details, all of it. These are indulgences I allow myself because later when I reread what I've written, I will find, amidst all this "stuff," a few phrases, images, bits of dialogue, and ideas worth keeping.

My subsequent drafts are very different from my first drafts. It's then that I labor over voice, plot, story arc, and extension of metaphors. I also read my work aloud to make sure that the language is efficient, rhythmic, and musical, and that it complements theme and character. Reading my work aloud also slows me down, forces me to reexamine each word.

As I'm working on these early drafts I ask myself a number of questions to make sure I'm on the right track, that these scenes have a good chance of becoming a story. I also ask my writing students to answer these questions about their work-in-progress.

1. Are your characters three dimensional, fully developed? Would you be able to have a conversation with them off the page?

2. Is genuine emotion evoked in the reader? Will your reader be moved to laughter, perhaps, or to tears?

3. What does the main character *want*? What is his/her goal? What is the conflict? Every protagonist must have a need, a dream, a scheme, a yearning.

4. What obstacles prevent your character from getting what he or she wants? Good fiction presents characters with desires they can't easily fulfill. Just consider *Romeo and Juliet*.

5. What are the stakes? Or think of it this way: why should this story matter, not only to the characters, but also to readers?

Writing Suggestions

1. Eidus claims that the inspiration for "Vito Loves Geraldine" came, in part, from her own life, specifically an experience she had "in an elevator with an older girl whom I'd seen a few times in the neighborhood." Like Eidus, select one person from your hometown whom you casually know. This can be a person from your high school, a summer job, your neighborhood, a local store, etc. For one to two pages, speak in this person's voice, creating a scene in which something important happens. Before writing, review Eidus's early-draft checklist (above) to help guide your work. Do your best to capture this person's voice through word choice and syntax. (Variation: Listen to a radio call-in show and select one caller whose voice, for you, suggests an interesting character. For one to two pages, write in this person's voice, doing your best to develop your memory of the caller into a complete character.)

2. Before beginning your next story, draw an illustration for each scene. Pay attention to character staging, background setting, as well as how these elements play into plot issues. Think of this as a movie storyboard or comic book panel, where one scene logically leads to the next. You don't need to be an artist to make this work—what matters is working visually through the overall arc of your story. Before beginning to write the story, lay your illustrations out on a table and use each drawing like magnetic poetry squares. Try removing the first scene and see how it affects the entire story. Try removing the last. Think of these illustrations as an alternative to outlining your story in writing and as an opportunity to work out the internal logic and any potential plots kinks. (Variation: Use images from advertisements or art and photography books as panels in the above assignment.)

3. Eidus refers to her story as a "romantic Bronx fairy tale." Retell a fairy tale, myth, or legend in a contemporary setting. For example, the movie *Pretty Woman* is a modern-day revision of the Cinderella story, as is the movie *Ever After*. George

Saunders's "The 400 lb. C.E.O." (from *CivilWarLand in Bad Decline*) is a retelling of the Beauty and the Beast tale. Feel free to break from the structure of the original fairy tale if it helps your story. Because the plot is suggested from an outside source, focus your attention on developing a believable, three-dimensional protagonist who will elicit reader sympathy. (Variation: Select your character and plot from one of the Brothers Grimm tales, which are a drastic shift in tone and content from the family-oriented Disney or Warner Brothers' versions.)

4. In the library, read the first sentences of ten or more stories. You can find dozens of short stories in anthologies (such as the *Best American Short Stories* and *Prize Stories: The O. Henry Awards* series), magazines (such as *The Atlantic Monthly* and *The New Yorker*), and literary journals (such as *The Georgia Review*, *The Paris Review*, and *Ploughshares*). Read only the first sentence. When you find one that intrigues you, take this sentence and finish the rest of the story yourself without having read any more of the original. After you've completed a rough draft, replace the first sentence with one of your own. Consider comparing the entire original story to your own, noticing key differences between the two.

> *Generally speaking, fictional characters have to be on a road that's*
> *going to lead toward some kind of interesting trouble.*
> —Charles Baxter

Section 3

⟨decorative flourish⟩

DISCOVERING STORIES THROUGH OBSERVATION AND RESEARCH

Elizabeth Graver

The Mourning Door

From *Ploughshares, Best American Short Stories 2001*,
and *O. Henry Prize Stories 2001*

The first thing she finds is a hand. In the beginning, she thinks it's a tangle of sheet or a wadded sock caught between the mattress cover and the mattress, a bump the size of a walnut but softer, more yielding. She feels it as she's lying, lazing, in bed. Often, lately, her body keeps her beached, though today the sun beckons, the dogwoods blooming white, the peonies' glossy buds specked black with ants. Tom has gone to work already, backing out of the driveway in his pickup truck. She has taken her temperature on the pink thermometer, noted it down on the graph—98.2, day eighteen, their thirteenth month of trying. She takes it again, to be sure, then settles back in, drifting, though she knows she should get up. The carpenters will be here soon; the air will ring with hammers. The men will find more expensive, unnerving problems with the house. She'll have to creep in her robe to the bathroom, so small and steady, like one of the pests they keep uncovering in this ancient, tilting farmhouse—powder post beetles, termites, carpenter ants.

She feels the bump in the bed the way she might encounter a new mole on her skin, or a scab that had somehow gone unnoticed, her hand traveling vaguely along her body until it stumbles, oh, what's this? With her shin she feels it first, as she turns over, beginning to get up. She sends an arm under the covers, palpates the bump. A pair of bunched panties, maybe, shed during sex and caught beneath the new sheet when she remade the bed? Tom's sock? A wad of tissue? Some unknown object (needle threader, sock darner, butter maker, chaff separator?) left here by the generations of people who came before? The carpenters keep finding things in the walls and under the floor: the sole of an old shoe, a rusted nail, a bent horseshoe. A Depression-era glass bowl, unbroken, the green of key lime pie. Each time they announce another rotted sill, cracked joist, additional repair, they hand an object over, her consolation prize. The house looked so charming from the outside, so fine and perfectly itself. The inspector said, Go ahead, buy it. But you never know what's lurking underneath.

She gets out of the bed, stretches, yawns. Her gaze drops to her naked body, so familiar, the thin freckled limbs and flattish stomach. She has known it forever, lived with it forever. Mostly it has served her well, but lately it seems a foreign, uncooperative thing, at once insolent and lethargic, a taunt. Sometimes, though, she still finds in herself an energy that surprises her, reminding her of when she was a child and used to run—legs churning, pulse throbbing—down the long river path that led to her cousin's house.

Now, in a motion so concentrated it's fierce, she peels off the sheet and flips back the mattress pad. What she sees doesn't surprise her; she's been waiting so hard these days, looking so hard. A hand, it is, a small pink dimpled fist, the skin slightly mottled, the nails the smallest slivers, cut them or they'll scratch. Five fingers. Five nails. She picks it up; it flexes slightly, then curls back into a warm fist. Five fine fingers, none missing. She counts them again to be sure. *You have to begin somewhere*, the books say. *You have to relinquish control and let nature take its course.*

She hears the door open downstairs, the clomp of workboots, words, a barking laugh. Looking around, she spots, on the bedroom floor, the burlap sack that held the dwarf Liberty apple tree Tom planted over the weekend. She drops the hand into the bag, stuffs the bag under the bed. Still the air smells like burlap, thick and dusty. She pulls on some sweatpants, then thinks better of it and puts on a more flattering pair of jeans, and a T-shirt that shows off her breasts. She read somewhere that men are drawn to women with small waists and flaring hips. Evolution, the article said. A body built for birth. Her own hips are small and boyish; her waist does not cinch in. Her pubic hair grows thin and blonde, grass in a drought. She doesn't want these workmen, exactly, but she would like them, for the briefest moment, to want her. As she goes barefoot down the stairs to make a cup of tea and smile at the men, she stops for a moment, struck by a memory of the perfect little hand; even the thought of it makes her gasp. The men won't find it. They're only working in the basement and the attic, structural repairs to keep the house from falling down.

In her kitchen, the three men: Rick and Tony and Joaquin. Their eyes flicker over her. She touches her hair, feels heavy with secret, and looks down. More bad news, I'm afraid, Rick tells her. We found it yesterday, after you left—a whole section of attic. What, she asks. *Charred*, he says dramatically. There must have been a fire; some major support beams are only three quarters their original size. She shakes her head. Really? But the inspector never—. I have my doubts, Rick says, about this so-called inspector of yours. Can you fix it? she asks. He looks at her glumly through heavy-lidded eyes. We can try, he answers. I'll draw up an estimate, but we'll need to finish the basement before we can get to this. Yes, she says vaguely, already bored. Fine, thanks.

Had she received such news the day before, it would have made her dizzy. A charred, unstable attic, a house whittled down by flames. She would have called Tom at work— You're not going to believe this—and checked how much money they had left in their savings account, and thought about suing the inspector and installing more smoke alarms, one in every room, blinking eyes. Today, though, she can't quite concentrate; her thoughts keep returning, as if of their own accord, to what she discovered in her bed. One apricot-sized hand, after thirteen months, after peeing into cups, tracking her temperature, making Tom lie still as a statue after he comes, no saliva, no new positions, her rump tilted high into the air afterward, an absurd position but she doesn't care.

After thirteen months of watching for the LH surge on the ovulation predictor kit—the deep indigo line of a good egg, the watery turquoise of a bad, and inside her own body, waves cresting and breaking, for she has become an ocean, or is it an oceanographer? *Study us hard enough*, the waves call out to her, *watch us closely enough, and we shall do your will*. She has noted the discharge on her underpants—sticky, tacky, scant. Egg white, like she's a chef making meringues or a chicken trying to lay. *Get to know your body*, chant the books, the Web sites, her baby-bearing friends, and oh she has, she does, though it's beginning to feel like a cheap car she has leased for a while and is getting ready to return.

She still likes making love to Tom, the tremble of it, the slow blue wash, the way they lie cupped together in their new, old house as it sits in the greening fields, on the turning earth. It's afterward that she hates. She can never fall asleep without picturing the spastic, thrashing tails, the egg's hard shell, the long, thin tubes stretched like IVs toward a pulsing womb. A speck, she imagines sometimes, the head of a pin, the dot of a period. The End—or maybe, if they're lucky, dot dot dot.

But the hand is so much bigger than that, substantial, real. Her own hands shake with relief as she puts on the tea water. Something is starting—a secret, a discovery, begun not in the narrow recesses of her body but in the mysterious body of her new old house. The house has a door called the Mourning Door—the realtor pointed it out the first time they walked through. It's a door off the front parlor, and though it leads outside, it has no stoop or stairs, just a place for the cart to back up so the coffin could be carried away. Of course babies were born here too, added the realtor, her voice too bright. Probably right in this room! After she and Tom moved in, they decided only to use the door off the kitchen. Friendlier, she said, and after all, they're concentrating, these days, on making life.

When she goes back upstairs, she takes the burlap sack and a flashlight to the warm, musty attic, where Tom almost never goes. With the flashlight's beam, she finds, in one dark corner, the section where the fire left its mark. She touches the wood, and a smudge of ash comes off on her finger. She tastes it: dry powder, ancient fruit, people passing buckets, lives lost, found, lost. She leaves the sack in the other corner of the attic, inside a box marked "Kitchen Stuff." Then she heads downstairs to wash her hands.

Three days later, she is doing laundry when she comes across a shoulder, round and smooth. She knows it should be disconcerting to find such a thing separated from its owner, a shoulder disembodied, lying in a nest of dryer lint, tucked close to the wall. But why get upset? After all, the world is full of parts apart from wholes. A few months ago, she and Tom went to the salvage place—old radiator covers, round church windows, faucets and doorknobs, a spiral staircase leading nowhere. Then, they bought two doors and a useless unit of brass mailboxes, numbers fifteen through twenty-five. Now she wipes her hands on her jeans and picks the shoulder up. It is late afternoon, the contractors gone, Tom still at work. She takes the shoulder up to the attic and puts it in the sack with the hand. Then she goes to the bedroom, swallows a vitamin the size of a horse pill, climbs into bed, and falls asleep.

Whereas before she had been agitated, unable to turn her thoughts away, now she is peaceful, assembling something, proud. But tired too—this is not unexpected; every day by four or five o' clock she has to sink into bed for a nap, let in dreams full of floaty shapes, closed fists, and open mouths. Still, most days she gets a little something done. She lines a trunk with old wallpaper, goes for a walk in the woods with a friend, starts to plan a lesson sequence on how leaves change color in the fall. Her children are all away for the summer, shipped off to lakes and rivers and seas. Sometimes she gets a "Dear Teacher" postcard: *I found some mica. We went on a boat. I lost my ring in the lake.* The water in the postcards is always a vivid, chlorinated blue. She gets her hair cut, sees a matinee movie with her friend Hannah, starts to knit again. One night Tom remarks—perhaps with relief, perhaps with the slightest tinge of fear—that she seems back to her old self.

In the basement, the men put in Lally columns, thick and red, to keep the first floor from falling in. They construct a vapor barrier, rewire the electricity. They sister the joists and patch the foundation. In her bedroom, she stuffs cotton in her ears to block the noise. She wears sweatpants or loose shorts now, and Tom's shirts. Each time she catches a glimpse of herself in the mirror, she is struck by how pretty she looks, her eyes so bright, almost feverish, her fingernails a flushed, excited pink.

She finds a second hand with five perfect fingers, and a second shoulder. She finds a leg, an arm. No eyes yet, no face. Everything in time, she tells herself, and at the Center for Reproductive Medicine they inject her womb with blue and she sees her tubes, thin as violin strings, curled and ghostly on the screen. They have her drink water and lie on her back. They swab gel on her belly, and she neglects to tell them that her actual belly is at home, smelling like dust and applewood, snoozing under the eaves. They say, Come in on day three, on day ten. They swab her with more gel and give her a rattle, loose pills in an amber jar. Tom goes to the clinic, and they shut him in a room with girlie magazines and take his fish. At home, while he is at the doctor's, she finds a tiny penis, sweet and curled. Tom comes home discouraged—rare for him. He lies down on the floor and sighs. She says, Don't worry, babe, and leans to kiss him on the arm. She would like to tell him about everything she has found, but she knows she must protect her secret. Things are so fragile, really—the earth settles, the house shifts. You put up a wall in the wrong place and so never find the hidden object in the eaves. You speak too soon and cause—with your hard, your hopeful words—a clot, a cramp. Things are so fragile, but then also not. Look at the ants, she tells herself—how they always find a place to make a nest. Look at the people of the earth, each one with a mother. At the supermarket, she stares at them—their hands, their faces, how neatly it all goes together, a completed puzzle.

She knows her own way is out of the ordinary, but then what is ordinary these days? She is living in a time of freezers and test tubes, of petri dishes and turkey basters, of trade and barter, test and track, mix and match. Women carry the eggs of other women, or have their own eggs injected back into them pumped with potential, four or six at a time. Sperm are washed and coddled, separated and sifted, like gold. Ovaries are inflated until they spill with treasures. The names sound like code words: GIFT, IUI, ZIFT. Though it upsets her to admit it, the other women at the center disgust her a little. They seem so desperate, they look so swollen, but in all the wrong places—their eyes, their chins, their hearts. Not me, she thinks as the nurse calls her name and she rises with a friendly smile.

One day she moves the burlap bag from the attic to the back of her bedroom closet. It's such a big house, and the attic is sweltering now, and soon the men will be working up there on the charred wood. Before, she and Tom lived in a tiny, rented bungalow and looked into each other's eyes a lot. She loves Tom; she really does, though lately he seems quite far away. Outside, here, is a swing set made of old, splintered cedar, not safe enough for use. But that same day she finds an ear in it, tucked like a chestnut under a climbing pole. The tomatoes are ripe now. The sunflowers she planted in May are taller than she is, balancing their heads on swaying stalks. In the herb garden, the chives bear fat purple balls. The ear, oddly, is downed with dark hair, like the ear of a young primate. She holds it to her own ear as if she might hear something inside it—the sea, perhaps, a heartbeat or yawn. It looks so tender that she wraps it in tissue paper before placing it in the bag.

One night on the evening news, she and Tom see a story about a girl who was in a car accident and went into a coma, and now the girl performs miracles and people think she's a saint. The news shows her lying in Worcester in her parents' garage, hitched to life support while pilgrims come from near and far: people on crutches, children with cancer, barren women, men dying of AIDS. Jesus, says Tom, shuddering. People will believe anything—how sick. But she doesn't think it's so sick, the way the vinyl-sided ranch house is transformed into a wall of flowers, the way people bring gifts—Barbie dolls, barrettes, Hawaiian Punch (the girl's favorite)—and a blind man sees again, and a baby blooms from a tired woman's torso, and the rest of the people, well, the rest sit briefly in the full lap of hope, then get in their cars and go home. The girl is pretty, even though she's almost dead. Her braid is black and shiny, her brow peaceful. Her mother, the reporter says, sponge-bathes her each morning and again at night. Her father is petitioning the Vatican for the girl to be made an official saint.

Days now, while the men work in the attic, she roams. She wanders around the house looking for treasures, and on the days when she does not find them, she gets in her car and drives to town, or out along the country roads. Sometimes she finds barn sales and gets things for the house—a chair for Tom's desk, an old egg candler filled with holes. One day at a yard sale she buys a sewing machine, though she's never used one. I'll give you the instruction book, the woman says. It's easy—you'll see. Also at this yard sale is a playpen, a high chair, a pile of infant clothes. The woman sees her staring at them. I thought you might be expecting, she says, smiling. But I didn't want to presume. As a bonus, she throws in a plump pincushion stabbed with silver pins and needles and a blue-and-white sailor suit. It was my son's, she says, and from behind the house come—as if in proof—the shrieks of kids at play.

That night, with Tom in New York for an overnight meeting, she sets up the sewing machine and sits with the instruction manual in her lap. She slides out the trap door under the needle, examining the bobbin. Slowly, following the instructions, she winds the bobbin full of beige thread, then threads the needle. She gets the bag from the closet. She's not sure she's ready (the books say you're never sure), but at the same time her body is guiding, pushing, *urging* her. Breathe, she commands herself, and draws a deep breath. She has never done this before, never threaded the needle or assembled the pattern or put together the parts, but it doesn't seem to matter; she has a sense of how to approach it—first this, then this, then this. She takes a hand out of the bag and tries to stitch it to an arm, but the machine jams, so she unwinds a length of thread from the bobbin, pulls a needle from the pincushion, and begins again, by hand.

Slowly, awkwardly, she stitches arm to shoulder, stops to catch her breath and wipe the sweat from her brow. She remembers backstitch, cross-stitch; someone (her mother?) must have taught her long ago. She finds the other hand, the other arm. Does she have everything? It's been a long summer, and she's found so much; she might be losing track. If there aren't enough pieces, don't panic, she tells herself. He doesn't need to be perfect; she's not asking for that. He can be missing a part or two, he can need extra care. Her own body, after all, has its flaws, its stubborn limits. What, anyway, is perfect in this world? She'll take what she is given, what she has been able, bit by bit, to make.

She stitches feet to legs, carefully doing the seams on the inside so they won't show. She attaches leg to torso, sews on the little penis. The boy-child begins to stir, to struggle; perhaps he has to pee. Not yet, my love. Hold on. She works long and hard and late into the night, her body tight with effort, the room filled with animal noises that spring from her mouth as if she were someone else. She wishes, with a deep, aching pain, that Tom were here to guide her hands, to help her breathe and watch her work. Finally—it must be near dawn—she reaches into the bag and finds nothing. How tired she is, bone tired, skin tired. She must be finished, for she has used up all the parts.

Slowly, then, as if in sleep, she rises with the child in her arms. She has been working in the dark and so can't quite see him, though she feels his downy head, his foot and hand. He curls toward her for an instant as if to nurse, so she unbuttons her blouse and draws him near. He nuzzles toward her but does not drink, and she passes a hand over his face and realizes that he has no mouth. Carefully, in the dark, she inspects him with both her hands and mind: he has a nose but no mouth, wrists but no elbows. She spreads her palm over his torso, and her fingers tell her that he has kidneys and a liver but only six small ribs and half a heart. Oh, she tells him. Oh, I'm sorry. I tried so hard. I found and saved and stitched and tried so hard and yet—

She feels it first, before he goes: a spasm in her belly, a clot in her brain, a sorrow so thick and familiar that she knows she's felt it before, but not like this, so unyielding, so tangible. Six small ribs and only half a heart. While she holds him, he twitches twice and then is still.

Carrying him, she makes her way downstairs. It's lighter now, the purple-blue of dawn. She walks to the front parlor, past the TV, past the old honey extractor they found in the barn. She walks to the Mourning Door and tries to open it. It doesn't budge, wedged shut, and for a moment she panics—she has to get out now; the weight in her arms keeps getting heavier, a sack of stones. She needs to pass it through this door and set it down, or she will break. Trying to stay calm, she goes to the laundry room and finds a screwdriver, returns to the door and wedges the tool in along the lock packet, balancing the baby on one arm. Finally the door gives, and she walks through it, forgetting that no steps meet it outside. Falling forward over the high ledge, she lands, stumbles, catches her balance (somehow, she hasn't dropped him) to stand stunned and breathless in the still morning air, her knees weak from landing hard.

Across the road, the sheep in the field have begun their bleating. A truck drives by, catching her briefly in its headlights. She lowers her nose to the baby's head and breathes in the smell of him. He's lighter now, easier now. *Depart*, she thinks, the word an old prayer following her through the door. *Depart in peace.* With her hands, she memorizes the slope of his nose, the open architecture of his skull. She fingers the spirals of one ear. Then she turns and starts walking, out behind the house to the barn, where a shovel hangs beside the hoe and rake. It's lighter now. A mosquito hovers close to her face. The day will be hot. Later, Tom will return. She buries the baby under a hawthorn tree on the backstretch of their land and leaves his grave unmarked. My boy, she says as she turns to go. Thank you, she says—to him or to the air—when she is halfway home. She sleeps all morning and gardens through the afternoon.

That night (day sixteen, except she's stopped charting), she and Tom make love, and afterward she thinks of nothing—no wagging fish, no hovering eggs, no pathway, her thoughts as flat and clean as sheets. Tom smells like himself—it is a smell she loves and had nearly forgotten—and after their sex, they talk about his trip, and he runs a hand idly down her back. She is ready for something now—a child inside her or a child outside, come from another bed, another place. Or she is ready, perhaps, for no child at all, a trip with Tom to a different altitude or hemisphere, a rocky, twisting hike. They make love again, and after she comes, she cries, and he asks what, what is it, but it's nothing she can describe, it's where she's been, so far away and without him—in the charred attic, the tipped basement, where red columns try to shore up a house that will stand for as long as it wants to and fall when it wants to fall. Nothing, she says, and inside her something joins, or tries to join, forms or does not, and her dream, when she sleeps, is of the far horizon, a smooth, receding curve.

Graver on Where Stories Come From

Every once in a rare while, a story comes to me almost fully formed, a gift. These stories tend to be stranger than my other writing—shorter, less realist, more askew. They rise out of some murky, dream-soaked place, appearing, often, on the rim of sleep. "The Mourning Door" is such a story. I was making my bed one morning and came across a bump under the sheet, and with it, a first line: "The first thing she found was a hand."

The story came quickly. I wrote it in one sitting. Why this story? I'd been trying to get pregnant for a few months; I'd had a very early miscarriage; I live in a very old house. Those facts contributed to the story but do not equal it. Far more extreme, more dire than any facts contained in my life, "The Mourning Door" came to me line after line with a sort of urgency that made me want to follow its bidding. I did not stop to think about what tense to use, or whether or not to name my central character, or whether the story was "realist" or "fabulist," a modern-day fairy tale or the inner drama of a deluded soul. Later, in revising, I thought about these things as I tweaked and fiddled, polished and cut. But not a lot. The story felt like it had come straight from my stomach—or from, I suppose, my womb. I found it disturbing, but I was grateful for its presence. I didn't want to mess with it too much.

So what is it, this odd thing that I produced, filled, as it is, with body parts and dreamy findings, with clots and shudders, six small ribs and half a heart? Can I say what I—the urgent, writing part of myself, the part that moved, almost unthinking, from image to image, until a person of sorts was formed and failed—was trying to do? I can describe, perhaps, what I hope the story captures, and that is the strange, out-of-control feeling of trying to get pregnant, of bidding two bodies to make a third, in a process so hidden and mysterious—and, in these times of ours, so potentially subject to intervention and science—that it has, for me, all the elements of a fairy tale or myth: strange transformations, higher powers, a sense that the daily is transformed into something extraordinary. The soup pot is never empty; the eggs start talking; I'll huff and I'll puff and I'll blow your house down.

It is this mix of the daily, even the mundane, coupled with the extraordinary, that most interested me as I wrote the story. Everybody gets pregnant, almost everybody. Our mothers did. It's no big deal. And yet. The sperm penetrating, or not. The cells dividing, or not. The quite dazzlingly bizarre and surreal apparatuses of modern science, where bodies are incubators and sperm are, as I put it in the story, "washed and coddled, separated and sifted, like gold." It fascinated me. All my life, first as a child at imaginary play and then as a writer, I had made up characters, invented person after person; they could fill a town. Now, in mid-life, my husband and I wanted to make a real person. It should have been easier, more fun, than the painstaking work of writing a novel. But making a *person?* For real? It seemed an awesome task, at once similar to writing fiction and something entirely new.

Looking back, I can say this about the story. If the central character had been named, she would have felt too concrete and specific, a woman with too particular a past. If I had surrounded her with other women finding baby body parts, the story would have lost its sense of inner urgency, of dreamy, singular obsession. On the other hand, if the character's world had been entirely removed from the language of modern life and science and given the trappings of an *actual* fairy tale, the story would not engage with some of its most central issues and, oddly, it would lose some of its most fairy-tale-like images. In this way, it is a piece wholly rooted in its time.

If I had to locate "The Mourning Door" inside a literary "tradition," I would probably put it in the category of Magic Realism, which David Lodge defines as fiction where "marvelous and impossible events occur in what otherwise purports to be a realistic narrative." Such writing has, I think, a distinctive steadiness of tone, almost a flat-footedness. Nothing is shocking. Nothing is spectacular. An angel lands in the village, dirty and smeared. A man peers into a fish tank until he becomes one of the creatures on the other side. There is, Lodge observes, in writing of this kind, "always a tense connection between the real and the fantastic."

A tense connection. A fine line. Of this world but apart from it. The transformations of fairy tales but the intransigencies, losses, and solderings-on of real, lived life. This is what I was trying to do, though *trying* implies more conscious agency than I in fact felt. This is what my story was trying to do, I might say. And I was trying to help. I think the story has a happy ending, but not in an and-they-all-lived-happily-ever-after way; it is too steeped in loss and death for that. Still, I see the woman as having moved slowly through a painful process that is as much about dismantling her notions of creation as it is about creation itself. At the end, she is ready for the next moment, open to a wider range of possibilities, able to see further, to cling less hard.

Writing Suggestions

1. Write a scene in which your protagonist awakes to find something unusual at home—much in the way that the main character in "The Mourning Door" finds a hand as the story begins. Carefully consider the item your character finds and its dramatic effect. This item must somehow prove meaningful to the main character. How does it translate into story tension? How does it move the main character out of his or her regular daily routine? Were you to finish this story, how might it be resolved?

2. Write a story in which the main character desperately yearns for something or someone that ultimately does not arrive. How can this story develop tension? How can this story develop an ending that, though disappointing for the main character, provides meaningful resolution?

3. Take a story of your own that you've struggled with and rework the first scene to incorporate a dose of magical realism. Bring in a man with wings. Let lightning be captured in a bottle. Have someone dead return to the world. Does breaking the "laws" of reality offer new possibilities for this story? What is the difference between a story of magical realism (such as a story by Gabriel García Márquez) and one that's pure fantasy (J. R. R. Tolkein)? Which one offers your own style more opportunities for good writing?

4. Most professional writers agree: at the heart of writing is reading. Locate a book of fiction by a writer referenced anywhere in this book. A few examples: Ernest Hemingway, Amy Tan, F. Scott Fitzgerald, Eudora Welty, Edgar Allan Poe, Toni Morrison, John Updike, Flannery O'Connor, Louise Erdrich, Michael Chabon. Part of your own training as a writer is developing an awareness of the literature that came before. This can occur at a university creative writing program, in a writer's group, or entirely on your own. What is this writer up to? What techniques or fiction tactics are used? What similarities exist between your own writing and theirs? What lessons do they have to offer you?

> *If you stick too closely to your own experience, you have a built-in*
> *ceiling to that story. It's not going to go anywhere,*
> *or it's not going to go as far as it could.*
> —Daniel Wallace

Julianna Baggott

Dr. Ishida Explains his Case

Historical Note: On December 21, 1918, Dr. Norbu Ishida, a specialist in mental illness from Nagasaki, Japan, shot and killed Dr. George Wolff, his colleague at Sheppard-Pratt Hospital, a mental institution in Baltimore, Maryland.

I should dream at night of Dr. Wolff, the blood on the carpeted corridor, the morning sun, his hand gripping the leg of the cane chair. But I dream of my father. He keeps a sack of rocks on the floor of his cart. The cats mewl loudly. In life, he had good aim. His rocks hit the cats hard and direct. Their legs slipped out from under their bodies. At times, cats died all in one instant. In the dream, he cannot hit the cats. I can hear them cry. I can hear my father. He barks at them like a dog. And I can hear the glass jars of milk, covered by canvas to protect them from morning sun. The glass jars chime like the clocks at Sheppard-Pratt, the clocks that chimed above Dr. Wolff's body. In the dream, my father turns to me. I sit beside him in the cart. He stops barking. He has made a surrender. Now the cats crawl on my father like a moving coat. I am not a boy but a man sitting beside him in the cart, a grown man wearing my American clothing. He says, "Do not swallow these American coins, idiot son. They will only make you more foreign. They will announce you with a jingle when you walk into a room."

I am a handsome man in my own land. The women here cannot see it. Nurse Jacobs is blind to this fact. She has been blinded, like all nurses in their white skirts and white cornered hats, by men like Dr. Wolff. He is buried in his spotted bow tie. Everyone loved him. Their love came in great gusts like wind before storms. Even poor Nurse Jacobs was not immune. I told honorable judges, officers and the Lunacy Commission that Dr. Wolff was an evil force. But they did not believe *the Jap Murderer*. This is what they call me in the newspapers. The war is on. Their men are dying. And the soldiers who come back alive act from insanity—I have seen too many cases. As well, the city suffers crime and Spanish influenza. But still reporters have time to write that the Jap Murderer sits in his cell and only hums Japanese songs. They do not know that it is a lullaby, my father's killing tune.

I watch what they print as truth. They report my swelled head as a sign of paranoia. They say that because I have written plays, books, poetry, I am a paranoiac. If I

Some of the information about procedures, medications, and the direct quotes of doctors are taken from *Gatehouse: The Evolution of the Sheppard and Enoch Pratt Hospital, 1853–1986*, by Bliss Forbush and Byron Forbush, as well as *Baltimore Sun* articles from the coverage of the murder.

were not a gentleman, I would have told them details of all that I saw. Dr. Wolff molested Nurse Jacobs. His chambers and mine were separated by a wall. The wall was not firm throughout and a screwdriver made an easy hole through soft plaster near floorboards in my closet.

He molested me, as well, by telling everyone that I was a spy. A spy! What did I spy in this country? Only Dr. Wolff and Nurse Jacobs, alone, her feet, the stockings peeled, her hem dipping. A desperate act. And poor, poor Nurse Jacobs of fair skin, of delicate beauty, fine as a flower. I have written of poor, ruined Nurse Jacobs and her molestation in my own tongue.

The hospital staff should have spent more time on the patients than lies about me, gossip, rumors. I could always hear their forked tongues. I hate the way they all stared at me with their cow eyes. And what of the patients? I remember the ones who escaped—one to drown in a nearby pond, one self-poisoned by swallowing bichloride of mercury tablets purchased at a drugstore. If Dr. Wolff had not been distracted by his plot to molest Nurse Jacobs, couldn't these patients have been stopped from escaping? Couldn't we have saved their lives, if not their imbalanced minds?

But the staff is consumed with entertainments: light Swedish massage, billiards, bowling, a nine-hole golf course, tennis, concerts, the making of ornaments, stools, taborets. And these Americans so in love with baseball they have employed semi-professionals so that they can win games against the YMCA, the policemen and firemen! It is a mental sickness in itself.

I am not insane. It was a lawyer's desire to make me appear insane. I can confess to this now that the trial is over. My Honorable Wife would tell you, if she were here. My Honorable Wife would tell the honorable judges, the officers, the Lunacy Commission, that I am the most well respected specialist in the field of insanity in all of Japan, so well respected that my government sent me to America to exchange information on mental hygiene! (And where is Honorable Wife now? I receive no word. They stop my mail. These guards despise me. Is she alive? My children? Has Honorable Wife taken a bit of poison herself?) They did not believe that I was insane, in the end. How can a doctor be insane? It is not possible. Not possible.

But, yes, there was a mist. It came over my eyes. I did not falsify the mist in my testimony. I did not falsify the tunnel: it was like walking from bright sun into my father's covered cart where the milk grew warm if we did not go fast enough. If we did not go fast enough, the milk soured. The milk turned thick. It had skin. It became solid. It returned to the form of a body, the cow it came from. The cart was kept dark. Do not let the sun touch it! The cart was a dark tunnel that I walked through that morning. I did not remember the morning. I did not remember if I had washed my face, and usually I am tidy in appearance. I was in a state, yes. My voice was tight in my throat. Nurse Doroff asked if I was okay. "You sound shaky," she said.

I told that my throat was sore. "I am nearing sickness," I said to her cow eyes.

I had breakfast with Dr. Wolff, yes. I laughed with him about the iced walkway, and his father, the reverend, who had planned a visit. Dr. Wolff said, "There's little difference between a reverend and a doctor of mental illness when you get right down to it, Dr. Ishida. There's a barroom joke in there somewhere about the reverend's son who goes on to work in a mental institute. Isn't there?"

I said, "My father sold milk. Therefore I do not know."

Dr. Wolff laughed at me. He said, "Milk. There is something there, too. Something simple and pure in giving milk, nurturing. It's still part of what we try to do here. Am I right?"

I nodded pleasantly, but the son of a cow-man in Japan became a doctor of mental illness. This is a miracle. It did not let him marry well. No, he had to marry the daughter of a low level man. He had to marry Honorable Wife. In America, this is not understood. In America, a man can fall in love and follow his love with all of his heart. He can be free in this way. But I said nothing to Dr. Wolff, because in the breast of my coat I had a gun. By now he had already ruined Nurse Jacobs and I had already bought a pistol at a hardware store on Gay Street. The man did not want to sell it to me. He did not want to place it in my hands for me to feel its weight. He was afraid of me. He tried to discourage the purchase. He said to me, "It's expensive, you know. It costs a lot of money. Too much, if you ask me." But I have money. I put it on the counter and he couldn't do anything but package the gun and hand it to me.

Dr. Wolff walked ahead of me into the conference room. The staff looked at me when I entered the room. It was not because they know that there was a pistol in my pocket. No. My father is wise in the dream. I have swallowed something American, not coins, but something unknown. I have swallowed it, wildly, as my father swallowed milk when the cart became ripe. He drank like a man of lust until it ran down his chin onto his shirt. "Drink," he said to me. "Drink. Drink! This milk is money. Drink before it curdles." This American thing that I have swallowed makes them turn and watch me. They know that I do not belong here. I am Japanese and worse I am Onobori-san, a peasant from the country. I still wear the smell of bad milk. It is in my bones.

The conference room was too warm. It was winter, but the heat made the room tight with the odor of bodies. The radiators ticked. The windows were large. The sun poured in. I do not recall the topics discussed. I only know that Dr. Wolff left early. He did this. He had a habit of checking his watch, excusing himself and departing with a warm smile. Dr. Brush nodded to him. He was proud of him. Dr. Wolff deceived everyone to think he was a man of purpose. They believed that he had somewhere important to go. He had wide brown eyes. His eyebrows slanted down in an expression of deep sadness. And yet he was cheerful. He called everyone by their name. Nurse Doroff, he called her Kippy. Her name is Katherine. I called her Nurse Doroff.

But some people Dr. Wolff made nervous. Poor Nurse Jacobs, for example. She was not there that morning, but I had noted that after her molestation—days had passed, nearly a week—there was more flutter in her hands as if they were overtaken by birds whenever he walked into the room. She was frightened of Dr. Wolff—not in love with him. There is a difference. And I know this difference. Please recall that I am trained at discovering mental states.

I excused myself as well, walked quickly to the hallway, pulled the gun from my coat and here I stopped a moment. My vision of the tunnel collapsed to the sight of Dr. Wolff's wide back. I called out in Japanese words of honor. My neck felt tight with blood, my face pulsing. I could not shoot Dr. Wolff in his wide back. I am a gentleman. He turned at the sound of my loud voice. His eyes fell on the gun and grew large. He raised one arm as a shield, because he knew that I was going to kill him and he knew why. The gun went off, hammering in my hand, again and once more, and Dr. Wolff's face was gone. He folded over the bullet in his stomach and fell to the hall floor, to bleed on the carpeted corridor. His hand grasped the leg of a cane chair until it stopped. And his hand was loose.

The aged Dr. Dunton began to yell, "Ishida has shot Wolff!" And only then I knew that I had succeeded, only then. I was defending the honor of Nurse Jacobs, the poor, pale beauty, and two countries, two nations! But Nurse Jacobs did not see it. I can only think of her now as a vision running into the snow storm after her molestation, small quick steps like Honorable Wife, away from Dr. Wolff's room, away from me, that one evening of snow.

But I do not think of it. To pass the hours, I go over procedure: Arriving at the Hospital, the patient is greeted and assisted from his automobile. When not playing cribbage in the parlor, Nurse Doroff will do this task. Now that most of the men have gone to war, Nurse Doroff will even take over a patient who is violent. Nurse Doroff is gifted at cribbage and built like ox. No Japanese woman would move like Nurse Doroff without disgrace. Anthropometric measurements are taken. Here, I must touch the patients. They do not trust me. The patient is shown to his room, a small bed, where he prepares for further examination. Straps are available. This is a comfort to me, to know they are there, even if not needed. The patient's case is discussed in a doctor's conference shortly after admission. Dr. Wolff's bow tie bobbed at his throat when he spoke. Later, the physician conducts complete physical and mental examinations. The patients eye me hatefully. As part of the patient's treatment, a lumbar puncture may be administered by the physician. This is for their own well-being. There can be too much fluid, too much pressure, and sometimes it is the only way to relieve. Hydrotherapy is an excellent means to quiet a violent patient, many faucets turned on at the same time. The room echoes. In the meantime, the patient's relatives give his history to the physician. Dr. Brush has said, "Dr. Ishida, your English isn't yet perfect. It makes the families uncomfortable." And so I am not allowed. My English is excellent. It was better than the translator called into the trial. Dr. Brush does not tell the truth, that they despise me. A nurse monitors the patient's blood pressure. Sometimes this is Nurse Jacobs. She leans over the patient. She holds her breath to hear the beats. Her lips purse as she counts. A nurse assists a doctor in administering salvarsan. Nurse Jacobs, steady, steady, she lifts the tubing. Sometimes I brush against her, an accident. A wet sheet pack is administered as relief. The patients are wrapped like Egyptians I have seen in American curiosity museums. Here Nurse Jacobs touches their foreheads, looks deeply into their eyes. The patient is seen in the physician's office. Not until the whole staff becomes familiar with his condition and agrees that he is able to return home will he be discharged. How many patients have I kept against their will? We keep them as I am kept now.

Do I believe in cures? Do I believe that someone should return home? (Did I ever intend to go home to my island? America is an elixir to me. It can make you dizzy. Your head can ring here. Your heart can pound loudly in your chest. Anyone can hear it. Anyone. Here, I walked dizzy, ringing, pounding, in love with Nurse Jacobs. Only here could I exist in this state.) And what would I return home to? Honorable Wife, children, wards of insane, clawing, diseased. I would be the cow-man's son who rose up but is still the cow-man's son. And there is nothing I can do to help the patients. No one understands the mind. This business is a prank run by pranksters. We know nothing. We set the nozzles on full blast, wrap them in cold sheets, puncture their spines, decreasing their abundant fluids. We hope for cures that don't come. The patients' minds have turned and even my father knows that you cannot make sweet milk from what is already sour.

Dr. Brush, in his quietest moments, when he sits alone at the end of the day, knows this to be true. We all do, but never speak of it. Of course, I am concerned about what Dr. Brush thinks of me. After the trial, the Japanese doctors present stepped away from me. I became unclean. They made their distance. But Dr. Brush looked at me. He stepped toward me and said, "Doctor." That's all, not my name, and then he shook his head. Perhaps he believes that the Nipponese are devils. He agrees that the whole awful affair has a veil of Oriental mystery, just like the newspapers say. And didn't he always suspect Ishida of something? The newspapers do not like that I exude manners, that I am overly polite, too solicitous, always asking about welfare of others. And perhaps they are right. It was a fault. Although I tried to stop bowing, it proved impossible.

Dr. Brush preferred Dr. Wolff. And I always tried to grind sesame seeds, gomasuri, which is to say that I wanted to please him. When I went into Dr. Brush's office to complain about Dr. Wolff in a quiet manner, Dr. Brush scoffed at me. Dr. Brush has a very small mouth, a pointed nose. His light hair and sharp eyes, high collar and reedy body. He said that I was too serious, that Dr. Wolff jokes with the nurses a bit. He admitted that Dr. Wolff might even be too friendly, but he is a good soul. Wasn't Dr. Brush confessing that occasionally things happen and that he overlooks them? Wasn't he saying that in his day he was as drawn to molestation as Dr. Wolff? I believe that there was a nurse once, maybe, for Dr. Brush, perhaps when he was a young man. And she was spirited. And he enjoyed her. Or perhaps she was delicate like Nurse Jacobs, easily deceived. Now, I hope that Dr. Brush dreams of the nurse of his youth, that they are driving, and he puts his hand on her knee and his hand feels hot and then wet. He pulls his thin hand away and it's bloody. Perhaps he blames this on Ishida, the Jap. And he wakes up in sweat, saying, *You can't trust them. Any of them.*

I read in the newspaper that Dr. Brush wrestled the gun from me. The pistol was cocked for another shot, and Dr. Brush charged forward and took my arm. He says that he led me into his office, and there I resisted and he had to strong-arm the pistol from me. Wasn't it Dr. Brush who wrestled when young? Didn't he once tell me that he was Metal Boy at the St. James School for Boys? I can hear him saying, *I handled the wiry Nip, I tell you.* Dr. Brush is a brute, an American brute. He can speak like a man of science—his articles: "Hysterical Insanity," "Insanity and Arrested Development," "An Analysis of One Hundred Cases of Acute Melancholia,"—but it is an act. He once said, "There are some who can lead the strenuous life, but many there be who must go softly all their days lest disaster over take them." And now does he think I'm weak? Does he think I'm no better than a patient being sprayed, naked, in a shower?

In truth, I stepped into Dr. Brush's office and the mist, the tunnel cleared. I looked at the breathless man with his flushed cheeks, his narrow shoulders and pale brow. He said, "Why did you do it, Dr. Ishida? Why?" He took the gun from my hand with ease. My hands were soft then. I spoke to him in Japanese. I said, "In my homeland, I am a great man who believes in honor."

As a boy, I was not rich. My father had cows and carted milk to neighbors for pay, for exchanges. My father collected cats and he killed them. I have eaten a cat. This is true. It is what they say of us and, for me, it is true. We never ate the cows. In America there are so many cows to eat. And as my father killed the cats he hummed a song. I only know the tune. It is a soft nursery song, but it is a killing song, too, for me. My father told me that I was his idiot son. He told me that I knew nothing of the world. He told me that the neighbors sometimes wanted to kill him because of the sweetness of the cow milk, and they wanted to take his body and put it in the river.

"And one day," he warned me, "if you look into my eyes and it is not me but someone like me, know that the neighbors have killed me and put my body in the river so that they can partake of your mother and the sweet cows." My father gave me a sign that only we would know. We would touch our noses with our smallest finger. But my father became suspicious of me. He accused me of telling the neighbors about our sign and he beat me.

When I grew up, I became a doctor of mental illness. This is possible only because of the great thinker Fukuzawa Yukichi and his ideas on the problems with hierarchy and class. Without his thoughts, I would be working with cows because I was born of a cow-man. But I did not become a cow-man. In America this is a plain truth, not a miracle: I became a doctor. After this, I returned to my village to diagnose my father as a paranoiac, and quite luckily, I found an asylum for him. Mother was dead. My brother took over the cows, and my father died a year later in a hospital bed. He was buried in the ground not thrown to the river. Perhaps the milk made my father crazy with its sweetness. Perhaps Nurse Jacobs made me crazy for a time, for just a brief time, with her beauty.

Here, when my mind walks to this spot, like a field edging to a steep cliff that I am drawn to, I go over medications and their possible uses. Stramonium is useful in containing mania. Digitalis and conium for melancholia. Chloral hydrate is a fine sedative . . . But it is only a matter of time before I am back again. I hear the man in the cell next to mine. He groans when he urinates and it reminds me that Dr. Wolff and I shared a common wall. On my knees inside my closet, the sounds were clear. Nurse Jacobs's voice was soft. I could only see shoes: Dr. Wolff's wingtips, her square-toed nurse shoes. Dr. Wolff had been with another nurse once, a ruddy young woman. I didn't care for her. But this was not the frumpy chatterbox who threw herself at Dr. Wolff. This was Nurse Jacobs. I could tell from her shoes, her bell voice ringing. She said, "George, do you think?"

And he said, "Yes, I think so, Billie." He called Nurse Jacobs by her first name like all of the nurses. I do not like this boldness. "You weigh on my mind all day long. I'm no longer a kid. I need to settle down. I love you."

This is against policy. This is deception. Dr. Wolff was thirty-five years old, true, but he was not going to settle down with poor Nurse Jacobs. Dr. Wolff did not love Nurse Jacobs, not the way that I love Nurse Jacobs. He cannot understand what it is to be born in a box to break from the box to find yourself in another box. He doesn't know then what it is like to be shipped to America—dizzy, ringing, pounding. He did not love Nurse Jacobs because he was not able to love her the way one should love her. And it is part of our policy not to deceive: "Patients should never be brought to the Asylum by deception, they almost always suspect the deception and it invariably has a bad effect more or less permanent. They learn on arrival that the Sheppard is not a hotel or watering place, and are very apt to feel that the medical officer and others connected with the institution are parties to the deception, and decline to give them their confidence, so necessary to the successful dealing with their cases." Therefore, do you see how Dr. Wolff was lying, and how these lies would create a mental damage on poor Nurse Jacobs? She is fragile.

The shoes were nearly touching, tips to tips. I stayed crouched, my eye to the hole, my own sour breath filling the closet. I watched the shuffle. Why did Nurse Jacobs go to him? I wanted to take her shoulders and shake them in my strong hands. Sometimes I needed to do this to Honorable Wife. I needed to get her to stop her talk, to stop her singing chatter. Now I tried to be calm. I tried to tell myself that no one can understand taste, like the old saying: some prefer nettles. But I heard her voice rise up, and I knew that he was taking her. I saw her hem dip. He had unbuttoned her uniform. It must have fallen over her shoulders. I envisioned her full breast, bare, and her long creamy neck. I stood, brushed myself off, and walked to his office door.

I knocked and said, "Pardon, Dr. Wolff. I need to discuss a case. It is urgent."

But there was no response.

I said, "Dr. Wolff, I need to talk to you. This case needs immediate attention." I had no case in mind, but each case needed attention. It is the sad truth of our business.

He cleared his voice. "I cannot talk now, Dr. Ishida. I'm busy and feeling ill. Please don't disturb me."

It took me by such surprise, his rudeness! And now there was nothing I could do. I considered a fire, but, no, it would shame me if it were found to be false. And setting a real fire? I couldn't endanger the life of Nurse Jacobs. What if Dr. Wolff kept her hostage there and her pale skin turned to char? And so I could do nothing. I turned from the door and heard Nurse Jacobs, soft laughter, Dr. Wolff hushing her. You see how she was deceived. I went to my office and watched their feet, bare now, then to the sofa, gone.

When I stood, I felt dizzy. I was humming the killing tune. The window was a blur of snow. I heard heels in the corridor. I opened my door and watched Nurse Jacobs struggle into her coat as she walked briskly down the hall. "Nurse Jacobs! Excuse me. Forgive me for calling out!"

She turned. Her smile faded. She rubbed her arms, bracing for the cold. I caught up to her—her risen bony nose, her thick lashes and gaping eyes, her pointed chin, and honey hair. She is nothing like my Honorable Wife. I never loved Wife. I took her only with a covered face. And here was Nurse Jacobs, her pink cheeks. I imagined she was bleeding now, no longer pure. I said, "You didn't answer me about the theatre. I have an additional ticket. Do you want to accompany me?"

"No," she said. "I did answer you, Dr. Ishida. I told you, remember? I can't."

"Oh, no, I didn't remember."

She turned to go.

"You can't go out in this weather," I told her. "There is a storm."

"Dr. Ishida," she said. "Please don't take my arm like that."

And I realized then that I had taken her by the arm.

Her hand was now on the knob of the door leading outside. She said, "I have to go back to the house." The nurses lived together.

"I see. Can I walk you?"

"No. Please don't. Look," she said, glancing up the empty corridor. "I have someone that I'm sweet on."

"A soldier?"

"No, not a soldier. You know who it is, Dr. Ishida."

"I'm sorry I don't." My face was hot now.

"Don't tell anyone. Please."

She turned the knob. The door opened, a gust of cold, snow. I walked out into it after her and bowed, but she scurried on, down the walkway toward the gatehouse. I watched until her gray coat was lost to me in the white.

Today, again, I hum the killing song in my cell, wondering if Nurse Jacobs will come to visit, if she will appear in her white uniform and cornered hat and confess to me that Dr. Wolff stole her honor and that I restored it, and she is thankful. I can wait for her. I am as patient as moss. I can see from my cell window a distant tree. The blossoms have fallen beneath it and the ground is white, like snow, like milk. I want to tell poor Nurse Jacobs that I tried to go to the police, after the snowstorm, to get a warrant for Dr. Wolff's arrest, but they explained that it was not in their juris-diction. I want to tell her that I wrote a play for her and that I want her to be the star in the production. I want to tell her, in a hush voice, that Wife may have killed her-self, that I have not gotten word, but that sometimes shame can be heavy, and it is only a courtesy to kill oneself. I want to tell her that perhaps I can prove again that I am in need of psychiatric care, and she can be a nurse at the facility where they take me, and she can help me return to health. I want to tell her, and only her, that my father was not mentally well before his death. The last time I saw him strapped to his hospital bed, I touched my smallest finger to my nose, but he did not recognize the gesture, and now I wonder if it was my father in the bed. Or is my father alive? Does he know that I have killed Dr. Wolff and am being held in an American jail? Does he want to kill me, out of shame, out of hate, out of mercy? My father was a para-noiac. I want to tell Nurse Jacobs that I know how to falsify this condition, and the two of us can be together. I want her to know that I will overlook the fact that she has been ruptured by Dr. Wolff. He is dead!

Baggott on the Role of Research in Fiction

Let's begin with the obvious: it helps, in being a writer, if you've seen the world—Peru and someplace vaguely Russian-sounding—especially if you've fought in a war there. Like Ernest "Papa" Hemingway. It helps if, during that war, you had to kill a man at close range. If you haven't been in a war then you can easily make up for it by hunting big game in Africa wearing a pith helmet or, at the very least, knocking off a squirrel with a BB gun.

Now, all of this being said, I haven't done any of the above. I don't even own a BB gun. In fact, the only thing I've done of note, besides writing books, is give birth to smaller more promising versions of myself—meaning I've had some kids. Giving birth was, for me, more animalistic than I'd ever imagined. It shocked me. I wasn't prepared for it. A body coming out of my body—who could prepare me for that? For a long time, I wrote about what results from giving birth: families. This consumed me. It turns out I had much to say on the subject, things quite tender, ironic, and twisted.

Eventually, I decided to write my own family's history—my grandmother was raised in a house of prostitution in the 1920s and 30s; her mother was the madam. The result was my third novel, *The Madam*. When I mention this, writers often tell me how very lucky I am to have come from such stock. It is a writerly gift to have whoring descendants—perhaps it's even on par with big-game hunting. But I would like to add that everyone comes from fascinating stock. In some families there's a big internal campaign to whitewash the past, but if you pick at the paint chips, I guarantee that you'll find some exquisite oddity beneath.

In writing *The Madam*, I fell in love with research. A bully, really, research doesn't allow the author complete authority. Its insistence on accuracy manhandles plot and character. This bullying, this manhandling, was especially good for me. I became a servant again, which, in my opinion, is what a writer should be. Incapable of forcing my characters to do what I wanted them to, I had to follow. Research rewarded me. I found a grainy photo of an elephant working on a Miami dock in the early 1930s, a blind woman with a Bible and a Braille machine resting on her knees, a carnival poster of "The Mule-Faced Woman." I used all of them and many more.

I also learned that if you rely on research, you don't have to do as much inventing. I'm not saying that I'm lazy, because there's still much inventing to do once you've got the research in hand. And I'm not saying that I've run dry on my personal stories. But, frankly, I haven't really lived a very interesting life or at least it isn't all that extremely interesting to me. In fact, I'm ashamed to admit it, but I had a very happy childhood. The fact of the matter is that the world is filled with real, true, fascinating tales. I didn't have to spin them from air.

Once I'd finished writing *The Madam*, I went in search of strange histories, ones hidden in obscure books. I became weirdly territorial about my obscure books. In fact, there's one I've been renewing from the library every month for two years. (Have I just admitted to something illegal?) I am so territorial that I would try, right now, to weasel around using the actual name of the book that I used for most of my research for the short story "Dr. Ishida Explains his Case," but I've already made public note of it. And there's no real need for weaseling or claim-staking. Obviously I know that no one cares about my obscure books, and I don't own the history of a certain Baltimore mental institution, but there are these moments of pure high that a researcher gets when coming across their singular definition of pure gold. And the small mention of *Dr. Ishida Murdering Dr. Wolff* in *Gatehouse: The Evolution of the Sheppard and Enoch Pratt Hospital, 1853–1986*, by Bliss Forbush and Byron Forbush (I've said it), was such a moment. It made me dizzy and giddy, so overjoyed that I clutched the book to my chest and thought, mine mine mine!

But just finding the pure gold isn't enough. I wasn't researching so that I could simply present my findings. I was writing a story, and so there was still an entire invention that had to take place. I had Gatehouse to help me slip inside of Sheppard Pratt in 1917—the light Swedish massage and billiards, the lumbar punctures and straps, article titles: "Hysterical Insanity," "Insanity and Arrested Development," "An Analysis of One Hundred Cases of Acute Melancholia."

I had the *Baltimore Sun* articles for profiles on Ishida and Wolff as well as the terminology of the era—the Lunacy Commission and the Jap Murderer. I had studied Japanese culture years ago and went back to look over some old marked-up texts. I went online and dug up translations of Japanese idioms.

At first I was simply gathering details and whittling them to the most essential. What to keep—it's personal taste as well as developing a sense of what will translate into good writing. I went for details, specifics, especially things that expanded the senses. The season allowed for snow so Nurse Jacobs could disappear into it; Dr. Ishida had a fear of being perceived as insane: "no better than a patient being sprayed, naked, in a shower"; his testimony about the mist that settled over his eyes during the murder was evocative; and even the tiny detail that Dr. Wolff grips a cane chair while dying was important to building a real world inhabited by real people. This is always the writer's charge, whether using a true story or not.

When I began writing the first draft, I decided on first person from Ishida's point of view. It seemed the clearest way to the heart of the story. I had whittled my details and now I was arranging them in the narrative. I used a structure of hinting and then elaborating, hinting and then elaborating. There are many things that Ishida mentions and drops and then circles back around to again—his own father, the murder scene, his Honorable Wife, Nurse Jacobs. I was trying to stay true to his state of mind. At first, he's defending Nurse Jacobs, then he admits he's in love with her, and finally it's clear that he still hopes to have her. He is breaking down.

But I should admit that the first draft of this story was distant. It was a sad, boring, stiff little story of some irrelevant scandal from a long time ago. Ishida wasn't fully realized. He lacked depth. I had the details in place. I felt I knew his world and, in part, his motive of jealousy, but I didn't really know why he'd gone crazy to begin with. I looked at his photo. I stared at him. I reread the testimonies, and finally I decided to leave him alone.

Instead I turned my attention to Wolff. He was easier to understand. In fact, I was struck by him. He was handsome and sweet-eyed. He wore that bow-tie and he was a little soft-looking, comfortable, jovial. And then I thought: *Wolff was what Ishida wasn't.* This seemed key to understanding Ishida. And then I read that Wolff's father was a reverend. This was a good solid detail that could be worked in casually, over lunch, and what did Ishida's father do for a living? This simple question broke the story wide open.

The first paragraph of this story came last.

I should dream at night of Dr. Wolff, the blood on the carpeted corridor, the
morning sun, his hand gripping the leg of the cane chair. But I dream of my father.
He keeps a sack of rocks on the floor of his cart. The cats mewl loudly. In life, he had
good aim. His rocks hit the cats hard and direct. Their legs slipped out from under
their bodies. At times, cats died all in one instant. In the dream, he cannot hit the
cats. I can hear them cry. I can hear my father. He barks at them like a dog. And I
can hear the glass jars of milk, covered by canvas to protect them from morning sun.
The glass jars chime like the clocks at Sheppard-Pratt, the clocks that chimed above
Dr. Wolff's body . . .

For five years, my husband and I ran a boarding house. (I suggest running a boarding house if you can't go to Peru or somewhere Russian-sounding; in this way, these places can, in part, come to you.) One of our boarders was a Korean man whose father sold milk. I know that he sold milk because I asked a lot of questions. Asking a lot of questions is a huge part of my creative process. Writing down and storing answers to questions in drawers and folders and boxes is another huge part of my creative process.

Once I understood Ishida's childhood and his paranoid father and the legacy of that paranoia, then the story came together. It made sense emotionally. It became charged.

I am now addicted to research. Out of the last twenty-eight poems I've written, twenty-seven have been written in the voices of historic women. My office has been overtaken by clippings and photocopies and boxes of answers to questions, and buried beneath it all, that obscure book I refuse to return to the library.

I suppose there will be a time when I feel the need to write something closer to my own contemporary existence. (Oh, but wouldn't the good doctors of Sheppard-Pratt say that I'm still airing my own soul by taking on these voices in history, that in each chosen detail I'm revealing my own psyche?) But for now, I want to write in the service of language. I want to reclaim the dismissed. I want to raise up these lost voices—the number of them is infinite. It's an overwhelming task, but less so if more of us set to it. (If only it were mandatory . . . .) I suffer from the firm belief that each of our obscure lives is endlessly worthy of being written down—whether big-game hunting or birthing or, quite simply, our hearts' quiet seizing.

Writing Suggestions

1. Write the first scene for a story that is set during a historic period—say, the summer of 1985, 1990, 1995, or 2000. To complete this assignment, as a class, develop a list specific details that would situate the scene in that summer. Consider popular music, movies, TV shows, fashion styles, hair and make-up styles, news events, slang, celebrity gossip, video games, books, etc. This story can be about anything you like, but if you're stuck for a topic, consider conflicts or problems you experienced during the summer in question. How can your own experience become the window into a story? The goal of this assignment is to texture a story with historic detail while at the same time establishing character and plot. What details best define the era? Where would you go to gather other details to develop this story? As always, effective details will not only establish a sense of place and time but also will contribute to characterization and plot.

2. The best stories are ones that have a high degree of verisimilitude. Like Julianna Baggott, unless you have been to Peru or some vaguely Russian-sounding place, research is a good alternative for discovering authoritative details. Choose a famous event (murder, robbery, tragedy, love story, sacrifice, triumph, mystery) that happened more than fifty years ago and find out all you can about it. Use the Internet, libraries, bookstores, local authorities, museums, etc. Select a set of characters and a primary conflict from your findings, then sketch out the plot of your story using as many true details as you can. One warning about using real-life events to fuel your fiction—just because something actually happened does not mean it needs to happen in your story. Once you begin writing, that story is yours and you can fill

in any gaps with imagination, research, or a combination of the two (as happened in Charles Frazier's Civil War book *Cold Mountain*, Jane Mendelson's novel *I Was Amelia Earhart*, or the movies *Titanic* and *Pearl Harbor*).

3. Clearly Baggott worked to find the right names for her characters in "Dr. Ishida Explains his Case"—names that have associative powers that speak to character, attitude, style, dress, and even socioeconomic background. Read the following short descriptions and come up with an appropriate first and last name for each. Pick names that have strong or subtle influences on how a reader reacts to them.

   - a spinster heiress who lives alone in a mansion with forty cats
   - an ex-prize fighter who now is a social worker
   - a white-collar boss who vents his anger upon his employees
   - a teenager who spends more time on a surfboard than at school
   - a bitter woman who secretly works to undermine her brother's successes

   Now take any story of yours that you've felt never reached its fullest potential, and using the above explanation, radically change the name of your protagonist. Does this affect dialogue? Does it help you reenvision possibilities for your story? Consider changing other character names in the story, too, which necessitates reimagining character background, motivation, speech patterns, and attitudes.

4. In your local library, roam a nonfiction section that you've never spent much time in before. Locate a book that calls out to you the way Baggott "heard" her book. Read through it at your leisure, making note of what character and story ideas the book suggests. Select whichever ones interest you most and use those as the impetus for a future story. Remember that story ideas are everywhere: evening news stories, soap operas, magazine advertisements, laundromat gossip, etc.

> *Advice to young writers who want to get ahead without any*
> *annoying delays: don't write about Man, write about a man.*
> —E. B. White

PART
TWO

~~~

On Writing

Writing fiction doesn't have any clear hierarchy. You can't say that
you must understand plot before dialogue, description before point
of view, or even beginnings before endings. There's no rational order
or sequence in which those elements must be learned.
*They're **all** necessary.*
—Jerome Stern

Introduction

For the purposes of this book, we, the editors, have divided these aspects of writing fiction—**On Prewriting** and **On Writing**—into separate categories, though for many writers the activities of prewriting and writing overlap. In **On Prewriting**, you will find commentaries to help generate fiction ideas and get raw story material down on paper. The commentaries and corresponding exercises in this section are designed to help you generate, explore, and develop ideas long before you write the first draft of a story.

No writer begins the first scene without at least some vision of the story he or she hopes to write. But rarely do writers begin the first scene with a fully realized vision for the entire story. In truth, many writers learn about their characters and stories through the process of writing and even more so through the careful act of revision.

After completing the **On Prewriting** exercises, you probably have some idea about a story you wish to write—even if it is still a vague idea shrouded in the fog of inspiration. Perhaps, on scraps of notebook paper, you've compiled details about a compelling character. Or perhaps you have the glimmer of an opening scene. Better yet, you have the glimmer of both a first and a second scene. Maybe you have only this: the ability to hear the crystalline voice of a main character in your head. The stories, commentaries, and exercises in this section, **On Writing**, will help you take early inspiration and develop it into a draft of a story.

A successful short story requires a writer to simultaneously accomplish many tasks of fiction. A story's beginning establishes character, setting, and point of view, while at the same time releasing the mechanisms of plot and constructing successful scenes. In the sections that follow, we've asked sixteen writers to explain, individually, the essential elements of craft. These stories and commentaries will help you understand the role each element plays in the construction of a story. Moreover, these commentaries and their corresponding exercises will help you develop your prewriting ideas into the stuff of successful fiction.

Section Four: Story Structure and the Fundamentals of Plot

Alice Mattison discusses the overall structure of a short story, while three other writers (John McNally, Aaron Gwyn, and Jarret Keene) discuss its individual pieces: beginnings, middles, and ends, respectively, paying special attention to how each contributes to the greater aim of plot. There are many ways to conceptualize the structure of fiction, such as the example of rising action, the movement toward internal change, and the visual model of Freytag's Pyramid. Still, even while describing one component of story structure, all four writers reveal how interconnected these components are to the overall framework of successful fiction.

Section Five: Developing Characters

Of all the elements of fiction, few prove as difficult as the development of fully realized characters. Many beginning writers make the mistake of writing a draft before they understand their characters. The novelist Anthony Trollope, who also wrote short stories, once said, "A novelist's characters must be with him as he lies down to sleep, and as he wakes from his dreams. He must learn to hate them and to love them." To help you flesh out the specific history, personality, and interior life of your characters, we include two commentaries on characterization: one on composing "true" characters and another focusing on developing their emotional life. Lorrie Moore's commentary on "Debarking" exhibits her technique for breathing life into characters through sensitivity to public and private life. Amy Bloom, a fiction writer and a psychotherapist, further explains the process of developing psychologically complex characters.

In a short story, characterization often directly relates to the development of story tension. A story's conflict or dramatic problem must contain the potential to shake a character to his or her core. Without this intimate connection between a character's personality and the events represented in a story, there can be no compelling tension. In his commentary on "Nap Time," Tom Franklin offers advice for building tension in a domestic plot as well as for stories in general. By explaining his personal method of creating and manipulating story tension, he discusses how the needs and personalities of his characters intersect with plot, thereby demonstrating the way that careful investigation of character often suggests conflict.

Section Six: Choosing a Point of View

The five most common point of view choices are explored in essays by Michael Knight (first person), Adam Johnson (second person), Judith Claire Mitchell (third person limited), Lee K. Abbott (third person omniscient), and Josh Russell (third person objective). In many ways, point of view selection is as important as populating your story with believable characters because point of view defines the window through which readers view the fictional world. How do you choose the appropriate point of view? As fiction writer Nancy Kress says, "Your choice will depend on the total effect you want your story to have."

Section Seven: Scene Construction

John Updike believes, "Fiction is nothing less than the subtlest instrument for self-examination . . . that mankind has invented yet." In a short story, meaning is not developed from just the invention of character and plot. A short story can have character and plot, but not meaning. Meaning, in part, comes from the careful moment-by-moment development of a scene.

In this book, we examine the most important aspects of scene construction. In his commentary on "Palm Wine," Reginald McKnight examines ways to create effective settings in fiction through detail and emotional landscape. George Singleton discusses how time works in short stories—exposition, flashbacks, pacing, scene length, summary, and transitions. Keith Lee Morris explores the potential of dialogue and how it advances plot, creates characterization, and adds to story tension.

Section Eight: The Short-Short Story

Lastly, Tom Hazuka reveals how the elements of the traditional story are compressed and utilized in pieces of extremely short fiction, often called short-shorts, flash fiction, or micro-fiction. Hazuka, an expert on the form, offers advice and tips on assembling this unique short story that has recently seen a rise in popularity. He also offers a sampling of five short-shorts to demonstrate their dramatic range and possibilities.

Writing the First Scene: Essay and Writing Suggestions

Make no mistake: the first scene can be the most difficult to write.

It can be difficult because you, the writer, need to fully imagine not only the characters and the setting, but also the plot. Because of this need, many writers explore the story through notes and journal writing before taking a stab at the first scene. Some writers make a tentative outline; others thoroughly investigate their characters' personalities. Experienced writers know this: it's much easier to approach the first scene with well-defined characters, snippets of dialogue, an outline, and perhaps a list of descriptive phrases.

Writing first scenes can also prove rewarding: you are turning an idea into an actual story. You are finally pushing beyond the process of prewriting and are creating sentences and scenes that, after revision, other people will read. You are creating fiction.

To help you through the process of writing the first scene, we've assembled a list of qualities shared by many traditional first scenes. This list is by no means complete or universal, but it is simply a guide to help you understand the role of the first scene as it relates to the rest of the story. A good first scene creates the context out of which the rest of the story will grow. If you have a successful first scene, you're more likely to have a successful second scene and, ultimately, a successful story.

We should also point out that short story writers are always looking for new ways to tell a story. In some cases, writers will deviate from or adapt the qualities most often found in a first scene. If you find yourself in this group—leaving out or altering those aspects commonly found in a first scene—ask yourself, how will such decisions affect the rest of your story? Or, how will your decisions contribute to the creation of a satisfying story? Writers who successfully experiment with structure often are conscious how such experimentation will affect the final story.

As you explore these elements common to first scenes, imagine how your first scene might work once you draft it out on paper. Take notes. Write out sentences you might later include. Experiment by writing a first paragraph. Perhaps ideas will burn so brightly, you'll need to take a break from reading this essay and write an entire page. That's what this list is designed to do: not only define a first scene, but also inspire you to work on one of your own.

External Change

Most stories do not focus on the regular, daily life of a character. Few stories are more boring than one in which a character gets up, goes to work, has lunch, talks with his friends, then comes home—following more or less the general routine of his life. For the most part, stories are about the departure from the mundane. They are about moments of significance that rise above the background noise of common existence. Short stories describe situations that characters will remember fifteen, twenty, even thirty years into the future.

To this end, most fiction begins with an external change—a dramatic event that allows life to take on increased meaning and, quite often, tension. Nick Carraway (of *The Great Gatsby*) begins his story by moving to New York—the move, of course, being a significant external change. Holden Caulfield (the narrator of *The Catcher in the Rye*) begins his story by leaving prep school to return home. At the start of "This Is What It Means to Say Phoenix, Arizona," Victor Joseph, the main character, learns that his father has recently died of a heart attack. In this way, story beginnings often take main characters out of the comforts of regular life and set them on the course toward meaningful situations.

Many stories situate the external change right on the first page—perhaps not in the first sentence but in the first few paragraphs. In the following example, the opening two paragraphs from Stacey Richter's shocking short story, "The Beauty Treatment," notice how effectively the story establishes this external change. Notice, too, that the external change is not an impression or an attitude; it is an action. It is something that

could be easily dramatized if this short story were transformed into a play or a film. It
is *external* action.

> She smiled when she saw me coming, the Bitch, she smiled and stuck her fingers in
> her mouth like she was plucking gum out of her dental work. Then, with a little pout,
> like a kiss, I saw a line of silver slide toward my face. I swear to God, I thought she'd
> pried off her braces. I thought she'd worked one of those bands free and was holding it
> up to show me how proud she was to have broken loose of what we referred to, in our
> charming teenage banter, as oral bondage. The next thing I know there's blood all over
> my J. Crew linen fitted blouse, in edelweiss—a very delicate, almost ecru shade of
> white, ruined now. There's blood all over the tops of my tits where they pushed out my
> J. Crew edelweiss linen shirt and a loose feeling around my mouth when I screamed.
> My first thought was Fuck, how embarrassing, then I ran into the girls' room and saw
> it: a red gash parted my cheek from my left temple to the corner of my lip. A steady
> stream of blood dripped off my jawline into the sink. One minute later, Cyndy Dash-
> naw found the razor blade on the concrete floor of the breezeway, right where the Bitch
> had dropped it.
>   Elizabeth Beecher and Kirsty Moseley run into the bathroom and go Oh my
> God, then drag me screaming hysterically, all three of us screaming hysterically, to
> Ms. B. Meanwhile, the Bitch slides into her Mercedes 450SL, lime green if you can
> believe that—the A-1 primo daddy-lac of all time—and drives off smoking Kools.
> I'm in the nurse's office screaming with Ms. B. calmly applying pressure and order-
> ing Mr. Pierce, the principal, to get in gear and haul my ass to the emergency room.
> This is what you get from watching too much TV, I'm thinking, and believing your
> workaholic father when he tells you during one of his rare appearances that you're
> the Princess of the Universe to which none can compare. And then watching
> teenage girls from Detroit on Montel, for God's sake—the inner city—froth and brag
> about hiding razors under their tongues and cutting up some ho because she glanced
> sideways at the boyfriend: I mean, help me. This is the twentieth century. My father's
> a doctor. The Bitch's father is a developer who's covered half of Scottsdale with
> lifestyle condos. We consume the most expensive drugs, cosmetics, and coffee known
> to man. Tell me: what was she thinking?

In other stories, however, the external change doesn't appear in the first scene. It
can happen shortly after the story has begun: Huck Finn, for example, as the novel
begins, discovers that his abusive father, Pap, has returned to town. It is that change,
the drunken return of Pap, that sets *The Adventures of Huckleberry Finn* into motion.
Still in other stories, the external change occurs shortly before the first scene: in Tim
O'Brien's short story "The Things They Carried," the main character, Lt. Jimmy Cross,
has already left for Vietnam before the opening of the story—the move to Vietnam, in
this case, being the most important external change. As a rule of thumb, the external
change happens in the general vicinity of—slightly before, during, or slightly after—
the first scene.

Although some stories present the external change as a large, easily identifiable
event—the move to New York, the return of an abusive father, an angry girl with a razor
under her tongue, the involvement in the Vietnam War—other stories present the
external change with subtlety. An external change may be something as minor as a bad
day at work, a troubling phone call received on the drive home, the news that one's
mother is getting married again. In John Updike's short story "A & P," the external

change is nothing more than three attractive girls entering a grocery store wearing only bikinis. In Richard Ford's story "Communist," the initial change is the return of the mother's old boyfriend after being absent many months. Even more subtly, in Raymond Carver's story "What We Talk About When We Talk About Love," the initial change is the introduction of a particularly touchy topic, that of previous marriages and the elusive nature of love itself. The initial change, then, is a break however small from the regular routine of a character's life.

Character Explication

Hardly any short stories attempt to cover a character's entire life. Even in novels, this is rare. (One notable exception is the French novel, *Madame Bovary*, which begins with her childhood and ends with her death.) Most stories limit themselves to a year, a week, a day, even an hour. A story, for example, might begin the first day of spring and end the first day of summer. In fiction, then, character explication provides the necessary background information to interpret the action included in the story.

Character explication, in its most basic form, is the history of a character up until the story begins. If a plot is to be successfully enacted upon a character, it must affect the character at a deep level. If we, as readers, are to care about a character, we must understand a character's personal history as well as his or her personality. Character explication, then, is an essential element of most stories because it provides a context for the character, an impetus for the plot, and a means by which readers understand a story's action as significant.

Let's take another look at the opening paragraphs of Stacey Richter's "The Beauty Treatment." On the surface, it appears as if the story is primarily concerned with action, namely creating a brutal external change that will begin the story. But on closer examination, it's clear that the story is also working very hard to define the main character and her situation. Many sentences, in addition to creating action, also reveal a great deal about the personality and lifestyle of the narrator. Reread the following sentences, pulled from those paragraphs. This time, however, pay special attention to how they also define the narrator as a young woman, accustomed to money and privilege, who often relies on her "beauty" and "style" to establish a place for herself with the "popular girls" in high school.

- The next thing I know there's blood all over my J. Crew linen fitted blouse, in edelweiss—a very delicate, almost ecru shade of white, ruined now.
- Elizabeth Beecher and Kirsty Moseley run into the bathroom and go Oh my God, then drag me screaming hysterically, all three of us screaming hysterically, to Ms. B. Meanwhile, the Bitch slides into her Mercedes 450SL, lime green if you can believe that—the A-1 primo daddy-lac of all time—and drives off smoking Kools.
- This is what you get from watching too much TV, I'm thinking, and believing your workaholic father when he tells you during one of his rare appearances that you're the Princess of the Universe to which none can compare.
- My father's a doctor. The Bitch's father is a developer who's covered half of Scottsdale with lifestyle condos.
- We consume the most expensive drugs, cosmetics, and coffee known to man. Tell me: what was she thinking?

In this way, Stacey Richter creates an extremely effective first scene, one that simultaneously delivers an external change while slipping in bits of character explication. But not all stories deliver external change and character explication simultaneously.

In Janice Eidus's "Vito Loves Geraldine" (included in **On Prewriting**), the story begins with an extended section of character explication and then slowly, after two pages, works toward the moment of external change. As you read the opening to this story (reprinted below), notice how these paragraphs primarily define Geraldine's personality as well as the characters around her. The external change will come later, when Geraldine goes on her first date with Vito. But the story doesn't begin with that date. It begins with tightly drawn sentences designed to introduce readers to the main character of the story.

> Vito Venecio was after me. He'd wanted to get into my pants ever since tenth grade. But even though we hung around with the same crowd back at Evander Childs High School, I never gave him the time of day. I, Geraldine Rizzoli, was the most popular girl in the crowd, I had my pick of the guys, you can ask anyone, Carmela or Pamela or Victoria, and they'll agree. And Vito was just a skinny little kid with a big greasy pompadour and a cowlick and acne and a big space between his front teeth. True, he could sing, and he and Vinny Feruge and Bobby Colucci and Richie DeSoto formed a doo-wop group and called themselves Vito and the Olinvilles, but lots of the boys formed doo-wop groups and stood around on street corners doo-wopping their hearts out. Besides, I wasn't letting any of them into my pants either.
>
> Carmela and Pamela and Victoria and all the other girls in the crowd would say, "Geraldine Rizzoli, teach me how to tease my hair as high as yours and how to put my eyeliner on so straight and thick," but I never gave away my secrets. I just set my black hair on beer cans every night and in the morning I teased it and teased it with my comb until sometimes I imagined that if I kept going I could get it high enough to reach the stars, and then I would spray it with hairspray that smelled like red roses and then I'd stroke on my black eyeliner until it went way past my eyes.

As a general rule, characters are clearly defined in the first third of a story because this information is essential for readers to understand and interpret a story. Imagine how difficult it would be to continue reading "Vito Loves Geraldine" if we didn't have a close personal understanding of its main character. Or consider this: "The Beauty Treatment" would be a less powerful story if we, as readers, didn't understand that the narrator's identity and self-esteem were bound up in her appearance and then, on the first page, her beauty is taken away.

Most first scenes dance between creating action and defining characters. If readers aren't presented with an intimate portrait of a story's main character, readers will have no means to understand the action. In short, a character's past often allows readers to understand the important relationship between character and plot.

There are a number of ways to include character history in your story. Perhaps it is best to work with your first scene over many days, striving to find the most effective methods to define your characters.

To get you started, below are the most common methods:

- Flashback: a story can include a complete scene or scenes, dramatizing past events.
- Exposition: the narrator explains the history of a character's life.

- Dialogue: through dialogue, a character's past and personality is revealed.
- Detail: the details and setting, if properly described, often reveal a character's lifestyle and social standing.
- Voice: the way a character speaks reveals a good deal about his or her past. This can be particularly effective with first person narration.

In Media Res

Just as most stories don't begin at the start of a character's life, most stories don't begin at the true origin of the problem or conflict. In *The Adventures of Huckleberry Finn*, it is clear that Huck's father, Pap, has been gone for years, and though the novel doesn't include such scenes, it's highly likely that Huck wondered what had happened to his father, both missing and fearing him. But the novel doesn't begin with Pap's departure, nor does it begin by describing those days on which Huck sits wistfully beside the river as he considers what might have happened to Pap. No, the novel begins with action— Pap's return home. But behind this action are the feelings of loss, regret, perhaps longing, as Huck learns what it is like to be raised an orphan.

Likewise, in "The Beauty Treatment," the problems didn't begin on the day "the Bitch" arrived at school with a razor under her tongue. Absolutely not. Even from a casual reading of the story's first scene, a reader can't help but notice that the narrator and "the Bitch" were once friends. How else would she know that "the Bitch's" father is a developer, that she drives "the A-1 primo daddy-lac of all time," and the brand of cigarettes she smokes? More importantly, how would she know that "the Bitch" has been learning about inner-city life on *Montel*, longing to shake off the sanitized lifestyle of the Scottsdale suburbs? We can safely assume that not long ago these friends had a falling out. The tension of their damaged friendship had been simmering until the day "the Bitch" arrives with the razor blade. The action with the razor blade begins the story, but the tension has been building for months, a pressure cooker just waiting to burst. Once it does we have the beginning of a story.

In addition to character explication, stories usually offer a brief history of the conflict or problem behind the action depicted in the first scene. In *The Great Gatsby*, Nick Carraway explains that he has grown tired of the safety and seclusion of the Middle West before looking for excitement in New York. Similarly, Holden Caulfield, in *The Catcher in the Rye*, hints that he has been unable to recover from the death of his brother, Allie, a condition that has indirectly contributed to his dismissal from two previous prep schools and from Pencey, the school he leaves as the novel begins.

For most new writers, this can present one of the most difficult aspects of writing a first scene, namely discovering the relationship between the external change and the tension behind it. To put this another way, to write a first scene—one that occurs *in media res*—you need to know why these events matter to the main character. It's not just a girl at school who is attacked by a random stranger with a razor. No, the girl also is in love with her beauty. She's imagined a future in which her good looks open many doors. Oh, and then there's this: she also knows her attacker. They used to be friends until "the Bitch" grew tired of the suburbs, with its consumerism and sterilized emotions, and began to hate the good-looking girl for what she now represents.

At this point, we no longer have just an external change. Nor do we have just a character. We have three elements of a story triangulated into a first scene: an external change that is tied to a specific character as well as to an interesting yet tense backstory. We have all the structural elements necessary to begin a first scene.

Character Motivation, Pacing, Rising Tension, and Causality

These three elements—external change, character explication, and *in media res*—are key aspects to drafting the first scene of a story. Other aspects of drafting and constructing stories are covered in **On Writing**. But before ending this essay, we would like to discuss a few other general truisms about first scenes, if only briefly.

Character Motivation

■ Focus on what your character needs. Behind most fictional characters burns a deep need at the center of their personality. Nick Carraway (of *The Great Gatsby*) yearns to discover a life for himself outside the comfortable world of his family. Since the death of his younger brother, Holden Caulfield (of *The Catcher in the Rye*) needs help putting his life back together and ending the destructive cycle of grief. The narrator in "The Beauty Treatment" needs to value something in herself other than beauty, though she will also need to forgive "the Bitch" if she is ever going to feel whole again. Such needs are never simple and often are a conduit through which we pass into the center of a character's heart.

Pacing

■ The first scene of a story establishes many things: point of view, setting, tone, and prose style. But one of the overlooked elements established with the first scene concerns pacing. As a general rule, if your first scene is relatively short, you are indicating that the story that follows will include many subsequent short scenes; whereas, if your first scene is long, you are indicating just the opposite. Rarely do you find a story with an initial scene lasting five pages only to be followed by three single-page scenes before ending.

Rising Tension

■ Other commentaries in this textbook will discuss the structure of beginnings, middles, and endings, but what you need to know now as you craft your first scene is this: Tension rises gradually in a short story, like a symphony that slowly crescendos toward a powerful final movement. For your first scene, you want some tension. But you also want to leave room for this tension to expand and deepen. You have to leave room to up the ante.

Freytag's Pyramid illustrates this point. As we've said before, other contributors will discuss these elements in more detail. But for now, notice how the external change is a departure from a character's regular life, and beyond that, notice the gradual slope of rising tension, leading to the climax. The job of the first scene, therefore, is not to bring the action to a boiling point, but to guide the action gradually so that eventually it reaches a moment of importance.

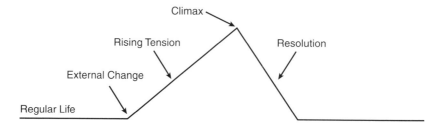

Causality

■ In general, the events presented in the first scene *cause* subsequent action to occur. Fiction is an art that examines causality. So as you write your first scene, ask yourself: is this the type of scene that will *directly cause* subsequent scenes? Will your characters be inclined to respond to this scene with action? As a rule of thumb, you should be able to link most scenes in a short story by using the word *because*. Here is a causal analysis of *The Adventures of Huckleberry Finn*: *Because* Huck's abusive father, Pap, returns home, Huck seeks to avoid him. *Because* Huck avoids him, Pap imprisons Huck in an island cabin. *Because* Huck is kept prisoner, he devises a means of escaping. *Because* Huck doesn't want Pap to find him again, he fakes his own death and, after finding a canoe, begins his trip down the Mississippi. And so on.

In your story, can you show the line of causality, connecting the scenes with the word *because*, starting with the first scene and progressing forward?

Get the First Scene Right

First scenes are fun to write. They're the point at which ideas become fiction. But hardly anyone gets the first scene right the first time through. Writing the first scene is an act of discovery: it's the time during which you finally see your characters in action. Quite often, the first time you tell a story, you are telling it to yourself, and each subsequent time, you are learning how best to convey it to someone else. So if you find your first scene isn't perfect the first time through, don't be afraid to rewrite it. Start with new sentences. Or begin at a different place in the action.

A first scene is a powerful moment in fiction. It is the spring that powers the rest of your story. It introduces the characters. It presents that drama that, through causality, will create the rest of the scenes. So before you move on to a second or third scene, do your best to wind this scene tight and sure so that your story keeps ticking away until the very last sentence.

Section 4

STORY STRUCTURE AND THE FUNDAMENTALS OF PLOT

John McNally

The New Year

From *North American Review* and *Troublemakers* (winner of the John Simmons Short Fiction Award)

At midnight, party horns blow obscenely, strangers kiss with tongues, and champagne corks fire perilously across the smoky room like a barrage of SCUD missiles. No one here has ever heard of "Auld Lang Syne," so what they do instead to celebrate the new year is blast the first few tracks off Ozzy Osbourne's *Blizzard of Ozz*.

Two hours later, half the people have gone home, fearing the approaching snowstorm. The remaining half have coupled, staking out for themselves every bedroom, hallway, and closet in the house. Here and there, men and women copulate—some, discreetly; others as if auditioning for the victim role in a slasher film: lots of panting, then moans, then a high-pitched squeal followed by a howl or scream, then nothing at all.

Dead, Gary thinks.

This is how he entertains himself: absorbing the reality around him and turning it into something other than what it is, something menacing. Only he and Linda remain among the flotsam of the party—cigarette butts rising like crooked tombstones out of bowls of salsa; a slice of pizza dangling like a limp hand over the edge of the coffee table—and Gary, lost in his own private world of the macabre, is listening for the next rising moan, the next victim, when Linda, joint in one hand, vodka tonic in the other, tells Gary that she's pregnant.

"I'm keeping it, too," she says, meeting Gary's eyes and smiling wildly, as if announcing an extravagant purchase she cannot afford, like alligator shoes or a raccoon coat, challenging Gary to tell her *No, You'll have to take it back*.

Gary dips his hand into the ice bucket, scoops out the last pitiful shards of ice, and deposits them into a tall glass. With the assortment of leftover liquor, he mixes himself what he thinks is in a Harvey Wallbanger, a name his father uses freely for all occasions, exclamations of surprise and scathing insults alike, the way another man might say *Great Scott!* or *Son of a bitch!* Gary sips the drink tentatively, squinting at Linda while he does so. The first concert he ever took her to was Megadeth in Omaha, and he wants to ask her if that had been the night, in a dark and cavernous loading dock at Rosenblatt Stadium, that he'd unceremoniously knocked her up, but he is having a difficult time summoning the proper words, let alone stringing them into a meaningful sentence.

"Do you mind?" he asks and picks up the four-foot bong he had packed earlier in the night but had somehow forgotten about. He holds it to his mouth as if it were a saxophone, and while Linda leans over to light the bowl, Gary sucks hard on the tube. He inhales for what seems an impossibly long time, and when he finally exhales, he tilts his head back so as not to blow smoke in the face of his girlfriend who is carrying his child.

Over their heads and scattered about the room float swollen clouds of marijuana smoke, thick as doom, and though Gary has long since run out of breath, smoke continues to leak from his nose and mouth. He's been working out daily at the gym, and he's amazed at how much his lung capacity has improved in just two short weeks.

"Wow," he says, amazed at *everything*—the pending baby, his new lungs—and it's the word *wow*, this last puff of smoke streaming from his mouth when he speaks, that triggers the smoke alarm. The alarm is deafening, piercing Gary's consciousness, one steady shriek after another, like a knife thrust repeatedly into his head, and though Gary wants nothing more than to stop the noise, he has no idea where to start looking.

Four men instantly appear from each corner of the house. They arrive like Romans, bedsheets draped around hips and torsos. One man stands on a chair, disappearing into a head of smoke, and when he rips open the smoke alarm's casing and yanks free the battery, along with the two wires the battery had been connected to, the noise mercifully stops.

The man steps off the chair, looks Gary in the eyes, and says, "What the fuck?"

Gary shrugs. He's still holding the bong, resting it against his shoulder as if it were a rifle. Then he tips the bong toward Linda, points the smoking barrel at her stomach, and says, "She's pregnant."

At this news, women emerge one by one from the darkest chambers and alcoves of the house. Some are barely dressed, wearing only underthings. Others wear long hockey jerseys or concert T-shirts that belong to the men they have chosen for the night. They surround Linda and gently prod her belly. *How far along are you?* they ask. *Is it a boy or a girl?* They move in closer and closer, confiscating her vodka tonic, relieving her of the roach pinched between her thumb and forefinger, until Linda becomes the nucleus, the Queen Bee of the party, pleasantly crushed by a circle of women who "ooooo" and "ahhhh" against her stomach and buzz with spurious tips on prenatal care.

Gary backs away from the chatter and smoke. As soon as he is outside, he bolts for his car. His coat, he realizes, is somewhere in the house, but it's too late now. If he returns, Linda will see him and want to leave as well, and what he wants now is to be alone. What he *needs* is to think.

Inside the Swinger, where everything is ice-cold to the touch, Gary starts the engine, then rubs his hands together, blowing frequently into the cave of his cupped palms. "Harvey Wallbanger!" he yells. "It's friggin' *cold*." He yanks the gearshift into drive and pulls quickly away from the party, heading for the unmarked road that will take him home.

Only after putting a safe distance between himself and the party does Gary allow himself to entertain the otherwise unthinkable, that Linda is pregnant. He says it aloud, trying out the feel of it. "So," he says. "You're pregnant." Then he laughs. He laughs until his throat burns and the windows fog up all around him. "Pregnant," he says, clearing a swatch of windshield. "Yow!"

Other girls he's known have called it *prego*, like the spaghetti sauce, or *preggers*, which sounds to Gary like something made by Nabisco, a new brand of snack cracker. He can't stop shivering, and the convulsions come stronger each time he thinks of Linda walking around with a smaller, mucousy version of himself inside her. *Inside her.* The very idea! A person inside of a person! Now that he really thinks about it, pregnancy makes no sense whatsoever, a horror movie where a living organism grows and grows, until, finally, it bursts through an innocent victim's stomach, a terrible surprise for everyone.

Truth is, Gary knows less than squat about the finer points of the subject. He'd slacked off in Sex Ed, unable to stop himself from laughing out loud at words like *fallopian tube* and *mons glans*. And the textbook, with its floating orbs and scary cross-sections, was like some kind of underground Science Fiction comic book, where body parts looked extraterrestrial, and their corresponding names, like *vas deferens*, were obviously chosen for haunting effect. The one time he ever even remotely touched on the subject of pregnancy was with a kid he knew named Jim Davis.

It had been a peculiar friendship from the start, one that had materialized between seventh and eighth grade because all of Jim's real friends had gone away for the summer, and because Gary seemed the least harmful of prospects. The subject had come up in regard to Jim's mother, who was much younger than Gary's mother, and who doted on her son in ways that Gary's mother had never doted on him. Jim and his mother played this game, acting as if Gary were not among them: mother and son whispering, pinching each other, always telling the other one how cute they were. Gary never knew where to look, what to do, so he would stand off to the side, rearranging the fruit-shaped magnets and family photos on the refrigerator: a pineapple in lieu of a toddler's head, a giant banana sprouting from their schnauzer's butt.

One day, after a game of eight-ball in their basement, Jim Davis made a confession that he had once tasted an eighteen-year-old girl.

Gary imagined a fork and knife, a dash of salt. "When was this?" he asked.

"Birth," Jim said.

Gary leaned his head sideways, scratched the inside of his ear with the tip of the pool cue.

What Jim Davis was claiming was that when he was born, he kept his tongue out the whole time, and even now, twelve year later, he remembered how it tasted.

"You want to know what it's like?" he said. "Go home and lick two hot slices of liver. I'm telling you, man, that's it. I shit you not, my friend."

Gary is on the unmarked road now, and since he is driving into the storm, it's significantly worse here than it had been on the highway. Visibility is zip. The wind has picked up, and snow swirls about the highway like smoke from a fog machine, not at all unlike the opening of that Megadeth concert three months ago. *Liver*, Gary thinks. He never touches the stuff. Gary squints for better vision. For stretches as long as fifteen seconds he can see one or two car-lengths ahead, whips of snow wiggling snake-like from one side of the road to the other, but soon they dissolve into dense sheets of white that repeatedly slap the windshield, and Gary cannot see more than a foot beyond his head-lights. He doesn't want a child. Earlier that evening, in fact, he was devising a strategy for breaking up with Linda. Strategy is everything when it comes to breaking up, and what he always strives for is to find a way to make it look like his girlfriend's idea, and not his. You have to flip-flop the argument, twist words, drag the murky past for minor infractions. It's an ugly way to conduct business, but sometimes you have to jumpstart the end of a relationship, otherwise it'll just rot and stink up the rest of your life.

He knows he should ask for advice on this one, but he doesn't know who to turn to. Gary's father has his own problems right now: the man hasn't spoken a word to anyone in two weeks. And besides, Gary was cured years ago of asking his father anything about sex after the day his father pulled him aside to warn him about transmittable diseases.

"In the old days," his father began, "when I was your age, if you had the clap, the doctor would make you set your thing onto a stainless-steel table. You know what I'm talking about, right? Your *thing*. Your Howard *Johnson*. So you'd do what the man said. You'd slap it down for him to look at, and after you told him what was wrong, he'd reach into a drawer and pull out a giant rubber mallet, and then he'd take that mal-let and hit your thing as hard as he could with it, and that would be that. Believe you me, son, you'd be damn particular from that point on where you went sticking man's best friend."

Gary is imagining his own thing getting whacked with a rubber hammer when someone or something steps out in front of his car. He is doing sixty or seventy miles-per-hour, the road is slick, and he touches his foot to the brake only after he has hit whatever it is that crossed his path. People claim that these moments always occur in slow-motion, but Gary is so stoned, the opposite is true: everything speeds up. One sec-ond he is thinking about his thing getting whacked; the next, he is lying with his head on the horn of his car. He has no idea how much time passes before he lifts his head and steps outside, but it's still dark when he does so, and the falling snow, sharp as pins, has thickened.

Gary hugs his arms and limps to the front of what's left of the Swinger. What he hit was the largest deer he's ever seen: a twelve-point buck. A gem of a kill if he were a hunter, which he's not—the only non-hunter, in fact, in a long line of men who pre-fer oiling their rifles and shitting in the woods to smoking dope and listening to Ratt. The deer, apparently, had slid all the way up onto his hood, smashed the windshield, then slid back down after Gary, either semi- or unconscious, brought the car to a stop. It lay now in front of the Swinger, its black eyes eternally fixed on something far, far away. Clots of fur sprout from the tip of the crumpled hood, as if the car itself is in the first stages of metamorphosis.

Gary licks his lips and tastes blood. No telling the damage he did to his face when his head hit the steering wheel. For all Gary knows, his forehead is split wide open and his nose, through which he can no longer breathe, is permanently flattened. He may have a concussion, too, his brain puffy, slowly inflating with blood. But far more press-ing than any physical damage is the sub-zero temperature. His entire body is starting to stiffen. He shuffles from foot to foot to keep warm. He rubs his bare arms and yells *Fuck* over and over. "Fuck, fuck, fuck."

Years ago he read a wilderness story in which a man stuck out in the freezing cold sliced open the carcass of a dead animal and crawled inside to keep warm. It was a bear, Gary remembers, and the man stayed inside of the bear until someone discovered him in there. Gary craves warmth, he's willing to make deals with a higher power, but he'll be goddamned if he's going to hang around inside of a dead deer and wait for his worthless friends and neighbors to find him. Besides, it's a small town, word travels fast, and he can't imagine any girl ever wanting to date him after hearing where he'd been. The girls he knows, they'll overlook the fact that you've slept with the town hosebag, but there is always a line, and sleeping inside of anything dead is clearly on the other side of it. Gary's about five miles from home—walking distance, really—close enough, he decides, to make a go of it, even without a coat.

Gary starts to jog, but his legs aren't working quite right. It's as if he's running on stumps instead of feet. He suspects a bone somewhere has snapped in two, so he works on the basics of walking instead, just keeping one foot in front of the other. He hugs himself the whole way, hands secured under his armpits. He'll have to wake his father when he gets home so they can tow the car before sunrise and avoid getting a ticket. He'd prefer not bothering him at all, but he sees no way around it. Gary's mother left home a year ago, and for a while Gary thought that this was the worst thing that could possibly happen to his father. Then, two weeks ago, his mother surprised everyone and married his father's best friend, a man named Chuck Linkletter. And that's when his father quit talking. He quit going to work at the gas station he owns, and he has quit taking calls. He has, it seems to Gary, quit altogether, like an old lawnmower.

Gary's ears and fingertips throb, and the snow pelting his face temporarily blinds him. His eyebrows are starting to ice over and sag, as are the few sad whiskers on his upper lip, a mustache Gary's been closely monitoring these past few months. He wishes he had taken the bong from the party. He'd be standing in the middle of the road right now, his back to the storm, lighting a fresh bowl. And then everything wouldn't seem so bad—Linda's news, his car, the pain.

When he finally reaches his house, shivering his way inside, he collapses next to the sofa.

"Oh. My. God," he says. "I made it." His voice, a croak in the dark, sounds like the voice of nobody he knows. Now that he's home and out of the cold, he's thinking maybe he won't wake his father after all—towing the car no longer seems so dire—but then the light in his father's bedroom comes on, the door swings opens, and his father appears as if from one of his own nightmares: sleepy but crazed, thin hair crooked atop his head like bad electrical wiring. This is how the man has looked ever since learning the news of the marriage, and though Gary is starting to wonder if he should seek professional help for his father, they live in a town of two hundred, and the only people around who claim to be professionals of anything either strip and refinish wood work or groom dogs.

Gary himself holds no grudge against his mother. As far as he's concerned, she's been a good mom. When Gary was in the third grade and his father refused to bring him a cat from the pound, his mother took Gary outside with several spools of thread. "You have to use your imagination," she'd told him. It was summer, and while Gary captured a few dozen grasshoppers, holding them captive inside of a Hills Brothers coffee can with holes punched in the plastic lid, his mother made several dozen miniature nooses with the thread. "Here," she said. "Let's see one of them." Gary gently pinched a grasshopper and held it up for his mother while she slid a noose over the insect's torso, then tightened it.

"What's his name?" she asked.

"Fred Astaire," Gary said.

Later, while Gary walked thirty or so of his grasshoppers down the street, old man Wickersham stepped down from his front stoop, stopped Gary, and asked him what he was doing.

"I'm taking my pets for a walk."

"Oh," the old man said.

Near the end of summer Gary had caught several hundred bumblebees, and over the next month, using his mother's tweezers and suffering through one painful sting after another, Gary managed to tie each surviving bee to one of his mother's nooses, and when he finished, he took all of them out for a stroll. The bees droned overhead, following him like a dark cloud. Old Man Wickersham burst out of his house, yelling, "My God, son, they're after you," and Gary, not realizing the old man meant the bees, let go of the strings and took off running. For days after that, people in town—and as far away as North Platte—reported getting tickled by mysterious airborne threads.

"Dad," Gary says now. "I totaled the car. We should probably tow it home before the police find it." Then Gary tells his father the story, omitting the pregnant girlfriend, the endless kegs of Old Style, and the four-foot bong. What he focuses on is the deer.

"You should see this thing," he said. "It's gargantuan. A twelve-pointer. Swear to God, I thought I slammed into a bulldozer."

His father puts on a coat and disappears through a door in the kitchen that leads into the garage, reappearing seconds later carrying an ax.

Gary, unable to stop quivering, the night's deep freeze still trapped in his bones, slips on leather gloves, zips himself into his father's wool trenchcoat, and pulls on a ski-mask that covers his entire head except for his eyes and mouth. They take the new pickup, Gary's father skillfully navigating the vehicle at high speeds through miles of virgin snow. Amazingly, they cover in less than ten minutes the distance it took Gary an hour-and-a-half to travel on foot.

His father parks in front of the dead deer and the demolished car, illuminating the scene with the pick-up's high-beams. The deer is already dusted with snow. Outside, towering over the carcass, Gary's father reaches down, takes hold of the base of the rack, and lifts the deer's head. He jiggles the head a few times, then crouches to get a better look.

"What do you think?" Gary asks through the ski-mask. "Should we drag it by the horns or just back it ass-first into the ditch?"

His father doesn't answer. He walks to the pick-up. He returns with the ax, lifting it over his head and taking aim.

"Dad," Gary says. "What are you doing?"

The blade comes down hard, slamming into the deer's neck. The deer's head rises off the ground, as if looking up to Gary for help, but it's the force of the blow causing it to do this, and the head falls quickly back into the snow. His father swings a second time, then a third, each time hitting a different part of the animal, though keeping within the general vicinity of the neck. It slowly creeps up on Gary that what it is his father is trying to do is chop off the deer's head. "The car," Gary says. "Maybe we should, like, shift our focus?" He points at the Swinger, but his father plants his foot onto the deer's ribs, jerks free the ax, then lifts it again. Each time his father lands a blow, Gary's fingertips and ears throb, a jolt of pain pulsing through the thousands of miles of nerves that twist and wind throughout his own body. In a few weeks, when Doctor Magnabosco asks Gary why he waited until the frostbite had progressed to this point before seeking help—this critical point, he'll add for effect—Gary will have no idea where to begin, nor will he know how to tell the story of this night in such a way that his father won't end up looking like a madman, and so Gary will simply shrug.

Gary watches his father through the tiny slits of the ski-mask, and still unable to breathe through his nose, he starts gasping for air. His father is crying. He keeps slamming the ax into the deer, each strike harder than the last, and Gary realizes that he, too, is crying. He chokes out one breath after another, large plumes of air, ghostly in the truck's headlights, spewing from his mouth. He's about to say something to his father, a word or two of consolation, when a car approaches, slowing at the sight of them. The car hits its own high-beams to see what's the matter, and what they see is a wrecked car, a dead deer, a weeping man holding an ax, and another man wearing a ski mask and a trenchcoat, glaring back into the eyes of the driver. In this moment, seemingly frozen in time, Gary spots Linda in the backseat, mittened hands cupped over her mouth. He starts walking toward the car, but the high-beams blink off and the car speeds away, disappearing into thick swirls of snow, the red glow of taillights dissolving into two pinpoints, then nothing.

When Gary turns back to his father, he sees that the deer's head has finally come detached. His father lifts the head by the rack and carries it to the pick-up where he heaves it up and over, into the bed. As for the other carnage—the headless deer, the wrecked car—they leave it all behind.

Once they are inside the truck's cab and on their way home, Gary experiences a surge of adrenaline, a genuine rush, and he can't wait to call Linda. He wishes he could hug his father, he wishes he could say, *Shit, man, what the hell just happened back there?* but his father is driving more cautiously now, both hands on the steering wheel, and any impulsive move on Gary's part may cause his father to drive them into a snowdrift.

Why another man's misery—his dad's, in particular—inspires Gary to want to call Linda and make amends, he's not sure, but he feels suddenly pumped, as though he has just had a great workout at the gym, his best workout ever. He feels almost possessed, but possessed by what he doesn't know. He's still too messed-up to put his finger on it, to understand how one thing in his life could possibly be connected to another, but after he gets some sleep, he's going to call Linda and tell her that he has come to a decision. He, too, wants to keep the child.

"Fuckin' ay, Dad," Gary says. "We took the bull by the horns, didn't we? And now we're bringing home the head to prove it."

His father laughs. His mood has taken a dramatic turn for the better. He is chipper, even. "We'll mount it," his father says. "We'll mount it and we'll send it to your mother and that son of a bitch she married for a wedding present. What do you say? You want to give me a hand with it tonight?"

"Tonight?" Gary asks. The sun is about to rise. Tonight, as far as Gary can tell, is over. It's already tomorrow. "Don't we have to get it taxidermied first?"

"Oh no," his father says, smiling. "Not this one. They'll get it just like this, nailed to a sheet of plywood. And I want to ship it off, lickety-split. I want to Fed-Ex this baby right to their front porch. I'll show those two Harvey Motherfucking Wallbangers I mean business."

Gary removes his ski-mask and touches his face experimentally. His flesh is disconcertingly spongy, and each time he presses down on his cheek or forehead, he leaves behind the soft imprint of his fingertip. "I think I'll pass," he says. "I'm sort of beat."

"Suit yourself," his father says. "But mark my words, this is going to be the highlight of the year. You can bet your ass on that."

Gary nods. He reassures himself that all of this is a good sign. At least his dad's talking again. Surely that's a step in the right direction.

They drive the rest of the way home in silence, the deer's head rolling around behind them, antlers clawing the truck's bed. Though the storm has ended and the sun is peeking over the tree-line, the wind is still fierce, and Gary stares blankly at the snow whirling across the highway. His surge of adrenaline is on the wane now, the rush of exhilaration over. He's falling asleep, slipping into that precarious crack between consciousness and unconsciousness, but for a moment, before he drifts completely away, Gary pretends that he and his father have been in a fatal collision, and that although dead, they are still puttering along in the pick-up, maneuvering it through swirling clouds instead of snow, and they are having the best time they've ever had together, father and son floating high above the rural roads and farms, two men no longer of this Earth.

McNally on Story Beginnings

Frank Conroy, my writing teacher in graduate school, said that the beginning of a story contains an implied contract that the author makes with the reader.

How can I tell when an author has violated this contract? It's simple. One minute I'm reading; the next, I'm pissed off. If it's a published story, I'll toss it aside. If it's a student's story, I'll circle where I believe the contract was broken and put my comments in the margin.

In truth, this contract varies from story to story, but on the first page, sometimes even the first sentence, the author establishes the tone, voice, style, point of view, and psychic distance. Here's a definition of the contract: it requires that these elements remain consistent throughout the story.

Consider *tone*. Let's say an author has written a humorous story about an Italian-American family, in which the vast majority of the humor grows out of honest, believable situations. Therefore, the humor is primarily organic—it is part of the characters' lives. Now, let's say that on page twelve a son and father get into an argument, the morning after which the son finds the head of a horse in his bed. The reader wonders, *What the hell just happened?*

This example is extreme, of course, but here's the point: the author parodied a scene from *The Godfather*, and the humor shifted abruptly from organic to authorial.

By authorial, I mean that the author's hand moved into the story to insert a comic moment. It's inconsistent with the rest of the humor.

I don't want to belabor the necessity for internal consistency in each story element, but the same is true for voice, style, point of view, and psychic distance. A violation of style might be a story whose first half reads like Hemingway (spare prose that employs a simple syntax) and whose second half reads like Faulkner (lush prose with syntax that bends and twists). Unless there's some logical reason for the switch in style, readers are likely to feel confused or, worse, angry.

The beginning of each story also establishes psychic distance, the relationship between the reader and the events in the story, and, more importantly, the relationship between the reader and the story's narrator. I have come to believe that psychic distance is one of the most important elements of fiction writing and it is established on the first page of a story.

The first sentence below is an example of the greatest distance the reader can feel to the story's events. Each subsequent sentence brings the reader closer to both the events and the characters. After each example, in italics, you'll find a brief explanation.

1. **It is August 4, 1977, and it's snowing.** *This sentence is pure exposition. There is no character, no precise setting, only information. The reader attaches him- or herself to a sentence such as this one almost entirely on an intellectual level. If the reader happens to respond on an emotional level, it's because of some personal connection to August 4, 1977, or some memory of snow, but not because of any emotionally resonant moment in the story.*

2. **A large man walks out of a restaurant and into the snowy night.** *If you think of this sentence in terms of a scene in a movie, it might be the opening shot, perhaps a bird's-eye view of the scene, filmed from a helicopter. Neither the man nor the bar is specific. The details are general in nature, unspecific.*

3. **Joe Worthington steps out of the Sunset Bar and Grill and shivers.** *Aha! Now we have specifics. These specifics, in turn, give the reader a sense of personality and place. The Sunset Bar and Grill has more character than "a restaurant." As a result, the reader starts feeling closer to the scene.*

4. **Joe Worthington, stepping out of the Sunset Bar and Grill, thinks about how horribly cold it is.** *For the first time, the reader is privy to Joe's internal thoughts. This is significant because the reader now has a consciousness to hook into. The fictional world is no longer viewed objectively; it is being filtered, at least in part, through Joe's point of view.*

5. ***Damn, it's cold,*** **Joe Worthington thinks, stepping out of the Sunset Bar and Grill.** *The difference between # 5 and # 4 is that the reader is now privy to Joe's direct internal thought. We are more fully inside his head. We are probably more likely to have a visceral response to what Joe thinks and what he does.*

6. ***Damn, it's cold!*** *In terms of psychic distance, this is as close as we can get. We are directly inside Joe's head. In #5 above, we still felt the presence of the author who provides "Joe Worthington thinks." Not here. If the story were to continue in this vein, we'd call it "internal monologue."*

The issue isn't whether feeling close is better than feeling removed. (Ernest Hemingway's "The Killers" effectively begins from a psychic distance that is very removed.) The issues are two-fold. One: How well does the author control shifts in psychic distance? Two: Is the author using psychic distance to the story's best advantage?

As for control, John Gardner, a noted teacher of creative writing in the 1970s and 1980s, insists that you shouldn't jump around from, say, #6 to #3 to #5 to #1, and so on. The reader would never feel grounded. Here's a film metaphor: Imagine a movie that jumps from an intense close-up to a bird's-eye view to a medium-shot, and so on. You'd be so distracted by the randomness of the filmmaker's decisions that you'd have a difficult time paying attention to the story, let alone feeling anything for the story's characters. The same is true for fiction. Control instills confidence in readers.

The level of psychic distance at which you begin your story should be the closest you're allowed to go throughout the course of your story. In other words, if you begin your story at #3, you could employ levels #4, #5, and #6, but not #1 or #2. Doing so would be too jarring to the reader, a violation of the contract. And if you begin your story at #6, well, you'd be stuck at #6 for the rest of the story. What you need to know is that one choice may severely limit you (remaining at #6 throughout, for instance), but your choice really rests on what you're trying to accomplish in your story.

Your fiction-writing course could easily be titled "The Art of Manipulation" since what you're graded on at the end of the semester is, in large part, your skill as a manipulator. It's as simple—and as difficult—as that.

I should note here that the reader/writer contract in a novel, as opposed to in a short story, tends to be established at the beginning of each chapter, which is why you're likely to read books that do, in fact, change voice, style, or even point of view throughout, but it's been my experience that many writers remain faithful to whatever contract they've established for each chapter. Some longer short stories or novellas may change voice, style, and point of view, too, but usually the author has broken the story into sections. In such instances, the author has carefully prepared the reader to read the story a certain way. The section breaks are like posted warning signs that the rules might change.

Perhaps the primary benefit to sticking with a contract is that the reader won't be jarred out of the story, that the story will maintain what Gardner called "the vivid and continuous dream inside the reader's mind." Sure, you can break all the rules you want, but it's a rare occasion, in my experience, that a broken rule results in greater gains than that which is lost. Such stories usually become one-trick ponies, accomplishing little more than being a showcase for a writer to yell, "Look, I've broken the rules!" as if no one in the long history of writing had ever thought to break the rules.

More than once, I've been asked by new writers, "Do you *really* think about all of these things before you write?" I believe this is their fear, that attention to craft takes the fun out of writing.

I explain to them that it's like playing pool: you work on a bank shot, you watch other players far better than you, and you spend countless hours thinking about the shot. And then one night you run the table. You've *internalized* what you need to do, and you simply do it. The more stories you work on, the more you read, the more you think about craft as a beginning writer, the more your stories will eventually do these things on their own, without your constant conscious attention.

For me, stories often start with character. Or they start with a haunting image that leads me to character. "The New Year" was one of those stories.

I wrote the first draft very quickly. It was the first story I wrote where I was hyper-conscious of establishing a particular contract with the reader—a contract I found helpful because it allowed me to achieve certain things later in the story. Here are the first three paragraphs—the contract, as it were:

> At midnight, party horns blow obscenely, strangers kiss with tongues, and champagne corks fire perilously across the smoky room like a barrage of SCUD missiles. No one here has ever heard of "Auld Lang Syne," so what they do instead to celebrate the new year is blast the first few tracks off Ozzy Osbourne's *Blizzard of Ozz*.
>
> Two hours later, half the people have gone home, fearing the approaching snow-storm. The remaining half have coupled, staking out for themselves every bedroom, hallway, and closet in the house. Here and there, men and women copulate—some, discreetly; others as if auditioning for the victim role in a slasher film: lots of panting, then moans, then a high-pitched squeal followed by a howl or scream, then nothing at all.
>
> *Dead*, Gary thinks.

You'll notice that I don't introduce any specific characters in the first two paragraphs. The point of view, as it turns out, is coming from some authorial voice, a voice hovering far above any individual character. It's not until the third paragraph that Gary is introduced, and I dip into his head for an internal thought, a single word: *Dead*. I made a conscious decision to begin the story this way for several reasons.

1. Gary is the story's main character. He's the one whose perspective we're eventually privy to. The problem is, Gary isn't the brightest guy in the world, so if the story had been written from an extremely close third person—that is, a point of view limited strictly to Gary's insights and perspective—the story would probably lack a subtext. For me, the subtext is the deeper and murkier and most interesting element of a story. Gary is unable to understand the subtext or the greater meaning of his life. He only has a surface understanding of his life, and so my fear was that without some psychic distance, the story would not reveal his true personality or true problems.

2. Gary is both stoned and drunk. Imagine how insufferable the story would be written entirely from psychic distance level #6, the internal monologue. The story would be utterly incomprehensible. Richard Yates, whose novel *Disturbing the Peace* tries to capture the state of mind of a manic-depressive slipping into the manic state, said the tricky thing was to write about mania while maintaining lucidity and to capture that state of mind in clear and precise language. I don't know if I entirely accomplished this in "The New Year," but early on I wanted to establish a means of narrating the events so as to tell Gary's story with lucidity.

3. The first paragraph sets the story's tone, mildly ironic and deadpan.

After I established the first-page contract, the rest of the story fell into place. Each story teaches the writer a different lesson about craft, and one thing I learned writing

"The New Year" was how the contract I established at the beginning of a story affected everything that followed it, whether or not I, as its writer, was conscious of it. The last sentence of "The New Year" moves from inside Gary's head outward, back to the authorial voice that began the story. I didn't plan this. There is no way I could have ended this story with its current final sentence had I established a different tone and psychic distance at the beginning of the story. But since I didn't *plan* to end the story with this kind of voice, the story apparently took on a life of its own. Rather than hindering me, understanding the contract made me aware of possibilities. It opened up a larger world at the end of the story.

Writing Suggestions

1. Write the first paragraph to a new story where you have extremely close psychic distance to the protagonist—see McNally's examples above for how to do this. Then redraft the same scene with a medium amount of psychic distance between you and the character. Lastly, redraft the paragraph again with a great deal of psychic distance. Which is easiest to create? How does altering the psychic distance change the story you're telling?

2. Referring to the **Writing the First Scene** introduction (pages 61–62), write the first scene to a story in which the main character receives troubling news from home. How will you include each of these elements in a first scene? How can the first scene cause subsequent scenes to happen? What does the pacing about the first scene suggest about how scenes, in general, will be handled in your story?

3. Revisit one of your own stories. Which of the elements from the **Writing the First Scene** essay (External Change, Character Explication, *In Media Res*, pages 62–68) do you see expressed in your first scene? Develop a means to strengthen each of these elements by revising the scene. Which first scene works better—the original draft or the revised draft? Why?

4. At the local newsstand, find a magazine that publishes short stories, such as *The Atlantic Monthly*, *Esquire*, *Harper's Monthly*, or *The New Yorker*, or a literary journal, such as *The Georgia Review*, *Glimmer Train*, *McSweeney's*, *Ploughshares*, *The Yale Review*, and *Zoetrope*. Read the first scene of a handful of stories. Pay attention to how psychic distance is situated in the story. How are the structural elements (from **Writing the First Scene**, pages 61–68) used in these contemporary pieces?

> *I want stories to startle and engage me within the first few sentences, and in the middle to widen or deepen or sharpen my knowledge of human activity, and to end by giving me a sensation of a completed statement.*
> —John Updike

Aaron Gwyn

Of Falling

From *Louisiana Literature* and *New Stories from the South 2002*

George Crider was seven when Freddy was born, fifteen before his brother grew old enough to sit a horse. In the autumn, after their chores were done, the boys would ride bareback across the pasture to a persimmon grove, spend their afternoons climbing the thin trees for fruit.

One day the animal they were riding stepped in a sinkhole and bucked. George caught hold of its mane, but his brother was behind him and fell to the ground. The boy's arm broke the skin, and the bone jutted into dirt. He developed tetanus and in two weeks was dead. George blamed himself for this, as did his parents, and at the funeral, when he climbed into the grave and sought to open the casket, his father lost two teeth trying to retrieve him.

Three years later, grown to well over six feet, he slid a razor in his hip pocket, a change of clothes in his knapsack, and without saying good-bye, walked forty miles through the Quashita forest until he came to Highway 3, hitching across Oklahoma in the back of a cattle truck. He went to work in the oil field and bought a new car, kept a shotgun underneath his seat, sawed at the stock and barrel. One night he left for Louisiana and returned a week later with a Cajun woman, named Sadie, whom he had taken to wife.

Everyone thought George unflappable. He was tall and lean, with a hard, lean face and expressionless eyes. He did not talk about himself or his brother or his parents back in Shinewell, pastors of a Pentecostal church. He was quiet and felt no need to speak. The men he worked with respected him, for they knew he was strong and stubborn, and they would not have wanted to face him in a fight, fair or otherwise.

Then, in 1933, working the eighth floor of an oil derrick in Pontotoc County, scaffolding gave way and George fell 116 feet onto the bank of a saltwater pit.

He did not remember this. Not the fabric blowing against his limbs or the girders moving past or the platform where he'd stood traveling into sky. It took him nearly four seconds to reach the ground, but he could not recall them. For him there was only the eighth floor and the earth.

Through the years to follow, he would recount the incident for his wife: the stares of the men who found him, the ambulance and hospital, the doctor who examined him from top to toe as if he were a puzzle. He would tell her about watching the clouds change to ceiling tile, the sun to bright lamps and mirrors. He would tell about sandstone pressing into his back like shards of bone and then the cool of the sheets, the anesthetic.

Yet, stretched beneath the shadow of the derrick, George's first thoughts were not of family or friends, the condition of his soul, or whether he would be able to one day move his legs. His thoughts were not of the porch standing unfinished, the clothesline needing repair, the foundation wall that had shown signs of flaking just the day before. His thoughts were not of what he would lose in this world, gain or lose in the world hereafter.

Lying there with the sky weighing down and the wind moving over and across him, George had considered only the boards that had snapped beneath his feet. With his lower lip clenched between his teeth, he watched himself walk to where they lay at the side of the derrick and kick them to splinters.

The fall had broken both his arms, his legs, six of his ribs at their connecting points. His skull was fractured, and his sternum snapped in half. The doctor who admitted him said he would not live through the night.

He lived regardless. Through that night and the night after and the night after that.

The surgeons said it was a wonder; they said it was a phenomenon. One stood in the middle of his hospital room and pronounced it a miracle. And though he said George would never walk, he thought he might, one day, have a life of some kind.

In two years George was walking. In two more he had returned to work. By the time he reached his midthirties, George was spry as any roughneck in the state. He was promoted to foreman, and through the depression years, when many left to seek work elsewhere, George and his wife began to build a collection of antique glassware. If he chose, he could retire young, live comfortably off his pension and what he had invested in glass rarities.

George seemed much the same as before the fall. To see him pull to the curb in his burgundy Pontiac, step out and approach an antique shop—a tall, slender man, graceful as a dancer, with jet-black hair and eyes like drops of oil—you would not have thought he had fallen in his life. Not even from the height of a chair.

It was along this time, along the time George stacked his crutches in the rear of the closet and poured his vial of laudanum down the sink, that the dreams came.

They were not, as one would think, dreams of falling, the body released from its federation with the earth and betrayed to gravity. Neither were they dreams of impact. The dreams that visited George after his fall were of stillness.

In them, he would be lying in a field, feeling drops of sweat run into his eyes and pool around the sockets. When he attempted to raise his hand and wipe them, he could not. His ears itched, his face and neck. His body burned. He lay among the blades of grass, blinking into sky.

Soon there was a cloud. It was small at first. If he had been able, George could have retrieved a quarter from his pocket, held it at arm's length, and eclipsed the cloud entirely. But as it grew, he would have needed a fifty-cent piece, a silver dollar, and then, even with both hands outspread and extended in front of his face, wisps of gray would have bled the edges of his fingers.

There was nothing about the cloud to warrant fear. It was not boiling and black, or streaked with light. There was no rumbling and it gave no sound. This was not the type of cloud from which angels or prophets descend.

Only, lying there beneath it, George came to know death in the stillness of wide and all but empty sky.

He awoke screaming. He awoke on the floor. The doctors said such dreams were common among those who had fallen. They gave him pills of all sizes, but the dreams did not stop.

Then one night he awoke running through the house, glassware rattling the mahogany furniture. Sadie watched him from their doorway.

"Crider," she called, "you'll break everything we own."

She was right; several vases lay broken already.

When he wakened and was asked what he'd been dreaming, George went to his car and fell asleep across the seats. The next morning, he was sitting on the front stoop of Woolworth when the owner unlocked the doors.

George purchased four belts, fastened each to the other, and threaded them between his mattress and box springs. Each night he brought the ends together and buckled himself beneath his quilts.

Years passed in this way, with George awaking early every morning strapped to his bed. His wife began sleeping across the hall and, when they stayed in motels, made him reserve nonadjoining rooms.

Visitors seldom came, but when they did, Sadie would take them on a tour of their home. By then every surface in the house—sideboard, dining and coffee table, ottoman, divan—was covered in antique glass. Sadie had acquired the largest collection in Perser and was slowly overtaking Herbert Nasser and his wife, Vinita, who made claim of the largest in Oklahoma.

Her guests would follow her through the small, dark house, through the smell of must and old wood. There were two bedrooms, a bath, a small kitchen crowded with dining table and stove. None of the window blinds or curtains were open; Sadie feared those passing on the sidewalk would see inside. The worth of her collection was estimated at thirty thousand dollars.

"This piece is very old," she would tell her visitors, pointing to a candy dish. "I found it in a filling station outside Shreveport."

They nodded, ran their hands along its rim. "And this piece," Sadie said, "I didn't think the man would part with it."

They nodded again, looked to their watches.

She would conclude her tour by showing George's room, the straps on his bed. The guests looked at her husband. They wanted to know how long it had been, if he would mind telling the story of his fall.

He would tell it. He knew it by rote: the platform, the derrick, the hospital, the dreams. It took him only fifteen minutes.

When he finished, his audience shook their heads. Often they reached to squeeze his hand or touch him on the arm. Sometimes they turned to Sadie and forced a smile.

She smiled back, gestured to George.

"This is what I have to live with," she would tell them.

It was then 1957, the year Oral Roberts took a tent across the Midwest, bringing his revival to the lost and infirm. Sadie heard on the radio testimonies of those treated by Roberts. Some who had never walked made claim to walk. Some who had never seen claimed to see. Sharon Stilman was carried into his tent on a sheet and soon thereafter began a ministry of her own.

Sadie told her husband of this, and they drove 120 miles to a small town outside Tulsa, where for the past week Roberts had held a tent revival. They arrived late and sat toward the back.

George found much of the service consonant with what he had known from his childhood. There was a low stage and a choir on it, men in folding chairs dressed in ties and slacks and white shirts. There were rows of similar chairs for the audience, stapled pages containing a few hymns, sawdust on the floor, carpets down the aisles. Midway through, paper buckets with crosses stenciled on them were passed for offering.

After Roberts delivered a brief sermon, he asked those in need of healing to form a line to the left of the stage. He told them it did not have to be physical healing.

"There are three kinds of healing," he told them. "There is physical healing and emotional healing and healing of the spirit." He said God could perform all three.

Sadie leaned over, whispered to George. He shook his head. When she went to lean again, he rose from his seat and stepped in line.

Roberts sat at the edge of the stage with a handkerchief in one hand and a bottle of olive oil in the other. He was a young man: long nose, a long, smooth face. His hair was combed with tonic and laid back on his head. He wore a plain white shirt, a tie, gray slacks, polished black shoes. Between his legs stood a microphone tilted toward his mouth, positioned low on its stand.

Folks came and stood in front the stage, handed one of Roberts's assistants an index card on which was written their names and the names of their afflictions. These in turn were handed to Roberts.

George examined the blank card and the pencil he had been passed moments before. He looked to the evangelist who was addressing an elderly woman with braces on her legs.

"How long have you had this, sister?"

"I been this way since I was twenty-two," the woman told him.

Roberts dabbed oil into the palm of one hand and told her to come close. He leaned over the edge of the stage, put the hand to her cheek, and lifted the other toward the ceiling, praying into the microphone.

"Lord," he prayed, "deliver her."

The woman began to shiver; then her body became rigid and she fell backward to the ground. A man in a dark suit came and covered her legs with a blanket. Another member of the audience approached, handed up her card. George watched all this, feeling of a sudden as if someone had hollowed him.

He started to turn, but just then one of Roberts's assistants happened down the line. He noticed George's card was blank and touched him on the elbow, inquiring after his affliction.

George shook his head, tried to step around the man, but found himself blocked by a row of card tables piled with books and pamphlets.

The man looked askance, leaned toward him, and George quickly told the story of his fall. When he finished, the other's face had an amazed look. He took George by the arm, parted the crowd, and led him onto the stage. They stood to the side while Roberts prayed, and then the man went to the evangelist and whispered into his ear.

Roberts turned. He rose, took the microphone from its stand, and walked to George. The crowd quieted. Roberts's voice in the microphone was wet and very loud.

"Tell these people your name."

George shifted from one foot to the other. He brought a hand from behind his back and scratched at his nose. "George Crider," he said.

"And you had an accident?" Roberts asked.

"Yes."

"You fell?"

"Yes."

"How far?"

"One hundred sixteen feet."

Many in the crowd gasped; some called to God.

"And you were hurt?"

"Yes."

"How many bones did you break?"

"All of them," George said.

The preacher put his hand on George's shoulder.

"And what did the doctors say?"

George paused, looked down. "They told me I would never walk again."

There were a few moments of silence. Then the crowd began to stir and then to applaud. They cried in loud voices, and most all raised their hands. One man left his seat and began to run the aisles.

Roberts turned to face them. "Do you hear that?" he said. "The God that did this can do the same for you. The same God who caused this brother to walk after breaking every bone in his body can grant you your deliverance."

More folk left their seats and stepped in line. The preacher stood above them like an auctioneer.

George was led from the stage. He saw Sadie waiting for him near the ramp.

As he was about to walk away, the man who had discovered him asked if he would return the next night to give his testimony. George shook his head, took his wife by the arm, and escorted her from the tent.

It was more than twenty years before he would visit another faith healer. By then George had retired from his job and begun to collect his pension. He and Sadie traveled most the year, attending antique shows, conventions, fairs and galleries. They acquired piece after piece, and in the 1969 edition of *Carnival Glass Anthology*, there was a black-and-white photo of his wife standing next to a bookcase full of depression-era teacups.

But, however great Sadie's satisfaction, George's condition grew worse. His hands would often shake and occasionally his vision blur. The man slept only two or three hours a night, and at times would go days on no sleep at all, walking through his afternoons with a glazed look. He did not talk about the dreams or the ailments that made him unfamiliar to his body. He refused to go back to the doctors or turn to the God of his father. He refused to take the shotgun from under the seat of the car and place the barrel in his mouth. Regardless, he found himself polishing the weapon once or twice a month, breaking it over at the dining-room table to check the shells.

In Denton, Texas, one night, Sadie forced him into a revival meeting held by the Reverend R. T. Shorbach. She told George that life with him had caused her to need healing of the spirit. George watched his wife leave her seat, walk the aisle, and take her place at the end of Shorbach's prayer line. He retrieved a hymnal from beside his chair and began to flip the pages.

Shorbach was an older gentleman from Tyler, Texas, who clothed his body in immense black suits. He had fat features and a welcoming face, thick eyebrows, a sweep of gray hair. The preacher smelled of strong cologne and sweat.

He stood down from the platform with a microphone, laying hands on those who came through his line. In front of each, he would pray loudly, examining the ceiling as people fell away from his thick fingers to the arms of an assistant.

After a while, George could no longer watch. He walked to the lobby, found a rest room and then a vending machine. He put quarters in, but the candy caught in a loop of the wire that held it. When he came back to the auditorium, his wife stood before the massive preacher. George crossed his arms and watched from the wings.

His wife seemed small from the distance. She was a petite woman still, her silver hair pinned in an elaborate bun. George watched as Shorbach's hand came to her forehead, watched Sadie's arms rise. He continued watching as her body went suddenly rigid and she fell backward into the arms of Shorbach's assisistant. She was laid on the ground, covered with a blanket.

"Slain," Shorbach said over the swell of the organ, "slain in the Spirit."

The next night Sadie persuaded George to return to Shorbach's meeting, where she again approached the prayer line and soon lay sprawled on the floor.

A month later, in Biloxi, Mississippi, George would watch his wife fall from the hands of the Reverend Shorbach, and two months later in Little Rock, and six later in Atlanta. Sadie began keeping two schedules on her refrigerator, one of antique conventions, one of Shorbach's camp meetings. And several years later, when Sadie stepped from the prayer line in front of the man of God, he held the microphone away from his face and asked where he knew her from.

Sadie smiled, raised both hands, and braced herself for the fall.

Years passed. Numb years of sickness and pain. Sadie continued seeing Shorbach when the preacher came within driving distance of Perser. If George was too ill to take her, Sadie would phone a nephew to do so, and when he could not oblige, the woman closed the door to her bedroom and watched the broadcast on TBN.

In the past, George had been a quiet man; now he was utterly silent. He did not answer his wife's questions, and when visitors called, he would retreat to his work shed behind the house. He was in considerable pain but took nothing for it. His lower back had deteriorated, his shoulders and hips. Some mornings it would take him upward of an hour to rise from bed. The dreams, as ever, continued to shake him, and he spent much time weighing the benefits of life and death.

Then one evening, Sadie fell from the back porch. She was putting out bread for squirrels, and she slipped, snapping her leg below the knee. From the shed, George heard his wife's screaming. He managed to position her in the backseat of the car, drive her to the hospital. When they sent her home with a cast and crutches, it was George who helped her to bathe, brought her meals, took her from place to place.

"George," Sadie would say. "I need to go."

George would trundle in, assist her to the bathroom, stand outside the door waiting.

It was late that summer when the First Pentecostal brought in Leslie Snodgrass, an evangelist of fifteen, already known across Oklahoma and much of Missouri. People said amazing things of the boy. They claimed signs and wonders, miracles and healing and salvation of the lost. He preached repentance, prayed over the hopelessly ill. The young man came from a small town outside Tishomingo and had been preaching since the age of six. He was short and fair, very thin, but his voice was that of a man three times his years, and audiences watched him with an amazed look. The elders in the crowd would shout and sing, and sinners sat with whitened faces, sinking quietly in their seats. When Snodgrass ended his sermons, old and young alike would fall into the altars to seek mercy. He knelt among them and, when moved, stood to his feet and walked about, laying hands on the sick and troubled of spirit.

Sadie soon heard of this and began asking George to take her to one of these meetings. She wanted to see her leg heal quickly.

George had decided some time before he could not endure another service; he told his wife to find someone else. But Sadie was persistent, and in a matter of nights George found himself sitting along the rear wall of the church, listening to the young evangelist's words.

He watched with an expression no less amazed than those around him. It was indeed a sight to astonish. The boy moved like one possessed, his eyes tightly shut, wads of tissue clenched in his fists. There were hard men who had heard him preach and could not return to their former lives, but by this point George believed only in anguish, for that, he felt, was the truth of the world, and though entranced by the young man pacing the platform above him, he did not recover his faith.

The boy's sermon ended with an altar call, and the altars were soon full. George sat with open eyes, staring over the bowed heads. People knelt, wrestling with their spirits. Occasionally, an elder among them would raise his voice in travail. All prayed for what seemed a very long time, and then Snodgrass rose, approached the platform, and asked those in need of healing to come forward. Sadie began tugging at George's sleeve, wanting him to help her there.

George pulled her to her feet, positioned the crutches beneath her arms. She hobbled out into the aisle and began inching toward the altar, her husband following a few steps behind. They reached the row of people standing along the front of the sanctuary, found themselves a place at the far right. George made sure of Sadie, then leaned against the wall to take the weight from his back.

He watched Snodgrass make his way down the line. The boy had no microphone, no handkerchief or oil. He would stop and speak quietly with each, bow his head and whisper, sometimes laying a pale hand to the person's shoulder, his demeanor one of tranquillity, calm.

George was shocked to see the people remain standing. They did not fall; they did not quake or run the aisles. They stood their places with broken looks, the wise looks of the condemned.

George noticed his wife was also watching the boy, but her face held a bitter expression, more so the closer Snodgrass came. She seemed to understand that the evangelist would not lay hands to her forehead. He would not send her to the carpet, and no assistant would stand waiting with arms and a blanket. Sadie would leave just as she came, and realizing this, George began to chuckle quietly.

The boy came closer and Sadie's face grew harsher, and as Snodgrass was praying for the man next to her, she spun suddenly from the line, casting George derision as she turned.

George watched his wife go up the aisle, past the pew where they'd formerly sat, out the double doors into the lobby. A louder laugh escaped his lips, and when he turned back around, his face was cracked from smiling. Snodgrass stood in front of him.

George's laughter died, and he watched the evangelist with an anxious look, failing for a moment to blink or breathe. The boy was utterly ashen, and he walked sternly up, raised his hand, and placed it to the old man's chest, closing his eyes to mumble a few words. George did not catch them. Only, the moment they left the boy's lips, the audience beheld George Crider fall like lightning.

It did not seem so to George. To him his descent seemed to take a very long time. At first there was the feeling his legs had given way, his limbs wilted to nothing. He sensed his arm go numb and a terrific burst go off in his chest just to the left of where the boy had touched him. He felt warm there and very still and the air that buzzed about his ears was like fire.

There was time for George to consider many things before he struck the ground, to consider a time before dreams troubled his sleep, before an injury placed him in a hospital bed. He considered walking forty miles through the Quashita forest, under the pines and cedars of southeast Oklahoma, and then the time of his boyhood under the dense trees, before his brother had fallen, before he had a brother at all. He considered when it was only he and his mother and his father, when they would pick him off the ground, only a child of four years then, place him in the center of a patchwork quilt, and lift him, allowing him to leave the fabric for a moment before he sank back to its folds. They repeated this for what seemed like hours—though it could not have been so long—the thin child rising and falling, caught up, snapped into the air.

It was weightless, that sense, the stomach a rush, face and arms and legs prickling, the heart feeling as if it might split. Rising and falling, and again, and over. If it had always been like that, there would have been point in nothing else but to live in the instant when gravity first took hold and pulled you to its center.

George considered this of all things as he abandoned himself to the fall, unaware he would expire some sixteen inches above the carpet, that his body would strike the floor with a hollow sound.

Gwyn on Story Middles

Talking about middles is difficult. We want (as writers, as warriors, as lovers, as humans) to rush from one state to another—start to finish, beginning to end—and rarely do we have an understanding of the process that takes us from the first moment to the last. Aristotle tells us that drama (epic drama, at least) starts in the middle of things: *in medias res*. This is how we begin: as close to conflict as possible, *in the midst* of conflict, inhabiting that space of chaos and turmoil, of tension.

For example, a story doesn't begin when a character is born. At least, not most stories. Rather, stories begin with a dramatic moment, a scene in which something interesting happens to a character. Or more specifically when a dramatic event—such as a move to a new city, the beginning of an adulterous affair, or the loss of a parent—bumps a character out of his or her comfortable world. And suddenly, well, life is a little more interesting. This is where stories begin.

Endings also come to us rather naturally. There is a trajectory, and we follow it quite logically to its purposeful conclusion. The dramatic tension is resolved. The narrative questions, most of them, answered. The tension depleted. It is not particularly difficult to imagine the end of a story once we have imagined its beginning.

Here is the difficult part:

You have a story, and there is beginning, there is end, there is conflict and resolution of conflict. But the soul of the story is the middle. It is the long, difficult road that takes us, moment by moment, from beginning to end. This is enough to make one squirm. How do you imagine a dead-on perfect second scene after writing the first? And then how do you imagine a third and a fourth?

In "Of Falling," I did not know exactly what would happen in the middle when I wrote the first scene. I was, to some extent, relating the story of my great uncle, and I wanted to *get it all down*. I wanted to pull in as much of his life as I could. But then I got to a point (the Oral Roberts tent revival scene) where I simply got stuck. The real events of my uncle's life wouldn't work as the satisfying conclusion to a short story.

After the revival scene, I couldn't think of what to say, what could happen, whether that happening would seem forced, whether or not, at some day in the future, people who read my story—assuming there would be such people—would find it believable and interesting. They certainly would *not* if I didn't finish the story.

The problem was I psyched myself out. I was worrying too much about it, rather than just trying to write the thing.

I was in the middle.
I was pretty well stuck.

This is where an understanding of craft is important. Short stories—at least a lot of them—have common structures. I don't mean to say that there are only seven plots in the world because wholeheartedly I believe there's more, millions more. But from reading stories for years, I knew that stories begin with tension. Not only in the abstract, but *dramatic* tension, a problem that has been simmering for weeks or even years. And then one day, boom, there's a move to a new city, flirting becomes an affair, or a parent dies. Middles tend to take the tension *suggested* by the drama in the beginning of a story and amplify it. Middles raise the stakes. They raise the stakes *gradually*—one scene at a time.

Here's the thing.

When you're in the middle, you have to *be inventive*. You have to keep driving that big rig forward. You have to *take risks*. In my head, I'm thinking, you have to *bullshit*, but that's not entirely right. Because it's not all bullshit. It's more an educated guess of where the story should go next. And if you're wrong—don't sweat it—go back to the last place the story felt real and true, then start down the road again.

I don't know any other way to say it. A middle ups the ante. Or here's some practical advice: the middle of a story often makes things *worse* for your protagonist. That's how you build tension, by getting in touch with your sadistic side. You need to cause your character pain. Prick your character, see if he bleeds. Let's say, for example, on page one your main character—someone who's forty-five, maybe like your uncle—starts an affair. Then a few pages into it this character's wife becomes suspicious. And how do things get worse from there? Well, maybe he falls desperately in love, or maybe an incriminating photo appears in the paper, or maybe a dinner receipt is left in a pocket. A good middle begins to shake a character to his or her core.

You have stories to tell. That's why you want to be a fiction writer and not a poet (yawn) or an essayist (yawn—wink, wink—yawn). In "Of Falling," I "concocted" this whole narrative about the Sadie character becoming addicted to faith healers. I made it up. I left my uncle's "real" life in the dust. I took my best shot at how to raise the tension in the beginning with more scenes. Why?

Because I was stuck, remember?

But I'm a fiction writer (not a poet or an essayist), so when I get stuck, I lie.

And I tell some real whoppers.

And I do my best to make it all go down very smooth.

E. L. Doctorow says, "Writing a novel is like driving a car at night. You can see only as far as your headlights, but you can make the whole trip that way." And that's all you need when you're in the middle, with your back to the proverbial wall, and a deadline grinding your ass, and the pressure and insecurity kicking in. You need a sense that you can get to the end, scene by scene, sentence by sentence, or even word by word. And if you ever get lost, double back to the last place you recognize.

I mean this: don't be afraid to throw away some pages, to find the last honest sentence, and continue writing from there. It may take a few tries. Or a dozen. But you can get from the beginning to the end by building scenes, by developing a story's tension, by "lying" and by creating a lot of details so perfect you have to believe them. If you're stuck, ask yourself: what's going to happen to keep a reader interested?

Tell a story.

Just tell a friggin' story.

And be as smooth as you can.

Writing Suggestions

1. Consider this story outline: A thirty-year-old woman falls in love with her boss at the office. He's single, but he's secretly interested in someone else at work. What happens next? Jot down five plausible options for "what happens next" that really sock it to the protagonist, that poor (or maybe not?) woman. As Gwyn recommends in his commentary, be inventive and really throw the doors of your imagination wide open.

2. The next story you decide to write, consciously plan out the beginning and the end, but nothing about the middle. See if having the start and finish locked in (at least mentally decided on), and letting the middle just happen, as Gwyn suggests,

helps you write the story. Are you surprised by what your characters are doing? Is this part of the story as easy to write as the mapped-out parts?

3. Using Gwyn's "On Falling" as your story template, select a single scene in the middle of his story and rewrite it in your own voice and style, changing the situation to something far more dramatic or at least significantly different than what currently exists. How does swapping out this single scene change the rest of the story? Is it easier to revise/rework someone else's story than a draft of your own?

4. In this book, find a story you've not yet read. Read ONLY the first three pages, then, on a blank piece of paper, draft out what you think should happen next to amplify the existing tension in the following two scenes. How does the first section suggest the main purpose of the story? Feel free to compare your version to the original.

> It's the writer's job to stage confrontations, so the characters
> will say surprising and revealing things, and educate and
> entertain us. If a writer can't or won't do that, he should
> withdraw from the trade.
> —Kurt Vonnegut, Jr.

Jarret Keene

Son of Mogar

From *The New England Review*

Perched high above Hollywood Boulevard, my house borrows much of its dark atmosphere from the wreckage below. Here I have simulated a world from another era. There are clues: framed lithographs of gorillas; a portrait of a giant robot, a woman trapped in its pincers; a small jade dragon, fanged and hideous. This place is a shrine, really—a testament to my early years in the profession, and to a friend who remains a profound influence on my life. Growing up in Hollywood, I met a lot of intriguing people, but none compares to Hirose, who moved here from Japan to work as a suit actor. Dead ten years now, he is an obscure champion. Today one might accidentally discover his films on an on-line horror fanzine. Sometimes a brief segment of his work pops up in a prime-time sit-com, where it is disrespected, ridiculed. The fading of Hirose's star is hard for me to accept, because the man looms so large in my memory. I write this in remembrance of the father I almost had.

Hirose trained to be a bomber pilot when he was sixteen. In the battle of Midway, his plane was hit by a Grumman F6F Hellcat. He saw the bullet make a tiny entrance, but the exit was larger than a softball. Wind violently rushed in through that hole, rattling the cabin and scattering his flight documents. He gripped the controls and turned the plane around. He executed a perfect landing with a damaged engine, then went immediately to a noodle house near the base. He drank wine and paid for a tattoo of a woman fornicating with an octopus.

After the war, Hirose secured a job as a driver in the motor pool of the Occupation Forces. He was amazed by the Americans and their emphasis on specialization. In Japan, versatility was considered an indispensable trait. He was scolded for changing a tire. "For tire problems there are tire men," the officer said. "Stick to the steering wheel." A few years later, Hirose was arrested by the American military police for speeding, thrown in jail, and fired.

He bummed around on his savings until he saw an ad for a one-year training school for actors, after which he found work with Imamura Pictures. Soon he landed small parts in various samurai flicks and later in big-budget war epics. Highly regarded by important directors, he was frequently cast, appropriately enough, as a bomber pilot.

One day Imamura's casting director, Endo, invited Hirose to privately screen a print of the 1933 *King Kong*. Having seen few if any American productions, Hirose was dazzled by the eerie power of model animation. The giant ape seemed truly alive! Yet even as a young man in his teens, he recognized the cost and time that such effects demanded. He was sure that he could do a better job than a poseable toy and a stop-motion camera. Indeed, the movie kindled something pure and atavistic inside him. He was stricken with the urge to climb skyscrapers, swat at fighter planes, clutch women like Fay Wray. But he needed a mask, a costume. The idea took shape in his mind just as the projector sputtered its last fragments of light. Hirose convinced his friend Endo to approve the research and development of a suit for a picture entitled *Mogar, the Monster-God!*

First there were the sketches. Working with artists in the costume department, Hirose made the creature's face tight, compact, brutal. During the construction phase, he asked for a wire-controlled tail and a low center of gravity. Despite the latter, the original design was still too top heavy, and the test for walking in the suit ended ignobly, with Hirose falling and breaking the proto-Mogar's jaw. The second design lacked a sufficient number of breathing holes and was difficult to remove. Finally the suit was ready, according to Hirose's specifications. Mogar resembled a bipedal dog with reptilian features, or rather a gigantic mutant terrier with scales.

He approached his role with enthusiasm and diligence. Frequently, he visited the zoo to study the movements of animals, theorizing how to best portray a radioactive creature from a mysterious, uncharted island. Inside the suit, it was very dark, lonely and isolated, and obviously more cramped than the bomber cabin he had inhabited during the war. Each morning, before heading to the studio, he meditated for a full hour. He choreographed all the monster battles well in advance, advising the set builders where to place the miniatures. He was even involved in the script and came up with the twist of having the scientist's daughter steal the oxygen destroyer.

When it came time to shoot, the production tested his physical limits. In the samurai pictures, he had worked summer days in full armor; the suit itself was not a problem, dehydration never a concern. But now the studio lighting caused him to swoon. The sensitivity of film was terribly slow at that time, and shooting a movie required severe brightness. The director used ten-kilowatt lights and the surface of the latex suit softened to the point of melting. Hirose's sweat evaporated; salt leaked from his pores. He had to move rapidly so that the speed could later be slowed down, creating the effect of an immense and naturally plodding Mogar. Fortunately, principal photography was completed in less than three months. Imamura Pictures initiated a marketing and distribution campaign. Meanwhile, they had the negative stored in a warehouse.

But the warehouse burned down.

Soon after, a competing film company began production on its own giant-monster flick. Relying on a similar rubber suit instead of model animation, the movie prompted a sensation at home and overseas. Hirose was devastated. He quit Imamura and worked sporadically in a bowling alley. He drank heavily. He paid for another tattoo. At the age of twenty-five, he felt washed up. It was agonizing to have been beaten to the punch, robbed of his personal vision. He had nearly suffocated, was almost hospitalized, and for what?

Meanwhile, Hirose's friend Endo married an American correspondent and moved here to California. He found a job as a stagehand for a small production company. Four years later, he had ascended to the position of special effects director, working on genre cheapies like *Zombie Ranch* and *Bride of Robot Spider*. He came across a script for a killer gorilla movie, which called for a suit actor. He thought of his friend Hirose and wondered what had happened to the talented young man. In a fit of nostalgic curiosity, he wrote a letter to the heads at Imamura. He received a saddening reply. The actor had hit the skids. He lived in a seedy district and refused to gain steady employment. Tattoos now covered his body. Endo felt somehow responsible. Perhaps he could have pushed harder for a release date on *Mogar*, in time to have made his young friend a star. Endo bought Hirose a one-way, third-class ticket to the States. The year, 1957.

I was ten years old and a Hollywood orphan. My father, who is best remembered for his role as the comical, cross-dressing pirate in *Black Mast*, had died in an alcohol-related car wreck when I was a baby. My mother, successful in her own right, was an amphetamine addict and eventually went psychotic, garroting her hairstylist with a belt and running over a producer with her silver Corvair. A well-intentioned and elderly vocal coach named Polly Steckler adopted me shortly after my mother entered the asylum.

Polly was gray-haired, round, a cat-lover. We lived in a cottage tucked away in the back of the lot where she gave lessons. I can remember her sitting opposite B-movie starlets, her bosom rising up and down, trying to get her pupils to speak from their diaphragms. She possessed a beautiful voice herself, and the actresses, before leaving, always kissed her on the cheek. Devoted to me as any mother could have been, she packed me lunches for school and inquired about my homework.

Polly taught into the evening, and so I'd wander the studio lot. I loved the sound stages, those great caverns of darkness as big as aircraft carriers. In the hours before dinner, while the actors were on set, I'd mess around in the makeup department, applying pancake powder, mascara, false eyelashes, and lipstick and studying my face in the bulb-lined mirrors. Then I'd go to the set and pester the prop man, Dexter. He had everything that might be needed in a scene. Phones, lamps, cut flowers, whatever. Drinks, too: coffee, tea, soda, even booze, and yet he never let me so much as taste the liquor. Looking back on it, everyone at the studio was very protective of me. I had been adopted not only by Polly, but by the stagehands, directors, assistants, other actors, the entire studio. That year, I became especially close to Hirose, though at first I saw him as peculiar and possibly dangerous. Gradually, he grew into a sort of father.

His gorilla suit was sophisticated for its time. It sported chest bladders and leather skin and was covered in genuine animal hair. I first met him on the set of *Drums for the Death-Ape*, a box-office turkey, which is now something of a cult classic, mostly due to the prolonged and titillating scene in which the murderous gorilla strips actress Lora Romero down to her undergarments and ties her to a sacrificial altar. Hirose was in the suit, mask and everything, preparing for the director's next move, when he must have seen me reach for one of Dexter's props, a whiskey flask.

"Do not drink that," he said, voice muffled, his furry hand taking the flask. "It will turn you mindless."

I mumbled a *yes, sir* and walked over to the standby painter's gear and pretended to rummage. I wiped away my makeup, sick with embarrassment and fear.

Hirose had scared me; it was unnerving to have been reprimanded by a gorilla. He must have felt bad, because minutes later he asked me—this time without the mask—to help mend his suit, which he'd torn in a poorly choreographed fight with a knife-wielding voodoo priestess. I saw that he was Japanese and asked if he knew any kamikazes. He said yes, many of his childhood friends had been trained as zero pilots and lost their lives. Taro, for instance, who died in a futile effort to crash his plane into the U.S.S. Archerfish, hitting only water. Early on Hirose struggled a bit to learn English, but he was always understandable and entertaining. For the rest of the day, as the electricians wasted time arguing over whether to use an existing source or an independent generator, I helped my new Japanese friend stitch his suit.

He told war story after war story. He related Mogar's awful fate. I recall that I had to thread the needle because his hands shook slightly.

"What's it like?" I asked. "To act like a gorilla."

"It is a freedom," he said. "I do what I want and no troubles for me."

Hirose was a perfectionist, and when he failed to meet his own impossible standards, he drank, although never in my presence. He drank by himself, because he was a foreigner, and Japanese at that. He lived in a trailer on the studio lot, out near the animal-training grounds. I was his first real American friend.

He kept in shape, playing handball with some of the lanky black carpenters in the late afternoon, and on the weekends he'd lift dumbbells. He'd wake me at sunrise to time him on his early morning runs around the studio's parking lot. He'd tap my window and say, "Get up, get up! Let us run!" I'd rub sleep from my eyes, run a comb through my hair, change, and tie on some tennis shoes.

To simulate the conditions of a monster suit, he'd wear three tees, a sweatshirt, a heavy coat and pull sweat pants over a pair of jeans. I'd yell *go!* and hit the stop watch, and he'd practically sprint the entire distance. In retrospect, I'm surprised he didn't give himself a heart attack. We had the parking lot measured, and he could run five-minute miles one after the other, like a machine. Afterwards, I'd help him remove all those layers so he could shower, and then we'd head to the studio's cramped cafeteria for breakfast. "Heart and lungs must be strong," he'd say, sipping his hot tea. "Else the monster is sickly." After a tiny bowl of oatmeal and some fruit, we'd walk to the gym for a quick series of pull-ups, push-ups, and sit-ups. He'd rip right through them. If I did some, he'd buy me an ice cream and a comic book at the studio's soda fountain after school let out.

One day he picked me up in his Cadillac and disclosed some spectacular news. The studio had cast him to star in an upcoming giant-monster movie. A larger production like this meant more screen-time and more money. In addition, the slightly higher cost of such a project might, one would hope, translate into a better film. Happy and garrulous, he puffed dramatically on a cigar. "I owe you everything," he said. "You have helped me with English, with my physical fitness. You are my best friend. Here is a token." He handed me a small statue, an ivory dragon, and cranked the radio.

"Thank you," I said over the blare. "And congratulations."

Unimpressed, Polly sat in her chair, patching a pair of my jeans, glasses angled against her nose. "I suppose it's an enjoyable way to make a living," she remarked. "In the absence of creative talent, one can always release the destructive tendencies." She didn't look up, but persisted in working her needle. I can't really blame Polly. Like most people, she perceived no decorum or technique in Hirose's performances. As a vocal instructor and former concert singer, she believed very much that these things must be self-evident in order to call oneself an artist or craftsman.

I paused, puzzled by her sardonic note. Ice cream melted down my hand. "You don't think Hirose is creative?"

"It seems rather nasty to break things."

"Nasty?"

"Cruel. Savage. Inhuman."

"Yes," I said. "That's what I like about Hirose. He's inhuman."

Being a top-notch suit actor was not easy. Even if you were in peak condition, even if you were strong enough to effectively maneuver in the suit, you still had to be able to perform stunts as well. In *Vaporize All Dinosaurs!* Hirose executed a dangerous underwater scene, using scuba equipment inside the costume. A cart was placed on rails on the bottom of a pool and towed by a rope tied to a truck. Hirose rode on the cart, his head below the surface. But the truck accelerated too quickly. He gradually rose out of the water, which rushed fiercely against his face. By some miracle, he retained his scuba mouthpiece. Had it been knocked away in the torrent, he surely would have drowned. Again, as a dinosaur, in *Planet of the Burrowing Lizards*, he was buried alive under a mountain of dirt and had to emerge on cue to combat a gargantuan moth. As a gravity-defying alien in *Martian Conquest*, he was hooked with wires, attached to a crane, and swung about wildly until he banged against a boom microphone and smashed the catering table.

His suits had to be regularly patched. He owned three: gorilla, dinosaur (T-Rex), and a metallic alien, which also doubled as robot duds. For repairs, he used anything and everything, from resin, fiberglass, and gelatin to urethane, tar, and chewing gum. If a suit became too worn and he had money saved, he'd replace it, buying a new, custom-made one from a designer in Oregon. Occasionally, the studio loaned out Hirose to star in another company's A picture, in which case a lavish outfit was provided by the company's special effects or costume department for him to work in. Such a deal was rare, however. Although they paid him a pretty salary, Hirose was contracted to a small production company that specialized in B-grade films, and the terms of the agreement dictated that he supply his own equipment. He didn't mind; he coveted his suits and preferred working in them. They gave him a feeling of independence insofar as he didn't have to rely on anyone, any studio, to transform him into a credible monster. He especially prized his gorilla suit. Once, I crept into his trailer and caught him talking to it, as if the hairy, lifeless thing in his arms was a woman. He brushed it carefully, lovingly, with his fingertips. "Darling," he told it. No doubt he'd been drinking.

It was after an all-you-can-eat buffet in Hollywood that he drove out to the beach, where he liked to practice some slow, deliberate, rudimentary judo he'd picked up in the Japanese Imperial Navy. He stood in the soft sand, poised, right leg drawn, as if to execute a kick. He performed peculiar motions with his arms. The sun allowed itself to melt into the Pacific. Sea gulls called, swooping down across the surf. I collected shells and poked a dead crab with a stick, flipping it over to reveal its underside. After a while, it grew dark, and Hirose turned on the car's headlights. We sat on the hood, listening to the waves, waiting for the stars to emerge. That night, Hirose told me about the flight deck of the battleship Shinano. It was covered with a mixture of concrete and sawdust, to provide traction for landing gears. More importantly, the Japanese Navy had installed twelve arresting cables that went up and down by compressed air and were supposed to snag planes and keep them from rolling off the battleship. Also, there were huge barrier nets in case aircraft missed the cables. "The metal nets stopped you," he said. "But they crushed your wings. Bent propellers like noodles.

"Let me say that I knew a young man assigned to the Shinano. He found below deck a jade propeller. The young man attached the propeller to his fighter plane and never lost in combat. He was forever victorious. He exploded many enemies. Nothing could touch him, not even machine guns. Also, the propeller allowed him to speak with the ghosts of dead pilots, and they forgave him. But the young man had a jealous friend, who wanted the propeller for himself. One night, this friend secretly switched propellers. The next morning the young man took off, immediately crashed and died.

"The jealous friend flew through the air like an invincible bird. He avoided sneak attacks, and his bullets struck every target. He defeated all his enemies and returned to the Shinano to land his plane. He descended so quickly that the arresting cables missed the plane. The nets were ready to stop him, but the jade propeller cut right through the metal, like it was tissue, and the jealous friend rolled his plane off the deck and into the water and he drowned. Today the skeletons of the young man and his jealous friend lie at the bottom of the ocean next to a propeller that glows green."

Hirose was silent then and so was I. The stars began to appear. He asked if I wanted to drive back to the studio, and I said yes. Hirose sat in the passenger seat, scanning the radio. He located Bo Diddley's "I'm a Man," and gave it a little volume. He tapped the dash all the way home. I drove with utmost care, to show that I was mature enough for the task. I remember thinking I'd heard one of his greatest war stories, even if I didn't quite grasp its meaning. I looked up to Hirose as a man, because he was one, like Diddley sang—physical and contemplative, tough but romantic, brave yet vulnerable. Of course, up to this point, I had every reason to admire him—he was at the top of his game.

"Can anything hurt you?" I asked, making the turn up the freeway entrance ramp. He said, "Only myself."

Diddley's song stuttered to a halt, and then a spot came on, a plug for what was arguably Hirose's finest, most impressive accomplishment, *The Day the Earth Ruptured!*, in which a giant-iguana obliterates all the major cities of the world.

For a short while, Hirose dated a bony, beehive-haired stenographer named Joyce. He'd met her in the downtown courthouse, where he planned to protest a speeding ticket, and, I imagine, he was captivated by her sunny aura of healthy all-Americaness, her pageant beauty, her thick makeup and conical breasts.

He said to me, "I have met an angel."

"Does she know you're a giant-monster?" I asked.

He winked. "Not something you tell a pretty girl right off the bat."

They went out on a few dinner dates, and I remember thinking they looked good together. I had apprehensions, of course. I surmised that she was a vapid gold-digger with an unnatural affinity for Cadillacs, and she did, in fact, utter remarks that suggested a dearth of brain cells, but I didn't dare discourage my friend. Even a child such as myself could recognize that people need other people to lessen the perpetual ache of loneliness. With Joyce beside him, Hirose acted like the world was boundless and bubbling with possibilities. Their relationship seemed to be progressing just fine, but then Hirose did the unthinkable and took Joyce to see *The Day the Earth Ruptured!* in hopes of impressing her. The movie was sneaked at the Cornell Theatre in Burbank, and after the show they had coffee at the Smoke House. Much to Hirose's dismay, Joyce said she didn't want to see him anymore. "If that's the kind of picture you make," she told him, "I don't think this relationship is going to work out." She wanted him to star in movies like *Show Boat*. Hirose tried to explain the unfeasibility of producing that kind of movie in five days for under $50,000, but she'd made up her barely functional mind. He never saw his angel again.

In the days that followed, Hirose feigned ambivalence, joking that at least he'd gleaned something from being dumped: to abstain from women whose hairstyles incited more sheer terror than his suits. But I could sense that he'd been wounded. One evening after a grueling non-union shoot—in which the 142-pound Hirose had nearly given himself a hernia carrying the 100-pound actress Lori Paget across a gopher hole–ridden field out near the Santa Anita Racetrack—we returned to his trailer to relax with steaming cups of green tea and a few slow-paced games of checkers. With the windows open, it felt like another warm, spring evening on the periphery of Hollywood. We listened to radio turned low, hoping to catch a decent R&B number, or at least a radio spot for one of Hirose's movies. Moths battered themselves against the screens, and in between moves Hirose would blow cigarette smoke on them. Point blank, I asked, "Did Joyce break your heart?"

He shrugged. "I can no longer be injured," he said. "My heart died many years ago." He looked visibly irritated as he exhaled another plume into the frenzy of moths. And so the subject was dropped and never broached again.

The relationship between Hirose and Endo was a mysterious and complex one. As soon as he'd found Hirose employment with the studio, Endo had jumped ship and signed to the studio's lesser competitor, the Santa Monica–based National Releasing Company, which specialized in buying the rights to Italian sword-and-sandal flicks, producing stories around the special effects sequences, and selling the results in packages, as double-features, to drive-ins across the country, from Arkansas to Pittsburgh. Endo's job involved fashioning new films out of the Italian footage. From what I gathered, he was highly critical of Hirose's profession, and whenever the two came together, Endo urged his younger countryman to give up suit-acting and move into production work.

One afternoon, on the set of another automaton-gone-amuck movie, I spotted Endo, talking with Polly near the sound equipment. I approached Hirose to tell him what I thought was good news—someone was here to visit him! But Hirose remained cool, his voice betraying displeasure: "Endo despises what I'm doing, the direction I'm taking. He hates everything about me." Bewildered, I said nothing.

Back in Hirose's trailer, as I toweled the sweat of his performance from his neck and back, the door opened and in walked Endo, smiling. He was in good shape, tanned, dressed in an electric blue jacket and a black turtle-necked top.

"Hello there, Hirose," he said. "I really like your new movie. The suit looks great."

Hirose, drily, replied, "Thanks, I'm so glad you *like* it."

"No, really," Endo said, unruffled. "It's a great effects team you have here. Lots of energy and intelligence." He gestured in my direction, indicating that I was a crucial cog in the larger mechanism that was Hirose's greatness.

Feeling awkward in my silence, I blurted out, "Yeah. Lots of energy."

Endo tried his best to be just another effects-member-in-the-trenches, to abandon his successful persona, but Hirose showed only disdain. I was stunned; I'd expected open displays of affection, or at least the mutual warmth of longtime friendship. Had they fallen out recently? Had Endo disparaged Hirose's latest performance? The tension was unbearable, so I went to join the crew outside for snacks and soft drinks.

I re-entered the trailer half an hour later and everything had changed. Hirose was smoking and smiling, totally absorbed in Endo's plan to repackage a Spanish gangster movie. It was mind-boggling: detachment and disregard one minute, enthusiasm about forthcoming projects the next. What did these two Japanese friends really think about the other?

One day I found myself in line for groceries, standing next to Endo. I asked him to translate what my friend Hirose had meant when he said his heart had died. Endo nodded grimly. He invited me to dinner at his ritzy house in the Topanga Canyon, where he described Hirose's wartime ordeal in hideously altered Technicolor, sparing no miserable detail, until I could imagine, projected on the screen in my mind, the wasteland that was once a place enveloped in a spectral cloak of radiation. Hirose's family were among the casualties at Hiroshima. This came as a shock to me. I'd understood, of course, that Hirose had no family in the States, but he'd never mentioned anything about the Bomb. Suddenly Hirose's life story expanded to cinematic proportions. Doomsday pictures coruscated through my mind, like those prompted by the psychotic ravings in a radio spot or a promo trailer for one of Hirose's movies.

"Hirose showed up hours later," said Endo. "He suffered what no man should suffer."

Hirose searched the makeshift hospitals that were pitched along the waterways, hoping to chance upon a surviving family member. He gained entry into the camp closest to the bombsite, where his younger sister was sleeping in a cot. Her face was bandaged and her fingernails had turned black. Hirose sat by her bedside until she lost consciousness the next morning and her heart stopped. He later learned that his family had died in the blast, their bodies crushed beneath the rubble of their homes.

"Hirose is a man full of pain," Endo told me. "He goes crazy from time to time. He drinks too much and he hurts others."

"He's never hurt me," I said.

Endo nodded. "I believe you. But I've had to deal with his wretchedness for too long, and I see him differently. He is under the death spell. Because he has known death, he thinks he must suffer a life of grief. He is a masochist. He derives pleasure from reliving the event over and over again. I tell him, 'Hirose, leave the past and look to the future.' But he doesn't listen. He refuses to embrace the present. He chooses instead the nightmare of history."

I had been abandoned, too, but my abandonment was brought on, for the most part, by my parents' poor, or rather all-too-human, choices and not through any cosmic irrationality like war. I wasn't forced to observe helplessly as some real-life fission-powered nightmare suddenly killed everyone close to me. I'd always figured that, since we were both lacking an immediate family, we shared a similar alienation and grief. But there was a chasm of difference between our circumstances; they were separate and mutually exclusive. I had an entire community of showbiz professionals to support me, like Polly and Dexter. Hirose had no one, except for me, a little kid. It's not that I compared our respective traumas and determined mine was insignificant. Simply, I perceived his sadness as being too much for one man alone to carry around. At only twelve years of age, I could sense that Hirose's sorrow isolated and threatened to destroy him.

I never told anyone this, but sometimes Hirose would visit Endo in Santa Monica, and while he was away, I'd sneak into his studio trailer. Under the mattress, he hid Betty Page bondage mags, which I'd often swindle and swap with the cameramen for comics. Beneath the sink, next to the cleansers, he stored his liquor, mainly vodka. Cigarettes were stashed in the medicine cabinet. I'd go through his closet and pull out the suitcase that contained all his Japanese-inscribed medals. In a shoebox, he kept a messy pile of photos taken during the war. Pictures of him, smiling, in uniform, walking the streets of Tokyo, or on the deck of the Shinano, looking out on the water. A wide-angle shot of him, flight-geared, helmeted, standing with his teenaged crew, all of them smoking cigarettes and wearing the same serious—or was it frightened?—expression, the bomber squatting ominously in the background. His suits hung in the kitchen walk-in, the driest and coolest part of the trailer.

I'd strip down to my underwear and step into one of these things and pull the top up and over my head. Through the eye slits, I'd see myself in the full-length mirror. I felt invulnerable, blameless. As if I could lay waste to anything and not be held accountable. I stood outside of convention, beyond good and evil. I'd pretend that Hirose's trailer was a metropolis and that I was Mogar. Sofa pillows were tanks; I'd throw them around. I'd scale the La-Z-Boy like it was a skyscraper, emit banshee screams, and thump my chest before falling to my doom. I'd imagine these and other scenes for hours, until I worked up a sweat and became exhausted. I was always careful to place the suits back on their hangers. Polly figured something was going on when I got busted at school for smoking.

"Where did you get the cigarettes?" she asked.

"I stole them from Hirose," I said.

She gave me a serious look. "No more. Don't take things from that poor man."

"Why is he 'poor'?"

She sighed. "He must always play a monster."

The studio personnel may have looked down on Hirose's profession, but they admired his work ethic. In spite of his Japaneseness, his stoicism made them feel petty, his commitment made them feel weak. He never complained, always showed up early and left late. He was quiet, polite, approachable, intelligent, forbearing. Indeed, people were mesmerized by the ease with which he went from "mild" to "wild." I loved to watch him on the sets, the way he would disappear into roles. Like Orson Welles in *Citizen Kane*, he could explode into a rampage at a moment's notice. He became a savage whirlwind, snapping power lines, careening through a gauntlet of laser cannons, mowing down chemical refineries, piledriving lobster-clawed behemoths. Nothing stood in his path. His demolitions were exhaustive and oddly therapeutic, not just for himself but the audience as well. An instinctual actor, he nonetheless had a definite if somewhat limited intellectual understanding of what he was doing.

Hirose got me interested in special effects, at first by encouraging me to observe his repair work. Eventually, I fixed his suits, and when I wasn't in school, I was his personal assistant on the set. I turned eighteen, and the studio hired me. I mostly worked on miniatures, scaled-down recreations of cities. Hirose believed well-constructed, well-placed miniatures were essential to an effective giant-monster performance. He worked closely with set builders and directors to ensure that there was sufficient room for the choreographed tussles and no screw-ups. Still, things went wrong. Now and again, the staff would pull the rope too soon, collapsing the building before Hirose made his approach, pelting him with debris. Or else the pyrotechnics would be too fierce, and his suit would catch fire. Model tanks and airplanes would assault him after the scene had already been shot, as he was taking off his costume. The other suit actor would drop-kick him at the wrong moment. In spite of all this, Hirose was both patient and forgiving, a far cry from his screen presence.

Yet wearing the suit, day after day, movie after movie, eventually took its toll. During the shooting of *The Plastic Eaters*, Curtis Bennington, the director, pressured him to dance a jig after thrashing the Atomic Avenger. Bennington was an anemic, effete, pipe-smoking Hollywood has-been, a real hack, who dressed like a beatnik from one of those campy, teen exploitation flicks, with shades and beret. In any case, Hirose adamantly refused to dance. Usually, the two got along. But now Hirose maintained he was an actor, not a ballerina.

"Our hands are tied," said Bennington, shrugging his shoulders, signaling the best boy to fetch him another brandy. "The studio wants to market *The Plastic Eaters* as a children's movie. This thing has got to be lighter in tone. It's too disturbing—there's a lot of nuclear paranoia going on here, man."

Hirose, dinosaur garbed, grabbed the bullhorn, stepped in front of the hapless director, and, inches from the man's face, shrieked, "I AM NOT TO BE A HAPPY CLOWN!"

As Bennington fell backwards, Hirose flung the bullhorn and stormed off to his trailer. The crew looked at each other in confusion. Someone—perhaps the camera operator—muttered the words "prima donna Jap." I suggested we break for lunch. We all looked at Bennington, who got up, adjusted his sunglasses, and cleared his throat. He nodded his approval. The best boy appeared with the brandy, and Bennington guzzled it before the kid had a chance to ask what had happened.

It wasn't long before the scandal made its way around the studio until it reached the company's secretary and gossip foreman, Susan Lychack—an excellent cook who always prepared a terrific spread of corned beef and Jewish dishes for the wrap parties—and she subsequently told the company's accountant who shuddered at the notion of spending another $1,000 dollars on an added day of principal photography. The producers summoned me to the their office and implored me to talk some sense into him, so that evening I knocked on Hirose's door. Outside, I heard the clink of bottles and the recorded twang of Chuck Berry's guitar. "Come in," he said.

Dressed in jeans and a plaid shirt, Hirose presented a bright smile. Tattoos slithered out from under his sleeves. He mock-punched my arm and gestured towards the sofa. "Please sit," he said. "Shall we dance to Chuck Berry?" He did a brief sing-along of "Too Much Monkey Business," after which he gave a sudden, sharp laugh: "Hah!"

I sat down and he brought me an iced tea. He lit a cigarette at the table. We looked at each other uncomfortably for a minute. Then he gazed at the empty TV screen, nervously flicking non-existent ashes. I chewed ice. Chuck Berry played on for the souls of the burger-munching teens. The trailer's spare furnishings gave the moment a procedural timbre. I tried to present the situation in a positive light. "Big, nasty creatures are no longer the rage," I said. "These days nothing is oversized. Everything is small and shows up in swarms: insects, spiders, killer bees. Look at Hitchcock and his pigeons. Or else you've got natural disasters, typhoons, tidal waves, earthquakes. There will always be a need for suit actors, but not in the same capacity. Now, see, little kids never tire of giant-monsters. So maybe children's entertainment offers another avenue for today's suit actor, you know? More employment opportunities? Kids can't watch *The Plastic Eaters* if it's all about Armageddon—"

"Hold a minute," he interrupted, exhaling smoke. "I do not agree. I cannot base my life's work on the fads and whims of babies. I am a suit actor because I have no choice, and so I must act with dignity. Not with dollar signs blocking my vision. No, no, I refuse to dance for money." He stood up to extinguish his cigarette. "I will pump gas instead."

"Fine," I said. I leaned forward to grab his arm. "Don't dance. But your principles won't make any difference. Bennington will simply get Pepe, the Mexican, to put on the suit. Bennington will film him doing the monster mash, and the scene will appear next month in drive-ins across the country. Your performance is already compromised."

He yanked his arm away. His face turned an angry red. "Not with my suit they won't!"

"Listen to yourself. The designer in Oregon manufactures the suit and sells it to other studios, other actors. It's not yours."

He picked up a chair and smashed it against the wall. The whole trailer shook. The record skipped. A picture frame went askew then fell, crashing to the floor.

Just as suddenly, he was restrained again. "I'm sorry," he said, brushing his hair back into place. "But I will not dance so that children will find me amusing. Let us go eat." He searched for his wallet.

"I only wish you further success," I said.

He threw me the keys to his Cadillac.

Bennington hired someone to don another Space Reptile costume, shot the dance scene, and included it in the final edit. Eventually, Hirose found out. He was livid. Emboldened by too much liquor, he broke into Bennington's home one night and threatened the director with a tire iron in front of his wife and children. Luckily, the studio heads arranged things so that no charges were filed. I promised everyone that I'd monitor the actor's behavior and intervene the next time I saw Hirose's fuse burning out. The damage had been done, however; from then on, the company labeled Hirose as a potential liability. They saw me as a babysitter, a kid who had to shoulder the responsibility of caring for an unstable veteran actor.

The Plastic Eaters scored a hit with the kids, spawning two sequels and a TV spin-off. Up to this point, giant-monsters suffered at the box-office; the genre seemed to be running out of steam. Because of the overplayed nuclear war concerns present in many of these movies, the plots for the most part were dull and formulaic. To limit production costs, the studio insisted that we use stock footage of Space Reptile and the Atomic Avenger leveling San Francisco and other cities. Even Bennington, an unimaginative and corner-cutting director, was not pleased. Thus, the movies ended up being nothing more than mish-mashes of clips from previous, already-screened movies. The studio kept churning out these special effects–deficient, ineptly scripted clunkers, and the tykes ate it up. I spent more time in the editing room than on the sound stage. I longed to return to miniatures. I had an overwhelming desire to construct a small metropolis, no matter how rickety or short-lived, no matter how cheap the materials. However, my aspirations were never fulfilled and my miniature-building skills languished.

Hirose, on the other hand, had entered a new phase of his career. Bit-by-bit, the hard facts of reality had penetrated his brain. Children's bad taste in cinema made it possible for him to draw a weekly salary. So he warmed to the idea of dancing. He put his pride on the shelf. Pushing fifty, he experienced the indignation of juggling boulders in his ape suit—in front of the camera no less! Mercifully, the series was cancelled after two seasons. Hirose continued to find work, albeit the kind that only the most hard-core sci-fi and horror fans could stomach. I'm talking grade Z. Worse, he picked up some more television gigs. As I grew older I could see that despite being in demand, Hirose's glory days in Hollywood were on the wane.

In my late teens, I started hanging out with the makeup department in between shoots and mastered tons of tricks: bald caps, hairwork, injury simulation, aging facials, and prosthetics. I even learned about kabuki, which impressed Hirose a great deal. By the mid-sixties, people in the industry began to take notice. Rival studios offered me lucrative salaries, signing bonuses, box-office percentages. They couldn't tempt me, because I felt guilty about Hirose; I wanted to improve his movies and make him look scary. Usually, he was pleased with my work. However, there was the time when I offered to add blood-tubing effects to his gorilla mask for the final showdown in the 1967 *Ape vs. Android*. He took offense. He had had it. He accused me of endeavoring to corrupt his aesthetic and philosophical beliefs. He claimed I was striving for offensive and immature goals.

"Blood and guts," he said, "will distort this film's message. It will contaminate my performance."

"I want to bring a sense of realism to your work."

"There is nothing *real* about an ape socking a robot," he insisted.

I saved the effects for what today would be considered an R-rated movie called *Gore-rilla*, which starred a Filipino suit actor, a newcomer named Cruz. Hirose had been offered the role, but after reading the script, passed on it because it was, as he said, "intended for shitheads." So the studio brought in Cruz for less than half of what they would've paid Hirose. From then on, he lost more and more work to actors like Cruz, guys who were willing to work for scraps. Also, the industry that Hirose had cut his teeth on here in the U.S. no longer played by the same rules, what with the sixties coming to a close, the dismantling of the factory system, the weakening of the Production Code. My friend found it difficult to adapt.

"Who is this Cruz person?" he once asked, after reading in the trades about a new movie, *Tentacles!*, slated for production. Hirose had not been offered the role. We were in the cafeteria, finishing breakfast. "He gets all the jobs but has no talent. The casting directors smoke grass! To play an octopus one needs to be ambidextrous. Cruz, you see, has a bad left arm."

"The tentacles are wire-controlled," I said, but then the expression on his face made it clear I'd given something away.

He narrowed his eyes. An uneasy period of silence. Then: "Why did you not tell me?"

"Tell you what?"

"That you were hired on this movie. That you are now Cruz's best buddy."

I fiddled helplessly with the silverware. "I'm not his buddy."

He shook his head. "Will the octopus require your makeup skills?"

"No," I said. "I've been promoted to special effects director."

"Oh, even *more* new developments. Tell me, after you signed on, did you ask the director to consider *me* for the part?"

"Yes."

"And what did he say?"

I looked down at the floor. "He said he wanted someone younger."

Hirose made no reply, but sat motionless, the paper splayed in his hands. He gently folded it, took a sip of tea, and left.

He avoided me for weeks.

I felt terrible. Hirose was, in fact, too old for his line of work. His choreography had become stale, his movements less convincing. He could not disassemble the Hoover Dam with the same mechanical efficiency, snatch a body with the same alien dexterity, savage a white woman with the same apelike conviction. No longer the consummate suit actor of yesterday, he refused to come to terms with the irrefutable fact of his advancing age. Why was he hanging on? After all, he had money saved. He could retire, take up gardening, travel, find a woman, relax. But he depended upon the ritual of performing in a suit. And yet people like Cruz threatened to render him and his performances obsolete. Twenty years Hirose's junior, Cruz had speed, superior strength, better mobility, increased stamina, all the necessary traits one must possess in order to wear a cumbersome octopus outfit. With all my heart, I had wished, hoped, and prayed for Hirose to cinch that role, but the producers and casting agents called the shots. I only had a say in matters pertaining to special effects.

Eventually, the studio's financial backers heard grumblings that Hirose was having trouble working in the suits. He fainted a few times during a crucial week of shooting, delaying the schedule and costing producers money. They called us in to talk, and as soon as we showed up at the office and sat down at the conference table across from these blank-faced executives and their garish ties, we both knew the score: they wanted Hirose to retire.

Hirose stood up and said, "I'm not going to retire."

In his adamance, he had spilled his Styrofoam cup of coffee, causing hot, black liquid to shoot towards the laps of panicky executives. One of them had the presence of mind to absorb the stream with some napkins. When the president of the company, Jim Osterberg, realized that the threat had been averted, he replied, "We don't want you to leave. However, we feel it's time to renegotiate. Everyone in this business knows your talent is incomparable. You have reached a level of experience that most of us can only dream of attaining. But twelve movies per year is too much strain for a man your age, in spite of all that you bring to the sets. Maybe now is when you should start thinking about the future. We want to give you a chance to ponder life outside the world of rubber suits and the spotlight. Now, if we were to trim down your workload to, say, six movies—"

"No," Hirose said, shaking his head, arms crossed. "I am perfectly healthy. The problem is that the suits need better ventilation." He looked directly at them, but not with defiance. Instead, his face took on the qualities of a petulant child, and for a moment I thought he might burst into tears.

Osterberg sighed. "I was afraid you might take it badly. Your health isn't the issue, Mr. Kumata. Monster movies are bombing big-time at the box-office. It's all been done: giant-lizards, giant-apes, giant-crabs, giant-amoebas, giant-chickens. Unless someone comes up with an original concept, we simply can't risk investing in sci-fi-horror while blaxploitation and martial arts flicks continue to make money. And since you're neither black nor a black belt, this means we don't need to rely on a suit-actor so heavily. We hate to force phased retirement on you, but our hands are tied. The giant-monster has fallen on evil days."

Following this, I tried to console Hirose by treating him to a seafood platter at Lindsey's. He picked spiritlessly at his fried clams and made short, perfunctory attempts at conversation. I did my best to steer away from movie-making, but I inadvertently blundered into describing a new, experimental recipe for realistic-looking internal fluids and organic structures.

Having heard enough of my prattle, he put down his fork.

"What will I do now?" he said, miserably.

I told him I did not know.

For the remainder of the sixties, Hirose picked up extra work—mostly no-budget features that paid little. Of course, money wasn't a concern for Hirose; he'd saved a good deal of his earnings. It was the work that mattered, that gave his life purpose. From time to time, I'd stop by his trailer with a gift of vodka, for which he'd sheepishly thank me, and we'd discuss the latest developments regarding the industry and the fading genre of giant-monsters. He was always happy to see me. However, my visits became less frequent; after all, I had my own career to tend to: I was twenty-years-old now.

During the seventies, things got worse for Hirose. The blockbuster was back, and B-movie industry took a nosedive, displaced by high-concept, high-priced extravaganzas. It was a trend, like disco music and bell bottoms. Every two-bit producer in tinsel town wanted a *Star Wars*, his very own *The Godfather*. Nobody wanted another *The Plastic Eaters*. Drive-ins, the teenage passion pits, were closing across the country, the looming screens torn down to make room for shopping malls. As a result, company policy suddenly changed, and the studio ended up retaining the production crew but firing the actors, all thirty of them, Hirose included. They gave him a gold watch. He found himself jobless at age fifty.

"This is my saddest day," he said, stuffing his suitcase with aloha shirts and khakis.

"Hardly," I said. "Just wait. You're going to enjoy retirement."

With little fanfare, he packed up his few belongings and took up residence in Endo's garage. Because her pupils were let go, Polly, too, was unemployed. She moved to Florida to spend her remaining days shuffleboarding, ingesting various medications, clipping coupons. A remarkable woman, she called me every Sunday until her death a few years ago. Anyway, having no reason to be loyal to the studio, I quit and began freelancing for the majors. I immediately established a reputation. I married a stuntwoman and during our few years together we lived in a pricey house in Beverly Hills. As for Bennington, Osterberg, and the others, I have no idea, nor do I care.

After being canned, Hirose auditioned for roles, but nothing ever came of it. It didn't help matters that the encroaching presence of digital technology put everyone out of work, and not just suit actors, but also go-motion experts, animatronic specialists, puppeteers. Not only did Hirose fail to impress directors, he failed to impress himself. Consequently, he hit the bottle more forcefully. He started hanging out in creepy, gross-out bars on Sunset. He got into fights. He was arrested twice for being drunk and disorderly. Tired of posting bail, Endo kicked him out.

Hirose was rotting away in a filthy, prostitute-harboring motel when I landed him a menial gig with one of my effects teams. It was humiliating work, I see that now. I had him making bug guts, paying him to take part in something that at one time he'd been entirely opposed to. It wasn't long before he started showing up intoxicated, unable to perform the simplest tasks. He left, and I never saw him alive again. I kept in touch with Endo, who every few months would invite me to lunch and bring me up to date on Hirose. Although plagued by deteriorating health, he'd managed to find satisfactory housing in downtown San Francisco. I had always intended to pay him a visit, but my busy career made it hard to plan a trip outside the Los Angeles area.

Ten years ago Endo called to say Hirose had died of cancer. I paid for the funeral, which was very small, and for the meager headstone that marks his grave. Besides Endo and myself, Dexter and Cruz were in attendance and appeared earnestly doleful. The priest muttered some religiously fitting words and tossed dirt on Hirose's casket. Afterwards, we all went out for drinks and struggled to recall what it was that made the Japanese man seem, on the one hand, so touchingly sensible, and on the other, so willingly lost.

I see my own fate in Hirose's story, and, inevitably, a computer programmer—some whiz-kid genius with a college degree and a filmic memory that goes back only as far as Steven Spielberg and George Lucas—will render me obsolete, useless. Late at night, safe in the present, comfortable in my spacious home that looks down on the broken and the confused, I drink Chianti and imagine this young man, motivated by vague loyalty and subtle remorse, building a shrine to me and my antiquated ways. Similar to the one I've built here, in honor of a man who channeled his pain and anger into a genuine if somewhat critically derided art form. Indeed, I can see the young man now, asleep in his house of luxury, surrounded by the relics and replicas of a world he helped devise and then destroy. He dreams of an enormous creature that, upon being awakened by the reverberations of man's arrogance, is forced to confront a shrunken metropolis, a city marvelous in its intricacies, yet obscene in the magnitude of its unconscious folly.

Keene on Story Endings

What's in an ending?

Godzilla movies always end with a bang. Inevitably, the giant radioactive lizard beats the hell out of Megalon, Mothra, MechaGodzilla, Cosmic Monster, King Ghidorah, King Kong, and many others. Godzilla triumphs even when completely surrounded by his rogues gallery, when the odds are stacked against him. Once an enduring symbol of man's folly regarding nuclear testing, Godzilla now represents the endurance of pop-cultural mythmaking. Thus, the end remains the same. And the open-endedness—or cliffhanging element—of each movie is crucial to Godzilla's mythic power. He is eternal, unbeatable, resurrected. Just like, well, God.

Godzilla movie endings gave me the idea for "Son of Mogar." Having watched countless giant-monster flicks as a kid, I set out to compose the definitive Godzilla story, the final chapter. I wanted my story to conclude with an evocative whimper instead of a sudden bang. I wanted a quiet elegy that would sneak up on readers and steal their breath away. And I wanted to pay tribute to and yet simultaneously deconstruct the myths at the heart of the Toho Studios creation.

In this case, I knew how the story would begin and end before I typed the first sentence: A lonely, abandoned FX guy sitting in his crumbling Hollywood mansion a la Sunset Boulevard, sipping wine, watching old reels, and dreaming of a giant radioactive monster. I didn't write the ending first, but I kept the image in my head as I began constructing the piece.

I borrowed from several templates, primarily *Ed Wood* and *The Unforgiven*. The story of an aging underdog confronted with his own limitations and mortality is compelling, but it's been done many times over. The trick was in finding a fresh approach, original characters and a unique setting. Believe it or not, I'd encountered Godzilla-related fiction before, but never from the point of view of a suit actor. And, of course, there aren't many Japanese-American characters, at least not in contemporary American fiction. The setting of an old B-movie studio lot seemed new to me as well. So I put the three things together and hoped to tell a good yarn.

Naturally, there were literary touchstones as well: George Saunders's *CivilWarLand in Bad Decline*, Lorrie Moore's *Self-Help*, the fantastical stories of Steven Millhauser. Indeed, I wanted "Son of Mogar" to have all the postmodern pizzazz that these writers so effortlessly wield. For instance, if you've ever reached the end of a Millhauser story, then you know what it's like to have your mind dazzled, your heart softly destroyed. A Millhauser ending lingers in your head like radioactive fallout after a nuclear explosion. It leaves a permanent mark.

This is precisely the effect I wanted to achieve with "Son of Mogar." Of course, I'm not completely sure if I managed it. I never will be. But the story was published in *New England Review*, nominated for a Pushcart Prize, and has been reprinted in a few anthologies. So, hey: It's most likely a pretty damn good story. Regardless, I did my best and tried to be honest, and that's what counts in the long run.

Consequences

The end is where everything comes together. It has to come together, otherwise the story doesn't work and the plot is deformed. The end of a work is the shortest part. Yet in many ways it's the most important to get right. A well-written beginning will get a reader's attention, a smooth plot will keep him along for the ride, but if you botch the end—if you swerve unexpectedly into a tree and dump the reader into an uncomfortable lawn in an unfamiliar neighborhood—well, then he's not just going to dislike your story. He will, in all likelihood, swear a blood oath never to pick up another story of yours again.

The end is distinct from the climax, of course. The climax is the part where the wife leaves her husband, or the bad guy gets decapitated, or the child makes the terrible discovery that his pet turtle is dead. The climax is the point at which the story's tension breaks, and the answer to our dramatic question is answered. The consequences must then be presented, and it's here that closure becomes key.

The end is about consequences: What happens after the climax? How do the characters carry on? What have they learned from the experience? These questions demand answers. At least some of them.

In "Son of Mogar," Hirose, the story's true protagonist, is finally destroyed by forces outside of his control, forces put into motion by the Bomb. Forever cursed to reenact the destruction of his family, Hirose can only be set free by death. Ultimately, the technology that gave birth to Mogar's anger and Hirose's agony has been replaced by a faster, stronger, deadlier technology—with this transformation playing out against the shifting landscape of a B-movie Hollywood. And these revelations flicker through the narrator's mind as he finally puts Hirose's ghost to rest.

Of course, these revelations occur more in the reader's mind than they do on the page. A good ending should only suggest thematic ideas; it should never dictate. "Son of Mogar" is, at its core, an anti-nuclear proliferation story. If I'd made this too obvious, it would've distracted, I think, from the emotional power of Hirose's tragedy. And if I'd told you as much at the beginning, I wouldn't have expected you to read the story all the way through. So when you're dying to let readers know what your story is "really about," you should always refrain from doing so. Yes, this is a rule: No didacticism.

When it comes to storytelling, emotion trumps ideology every time. Readers need to feel the consequences; they don't need to be spoon-fed what you think the story is supposed to be saying. Go ahead and bury the "meaning" a bit. Leave a few clues exposed for the reader to assemble on his own. Use imagery and metaphor to get your message across. Never preach. Keep it short and sweet.

Then again, don't bury it too deeply. Leave enough so that folks have something to work with. Don't make it too hard for them; they're readers, not *mind* readers.

Basically, you don't want to insult your readers or talk down to them. Give them some credit. The best way to do this is by thinking visually or symbolically about the character. Determine how he's dealing with the consequences, then communicate that emotion via action, a gesture, a bit of dialogue. Don't get too symbolic or elliptical. Pretension is worth risking but not worth achieving. Keep to the old adage: Show, don't tell.

The Inevitable End

On a certain level, an ending should feel inevitable yet unexpected. Sounds impossible, doesn't it? Well, admittedly, it's not easy. The best way to make it happen, though, is to keep writing and rewriting. Eventually, you'll settle on just the right tone and, if necessary, the appropriate twist that, when looking back on it, you'll say, "That's the only ending that makes sense." With any luck, readers will say the same thing.

I suppose there are an infinite number of ways to end a story. But from reading hundreds of short stories in graduate school, I came to understand that most stories close with some type of elegy, epiphany, or "O. Henry" surprise ending. An elegy is a lament for what is lost—the dead, a missing parent, or a failed love. An epiphany is a sudden comprehension or realization. An O. Henry ending usually offers an unexpected but satisfying twist. "Son of Mogar," clearly, is an elegy, although I'm sure it could be argued that the narrator's last few paragraphs suggest he's undergoing an epiphany. However you want to split hairs, if your ending feels right, then go with it.

Slice-of-life endings are valid, too, though I can't really recommend them. If you find yourself writing a story with no climax and no consequences, then you're writing a slice of life. Short story writer Raymond Carver is often accused of being a slice of lifer, but this is far from the case. All of his stories have powerful plots that motor along beneath the realistic characterization and dialogue of his blue-collar tales.

Make sure your final paragraphs match up with the story's central conflict. For example, if you're writing a coming-of-age tale, then striking an elegiac note at the end isn't going to work. And if you're writing about the deteriorating health of an impoverished artist who lives in a rabbit warren, then forcing the protagonist to undergo an epiphany is probably not the best tact. You see, with endings, there really aren't that many choices. A story's plot (coming of age, death and dying, forbidden romance, etc.) ultimately limits your options. The closer you come to understanding what your story is about, the less lost you'll be as you finally bring down the curtains. You'll recognize the right ending when you get there.

Dead Ends

There's a rule that often gets floated around writing workshops: Don't kill off your main characters. The idea being that a lot of genre fiction ends with bad guys brought to justice or the narrator discovering that he's already dead. (Shades of Ambrose Bierce and *The Sixth Sense*!) I understand why the rule is in place; I just don't believe in rules when it comes to creative writing. (Except for the one about preaching to the reader!)

Of course, I don't think every story should end with your protagonist's brains blown out. But you shouldn't automatically eliminate any of the already limited choices you have, either. If you feel your main characters have to die, fine: Go ahead and kill 'em all. Just make sure it's in keeping with the overall tone and direction of the story. If the tone is dark and somber and foreboding, then it's probably OK to spill some blood. If the tone is shiny and happy and romantic, then snuffing the young lovers at the end is going to seem like a cruel prank. If the ending is inevitable, then it's just that.

Creating a character specifically for the purpose of slaughtering is a tad cruel, too. Wait until the story plays out before bringing the knife to his throat. Who knows? Maybe you'll like him enough to keep him around for another story.

Killing a main character isn't as easy as it seems, either. Think about some of your favorite short stories. How many of them end with the protagonist dead? I can only think of a few: Thom Jones's "I Want to Live!," Flannery O'Connor's "A Good Man Is Hard to Find," and Hemingway's "The Killers." (Even in this last case, it's implied that one of the characters dies. The death occurs "off-screen," thus making it more "literary." What concerns most literary writers is moment-by-moment character change, more so than the specifics of a colorful death.) Plenty of genre stories end with death, of course. So if you enjoy killing characters, you might want to eschew the "literary writer" label.

Inspiration

I found myself reading over and over again the endings to many of my favorite short stories during the construction of "Mogar." Raymond Carver's "Cathedral" has a breathtaking finale, as do many of his other works: "What We Talk About When We Talk About Love," "Fat," "So Much Water So Close to Home." The last few sentences of each of these are spare, lean, and yet they communicate a lot of information. They "telegraph" ideas that the characters and plot have been working toward throughout the story.

My advice for when you're struggling to discover just the right sentences to wrap things up? Immerse yourself in the modern story masters: Raymond Carver, James Joyce, John Cheever, Thom Jones, Denis Johnson, Lorrie Moore, Mary Gaitskill, Richard Ford, John Updike, Louise Erdrich, Joyce Carol Oates, Michael Chabon. Stealing is okay and sometimes necessary, I guess, as long as you don't plagiarize. Honor the masters, and they will always reward you, even if it's simply on the level of language and style.

The real reward is in writing your way to the end of a story. Once you get there and you're faced with the challenge of devising the perfect conclusion, don't wade in like an angry Godzilla among the skyscrapers. Instead, take a deep breath, reflect, and write and rewrite your way home.

Writing Suggestions

1. Consider the following story outline. A community college student meets some-one of the same age; they hit it off and fall in love. An old flame comes into the picture and mucks things up for the first two. What happens next? Recalling the three types of endings that Keene points out in his commentary (elegy, epiphany, and surprise ending), write three one-page scenes that each end the story using one of the available options. After you decide who your protagonist is (the college stu-dent or the other lover, or perhaps even the old flame), stick with that point of view for all three endings. Which of your three versions seems the most effective? The least plausible?

2. There's no one right way to write a story, so try writing one backwards. Start with an ending—write that entire scene, whatever it is—then write the scene leading up to that, then the scene before that, etc., until you reach a place that starts off the chain of events. How is constructing a story this way different from starting at the beginning? Does this way give you a clearer goal to work for since you know exactly where your story needs to end up? How can writing a story backwards enable you to layer in details and work with foreshadowing?

3. Taking your cue from writing suggestion #1 above, try this same technique on a story of yours that seems to fizzle out rather than finish strongly. Decide which type of ending (elegy, epiphany, or surprise ending) yours seems most like, then rewrite the ending in the other two options. Which seems strongest? Does rethinking the ending give you a way to revise your original one such that it becomes more satis-fying? Don't be afraid to write a page or even a few pages that likely won't be in the final product—if writing these new pages helps you see your story more clearly, thus enabling you to make the story better, it's worth it.

4. Clearly, Keene's story emerges from a strong interest in B-movies. Take one of your own interests—reading Batman comics, shopping at the mall, running in marathons, etc.—and use it as the source material for your next story. Think about how you might approach this unusual topic in fiction. Should your protagonist be deeply involved or an outsider? Should your interest be the main thrust or simply part of a well-developed background? Though you might consider yourself an expert in your area of interest, you might find the need to hit the library or do some serious Internet research in order to write an authoritative, effective story.

> *The great Japanese film director Akira Kurosawa said that to be*
> *an artist means never to avert your eyes, and that's the hardest*
> *thing, because we want to flinch.*
> —Robert Olen Butler

Alice Mattison

In Case We're Separated

From *Ploughshares* and *Best American Short Stories 2002*

"You're a beautiful woman, sweetheart," Edwin Friend began. His girlfriend, Bobbie Kaplowitz, paid attention: Edwin rarely spoke up and complimented her. He tipped his chair against her sink and glanced behind him, but the drainboard wasn't piled so high that the back of his head would start an avalanche today. He took a decisive drink from his glass of water and continued, "But in that particular dress you look fat."

It was a bright Saturday morning in October 1954. Edwin often visited Bobbie on Saturday mornings, and she had dressed up a little, anticipating. Now she didn't bother to speak. She reached behind to unfasten the hook and eye at the back of her neck, worked the zipper down without help, stepped out of the dress, and in her underwear took the sharp scissors. She cut a big piece of brown wrapping paper from a roll she kept next to the refrigerator, while Edwin said several times, "What are you doing?"

Bobbie folded the dress, which was chestnut brown with a rust and cream-colored arrowlike decoration that crossed her breasts and pointed fetchingly down. She set the folded dress in the middle of the paper, wrapped and taped it, and addressed the package to her slimmer sister in Pittsburgh. Then she went into the bedroom and changed into something seriously gorgeous.

"Come, Bradley," she called, though Edwin would have babysat, but Bradley came quickly. He was a thin six-year-old with dark curls and the habit of resting his hands on his hips, so from the front he looked slightly supervisory and from the back his pointed elbows stuck out like outlines of small wings. They left Edwin looking surprised. At the post office, a considerable walk away, the clerk said the package had to be tied with string, but lent Bobbie a big roll of twine and his scissors. Bobbie was wearing high-heeled shoes, and she braced herself on the counter with one gloved hand. She was short, and the shoes made her wobble. She took the end of the twine in her mouth, grasped it between her teeth, and jerked her head back to pull it tight. It was brown twine, now reddened with her lipstick, and its taste was woody and dry. Fibers separating from the twine might travel across Bobbie's tongue and make her gag. For all she knew, her poor old teeth might loosen.

Much was brown: the twine, the paper around the package (even the dress inside, if one could see it), and the wooden counter with its darkened brass decorations. The counter was old enough to have taken on the permanent sour coloring possessed by wooden and metal objects in Brooklyn that had remained in one place—where any hand might close upon them—since the century turned. But Bobbie's lipstick, and the shoes she'd changed into, and her suit—which had a straight skirt with a kick pleat—were red. She wore a half-slip because she was a loose woman. Joke. Edwin's hands always went first to her bare, fleshy midriff. Then he seemed to enjoy urging the nylon petticoat down, sliding the rubber knobs up and out of the metal loops that attached her stockings to her girdle, even tugging the girdle off. She never let him take off her nylons because he wasn't careful.

Bobbie tied a firm knot. Then she changed her mind. She poked the roll of twine and the scissors toward the clerk with an apologetic wave, called to Bradley—who was hopping from one dark medallion on the tile floor to the next, flapping his arms—and went home. As Bobbie walked, one eye on Bradley, the package dangled from her finger on its string like a new purchase. At home she found Edwin taking apart her Sunbeam Mixmaster with her only tool, a rusty screwdriver.

"Didn't you say it wasn't working?" Edwin asked.

"There's nothing wrong with it. I didn't say anything."

Edwin was married. He had told Bobbie he was a bachelor who couldn't marry because he lived with his mother, who was old, silly, and anti-Semitic. But his mother lived in her own apartment and was not silly or anti-Semitic, as far as he knew. Edwin had a wife named Dorothy, a dental hygienist. She'd stopped working when their first child was born—they had two daughters—but sometimes she helped out her old boss. Now, fumbling to put Bobbie's mixer back together, Edwin began to wonder uneasily whether it wasn't Dorothy, dressing for work in her uniform, who happened to mention a broken mixer. He had never confused the two women before in the years he'd been Bobbie's boyfriend.

Edwin's monkey business had begun by mistake. He was a salesman for a baking supply company, and Bobbie was in charge of the payroll at a large commercial bakery. Though Edwin didn't wear a ring, he believed that everyone in the firms through which he passed assumed he was somebody's husband. However, a clerk in Bobbie's office had moved to Brooklyn from Minneapolis. When this young woman, who had distinctive habits, asked him straight out, Edwin misheard the question and said no. He had heard, "Mr. Friend, are you merry?"

Edwin was good-natured but not merry, and the question puzzled him until he found himself having lunch with Bobbie, to whom the young woman from Minneapolis had introduced him. He realized that he was on a date. Bobbie seemed eager and attractive, while Dorothy liked to make love about as often as she liked to order tickets and go to a Broadway show, or invite her whole family for dinner, and with about as much planning. Not knowing exactly what he had in mind, Edwin suggested that Bobbie meet him for a drink after work, nervous that she'd refuse anything less than dinner and a movie. But she agreed. Drinking a quick whiskey sour in a darkened lounge, she suggested that next time he come to her house. So his visits began: daytime conversations over a glass of water or a cup of coffee; suppers followed by bed. Bobbie was always interested. She only needed to make sure Bradley was sleeping.

Bobbie rarely spoke of her marriage. Her husband had been a tense, mumbly man, a printer. He'd remained aloof from her family. At first he said she was nothing like her crude relatives. "I felt refined, but I didn't like it," Bobbie told Edwin. Later her husband began to say she was *exactly* like her family, and at last he moved her and Bradley, an infant, into a dark two-room apartment where nothing worked and there was hardly ever any hot water. He said he slept at his shop, and at first he brought her money, but soon that stopped. "I didn't have enough hot water to bathe the baby," Bobbie said.

"Let alone my whole self." Edwin imagined it: naked Bobbie clasping a thin baby and splashing warm water on herself from a chipped, shallow basin. She'd moved back with her mother and got a job. Eventually she could afford the apartment on Elton Street where Edwin now visited her. When Bradley was two, she had taken him on the train to Reno, lived there for six weeks, and come home divorced, bringing her sisters silver pins and bracelets with Indian designs on them, arrows and stylized birds.

Bobbie's family wouldn't care much that Edwin wasn't Jewish, she assured him, and they'd understand that he couldn't be around often because of his mother. But they did want to know him. So Edwin had consented to an occasional Sunday lunch in Bobbie's kitchen with her mother or one of her sisters, eating whitefish and kippered salmon and bagels off a tablecloth printed with cherries, and watching the sun move across the table as the afternoon lengthened and he imagined Dorothy wondering. After the bagels they'd have coffee with marble cake from Bobbie's bakery. He'd tip his chair against the porcelain sink and consider how surprised his wife would be if she knew where he was, being polite to another woman's relatives. His own house was bigger and more up-to-date.

Dorothy would be even more surprised if she knew, right now, that Edwin was in the same kitchen, less sunny in the morning, fixing a mixer that wasn't broken. Edwin would have preferred to be a bigamist, not a deceiver. When he reassembled the mixer, it didn't work. He left the bowls and beaters and took the big contraption home in the trunk of his car. He'd work on it when Dorothy was out. She had promised Dr. Dressel, her old boss, a few hours in the coming week.

The day Edwin carried off the mixer, Bobbie's sister Sylvia and her kids, Joan and Richard, rang Bobbie's bell after lunch because they were all going to the Hayden Planetarium. Sylvia, a schoolteacher, had said, "Bradley's ready," as if she'd noticed blanks in his eyes where stars and planet belonged. Her own kids had often been to the planetarium. So the sisters walked to Fulton Street, urging along the children, who stamped on piles of brown sycamore leaves. Climbing the stairs to the elevated train, Bobbie was already tired. She'd have changed her shoes, but she liked the look of the red heels. They waited on the windy platform, Joan holding Bradley's hand tightly. She and Richard were tall, capable children who read signs out loud in firm voices: NO SPITTING. MEET MISS SUBWAYS. They had to change trains, and as the second one approached, Sylvia said, "Does Bradley know what to do in case we're separated?"

"Why should we get separated?" said Bobbie.

"It can always happen," she said as the doors opened. The children squeezed into one seat, and Sylvia leaned over them. She had short curly hair that was starting to go gray. "Remember," she said, "in case we get separated, if you're on the train, get off at the next stop and wait. And if you're on the platform, just wait where you are, and we'll come back for you. Okay?"

Joan and Richard were reaching across Bradley to slap each other's knees, but Bradley nodded seriously. Bobbie rarely offered directives like that, and he probably needed them, yet she felt irritated. At the planetarium, Bradley tried to read aloud words on the curved ceiling that was covered with stars. The theater darkened. While the stars revolved swiftly, a slightly spooky voice spoke of a time so far back that Bobbie felt disjointed from herself: she in her red suit would surely never happen. Anything at all might be true.

Then Bradley whispered something. "Do you have to go to the bathroom?" Bobbie asked. "I can't go in with you." If Edwin would marry her, he'd be there to take Bradley to the bathroom! The size of Bobbie's yearning, like the age of the stars, was suddenly clear. But Bradley shook his head. "No. No. I can't remember what I do if you get off the train without me."

"I wouldn't do that, honey," she said, but of course he continued to worry. She could feel his little worry machines whirring beside her.

"You scared him," she said to Sylvia later, as they shuffled toward the exit with the crowd. "About being lost on the subway."

"He needs to know," Sylvia said, and Bobbie wondered if Sylvia would be as bossy if she didn't have a husband, Louis—an accountant, a good man; although Sylvia said he was quick in bed.

They spent an hour in the natural history museum—where Joan held Bradley's hand, telling him what Bobbie hoped were nonfrightening facts—before taking the long subway ride home again. At the stop before theirs, Bradley suddenly stood and ran toward the closing doors, crying out. Richard tackled him, knocking him to the dirty floor, and Bobbie took him on her lap. Bradley had thought a departing back was hers. "Oh, sweetie," she said, brushing him off and kissing him. She carried him as far as the stairs.

"Well, I shouldn't have said anything," said Sylvia as they reached the sidewalk and turned toward home. The train's sound grew faint behind them.

Bobbie said nothing. If she agreed, Sylvia would change her mind and defend what she'd said after all. Bobbie glanced back at the three kids, who were counting something out loud in exultant voices—passing cars, maybe. "Seven! No, nine!"

"I have chopped meat," said Sylvia at last, when their silence had lasted for more than a block. "I'll make mashed potatoes. Lou will drive you later, okay?"

"That would be nice," said Bobbie. They reached the corner of Sylvia's street and turned that way.

"Unless you have a date?" Sylvia added.

But it was cruel to make Bobbie say what was apparent. "No such luck."

"That guy has a problem," said Sylvia. "It's Saturday night!"

"Edwin says I look fat in that brown dress," Bobbie said. She never let herself think about Saturday nights. Edwin said his mother cooked corned beef and cabbage then, and minded if he went out. "Remember that dress? With the design down the front?"

"That gorgeous dress!" Sylvia said. "To tell the truth, you do look a little hefty in it, but who cares?"

In the dark, Bobbie cried. She hoped her sister would notice and maybe even put an arm around her, but that wasn't their way. Maybe Sylvia did notice. "I'll make a nice salad. You like salad, don't you?" she said soothingly.

Edwin's house was empty when he came home on Tuesday. Dorothy was working, and the girls were at a neighbor's. He spread newspaper on the dining room table and fixed Dorothy's mixer, the one that had been broken in the first place. It was not badly broken. A wire was loose. Then it occurred to him that mixers looked alike, with bulbous arms to hold the beaters, and curved white bases on which bowls rotated. He'd brought Dorothy's fixed mixer out to his car, then returned and put Bobbie's broken one on the sheet of newspaper.

He jumped when he heard Dorothy and the girls arriving, but there was nothing to worry about. Dorothy asked, "Did you fix it?" and Edwin truthfully said, "Not yet." She stood behind him watching as he took apart Bobbie's mixer. By this time it was hard to remember that the broken mixer was the one he had broken himself, not the one Dorothy had reported broken, and he listened attentively while she told him what she'd been about to mix when it didn't work. As he listened, his back to his wife, he suddenly felt love and pity for her, as if only he knew that she had a sickness. He looked over at Dorothy in her thin white hygienist's uniform, her green coat folded over her arm. She had short blond hair and glasses.

The girls had begun to play with a couple of small round dentist's mirrors that Dorothy had brought from Dr. Dressel's office. Mary Ann, the younger one, brought her mirror close to her eye. "I can't see anything," she said.

"Wait a minute," said Eileen. Her light hair was in half-unraveled braids. Eileen turned her back on Edwin and Dorothy and positioned her mirror just above her head. "I'm a spy," she said. "Let's see . . . oh, Daddy's putting poison in the mixer." Eileen would say anything.

"I'm a spy, too," said Mary Ann, hurrying to stand beside her sister and waving her mirror. "Show me. Show me how to be a spy."

Edwin couldn't fix Bobbie's mixer, and it stayed broken, on a shelf in Edwin and Dorothy's kitchen, for a long time. Meanwhile, Dorothy's working mixer was in the trunk of Edwin's car, and it was a natural thing to pretend it was Bobbie's and take it to her house the next time he visited.

On many Thursdays Edwin told Dorothy a story about New Jersey, then arranged a light day and drove to Brooklyn to visit Bobbie. Bobbie prepared a good dinner that tasted Jewish to Edwin, though she said she wasn't kosher. Little Bradley sat on a telephone book, and still his face was an inch off the plate, which he stared at, eating mostly mashed potatoes. "They're better the way Aunt Sylvia makes them, with the mixer," Bobbie said on this particular Thursday, the Thursday on which Edwin had brought her his wife's Sunbeam Mixmaster and pretended it was hers.

"I'm sorry I couldn't bring it sooner, babe."

"Oh, I didn't mean that. I just don't bother, the way Sylvia does."

Edwin watched Bradley. With the mental agility born of his mixer exchange, Edwin imagined carrying Bradley off in similar fashion and replacing him, just temporarily, with talky Eileen. If her big sister was out of the way, Mary Ann would play with Bradley, while Bobbie would enjoy fussing with a girl.

"What are you thinking about?" said Bobbie.

"I wish I could take Bradley home to meet my mother."

"Take both of us. She won't be against Jewish girls once she sees me," said Bobbie. "I don't mean I'm so special, but I don't do anything strange."

She hurried to clean up and put Bradley to bed, while Edwin, who hadn't replied, watched television. He couldn't help thinking that his family was surely watching the same show, with Groucho Marx. Over the noise of Groucho's voice and the audience's laughter, Edwin heard Bobbie's voice now and then as she read aloud. "'Faster, faster!' cried the bird," Bobbie read. Soon she came in, and Edwin reached for her hand, but she shook her head. She always waited until Bradley was asleep, but that didn't take long. When she checked and returned smiling, Edwin turned off the set and put his hands on her shoulders, then moved them down her back and fumbled with her brassiere through her blouse. Dorothy wore full slips. Edwin pulled Bobbie's ruffled pink blouse free and reached his hand under it. Even using only one hand, he'd learned that if he worked from bottom to top, pushing with one finger and pulling with two others, he could undo all three hooks of her brassiere without seeing them. In a moment his hand was on her big round breast, and she was laughing and opening her mouth for him, already leading him toward her bed.

Edwin forgot that Dorothy had promised Dr. Dressel she'd work Saturday morning. As he dressed in Bobbie's dark bedroom on Thursday night, she asked, "Will you come Saturday?"

"Sure, babe," he said. He had fallen asleep, but he could tell from Bobbie's voice that she'd remained awake, lying naked next to him. He leaned over to kiss her, then let himself out, rubbing his hand on his lips and checking for lipstick stains.

But on Saturday he had to stay with Eileen and Mary Ann, then pick up Dorothy at Dr. Dressel's office. He was more at ease with the girls in the car than at home. Made restless by his broken promise to Bobbie, he left too early, then had to look after his children in the dentist's waiting room. He didn't know how to braid Eileen's hair, and it had not been done that morning; Edwin noticed as he reread the dentist's posters, which urged him to eat carrots and apples, that one of yesterday's rubber bands still dangled off Eileen's mussed hair. He called to her and tried to remove the band without pulling. "You're hurting me," she said, though he didn't think he was.

At last Dorothy came out in her coat. "I heard them whooping it up," she said, but she sounded amused. She took two rubber bands from the receptionist's desk and swiftly braided Eileen's hair. Leaving the car where it was, they walked to a nearby luncheonette. Dorothy took Edwin's hand. Sometimes she spoke to him in baby talk; it was a kind of game. "I am going to teach you how to bwaid hair," she said. But he didn't know how to answer, so she spoke again, now taking his part, in a gruff voice like the Three Bears. *How on earth do you braid hair?* He let go of her hand and put his arm around her shoulders as she answered with elaborate patience, "Well, first you make a center part . . . " Edwin imagined Bobbie watching them, not jealously. "Squeeze," the imaginary Bobbie said, and Edwin squeezed his wife's taut shoulder through the green coat.

Bobbie didn't use her mixer often. She was not sufficiently interested in its departure and return to put it away, so she left it on the extra chair next to the kitchen table where Edwin had put it. On Saturday morning she put on makeup and stockings, but he didn't come. Ordinarily, if Edwin didn't appear by a quarter to ten, Bobbie took Bradley out, rather than brooding. This Saturday, though, Bradley had a cold. To distract herself, Bobbie called Sylvia, who asked, "Does he have a temperature?" Bobbie's thermometer was broken, so Sylvia brought hers over. Bobbie made coffee. Bradley sat on the floor in his pajamas, wiping his nose on his sleeve while putting together a jigsaw puzzle, a map of the United States.

Bobbie offered Sylvia a cookie, and she and Bradley said together, "Before lunch?" but then everyone took a Mallomar, since Bobbie said a cookie might cheer her up. Bradley licked his fingers and then placed Florida in the puzzle correctly.

"Edwin didn't come by today?" Sylvia said, playing with her spoon.

"Sometimes he's busy on Saturdays."

"You need more."

"I manage," Bobbie said. If Sylvia knew all Edwin's ways, she thought, she wouldn't object to him. "He's worth it."

Sylvia laughed, stretching her arm and actually taking a second cookie. "Oh, I know what you mean," she said. She interrupted herself to supervise Bradley's placement of California. "I know what you see in your Edwin. I see the way he looks at you."

"When you've been married a long time," Bobbie said, "I guess it's not so exciting."

Sylvia laughed. "I know how you feel," she said again, not scolding.

"You mean you felt that way about Lou once."

"Well, I suppose."

"What *did* you mean?" Bobbie asked.

"Oh, I shouldn't say anything," Sylvia said. She tipped the bowl of her spoon with one finger, making the handle rise.

"He's not listening," Bobbie said, tilting her head toward Bradley. "You mean—someone?"

"Someone I met at an in-service course."

"Another teacher? A man."

"He teaches at Midwood."

"A high school teacher. You—have feelings?" Bobbie said.

"Did this ever happen to you?" Sylvia said, now glad—it seemed—to talk. "At night, you know, picturing the wrong person?"

Bobbie thought she knew what Sylvia meant. She wasn't sure what an in-service course was, whether it consisted of one occasion or several. "How many times have you seen him?"

"Wait a minute," said Sylvia, but then she crouched on the floor. "Doesn't Colorado belong where you put Wyoming, Bradley?" Wyoming was nice and tight. "Could the map be wrong?"

"Did you have lunch with him?"

"Oh, I'm exaggerating, it's nothing," Sylvia said. She remained on the floor, helping Bradley with a few more states. Then she got up, reaching out a hand to steady herself on the extra chair. She gave the Mixmaster a pat. "Hey, you didn't just buy this, did you?"

"No, I've had it for a while."

"I might have been able to get you a discount. A client of Lou's . . . "

"I bought it last year."

"Oh, right." Sylvia seemed to expect Bobbie to explain why the mixer was on the chair, so Bobbie told in full the story Sylvia had heard only in part: the story of the dress, the walk to the post office, and her return to find Edwin fixing a mixer that wasn't broken.

"He took it home? Why did he do that?" Sylvia asked.

"At home he has tools."

"Maybe he took it to a repair place."

"Oh, no. I'm sure he fixed it himself," said Bobbie.

"You're sure he brought back the same mixer?"

"You mean he bought me a new one? I hope not!" Bobbie said.

"Or he could have bought a used one," said Sylvia.

"Oh, stop being so suspicious." She liked the more tremulous Sylvia who had spoken of the teacher from Midwood High School. She wasn't ready, yet, for the usual Sylvia. "Of course it's mine."

But as she spoke, as she insisted it was hers, Bobbie suddenly sensed that the mixer on the chair might never have been in her house before, and then, looking hard, she was certain. It was the same, but somehow not the same. It had been cleaned differently, maybe with a sponge, not a dishrag. But that thought was ridiculous. It had been handled in a way that was not Jewish. An even more ridiculous thought.

Bradley had abandoned the puzzle and left the room. Maybe Sylvia would say more. "Did you have lunch with him?" Bobbie asked again.

But Sylvia would not be deterred. "Maybe Edwin has another girlfriend," she said, "and this is her mixer. Hey, maybe he has a wife!" She gave a short laugh.

"He has a mother . . . " said Bobbie. His mother didn't sound like someone who'd plug in a mixer and mix anything. She now remembered that the metal plate with the Sunbeam insignia on her mixer was chipped. She looked, and this one was whole. She looked again. "I *trust* Edwin," she said.

"I know you do. Boy, that would be something," Sylvia said. "If it turned out Edwin was married."

But Bobbie was experiencing one of those moments when one discovers the speed of thought by having several in an instant. First she felt ashamed of being stupid. Of course there had been plenty of hints that Edwin was married. Once she allowed herself to consider the possibility, she was sure it was so. Bobbie didn't need to know whose mixer it was to know that Edwin was married. Then, however, Bobbie felt something quite different. It wasn't anger at Sylvia, at her sister's gossipy curiosity.

She was not angry at Sylvia. She felt sorry for Sylvia, a little superior to Sylvia. All her life, Bobbie had known that Sylvia was smart, so Bobbie must be smart too, even Bobbie who carried her clothing back and forth to the post office. Once they knew Edwin was married, Sylvia would imagine there was only one way to behave—to laugh bitterly—but Bobbie understood that there were two.

That there were two different ways to think about Edwin's marriage—like thinking about the stars, which might be spots of light, close together, and might be distant, wild fireworlds—struck Bobbie with almost as much force as her sorrow. Sylvia's way would be to laugh bitterly and tell everyone the story. Edwin's marriage might be a bad joke on Bobbie, but then Edwin would no longer tip his chair against her sink, or walk her to her bed while his hands grasped all of her body he could reach under her loosened clothes. His marriage might be a bitter joke—or it might be something Bobbie just had to put up with.

Bobbie would never marry Edwin, but Bobbie had the mixer that worked. She stood and plugged it in, and it made its noise. The years to come, during which she'd keep Edwin's secret, not letting him know she knew—because it would scare him away—and not letting her sisters know she knew—because they'd scream at her to forget him—became real in her mind, as if she could feel all their length, their loneliness, at once. She would be separated from Edwin, despite Thursday evenings and Saturday mornings. Bobbie turned off the mixer and wept.

"Oh, of course he's not married," Sylvia said, and Bobbie didn't say that wasn't why she was crying. "Me and my big mouth, as usual," Sylvia continued. She stood up and put her arms around Bobbie, and then the sisters were hugging and smiling. "Edwin married," Sylvia said. "If there's one man on earth who couldn't manage being a two-timer, it's Edwin. Sorry, baby, I love the guy, but that swift he's not." And she went on and on, hugging her sister and calling her baby. Baby! The unaccustomed sweetness, like the cookie, comforted Bobbie for a while. Maybe she and Sylvia both had secrets, like Edwin. Maybe life required secrets. What an idea.

Mattison on Story Structure

Like many other writers, when I'm working on something new I often feel that it exists somewhere already and must be found, like an overgrown trail in a forest that I rediscover step by step, groping in the undergrowth for a little space that might open into a path. "In Case We're Separated" was the first story I wrote after completing a novel. With a long hard task done, I felt free, and for several weeks I jotted down notes in a black composition book about future projects, especially a collection of connected short stories.

I'd written connected stories before. That first time, I didn't know I was doing it. A minor character in one story, Ida, interested me, so I wrote two stories about her. After that came one about people I thought had nothing to do with Ida, but when a new character entered a room, I recognized him: he was Ida's lover! And so it went.

This time, for the first time, I decided before I began that I would write a group of stories. Writing connected stories had been fun—easier than a novel, and satisfying, because I could follow my imagination where it happened to go. I wanted to do it again. Also, the characters coming to mind seemed to know one another: they were related. These stories would be closer to my own life than those I'd written before. They wouldn't be autobiographical—nothing in "In Case We're Separated" happened to anyone I know. But they would all concern one extended family, and it would resemble my mother's side of my family. My mother was one of five sisters and a brother who grew up in Brooklyn, New York, in the first decades of the twentieth century. They were Jewish, but not particularly observant. When I was growing up, my grandmother and three of my aunts, with their husbands and children, lived near us in East New York. One aunt was divorced, and for a long time she had a mysterious boyfriend. The family I wrote about—eventually in thirteen stories—is just like that, but there the similarities end. I didn't write about my mother and aunts or my actual cousins.

Yet the life in "In Case We're Separated"—the way people spend their time, the way they talk, what they think is important—is the life I grew up with, and the story is set in the 1950s, when I was a girl. Maybe all writers fear that the life they know best is not exciting, too ordinary. It's sometimes disconcerting to write about what's closest, and when I began these new stories I vowed to keep them close to myself whether that made me uncomfortable or not. In the notebook I wrote that when I'd written the book of intersecting stories, "there was something direct, corny, and simple I was running away from. Now's the time to go back to it."

There's another whole sentence—written in purple ink with a circle around it—in the black notebook's mess of words and half sentences: "In this book is the intersection of the Jewish girl and literature." I lived at home when I was in college, taking the subway and bus to Queens College. I majored in English and planned to be a poet and an English teacher. I read poems to remind myself that people besides me cared about feeling, experienced ambivalence, or were carried away by beauty. Home life was not terrible at all, but my parents and relatives seemed relentlessly practical, sensible, and rational (except for one aunt who told enthralling stories and almost admitted having an inner life). I was rescued by literature as a young woman, and now I wanted my new stories to be rescued by it, too. I wanted to write plainly and simply—and also to play, to fool around, as poetry does.

I decided, for no reason I could name, that each story would use six of something in a manner comparable to the use of six words in the sestina, an Italian Renaissance poetic form. For a sestina, the poet selects six words and then, in each six-line stanza, uses one of the six at the end of each line. If the six ending words in the first stanza are numbered 1, 2, 3, 4, 5, 6, then in the second stanza those words are used in the order 6, 1, 5, 2, 4, 3. In Elizabeth Bishop's "Sestina"—to mention just one striking example—the repeated words are "house," "grandmother," "child," "stove," "almanac," and "tears." In my stories, I decided, I'd use not six words over and over, but six fictional elements, six objects or topics or situations—or, to use a literary term, six tropes. Before writing, I'd choose my six tropes. Then I'd include each of them, in the order prescribed by the sestina form, in each story, as if each story were one stanza of a gigantic sestina.

I spent a couple of months making lists of what the six tropes might be, looking forward to the intriguing task of including them in stories (which proved less difficult than I expected). "Song?" I wrote. "Zipper?" "Tortoise?" When I thought of one that was right, I usually knew right away. Eventually I had the six: a glass of water, a sharp point, a cord, a mouth, an exchange, and a map. I don't expect the reader to notice or think about these tropes when reading the stories, although I suppose that when the book—which will be called *Brooklyn Sestina*—comes out, someone will notice that there are quite a few glasses of water in it. I plan to include a sentence of explanation at the end. Reading the stories individually, there's no way to tell what game I'm playing, and I only describe it here because it explains how I wrote "In Case We're Separated." If you look, you can see that I was excited, writing this first story, and used four of the tropes right away. Edwin drinks a glass of water and Bobbie uses the sharp scissors. She borrows cord at the post office and puts it into her mouth. In subsequent stories, I usually waited to use the tropes, and often they provided me with important plot turns. The exchange is the trope that matters most this time, and Edwin's replacement of Bobbie's mixer with Dorothy's is the center of the story: as I made up the plot, it helped to know that an exchange would take place. The map comes at the end—it's Bradley's jigsaw puzzle of the United States.

At this point I knew something about each story I was going to write, but not much. It's a little mysterious how a fiction writer moves from that state of mind to the state of mind in which a story emerges. Many of us begin to write without knowing what will happen in the story, setting down—at least in the first draft—whatever comes to mind, trusting that something good will turn up eventually.

But there's knowledge we need before we begin, if the story we end up with will have any merit. There are no rules for writing stories: no sooner does a writer decide that in every good story a character changes, or in every good story there must be a conflict, than a fine story will come to mind in which nobody changes or there is no conflict. Yet there's a great deal of difference between a good story and a bad one, or a good story and a random recitation of events. We all tell stories every day, stories that might be titled "What Made Me Late," "How She Found Out," or "Wait Till I Tell You What He Did." As we know from boring parties, though, not all those stories are worth telling, not all are clear, not all arrive at a satisfying conclusion. A story need not include conflict or change, but it needs something that will make you feel, when you reach the end, that what you've just heard or read is indeed a story, a finished work that has a reason for being told and heard.

Fiction writers can't study instructions to learn to write good stories. What we can do is make ourselves so familiar with good writing that we'll come to crave it, so alert to language that we'll sense when to embellish and when to stop, when to let a character speak and when to make silence do the work. We need to take so much delight in a satisfying structure that we develop a feel for when to draw out a scene and when to cut it short, when to give away what happened, and when to keep the reader guessing. Learning to write fiction is slow, gradual, and indirect: we need to read not just contemporary stories but stories, poems, novels, and other books written centuries ago or in distant places. It's helpful for fiction writers to learn the rules for formal poetry, meter and rhyme and use of sound, which will teach us to hear language, to feel the words we use physically. It's helpful to learn a foreign language, if only to make us more aware of our own, or to look at painting and sculpture, so as to see visual artists making choices about shape, balance, and surprise. When I describe writing this story, I talk about little more than daydreaming. To become fiction writers, we must prepare ourselves to be good daydreamers.

But sometimes the daydream is slow to come. When I finally sat down and began "In Case We're Separated," I didn't feel as cheerful as I had making up lists of tropes. My husband was spending a year in graduate school, and I lived with him in Somerville, Massachusetts, about half the time, in an apartment I didn't like, writing in a back room that I swear was haunted. The day I began the story, he was in the living room with a classmate studying for an exam, and as I wrote the first paragraph, setting down on paper the people I saw in my mind, I tried to lose myself in the pleasure of words rather than hearing my husband and his classmate discuss economics. I liked the opening paragraphs I wrote that day, in which Bobbie takes her dress to the post office—but then I was stuck for days. I had no idea what would happen next.

Finally, one afternoon I went out with the black notebook and kept walking until I emerged from the maze of hilly little streets where we lived, to an avenue with bustle and people and a coffee shop. I drank coffee and watched people out the window. The store also sold chocolate, which smelled wonderful. Now I wrote in the notebook, in green ink, "This feels much better!" In the same green ink, I began to write speculative sentences and questions about the story. I hadn't yet found my trail through the woods, but at last I was exploring instead of sitting silent and miserable. As I often do, I asked myself questions, hoping to think of an incident that would make a story, that would make what came before feel complete. It's helpful to ask, "Well, what could happen?"

If you're writing about a quarrel between two people in a car, for example, it's useful to think of half a dozen incidents that could happen to people driving. They could get lost. They could have a breakdown, be stopped for speeding, encounter bad weather. They could stop because of something they see—what? a stranded motorist? an ice cream stand? an antique store? And then what might happen? And then what?

Thinking of Bobbie, I wrote "Her job?" Then, "He could give her . . . furniture . . . chocolate . . . " "She's at her sister's house?" If you can speculate freely about characters, eventually you'll arrive at some incident that would work for your story, would round it out and complete it. If your story is comical, you probably don't want your characters to die in an automobile accident; if it's about people who misunderstand each other, getting lost might be just the thing. Writing this story, after two pages of questions I finally jotted down some useful notes. "He tries to fix something. Breaks it worse. Mixer?" And then (since I knew there would be an exchange in the story), "Takes hers and exchanges it with his wife's." Among the next notes are "Bobbie and Sylvia and children go to museum. Edwin and Dorothy and daughters. He brings other mixer. Scene with Bradley. Sylvia figures it out." I'd found my trail through the woods, and now the answers came more easily. After that day, I knew what would happen, and I could write.

Of course, what gives a story interest is not just what happens but the way it's written, the way words reveal feeling. As I tried to make the sentences in this story smoother and more precise, I gradually understood how Bobbie would deal with the truth she discovered. In revision, parts of the story grew longer, more detailed, as I saw the need to say more about Dorothy or Sylvia. It's often painful to realize during revision that what seemed like the right plan for the story isn't right after all, that you have to start over. That didn't happen to me this time, but it's happened often enough: the slow realization, if I can make myself pay attention to my own nagging discomfort as I read, that I haven't told the fictional truth after all, that something different happened to these characters. It takes practice and confidence to learn to recognize mistakes without giving up on the whole story, and sometimes there's no way to discover what works and what doesn't except by showing it to others. I worked on this story for a year or so, helped by the half dozen friends who always read and comment on my work, and once by a magazine editor who didn't buy the story but took the time to explain her difficulties with it. My habit is to print out a story, make changes in pen, then retype it on a blank screen if the changes are at all extensive, and print it out again. My brains are in my fingers: when I retype I often learn what I should write. This story wasn't as hard to finish as some, but it was hard enough. In the drawer where I keep finished stories are thirteen drafts of "In Case We're Separated."

Writing Suggestions

1. Many stories can be boiled down to one of two underlying story structures: someone comes to town, or someone goes to a new place. Write a one-page scene in which a long-lost friend or family member returns. Imagine what it would be like

to see that person again. How has the person changed—in appearance, attitude, or speech? What details stand out most strongly? What effect does his or her return have on you? Consider how these two plot archetypes come into play in the stories in this book. Consider such stories as "Unheard Music" and "Palm Wine."

2. Following Mattison's general example of using her own family as a model for fiction, select a photograph (not of yourself) from a family album and write the story of that photograph's protagonist. Consider a photograph of relatives you've only met once or twice. Imagine ways this photograph might suggest a conflict. Look for clues about character's personality in facial expressions, clothing, and body language. (Variation 1: Select two or three photographs from a family album and tell the story that connects the images. Variation 2: Select photos instead from a magazine or newspaper.)

3. Reread a story you've recently written. Look for images that hold emotional meaning (a wedding ring, a favorite shirt, an audio CD, the reflection of the moon off a pond). Perhaps brainstorm, like Mattison does, to generate new images. Consider ways to artfully repeat one or more of these images to help texture a story and suggest a thematic meaning, such as the Mixmaster in "In Case We're Separated." Readers will remember the original emotion associated with the image each time it is repeated.

4. At home, keep a journal for one week in which you record gestures and body language used by your family, friends, and co-workers—gestures that communicate nonverbal meaning and emotion. Revisit your stories to see if you can include these, or similar gestures, as a way of further developing scenes. (For a model, reread the first three pages of Mattison's story, "In Case We're Seperated," paying particular attention to physical movement.) In fiction what messages can be more effectively communicated through gesture than through dialogue?

One doesn't write stories about people who are comfortable in
their skins. You have to have trouble to write a story. If you don't
have trouble, you don't have a story.
—Tobias Wolff

Section 5

Developing Characters

Introduction

Turning Ideas Into Characters: Essay and Writing Suggestions

All characters begin as ideas. They begin as glimpses, a slice of personality, a voice whispering in your ear. They are crafted and carefully sculpted from the raw material of experience and imagination, revealing themselves to authors over time. The difficult work of writing fiction is, in part, developing the idea for a character, piece by piece, until the idea becomes a character richly imagined, so compelling as to immediately capture a reader's attention.

Humbert Humbert, the middle-aged narrator of Vladimir Nabokov's classic novel, *Lolita*, announces his presence with such surety and exactness, we find it difficult to believe that Humbert never existed, that his voice was, in fact, invented. Or rather that Humbert doesn't exist. He is an extension of the author's gifted and generous imagination. For us, Humbert—a delusional, erudite, elegant, pedophile—has been and always will be attached to the object of his sick affection, the young girl named Lolita.

Listen to how clearly and fully Humbert announces himself as the novel begins:

> Lolita, light of my life, fire of my loins. My sin, my soul. Lo-lee-ta: the tip of the tongue taking a trip of three steps down the palate to tap, at three, on the teeth. Lo. Lee. Ta.

Before the flint of Humbert's narration sparked across the page, there was an author, Vladimir Nabokov, performing the mundane and difficult task of imagining the character. Before Humbert's voice flamed into existence, there was merely the idea for a character. There might have been a morning when Vladimir Nabokov—and we're guessing here—had the idea to construct such a character: a pedophile, let's say, who also has a generous, even artistic understanding of the human condition. This is the idea that would become Humbert. Humbert is not yet a character, a glimmer of personality, perhaps a hint of his mercurial voice. Sometime after alighting on this idea, Vladimir Nabokov must've begun the difficult work of transforming the idea for a character into a character itself.

There is nothing particularly glamorous about this aspect of writing fiction. It is part of the hard work required before the real writing begins.

Towards the beginning of each semester, we ask each of our workshop students to return to class with a well-developed character in mind for a story. Most students return with the ideas for characters, rather than characters themselves: a man whose wife is leaving him, a woman taking a new job, a young boy who learns his parents will divorce.

Usually there's some lifeblood here, some genuine emotion and personality. Most students, though, don't understand they only have the "idea" for a character. Such ideas, to a new writer, can "feel" as real as a developed character. It's only as class progresses, as we work through exercises, that students slowly take the idea and turn it into a richly developed character.

Ernest Hemingway believed that a writer must be an expert on the lives of his or her characters. Simply put, the writer must know them better than the characters know themselves. Of course, all of this information will not end up in the story. But the information is important nonetheless. Only after an author fully understands his or her characters will that author finally know how to craft the story. This approach to writing is often called Hemingway's Iceberg Theory of Fiction.

After the publication of his novel *The Old Man and the Sea*, Ernest Hemingway explained this theory in an interview published in the literary journal, *The Paris Review:*

> I always try to write on the principle of the iceberg. There is seven-eighths of it underwater for every part that shows. Anything you know you can eliminate and it only strengthens your iceberg. It is the part that doesn't show. If a writer omits something because he does not know it then there is a hole in the story.

In straightforward terms, Hemingway is saying that he needs to explore the full lives of his characters before he is able to write their stories. Short stories, like icebergs, reveal only a small portion of their overall structure. Also like icebergs, short stories rely on an invisible mass hidden beneath the surface. For short stories, that invisible mass is the exploration of character and situation. It is the difficult task of turning the "idea" for a character into the genuine article.

Other contributors to this book will discuss the more subtle and complex aspects of character creation: psychological realism, public and private lives, and the illusion of life as it is presented on the page. But for now, we are only talking about the most basic elements, transforming an idea into a character.

Below are twenty questions you can use to guide character development. Some are rather easy—about names and style of dress—and you will know the answers right away. But others will prove more difficult. They might even stump you. For a time, you may even believe you don't know your character well at all. But here's what is happening: in such moments, you have found the boundaries of your knowledge. You have found a border beyond which you have not yet imaged a life for your character.

Here's what to do when stumped: take an educated guess. You already have a piece of this character. Use that knowledge as the starting point, from which you will explore, build out, and *imagine* a more fully developed character. The knowledge you have will suggest a path to follow. Answer each question fully. If your first attempt to answer a question doesn't seem right—if it rings false or incomplete—go back and create a new answer until you strike upon the one that, with the surety of intuition, feels true and complete.

Twenty Questions to Develop a Character:

1. What is your character's name? What sounds right for this character? What fits? What does this name suggest about your character's personality? Does your character use

his/her given name or a nickname? If so, why? Has your character ever had a nickname? (Note: For stories with unnamed characters, like Elizabeth Graver's "The Mourning Door," it's helpful for the author to know the name even though it's not used.)

2. If you were going to buy a casual outfit for this character, what would you buy? What image does he/she cultivate? What does this image say about him/her?

3. If your character could have three wishes granted, what would they be?

4. Likewise what three things does your character most want NOT to happen to him/her?

5. If you were to enter this character's bedroom for the first time, what would you notice? Name four objects that immediately stand out. What are the dominant colors of the room? What sounds do you hear? If you were to spend an hour snooping in this room, would you find anything hidden? If so, what?

6. What obsessions does your character have?

7. Describe your character's belief system—or lack of belief system—and sketch out how he or she came to believe these things.

8. Late at night, you are talking to your character, perhaps after having a few drinks. There's a good honest mood moving between the two of you. Finish each of these sentences in the voice of your character:

   - "To understand me, you first need to understand . . . "
   - "I don't usually tell anyone this, but when I was a kid . . . "
   - "If I had a million dollars, I would . . . "

9. Where does your character work? What specifically is his/her job? How does your character feel about this job? How long has he/she worked there?

10. Describe your character's average Wednesday. Where is your character at 8 a.m., 10 a.m., noon, 3 p.m., 6 p.m., and 10 p.m.? How does this compare to an average Saturday?

11. How much money does your character have in the bank or in investments? Where did this money come from?

12. What are your character's most substantial character flaws or shortcomings in personality? Does he or she recognize them?

13. What are your character's most significant character strengths?

14. Does your character have any brothers or sisters? If so, which one is his or her favorite, and why? If your character only has one sibling, what does your character like best about this person, and like least?

15. How many close friends does your character have? Name them.

16. Who is your character's closest friend and why? Describe their history as friends.

17. What is the worst thing your character has ever done?

18. Describe your character's relationship with his/her parents?

19. If your character were to die today, what would he or she most like to be remembered for? What would other people actually remember him or her for?

20. List three things about your character that will most likely NOT be included in your story.

Creating a complex character is just one way to begin developing a short story. But it's one that many authors repeatedly use. The short story writer, Thomas E. Kennedy, advises new writers: "Just follow the character through a day. What you come up with might not be pages that you'll use, but might lead you into the place where the story starts."

Lorrie Moore

Debarking

From *The New Yorker*

Ira had been divorced for six months and still couldn't get his wedding ring off. His finger had swelled doughily—a combination of frustrated desire, unmitigated remorse, and misdirected ambition was how he explained it. "I'm going to have to have my entire finger surgically removed," he told his friends. The ring (supposedly gold, though now that everything he had ever received from Marilyn had been thrown into doubt, who knew?) cinched the blowsy fat of his finger, which had grown twistedly around it like a fucking happy challah. "Maybe I should cut the whole hand off and send it to her," he said on the phone to his friend Mike, with whom he worked at the State Historical Society. "She'd understand the reference." Ira had already ceremoniously set fire to his dove-gray wedding tux—hanging it on a tall stick in his back yard, scarecrow style, and igniting it with a Bic lighter. "That sucker went up really fast," he gasped apologetically to the fire marshal, after the hedge caught, too—and before he was taken overnight to the local lockdown facility. "So fast. Maybe it was, I don't know, like the residual dry-cleaning fluid."

"You'll remove that ring when you're ready," Mike said now. Mike's job approving historical-preservation projects on old houses left him time to take a lot of lenient-parenting courses and to read all the lenient-parenting books, though he had no children himself. He did this for project-applicant-management purposes. "Here's what you do for your depression. I'm not going to say lose yourself in charity work. I'm not going to say get some perspective by watching our country's news every night and contemplating those worse off than yourself, those, say, who are about to be blown apart by bombs. I'm going to say this: Stop drinking, stop smoking. Eliminate coffee, sugar, dairy products. Do this for three days, then start everything back up again. *Bam.* I guarantee you, you will be so happy."

"I'm afraid," Ira said softly, "that the only thing that would make me happy right now is snipping the brake cables on Marilyn's car."

"Spring," Mike said helplessly, though it was still only the end of winter. "It can really hang you up the most."

"Hey. You should write songs. Just not too often." Ira looked at his hands. Actually, he *had* once got the ring off in a hot bath, but the sight of his finger, naked as a child's, had terrified him and he had shoved the ring back on.

He could hear Mike sighing and casting about. Cupboard doors closed loudly. The refrigerator puckered open then whooshed shut. Ira knew that Mike and Kate had had their troubles—as the phrase went—but their marriage had always held. "I'd divorce Kate," Mike had once confided, "but she'd kill me."

"Look," Mike suggested, "why don't you come to our house Sunday for a little Lent dinner. We're having some people by, and who knows?"

"Who knows?" Ira asked.

"Yes—who knows."

"What's a Lent dinner?"

"We made it up. For Lent. We didn't really want to do Mardi Gras. Too disrespectful, given the international situation."

"So you're doing Lent. I'm unclear on Lent. I mean, I know what the word means to those of us of the Jewish faith. But we don't usually commemorate these transactions with meals. Usually there's just a lot of sighing."

"It's like a pre-Easter Prince of Peace dinner," Mike said slowly. "You're supposed to give things up for Lent. Last year, we gave up our faith and reason. This year, we're giving up our democratic voice, our hope."

Ira had already met most of Mike's *goyisheh* friends. Mike himself was low-key, tolerant, self-deprecating to a fault. A self-described "ethnic Catholic," he once complained dejectedly about not having been cute enough to be molested by a priest. "They would just shake my hand very quickly," he said. Mike's friends, however, tended to be tense, intellectually earnest Protestants who drove new, metallic-hued cars and who within five minutes of light conversation could be counted on to use the phrase "strictly within the framework of."

"Kate has a divorcée friend she's inviting," Mike said. "I'm not trying to fix you up. I really hate that stuff. I'm just saying come. Eat some food. It's almost Easter season and—well, hey, we could use a Jew over here." Mike laughed heartily.

"Yeah, I'll reënact the whole thing for you," Ira said. He looked at his swollen ring finger again. "Yessirree. I'll come over and show you all how it's done."

Ira's new house—though it was in what his real-estate agent referred to as "a lovely, pedestrian neighborhood," abutting the streets named after Presidents, and boasting instead streets named after fishing flies (Caddis, Hendrickson, Gold-Ribbed Hare's Ear Road)—was full of slow drains, leaky gas burners, stopped-up sinks, and excellent dust for scrawling curse words. *Marilyn blows sailors.* The draftier windows Ira had duct-taped up with sheets of plastic on the inside, as instructed by Homeland Security; cold air billowed the plastic inward like sails on a ship. On a windy day it was quite something. "Your whole house could fly away," Mike said, looking around.

"Not really," Ira said lightly. "But it *is* spinning. It's very interesting, actually."

The yard had already grown muddy with March and the flower beds were green-ing with the tiniest sprigs of stinkweed and quack grass. By June, the chemical weapons of terrorism aimed at the heartland might prove effective in weeding the garden. "This may be the sort of war I could really use!" Ira said out loud to a neighbor.

Mike and Kate's house, on the other hand, with its perfect lines and friendly fussi-ness, reeking, he supposed, of historical-preservation tax credits, seemed an impossible dream to him, something plucked from a magazine article about childhood memories conjured on a deathbed. Something seen through the window by the Little Match Girl! Outside, the soffits were perfectly squared. The crocuses were like bells, and the Siber-ian violets like grape candies scattered in the grass. Soon their prize irises would be gor-geously crested cockatoos along the side yard. Inside, the smell of warm food almost made him weep. With his coat still on, he rushed past Kate to throw his arms around Mike, kissing him on both cheeks. "All the beautiful men must be kissed!" Ira exclaimed. After he'd got his coat off and wandered into the dining room, he toasted with the champagne that he himself had brought. There were eight guests there, most of whom he knew to *some* degree, but really that was enough. That was enough for everyone. They raised their glasses with him. "To Lent!" Ira cried. "To the final days!" And, in case that was too grim, he added, "And to the Resurrection! May it happen a little closer to home next time! Jesus Christ!" Soon he drifted back into the kitchen and, as he felt was required of him, shrieked at the pork. Then he began milling around again, apologizing for the crucifixion. "We really didn't intend it," he murmured. "Not really, not the killing part? We just kind of got carried away? You know how spring can get a little crazy, but, believe me, we're all really, really sorry."

Kate's divorced friend was named Zora and was a pediatrician. Although no one else did, she howled with laughter, and when her face wasn't blasted apart with it or her jaw snapping mutely open and shut like a pair of scissors (in what Ira recognized as post-divorce hysteria: "How long have you been divorced?" he later asked her. "Eleven years," she replied) Ira could see that she was very beautiful: short black hair; eyes a clear, reddish hazel, like orange pekoe tea; a strong aquiline nose; thick lashes that spiked out, wrought and black as the tines of a fireplace fork. Her body was a mixture of thin and plump, her skin lined and unlined, in that rounding-the-corner-to-fifty way. *Age and youth,* he chanted silently, *youth and age, sing their songs on the very same stage.* Ira was working on a modest little volume of doggerel, its tentative title "Women from Venus, Men from Penis."

Like everyone he knew, he could discern the hollowness in people's charm only when it was directed at someone other than himself. When it was directed at him, the person just seemed so totally *nice.* And so Zora's laughter, in conjunction with her beauty, doomed him a little, made him grateful beyond reason.

Immediately, he sent her a postcard, a photograph of newlyweds dragging empty Spam cans from the bumper of their car. He wrote: *Dear Zora, Had such fun meeting you at Mike's.* And then he wrote his phone number. He kept it simple. In courtship he had a history of mistakes, beginning at sixteen with his first girlfriend, for whom he had bought at the local head shop the coolest thing he had then ever seen in his life: a beautifully carved wooden hand with its middle finger sticking up. He himself had coveted it tremulously for a year. How could she not love it? Her contempt for it, and then for him, had left him feeling baffled and betrayed. With Marilyn, he had taken the other approach and played hard to get, which had turned their relationship into a never-ending Sadie Hawkins Day, with subsequent marriage to Sadie an inevitable ruin—a humiliating and interminable Dutch date.

But this, the Spam postcard and the note, he felt contained the correct combination of offhandedness and intent. This elusive mix—the geometric halfway point between stalker and Rip van Winkle—was important to get right in the world of middle-aged dating, he suspected, though what did he really know of this world? The whole thing seemed a kind of distant civilization, a planet of the apings: graying, human flotsam with scorched internal landscapes mimicking the young, picking up where they had left off decades ago, if only they could recall where the hell that was. Ira had been a married man for fifteen years, a father for eight (poor little Bekka, now rudely transported between houses in a speedy, ritualistic manner resembling a hostage drop-off), only to find himself punished for an idle little nothing, nothing, nothing flirtation with a colleague, punished with his wife's full-blown affair and false business trips (credit-union conventions that never took place) and finally a petition for divorce mailed from a motel. Observing others go through them, he used to admire midlife crises, the courage and shamelessness and existential daring of them, but after he'd watched his own wife produce and star in a fabulous one of her own he found the sufferers of such crises not only self-indulgent but greedy and demented, and he wished them all weird unnatural deaths with various contraptions easily found in garages.

He received a postcard from Zora in return. It was of van Gogh's room in Arles. Beneath the clock face of the local postmark her handwriting was big but careful, some curlicuing in the "g"s and "f"s. It read, *Had such fun meeting you at Mike's.* Wasn't that precisely, word for word, what he had written to her? There was no "too," no emphasized *you*, just exactly the same words thrown back at him like some lunatic postal Ping-Pong. Either she was stupid or crazy or he was already being too hard on her. Not being hard on people—"You *bark* at them," Marilyn used to say—was something he was trying to work on. When he pictured Zora's lovely face, it helped his tenuous affections. She had written her phone number and signed off with a swashbuckling "Z"—as in Zorro. That was cute, he supposed. He guessed. Who knew? He had to lie down.

He had Bekka for the weekend. She sat in the living room, tuned to the Cartoon Network. Ira would sometimes watch her mesmerized face, as the cartoons flashed on the creamy screen of her skin, her eyes bright with reflected shapes caught there like holograms in marbles. He felt inadequate as her father, but he tried his best: affection, wisdom, reliability, plus not ordering pizza every visit, though tonight he had again caved in. Last week, Bekka had said to him, "When you and Mommy were married, we always had mashed potatoes for supper. Now you're divorced and we always have spaghetti."

"Which do you like better?" he'd asked.

"Neither!" she'd shouted, summing up her distaste for everything, marriage *and* divorce. "I hate them both."

Tonight, he had ordered the pizza half plain cheese and half with banana peppers and jalapeños. The two of them sat together in front of "Justice League," eating slices from their respective sides. Chesty, narrow-waisted heroes in bright colors battled their enemies with righteous confidence and, of course, laser guns. Bekka finally turned to him. "Mommy says that if her boyfriend Daniel moves in I can have a dog. A dog and a bunny."

"*And* a bunny?" Ira said. When the family was still together, the four-year-old Bekka, new to numbers and the passage of time, used to exclaim triumphantly to her friends, "Mommy and Daddy say I can have a dog! When I turn eighteen!" There'd been no talk of bunnies. But perhaps the imminence of Easter had brought this on. He knew that Bekka loved animals. She had once, in a bath-time reverie, named her five favorite people, four of whom were dogs. The fifth was her own blue bike.

"A dog *and* a bunny," Bekka repeated, and Ira had to repress images of the dog with the rabbit's bloody head in its mouth.

"So, what do you think about that?" he asked cautiously, wanting to get her opinion on the whole Daniel thing.

Bekka shrugged and chewed. "Whatever," she said, her new word for "You're welcome," "Hello," "Goodbye," and "I'm only eight." "I really just don't want all his stuff there. His car already blocks our car in the driveway."

"Bummer," Ira said, his new word for "I must remain as neutral as possible" and "Your mother's a whore."

"I don't want a stepfather," Bekka said.

"Maybe he could just live on the steps," Ira said, and Bekka smirked, her mouth full of mozzarella.

"Besides," she said, "I like Larry better. He's stronger."

"Who's Larry?" Ira said, instead of "bummer."

"He's this other dude," Bekka said. She sometimes referred to her mother as a "dudette."

"Bummer," Ira said. "Big, big bummer."

He phoned Zora four days later, so as not to seem pathetically eager. He summoned up his most confident acting. "Hi, Zora? This is Ira," he said, and then waited—narcissistically perhaps, but what else was there to say?—for her response.

"Ira?"

"Yes. Ira Milkins."

"I'm sorry," she said. "I don't know who you are."

Ira gripped the phone and looked down at himself, suddenly finding nothing there. He seemed to have vanished from the neck down. "We met last Sunday at Mike and Kate's?" His voice quavered. If he ever actually succeeded in going out with her, he was going to have to take one of those date-rape drugs and just pass out on her couch.

"Ira? Ohhhhhhhhhh—Ira. Yeah. The Jewish guy."

"Yeah, the Jew. That was me." Should he hang up now? He did not feel he could go on. But he must go on. *There* was a man of theatre for you.

"That was a nice dinner," she said.

"Yes, it was."

"I usually skip Lent completely."

"Me, too," Ira said. "It's just simpler. Who needs the fuss?"

"But sometimes I forget how reassuring and conjoining a meal with friends can be, especially at a time like this."

Ira had to think about the way she'd used "conjoining." It sounded New Age-y and Amish, both.

"But Mike and Kate run that kind of home," she went on. "It's all warmth and good-heartedness."

Ira thought about this. What other kind of home was there to run, if you were going to bother? Hard, cold, and mean: that had been his home with Marilyn, at the end. It was like those experimental monkeys with the wire-monkey moms. What did the baby monkeys know? The wire mother was all they had, all they knew in their hearts, and so they clung to it, even if it was only a coat hanger. *Mom.* So much easier to carve the word into your arm. As a child, for a fifth-grade science project, in the basement of his house he'd tried to reproduce Konrad Lorenz's imprinting experiment with baby ducks. But he had screwed up the incubation lights and cooked the ducks right in their eggs, stinking up the basement so much that his mother had screamed at him for days. Which was a science lesson of some sort—the emotional limits of the *Homo sapiens* working Jewish mother—but it was soft science, and therefore less impressive.

"What kind of home do *you* run?" he asked.

"Home? Yeah, I mean to get to one of those. Right now, actually, I'm talking to you from a pup tent."

Oh, she was a funny one. Perhaps they would laugh and laugh their way into the sunset. "I *love* pup tents," he said. What was a pup tent, exactly? He'd forgotten.

"Actually, I have a teen-age son, so I have no idea what kind of home I have anymore. Once you have a teen-ager, everything changes."

Now there was silence. He couldn't imagine Bekka as a teen-ager. Or, rather, he could, sort of, since she often acted like one already, full of rage at the second-rate servants whom life had hired to take and bring her order.

"Well, would you like to meet for a drink?" Zora asked finally, as if she had asked it many times before, her tone a mingling of weariness and the cheery pseudo-professionalism of someone in the dully familiar position of being single and dating.

"Yes," Ira said. "That's exactly why I called."

"You can't imagine the daily drudgery of routine pediatrics," Zora said, not touching her wine. "Ear infection, ear infection, ear infection. Wope. Here's an exciting one: juvenile-onset diabetes. Day after day, you have to look into the parents' eyes and repeat the same exciting thing—'There are a lot of viruses going around.' I thought about going into pediatric oncology, because when I asked other doctors why they'd gone into such a depressing field they all said, 'Because the *kids* don't get depressed.' That seemed interesting to me. And hopeful. But then when I asked doctors in the same field why they were retiring early they said they were sick of seeing kids die. The kids don't get depressed, they just die! These were my choices in med school. As an undergraduate, I took a lot of art classes and did sculpture, which I still do a little to keep those creative juices flowing! But what I would really like to do now is write children's books. I look at some of those books out in the waiting room and I want to throw them in the fish tank. I think, I could do better than that. I started one about a hedgehog."

"Now, what's a hedgehog, exactly?" Ira was eying her full glass and his own empty one. "I get them mixed up with groundhogs and gophers."

"They're—well, what does it matter, if they're all wearing little polka-dot clothes, vests and hats and things?" she said irritably.

"I suppose," he said, now a little frightened. What was wrong with her? He did not like stressful moments in restaurants. They caused his mind to wander strangely to random thoughts, like "Why are these things called *napkins* rather than *lapkins*?" He tried to focus on the visuals, on her pumpkin-colored silk blouse, which he hesitated to compliment her on lest she think he was gay. Marilyn had threatened to call off their wedding because he had too strenuously admired the fabric of the gown she was having made; then he had shopped too long and discontentedly for his own tuxedo, failing to find just the right shade of "mourning dove," a color he had read about in a wedding magazine. "Are you homosexual?" she had asked. "You must tell me now. I won't make the same mistake my sister did."

Perhaps Zora's irritability was only job fatigue. Ira himself had creative hankerings. Though his position was with the Historical Society's human-resources office, he liked to help with the society's exhibitions, doing posters and dioramas and once even making a puppet for a little show about the state's first governor. Thank God for meaningful work! He understood those small, diaphanous artistic ambitions that overtook people and could look like nervous breakdowns.

"What happens in your hedgehog tale?" Ira asked, then settled in to finish up his dinner, eggplant parmesan that he now wished he hadn't ordered. He was coveting Zora's wodge of steak. Perhaps he had an iron deficiency. Or perhaps it was just a desire for the taste of metal and blood in his mouth. Zora, he knew, was committed to meat. While other people's cars were busy protesting the prospect of war or supporting the summoned troops, on her Honda Zora had a large bumper sticker that said, "Red meat is not bad for you. Fuzzy, greenish-blue meat is bad for you."

"The hedgehog tale? Well," Zora began, "the hedgehog goes for a walk because he is feeling sad—it's based on a story I used to tell my son. The hedgehog goes for a walk and comes upon this strange yellow house with a sign on it that says, 'Welcome, Hedgehog: This could be your new home,' and because he's been feeling sad the thought of a new home appeals to him. So he goes in and inside is a family of alligators—well, I'll spare you the rest, but you can get the general flavor of it from that."

"I don't know about that family of alligators."

She was quiet for a minute, chewing her beautiful ruby steak. "Every family is a family of alligators," she said. (Later, she would tell him that she'd been "emotionally incested" by her father. "But you turned out so well!" Ira would exclaim. "Daughters who are close to their fathers turn into achievers," Zora said. "That's been statistically shown!")

"Alligators. Well—that's certainly one way of looking at it." Ira glanced at his watch.

"Yeah. To get back to the book. It gives me an outlet. I mean, my job's not terrible. Some of the kids are cute. But some are impossible, of course. Some are disturbed, and some are just spoiled and ill-behaved. It's hard to know what to do. We're not allowed to hit them."

"You're 'not allowed to hit them'?" He could see that she had now made some progress with her wine.

"I'm from Kentucky," she said.

"Ah." He drank from his water glass, stalling.

She chewed thoughtfully. Merlot was beginning to etch a ragged, scabby line in the dried skin of her bottom lip. "It's like Ireland but with more horses and guns."

"Not a lot of Jews down there." He had no idea why he said half the things he said. Perhaps this time it was because he had once been a community-based historian, digging in archives for the genealogies and iconographies of various ethnic groups, not realizing that other historians generally thought this a sentimental form of history, shedding light on nothing; and though shedding light on nothing didn't seem a bad idea to him, when it became available he had taken the human-resources job.

"Not too many," she said. "I did know an Armenian family, growing up. At least I *think* they were Armenian."

When the check came, she ignored it, as if it were some fly that had landed and would soon be taking off again. So much for feminism. Ira pulled out his state worker's credit card and the waitress came by and whisked it away. There were, he was once told, four seven-word sentences that generally signalled the end of a relationship. The first was "I think we should see other people" (which always meant another seven-word sentence: "I am already sleeping with someone else"). The second seven-word sentence was, reputedly, "Maybe you could just leave the tip." The third was "How could you forget your wallet again?" And the fourth, the killer of all killers, was "Oh, look, I've forgotten my wallet, too!"

He did not imagine that they would ever see each other again. But when he dropped her off at her house, walking her to the door, she suddenly grabbed his face with both hands, and her mouth became its own wet creature exploring his. She opened up his jacket, pushing her body inside it, against his, the pumpkin-colored silk of her blouse rubbing on his shirt. Her lips came away in a slurp. "I'm going to call you," she said, smiling. Her eyes were wild with something, as if with gin, though she had only been drinking wine.

"O.K.," he mumbled, walking backward down her steps in the dark, his car still running, its headlights bright along her street.

The following week, he was in Zora's living room. It was beige and white with cranberry accents. On the walls were black-framed photos of her son, Bruno, at all ages. There were pictures of Bruno lying on the ground. There were pictures of Bruno and Zora together, the boy hidden in the folds of her skirt, Zora hanging her then long hair down into his face, covering him completely. There he was again, naked, leaning in between her knees like a cello. There were pictures of him in the bath, though in some he was clearly already at the start of puberty. In the corner of the room stood perhaps a dozen wooden sculptures of naked boys that Zora had carved herself. "One of my hobbies, which I was telling you about," she said. They were astounding little things. She had drilled holes in their penises with a brace-and-bit to allow for water in case she could someday sell them as garden fountains. "These are winged boys. The beautiful adolescent boy who flies away. It's from mythology. I forget what they're called. I just love their little rumps." He nodded, studying the tight, sculpted buttocks, the spouted, mushroomy phalluses, the long backs and limbs. So: this was the sort of woman he'd been missing out on, not being single all these years. What had he been thinking of, staying married for so long?

He sat down and asked for wine. "You know, I'm just a little gun shy romantically," he said apologetically. "I don't have the confidence I used to. I don't think I can take my clothes off in front of another person. Not even at the gym, frankly. I've been changing in the toilet stalls. After divorce and all."

"Oh, divorce will do that to you totally," she said reassuringly. She poured him some wine. "It's like a trick. It's like someone puts a rug over a trapdoor and says, 'Stand there.' And so you do. Then *boom.*" From a drawer in a china hutch, she took out a pipe, loaded it with hashish from a packet of foil, then lit it, inhaling. She gave it to him.

"I've never seen a pediatrician smoke hashish before."

"Really?" she said, with some difficulty, her breath still sucked in.

The nipples of her breasts were long, cylindrical, and stiff, so that her chest looked as if two small plungers had flown across the room and suctioned themselves there. His mouth opened hungrily to kiss them.

"Perhaps you would like to take off your shoes," she whispered.

"Oh, no," he said.

There was sex where you were looked in the eye and beautiful things were said to you and then there was what Ira used to think of as yoo-hoo sex: where the other person seemed spirited away, not quite there, their pleasure mysterious and crazy and only accidentally involving you. "Yoo-hoo?" was what his grandmother always called before entering a house where she knew people but not well enough to know whether they were actually home.

"Where *are* you?" Ira said in the dark. He decided that in a case such as this he could feel a chaste and sanctifying distance. It wasn't he who was having sex. The condom was having sex and he was just trying to stop it. Zora's candles on the night-stand were heated to clear pools in their tins. They flickered smokily. He tried not to think about how, before she had even lit them and pulled back the bedcovers, he had noticed that they were already melted down to the thickness of buttons, their wicks blackened to a crisp. It was not good to think about the previous burning of the bedroom candles of a woman who had just unzipped your pants. Besides, he was too grateful for those candles—especially with all those little wonder boys in the living room. Perhaps by candlelight his whitening chest hair would not look so white. This was what candles were made for: the sad, sexually shy, out-of-shape, middle-aged him. How had he not understood this in his marriage? Zora herself looked ageless, like a nymph, with her short hair, although once she got his glasses off she became a blur of dim and shifting shapes and might as well have been Dick Cheney or Lon Chaney or the Blob, except that she smelled good and, but for the occasional rough patch, had the satiny skin of a girl.

She let out a long, spent sigh.

"Where did you go?" he asked again anxiously.

"I've been right here, silly," she said, and pinched his hip. She lifted one of her long legs up and down outside the covers. "Did you get off?"

"I beg your pardon?"

"Did you get off?"

"'Get off'?" Someone else had asked him the same question once, when he stopped in the jetway to tie his shoe after debarking from a plane.

"Have an orgasm. With some men it's not always clear."

"Yes, thank you. I mean, it was—to me—very clear."

"You're still wearing your wedding ring," she said.

"It's stuck, I don't know why—"

"Let me get at that thing," she said, and pulled hard on his finger, but the loose skin around his knuckle bunched up and blocked the ring, abrading his hand.

"Ow," he finally said.

"Perhaps later with soap," she said. She lay back and swung her legs up in the air again.

"Do you like to dance?" he asked.

"Sometimes," she said.

"I'll bet you're a wonderful dancer."

"Not really," she said. "But I can always think of things to do."

"That's a nice trait."

"You think so?" and she leaned in and began tickling him.

"I don't think I'm ticklish," he said.

"Oh." She stopped.

"I mean, I probably am a *little*," he added, "just not a lot."

"I'd like you to meet my son," she said.

"Is he here?"

"Sure. He's under the bed. Bruny?" Oh, these funny ones were funny. "No. He's with his dad this week."

The extended families of divorce. Ira tried not to feel jealous. It was quite possible that he was not mature enough to date a divorced woman. "Tell me about his dad."

"His dad? His dad is another pediatrician, but he was really into English country dancing. Where eventually he met a lass. Alas."

Ira would put that in his book of verse. *Alas, a lass.* "I don't think anyone should dance in a way that's not just regular dancing," Ira said. "It's not normal. That's just my opinion."

"Well, he left a long time ago. He said he'd made a terrible mistake getting married. He said that he just wasn't capable of intimacy. I know that's true for some people, but I'd never actually heard anyone say it out loud about themselves."

"I know," Ira said. "Even Hitler never said that! I mean, I don't mean to compare your ex to Hitler as a *leader*. Only as a man."

Zora stroked his arm. "Do you feel ready to meet Bruno? I mean, he didn't care for my last boyfriend at all. That's why we broke up."

"Really?" This silenced him for a moment. "If I left those matters up to my daughter, I'd be dating a beagle."

"I believe children come first." Her voice now had a steely edge.

"Oh, yes, yes, so do I," Ira said quickly. He felt suddenly paralyzed and cold.

She reached into the nightstand drawer, took out a vial, and bit into a pill. "Here, take half," she said. "Otherwise we won't get any sleep at all. Sometimes I snore. Probably you do, too."

"This is so cute," Ira said warmly. "Our taking these pills together."

He staggered through his days, tired and unsure. At the office, he misplaced files. Sometimes he knocked things over by accident—a glass of water or the benefits manual. The buildup to war, too, was taking its toll. He lay in bed at night, the moments before sleep a kind of stark acquaintance with death. What had happened to the world? It was mid-March now, but it still did not look like spring, especially with the plastic sheeting duct-taped to his windows. When he tried to look out, the trees seemed to be pasted onto the waxy dinge of a still wintry sky. He wished that this month shared its name with a less military verb. Why "March"? How about a month named Skip? That could work.

He got a couple of cats from the pound so that Bekka could have some live pet action at his house, too. He and Bekka went to the store and stocked up on litter and cat food.

"Provisions!" Ira exclaimed.

"In case the war comes here, we can eat the cat food," Bekka suggested.

"Cat food, heck. We can eat the cats," Ira said.

"That's disgusting, Dad."

Ira shrugged.

"You see, that's one of the things Mom didn't like about you!" she added.

"Really? She said that?"

"Sort of."

"Mom likes me. She's just very busy."

"Yeah. Whatever."

He got back to the cats. "What should we name them?"

"I don't know." She studied the cats.

Ira hated the precious literary names that people gave pets—characters from opera and Proust. When he first met Marilyn, she had a cat named Portia, but he had insisted on calling it Fang.

"I think we should name them Snowball and Snowflake," Bekka said, looking glassy-eyed at the two golden tabbies. In the pound, someone with name-tag duty had named them "Jake" and "Fake Jake," but the quotation marks around their names seemed an invitation to change them.

"They don't look like a snowball or a snowflake," Ira said, trying not to let his disappointment show. Sometimes Bekka seemed completely banal to him. She had spells of inexplicable and vapid conventionality. He had always wanted to name a cat Bowser. "How about Bowser and Bowsee?"

"Fireball and Fireflake," Bekka tried again.

Ira looked at her, he hoped, beseechingly and persuasively. "Are you *sure*? Fireball and Fireflake don't really sound like cats that would belong to you."

Bekka's face clenched tearily. "You don't know me! I only live with you part time! The rest of the time I live with Mom, and she doesn't know me, either! The only person who knows me is me!"

"O.K., O.K.," Ira said. The cats were eying him warily. In time of war, never argue with a fireball or a fireflake. Never argue with the food. "Fireball and Fireflake."

What *were* those? Two divorced middle-aged people on a date?

"Why don't you come to dinner?" Zora phoned one afternoon. "I'm making spring spaghetti, Bruny's favorite, and you can come over and meet him. Unless you have Bekka tonight."

"What is spring spaghetti?" Ira asked.

"Oh, it's the same as regular spaghetti—you just serve it kind of lukewarm. Room temperature. With a little fresh basil."

"What should I bring?"

"Perhaps you could just bring a small appetizer and some dessert," she said. "And maybe a salad, some bread if you're close to a bakery, and a bottle of wine. Also an extra chair, if you have one. We'll need an extra chair."

"O.K.," he said.

He was a little loaded down at the door. She stepped outside, he thought to help him, but she simply put her arms around him. "I have to kiss you outside. Bruny doesn't like to see that sort of thing." She kissed Ira in a sweet, rubbery way on the mouth. Then she stepped back in, smiling, holding the door open for him. Oh, the beautiful smiles of the insane. Soon, he was sure, there would be a study that showed that the mentally ill were actually better-looking than other people. Dating proved it! The aluminum foil over his salad was sliding off, and the brownies he had made for dessert were still warm underneath the salad bowl, heating and wilting the lettuce. He attempted a familiar and proprietary stride through Zora's living room, though he felt neither, then dumped everything on her kitchen table.

"Thank you," she said, and placed her hand on the small of his back. He was deeply attracted to her. There was nothing he could do about that.

"It smells good," he said. "You smell good." Some mix of garlic and citrus and baby powder overlaid with nutmeg. Her hand wandered down and stroked his behind. "I've got to run back out to the car and get the appetizer and the chair," he said, and made a quick dash. When he came back in, handed her the appetizer—a dish of herbed olives (he knew nothing about food; someone at work had told him you could never go wrong with herbed olives: "Spell it out. H-e-r b-e-d. Get it?")—and then set the chair up at Zora's little dining table for two (he'd never seen one not set up for at least four), Zora looked brightly at him and whispered, "Are you ready to meet Bruny?"

Ready. He did not know precisely what she meant by that. It seemed that she had reversed everything, that she should be asking Bruno, or Bruny, if he was ready to meet *him*. "Ready," he said.

There was wavery flute-playing behind a closed door down the hallway. "Bruny?" Zora called. The music stopped. Suddenly a barking, howling voice called, "*What?*"

"Come out and meet Ira, please."

There was silence. Nobody moved at all for a very long time. Ira smiled politely. "Oh, let him play," he said.

"I'll be right back," Zora said, and she headed down the hall to Bruno's room, knocked on the door, then went in, closing it behind her. Ira stood there for a while, then he picked up the Screwpull, opened the bottle of wine, and began to drink. After several minutes, Zora returned to the kitchen, sighing, "Bruny's in a little bit of a mood." Suddenly a door slammed and soft, trudging footsteps brought Bruno, the boy himself, into the kitchen. He was barefoot and in a T-shirt and gym shorts, his legs already dark with hair. His eyebrows sprouted in a manly black V over the bridge of his nose. He was not tall but he was muscular, broad-shouldered, and thick-limbed. He folded his arms across his chest and leaned against the wall with weary belligerence.

"Bruny, this is Ira," Zora said. Ira put his wineglass down and extended his hand. Bruno unfolded his arms, but did not shake hands. Instead, he thrust out his chin and scowled. Ira picked up his wineglass again.

"Good to meet you. Your mother has said a lot of wonderful things about you."

Bruno looked at the appetizer bowl. "What's all this grassy gunk all over the olives." It was not really a question, so no one answered it. Bruno turned back to his mother. "May I go back to my room now?"

"Yes, dear," Zora said. She looked at Ira. "He's practicing for the woodwind competition next Saturday. He's very serious."

When Bruno had tramped back down to his room, Ira leaned in to kiss Zora, but she pulled away. "Bruny might hear us," she whispered.

"Let's go to a restaurant. Just you and me. My salad's no good."

"Oh, we couldn't leave Bruno here alone. He's only sixteen."

"I was working in a steel factory when I was sixteen!" Ira decided not to say. Instead, he said, "Doesn't he have friends?"

"He's between social groups right now," Zora said defensively. "It's difficult for him to find other kids who are as intellectually serious as he is."

"We'll rent him a movie," Ira said. "Excuse me, a *film*. A foreign film, since he's serious. A documentary. We'll rent him a foreign documentary!"

"We don't have a VCR."

"You don't have a VCR?" At this point, Ira found the silverware and helped set the table. When they sat down to eat, Bruno suddenly came out and joined them. The spring spaghetti was tossed in a large glass bowl with grated cheese. "Just how you like it, Brune," Zora said.

"So, Bruno. What grade are you in?"

Bruno rolled his eyes. "Tenth," he said.

"So college is a ways off," Ira said, accidentally thinking out loud.

"I guess," Bruno said.

"What classes are you taking in school, besides music?" Ira asked, after a long awkward spell.

"I don't take music," Bruno said with his mouth full. "I'm in All-State Woodwinds."

"All-State Woodwinds! Interesting! Do you take any courses like, say, American history?"

"They're studying the Amazon rain forest yet again," Zora said. "They've been studying it since preschool."

Ira slurped with morose heartiness at his wine—he had spent too much of his life wandering about in the desert of his own drool; oh, the mealtime games he had played on his own fragile mind—and some dribbled on his shirt. "For Pete's sake, look at this." He dabbed at it with his napkin and looked up at Bruno with an ingratiating grin. "Someday this could happen to you," Ira said, twinkling in Bruno's direction.

"That would never happen to me," Bruno muttered.

Ira continued dabbing at his shirt. He began thinking of his book. *Though I be your mother's beau, no rival I, no foe, faux foe.* He loved rhymes. They were harmonious and joyous in the face of total crap.

Soon Bruno was gently tapping his foot against his mother's under the table. Zora began playfully to nudge him back, and then they were both kicking away, their energetic footsie causing them to slip in their chairs a little, while Ira pretended not to notice, cutting his salad with the edge of his fork, too frightened to look up. After a few minutes—when the footsie had stopped and Ira had exclaimed, "Great dinner, Zora!"— they all stood and cleared their places, taking the dishes into the kitchen, putting them in a messy pile in the sink. Ira began halfheartedly to run warm water over them while Zora and Bruno, some distance behind him, jostled up against each other, ramming lightly into each other's sides. Ira glanced over his shoulder and saw Zora step back and assume a wrestler's starting stance as Bruno leaped toward her, heaving her over his shoulder, then ran into the living room, where, Ira could see, he dumped her, laughing, on the couch.

Should Ira join in? Should he leave?

"I can still pin you, Brune, when we're on the bed," Zora said.

"Yeah, right," Bruno said.

Perhaps it was time to go. Next time, Ira would bring over a VCR for Bruno and just take Zora out to eat. "Well, look at the clock! Good to meet you, Bruno," he said, shaking the kid's large limp hand. Zora stood, out of breath. She walked Ira out to his car, helping to carry his chair and salad bowl. "It was a lovely evening," Ira said. "And you are a lovely woman. And your son seems so bright and the two of you are adorable together."

Zora beamed, seemingly mute with happiness. If only Ira had known how to speak such fanciful baubles during his marriage, surely Marilyn would never have left him.

He gave Zora a quick kiss on the cheek—the heat of wrestling had heightened her beautiful nutmeg smell—then kissed her again on the neck, near her ear. Alone in his car on the way home, he thought of all the deeply wrong erotic attachments that were made in wartime, all the crazy romances cooked up quickly by the species to offset death. He turned the radio on: the news of the Middle East was so surreal and bleak that when he heard the tonnage of the bombs planned for Baghdad he could feel his jaw fall slack in astonishment. He pulled the car over, turned on the interior light, and gazed in the rearview mirror just to see what his face looked like in this particular state. He had felt his face drop in this manner once before, when he first got the divorce papers from Marilyn—now, *there* was shock and awe for you; there was *decapitation*— but he had never actually seen what he looked like this way. So. Now he knew. Not good: stunned, pale, and not all that bright. It wasn't the same as self-knowledge, but life was long and not that edifying, and one sometimes had to make do with these randomly seized tidbits.

He started up again, slowly; it was raining now, and, at a shimmeringly lit intersection of two gas stations, one QuikTrip, and a KFC, half a dozen young people in hooded yellow slickers were holding up signs that read "Honk for Peace." Ira fell upon his horn, first bouncing his hand there, then just leaning his whole arm into it. Other cars began to do the same, and soon no one was going anywhere—a congregation of mourning doves, but honking like geese in a wild chorus of futility, windshield wipers clearing their fan-shaped spaces on the drizzled night glass. No car went anywhere for the change of two lights. For all its stupidity and solipsism and self-consciously scenic civic grief, it was something like a gorgeous moment.

Despite Bekka's reading difficulties, despite her witless naming of the cats, Ira knew that his daughter was highly intelligent. He knew it from the time she spent lying around the house, bored and sighing, saying, "Dad? When will childhood be over?" This was a sign of genius! As were other things. Her complete imperviousness to the adult male voice, for instance. Her scrutiny of all food. With interest and hesitancy, she studied the antiwar signs that bestrewed the neighborhood lawns. "'War Is Not the Path to Peace,'" she read slowly aloud. Then added, "Well—duh."

"'War Is Not the Answer,'" she read on another. "Well, that doesn't make sense," she said to Ira. "War *is* the answer. It's the answer to the question 'What's George Bush going to start real soon?'"

The times Bekka stayed at his house, she woke up in the morning and told him her dreams. "I had a dream last night that I was walking with two of my friends and we met a wolf. But I made a deal with the wolf. I said, 'Don't eat me. These other two have more meat on them.' And the wolf said, 'O.K.,' and we shook on it and I got away." Or, "I had a strange dream last night that I was a bad little fairy."

She was in contact with her turmoil and with her ability to survive. How could that be anything less than emotional brilliance?

One morning she said, "I had a really scary dream. There was this tornado with a face inside? And I married it." Ira smiled. "It may sound funny to you, Dad, but it was really scary."

He stole a look at her school writing journal once and found this poem:

> Time moving
> Time standing still.
> What is the difference?
> Time standing still is the difference.

He had no idea what it meant, but he knew that it was awesome. He had given her the middle name Clio, after the Muse of history, so of course she would know very well that time standing still *was* the difference. He personally felt that he was watching history from the dimmest of backwaters—a land of beer and golf, the horizon peacefully fish-gray. With the windows covered in plastic sheeting, he felt as if he were inside a plastic container, like a leftover, peering into the tallow fog of the world. *Time moving. Time standing still.*

The major bombing started on the first day of spring. "It's happening," Ira said into Mike's answering machine. "The whole thing is starting now."

Zora called and asked him to the movies. "Sure," Ira said. "I'd love to."

"Well, we were thinking of this Arnold Schwarzenegger movie, but Bruno would also be willing to see the Mel Gibson one." *We.* He was dating a tenth grader now. Even in tenth grade he hadn't done that. Well, he'd see what he'd missed.

They picked him up at six-forty, and, as Bruno made no move to cede the front seat, Ira sat in the back of Zora's Honda, his long legs wedged together at a diagonal, like a lady riding sidesaddle. Zora drove carefully, not like a mad hellcat at all, as for some reason he had thought she would. As a result, they were late for the Mel Gibson movie and had to make do with the Schwarzenegger. Ira thrust money at the ticket-seller—"Three, please"—and they all wordlessly went in, their computerized stubs in hand. "So you like Arnold Schwarzenegger?" Ira said to Bruno as they headed down the red-carpeted corridor.

"Not really," Bruno muttered. Bruno sat between Zora and Ira, and together they passed a small container of popcorn back and forth. Ira jumped up twice to refill it out in the lobby, a kind of relief for him from Arnold, whose line readings were less brutish than they used to be but not less brutish enough. Afterward, heading out into the parking lot, Bruno and Zora reënacted body-bouncing scenes from the film. When they reached the car, Ira was again relegated to the back seat. "Shall we go to dinner?" he called up to the front.

Both Zora and Bruno were silent.

"Shall we?" he tried again, cheerfully.

"Would you like to, Bruno?" Zora asked. "Are you hungry?"

"I don't know," Bruno said, peering gloomily out the window.

"Did you like the movie?" Ira asked.

Bruno shrugged. "I don't know."

They went to a barbecue place and got ribs and chicken. "Let me pay for this," Ira said, though Zora hadn't offered.

"Oh, O.K.," she said.

Afterward, Zora dropped Ira at the curb, where he stood for a minute, waving, in front of his house. He watched them roll down to the end of the block and disappear around the corner. He went inside and made himself a drink with cranberry juice and rum. He turned on the TV news and watched the bombing. Night bombing, so you could not really see.

A few mornings later was the first day of a new month. The illusion of time flying, he knew, was to make people think that life could have more in it than it actually could. Time flying could make human lives seem victorious over time itself. Time flew so fast that in ways it failed to make an impact. People's lives fell between its stabbing powers like insects between raindrops. "We cheat the power of time with our very brevity!" he said aloud to Bekka, feeling confident that she would understand, but she just kept petting the cats. The house had already begun to fill with the acrid-honey smell of cat pee, though neither he nor Bekka seemed to mind. Spring! One more month and it would be May, his least favorite. Why not a month named Can? Or Must! Well, maybe not Must. Zora phoned him early, with a dour tone. "I don't know. I think we should break up," she said.

"You do?"

"Yes, I don't see that this is going anywhere. Things aren't really moving forward in any way that I can understand. And I don't think we should waste each other's time."

"Really?" Ira was dumbfounded.

"It may be fine for some, but dinner, a movie, and sex is not my idea of a relationship."

"Maybe we could eliminate the movie?" he asked desperately.

"We're adults—"

"True. I mean, we are?"

"—and what is the point, if there are clear obstacles or any unclear idea of where this is headed, of continuing? It becomes difficult to maintain faith. We've hardly begun seeing each other, I realize, but already I just don't envision us as a couple."

"I'm sorry to hear you say that." He was now sitting down in his kitchen. He could feel himself trying not to cry.

"Let's just move on," she said with gentle firmness.

"Really? Is that honestly what you think? I feel terrible."

"April Fool's!" she cried out into the phone.

His heart rose to his throat then sank to his colon then bobbed back up close to the surface of his rib cage where his right hand was clutching at it. Were there paddles nearby that could be applied to his chest?

"I beg your pardon?" he asked faintly.

"April Fool's," she said again, laughing. "It's April Fool's Day."

"I guess," he said, gasping a little, "I guess that's the kind of joke that gets better the longer you think about it."

He had never been involved with the mentally ill before, but now more than ever he was convinced that there should be strong international laws against their being too physically attractive. The public's safety was at risk!

"How are you liking Zora?" Mike asked over a beer, after they'd mulled over the war and the details of Dick Cheney's tax return, which had just been printed in the paper. Why wasn't there a revolution? Was everyone too distracted with tennis and sex and tulip bulbs? Marxism in the spring lacked oomph. Ira had just hired someone to paint his house, so now on his front lawn he had two signs: "War Is Not the Answer" in blue and, on the other side of the lawn, in black and yellow, "Jenkins Painting Is the Answer."

"Oh, Zora's great." Ira paused. "Great. Just great. In fact, do you perhaps know any other single women?"

"Really?"

"Well, it's just that she might not be all that mentally *well*." He thought about the moment, just the night before, at dinner, when she'd said, "I love your mouth most when it does that odd grimace thing in the middle of sex," and then she contorted her face so hideously that Ira felt as if he'd been struck. Later in the evening, she'd said, "Watch this," and she'd taken her collapsible umbrella, placed its handle on the crotch of her pants, then pressed the button that sent it rocketing out, unfurled, like a cartoon erection. Ira did not know who or what she was, though he wanted to cut her some slack, give her a break, bestow upon her the benefit of the doubt—all those paradoxical clichés of supposed generosity, most of which he had denied his wife. He tried not to believe that the only happiness he was fated for had already occurred, had been with Bekka and Marilyn, when the three of them were together. A hike, a bike ride—he tried not to think that this crazy dream of family had shown its sweet face just long enough to torment him for the rest of his life, though scarcely long enough to sustain him through a meal. Torturing oneself with the idea of family happiness while not actually having a family, he decided, might be a fairly new circumstance in social history. People had probably not been like this a hundred years ago. He imagined an exhibit at the society. He imagined the puppets.

"Sanity's conjectural," Mike said. His brow furrowed thoughtfully. "Zora's very attractive, don't you think?"

Ira thought of her beautiful, slippery skin, the dark, sweet hair, the lithe sylph's body, the mad, hysterical laugh. She had once, though only briefly, insisted that Man

Ray and Ray Charles were brothers. "She is attractive," Ira said. "But you say that like it's a good thing."

"Right now," Mike said, "I feel like anything that isn't about killing people is a good thing."

"This may be about that," Ira said.

"Oh, I see. Now we're entering the callow, glib part of spring."

"She's wack, as the kids say."

Mike looked confused. "Is that like wacko?"

"Yes. But not like *Waco*—at least not yet. I would stop seeing her, but I don't seem to be able to. Especially now, with all that's happening in the world, I can't live without some intimacy, companionship, whatever you want to call it, to face down this global insanity."

"You shouldn't use people as human shields." Mike paused. "Or—I don't know—maybe you should."

"I can't let go of hope, of the illusion that something is going to come out of this romance. I'm sorry. Divorce is a trauma, believe me, I know. It's death within life! It's pain is a national secret! But that's not it. I can't let go of love. I can't live without some scrap of it. Hold my hand," Ira said. His eyes were starting to water. Once, when he was a small child, he had got lost, and when his mother had finally found him, four blocks from home, she'd asked him if he'd been scared. "Not really," he had said, sniffling pridefully. "But then my eyes just suddenly started to water."

"I beg your pardon?" Mike asked.

"I can't believe I just asked you to hold my hand," Ira said, but Mike had already taken it.

On the bright side, the hashish was good. The sleeping pills were good. He was walking slowly around the halls at work in what was a combination of serene energy and a nap. With his birthday coming up, he went to the doctor for his triannual annual physical and, having mentioned a short list of nebulous symptoms, he was given dismissive diagnoses of "benign vertigo," "pseudo gout," or perhaps "migraine aura," the names, no doubt, of rock bands. "You've got the pulse of a boy, and the mind of a boy, too," his doctor, an old golfing friend, said.

Health, Ira decided, was notional. Palm Sunday—all these *goyim* festivals were preprinted on his calendar—was his birthday, and when Zora called he blurted out that information. "It is?" she said. "You old man! Are you feeling undernookied? I'll come over Sunday and read your palm." Wasn't she cute? Damn it, she was cute. She arrived with Bruno and a chocolate cake in tow. "Happy birthday," she said. "Bruno helped me make the frosting."

"Did you, now?" he said to Bruno, patting him on the back in a brotherly embrace, which the boy attempted to duck and slide out from under.

They ordered Chinese food and talked about high school, advanced-placement courses, homeroom teachers, and James Galway (soulful mick or soulless dork, who could decide?). Zora brought out the cake. There were no candles, so Ira lit a match, stuck it upright in the frosting, and blew it out. His wish was a vague and general one of good health for Bekka. No one but her. He had put nobody else in his damn wish. Not the Iraqi people, not the G.I.s, not Mike, who had held his hand, not Zora. This kind of focussed intensity was bad for the planet.

"Shall we sit on Bruno?" Zora was laughing and backing her sweet tush into Bruno, who was now sprawled out on Ira's sofa, protesting in a grunting way. "Come on!" she called to Ira. "Let's sit on Bruno."

Ira began making his way toward the liquor cabinet. He believed there was some bourbon in there. He would not need ice. "Would you care for some bourbon?" he called over to Zora, who was now wrestling with Bruno. She looked up at Ira and said nothing. Bruno, too, looked at him and said nothing.

Ira continued to pour. At this point, he was both drinking bourbon and eating cake. He had a pancreas like a rock. "We should probably go," Zora said. "It's a school night."

"Oh, O.K.," Ira said, swallowing. "I mean, I wish you didn't have to."

"School. What can you do? I'm going to take the rest of the cake home for Bruny's lunch tomorrow. It's his favorite."

Heat and sorrow filled Ira's face. The cake had been her only present to him. He closed his eyes and nuzzled his head into hers. "Not now," she whispered. "He gets upset."

"Oh, O.K.," he said. "I'll walk you out to the car." And there he gave her a quick hug before she walked around the car and got in on the driver's side. He stepped back onto the curb and knocked on Bruno's window to say goodbye. But the boy would not turn. He flipped his hand up, showing Ira the back of it.

"Bye! Thank you for sharing my birthday with me!" Ira called out. Where affection fell on its ass, politeness might rise to the occasion. Zora's Honda lights went on, then the engine, and then the whole vehicle flew down the street.

At the cuckoo private school to which Marilyn had years ago insisted on sending Bekka, the students and teachers were assiduously avoiding talk of the war. Bekka's class was doing finger-knitting while simultaneously discussing their hypothetical stock-market investments. The class was doing best with preferred stocks in Kraft, G.E., and G.M.; watching them move slightly every morning on the Dow Jones was also helping their little knitted scarves. It was a right-brain, left-brain thing. For this, Ira forked over nine thousand dollars a year. Not that he really cared. As long as Bekka was in a place safe from death—the alerts were moving from orange to red to orange; no information, just duct tape and bright, warm, mind-wrecking colors—turning her into a knitting stockbroker was O.K. with him. *Exploit the system, man!* he himself used to say, in college. He could, however, no longer watch TV. He packed it up, along with the VCR, and brought the whole thing over to Zora's. "Here," he said. "This is for Bruno."

"You are so sweet," she said, and kissed his ear. Possibly he was in love with her.

"The TV's broken," Ira said to Bekka, when she came that weekend and asked about it. "It's in the shop."

"Whatever," Bekka said, pulling her scarf yarn along the floor so the cats could play.

The next time he picked Zora up to go out, she said, "Come on in. Bruno's watching a movie on your VCR."

"Does he like it? Should I say hello to him?"

Zora shrugged. "If you want."

He stepped into the house, but the TV was not in the living room. It was in Zora's bedroom, where, spread out half naked on Zora's bedspread, as Ira had been just a few days before, lay Bruno. He was watching Bergman's "The Magic Flute."

"Hi, Brune," he said. The boy said nothing, transfixed, perhaps not hearing him. Zora came in and pressed a cold glass of water against the back of Bruno's thigh.

"Yow!" Bruno cried.

"Here's your water," Zora said, walking her fingers up his legs.

Bruno took it and placed it on the floor. The singing on the same television screen that had so recently brought Ira the fiery bombing of Baghdad seemed athletic and absurd, perhaps a kind of joke. But Bruno remained riveted. "Well, enjoy the show," Ira said. He hadn't really expected to be thanked for the TV, but now actually knowing that he wouldn't be made him feel a little crestfallen.

On the way back out, Ira noticed that Zora had added two new sculptures to the collection in the living room. They were more abstract, made entirely out of old recorders and wooden flutes, but were recognizably boys, priapic with piccolos. "A flute would have been too big," Zora explained.

At the restaurant, the sound system was playing Dinah Washington singing "For All We Know." The walls, like love, were trompe-l'oeil—walls painted like viewful windows, though only a fool wouldn't know that they were walls. The menu, like love, was full of delicate, gruesome things—cheeks, tongues, thymus glands. The candle, like love, flickered, reflected in the brass tops of the sugar bowl and the salt and pepper shakers. He tried to capture Zora's gaze, which seemed to be darting around the room. "It's so nice to be here with you," he said. She turned and fixed him with a smile, repaired him with it. She was a gentle, lovely woman. Something in him kept coming stubbornly back to that. Here they were, two lonely adults lucky to have found each other, even if it was just for the time being. But now tears were drizzling down her face. Her mouth, collecting them in its corners, was retreating into a pinch.

"Oh, no, what's the matter?" He reached for her hand, but she pulled it away to hide her eyes behind it.

"I just miss Bruny," she said.

He could feel his heart go cold, despite himself. Oh, well. Tomorrow was Easter. Much could rise from the dead. Yesterday had been "Good Friday." Was this all cultural sarcasm—like "Labor Day" or "Some Enchanted Evening"?

"Don't you think he's fine?" Ira tried to focus.

"It's just—I don't know. It's probably just me coming off my antidepressants."

"You've been on antidepressants?" he asked sympathetically.

"Yes, I was."

"You were on them when I first met you?" Perhaps he had wandered into a whole "Flowers for Algernon" thing.

"Yes, indeedy. I went on them two years ago, after my 'nervous breakdown.'" Here she raised two fingers, to do quotation marks, but all of her fingers inadvertently sprang up and her hands clawed the air.

He didn't know what he should say. "Would you like me to take you home?"

"No, no, no. Oh, maybe you should. I'm sorry. It's just I feel I have so little time with him now. He's growing up so fast. I just wish I could go back in time." She blew her nose.

"I know what you mean."

"You know, once I was listening to some friends talk about travelling in the Pacific. They left Australia early one morning and arrived in California the evening of the day before. And I thought, I'd like to do that—keep crossing the international date line and get all the way back to when Bruno was a little boy again."

"Yeah," Ira said. "I'd like to get back to the moment where I signed my divorce agreement. I have a few changes I'd like to make."

"You'd have to bring a pen," she said strangely.

He studied her, to memorize her face. "I would never time-travel without a pen," he said.

She paused. "You look worried," she said. "You shouldn't do that with your fore-head. It makes you look old." Then she began to sob.

He found her coat and drove her home and walked her to the door. Above the house, the hammered nickel of the moon gave off a murky shine. "It's a hard time in the world right now," Ira said. "It's hard on everybody. Go in and make yourself a good stiff drink. People don't drink the way they used to. That's what started this whole Iraq thing to begin with: it's a war of teetotallers. People have got to get off their wagons and high horses and—" He kissed her forehead. "I'll call you tomorrow," he said, though he knew he wouldn't.

She squeezed his arm and said, "Sleep well."

As he backed out of her driveway, he could see Bruno laid out in a shirtless stupor on Zora's bed, the TV firing its colorful fire. He could see Zora come in, sit down, cud-dle close to Bruno, put her arm around him, and rest her head on his shoulder.

Ira brusquely swung the car away. Was this *his* problem? Was he too old-fashioned? He had always thought he was a modern man. He knew, for instance, how to stop and ask for directions. And he did it a lot! Of course, afterward, he would sometimes stare at the guy and say, "Who the hell told you that bullshit?"

He had his limitations.

He had not gone to a single seder this week, for which he was glad. It seemed a bad time to attend a ceremony that gave thanks in any way for the slaughter of Middle-Eastern boys. He had done that last year. He headed instead to the nearest bar, a dank, noisy dive called Sparky's, where he had often gone just after Marilyn left him. When he was married he never drank, but after the divorce he used to come in even in the mornings for beer, toast, and fried side meat. All his tin-pot miseries and chickenshit joys would lead him once again to Sparky's. Those half-dozen times that he had run into Marilyn at a store—this small town!—he had felt like a dog seeing its owner. Here was the person he knew best in life, squeezing an avocado and acting like she didn't see him. *Oh, here I am, oh, here I am!* But in Sparky's he knew he was safe from such unex-pected encounters. He could sit alone and moan to Sparky. Some people consulted Mar-cus Aurelius for philosophy about the pain of existence. Ira consulted Sparky. Sparky himself didn't actually have that much to say about the pain of existence. He mostly leaned across the bar, drying a smudgy glass with a dingy towel, and said, "Choose life!" then guffawed.

"Bourbon straight up," Ira said, selecting the barstool closest to the TV, from which it would be hardest to watch the war news. Or so he hoped. He let the sharp, buttery elixir of the bourbon warm his mouth, then swallowed its neat, sweet heat. He did this over and over, ordering drink after drink, until he was lit to the gills. At which point he looked up and saw that there were other people gathered at the bar, each alone on a chrome-and-vinyl stool, doing the same. "Happy Easter," Ira said to them, lifting his glass with his left hand, the one with the wedding ring still jammed on. "The dead are risen! The damages will be mitigated! The Messiah is back among us squeezing the flesh—that nap went by quickly, eh? May all the dead arise! No one has really been killed at all—O.K., God looked away for a second to watch some 'I Love Lucy' re-runs, but he is back now. Nothing has been lost. All is restored. He watching over Israel slumbers not nor sleeps!"

"Somebody slap that guy," said the man in the blue shirt down at the end.

Moore on Breathing Life into Characters

Shortly after this story first appeared in *The New Yorker*, I received mail from faraway readers who said, "This character was me," or, "these characters are composites of about four different people I know." Which is usually what the author of a story feels herself, so it was curious to be once again reminded that giving the reader the experience of the author's own relationship to a story can be part of what makes a narrative powerful. One hopes to breathe life into the characters who speak and think and move about on the page, because life is, in part, where they've come from, and the real world is the fiction to which their fictional world is referring. To some extent.

In this story I was interested in making two incongruous things intersect, or at least making them sit side by side: post-divorce middle-aged dating and a shocking war beginning on the other side of the globe. All that these two subjects have in common is that they are American and create high levels of anxiety within the protagonist. Making public events coexist with private ones in the consciousness of a character is not usually recommended by anyone (not editors, not teachers, not other writers, not even me). Incongruous subjects, or subjects asymmetrical in proportion, often compete and cancel each other out—and I did anticipate and in fact receive editorial feedback to that effect. "What is the war in Iraq doing in this story?" was the gist. Well, I thought, what *is* the war in Iraq doing in the world? I felt the necessity of it as a backdrop in my character Ira's life because it was indeed a backdrop in all our domestic American lives at the time (and it continues at this writing) and I wanted that circumstance registered, in all its uneasiness and cruel absurdity. This is how we live, the story means to demonstrate. If the political and personal components of the story reside together in the same pages a bit nervously, that discomfort is intended to express those components of our actual lives that do actually exist in uncomfortable proximity, in that same jittery, implausible dynamic. Realism includes surrealism.

Of course, if one fails artistically, one will be attacked politically. Which, given one's (mine) fluctuating skills, is not always preventable. Still, one (you) must be careful to concentrate and not be casual in one's imagining. One (we) must—if we feel we must (this is not a recommendation, only a piece of permission)—try to hold large and small worlds together on the same page when it is simply the truth. Still, weaving the fabric of this truth may feel clumsy or botched. There are times that I fear that all the large and small themes of my work are held together by a kind of cheap Scotch tape. I despair of the narrative ever coming together in an organic whole. It is not a new feeling. History has insinuated itself—in a mediated way (as we safe citizens tend to experience it)—in other work of mine. I have written short stories before that briefly bring the horrific but distant world of war right into a love story that is taking place fairly peacefully somewhere else. In one story ("Beautiful Grade") the bombings of Belgrade, Berlin, and Hiroshima make their appearance at an otherwise sedate dinner party. In another story ("The Jewish Hunter") the specter of the Holocaust suddenly emerges in a love story occurring in the contemporary American Midwest. In still another story ("What You Want to Do Fine") I tried, not for the last time, to write about two lonely, troubled people who are romantically involved, as a war in the Middle East is beginning to brew. There were times in writing "Debarking," in fact, when I thought, "Haven't I written this before?" Different President Bush, different lovers—but the same Iraq. Story writing repeats itself because the world repeats itself.

One has to be true to what one sees and hears and knows. If you try to make your characters see, hear, or know absolutely no less than you do, you will fall on your face. But that high-minded, uncondescending, and futile attempt will give characters real juice as well as allow the story to bear intelligent if botched witness to the world. Which is also botched. Art is made from it anyway.

Writing Suggestions

1. Characters in good fiction are rarely one dimensional, as they were in old spaghetti westerns where the bad guy wore all black and the good guy wore all white. In less than one page, write a detailed scene introducing an antagonist who has one or more redeeming qualities. In less than one page, do the same for a protagonist who has one ore more character flaws. Do these characters feel more real than those you've created before? Think about characters from TV or movies who have deep and sometimes conflicting levels: Hannibal Lecter (Anthony Hopkins) from *The Silence of the Lambs*, Tony Soprano (James Gandolfini) from *The Sopranos*, Leticia (Halle Berry) in *Monster's Ball*, Vivian Ward (Julia Roberts) in *Pretty Woman*, Frank Abagnale Jr. (Leonardo DiCaprio) in *Catch Me If You Can*, Melvin Udall (Jack Nicholson) in *As Good As It Gets*, Annie Wilkes (Kathy Bates) in *Misery*. Complex characters are often a combination of higher (or generous) impulses and lower (or selfish) impulses. Strive to make all of your main characters as dynamic, conflicted, and memorable as these.

2. Moore went against standard writer maxims in "Debarking" by juxtaposing private lives against public events. Take an event in twentieth-century history—such as the stock market crash of 1929, the release of Walt Disney's *Snow White* (the first full-length animated feature), Pearl Harbor, the shooting of J. F. K., Rosa Parks's famous bus ride, the Beatles appearing on *The Ed Sullivan Show*, the Apollo 11 moon landing—and, using this as the backdrop, develop a story that focuses on a

character's private life, paying particular attention to how the public events impact the character's life. How can using a specific historical setting create opportunities for a character's identity to more fully emerge?

3. Make a list of twenty specific things you wish had happened to you in your early teens but didn't. Comb through that list for the most interesting three. Now revisit one of your own stories. Add in one or two of these unfulfilled childhood dreams to your protagonist's makeup—work them in via backstory, exposition, another character's dialogue, or any other suitable means. Do specific details like dreams (or phobias, or career aspirations) help round out a character and make him or her memorable? What else might you take from your own life to help make characters develop on the page?

4. Lorrie Moore is often cited as being both one of the most accomplished short story writers of her generation and one of the best teachers of creative writing. Moore works—as do many writers of fiction—at a university. In her case, it is the M.F.A. program at the University of Wisconsin. Make a list of your favorite contributors to this book. Check their biographical information in Appendix A. Using online resources, explore the writing program where they work, noting classes offered, biographies of creative writing faculty, areas of study, etc. Would such a creative writing program serve your goals as a writer? What sort of self-motivated personal study or nonuniversity organizations or groups might help you become a better, more polished writer?

> *A story is a way to say something that can't be said any other way,*
> *and it takes every word in the story to say what the meaning is.*
> —Flannery O'Connor

Amy Bloom

By-and-By

From Ms. *Magazine*

Every death is violent.

The iris, the rainbow of the eye, closes down. The pupil spreads out like black water. It seems natural, if you are there, to push the lid down, to ease the pleated shade over the ball, to the lower lashes. The light is out, close the door.

Mrs. Warburg called me at midnight. I heard the click of her lighter and the tiny crackle of burning tobacco. Her ring bumped against the receiver.

"Are you comfortable, darling?"

I was pretty comfortable. I was lying on her daughter's bed, with my feet on Anne's yellow quilt, wearing Anne's bathrobe.

"Do you feel like talking tonight?"

Mrs. Warburg was the only person I felt like talking to. My boyfriend was away. My mother was away. My father was dead. I worked in a felafel joint on Charles Street where only my boss spoke English.

I heard Mrs. Warburg swallow. "You have a drink, too. This'll be our little party."

Mrs. Warburg and I had an interstate, telephonic rum-and-Coke party twice a week the summer Anne was missing. Mrs. Warburg told me about their problems with the house; they had some roof mold and a crack in the foundation, and Mr. Warburg was not handy.

"Roof mold," she said. "When you get married, you move into a nice pre-war six in the city and let some other girl worry about roof mold. You go out dancing."

I know people say—but it's not true—you see it in movies, cascades of hair tumbling out of the coffin, long curved nails growing over the clasped hands. It's not true. When you're dead, you're dead, and although some cells take longer to die than others, after a few hours everything is gone. The brain cells die fast, and blood pools in the soft, pressed places: the scapula, the lower back, the calves. If the body is not covered up, it produces a smell called cadaverine, and flies pick up the scent from a mile away. First, just one fly, then the rest. They lay fly eggs and ants come, drawn to the eggs, and sometimes wasps, and always maggots. Beetles and moths, the household kind that eat your sweaters, finish the body; they undress the flesh from the bone. They are the clean-up crew.

Mrs. Warburg and I only talked about Anne in passing and only about Anne in the past. Anne's tenth birthday had a Hawaiian theme. They made a hotdog luau in the backyard and served raspberry punch; they played pin-the-lei-on-the-donkey and had grass skirts for all the girls. "Anne might have been a little old for that, even then. She was a sophisticate from birth," Mrs. Warburg said. I was not a sophisticate from birth. I was an idiot from birth, and that is why when the police first came to look for Anne, I said a lot of things that sounded like lies.

Mrs. Warburg loved to entertain; she said Anne was her mother's daughter. We did like to have parties, and Mrs. Warburg made me tell her what kind of hors d'oeuvres we served. She was glad we had pigs-in-blankets because that's what she'd served when she was just starting out, although she'd actually made hers. And did one of us actually make the marinara sauce, at least, and was Anne actually eating pork sausage, and she knew it must be me who made pineapple upside-down cake because that was not in her daughter's repertoire, and she hoped we used wine glasses but she had the strong suspicion we poured wine out of the box into paper cups, which was true. I told her Anne had spray-painted some of our third-hand furniture bright gold and when we lit the candles and turned out the lights, our apartment looked extremely glamorous.

"Oh, we love glamorous," Mrs. Warburg said.

In the Adirondacks, the Glens Falls trail and the old mining roads sometimes overlap. Miles of trail around Speculator and Johnsburg are as smooth and neatly edged as garden paths. These are the old Fish Hill Mining Company roads, and they will take you firmly and smoothly from the center of Hamilton County to the center of the woods and up the mountainside. Eugene Trask took Anne and her boyfriend, Teddy Ross, when they were loading up Teddy's van in the Glen Falls parking lot. He stabbed Teddy twice in the chest with his hunting knife, and tied him to a tree and stabbed him again, and left him and his backpack right there, next to the wooden sign about No Drinking, No Hunting. He took Anne with him, in Teddy's car. They found Teddy's body three days later and his parents buried him two days after that, back in Virginia.

Eugene Trask killed another boy just a few days before he killed Teddy. Some kids from Schenectady were celebrating their high school graduation with an overnight camping trip, and when Eugene Trask came upon them, he tied them all to different trees, far enough apart so they couldn't see each other, and then he killed the boy who'd made him mad. While he was stabbing him, the same way he stabbed Teddy, two sharp holes in his heart and then a slash across his chest, for emphasis, for something, the other kids slipped out of their ropes and ran. By the time they came back with people from town, Eugene Trask had circled around the woods and was running through streams where the dogs could not catch his scent.

The heart is really two hearts and four parts: the right and the left, and the up and the down. The right heart pumps blood through the lungs, the left through the body. Even when there is nothing more for it to do, even when you have already lost ten ounces of blood, which is all an average-sized person needs to lose to bring on heart failure, the left heart keeps pumping, bringing old news to nowhere. The right heart sits still as a cave, a thin scrim of blood barely covering its floor. The less air you have, the faster the whole heart beats. Still less and the bronchioles, hollow, spongy flutes of the lungs, whistle and squeeze dry until they lie flat and hard like plates on the table, and when there is no more air and no more blood to bring help from the furthest reaches of the body, the lungs crack and chip like old china.

Mrs. Warburg and I both went to psychics.

She said, "A psychic in East Cleveland. What's that tell you?" which is why I kept talking to her even after Mr. Warburg said he didn't think it was helping. Mrs. Warburg's psychic lived in a run-down split-level ranch house with lime-green shag carpeting. Her psychic wore a white smock and white shoes like a nurse, and she got Mrs. Warburg confused with her three o'clock, who was coming for a reading on her pancreatic cancer. Mrs. Warburg's psychic didn't know where Anne was.

My psychic was on West Cedar Street, in a tiny apartment two blocks away from us on Beacon Hill. My boss's wife had lost a diamond earring and the psychic found it, she said. He looked like a graduate student. He was barefoot. He saw me looking down and flexed his feet.

"Helps me concentrate," he said.

We sat down at a dinette table and he held my hands between his. He inhaled and closed his eyes. I couldn't remember if I had the twenty dollars with me or not.

"Don't worry about it," he said.

We sat for three minutes, and I watched the hands on the grandfather clock behind him. My aunt had the same clock, with the flowers carved in cherrywood climbing up the maple box.

"It's very dark," he said. "I'm sorry. It's very dark where she is."

I found the money and he pushed it back at me, and not just out of kindness, I didn't think.

I told Mrs. Warburg my psychic didn't know anything either.

The police came on Saturday and again on Monday, but not the same ones. On Monday it was detectives from New York, and they didn't treat me like the worried roommate. They reminded me that I told the Boston police I'd last seen Anne at two o'clock on Thursday, before she went to Teddy's. They said someone else had told them Anne came back to our apartment at four o'clock, to get her sleeping bag. I said yes, I remembered, I was napping and she woke me up, because it was really my sleeping bag, I lent it to her for the trip. Yes, I did see her at four, not just at two.

Were you upset she was going on this trip with Ted? they said.

Teddy, I said. Why would I be upset?

They looked around our apartment, where I had to walk through her little bedroom to use the bathroom and she had to walk through my little bedroom to get to the front door, as if it was obvious why I'd be upset.

Maybe you didn't like him, they said.

I like him, I said.

Maybe he was cutting into your time with Annie.

Anne, I said, and they looked at each other as if it was very significant that I had corrected them.

Anne, they said. So maybe Teddy got in the way of your friendship with Anne?

I rolled my eyes. No, I said, we double-dated sometimes, it was cool.

They looked at their notes.

You have a boyfriend? they said. We'd like to talk to him too.

Sure, I said, he's in Maine with his family, but you can talk to him.

They shrugged a little. Maine, with his parents, was not a promising lead. They pressed me a little more about my latent lesbian feelings for Anne and my unexpressed and unrequited love for Teddy, and I said that I thought maybe I had forgotten to tell the Boston police that I had worked double shifts every day last week and that I didn't own a car. They smiled and shrugged again.

If you think of anything, they said.

It's very dark where she is, is what I thought.

The police talked to me and they talked to Rose Trask, Eugene's sister, too. She said Eugene was a worthless piece of shit. She said he owed her money and if they found him she'd like it back, please. She hid Eugene's hunting knife at the bottom of her root cellar, under the onions, and she hid Eugene in her big old-fashioned chimney until they left. Later, they made her go up in the helicopter to help them find him, and they made her call out his name over their loudspeaker: "Eugene, I love you. Eugene, it will be okay." While they circled the park, which is three times the size of Yellowstone, she told the police that Eugene had worked on their uncle's farm from the time he was seven, because he was big for his age, and that he knew his way around the woods because their father threw him out of the house naked, in the middle of the night, whenever he wet his bed, which he did all his life.

Mrs. Warburg said she had wanted to be a dancer and she made Anne take jazz and tap and modern all through school but what Anne really loved was talking. Debate Club, Rhetoric, Student Court, Model U.N., anything that gave you plenty of opportunity for arguing and persuading, she liked. I said I knew that because I had lived with Anne for three years and she had argued and persuaded me out of cheap shoes and generic toilet paper and my mother's winter coat. She'd bought us matching kimonos in Chinatown. I told Mrs. Warburg that it was entirely due to Anne that I was able to walk through the world like a normal person.

Mrs. Warburg said, "Let me get another drink."

I lay back on Anne's bed and sipped my beer. Mrs. Warburg and I had agreed that since I didn't always remember to get rum for our parties, I could make do with beer. Anne actually liked beer, Mrs. Warburg said. Mr. Warburg liked Scotch. Mrs. Warburg went right down the middle, she felt, with the rum-and-Coke.

"Should we have gone to Teddy's funeral?" she said.

I didn't think so. Mrs. Warburg had never met Teddy, and I certainly didn't want to go. I didn't want to sit with his family, or sit far behind them, hoping that since Teddy was dead, Anne was alive, or that if Anne had to be dead, she'd be lying in a white casket, with bushels of white carnations around her, and Teddy would be lying someplace dark and terrible and unseen.

"I think Anne might have escaped," Mrs. Warburg said. "I really do. I think she might have gotten out of those awful mountains and she might have found a rowboat or something, she's wonderful on water, you should see her on Lake Erie, but it could be because of the trauma she doesn't—"

Mr. Warburg got on the line.

"It's three o'clock in the morning," he said. "Mrs. Warburg needs to sleep. So do you, I'm sure."

Eugene Trask and Anne traveled for four days. He said, at his trial, that she was a wonderful conversationalist. He said that talking to her was a pleasure and that they had had some very lively discussions, which he felt she had enjoyed. At the end of the fourth day, he unbuckled his belt so he could rape her again, in a quiet pine grove near Lake Pleasant, and while he was distracted with his shirttail and zipper, she made a grab for his hunting knife. He hit her on the head with the butt of his rifle, and when she got up, he hit her again. Then he stabbed her twice, just like Teddy, two to the heart. He didn't want to shoot her, he said. He put her bleeding body in the back of an orange Buick he'd stolen in Speculator, and he drove to an abandoned mine. He threw her down the thirty-foot shaft, dumped the Buick in Mineville, and walked through the woods to his sister's place. They had hamburgers and mashed potatoes and sat on Rose's back step and watched a pair of red-tailed hawks circling the spruce. Rose washed out his shirt and pants and ironed them dry, and he left early the next morning, with two meatloaf sandwiches in his jacket pocket.

They caught Eugene Trask when one of his stolen cars broke down. They shot him in the leg. He said he didn't remember anything since he'd skipped his last arraignment two months ago. He said he was subject to fits of amnesia. He had fancy criminal lawyers who took his case because the hunt for Eugene Trask had turned out to be the biggest manhunt in the tristate area since the Lindbergh baby. There were reporters everywhere, Mrs. Warburg said. Mr. Feldman and Mr. Barone told Eugene that if he lied to them they would not be able to defend him adequately, so he drew them maps of where they could find Anne's body, and also two other girls who had been missing for six months. Mr. Feldman and Mr. Barone felt that they could not reveal this information to the police or to the Warburgs or to the other families because it would violate lawyer-client privilege. After the trial, after Eugene was transferred to Fishkill Correctional Facility, two kids were playing in an old mine near Speculator, looking for garnets and gold and arrowheads, and they found Anne's body.

The dead body makes its own way. It stiffens and then it relaxes and then it softens. The flesh turns to a black thick cream. If I had put my arms around her to carry her up the gravel path and home, if I had reached out to steady her, my hand would have slid through her skin like a spoon through custard, and she would have fallen away from me, held in only by her clothes. If I had hidden in the timbered walls of the mine, waiting until Eugene Trask heard the reassuring one-two thump of the almost emptied body on the mine-car tracks, I might have seen her as I see her now. Her eyes open and blue, her cheeks pink underneath the streaks of clay and dust, and she is breathing, her chest is rising and falling, too fast and too shallow, like a bird in distress, but rising and falling.

We are all in the cave. Mrs. Warburg went back to her life, without me, after Anne's funeral that winter (did those children find her covered with the first November snow?), and Mr. Warburg resurfaced eight years later, remarried to a woman who became friends with my aunt Rita in Beechwood. Aunt Rita said the new Mrs. Warburg was lovely. She said the first Mrs. Warburg had made herself into a complete invalid, round-the-clock help, but even so she died alone, Rita said, in their old house. She didn't know from what. Eugene Trask was shot and killed trying to escape from Fishkill. Two bullets to the heart, one to the lungs. Mrs. Warburg sent me the clipping. Rose Trask married and had two children, Cheryl and Eugene. Rose and Cheryl and little Eugene drowned in 1986, boating on Lake Champlain. Mrs. Warburg sent me the clipping. My young father, still slim and handsome and a good dancer, collapsed on our roof trying to straighten our ancient TV antenna, and it must have been Eugene Trask that pulled his feet out from under him, over the gutters and thirty feet down. Don't let the sun catch you crying, my father used to say. Maybe your nervous system doesn't get the message to swallow the morning toast and Eugene Trask strangles you and throws you to the floor while your wife and children watch. Maybe clusters of secret tumors bloom from skull to spine, opening their petals so Eugene Trask can beat you unconscious while you're driving to work. Everyone dies of heart failure, Eugene Trask said at his trial.

I don't miss the dead less, I miss them more. I miss the tall pines around Lake Pleasant, I miss the brown-and-gray cobblestones on West Cedar Street, I miss the red-tailed hawks that fly so often in pairs. I miss the cheap red wine in a box and I miss the rum-and-Coke. I miss Anne's wet gold hair drying as we sat on the fire escape. I miss the hotdog luau and driving to dance lessons after breakfast at Bruegger's Bagels. I miss the cold mornings on the farm, when the handle of the bucket bit into my small hands and my feet slid over the frozen dew. I miss the hot grease spattering around the felafel balls and the urgent clicking of Hebrew. I miss the new green leaves shaking in the June rain. I miss standing on my father's shiny shoes as we danced to the Tennessee Waltz and my mother made me a paper fan so I could flirt like a Southern belle, tapping my nose with the fan. I miss every piece of my dead. Every piece is stacked high like cordwood within me, and my heart, both sides, and all four parts, is their reliquary.

Bloom on Creating Dynamic Characters

It took me a long time to write this story. Even now, I don't have any wish to reveal it or myself, to say this: this is true, this I made up whole cloth, this I wove from a mote that resembles reality. And, fortunately, no story rises or falls on the facts. Getting the facts wrong can be disastrous; getting them right won't save you.

That's particularly fortunate because writers lie. They lie when they tell you the work's autobiographical (because memory itself is a shocking liar, a transformer, a patchwork artist; memory is the greatest living novelist). They lie when they tell you it's not autobiographical (right, I have never known love, loss, longing, or lust, as my characters and everyone else on earth, have). The lie is only partially conscious, I think; I can only speak for my own defended, deceptive self. The other part is not only unconscious, but inevitable. It takes three years—or five, or twenty—after a story's done, to understand it and to know what one has really written. Suddenly I can see that the pretty, brittle, indifferent English mother who so resembles an admired aunt, looks, or seems, on closer, long, later introspection much more like my own cuddly, attentive, and American mother. And the withdrawn, adulterous Midwestern pianist, the middle-aged man desperately pursuing a teenage girl, and the heartsick, dutiful young basketball player are more portraits of the author than any character that looks the slightest bit like me.

Readers do not read to know more about the writer. No one cares about the facts of your life, your musical preferences, or your longing for whoever it is that dominated your life in eleventh grade. Readers care about a good story that keeps their interest, and characters that move them. This is all about writing a good sentence and learning something about rhythm and pace; it is not about revealing how and why you hate your father or how much you miss your late mother.

Which is why, in the end, as hard as it is, it's a lot easier to write and talk about technique and craft than it is to tell the truth about the heart of any story. The word-by-word, sentence-by-sentence bricklaying is the only part of the story I have control of. I make up my characters (see previous disclaimer) and get to hear and see them in my head, on an internal audio-visual system that comes in clear as a bell about twice a week, late at night, and crammed with static most of the time. You have to do more than invite them in and describe them. In fact, describing them might be one of writing's great time-wasters (excessive research and e-mail being the others). You have to become them. The question is not what would *she*—fat, tired paleontologist—do? It is: what would I, becoming her, poured into her body and soul, do, think, feel, and see in this world? Everything else is reporting about a made-up character. What I am trying to describe (even though it sounds goofy and more mystical than I would want) is more like such a deep empathetic leap to another, even a made-up other, that in the moment, you feel more like the character than like yourself. Write from there.

These characters and their overheard remarks and hastily observed gestures lead me to their actions, to what I hope will become plot. I can keep them coming and going, hitchhiking to Alaska, buying nectarines in Norwich, and slinging falafel in Boston, but in the end, as in life, people only do what is in their natures to do. We are revealed not by what happens to us, but what we make of what happens to us. My characters' natures are shaping and declaring themselves before I can fully account for them.

And that leaves the word, for which I am totally, fearfully, and happily, accountable. "Green" rather than "verdant"—although occasionally, yes to verdant, which is such a lush mix of "ardent" and "verde" that it sometimes transcends the way it can't help being interior-decorator fancy and slightly Emily Dickinson-ish. In this story "tiny crackle of burning tobacco" because what we hear, on the phone, takes the place of what we see. "Hot dog luau" instead of "party" because first of all, party is implicit in that sentence and to write it is to be redundant and even more importantly, Mrs. Warburg's need to remember it and tell it and the narrator's need to hear, see, and painfully embrace every detail of that party is their bond.

There are three narrative lines—the narrator's story of that summer and fall, the narrator's story of life afterwards, and the more distanced voice that tells us what happens to the body, at the end of life. The information for one strand, about the body's decomposition, came from anatomy books and the websites of people who enjoy not only anatomy texts, but medical examinations and true crime, as well. The pursuit of that information felt, always, like an extension of the life of the story's narrator. I came to the three strands because I could not bear, as the narrator cannot, to tell the story straightforwardly. I didn't plan the three tiers, although I believe that any good story has to have at least two.

Will Durant, the American historian and philosopher, described human history as consisting of life on the riverbanks: cooking, cleaning, making love, living, and dying, and of the river, bloody and terribly: combat, famine, destruction, that runs between the banks. I think that the best stories are like this, life on the banks and the river rushing between, a city of story and a second story which runs, like a web of tunnels, beneath it. I couldn't make it less terrible and I didn't want to make it less terrible. I wanted to make it real and plain, without allowing it to become the most significant moment in the story. And because I couldn't bear to let the violence be the point, the voice of the narrator became bigger, her dark, loving fatalism shaped the rest of the story, which is the why and the how of Eugene Trask becoming, not a symbol of violence, or of bad men, but of the hand that life deals, the unknowable and the thing one has to face, in order to have the dance with one's father, the pleasure of summer, the beauty of the hawks. And the language of the end builds in a rush of adjectives, in language that moves breathlessly, sentence after hurried sentence, with simple adjectives because I wanted to give the language the moment to burst, to be the river sweeping over the banks, taking the living and the dead with it.

Writing Suggestions

1. Write a scene in which a character has recently learned of his father's death. Only, you cannot mention the father, nor death. Nor can you mention anything directly related to death, such as a memorial service, funeral home, or mourner's garments.

In your scene, try to evoke the emotional landscape of grief and loss simply through the careful use of details, tone, and word choice. Let's say your character is eating breakfast, walking alone to school, or driving to the bank. What would this character notice as opposed to what a character who just met the love of his life notice? How would a grieving character use language? What words would he use? How might this character's actions betray his emotional life? How can the scene use small, specific details to signify the inner change?

2. Contact a relative who is at least ten years older than you and ask her to tell you about a period of her life that changed her irrevocably. Use this as the basis for a short story. Make sure to point out to your relative that, as you convert this to fiction, you will necessarily change the names, the locations, and many of the details for dramatic effect.

3. Amy Bloom claims: "I make up my characters . . . and get to hear and see them in my head." In a story you're currently working on, select the three most important characters for the following exercise. Using a blank piece of paper for each character, "speak" in that character's voice using first-person point of view for each, as though you are writing that character's diary. Use these phrases to start each paragraph.

   - "One thing that I rarely tell people about myself is . . . "
   - "If people really understood my feelings, they would know that . . . "
   - "The worst thing I really did to someone else is . . . "
   - "What I most want out of life is to . . . "
   - "The reason I really love (this character's favorite movie, book or song) is . . . "
   - "So far the best thing I have ever done in my life is . . . "

The goal here is not to create more dialogue for your story. Nor is it to understand how your characters speak, though that might be an added benefit. The goal here is to push yourself to a better understanding of these characters. Don't stop writing until each character reveals at least two significant (and new) pieces of information.

4. Using the Internet, the library, or personal observations, develop the specificity of details in a story you've recently completed or are presently writing. The use of such details not only textures a story, but also reveals the specific world of your characters. For example, if in your story, your original sentence is, "Steve placed his hands nervously on the counter," you might consider changing your sentence to one of the following, depending on the world your character, Steve, inhabits: "Steve placed his hands nervously on the marble counter veined with gold," or "Steve pressed his hands against the chipped tile counter scarred with cigarette burns." Each of the revised sentences not only presents a more vividly imagined world but also suggests an emotional atmosphere for the story. For another example, Jarret Keene, while writing his story, "Son of Mogar," used research to authoritatively describe the equipment of a suit actor at a movie studio: "His gorilla suit was sophisticated for its time. It sported chest bladders and leather skin and was covered in genuine animal hair."

*Ask yourself what characters want, what they're afraid of, what's
at stake in the story, what they stand to gain or lose, and in some
sense what kind of emotional modality they're living in. It keeps a
story from becoming frigid.*
—Charles Baxter

Tom Franklin

Nap Time

From *The Georgia Review* and *New Stories from the South 2005*

The baby was finally down, so the parents took a nap, too.

But they couldn't sleep.

Her husband said, "Listen how quiet."

They listened. It was late in the evening and the walls of the room were colored red by the sun through the red drapes, drapes she hated but hadn't yet replaced. The landlord had told them they could make any cosmetic changes they wanted. But nothing came off the rent, he'd said.

"How long does it normally last?" her husband asked.

"Two or three months, according to the book. Didn't you read it?"

"Not yet." He rubbed his eyes with the heels of his hands and they were quiet. Except for their socks, both were naked, thinking they might have sex before their nap. Until now, they'd mostly been too tired to try, and when they had, she'd been too sore.

Then she said, "When he's screaming like that and you've been carrying him all night, swinging him till you can't feel your arms, do you ever think about, like, dropping him? Just letting him fall out of your hands?"

Her husband didn't answer, and she thought she'd said the wrong thing.

But he took a breath. "Yeah," he said. "Sometimes I do. Sometimes I think about dropping him on the porch." Which was concrete.

She propped up on an elbow. "Really? God, I'm relieved to hear you say that. I've been thinking I'm the worst mother imaginable."

For a while, neither said anything.

Then, "Sometimes," he said, "I go farther with it."

"Farther? How?"

"I'll be driving, like on the interstate, and he'll be screaming, and I'll think, what if I were to sling him out the window. Car seat and all."

She didn't say anything. She wished it were darker in the room.

He looked at her. "You must think I'm terrible."

She leaned and kissed his shoulder blankly. "No, of course not." She sat up, her elbows orange in the light, band-aids on her nipples, and reached for her cigarettes and shook one out of the package. "The other day I thought—" She lit the cigarette.

"Tell me."

"I was carrying him, I'd been lugging him around in that colic hold for two hours and he was crying, crying, crying. Nothing would make him stop, and I was so exhausted. I'd walked around the house so many times I'd started doing it with my eyes closed, counting my steps, and he still kept crying." She drew on her cigarette. "I went through the kitchen for like the thousandth time, and I thought, god, of putting him in the microwave."

He moved his feet under the sheets. "We did that to a hamster when I was a kid."

"Really?"

"Yeah. My brother was at school and I was home sick. I wasn't really sick, I'd pretended to have a stomachache. Me and my little sister took his hamster out of its cage and I held it under the faucet. We wanted to see what it looked like wet. But when we did it, we realized mostly all it was was hair, the little body was only as big around as your finger. We thought, he'll know we did this. So I put the hamster in the microwave." He hesitated.

She could feel him breathing. "What happened?"

"It started steaming, so we took it out. It seemed fine at first. Then, about two weeks later, it grew this huge tumor on its neck. It kept crawling in a circle in the cage until it finally stopped under the little Ferris wheel and laid there breathing hard. In the morning it was dead."

"God," she said. She looked at her cigarette and dropped it in the Diet Coke can on the table beside the baby book. She'd quit smoking when she learned she was pregnant, and except for New Year's Eve and Mardi Gras and two or three other nights she'd been vigilant. With drinking too. But when the baby came she'd had problems breastfeeding, her milk ducts infected, oozing thick green pus, the baby almost malnourished, screaming so loud in the doctor's office the nurses had to yell to hear each other. So she'd been forced to use bottles and thought, Why not smoke? But she didn't enjoy it anymore.

"Did your brother ever find out?" she asked, lying back.

"No. I told my sister if she ever blabbed, I'd put *her* in the microwave. To this day she won't use one." He gave a dry laugh.

She looked over at him for a long time, taste of nicotine in her mouth and nose. Then she said, "Okay. I've got one." She put her arms under the covers, felt his foot brush against hers. "Growing up, I knew this girl who was murdered. Somebody grabbed her off the street while she was walking home from the pharmacy where she worked after school. It was almost dark. They found her body in the woods half a mile from this dirt road she'd never been on in her life. She'd been hit in the forehead with some kind of hammer. She was dead. My best friend's older sister."

"You never told me that," he said. "Did they find out who did it?"

"The police went crazy looking. They were interviewing everybody they could find. They stopped people on the street and went door to door, but all they ever got was that somebody might've seen a pickup. Then one night, it was a week after the funeral, I had this dream. I dreamed I was her, and I was walking home from the pharmacy. Wear-

ing the same green pastel dress she'd had on. I knew it was me, but I was her, too, somehow. And I knew what was going to happen, but I couldn't stop it. I turned around and
this truck had pulled up beside me, a blue pickup truck. The door opened and this guy
I sort of knew was driving it. He was our preacher's son's friend, who'd been kicked out
of the marines. I knew not to get in the truck with him, but he showed me that he had
a joint, and so I got in anyway. We drove without saying anything. His radio was playing Dylan, but I can't remember what song. He turned on a county road and kept driving. I couldn't remember his name but he had cute sideburns and a cute little chin. I
liked the way his Adam's apple bobbed and the way he smoked his cigarette. The way
it looked in his fingers. Then he turned onto the dirt road."

Her husband had rolled to face her. He put his hand on her stomach, which was
softer than before, the skin loose and cool.

"He stopped the truck right where all the police cars and the ambulances would
be later," she said. "We got out and he took my hand and led me into the woods. On a
path I hadn't even seen. We walked for a long time, holding hands, till you couldn't
hear any cars anywhere. You couldn't hear anything. We smoked the joint and he
started unbuttoning my dress. I let him. I was buzzing all over. I let him do whatever he
wanted—"

"What'd he do?" He was moving his hand on her stomach, going lower. She could
feel him getting hard against her leg.

"I let him, you know."

"Did you like it?"

She shifted her hips. "Yes," she said. "I liked it."

He said, "Then what happened," as his hand opened her thighs.

"He took this hammer out of his pocket," she said, "and I shut my eyes, and he hit
me right here—" She touched herself at the bridge of her nose. "And I woke up panicked, with this splitting pain in my forehead."

He moved his hand gently into place. "Was it him? Was it the preacher's son's
friend?"

"I don't know. Nobody was ever arrested."

He began to rub her with the pad of his thumb, the way she liked. "Did you tell
anybody?"

"No," she said, her eyes closed, "I never told anybody . . . ."

He whipped the sheet up and in the tented air rolled on top of her. When the sheet
had floated back down around them he was already edging in in his familiar way. He
went slowly and she stretched her legs so exquisitely her hips popped and when he murmured against her neck did it feel good she could only nod and raise her knees. She was
climbing in the truck again and there he was, holding his cigarette in his fingers. He
offered it to her across the long bench seat which had a quilt over it, and she took the
cigarette and put it to her lips and sucked in the good-tasting hot smoke. Drive, she
told him.

But something was wrong. She opened her eyes.

"Listen," she said.

In his room, across the hall, behind the closed door, the baby was silent.

Franklin on Story Tension

The idea for "Nap Time" came to me after listening to friends describe dealing with their colicky baby, how they'd had to carry him around the house in a "colic hold" at certain times of the day or else he'd scream and scream. This went on, they said, for *months*. I'd also heard, from another friend, how his wife hadn't been able to breastfeed their daughter, how my friend's wife's nipples grew raw and scabbed-over, bottles of formula her only option. Our daughter was two at the time, but she'd been a relatively easy baby, a fair sleeper, good breastfeeder, and an all-around good-natured, charming girl. Still, she'd had her moments of sublime brattiness, and when she threw tantrums or "acted out" (as the baby books call it), I would, at times, have fantasies of violence, and feel very, very, very guilty about them. I never told anybody this.

I saw the storyline or the plot rising out of the personality of my characters. Their needs, their desires became, in effect, the plot itself. For me, plot is often an extension of what a character wants. Character definition and story tension are related: one can give rise to the other. I intended the story's original plotline to be simple—in one brief scene, a husband and wife with a colicky baby would get more and more outrageous and explicit in their fantasies of hurting or killing their child, one-upping one another until they were crazed and horribly specific about what they wanted to do. At the end of the story, the baby would wake from its nap and cry, snatching them back to their sleepless, sexless lives.

As planned, the first draft began with the wife's admission of wanting to drop their baby, and the husband's of wanting to toss him out the car window. When it got to the part where the wife admits that she's considered sticking the baby in the microwave, I fully expected the husband to go further with a like example, such as wishing he could stuff the baby in the clothes dryer. But here, unexpectedly, the story veered, and I was surprised when the husband told of once having put a hamster into the microwave. A student had once told me a similar thing, and all the details—the hamster steaming, the tumor—came from him. For some reason, this detail helped me see further into my character and into the story itself. Using this information felt right.

For me, characters taking on lives of their own is the best, rarest delight of writing. (And, of course, when characters act on their own, it's simply the writer's subconscious taking over.) In retrospect, it's better in the story that the microwave-hamster anecdote occurred; otherwise, I'd have a one-note story, the escalation of a single idea its only movement. In order for the story's tension to rise, I had to see deeply into my characters: I had to know them. Fantasies of violence lead the couple to memories of real violence, which oddly brings them closer sexually, which, I knew, was what my characters most needed in this time of domestic stress.

The surprise of the conversation veering off elevates the tension: you're suddenly on different ground. Only through exploring my character's impulses was I able to uncover this moment.

Now, with the husband having changed the subject from that of fantasies of harming their baby to another, actual instance of violence (dead hamster), it's the wife's turn to respond. It didn't seem right (as I drafted it) for her to return to the idea of hurting the baby, though. That had already been done. But it seemed natural, in such a conversation, that she would reveal something, too. Reciprocate. So she tells the story of her sister's friend's murder, which (though I hadn't thought of it in years) is based on something someone told me long ago; I changed some details, but the real events are close to the ones I used in "Nap Time." In a way, it shocked me that this was what the wife in the story said, but—at the risk of sounding artsy—by that point the couple was talking among themselves, and it was almost as if I were listening. After bringing both characters to unexpected confessions, it was just a matter of closing the story out the way I'd planned, with the baby's crying defusing the tension between husband and wife.

The first time I read "Nap Time" to an audience, when I read the wife's confession about considering dropping the baby, I was shocked at the audience's reaction: they laughed. When the husband makes his similar confession, the concrete porch, they laughed harder. And they laughed at the microwave part, too. Reading, I thought, *Who are these sickos? This isn't funny.* Each subsequent audience has reacted relatively the same. They stop laughing, however, when she recounts the murder of her friend's sister. From there on it's dead silent.

When T. R. Hummer, editor of *The Georgia Review*, accepted the story for publication, he had only one editorial suggestion, for which I would like to publicly thank him. My original last line was: "In his room, across the hall, behind the closed door, the baby was starting to cry." Mr. Hummer suggested that I change the final clause to, " . . . the baby was silent." I knew his point: keeping the baby quiet turns the story darker, raises the tension one more crank.

~~~~~

Writing Suggestions

1. Write the first scene of a story between two characters in which the tension of the story is immediately defined: two lovers breaking up, an office worker being reprimanded by the boss, a mother who is disappointed with her teenaged son. Allow dialogue to carry the majority of the scene. Use as little description as possible. How will the characters' voices change as the scene progresses? How can the dialogue contribute to the growing conflict? How can tense dialogue remain realistic without creating melodrama? How can a few well-placed physical gestures (such as nervously twisting a wedding band around a ring finger) contribute to the meaning of the conversation?

2. Write a story that takes the form of nonfiction writing, such as a piece of newspaper journalism, a freshman essay, an interview, a set of diary entries or letters, or an article for *Rolling Stone*. How can a story both accomplish the traditional role of fiction—developing character, plot, and conflict—while at the same time accomplishing the requirements of the essay, interview, diary entries, etc., that it claims to be? Do these fixed forms of nonfiction open up new possibilities for character exploration? How does language in these forms of nonfiction operate differently than in most forms of short fiction? Or does it?

3. Take a story of yours that despite being done still has unrealized potential, then figure out what tensions are in operation. What do these characters want or desire, and how is this related to the plot? Take the stakes and really kick them through the roof. If your protagonist is in danger of losing a bonus at work, up that to losing a job. If it's losing a job, make it losing the house, car, and clothes off his or her back. Or even put the protagonist in life-threatening danger. Does this new obvious tension help out your story? If not, try a more subtle tension—emotional or psychological. Be willing to experiment with new ideas in order to make your story more realized and your readers more interested.

4. High school English classes often discuss tension, or conflict, as man vs. man, man vs. self, man vs. society, or man vs. nature. Which of the stories from this book have appealed to you most? What type of conflicts did those stories have? Are you mostly interested in internal or external tension in a story? Which single story from this book did you find most compelling? Does this story or do any of the stories have more than one clear tension? Being aware of your own interests and tendencies will allow you to write different types of stories more easily when you feel that you need a change.

> *I don't think of myself as a naturally gifted writer when it comes*
> *to using language. Consequently, I try every which way*
> *with a sentence, then a paragraph, and finally a page,*
> *choosing words, selecting pace (I'm obsessed with that,*
> *even the pace of a sentence).*
> —Joseph Heller

Section 6

~~~~~~

CHOOSING A POINT OF VIEW

Introduction

Point of View

Point of view is often oversimplified to mean the selection of pronouns in a piece of fiction—is the main character identified as "I" (first person), "you" (second person), or "he" or "she" (third person)? But point of view represents a far more complicated relationship in the story. It is the lens through which readers enter the fictional world. First person can offer a type of intimacy that is difficult to duplicate in third person. Likewise, third person can offer a narrative flexibility impossible to duplicate in either first or second person.

Because point of view selection defines the relationship between the narrator and the main character, it is crucial to understand some of the benefits each option offers you.

First Person

Perhaps the most natural point of view construction is first person because of most writers' previous experience with it (through letters, diaries, and essays). There is no distinction between narrator and main character in first person because with this point of view choice, they are the same. It is the only point of view choice in which the narrator is included as a character within the story.

For readers, the vocal quality of a first-person narrator invites them into the world of the story. As opposed to stories in third person, a first-person story can reveal much about the character through the use of narrative voice. Michael Knight's commentary on first person explores the way a first-person voice can be used to construct a story, but can also be the means to identify a character.

Second Person

The least common point of view selection is second person, which places "you" as the main character in the story. As explored in Adam Johnson's commentary on second person, short story authors can use "you" for distinct effects. For example, a second-person short story can be arranged as a set of directions, much like a self-help magazine article, in which the reader participates in crucial decisions. In contrast, another type of second-person story, such as a letter written to someone, makes the "you" both the main character and the primary audience of the story. Lastly, a second-person story can also be a first-person story in disguise, particularly when a narrator has difficulty speaking about uncomfortable events in his or her life.

Third Person

As with second person, third-person point of view represents a distinct relationship between the narrator and the main character. This relationship is so complex that three writers were asked to explore how third-person point of view was uniquely used in their own stories. Lee K. Abbott examines third-person omniscient in his commentary on "One of *Star Wars*, One of *Doom*," explaining how omniscience allows the narrator access to the minds of many characters. In Josh Russell's commentary on third-person objective for "Yellow Jack," he explores how third person in this particular case can be used to purposefully distance the reader from the events of the story. Lastly, Judith Claire Mitchell, in her commentary on "A Man of Few Words," explores the most commonly used variation of third-person construction, third-person limited, in which the narrator reveals the fictional world through the perspective of a single character.

Many authors feel that point of view selection is one of the most important and complex choices presented in the writing of any short story. Edgar Allan Poe's "The Tell-Tale Heart," a classic first-person work, would be an entirely different story if rendered in third person. Likewise, Nathaniel Hawthorne's famous third-person story, "Young Goodman Brown," would lose much of its mystery if it were told in first person.

Michael Knight

Gerald's Monkey

From *Playboy* and *Dogfight and Other Stories*

Gerald wanted a monkey and Wishbone said he could get it for him. Wishbone had a man on the inside. The three of us were burning out badly rusted floor sections of a tuna rig called *Kaga* and welding new pieces in their place, patchwork repairs, like making a quilt of metal. A lot of Japanese fisheries were having ships built in the states; labor was cheaper or something. This hold was essentially a mass grave for marine life and it stunk like the dead. The smell never comes out, Gerald told me, even if you sandblasted the paint off the walls. The door to the next room had been sealed, so there was only one way in, an eight-by-ten-foot square in the ceiling, and it was almost too hot to draw breath. They seemed connected somehow, the heat and that awful smell, two parts of the same swampy thing.

"Will it be a spider monkey?" Gerald said.

Wishbone shut down his burner and looked at Gerald.

"I don't know. My Jap gets all the good shit. It'll eat bananas," Wishbone said, "it'll scratch its ass. Shit, Gerald, *Will it be a spider monkey?*"

"Spider monkeys make the best pets," Gerald said.

"Gerald, what the hell do you want with a monkey?" I said. Gerald started to answer, paused in his burning, white sparks setting around his gloved hands, but Wishbone cut him off. He said to me, "Do not speak until you are spoken to, little man." His voice was muffled and deepened by his welding mask. "A monkey Gerald wants, a monkey Gerald gets. Now, run and fetch me some cigarettes."

He stood and stretched his legs. Wishbone was one large black man. With his welding mask down and black leather smock and gloves and long, thick legs running down into steel-toed work boots, he looked like a badass Darth Vader.

"Wishbone, can you read?" I said.

He snapped his mask up. His face was running with sweat and his eyes were bloodshot and angry. He was high on something. This was my second summer at my uncle's shipyard, and the best I could tell, Wishbone was always high.

"Did you speak, little man? I hope not."

I didn't say anything else, just pointed at the sign behind him—DO NOT SMOKE, painted in red block letters on plywood. The torches burn on a combination of pure oxygen and acetylene and sometimes tiny holes wear in the lines from use. The welding flames themselves generally burn off all the leaking oxygen and gas, but shut down the torches and give the gas a little time to collect in the air, then add a spark, and the world is made of fire. A spark is rarely enough but why test the percentages? There's a story around the yard about a guy who'd been breathing the fumes for hours with his torch unlit. When he went to fire it up, he inhaled a spark and the air in his lungs ignited. Afterward, he looked okay on the surface, nothing damaged, but his insides were charcoal, hollowed out by fire.

Wishbone glanced over his shoulder at the sign, looked back at me, shrugged. He reached under his smock and came out with a rumpled pack of Winstons. He put a bent cigarette between his lips, struck a match, and held it just away from the tip.

"This is my last cigarette," he said. "You have till I am finished to get your ass up from the floor and out to the wagon for a new pack. Let me be clear. If you are not back before I put my boot on this thing, I'm gonna beat you like a rented mule." He spoke real slow like I was his Jap connection and my English wasn't so good. "Do you understand?"

I got to my feet reluctantly. I didn't want him to know that I was afraid. I said, "Gerald, you need anything?" Gerald shook his head and gave me a wave.

I sidled to the ladder and climbed it slow and easy, no hurry, but once topside, I was gone, the fastest white boy on earth, dumping equipment as I ran, a jackrabbit, skirting welders and shipfitters on the deck, clanging down the gangplank, then up over the cyclone fence, headed for the supply wagon. It was ninety-five degrees out, wet July heat in lower Alabama, but after the hold, it felt good, almost cold. Goose bumps rose lightly on my skin.

Wishbone got off on razzing me. White kid, sixteen, owner's nephew, gone with the summer anyhow. I was his wet dream. We had worked together for a week last summer, my first time on a welding crew, and even then he had no patience for me. He ignored me for the whole week, just looked away whenever I spoke, concentrated on the skittering sparks and pretended I wasn't there. The cigarette runs were a new addition, but I didn't mind so much. Probably, he wouldn't have roughed me up, if I had refused to play along. He would have been fired, maybe jailed, and he knew it, but I wasn't taking any chances.

Summers at the shipyard were a family tradition. Learn the value of a dollar by working hard for it, that sort of thing. I'd drag myself home in the evenings, caked with filth, feeling drained empty, like I'd spent the day donating blood, and there my sister would be, fresh and blond and lovely, stretched languorously on the couch in front of the television. She'd have on white tennis shorts and maybe still be wearing her bikini top. She spent her summer days reading by the pool, her nights out with one boy or another. She had tattooed a rose just below her belly button by applying a decal and, letting the sun darken the skin around it.

"Give me the fucking remote," I'd say.

"Blow me."

She was eighteen, off to the university in the fall. Fifty-one days, I'd tell myself, that's all. It was usually evening by the time I got home and the last of the daylight would be slanting in through the banks of long windows, making everything look dreamy and slow. My sister would yawn and change the channel just to show me she could.

"I'm gonna sit down now, Virginia, and take off my boots and socks," I'd say. "You have until I am barefoot to hand it over or I will beat you like a rented mule."

She would smile pretty, adjust her position on the couch so she was facing me, draw her smooth knees up to her belly, get comfortable. She'd yell, "Mo-om," stretching the word into two hair-raising syllables, "Mom, Ford's acting tough again."

Gerald brought a monkey book to the shipyard, smuggled it in under his coveralls, and the two of us sat around on a break flipping through it. He was an older man, nearing fifty, his dark skin drawn tight over his features, worn to a blunt fineness. He had been working for my uncle almost twenty years. Wishbone lay on his back with his fingers linked on his chest, washed in the rectangle of light that fell through to us. He owned the traces of breeze that drifted down through the hatch. I had the book open across my knees, a droplight in one hand, my back against the bluish-white wall. Gerald was kneeling in front of me, watching for my reaction.

"See there?" he said. "See where it says about spider monkeys make the best pets?"

He reached over the book and tapped a page, leaving a sweaty fingerprint. I flipped pages, looking for the passage that he wanted, past capuchins and geurezas with their skunk coloring, past howler monkeys and macaques, until I came to the section on spider monkeys. I said, "Okay, I got it."

"Read it to me," he said.

I cleared my throat. "Spider monkey, *Ateles paniscus*, characterized by slenderness and agility. They frequent, in small bands, the tallest forest trees, moving swiftly by astonishing leaps, sprawling out like spiders, and catching by their perfectly prehensile tails. Their faces are shaded by projecting hairs, blah, blah, blah, ten species between Brazil and central Mexico . . . " I skimmed along the page with the droplight. "Okay, here we go. They are mild, intelligent, and make interesting pets. There it is, Gerald."

I tried to hand him the book, but he pushed it back to me.

"Look at the pitcher," he said. "Look at those sad faces."

In the middle of the page was a close-up photograph of two baby spider monkeys. Gerald was right about their faces. They did look sad and maybe a little frightened, their wide eyes full of unvoiced expression, like human children, their hair mussed as if from sleep, their mouths turned down slightly in a stubborn monkey frown.

"Don't nobody got a monkey," Gerald said.

"Michael fucking Jackson got a monkey," Wishbone said.

We turned to look at him. He hadn't moved, was still stretched in the light, legs straight as a corpse. I had thought he was asleep. Gerald said, "Michael Jackson's nobody I know."

"Michael Jackson has a *chimpanzee*, Wishbone," I said. "There's a difference."

Wishbone sat up slowly, drew in one knee, and slung his arm over it. He looked handsome, almost beautiful in the harsh sunlight, his eyes narrow, his smile easy, perspiration beaded on his dark face. He looked so mysterious, just then, I thought that if I could catch him in the right light, strike a match at an exact moment, I would see diamonds or something beneath the surface of his skin.

He got to his feet, walked over, and squatted in front of me. He snatched the book from my hands. "The food of the spider monkey is mainly fruit and insects." Wishbone enunciated each word carefully. He winked at Gerald, then leaned toward me until his face was close enough to mine that I could feel his breath on my cheeks. "In certain countries, their flesh is considered a delicacy." He closed the book and passed it to Gerald without taking his eyes from me. He rooted around under his coveralls, found what he was looking for, and dangled it in front of me. "You know the routine," he said, an empty cigarette pack between two fingers.

I took my time on Wishbone's errand. He hadn't given me a countdown so I thought I'd at least make him wait awhile for his nicotine. The shipyard was on skeleton crew since we lost the navy contract—four hundred people out of work at my uncle's company alone—and the *Kaga* was one of only three ships in for repairs, leaving seven drydocks empty, rising up along the waterfront like vacant stadiums. I wandered into the next yard over, yard five, thinking about Gerald's monkey. I wondered if Wishbone could actually get it for him or if that was just talk. I hoped he could for Gerald's sake. Cruel to lead him on. I had this picture in my head of Gerald at home in an easy chair, the television on in front of him and this spider monkey next to him on the arm of the chair, curling its tail around his shoulders. It was a nice picture. They were sharing an orange, each of them slipping damp wedges of fruit into the other's mouth.

I could hear the lifting cranes churning behind me, men shouting, metal banging on metal but yard five was still and quiet. Dust puffed up beneath my steps. The infrequent wind made me shiver. Two rails set wide apart, used for launching ships, ran down to the water's edge and I balanced myself on one and teetered down the slope to the water. A barge lumbered along the river with seagulls turning circles in the air above it.

When I was nine years old, my parents took me to the launching of a two-hundred-foot yacht, the *Marie Paul*, built here for a California millionaire. My family had been invited for the maiden voyage, and we mingled with the beautiful strangers under a striped party tent, which sheltered a banquet of food and champagne and where a Dixieland band fizzed on an improvised stage in the corner. There were tuxedos and spangled cocktail dresses along with the canary-yellow hard hats that my uncle required. The women from California wore short dresses, dresses my mother never would have worn, exposing tan and slender legs that seemed to grow longer when they danced.

One of these women proclaimed me the cutest thing in my miniature tuxedo and hard hat. She hauled me away to dance, my mother shooing me politely along despite my protests. We did the stiff-legged foxtrot that Mother and I did at home, the only dance I knew. "Loosen up, baby," the woman said, stepping away from me after only a few turns. "Dance like you mean it." She shimmied around me, overwhelmed me, the rustle of her dress and swish of her hair, her hands slipping over my arms and shoulders, her perfume and warm champagne breath, her brown thighs gliding together, her exposed throat and collarbone. This woman did the christening, shattering a bottle of champagne on the prow. The *Marie Paul* was the most magnificent thing I'd ever seen, with a sleek stern and muscular bow, like a tapered waist and broad chest. It was polished incandescent white with a swimming pool at the rear, a helicopter pad on the topmost deck, and four Boston Whalers to serve as landing craft strapped to the foredeck and covered with purple tarp. Workmen on overtime scurried in its shadow, double-checking. My dance partner was tiny beneath its bulk.

Ships are launched sideways, set on giant rollers and drawn down the tracks with heavy cable. When that one hit the water and careened to starboard, sending up a tidal wave of spray, I thought she would go under, that she would keep rolling, slip beneath the slow, brown water and go bubbling to the bottom. I screamed in panic and shut my eyes. My mother pulled me against her leg and said, "It's all right, Ford, honey. Look, it won't sink. See, it's fine." The *Marie Paul* found her balance, came swaying upright, thick waves rushing away from her on both sides, as if drawn ashore by our cheering. Tugboats motored in, like royal attendants, to push her out to deeper water.

I met my uncle on my way back from the supply wagon. He was giving three Japanese men a tour of the yard, all of them in business suits and yellow hard hats. When he spotted me, he yelled my name and waved me over. I stashed Wishbone's cigarettes in my pocket.

"I'd like you gentlemen to meet my nephew," my uncle said, slapping my shoulder. "He's learning the business from the ground up."

I wiped my palms on my coveralls and shook the hands that were offered. Each of the men gave me a crisp bow. They wore black leather shoes, recently filmed over with dust. Since last summer, I had grown three inches. I had my uncle's size, now, and both of us towered over them.

"Hard work," the oldest man said. He made his voice stern and gravelly, as if to imply that physical labor was good for you.

"Yes, sir."

"You better believe it," my uncle said. "No cakewalk for this boy."

My uncle was grooming me. He had no children of his own. Money-wise, my old man did all right as well, exploring the wonders of gynecology, but as I had thus far displayed a distinct lack of biological acumen in school, my parents viewed the shipyard as the best course for my future. My father's routine sounded considerably more pleasant, but I didn't argue.

"Ford, these gentlemen own the *Kaga.*" My uncle put his hands in his pockets and rocked back on his heels. "They're thinking about letting us build them another one. Wanted to see a work in progress."

"She's a fine boat," I said and they bowed again.

"*Arigato.*"

Normally, there was a cluster of men dawdling at the supply wagon but there were no customers now. No one wanted to be caught loafing. All around us, men were busy at their jobs—swarming on deck, unloading a hauling truck over by the warehouse—like a movie version of a bustling shipyard. The air had a faint tar smell and was full of wild echoes, the resolute clamor of progress, the necessary bang of making something from nothing. If you stepped back from it a second, weren't sweating in the guts of the thing, it was sort of heartening. You could almost see giant ships growing up out of the ground.

"Well," my uncle said. "Back to the grind, boy."

When I returned to the *Kaga* with Wishbone's cigarettes, I heard voices drifting up from the hold, and I knew that he and Gerald hadn't yet gone back to work. There was an unspoken understanding among the men, a costly one if my uncle got wind of it. The longer a ship stayed in drydock, the longer you had a job. My first summer at the yard, I was an industrious dervish, anxious to learn, eager to make a good impression. It wasn't long before I figured out why no one wanted me on their crew. If I worked too hard, they kept up, afraid that I might inform the higher powers. These men walked a fine line. The ships had to be repaired in reasonable time, of course, or there would be no business at all, but if they were finished too quickly, it might seem as if fewer men were needed, or the interval before the next ship arrived might be long enough that layoffs became necessary. The work had to be timed perfectly, not too slow or too fast, or the balance would be upset. It wasn't laziness that slowed the work, as my uncle complained, it was fear. Except Wishbone. I don't know what slowed him down. Wishbone wasn't afraid of anything that I could tell.

I took off my hard hat, belly-crawled to the hatch, and hung myself silently over to watch them. Gerald and Wishbone were on their backs with their feet propped against the far wall, passing a joint between them, its glowing tip visible in the semi-darkness. They were giggling like stoned schoolboys.

"Whadju tell him?" Wishbone was talking now, holding the joint between two fingers, blowing lightly on the coal. He dragged, offered it to Gerald, but Gerald waved it away.

"I said, 'Yo dumbass, standing on a trip wire and you want me to stay and *talk?*' Boy want somebody to keep him company while we wait for the EOC. Don't explode when you step on it, see. They blow when you step off, get the guy behind you, which in this case is me. I said, 'You crazy as you are dumb.'"

Gerald laughed a little, which got Wishbone started again. It took a minute for *him* to get himself back under control.

"You leave him?" he said, finally.

"Naw," Gerald said. "I stuck around a while. Guess I'm dumb as he was."

"Shit, Gerald," Wishbone said. "The Nam."

"It wasn't all bad," Gerald said. "Saw my first live monkey in Vietnam."

They stared quietly at the ceiling for a moment. The sun cast a spotlight beam that fell just short of where they lay, and I could see my shadow in the dusty light. I could feel the blood behind my eyes, could smell all those dead fish that had been there before us. I had been thinking about crashing angrily into the hold, doing an impersonation of my uncle, shouting, "Heads are gonna roll around here," and watching them scramble to their feet in panic, but I decided against it. I was already late with Wishbone's cigarettes. I stood and tiptoed away from the hatch. Then, I approached again, saying, "I'm back, fellas. Sorry it took so long," unnecessarily loud, making extra noise, the way you clomp around when coming home to a dark, empty house to give the burglars or ghosts or whatever time to clear out.

When I got home, finally, I walked around the side of the house to the pool, stripping as I went. My sister was stretched on a lounge chair in her American flag bikini, one knee up, and a boy her age was lying on his side on a second chair, watching her, two sweating glasses of Coke on the table between them. I must have been a strange sight in my boxer shorts, my body pale from hours below deck, forearms and face smeared with sweat and grime, like an actor in blackface only partly painted. They looked up when I passed, and Virginia started to say something, but I didn't give her a chance. I plunged into the clear water, cutting off the sound of her, and let myself glide, rubbing dirt from my arms and cheeks as I went, leaving a distinct, muddy trail in the water, like a jetstream. I floated to the surface in the deep end and hovered there, belly down like a drowned man, until I had to take a breath. The water was pure, cold energy on my skin.

"Mom's gonna kill you for not washing first," Virginia said.

"Mom's not gonna find out, is she." I paddled to the shallow end and stood looking her in the eyes. The pool was chest deep at this end, and my body felt almost weightless in the water.

"She might."

"She won't," I said.

I turned from her, convinced my point had been made. From the pool, our backyard sloped over a neatly cut acre to the sixteenth hole of a golf course. Marking the border between the two was a hedgerow of holly, red berries among the leaves like Christmas decorations. When we were kids, Virginia and I would hide beneath the diving board, submerged to the nostrils like alligators, and wait until a golf ball was shanked into our yard, then we'd swoop down on it and retreat to the pool. The golfer would wander over looking for his ball, and Virginia would hide it in her bathing suit, knowing he would never look in there, and we would give him our best innocent looks and tell him to try the next yard over. We didn't use the balls. They collected like fishtank gravel on the bottom of the pool. We just liked the thrilling mischief of the thing. Now, I could see natty golfers in the fading light and just barely, I could hear the sound of their club faces whisking through the grass, like whispered secrets.

"I'm Art." The boy with my sister was as tan as she was and his hair had been bleached almost white from days in the sun. "You must be the brother."

"You getting laid, Art?" I said without looking at him.

"There's an idea," he said. Virginia socked him in the arm and he winced. He was wearing floral print jams and a bulky diver's watch, one of those that's pressure tested to something ridiculous like six thousand feet.

Virginia said, "That's it. I'm getting Mom."

She stood and padded across the deck toward the sliding doors. I said, "That's a mistake, Virginia," but she kept walking, skipping a little over the hot pavement. She snapped her bikini bottom into place with two fingers as she went. "Bitch," I said. "Dyke, cunt, whore."

"Whoa now," Art said. "You shouldn't talk to your sister like that."

I climbed the four concrete steps from the pool. My body felt huge and slick and dangerous. It would do whatever I wanted. I walked over to Art, and he stood to meet me. We were almost the same height, and our bodies made a stark contrast, his browned and indolently soft, mine white like hard marble. I leaned into him, our faces inches apart, and gave him an evil wink. "Don't fuck with me, Art," I said. "Just don't." We looked at each other a moment longer before he sidestepped me and followed Virginia into the house.

My sister had a remarkable propensity for never appearing sleepworn. I didn't know what went on in that bathroom of hers before the lights went out, but she woke each morning in mint condition, emerging from bed as fresh as she went in, no puffy eyes, no crust around the mouth, not a hair mashed out of place by the pillow. She said it was because she never dreamed. But one night, not long after my meeting with Art, I was startled from sleep by something and jerked awake, heart fluttering, thinking I'm late for work, the house is on fire, whatever, to find my sister standing at the window in my room looking out.

"Jesus Christ, Virginia, you scared me shitless," I said. I rolled over to look at the clock. Five-thirty. The night crew at the yard would be getting off any minute. "Get the fuck outta here. I've got an hour left to sleep."

Virginia didn't answer right away. She was wearing her white knee length nightgown and the light coming through the window made her shape a silhouette beneath the fabric. Her hair was smooth and perfect on her shoulders. My room faced the golf course and I could see morning mist just above the ground.

"What the fuck, Virginia?" I said.

She turned toward me and I knew that she was asleep. Her arms hung loosely at her sides, her fingers curled up a touch. Her eyes were open but as distant as the moon. The world was pulling itself together outside. Sprinklers ticked sleepily on the golf course, the garbage truck ground its way down the street. I pictured Wishbone and Gerald, right then, finishing the first leg of a double shift, corning up from below deck, oiled with sweat, blinking at the dim morning like coal miners.

"Eighty feet," Virginia said.

"What?"

"It has to be eighty feet." Her voice was hushed but firm.

"Okay, Vee, no problem. Eighty feet." I got out of bed and put my hands on her warm shoulders and piloted her back down the hall to her room. She didn't resist and climbed into her bed, a fourposter with an embroidered canopy, when I showed it to her. I couldn't fall back asleep after that. I wondered what my sister was building in her dreams.

Gerald's monkey was on its way. Wishbone had contacted the Jap, and the wheels of black market commerce were turning as we spoke. I didn't know whether or not to believe him. It was true that the repairs on the *Kaga* were nearly finished and her crew was filtering back into town, so he could have been in touch with his connection, but I had trouble seeing how a drug dealer from Japan was going to get his hands on a monkey from Brazil. For Gerald's sake, I remained skeptical.

"Wishbone, where's your guy gonna come by this monkey?" I said.

We had finished welding two new plates into the deck and had one more to burn out and replace. The seams from the new plates ran along the floor like tiny, steel molehills. We were kneeling around three sides of a square, burning along white lines drawn in chalk, the heat between us enough to burn the hair from your arms without protection. I could feel the heat pressing against my clothes, could feel it on my tongue when I took a breath.

"What *is* that sound? It's almost like a woman," Wishbone said.

"You hear something, Gerald?"

Gerald chuckled behind his mask. Bootsteps echoed above us.

"All I'm saying is, according to Gerald's book, spider monkeys live in Central and South America." The metal beneath the tip of my flame bent and glowed molten orange. "Your guy's not going anywhere near South America."

Wishbone shut down his burner and waved at Gerald to do the same. Gerald and I screwed down the nozzles that controlled the gas, reducing the flames to tiny blue pinpoints. Wishbone lifted his mask and breathed in deeply through his nose.

"Listen here, little man, I don't ask questions." He narrowed his eyes at me. "I tell the Jap what I want, and he gets it. Simple as that. Like magic. That's why they call me Wishbone. You trying to discourage Gerald? Make him think his wish won't come true?"

At that, my skin prickled. I glanced at Gerald. His mask was still down, the bar of window over his eyes blurred by the heat, but I could tell he was watching us. We were directly beneath the hatch and I could see a block of clear sky above the ship. "Of course not," I said. "I just don't want him to get his hopes up unnecessarily."

"So you think Gerald can't work it out for himself, that it?" Wishbone said. "He's just some dumb nigger got to be looked after."

"Fuck you, Wishbone."

Wishbone leaned back on his elbows, his temples and neck tracked with sweat. He smiled, then, all the anger in his face suddenly gone, his features smooth with pure delight. That smile was the most terrifying thing I'd ever seen.

"You hear that, Gerald?" he said. "Nephew's pissed."

"Leave the boy alone, Wishbone," Gerald said, snuffing the flame on his torch and raising his mask. He looked tired. "You know he don't mean no harm."

Wishbone cocked his head and examined me a moment longer, still smiling that amused, unnerving smile. "What Gerald wants, Gerald gets," he said. He fished in his pocket and brought out his cigarettes. He shook the last three from the pack, snapped two of them at the filter, crumbling the grains of tobacco between his fingers and situated the remaining one between his lips. He said, "What do you think I want?"

For an instant, I thought about saying no, thought about telling Wishbone to go fuck himself, but I didn't. Something in me resisted the impulse. I don't know whether it was guilt over what Wishbone had said about Gerald or just plain fear or something else entirely, but I dropped my mask and shed my smock and gloves and made my deliberate way up the ladder and into the air.

Outside, the sun was lolling above the crooked tops of the cranes. It was a perfect day for sunbathing. I wondered if Virginia remembered her sleepwalking, remembered the dimensions that troubled her dreams. I walked over to the supply wagon, waving occasionally at one man or another who acknowledged my passing. I knew their faces but rarely did I know their names. Everyone knew me, though. The boss's nephew. The guy that ran the supply wagon saw me coming and had a pack of Winston Reds waiting for me when I arrived.

He smiled and shook his head and said, "Wishbone's daily bread." I forked over the two bucks, thanked him. I turned to retrace my steps across the yard. Right then, the ground rocked and I had to grab the counter for balance. The tremor didn't seem connected to anything, seemed to come from the earth itself, scattershot and violent, but I saw the source when I turned. For a second, less than a second, I could see the thing, a thick twisting chord of flame, growing up out of the *Kaga* like a vine.

Then it was gone, and I was running hard for the ship, dodging through the wedge of bodies that rushed down the gangplank and away from the explosion, I found Wishbone on deck, four men pinning his arms and legs, telling him, "Lie still, Bone. It's gonna be all right. Don't move." His eyes were squinched tight against the pain, his mouth wide open, his lips chapped looking, but he wasn't screaming. He was naked, his clothes disintegrated by the fire, and his skin was raw and crinkly allover, like the edges of burned paper. Several men were jetting fire extinguishers into the hold, white vapor billowing back, but the fire was already out. That sort of flame was a supernova, here and gone in a flash.

I caught one of the men by his shirtsleeve. "Where's Gerald?" I said. "Let me down there. Gerald's down there. Shut that thing off so we can see him."

He dropped the extinguisher and grabbed my arms.

"You don't wanna see him, son. Believe me."

I let him lead me away from the crowd and sit me down on a spool of heavy cable. My uncle had arrived on the scene by then, and he came over to where I was sitting. "You're okay, Ford?" he said. "What happened? Jesus Christ, your mother would've slit my throat if you'd been down there." He leaned close to me with his idea of a kind expression on his face.

"Gerald wants a monkey," I said.

"Of course he does," my uncle said. "You bet, pal."

My uncle drove me home early from work and dropped me at the front steps. I don't think he was ready to face my mother. I didn't tell anyone at home what had happened, just blew right past them, headed down the hall to Virginia's bed. I climbed in, unwashed, and jerked the covers to my chin. I had this crazy idea that my dreams would be safer there. Virginia came in eventually and said, "What the fuck do you think you're doing?" I didn't answer. Without opening my eyes, I slipped one hand free of the covers and gave her the finger and for some reason, that was enough. I could feel her standing there quietly for a minute or two, watching me. After a while, she said, "You look like a little kid," then she closed the door behind her and left me alone.

To hear Wishbone tell it, Gerald was the smoker. Pack a day at least, must've warned him a hundred times not to smoke around welding lines but he wouldn't listen. Gerald was an old-timer, set in his awful ways. I stood against the wall of my uncle's office a week or so after the accident and waited my turn to speak. My mother was beside me, her hand lightly at my elbow. To my surprise, I felt no anger at Wishbone's lying. The skin on his face was still whitish-pink in places, and his sleeves were buttoned to the wrist, covering his scalded arms, and he wore a newborn's light blue knit cap to protect his tender skull. His hands trembled and his eyes were rheumy, his vision blurred, he said, since the accident. He looked weak, vulnerable, afraid, squinting across the conference table at my uncle and the men from the insurance company. I felt sorry for him. I wanted to know what made him think I wouldn't expose him. All the shit he gave me. Maybe he thought I was afraid because he was black or that I was ashamed of being white when he wasn't. Maybe he thought his cigarette run had saved my life and I ought to be grateful, despite everything. But what I wanted to know more than anything was how he survived and Gerald didn't, because for an instant, the amount of time it took to burn away the flammable air, that hold was pure, white conflagration, molten gas, like the center of the sun. Nothing could have lived in there. But here was Wishbone telling these lies right in front of me, burned but alive, breathing in and out like the rest of us when he should have been dead. After things had settled down on the deck that day, I walked over to the hatch and looked in. Two policemen and some emergency personnel were milling around a lumped sheet of blue tarp covering what must've been Gerald's body. It's funny but the stink of all those rotting fish, that death smell, it was gone.

When my turn came to speak, I only had to answer one question—Ford, can you corroborate everything this man has just told us? After but a moment's hesitation, I lied. It wasn't something I'd planned. I'd planned on telling the truth, but in the space of that pause, I thought of Gerald wanting that monkey. He had died believing it would come, hoping for it, and that didn't sound so awful all of a sudden. And I thought of Wishbone, of what good it would do me to ruin his life, what sort of justice would be served. And, strangely, I thought of my sister, so far away from all this, troubled only by rare bad dreams.

"Yes, sir," I said. "He's telling the truth."

I looked at Wishbone, but he wouldn't meet my eyes. He was crying without making a sound. It turned out that he had been standing directly beneath the hatch when he struck the spark that brought the air to life. He had been lifted out by the force of the explosion, shot free of the hold like a cartoon spaceman. One minute, he was standing in a perfect square of yellow light with his friend before him, the next, he was riding a grim column of fire.

Knight on First-Person Point of View

Let me say right off that I almost never write stories drawn directly from the events of my life. What's more often the case is that the story itself is pure invention but the protagonist and I will share certain autobiographical elements or a particular way of looking at the world.

I did, however, write this story called "Gerald's Monkey," which is about a sixteen-year-old kid working a summer job at his uncle's shipyard in Alabama. He gets mixed up with a pair of older black men, Wishbone and Gerald, also employees, and he has an openly hostile relationship with his beautiful sister, Virginia. Both sets of interactions are important to the central issues in the story—race and class and manhood, in the most general sense—all of which I hope add up to a kind of coming-of-age for the protagonist that is richer and more intricate than the sum of its parts, though, for the record, I didn't have the slightest idea what sort of big-picture notions would underlie the narrative when I sat down to write. I was only interested in telling a story, and I think that's the case with most writers.

Now, it's true that I have a sister, though she's the younger sibling in real life, and while I can't recall a great deal of bickering between us, I'm sure we must have tangled sometimes, like the brother and sister in the story. It's also true that I worked summers at my uncle's shipyard in high school and college, and true that I was never entirely comfortable there because of my relationship to the boss, despite the fact that I very much liked and admired the men I worked with. The awkwardness cut both ways, I guess, though I can't think of a single thing anybody did to make me feel out of place. In fact, the men were by and large deferential, which might in and of itself have made me more aware of the differences between us. What I mostly feel, looking back, is ashamed that I didn't do a better job of fitting in.

On its face, then, the origins of this story likely are transparent. But there's this as well: One time in grad school I was at a party at my neighbor's house and he was giving me the tour. In the corner of a bedroom stood a tall, ornate cage. It looked like something from Japanese mythology. When I asked what it was, my neighbor said, "That's my roommate's. Gerald. He's got a monkey." I laughed and told him that Gerald's Got a Monkey would make a great title for a story. Obviously, the title morphed with successive rewrites but it seems to me now that that incident, despite the fact that I never met Gerald or saw a monkey anywhere in the house, is far more responsible as an impetus for the story than any of the specifics of my past. It started me fictionalizing in my head—who was Gerald and what kind of monkey and how did he get his hands on it in the first place?

Why those two things—the real Gerald's monkey and my experience at a shipyard—came to be linked in my mind, I honestly have no idea. There's no getting around the fact that a lot of what's important in any story happens in the subconscious and anyone who says otherwise is full of baloney. I do know that I'd always thought the yard would be a good place to set a story and now I had a first line and because of that line, two characters—three counting the narrator, Ford, this thinly veiled version of my young self—and there were some questions that needed answering, which, at the most basic level, is what happens in any story, right? Questions are posed early on, regarding plot, regarding character, which provide tension and narrative momentum, and they're answered over the course of the story in what the writer hopes is an artful way.

It might be argued that third person is the wiser choice when writing from personal experience, because it allows for greater distance, allows the writer to step back a little more easily from his or her recollection. But first person just felt natural here. Not only is there a literal connection between myself and the material but Ford's personality is bound up in and expressed by his conversational tone and in the contrast between his dialogue, which is mostly tough-guy lingo and teenage posturing, and his interior life, which is more thoughtful, more self-aware, and which, I hope, helps to expose his actual sensitivity and insecurity. In other words, the point of view is as important and revealing as the events themselves.

The risk with first person, it seems to me, especially when writing from personal experience, is that the point of view will overwhelm the narrative, will become too expository, that the writer will linger too long in the narrator's head and not long enough in the world he is attempting to create. This is doubly true of the first-person past tense because the past tense suggests that the material has been mulled over, processed, that the narrator has arrived at an understanding of these events before he or she begins the telling. The trouble is, when I read a story that opens with something like, "Everything changed on my sixteenth birthday," I get a little antsy right away. The tone is so deliberately explantory. Here is a narrator looking back on his life who not only recognizes the importance of the story he's about to tell but knows what's to be learned from it, and is gearing up to make sure I get it, too. I, for one, don't want to be spoonfed meaning in a piece of fiction, not only because I'm smart enough to figure things out by myself most times, but also because to pronounce meaning is generally to lessen its impact. I should probably add that I can think of a fair number of stories right this minute that begin along those lines and work just fine, though in every case the writer has the good sense to back away from the impositions of voice and point of view, to rely on image and action rather than explication.

Take Raymond Carver. There's a reason his story "Cathedral" turns up over and over in anthologies. "My eyes were still closed," he writes in the penultimate paragraph. "I was in my house. I knew that. But I didn't feel like I was inside of anything." The phrasing suggests that the narrator realizes that he's describing something important and the past tense lets us know that whatever it is, it's stayed with him for a while, kept on resonating long enough that he needs to get it off his chest but he never imposes his own interpretation of the events on his reader. To a certain extent, that happens anyway in first person, right? First-person narration is by nature limited to a single focus, to its narrator's ideas—however flawed—about how things happened, filtered through his or her own fears and desires. In Carver's case, the narrator is still reaching for the meaning rather than defining it, which lends the story mystery and power.

I wanted something similar from "Gerald's Monkey." It was important to tell the story in a young man's voice, to allow Ford himself to let us in on who he was, but I also wanted the kind of permanence and gravity conveyed by the past tense. By restricting his narration to the events of the story as opposed to an interpretation of the events, he comes off, I hope, similarly awed and mystified by what's happened this one summer in his life.

The hard thing about writing fiction from autobiography, at least for me, is that the actuality of the past and my understanding of it or lack thereof, nearly always gets in the way of what's best for the story. Facts are permanent. Memory, though imperfect, is pretty fixed as well. It makes sense that they would be difficult to alter. A standard response to workshop criticism: "But that's how it really happened." The thing is, how it really happened is beside the point. What's important is the story, the fiction, the artifice, and a big part of all that is point of view. Despite our surface similarities, Ford most defintely is not me and there were no Wishbones or Geralds at the yard when I was there—they aren't even composites, not conscious ones at least—nor were there any deadly accidents. My time was mostly uneventful and if I'd tried to write it the way it was it would look empty to anyone but me.

I know there are lots of writers who supposedly write from experience—Hemingway leaps immediately to mind—but I have the sense that critics and scholars make too much of the link between reality and fiction, that the actual connections are less significant than what's invented. When people tell me they're working on a novel about their eccentric grandmother or when my students want to write stories about their summer in Outward Bound, I'm often leery and try to encourage them to veer as far from the facts as possible. It's not that I discount their experience or even that I think it's not worth writing about. It's that everything you write will be informed by your experience whether you make it up or not. It's that life is mostly chaos on its face. Fiction, by nature, seeks not only meaning, not the kind of meaning we've gotten used to, the kind you can put in a brochure—Learn the value of teamwork and/or self-reliance on Outward Bound!!—but the kind that's too complicated to distill.

Writing Suggestions

1. Write a first-person scene in which the narrator is someone far different from yourself. Write from the perspective of a different gender and include an age difference of at least a decade. Write for a page or two and let this "I" say what's on his or her mind. If you're not sure how to speak authentically in this voice, see if you can write your way into it. Sometimes it takes a few pages to figure out how narrators speak when they're not thinly veiled versions of the author.

2. Find a story that interests you from one of these sources: the news, a style or entertainment magazine, a grocery store tabloid. Create a first-person narrator suggested by the events in this story. How would this narrator use language and description to retell the events in his or her own words? What events and details would this narrator include from the original story? What details would this narrator exclude? For help creating this character, refer to the essay, **Turning Ideas into Characters** (page 124–127). When you feel you know this character well enough to speak in that voice, write the story.

3. One of the advantages of the first person is the immediacy that comes from the act of witnessing. Take a story or scene of yours (rendered in either second or third person) and rewrite the first page in first person. This involves far more than switching every "he" to "I"—it necessitates a rethinking of perspective. What part of the experience can the "I" tell more clearly or with better effect than can a second- or third-person narrator? Remember that a first-person narrator not only witnesses but also responds to the events by telling a story. What might be the range of responses for the events of your story?

4. First person is one of the most popular choices for point of view. How many of your favorite stories—from this book or elsewhere—are written in first person? In your

opinion, what are the benefits of using first person over third person? What are the drawbacks? How is the use of first person in fiction different from the first person in memoir or in a personal essay?

> *It is terribly easy to write in first person; in fact, I think it's so easy that unless you're really gifted like Kaye Gibbons, you're going to use it in a cheap way. The first person point of view is incredibly plastic—it'll take you anywhere you want to go.*
> —Jim Grimsley

Adam Johnson

The Death-Dealing Cassini Satellite

From *New England Review* and *Emporium: Stories*

Tonight the bus is unusually responsive—brakes crisp, tires gripping—jockeying lane to lane so smoothly your passengers forget they're moving as they turn to talk over the seats, high heels dangling out into the aisle, teeth bright with vodka and the lemon rinds they pull from clear plastic bags in their purses. Some stand, hanging loosely from overhead handles, wrists looped in white plastic straps, smiling as their bodies lean unnaturally far with the curves. Off-balance, half-falling, this position has its advantages: hips flare and sway behind you, ribs thumb their way through fabric, and this it seems is the view you've grown used to, daring you to touch, poised to knock you down.

You don't even know where you're driving yet, but through breaks in the trees, you can see red and blues on the Parkway and know traffic cops are working the outflow of an I-High baseball game. The school is not a place you want to be near tonight, especially bumper-to-bumper with old teammates, especially as a nineteen-year-old go-nowhere who drives a charter bus for a cancer victim support group on Thursday nights. So you're banking a turn onto the Cascade Expressway instead—not an easy feat in a fifty-six-foot Blue Liner—when you catch a glimpse of Mrs. Cassini walking down the long aisle toward you, her figure vibrating in the overhead mirror, and you know you're in trouble. Her husband built the Cassini Satellite, the one powered by seventy-two pounds of plutonium, so you know what you're dealing with.

Your eyes double back from carloads of teenagers behind victory-soaped windows to the sight of Mrs. Cassini growing in the mirror: she's running the tips of her fingers across the green-black vinyl seat backs, and she's closing on you in a black Lycra cocktail dress that's Olympic time-trial tight. The streetlights through the bus windows are flashing across her torso, her arms and neck taking on the cobalt blue of barium dye, and even from here you can make out the bubble-gum ridges of her mastectomy scars.

All the other women seem to lean in her wake, as if she is their talisman, this woman who's walked through the flames, who's beat cancer three times. The old Blue Liner wants to wander in the fast lane.

Only when Mrs. Cassini reaches the front of the bus do you notice the flask in her hand. At the sight of your SAT study guides on the dash, she says, "Relax, Ben," and sloshes back some scotch. Amber traces down her chin, pauses at the base of her neck. She slips a tape into the deck and *Blue Danube* starts over the loudspeakers.

As she leans the backs of her legs against the dash, the door lever forces her closer to you, and the black wing of her pelvis glows an edgy green from the dash gauges. She stares at you hard—eyes rimmed a renal yellow, the color of canary diamonds—then lifts and places a heel in the pocket of seat between your legs. This move hitches her skirt high enough that you can see the white-clamped tip of her catheter dangling before you, and you're trying not to stare, but man . . .

Then Mrs. Cassini leans over, her hand like it's going for your belt loops, and you go limp, drop a hand from the wheel and give her room. "That's better, Benny," she says, and soon her strong chest is in your face—you're in the fast lane!—as she fumbles around on the far side of your captain's chair. She comes up with the microphone hand-set, the loopy cord bouncing in your face. When she's composed herself a little, you give the BlueLiner a quick burst of gas and watch the tip of that catheter circle into a tight orbit below her hem. Cassini smiles sideways at you.

You two've done this routine before.

Blue Danube kicks into gear, and across the women's faces in the mirror comes a certain serenity, like they're all picturing the slow-tumbling spaceships from *2001: A Space Odyssey*, a movie you thought was pretty sexual—all that docking and pod work —and which your dad said was a coded history of existentialism.

She lifts her flask high. "For my husband," she says into the mike, addressing the bus like a lounge singer. "Scholar. Diplomat. NASA scientist of the year." Here she *whoops* loud, and the women are swaying to the music just enough to make the bus woozy between lanes.

"He has a permit to buy weapons-grade plutonium, reserved parking at JPL. He wrote his name in the wet cement of Cape Canaveral's launch pad, but it's Thursday night, and he can't come within five hundred feet of his wife for four more hours."

The bus explodes, the women are in the aisles, some with their arms in the air, dancing and pirouetting homages to both the famous Cassini satellite and the weekly, six-hour Cassini restraining order.

Mrs. Cassini tosses the mike into your lap and from her glowing abandon, you're trying to guess the destination this week: Shocking the tourists at the Idanha Hotel? Maybe scar-strutting with the black ties at the Capitol Club or lobbying complimentary cocktails from the Westin convention staff.

Cassini moves closer, her lips just brushing your ear, and you want to close your eyes. "To the Cove, young captain," she mouths and you know there's both a difficult U-turn and some slumming ahead. But your shoulders start to loll to the music and soon you have the old BlueLiner waltzing through the backroads of Boise, a little too fast perhaps, though none of your passengers are very worried about crashing because they've all had cancer, and the motion of their bodies tonight seems to confirm both *Space Odyssey* theories.

At the Cove, you wheel the bus around in a crush of white gypsum and bottle caps, coming to rest under the yellow buzz of bug lights and a single beer sign humming blue enough that cars look stripped of their paint. The Cove through the windscreen is a square slump-block hut set off by its brighter parking lot, darkbordering pine, and backdrop of lake that's snowmelt still.

The women descend beside you, heels sinking in gravel, and make for the only door there is. They move past, winking, patting your shoulders, letting the sheen of their nylons run staticky along your forearm as you hold the door lever. There are some new faces in the Cancer Survivor's Club this week, but you don't have the energy to meet their eyes. You look to familiar faces instead, the veterans. It's pathetic, for sure, but they ladle love on you and you take it, these Thursday-night women who flirt with you, rub your shoulders, teach you to foxtrot. Judge Helen—the one who granted the restraining order—is the last to leave, and she already has her weekly Winston in her lips. She is a bigger woman with short, spiked hair who is not afraid to wear black spandex, and you like her for that.

They all cross the blue-yellow parking lot with a motion only cancer survivors can muster, a sexy, patient gait that comes with the knowledge bosses can't fire dying women, that cops won't cart them off, that bartenders don't tell bald women they've had too much. Through a door padded with red vinyl and brass studs, they disappear, and you are alone again.

Out stumble two men who turn back to stare at the red door in disbelief. One is wearing fishing gaiters. They look at each other, at the bus, strain a glance at the sky as if the weather might have something to do with the women they've seen and then backtrack, heads shaking, for an old Subaru by the Dumpster.

You shut the door, check your watch, and pull out a *Millers Analogies* workbook. The college entrance test is Saturday, and you're more than a year behind on everything. You put your feet up on the console and flip through the pages, a stream of letters and numbers that don't even register.

"I'll scream rape," comes from the back of the bus, singed with mock-play and the smell of tobacco.

"You know the rules, Mrs. Cassini. No smoking on the BlueLiner." You say this over your shoulder, feigning interest in antonyms in an effort not to encourage her. But you can feel her nearing, hear her slapping the overhead straps on the way, leaving them to swing in the dark behind her.

"I could have Helen throw away the key," she says and pauses, smoking. "I'm willing to bargain on your punishment, though."

"Cat-o'-nine-tails? Thousand licks, Mrs. Cassini?" Your voice is flat, disinterested.

"Benny, your tongue. You're lacking a refining, feminine influence."

"And you're the best I've got?"

She's standing beside you now, taking one step down toward the door so that she is lower, but farther, so she has to lean. "Oh, Ben. If you only knew how much control it takes to be a role model for you." She runs a hand through your hair in a circular motion that leaves her holding your earlobe. It's a thing your mother used to do. "Seriously, though, how's things? Stan okay?"

"You know Dad, he's sawing wood. I got a test coming up."

"Good, good. You study hard and I'll throw you a party." She taps the cigarette ash into her hand. "In the meantime, are you gonna help me get off?"

"Mrs. Cassini?"

She nods her head at the lever, and you swivel the doors open for her. "Relax, Benny. Go with things, okay? Live for me." She turns to leave, but on the last step stops and lifts her skirt for a full bare-ass flash before jumping down and trotting off toward the red vinyl of home, and you're left shivering with a knob in your hand. You know these women well. You know a side of them nobody sees, and Mrs. Cassini's been playing the flirting "auntie" for a long time. Back then, though, you were seventeen and your mom was on this bus. Now you're nineteen, a lot of things have changed, and it's fifty-fifty at best whether you'll even show for that test.

You swing the doors shut and set the lock, more to keep yourself on the bus than anything, but the static is still in your arm, smoke hangs in the air. Your dad has a small State Farm branch—which is why Mom was insured to the teeth and you're covered to drive a fifty-six-foot bus—but one time he took you with him to underwrite a warehouse, a windowless cinder building that stored marine batteries. Everything was primer gray except for the stacks of yellow cells with their red and green posts, but there was a pulse to that place that twitched like copper windings and made your mouth taste of zinc. You remember thinking this must be what it's like inside a hydroelectric dam, with stands of vibrating water behind the walls. This is what you feel now from the Cove, this draw.

You pick up your books and set them down.

Your mom once said cancer was the best thing on earth, that as long as it didn't kill you, you were going to *live*. When she and Cassini and the others started the club, they sat outside in your mom's cactus garden, drinking tea and sharing. It wasn't long before they started searching for stronger medicine and held rituals in the trees out back, events in the twilight where they buried their hopes and burned their fears in the group holes they'd dug. Except for a few veterans, the turnover rate in the club is pretty high, and you understand why green tea and empathy eventually yielded to Donna Karan dresses and a tang of vermouth.

The I-High school counselor, Mrs. Crowley, said writing an essay about struggling with your mom's death could open the doors of a lot of good colleges. You didn't jump at that idea. She said look at the big picture: it could help you get into medical school someday, where you could make a difference, where you could find a cure for what took your mother.

You told Mrs. Crowley she had something there, that working with radon and lab rats had always been a dream, but your real plans include asbestos. For some reason, you confessed to stealing your father's drill bits, to once lying about the reading on your mother's thermometer so you could go see *Forrest Gump* at the drive-in, admitted to sometimes eating her chemotherapy pills when she wasn't around. Mrs. Crowley said remember to turn in the combination for your locker and bring a photo of yourself to the SAT.

What you couldn't explain to Mrs. Crowley was that the real danger is in handling it too well. Managing loss is your father's business. He's pretty good at it. He got mom the best medical plan, the best doctors, the best palliative counselor. Dad knew the stages of grief and there were no surprises. Mom even died on schedule. Those doctors were amazing; they called it within a weekend.

Dad joined a support group and took up woodworking. He bought you a brass trumpet and a punching bag. Now he comes home from work, checks the Weather Channel—he's crazy about the weather—puts on a shop apron, and goes into the garage to build the look-alikes of colonial furniture that fill your house.

Sometimes he gets nostalgic on Sundays or has a few too many beers over dinner and tells you things about Mom when she was young. You've heard most of them many times, but once in a while he says something new, and you feel close to him for that. Your mom had a pony named Applejack when she was a girl. In college, her favorite movie was *The Andromeda Strain*. That, pregnant with you, she was in Albertson's supermarket when her water broke, and she calmly took a jar of pickles from the shelf, dropped it over the fluid on the floor, and moved on.

But even these moments of disclosure from your father seem expected in a way, and his power tools never seem to rattle him the way you'd think they might, the way the Blue Liner's big diesel can vibrate something loose in you that makes you forget where it is you are driving, makes you check and check the overhead mirror for her in row six. You think if Dad could have seen her on this bus one time, bright-eyed and destination bound, all those pieces from his replica projects wouldn't fit together so well.

You hear the thump of the red door and look out the windscreen to see a kid your age cross the lot with a white bucket of beer caps. He cuts around to the back dock, where he starts dumping them in the lake. It's dark and a long way off, but you think you know him from the baseball team, from before you quit. He leans against the rail and he pours slowly, watching the caps go down like all those green innings in a near-championship stadium. His name might be Tony. Finished, he spits on what is probably his own reflection and goes inside. When the door closes, though, there is a woman standing beneath the blue beer sign.

She crosses the lot, circling wide to avoid the floodlight. With calm, measured steps she walks around the far side of the bus, where she grabs a sapling with both hands and stares at her feet.

She's in trouble, about to be sick, but there's something about her shoulders, the way her ribs flare and trim toward her waist. She's younger, new to the club, and caught your eye in the mirror on the way over. You could tell she was drawn to the mood on the bus, the abandon, the acceptance of being out without her wig. For everyone on the BlueLiner, the worst has already happened, and this is how they can laugh and talk to one another across newly emptied seats. This is what your mother wanted: for everything to race on without her.

Now, she retches, the thin branches shaking above her. When her shoes and ankles get wet, you know you should look away, but there is something necessary in the sight. It makes you wish your mother could have shown this side, the alone-and-sick, slipping outside part of the deal, because all her strength, like your father's adaptability, did nothing to brace you for after.

Her heels shift in the gravel again, heading for the bus, where she shakes the locked doors. You find her seat, her purse, and at the cab, strip the towel off your captain's chair before levering open the door. With the bright lights behind, she is more than alluring. She is here and real.

She takes her bag from your hand. "Jesus," she says. "This stuff I'm taking."

"I'm Ben," you tell her. Inside you're feeling that pulse, and don't know what to say because somehow you're already beyond small talk. And even just talking means you're making an investment of some kind. It's like standing before a brass trumpet or boxer's bag: they promise to show you a lot more of yourself than a red face or sore hands, and you're unsure if you want to touch them for that.

You climb down to the last step and sit, so she's taller. "Here," you say, holding the towel in the air before her, and there's this thing between you so clear that she grabs the door molding for balance and places a foot in your hand. You begin with her calf, stroking down to the heel.

"Do you feel better?"

"Sue. I'm sorry, Sue."

"Do you feel better, Sue?"

"No, not really."

She has a Hickman port in her chest, a sort of gray button connected to a white tube that disappears into the skin below the collarbone. You know your cancers pretty well, and the Hickman's a bad sign. It's made so they can inject really strong drugs like vinblastine, chemicals that will burn out the veins unless they're pumped straight into the superior vena cava, straight into the heart. You can feel the slim bones of her foot through the towel. Vinblastine is made from the purple blossoms of the periwinkle plant. You want to push that button.

"I mean you're nice for this, but this medicine . . . "

"Ben."

"This medicine, Ben." She shakes her head.

You take her other foot when she offers, wanting to make her legs dry and clean. You want to tell her you understand, that you've tasted Cytoxan, that it made your fingernails loose and teeth hurt. The feeling like your molars have been pulled returns: platinum spark plugs have been screwed into your jaw, and for a moment, it's like when they'd crackle to life in the middle of the night, making you see blue on the inside of your eyelids. "It's okay," you tell Sue.

"What's okay?"

"Everything. It feels pretty bad now, I know, but it'll all work out."

She pulls her foot back.

Your voice is thinner even than Mrs. Crowley's, but still you say, "things'll be fine."

"I'm pretty fucked, thank you. I'm screwed."

She says this and hops once, slipping a shoe strap over her heel before walking away.

From your wallet you pull your entrance ticket to the SAT. The picture you glued to it doesn't look anything like you. You cut it out of your sophomore yearbook, a dull-faced goofy kid who has no idea what's coming, who doesn't suspect that no one in his family will take a photo for the next three years.

You follow the route Sue took through the cars, into the Cove.

Inside, things are about what you'd thought. Several women have corralled two wrecker drivers into a group jitterbug that has them spinning off balance from woman to woman, their eyes unsure where to land—avoiding chests and hairlines—while their hands clutch at waists as if for emergency brakes. Oblivious to the fast rhythm, Mrs.

Boyden dances with a small, older gentleman in a brown jumpsuit. They move like strangers on liberty, her fingers hooked in his collar, his hands gathering the fabric of her emerald dress like parachute cord, a move that smoothes where his head lay sideways on her sternum, listening, as if to the source of the softer music they seem to move to. There is no sign of Sue.

Nothing seems to involve you. You sit at the bar wanting ice water while the bartender watches the *Tonight Show* on a soundless set. The music and laughing seem to sweep past, and it is as still on this stool as afternoons when you pull one of your father's pine Louis XIV chairs into your mother's cactus garden and contemplate in the half-light where she might've dug her holes. Lately, though, this is a riskier proposition because after only a year, you're no longer so sure of what she hoped for and feared. If you wrote it, this is what your college essay would be about: Feeling for divots in a dark lawn with your toes. Renting movies like *The Fighting Seabees* with your father. Living in a house filled with cactus all winter, sleeping in a room made small by jade-green ribs and spines while the smell of hot saw blades from the garage blows in through the heat vent.

Sue takes the stool next to you, and she also is ignored by the bartender. You ignore her too. In front of you is a wall-length mirror littered with business cards, snapshots in cheap plastic frames, and several yards of dollar bills signed with red marker. There is a crisp five-dollar bill that says *Work-Battle-Battle-Win* in beautiful script; it was the motto of your I-High baseball team, a stupid ritual you chanted before every game.

At the end of the bar, like sisters, Judge Helen smokes and chats with a woman who has rad-therapy lines tattooed on her neck. If you catch her from the other side, where they took the lung, Judge Helen's smoking can be spooky. But from here, her ribs expand as she drags and exhales, her laugh comes with a rise in her chest.

If you were sick, you and Sue would be laughing like this. You're pretty sure you might even have her in the back of the bus right now. But if you were sick, there'd be a hell of an essay in it, and you'd probably be at Harvard. As your mind hovers over cancer and college and Sue on hot vinyl, your eyes wander the mirror, and there, framed by shoulder-length black hair, are the brown eyes of your mother.

This snapshot—taken by who, the bartender?—depicts your mother about to limbo under a pool cue held by her best friend, Mrs. Cassini, and another woman who's no longer in the club. The colors are washed out, the eyes red, and Mom's just starting to descend, her eyes reckoning the height of that bar. There is confetti in her hair and for now her breasts are whole, so you know this must be her thirty-eighth birthday, and that despite the sheer dresses, the snow outside the Cove is deep. Her friends have set the bar at a ridiculous height, a point from which no one could be expected to rise, and you're wondering where you were when this picture was taken. Everyone smiles. She is about to fall, yet there is a thrill in this, too. They all lean forward, breath held, and for this moment, it looks like she is going to make it.

You turn to Sue. "What do you want for your birthday?"

She doesn't miss a beat. "A fishing pole. Maybe a pass to the zoo."

"That's my mom," you say, nodding at the bank of pictures.

"Where?"

"Doing the limbo."

Sue doesn't know what to say. "She's pretty."

"You think so?"

"She was in the club?"

"She started it. That shot's from later, though, from her birthday. I was trying to remember if I got her anything that year. I might have forgot."

"And you're thinking, what are you supposed to get for the woman who'll lose everything?"

You shrug. "Judge Helen was telling a story one time on the bus, about how when it didn't look like she was going to make it, her sister sent away to one of those mail-order companies that specializes in this. It names stars after people. God, they were howling over that one, I mean, laughing up their drinks. An eternal dot in the sky named Helen. Actually, it was Helen B-63, that's how good business was."

Sue pauses. "Your mother, is she?"

"No."

"Good. That makes me feel a little better."

"I'm sorry, I meant she died last year."

"You mean, less than a year after that picture?"

"Ten months."

"Fuck," she says. "What am I doing around you people?"

Sue stares at the dull brass of the bar rail, and you feel for her, but can't get past that picture. The bartender is shaking glasses in soapy water. You tell him you want to take a look at something on his wall, and he looks at you like you've just asked for a key to the Ladies' room.

"Give him the damn picture, Bill," Mrs. Cassini says and she's right behind you once again this evening. "In fact, give him anything he wants. We'll start with the picture, six shots, and an order for five taxis at midnight."

"Mrs. Cassini, I got to drive that bus."

"Oh, be quiet, Ben. Listen to your Auntie Cassini for once," she says and slides onto the barstool next to you. It feels like being between the posts of a marine battery, as if you touched both these women at the same time, you'd see that blue light again.

You're handed a framed photo of your mother that's been wiped with a bar towel. Tequila appears, lime and salt. Cassini licks the back of her hand. Sue bumps you as she hooks a heel in a rung of your barstool to better brace herself. The salt and alcohol burn in your fingernails. Three rims touch in front of you, and as usual, life seems to be moving just beyond your control, but for the moment, the place you're headed feels good.

"To cancer," Cassini says. "A growth industry." And you all nearly spray your drinks with laughter. In the mirror, Sue's smooth head rolls back, a nautilus-curve. Her throat lifts and relaxes, and you drink too. A sharp, patient burn, like cactus, winters in your throat.

Sue is fine until the lime. She lifts it to her mouth but the smell of it triggers something in her that makes her stand up. She puts her hands on the bar. "Not again," she says, turning, pushing away the hand you offer.

"Let her go," Cassini says, anticipating your urge to follow. "She asked about you, you know. She'll be back."

"When?"

She passes you the salt. "Just a bit ago. Out back by the lake. I told her you were dead in the water."

"Great. Thanks."

"Stuck in a rut. Afraid to move on. Staring at your feet."

"Okay, I get it."

"It's true," she says and fumbles for a cigarette in her cocktail purse.

The bartender has the Weather Channel on now, and you glance at the bottle-necked shape of Idaho, seen from space. You are somewhere on that screen, you think. Idaho is blue, and Mrs. Cassini is in that blue next to you. So is your mother, somewhere. Your dad is watching this, you're sure, but what he sees is clear skies.

Mrs. Cassini lights a smoke, and you do another shot together.

"I also told her you were looking to get laid."

You lick the tequila off your teeth and shake your head. It's all you can do. "You're killing me, Mrs. Cassini."

"Who gets the pretty one's other shot?"

"Go ahead," you say.

"See, that's what I'm talking about. A rut. No zest. Your mom and I were pretty close. You know what she asked me? I mean at the end. She didn't say *look out for my baby* or any crap like that. She said, 'Keep things interesting for Ben.'"

"Life doesn't seem that thrilling right now."

"Trust me. The excitement never stops," she says, with a touch of bitterness.

Your mom's picture is surrounded by shot glasses. "That's easy for you to say."

"Oh, you can be a little bastard."

"I didn't mean it that way."

Mrs. Cassini puffs on her cigarette and looks at you. "You want a thrill?"

You meet her eyes.

"I'm serious. I'll give you a grade-A thrill, right here."

It's like you're standing in your backyard, and you can feel that spot where that hole is, feel all those fears and desires hot through your feet.

"Okay," you tell her.

Mrs. Cassini stamps out her cigarette on the bar. Then she takes your hand, wet with lime and alcohol, and places it under her dress. For a moment, nothing registers. The old man in the brown jumpsuit stands at the end of the bar, talking into a telephone. The Weather Channel now shows the whole northern hemisphere, all of Idaho lost under its curve, and then your fingers start to feel the inside of her hipbone, the moist heat from below. She guides your hand to the edge of a vinyl-smooth scar and traces it with your fingers downward to the edge of her pubic hair. You can't help it, you close your eyes.

It's not a dance your hands are in, but a mechanical tracing. You are guided to the other side of her navel, where there, soft and flat, is skin you feel as blue.

"It's on the other side now," she says and you open your eyes to meet a face without anger or sadness, and that holds you all the more for it. The strong bones of her fingers push yours hard against her skin, deep into the wall of her abdomen until you know it must hurt. "There," she says, rolling the tips of your fingers. "Do you feel it?"

There's nothing there you can make out, nothing but heat and resistance, a yellow, oily pressure. You pull your hand away.

"That's the new baby."

Your fingers are red and you rub them under the bar, wanting another taste of lime for the brass in your mouth.

"That sounded pretty bitter, didn't it? I don't know why I called it that."

There is nothing you can say to her.

You do the shot on the bar and order two more.

"That's my Benny."

The bartender pours the tequila without limes or salt and when he changes the TV to the late news, Mrs. Cassini yells, "What time is it?" She turns to you, excited, and runs her hand though your hair, shaking your head with your earlobe at the end. "Come on, young captain. It's time."

Waving her hand to the bar, she yells, "To the satellite!"

With that great pull of Mrs. Cassini, you let yourself be swept. Reaching for the bar, you barely manage to grab a portrait of your mother and down that shot.

Outside, the patrons empty onto an oil-planked T-pier, and drinks in hand, stroll above black water lightly pushed from a breeze farther out. The clatter and footsteps of those moving ahead seem to echo from landings across the lake a pitch higher, like the tin of old wire or metal that's been spun, and it feels good to be part of a group moving together to see a sight.

Mrs. Cassini is only a strong voice over the others, Sue, a glimpse through the shoulders ahead, and you follow at the edge, skeptical about what you'll find ahead, even though you get that feeling like you're safe behind the BlueLiner's wheel, like nothing bad can come within fifty-six feet.

At the end of the pier everybody looks up. You hear the soft thunk of a wrecker driver's Zippo, his eyes scanning the night above the hands that cup his smoke. Mrs. Boyden and the older man are together again, each with a hand to the brow as if the stars were too bright to consider straight on. Even the boy who might be Tony squints into the night, and the way he absently wipes his hands on his apron makes you see him as of an earlier version of your father, thinking of policies and premiums as he looks to the future, though covered each way for whatever comes.

"I told my husband I wanted to see the new satellite. Then this morning, *over break- fast,* he changes the sweep of its orbit with his laptop," Mrs. Cassini says, and guides us across the sky with her hand. "It'll be coming from Seattle and heading toward Vegas, with enough plutonium to make a glass ashtray of Texas."

Judge Helen coughs.

You look at everyone's faces and you know this is stupid. You can't put a restrain- ing order on a satellite the same way you can't change the path of a tumor. It's stupid to think you can just wave your hand and summons up something that doesn't care about any of us.

"There," Judge Helen says and points back and away from where everyone was looking. They all turn in unison but you.

"Yes," says Sue.

"Of course," says the kid in the apron, with all the battle-battle win optimism of a near-champion, and you look just to prove him wrong, because deep down you want to believe.

Twenty fingers guide you to it. At first it's too much to take in, all those stars. You wish your mother had thrown herself into something the last year of her life, like writ- ing a cookbook or sketching cloudscapes, so that you could make some of those recipes and see how they tasted to her, so you could look up and see what she saw. Overhead, though, is a sky splattered as laughed-up milk, about as shaped as the mass in Mrs. Cassini's belly. Until suddenly you say *of course*. It's that simple. You see it: the green light of the Cassini Satellite ticking its chronometer path toward Vegas. You remember the earth-shot on the Weather Channel and the thought that a satellite couldn't see you but you can see it feels pretty damn good. It makes you want to write *of course* on a ten-dollar bill in red ink.

Mrs. Cassini dives into the ice-cold lake and begins backstroking.

At the end of the pier, you hear Judge Helen whistling the *Blue Danube* and look up to see her balanced on a tall shoring post. She launches, extending, and executes a thunderous jackknife, the crowd throwing up whoops as people begin diving in.

The kid in the apron stands in disbelief, and you walk to him. It's not your father he looks too much like, but yourself. In his hands you place the picture.

"Hold this for me," you tell him. "It's important."

He angles the glass against the light off the lake to see. "Okay," he says.

You slip off your shoes, and barefoot, hop up to balance atop a post. From here you can see no more of the lake, but the women below are clear as they stroke and stretch as if doing rehab exercises. There will always be a reason not to jump in a cold lake, thousands of them, and a certain sense emerges from this. It's like the logic of getting a court order against a husband who spends his evenings watching TV in the basement. It's the desire to control anything you can.

Mrs. Cassini floats on her back in the cold water, facing the sky. She looks at you, then closes her eyes, floating. "I'm twice as alive as you are," she says softly, her voice so vital she almost sounds angry. Some women clap water in the air while others backstroke into deeper water, their arms lifting in graceful salute to a satellite that cannot see us, that for tonight at least, just passes on by.

You jump. One slow tumble in the air that unfolds into a sailor's dive, and you enter with your arms at your sides, chin out, barreling toward the beer caps awaiting below. You hadn't planned on hitting the bottom, but it's somehow not a surprise. The muted rustling of tin, when you make contact, is the exact sound of the BlueLiner's air brakes—the shh of compressed air releasing—and the flash of pain in your eyes is bright enough to fire your irises white.

Surfacing, you can feel the flap on your jaw and the warmth on your throat. You swim to Sue and kiss her, awkwardly, half on the nose.

"Easy there, bus driver," she says and has to smile, just her slick face showing.

"You shouldn't swim with a Hickman port," you say. "You could get an infection and die."

"And that kiss was any safer?"

"I suppose it wasn't much of a kiss."

"I think you gave me a fat lip."

"I can do better."

"Another one like that and I won't need the zoo pass."

"The fishing pole, then."

"Maybe it was the satellite," she says. "All that pressure to perform."

"They're watching us on the Weather Channel right now."

Sue gets a conspiratorial look on her face. "I saw at least three satellites up there. How many did you count?"

You're both treading water, breathing hard between phrases.

"They were fucking *everywhere*," you tell her.

"That Mrs. Cassini. I think the satellite she's talking about is halfway to Saturn."

Sue's treading water with you, and that's a good sign. You know you're going to kiss her again. You have a photo of your mother safe with a friend and a mild case of shock. You're immersed in ice water, losing blood fast, and still you feel an erection coming on, the kind you'd get when you were sixteen, appearing out of nowhere, surprising you with its awkward insistence on the terrifying prospect of joy ahead.

Johnson on Second-Person Point of View

When I was in graduate school, one of my mentors died. He was a person who'd offered me lots of personal wisdom, and I saw him as a model of how to be both confident and humble. One day, it seemed, he was just gone. Over the next couple months, I found it hard to write, and I realized I had to tackle this event in a short story. Looking at it through the cold lens of fiction, it seemed like it would be an easy story to write: a character cares about someone, then that someone disappears, and the character feels like hell. Maybe there'd be a deep epiphany at the end.

When I went to write the story, though, it proved more difficult. First of all, who was I fooling? The "character" wasn't just some character: he was me, or at least he was feeling what I felt, and I felt horrible—there was this hole in my life where a friend and teacher should have been, and it really mattered that I capture that emotion. Right away, I had a problem because my task bordered on nonfiction. I had to create a credible character who would feel exactly what I wanted him to feel. It would be like imagining a perfect friend and then introducing yourself to hundreds of people until you met the one that was already in your head.

One of the joys in life is getting to know another human. After an introduction with a stranger, all you know is a name, but over the course of a dinner or weekend, a full portrait emerges: you find connections, points of divergence, discover coincidences, yet still have the ability to surprise one another. This is also the experience a reader has: a character is met on the first page, and by the last, that character feels like family.

Ideally, this is the experience of the fiction writer as well. Characters, like good friends, have to be discovered and cultivated. There's no worse experience than going to a party, and on the way, your friends tell you all about someone they want you to meet. "Wait till you get a load of Ted," they say. "Ted's a writer, too. And he also grew up in California, where he was an all-state wrestler." You hear about Ted's car and dogs and how he volunteers to help troubled youth, and when you get to the party, you naturally hate Ted. So it is in reading, when a book summarizes the protagonist on the first page. So it is in writing, when the author (me) knows too much about the character.

So, like a fool, I started writing a story about a grad student whose teacher dies. Not only was that first try obvious and uninteresting, it didn't take advantage of the power of fiction: that all the facts of an experience can be changed and rearranged in order to capture the emotional truth of an experience. Plus, I had another problem: my first-person narrator was maudlin. He was mopey and sad, and all he did was complain about how much he missed his friend and how much his heart hurt. Not only did that do a disservice to the real emotion I felt, I plain-old didn't like the narrator of my own story.

I went back to the drawing board and made three changes. First, I lowered the age of the narrator from a 30-year-old graduate student to an 18-year-old headed for college. That made him more vulnerable and increased the reader's threshold for his emotional struggle. Second, instead of a young man struggling with the recent death of a friend, I made him struggle with the more distant death of a mother. The two felt like they had a similar emotional weight, and I was willing to trade the urgency of a recent death for the resignation of a past one. Finally, I interviewed someone who had survived cancer; she described how the value of life increases in the proximity of death, and she tried to explain the utter liberation that comes after you've accepted your own death, but then survive.

I put all these elements in the story, and threw in the Cassini Satellite. I was living in Florida at the time, and there was a controversy about the impending launch of the Cassini space probe, which was powered by 15 kilos of pure plutonium. I was all for a good space probe, but the newspaper said that if anything went wrong with the launch, there was enough radioactivity to give everyone in Florida cancer. The Cassini Satellite, for me, contained all the elements I was looking for: uncertainty and possibility, excitement and danger, randomness and control.

There was only one problem: the narrator still sounded maudlin. In a novel, there's a great deal of context for a character—the reader sees the protagonist in many situations and settings. In a story, however, a character who confesses his emotions for 15 pages seems wholly sentimental. I decided to change point of view to the third person, to gain some distance by having a "professional" narrator reveal the character's feelings for him, but they sounded even worse when discussed. I went back and forth: first to third, third to first, and so on. The American novelist and short story writer, Wallace Stegner once said, "point of view is the lever with which the writer moves the world." I wasn't even moving myself.

Then I tried the second person, and everything seemed to work.

The second person is a wily point of view. The "you" pronoun is difficult to work with because of its strange alchemy in our language: The second person is used to construct the imperative, as in "Come out with your hands up." It's also used, like the pronoun "one," to form general statements, like "You'll never know unless you try," or my favorite from grade school, "You shuffle your feet, you lose your seat." And just to confuse things, "you" is both singular and plural.

In fiction, the second-person point of view is used in a few different ways.

First, when the second person is used as a subject, it can make the reader feel like the agent of action and thus become the central character. This is especially effective when the reader is forced to become an unsavory character who does things most people wouldn't do, like the drug-dealing thug at the heart of Robert O'Connor's second-person novel *Buffalo Soldiers*. Second, when the second person is used as an object, it makes the reader feel like the recipient of action, as when a first-person narrator speaks to a "you" or a letter is written to "you." With the first line, the reader becomes involved in a long-standing yet unknown relationship.

The third use of "you" was the one I was after. The second person, for many people, is the pronoun they use when internally addressing themselves. At a party, when no one laughs at my joke, I'm liable to think, "You idiot. You've got to quit trying so hard or you'll never have any friends." This "you" is a private, unorchestrated voice that others never hear. The first person, on the other hand, is a public, constructed voice. All "I" speakers are aware of an audience, and some degree of their stories—the degree to which they're responsible for their roles in them—is devoted to managing how they're perceived by the reader. This creates an inherent tone of confession and rationalization—the tone that was killing my short story.

But the internal "you" doesn't come with that sense of audience, and therefore doesn't feel confessional. To me, the central character of "The Death-Dealing Cassini Satellite" is a young man whose story is too painful and complicated to tell, even though in his own head, he's telling it over and over. What I tried to create with the second-person point of view was the illusion that, rather than hearing a story, the reader had become privy to a deeply personal narrative that someone would never tell.

Writing Suggestions

1. Write the first scene in a story in which the narrator offers "how to" advice on performing an emotionally difficult situation, such as "How to Leave Your Boyfriend," "How to Lose Your Job," or "How to Survive a First Date." The "you" will be the main character in this scene. How can you, as a writer, combine a set of directions (the imperative usage of "you") with the voice of a second-person narrator, in which the scene not only depicts an important moment but also offers "advice"? How does this narrative style, compared to the narrative expression of first person, change the texture of the writing?

2. Johnson defines yet another use of second-person point of view, the recipient of action, "as when a first-person narrator speaks to a 'you' or a letter is written to 'you.'" Write a story framed as an extended letter in which the narrator (the "I") continually addresses the recipient of the letter ("you"). Before beginning, consider what types of stories lend themselves to the form of a letter. What is a best friend, a girlfriend, or a mother more likely to say in a letter than in person? What confidences or intimacies or emotions are more often revealed in writing than in conversation?

3. Johnson defines the third use of second person as "the pronoun [people] use when internally addressing themselves." Rewrite a scene you've previously written in first person into second person. How does the shift in point of view change the narrator's relationship to the character? Is the story more intimate? Is this particular scene more effective? How might the change in point of view also change the way a reader relates to the story?

4. In Johnson's commentary, he directs us to a novel-length example of second person, Robert O'Connor's *Buffalo Soldiers*. Go to your local library or bookstore and locate two of the following examples of second-person narratives. Notice how each

author uses the second person to a slightly different effect. Use the description in Johnson's commentary to distinguish one type of second-person narrator from another. Which examples do you find most effective? Why?

- "How to Date a Browngirl, Blackgirl, Whitegirl, or Halfie" (short story) in *Drown* by Junot Diaz
- "How to Talk to a Hunter" (short story) in *Cowboys Are My Weakness* by Pam Houston
- "You and the Boss" (short story) in *Slaves of New York* by Tama Janowitz
- *Bright Lights, Big City* (novel) by Jay McInerney
- *Self-Help* (story collection) by Lorrie Moore
- *Buffalo Soldiers* (novel) by Robert O'Connor

> *We need not spell out all the various possibilities of stylistic choice
> . . . it will be enough to simply suggest that each choice of style
> becomes a serious consideration. The writer must decide what
> point of view he will use, what diction level, what "voice," what
> psychic-distance range.*
> —John Gardner

Judith Claire Mitchell

A Man of Few Words

From *Scribner's Best of the Fiction Workshops, 1998*

Only minutes after he died at age seventy-eight Ike Grossbart had come to understand he could enjoy, one more time, a pleasure from his life. It was up to him to choose which pleasure that would be. Ike was surprised and grateful. He had been expecting earthworms and dirt. Instead—or at least first—here was a squirt of whipped cream to top off his time on earth.

He mulled over the various joys and delights he had known. He did not want to choose precipitously. But deciding was difficult, and made even more so by a conversation he'd had only hours before and could not shake from his head.

"Ike, remember the knishes they had at Zalman's in Flatbush?" his brother-in-law had asked. "Wouldn't you love one of those now?"

"One of those now would kill me," Ike had said. His voice was near gone. He'd never imagined he'd use up his voice over the course of his life as if it were ink in a pen. Thank goodness he'd been a man of few words. "All that salt and fat," he managed to rasp. "Anyway, the best knishes were from Dubin's."

"Dubin's?" Ike's daughter asked. "Was I ever there?"

His wife had looked up from her crossword puzzle. She was sitting in the recliner the orderlies had dragged in so she could spend nights in the hospital room. "What are you saying?" she said. "Are you saying the best knishes weren't from Yonah Shlissel's?"

Yonah Shlissel's. Of course. The two men murmured the name out loud, and sighed as if recalling the most beautiful woman they'd ever laid eyes on. It was a sigh of fond remembrance but also of regret. The beautiful woman was long gone, and Ike and his brother-in-law so old they had to be reminded she'd existed at all.

"What made that place so good?" Ike's daughter asked.

"I heard Yonah had a secret ingredient," his wife said. "Once I heard oil imported from the old country. Another time I heard potatoes from some farm out in Jersey."

"Nah, it was water they pumped in special," the brother-in-law said. He was the kind of man who had to let people know he was smarter than they were. Ike had never understood how his sister endured this man's blather. Nevertheless, she had, and so, though his sister was gone, the man remained family.

Ike had shrugged. "All I know is my wife is as usual right. No one matched Yonah Shlissel's potato knishes."

It was a few hours later—the brother-in-law gone home, the daughter in the cafeteria having a late-night snack, the Grossbarts asleep—that death came for Ike. *Yitzchak Ben Moshe*, death sang like a rabbi honoring a congregant by calling him to the pulpit to bless the Torah. Ike left the hospital room quietly, obediently. He was thankful he hadn't been asked to say goodbye to his wife; he could not imagine anything more difficult.

Now he wishes he could ask her advice. She'd been the wise one, the expert on emotions and pleasure and pain. "Life is so full of heartache and loss," she used to say to the kids. "Whenever the chance for happiness comes along, I want you to fill both hands."

Ike's hands are empty. It's not that there's a dearth of pleasures to choose from. He just doesn't know which one to pick. He considers weddings, his own, his son's. He considers Bar Mitzvahs, his own, his son's. Birthday parties, even days with the family at the beach. But knishes keep pushing these memories out of his head.

You are spending far too much energy chasing knishes away, he scolds himself. Don't be so frivolous. Food has always meant far too much to you.

Although he was gaunt when he died, he had the clogged arteries and overburdened heart of a fat man. He had always loved to eat. From growing up poor, he supposed. Columns of gingersnaps, spoonfuls of peanut butter, and the skins of barbecued chickens which he'd pull off the birds and roll in his fingers as if he were rolling a cigarette and then noisily slurp down the way the kids sucked spaghetti.

Jewish food, the food his mother used to make, was his weakness. He once encountered an anti-Semite who called Jews not kikes or sheenies but bagels. You goddamn Jew-bagel, he'd say. Ike had found it hard to take offense. After his second heart attack, only days before, he'd offered the floor nurse five dollars to sneak a bagel to him. I'm at death's door, he thought when she refused, what can it matter? Finally, when neither the nurse nor his wife were looking, his daughter brought him a jumbo deluxe from Weinstein's, the crusts sticky with brown onions and the soft toasted middle smeared with at least an inch of cream cheese. The two of them had shared it. It had been a foolish thing to do. His daughter was already fat enough and just look where it had gotten him. Still, that had been a nice moment, maybe as nice as any.

Can a dead man blush? Apparently, yes. Shame on you, he thinks. He will not go out a glutton, a pig. He'll select a meaningful moment of his life to enjoy again, a memory sweet enough to sustain him through eternity. If now is not the time for meaningful memories, then someone should tell him when is.

Yet as he reflects and ponders he realizes his difficulty in choosing is compounded by the number of precious memories that sustain him already. He has not made love to his wife in fifteen years, for instance, but now, when he thinks of her, he feels sated and sleepy as if they last lay together moments ago. He can taste her mouth, feel her soft, round belly and the breasts that, as if he had been granted a wish by a genie, had grown larger with each of the children she gave him. To seek even one more time with his wife strikes him as greedy and in a way, superfluous. She is with him still. Leave well enough alone, he thinks.

He considers, too, reliving the day his youngest was born—the boy, a son. As the baby came into the world, Ike had paced in the waiting room down the hall. He smoked a few packs of Luckies, ate three or four Hershey Bars. It was what men did in those days. He was glad for it. He had no interest in participating in birth the way fathers had to now—catching the baby, cutting the cord, seeing one's beloved wife open and as red as the meat of a plum. But to go back once again to the waiting room, that might be nice. To hear once again, *Mr. Grossbart, it's a boy.*

Yet just thinking about his son's birth causes the same explosion of pride beneath his ribs that he experienced forty-one years ago. An explosion he had not felt when his daughter had been born seven years prior. An explosion, he now realizes, not all that different from a minor heart attack. *Mr. Grossbart, it's a boy,* and his heart twisted like a wrung dishrag. He felt fear and pain; he felt small and inadequate—mortal. It was as if his body, aware that his head and his tongue were too stunned to thank God in words, began to express his awe and gratitude through trembling and aching and terror. And then, as if God heard and responded to his body's prayer—for that's what it had been, a prayer spoken by flesh and bones—Ike's heart had been soothed. Comfort and hope and optimism had rested on his shoulder like a reassuring hand.

It was the most powerful moment of his life. Perhaps for that reason he does not want to live it again. If his son could overhear these thoughts, Ike knows, he would feel only rejection. He would resent Ike's decision to choose a different moment to return to. He would not understand the love in this decision.

Other good days—the birth of his chubby, uncomplicated daughter, the day Hitler got his, the morning in the middle of the Depression when Ike found a twenty on a subway platform—none of those other good days have faded for him, either.

He is getting nervous now. What if there is only so much time in which to choose? Maybe a buzzer will go off soon. An egg timer might ring. He racks his brain. It's still full of knishes. Perhaps, he thinks, there's a reason for this.

So at last he decides, why not? Why not choose a Yonah Shlissel knish? That overstuffed pillow, yellow as gold, salty as sea air. Why not choose to relive the simplest pleasure of all? He'll have a knish, but before he does, he'll bow his head, recite the proper blessing so God will know he is thankful for even small pleasures. And then he will call it a day.

The Lower East Side has been given over to colored people. West Africans and Haitians and Jamaicans, dark-skinned Cubans. The buildings shake from drumming and radios and languages. The sidewalk is broken, and the street with its potholes resembles the soles of a poor man's shoes.

When Ike was a boy, the air here smelled of garlic pickles and sauerkraut. Now the air reeks from fumes expelled by idling delivery trucks and city buses. When Ike was a boy, the stores here sold felt derbies and fresh fish and used books. Now they sell knock-off designer sneakers, vinyl leather jackets, and T-shirts with dirty sayings across the front.

This is why he has avoided the area for decades. He feels discouraged now that he's here, a little down-hearted as he keeps walking east. He thinks about the other, better choices he could have made—even the day Kennedy squeaked by Nixon might have been better, even the first time he watched TV he felt more excitement. How about his first car, the gray Plymouth, that boat.

Then suddenly, his feet stop short. If he'd been the Plymouth, his brakes would have squealed.

"*Kinehora*," he whispers.

He is standing in front of Yonah Shlissel's. It's there—here—right where he left it, right where it ought to no longer be.

His no-good heart pounds. He hesitates. In his head, he counts to three, and on three he pulls open the dark heavy door. He steps tentatively into a vestibule with a wooden slat bench used not for sitting but for piling. Even now it's covered with stacks of Jewish newspapers and political pamphlets. He takes a breath. With a trembling hand, he turns the mock crystal knob of the next heavy door. He steps inside. It's the same. It's Yonah's.

If earlier that day his wife had challenged him to describe Yonah Shlissel's, Ike would have replied that he couldn't remember what he'd had that morning for breakfast, much less the interior of a restaurant he last saw fifty years ago. But seeing it now, he knows every detail is one hundred percent correct. The wooden floors, scuffed and warped. The round wooden tables, each with a waiter's pad shoved beneath one leg to quiet its rocking. He remembers that—yes—there were no windows, yes, the place was dimly lit, yes, the waiters ran about in clean white aprons and confided the customers' orders to Yonah in the kitchen as if they were passing along government secrets.

Is it an illusion? A gag? Ike knows hair continues to grow after death, but do dreams continue to spin? He reaches for one of the mints in the bowl by the cash register and chews it cautiously. It's stale. It tastes more like soap than mint. It's the same as ever. The mints, at least, are real.

And now here comes the frowsy, fat hostess in her polka-dot dress. She wears a brown wig meaning she is married, this battle-ax, maybe to Yonah himself. In those days the married women covered their hair when they went out in public. He'd nearly forgotten, but now he remembers and remembers, also, his mother's wig. He remembers it suddenly, fondly, and then with tears that shine but don't fall. His mother's wig also was brown, always askew, and so cheap he could see the stitches holding the strands to its net crown.

"Party of, what, only one?" The fat woman is annoyed. Ike remembers this woman now as clearly as he remembers the wobbly tables and soapy mints. When he was a child she frightened him. Now he is a 78-year-old dead man and she still gives him the heebie-jeebies.

Why is she so aggravated with him? Did his wish to return here disturb her own rest? Had she been forced to rouse herself, stretch her bare bones, tunnel up through six feet of beetles and ruin, all the while bobby-pinning that wig to her head, just so she could get to Yonah's in time to seat him, this negligible party of one?

"Poppa, why are they so grouchy here?"

"Did we come to make friends or have lunch?"

Yes, Ike thinks. Yes, he is only one. Yes, he's alone. We come in alone, go out the same way. God knows he wishes that wasn't how it worked. God knows already he misses his wife, wishes she were at his side. Or no, he doesn't wish that. That would be wishing her dead. He wishes he knew what one had the right to wish for under these circumstances. He might have wished not to go back into his life but forward into his death where his loved ones who'd left him might be waiting.

He says nothing, of course. He is too shy to speak, too tongue-tied. And what would be the point of philosophizing with Mrs. Shlissel? The woman has been dead at least half a century. To her nothing he could say about death would be news. To him every-thing about death—even the fact of it—is a revelation. It came as a shock. Of course all the time he knew. All his life he knew everyone gets old, sick, dies. It wasn't exactly top secret. But somehow all along he figured nobody really meant *him*. Not him, not little Yitzchak Grossbart. But of course, that's just who they meant. The proof was in the pudding. Here was little Yitzchak Grossbart standing in a building demolished dur-ing the Korean conflict talking away in his head to a fat dead lady.

She does not even look at him. She waddles to an empty table near the counter intending for him to follow. As he does he thinks that today a woman with such a rump would never wear that skinny cloth belt nor those big white polka dots. His daughter always wore big shirts that skimmed her tush, covered the thighs, and always they were black. "Am I ever going to see you in anything but mourning rags?" he'd once heard his wife ask. A similar comment would have hurt his son's feelings, but his daughter had laughed and said she liked to be comfortable and that black didn't show dirt. Maybe he should have said something then. He didn't mind a girl with a fanny on her. But it had not seemed proper. It had not seemed like something a father should say.

A waiter comes, places a wooden bowl filled with slices of bread—seeded rye, black pumpernickel, braided challah—onto the table. "You need time?" the waiter asks. Ike nods. He needs time.

He cranes his neck so he can see the long cases beneath the counter. A wall of food under glass. Kishka, kasha, kugel. Herring. Greek olives, black and wrinkled like the skin on the hands of the old man sweeping the floors. Lox as pink as flamingo, gefilte fish pocked and slimy, and rows of white fish still sheathed in their gold scales, their dead eyes like opals. And, then, in another case, meat. The salami and franks, the corned beef and pastrami, the tongue. Agents of death all looking as benign as a school-boy twiddling his thumbs.

The knishes have an entire compartment to themselves not in respect of any dietary law, but rather the same way royalty is given a private box in the concert hall.

Ike sighs. He truly is at Yonah Shlissel's again. It's a miracle and a blessing. It was, he thinks, a pretty good choice. It reminds him of his boyhood, his father, even of something his daughter had said when she'd split that bagel with him. She'd been violating not only the rules of his diet that day, but the rules of her own as well. She was perpetually starving herself, that one, never with any discernable results. She'd inherited his appetite and God knows whose metabolism.

"I'm so bad," she had said, but it was clearly a fine moment for her, maybe the moment she'd return to someday. She'd rolled her eyes and licked her fingers. "Oh, God," she'd said. "I've died and gone to Heaven."

His time is up; the waiter is back, tapping pencil against pad. "I haven't got all day, Mister," he says. "You want to order before it's tomorrow?"

Ike remembers the waiter now, too. Abrupt and arrogant. A Shlissel for sure. Always acting like there's somewhere more important he has to rush off to.

"Pardon me," Ike says. "One potato knish."

The waiter scurries off. Ike looks around at the other customers. Are they props, are they real men, or are they his comrades, other dead Jews who have chosen Yonah's? They are mostly old men, he sees. Many of them are reading *The Forward*. The newspapers smudge their fingers and conceal their faces. It's from seeing their hands that Ike knows the men are old. Brown spots stain old hands the way rust stains old cars.

When they were youngsters, he and his sister had called such hands old lady hands. Old lady hands, as if a man's hands never withered, never wrinkled, never became bent and blue with veins. After a bath, he and his sister would show their wrinkled, pruney fingers to each other. His sister's singsong taunt: *Yitzchak's got old lady hands.*

He'd held her old lady hands when she died. She'd passed a decade ago, beaten by the same ailment that got him years later . . . minutes earlier. A heart whose muscles sagged from working too hard for so many years until it could no longer beat, and slowly came to a stop. It was how hearts were designed, like old-fashioned windup toys.

He had held her hands and thought about singing her song back to her: *Look now who's got old lady hands.* Not as a taunt, of course. More like a lullaby. He hoped she'd remember the time they were so young they could bathe naked together, laugh at old age. *Wisenheimer,* she'd maybe have whispered. *Ishkabibble.* These were the worst things she'd ever called him. Much nicer than asshole, which is what his son used to call his daughter when she teased him too hard.

Ike had not sung to his sister. Something had stopped him. He'd worried she might not have remembered. It would have been terrible had she taken it wrong. So he'd kept quiet. What does one say at such moments? Is anyone so wise they know? Certainly not Ike, not someone like Ike. As his sister passed on, he squeezed her hands and thought, She looks so much like Mama. This had comforted him. Anyone in Heaven who took one look at his sister would know just who to direct her to.

Again there are tears in his eyes. He is able to blink them away. He tells himself to stop. You are squandering your moment, he thinks. It's supposed to be a moment of pleasure.

So he focuses on the task at hand. He prepares for the meal to come. He gets up, goes to the sink in the corner of the restaurant, washes his hands. In his own home he and his wife were never so observant, but here it seems fitting. He returns to his table and tears a piece of challah. He considers his life. He'd lived it as right as he knew how.

He loved his wife, had a daughter who was good-natured and smart, had a beloved son he could name after his father. He had grief and loss; he had modest pleasures and joys. He never would have asked for more but now he has been given more, just a little bit more. He recites the blessing for bread.

Twice a year his father took him to Delancey Street to buy a new suit. Once in the fall for Rosh Hashanah; again in the spring for Pesach. And then after, as a reward for not bellyaching during the fitting, his father would take him to Yonah Shlissel's. Just the two of them, father and son, twice a year. Just the men in the family.

Like the old men here now, his father hid behind a newspaper. Ike, six or seven, pretended the paper was a shield that made persons on either side of it invisible and invincible.

Six or seven, he ate his knish with his fingers. He peeled the thin crust apart and then, like the boy in the nursery rhyme, he stuck in his thumb. But he did not pull out a plum. He merely pulled out that same thumb coated with hot mashed potato. Nor did he say, What a good boy am I! He knew this was not something a good boy would do. He would not have done this in front of his mother. But his father, absorbed, never noticed.

His table manners were never what they should have been. He was the child of immigrants, unschooled and unsophisticated. If he'd grown up during his son's era instead of his own, he'd have blamed this shortcoming on his father. *I'd stick my thumb into a knish and you wouldn't say boo; how was I supposed to learn better? No wonder I was never asked to join a fancy men's eating club.*

No one cares about table manners at Yonah Shlissel's. Everyone here slurps, sighs, grunts, belches. We are descendants of peasants, Ike thinks not without pride. Children of immigrants, adventurers, survivors. And this is our reward for feeling no shame. This place of our people. This wonderful repast. Manna from Yonah's. Something his children have never tasted, will never taste.

His daughter would have loved it here. She would have run about, pressing her nose to the glass cases. *What's that? What's that? Let's try some of this.* He never brought her here, though he remembers one time taking her to that same children's clothing shop. His son was an infant with the croup, the Holy Days were around the corner, and the girl needed a new dress. Ike remembers sitting in a chair feeling useless and bored while his daughter emerged from the dressing room in one matronly purple dress after another, baby fat distorting the lines of each one, her head lowered—sulking only emphasized the double chins—and the saleslady shaking her head. "She has a bit of a belly, doesn't she?" the woman had said, and Ike had shrugged.

By the time his son was old enough both the clothing shop and Yonah Shlissel's were gone. It didn't matter. His son would have despised Delancey Street. His son despised his own heritage. It was too bad, then, that it had been his son who inherited Ike's face, the same face Ike had inherited from his own father. The huge ears that winged from the head and had been ridiculed even during Gable's heyday. The narrow horned beak rising between bushy brows, bestowing a cross-eyed and angry appearance. Those three faces repeated generation to generation had proclaimed, probably too loudly, their lineage. Those faces had gotten each of them beaten up, one time or another, by tough Catholic boys in prim navy blue uniforms.

Still, it had never occurred to Ike to try to change his face. He'd never really tried to change much about himself. When he married his wife he had warned her. He was not a plant who, with water and sunlight, would bloom and grow into a flowering thing of beauty. He was a homely hard-working, straightforward man who felt silly saying honeybunch or sweetiepie. He called his wife *fleegle*—Yiddish for chicken wing.

His son believed in change. His son changed his name from Grossbart to Garner. Then he changed his religion. "So what should we call him now?" Ike had asked his wife, "Mahatma Garner?" His son had changed even his face. His son had his ears pasted back. He had his nose shaved and trimmed as if it were a mustache rather than hard bone and cartilage.

The boy had shown up at their house one Sunday modeling the new face for them, preening like a woman in a hat. Ike had said nothing. He left the kitchen, shut the bedroom door with more noise than required. "It's my money," the boy hollered after him. "My face."

Ike lay on his bed, turned on a ball game with the remote. He closed his eyes.

He didn't object to the way his son spent his money. But the rest of what his son had hollered up at him . . . how could the boy think his face belonged to him only? When his son studied his new reflection, whose child did he see?

When his wife joined him in bed that night, Ike said, "You know, *fleegle*, sometimes, I catch a glimpse of myself in a mirror when I don't expect to, and I think, 'Hey, that guy looks like a member of my family.' I like that. I take pleasure in being from this family." A veritable speech, an outburst.

His wife had said, "And why are you telling this to me?"

"There's a point in telling him?" Ike never mentioned it again. He said nothing about it even though it hurt to look at that face. Revised, his son looked not like a Grossbart, not like a Garner, not like a Jew or the Hindu he claimed to be, but like an owl with a big round head, angry yellow brown eyes and, lost in the middle, a tiny snipped beak.

And yet, in the end, it was the boy who refused to look at Ike. During those terrible months after the boy's marriage ended and he'd moved back home, he refused to sit at the same table with Ike.

It was his table manners the boy objected to. "It's disgusting," Ike heard his son say. "He just sits there and shovels it in. No wonder he can't make conversation, with his mouth stuffed like that. It makes me sick. I'll eat in my room."

Like a servant, Ike's wife carried the boy's plate—the boy; the boy was thirty-six—up to his old bedroom where once again he was living, holed up like a hermit, the room a mess as it had been when he truly was a boy, all his clothes on the floor, dirty Kleenexes and rotted banana peels overflowing the trash basket, and the mattress he slept on bare, not a sheet, not even a pad, and yet this was where he wanted to be. Sometimes he did not come out for days, at least not while Ike was awake.

Sometimes the creak of floorboards, the snap of a light switch woke Ike before sunrise. He lay in bed and told himself that another father would get out of bed and go downstairs. Another father would pull up a chair, pour two strong drinks, get the kid to open up. *Talk to me, son, tell me what's wrong.* But after that, what does one say at such a time? Besides, as the father of this boy, Ike knew getting up and going downstairs would be futile. There was nothing anyone could say to this boy. Not even Ike's wife knew what to say. She'd say, "You want at least a mattress pad, honey?" and the kid would look at her like she'd accused him of child murder.

Ike had been grateful for whatever snippets of time his father had managed to give him. At Yonah Shlissel's, Ike sucked potato off his thumb. He blew air through his straw turning his glass of celery tonic into a bubbling cauldron. His father said nothing. Ike balanced on two legs of his chair and worked up some jokes, the funniest being a variation of an old one which, to set the stage, he now told his father. "Hey, Poppa." A grunt. "Poppa, what's black and white and red all over?" "What?" his father asked, still hidden behind the newspaper shield. Ike gave the answer. He gave it loud so his voice would penetrate newsprint and Yiddish. "A newspaper." "Mmm-hmmm," his father said. "Hey, Poppa." His father grunted. "Hey, Poppa. Over all red and white and black is what?" A second grunt. "The Jewish newspaper," Ike said. "Get it? On account of you read it backwards."

"Very good," his father said. "Be quiet. Eat your knish."

Whenever Ike felt sad because his father was not conversing with him, was not asking about school or laughing at Ike's jokes or telling a few of his own, then Ike would think the following: *the two men shared a companionable silence.*

From what radio show or dime novel he had gotten that phrase, he had no idea. But it made him feel better to think it. It was the way men behaved together. Not like his sister and mother who babbled endlessly, clucking chickens. Not like women. Men shared companionable silences.

But the silence he shared with his son had not been so companionable, and he thinks now of his grown son returned to the narrow bed of childhood where he keened like a lost goat, cried to Ike's wife what a terrible father Ike had been. Distant, his son wailed. Withholding.

Like a drill his son's voice bore through the walls of the house Ike had worked his whole life to pay off. Like a jackhammer, the voice of his son—his heir, his devisee— shattered walls into splintery fragments. It made Ike hate the house. It made him see it as flimsy and cheap. "He never played catch with me," Ike's son wept. Crash, a wrecking ball knocking down plaster. "He never took me fishing." Boom, a sledgehammer punching holes in the framing. "He never talked to me about women. How was I supposed to know what to do when Dinah got so unhappy?" Thirty-six and bleating like a goat. "Never once did he say he loved me."

"He's angry?" Ike asked when his wife came to bed.

"At the world," she said. "Don't take it personal."

"Did your parents ever say they loved you, *fleegle*?"

"I'd have dropped dead twice from shock, *fleegle*." She hesitated. "But since he wants to hear it, what could it hurt?"

He couldn't sleep. Had his own father ever tossed him a ball, ever taken him fishing? And he could only thank God his father had never talked to him about women. It would have been excruciating for both of them. His son had seen too many TV fathers on the TV sets Ike had bought through the years, the black-and-white consoles, the big screen colors, the miniatures you could hold in your hand as you lay on your naked mattress and bleated like a goat. Fathers in ties spouting philosophy whispered into their pasted ears by a team of professional writers.

Nobody fed Ike dialogue. Growing up nobody fed him delusions. His father had been too busy working double shifts in a factory to be a television father. A teacher in Poland, in Brooklyn Ike's father worked in a dye factory. He came home late and exhausted and his fingernails were tinted blue as the summer sky.

Ike got out of bed. He knocked on his son's bedroom door. No response. He went in anyway. "You really don't know I love you?" he asked. "I know I'm not the father you wanted, but you have to at least know I love you. You have to know that. You're my only son."

"How does a person know what he's never been told?" his son had said. His unfamiliar face was pressed into a bare pillow with a small tear in the side. Little white feathers floated from it, lighthearted and comical.

By the color of fingernails, Ike wanted to say. But he did what he had come to do. "I love you," he said.

"Too little too late," said his son.

The next time Ike saw his daughter, he felt obliged to ask her if she knew he loved her. She shivered and said, "Oh, Pop, please don't." She brought up the time he'd taken her to Delancey for that dress. "Remember how that heinous saleslady kept harping about how fat I was?" she said. She reddened a little. Ike was not sure if she was embarrassed or angry on behalf of the chubby little girl modeling purple. "And I was so miserable," she said, "until finally you jumped up and picked out that beautiful ivory smock with the shirred bodice and scalloped hem? And I remember thinking, My father knows how to make me look pretty. My father knows what I look like. No one else in this world saw me the way you did. That's how you told me you loved me."

Ike tried to remember the day. He remembered the chair he sat in, he remembered checking the clock on the wall, he remembered the ball game he wanted to get home for, to watch on TV.

"It was such a special moment for me," his daughter said, still red-faced, a girlish blush. "Really, the best. I have that dress still. Can you believe it? In a box in an attic, the way some women preserve their wedding gowns." She was looking at him smiling, expecting something.

"Still, I hope someday you get married," Ike said.

It was a nice speech she made. Maybe she'd make the same speech over his grave. Later that same day his memory finally dredged up the dress. He'd been impatient. He wanted to get home to that ball game, to his new baby boy. The ivory dress was the only one left on the rack she hadn't already tried on and rejected.

At last. The waiter has placed the knish before him. It sits on a pristine white plate. It glistens with oil. Ike pierces the center with the tines of his fork. From the pricks in its belly come perfume and heat.

He cuts off a piece with the side of his fork, carries it up to his lips. It is steaming. It is too hot to eat. He blows on it. His breath is not yet chill enough to cool it.

He could have brought the girl here. The day they picked out the dress, Yonah Shlissel's had still been standing. They could have walked here, her dimpled hand in his, and he could have bought her one of these potato dumplings, could have called her potato dumpling, a little joke between the two of them. He could have told her jokes.

It had never crossed his mind. Yonah Shlissel's had been for the men in the family. It had not crossed his mind. There was a ball game on TV he wanted to watch. He was waiting to take the boy. By the time the boy was old enough, Yonah Shlissel's was gone.

The boy would have hated it anyway. Even had he brought the boy here, the boy never would have returned on his own, certainly would not be here now.

Ike blows again on the knish. He thinks, I had a boy who heard nothing in silence that was rich with meaning, and a girl who heard everything in silence that was nothing but silence. Which child was more foolish?

Which child, he wonders, was he? He remembers visiting his own father weeks before the old man's death. His daughter, a teenager then, had come along. His father who lived in a not-so-hot neighborhood had complained he couldn't sleep. "It's the *blue-ers*," he grumbled. "Up all night playing their radios."

"What's that, a *blue-er*?" Ike's daughter had asked.

"Well, you can't call them *shvartzers* anymore," his father said. "They know what it means."

The girl had smiled. "We'll buy you ear plugs," she'd said. "You can't stop people from playing music. You know what God says. Make a joyful noise unto the Lord."

"He says, too, 'be silent and know that I'm God.'"

Ike had considered engraving those words on his father's headstone. He is certain the pleasure his father chose to reclaim had been silence. Perhaps the late hour when the kids on the street finally turned off their music. That moment of peace before sleep comes. Ike knows at least this much—his father had not returned here to the site of their twice-yearly father and son lunches. He has already scanned the room for blue fingernails, hoping, finding none.

In the reverent quiet of Yonah Shlissel's, Ike puts down his fork. It chimes when it touches the wooden table. The waiter looks up, comes over as if summoned. "Something wrong with your knish, mister?"

Ike gestures for the waiter to lean closer. "I think I made the wrong choice," Ike whispers.

The waiter clearly has never before heard such a thing. He frowns. "You can never go wrong with a Yonah Shlissel potato knish," he tells Ike.

"I completely agree, but I think maybe still I want something else."

"What do you mean something else? You already ordered."

Ike wishes again he knew the rules of wishing. Who makes the rules? Is there someone he can talk to? What is the point—this is what he wants to know—what point is there in experiencing again a joy from a life now complete? Better, one should be able to return and rectify an error. One should be allowed to meet with departed loved ones, brainstorm, figure out how to improve things for the grandchildren. Better yet, one should be able to hover over loved ones still living and guide them a little.

If he could do that, he'd return to his son, steer him towards simple pleasures. He is concerned that the boy will have no pleasurable moment to return to someday.

Not true, Ike thinks. He remembers his son as a child—baseball games, roller skates, Schwinns, picnics. Pleasure after pleasure. Sitting in sunlight. If Ike had made a mistake, it was not his failure to shout his love. It was his failure to teach the boy how to say, "Boy, oh boy, that sun feels good on the back, doesn't it?"

Now a short man, a bald-headed man in a stained apron is walking Ike's way. He is muscular and sweaty, a man with glittering eyes and a scowl, someone who, despite his scant height, Ike would not wish to anger or fight.

"I hear you don't like my food," the man says.

Yonah Shlissel, Ike thinks. He has never laid eyes on Yonah Shlissel before. He is in awe. It's like meeting a celebrity—Joe DiMaggio striding up to your table. At the same time, there's a part of him wanting to laugh. He is picturing the Shlissel family, this stunted chef, the fat woman in polka dots, the crotchety waiter.

"It's not that I don't like your food," Ike says. "God knows it's not that. It's just that I was thinking I need to be somewhere else."

"What, you got an appointment with Roosevelt to bring world peace?"

Ike shrugs, tries to smile as if he and Yonah were pals, joking.

"You got a cure for the common cold maybe? You have to run and share it with all of mankind?"

"You're the one with the cure for the common cold," Ike says. He means to be ingratiating, disarming. "Your matzo ball soup, right?"

It works. Yonah softens. "So, just to make conversation, where do you think you should be instead of my place?"

"There's this kid's clothing store around here," Ike says. "Somewhere near here. My daughter is trying on dresses. Or will be. Or might be. I don't know. I got to go there in case. I need to hand her an ivory smock."

"She can't pick out a smock herself?"

"She's a kid. She needs me to find it for her. She doesn't have the sense of herself that I do. You know what I mean."

Yonah shakes his head. "I'm not one for fashion. I'm a cook, plain and simple." He is considering. Then he says, "You'd rather hand a kid a dress than eat my food?"

"I want to see the look on her face," Ike says. "I want to say how pretty she looks."

At that Yonah laughs. It is not an especially pleasant laugh.

"All right, all right," Ike says. "You're right. It would never come out of this mouth. I've never been Mr. Smooth. But I want at least to look at her like . . ."

He wants to look at her with love this time. He doesn't want his daughter to end up the foolish one. But Yonah's laughter has made Ike self-conscious. He can't think. Words stop coming into his head. He can't form the thought. Just sits there and feels it and doesn't know how to say it.

Yonah sighs. "The customer," he says, "is not always right." He takes the white plate back to the kitchen.

Ike sits very still, not sure what to do next, aware that now he has nothing.

Then the waiter returns with two packages—white butcher paper, a bit oily, tied with red-and-white string, the kind of string that came wrapped around the box when Ike's wife brought bakery cake as a present for friends.

"From Mister Shlissel," the waiter says. He sounds crabby and put-upon. "Potato knish to go. He says you should give one to your daughter, she should know how good they are."

The waiter holds the packages out to Ike. Ike takes one in each hand.

Out on Delancey Ike walks past stores and loitering youth. He doesn't remember the name of the dress shop. Pinsky's, he thinks. Maybe Pincus's. He's not sure if he will find it or when or where. He has no idea what time it is, whether he sat in Yonah's for minutes or decades. He doesn't know what else to do now but walk. It's a nice enough day. The smell of the gift-wrapped knishes he carries is stronger than the bus fumes. The smell of good simple food envelops him. The promise of tasting it sometime soon gives him the strength to go on forever.

Mitchell on Third-Person Limited Point of View

Shortly before he died at the age of 78, my father began talking to ghosts. I don't mean that he attended séances or claimed that banshees were rattling chains in his hospital room. What I mean is he had animated conversations with people who were, according to documents on file with various state coroners, no longer living. Nevertheless, it was clear that, despite their bona fides, these dead people were as real to my father as the doctors and nurses wandering in and out of his room were to me. And just as I saw no reason to doubt the existence of a solemn nurse, so I saw no reason to doubt that my Uncle Seymour, officially dead since the early seventies, was standing next to my father's IV drip, smoking a cigarette because my father kept telling him to put it out.

The father I knew was a gentle soul, a good provider, devoted to his family. At the same time, he was almost pathologically taciturn, the kind of man who rarely initiated conversation, the kind of man who never expressed his emotions. Although, perhaps "never" is not strictly accurate; he once actually did use the word "love" in relation to me. This was in another hospital, when he'd just woken from a triple bypass to find me sitting at the foot of his bed. "Poor Judy," he said then, still woozy from anesthesia, so not quite himself. "Her father has never said he loved her."

Ten years later, my father had still never told me he loved me, but while his inability to discuss his feelings hadn't changed, other things had. For one, surgery could no longer offer him a few more years with us. For another, while I was once again sitting at the foot of his hospital bed, he was no longer musing about things he might have said to me. In fact, he no longer saw me at all.

While I conferred with the nurses, my father conversed with those ghosts. I never saw them, never heard them speak. Still, I knew they were there because my father talked to them with visible pleasure and uncharacteristic animation. He hung on to their every word. He made eye contact with them. That's how I knew my Aunt Hannah who died before I was born was sitting in a chair I might have otherwise described as being piled high with magazines. That's how I knew Uncle Seymour was standing by that IV drip, puffing up a storm.

Hospital psychosis, I was told. Something about confinement in a hospital causes patients to hallucinate wildly.

I didn't want to know that this was a predictable syndrome with a medical name. The truth is that I loved this time with my father. I loved seeing his face light up, loved hearing him chatter with his siblings. I'd never seen this side of him, didn't know the guy had it in him.

Of course, what I was really doing was waiting for my turn, waiting to see if my father would light up when my own childish ghost toddled into the room. But it turned out I was waiting in vain. Not once did my father engage with the ghost of Judy-past. Even though I was his first-born child, his only daughter, even though there I was, sitting right at the foot of his bed—not once, as far as he was concerned, did I enter that room.

One of the best things about being a writer is that you get to write the stories you want to read. And so, shortly after my father died, I wrote a story that takes place in a world where it's never too late for a father to tell his daughter he loves her. And I didn't write it from the point of view of that daughter, either. I already knew her story. It was the father's story I wanted to understand. But here was a man who wouldn't express himself, couldn't speak for himself. He needed my help. And, so, limited third person it was. My story would be limited to the perspective of one character.

When I sit down to write a first draft of a story I rarely ponder craft issues. Instead, I just start banging away at the keyboard. When I hit upon a first sentence that sounds right to my ears, rather than worrying about matters of tone or pacing or voice or narrative arcs or point of view, I focus all my energy on coming up with a second sentence that sounds right. Getting that second sentence, and then the third, is hard enough without throwing actual *thinking* into the mix. And that's what happened when I sat down to write "A Man of Few Words." I just plunged in.

It's only later, sometimes during revision, oftentimes not until the story is published, that I'm willing to analyze why I wrote it the way I did. Even then, I rarely analyze my own work unless I'm asked a specific question by a student or a reader or the editor of a creative writing textbook. But once asked, even though my choices were instinctive, intuitive, I usually find those choices fairly easy to justify or at least to explain. When a story works, it's because we've stumbled upon the right way to tell it. I think—I hope—that's what happened here.

Why didn't I write this story in first person, for instance? Well, the most compelling reason is fairly obvious. Basically, you can't describe your main character as being a man of few words and then have him blither on for a dozen pages or so. The general lesson? Limited third is a great point of view when your character is unable to tell his own story for whatever reason. Perhaps your character is shy like mine. Perhaps he's obnoxious. Or Russian. If this character's story is going to be told in a way that isn't tongue-tied or rudely off-putting or Cyrillic, he will probably need your help. Limited third is the way to offer that help.

But even had my story been titled "A Charming Man Who Never Shut Up for A Blessed Second," I wouldn't have opted for a first-person narrator. That's because my story is essentially a fantasy, a fable, a fairy tale, and fantasies, fables, and fairy tales are traditionally told in third person. Using that voice, the voice of the story-teller, gave the story a "once upon a time" aura. Because readers are used to, and therefore accepting, of a third-person narrator intoning, "Once upon a time there lived (or, in this case there died) a man who was granted one wish," it makes it easier, I think, for readers to buy into a dead guy wandering around heaven, learning nice little life lessons.

Which leads us to another reason I went with third rather than first, namely, that my main character is dead from the get-go. Now, I'm not saying you can't write a story in first person, dead. Alice Sebold did just that in *The Lovely Bones,* when she allowed a fourteen-year-old murder victim to tell her own story. Still, Sebold's feat notwith-standing, permitting a dead narrator to natter on about his or her adventures in heaven is a choice fraught with peril. One false move and your story becomes hopelessly senti-mental or clunkily gimmicky. In my case, I instinctively ran from both the challenges and the potential distractions of a story told by an angel. Relaying Ike Grossbart's tale through the matter-of-fact voice of a detached third-person narrator minimized the chances of my writing an overly precious story. That's because third person provides an intermediary voice, a more objective sensibility to put forth the main character's story.

So (I now realize) those are some of the reasons I went third, not first. But why third *limited?* Why not third-person objective, where we view each scene from a dis-tance? Why not third-person omniscient, where we are privy to the insights of a num-ber of characters?

Again, in my case, the Whole Truth is that I never consciously weighed the pros and cons of those options. Looking back now, I see that I was automatically reject-ing choices that wouldn't have worked for this particular story. This story clearly belongs to my main character, Ike. Accordingly, we don't need to know what the other characters are thinking. It doesn't matter, for example, why Ike's waiter is so arrogant. In fact, it doesn't even matter if Ike's waiter is a real person or just a vision produced by the last few flickers of Ike's fading synapses. Nor do readers need an omniscient narrator to explain the significance of these events: are Ike's perceptions accurate and how do they fit in with the greater scheme of things? Like so many short stories, this story is about a single individual's journey. All that matters are the steps that Ike, and only Ike, takes as he walks along the cracked sidewalks of his par-ticular heaven.

Here are some general principles of how third-person limited works: the narrator allows readers to see the story through the experience of one—and only one—charac-ter. The narrator also has a consistent and intimate relationship with the main char-acter and sticks to him like glue until the story is finished.

A story I discuss in workshops to exemplify limited third to my students is Tobias Wolff's "Bullet in the Brain." In that story, a book critic named Anders (and we know Anders is going to be a jackass the moment we learn what he does for a living) cannot resist ridiculing the hackneyed patter of two armed bank robbers, one of whom expresses his dislike for Ander's unsolicited review by shooting Anders in the head. This is how the story begins:

Anders couldn't get to the bank until just before it closed, so of course the line was endless and he got stuck behind two women, whose loud, stupid conversation, put him in a murderous temper. He was never in the best of tempers anyway, Anders—a book critic known for the weary, elegant savagery with which he dispatched almost everything he reviewed.

The story is told in limited third person; that is, everything is filtered through the sensibilities of our jaded protagonist. My students always understand that this is the perfect choice, point-of-view-wise, even if they can't articulate why. But they get it, they know that with such an unlikeable character a first-person narrative would have quickly grown oppressive, that like the murderous bank robber, the reader would not have been willing to put up with Ander's contemptuous voice for long. They recognize that the third-person narrative allows a more modulated, somewhat more reasonable, certainly a more poetic, voice to tell us the story. Meanwhile, the limited part of third-person limited keeps the story focused on Anders alone. Wolff never tells us anything that Anders himself doesn't know at least on some subconscious level. And yet, because this is third person, not first, Wolff is able to explore that subconscious, to clue us in on things that Anders would never willingly reveal to us. Wolff can even tell us about the tender memories Anders has long suppressed.

But enough about Tobias Wolff. Let's get back to me. The story I told you at the beginning of this essay—first person, daughter—may seem to be about my father, but in truth it was all about me: what I saw, what I felt, what I longed for as my father lay dying. My guess is that if my father had written about his own last days, his story would have differed significantly from mine. He might have gone for omniscient third so he could have told us not only his own thoughts, but also the thoughts of all those ghosts in the room. And if, say, the nurse had written the story, maybe she'd have opted for first person so she could report on other deaths she'd witnessed over the years. Or—who knows—maybe she'd have written a second-person story that began, "You're the most dedicated nurse in the world and all anyone ever says to you is, 'Your name's Canary?'"

Which speaks to the fact that there is no right or wrong point of view, per se. Each point of view choice offers certain options, certain benefits to both the story and its writer. Each point of voice choice allows a story to examine its characters and events from different perspectives, different angles.

But along with this, at times, I find dogmatic advice helpful as well: Figure out the story you want to write and before long, with luck and perseverance, it will become clear how it ought to be told.

So here's the lesson I really want to impart: learn to see and then to listen to the ghosts who come to your writing room. All our rooms are filled with them. The ghosts of our younger selves and the selves we imagine we will someday be; the ghosts of our lovers, our friends, our children; the ghosts of the future we dream of or dread; the ghosts haunting our imaginations, dwelling in our hearts, whispering in our ears; the ghosts tempting us, inviting us, sometimes begging us to tell their stories; the benevolent ghosts, the frightening ghosts, our guardian angels, our demons. Listen to them and then you'll know how to tell all your stories, because it's those ghosts who are the arbiters of point of view. And that, in the end, is the most important lesson I share with my students. And that is also the last, generous lesson I learned from a father who, though he never said so, loved me plenty.

Although, he did say so that one time, didn't he? "Poor Judy," he said. That was my dad saying I love you in his version of limited third.

Writing Suggestions

1. Referring to Mitchell's as an example, write a one-page scene in third-person limited where a single character is in a situation that he or she does not entirely understand. Limit yourself to the thoughts of the central character, mentioning nothing that is not present in the character's mind. How difficult is it to write about someone who is experiencing confusion without confusing the reader? Would a different point of view choice remedy the situation here?

2. Find an article in your local newspaper that interests you—a young man leaves for military service overseas, a politician is accused of lying, a local woman gives birth to quintuplets, a teenager protests the construction of a new strip mall, etc. Using the vantage point of third-person limited, create a story suggested by the events described in the newspaper. Pay special attention to developing the main character, because newspaper stories tend to report events without exploring the interior life of the person represented.

3. Refer back to your response to writing suggestion #1 from any of the other point of view commentaries—those by Michael Knight, Adam Johnson, Lee K. Abbott, or Josh Russell. Change the point of view in your response into third-person limited. How does this shift change your scene? Aside from simply changing pronouns, what other, more substantial changes are now required to complete the scene? How might you similarly rework a story of yours this way to good effect?

4. As Mitchell mentions in her commentary, Alice Sebold's runaway bestseller *The Lovely Bones* also uses third-person limited (dead), as does Mitchell in "A Man of Few Words." If you've already read Sebold's book, revisit it. If you haven't, locate a copy at your local bookstore or library and read the first chapter. What similar challenges did the authors encounter due to the point of view choice other than the obvious—the narrator being dead? Did they handle those problems in similar ways? How can a writer maintain reader interest in a deceased narrator telling his or her own story? (Variation: Instead of or in addition to Sebold's novel, you can also find third-person limited (dead) narrators in the novel *Ironweed* by William Kennedy and in the film *American Beauty*.)

> *The choice of point of view will largely determine all other choices*
> *with regard to style—vulgar, colloquial, or formal diction, the*
> *length and characteristic speed of sentences, and so on.*
> —John Gardner

Lee K. Abbott

One of *Star Wars,* One of *Doom*

From *The Georgia Review*

The slaughter hasn't started yet.

Tango and Whiskey, in fact, have just left bowling class at the Mimbres Valley Lanes off Iron Street. No one knows about the Intratec DC 9 or the Savage sawed-off double-barreled 12-guage. No one knows about Little Boy and FAT MAN, the propane tank bombs set up with egg timers and gallon gasoline cans. Even Mr. DeWine, who's famous for believing he knows everything about anything any kid does, doesn't know that right now, nearly nine in the morning, Tango and Whiskey are parking their cars, a black VW Golf and a blue Camry, in their assigned places in the student lot across from the gym. Sadly, Mr. DeWine can't even guess that in several minutes—maybe ten—Tango, Marlboro in hand, will stop Mike Richardson outside the cafeteria.

"Richardson, I like you," he will say. "Now, get out of here. Go home."

No, Mr. DeWine knows only that it's too early for lunch and that he has a mountain of civics exams to grade before seventh period. His gut is churning—too much coffee too early, he guesses—and, come four-thirty this afternoon, he'll be in his Jockey shorts in a room at the Red Roof Inn off I-10, listening to Ms. Petty—Ms. Leanne Elizabeth P., late of Tularosa—crying in the bathroom. Before or after—hell, often both—she cries in the bathroom: no one is listening to her, she sobs, no one values her opinion, she's a fireplug for all anyone cares. Just a truck or a root or a box of rocks. She'll be wearing a garter belt and seamed hose, the fetish wear Mr. DeWine drools over, and she'll be sitting on the closed toilet lid, sniffling and boohooing that even Mr. DeWine, the guy she's been screwing for the last ten months—Christ, probably the only heterosexual in this goddamn Land of Enchantment who can get from one to ten without using his goddamn fingers, a guy who regularly made her laugh right out loud—even he doesn't listen to her. No, that crumb just climbs on and hollers "Whoopee!"— not a "yes" or "no" or civilized phrase to go back and forth between them until, at 6:30, he says adios so he can hustle back before Sue Ellen, the wife, gets home from Pioneer Realty Associates.

So there is Mr. DeWine—Frank to his pals, Francis to the Social Security Administration and the DMV, Shitbird to the likes of Tango and Whiskey—in the hall, for eight minutes merely another cop-slash-cowboy obliged to herd Brianna (all forty of her) and Jason (the fifty or so he is) and Niki (the dozen she's turned out to be) into the right holding pens-slash-classrooms, to prevent them from stampeding over one another. He's got the "Declaration" to teach, for crying out loud. And attendance to take. A zillion announcements to make, plus homework to hand back—No, Tiffany, not on the curve—a whole briefcase of ideas he'd like to tell the world about if only the natives weren't so damn pimply and tall and loud, if only they didn't dress like lumberjacks and toddlers and thugs, if only they had more on their minds than Friday night and Duke Nukem and where to barf up that turkey sandwich.

The world? Fuck the world, he wants to say. Wants to stand in the center of the hall—right there, in fact, right where Colin is messing with Trisha who's messing with Erika who's messing with Misty who's probably wishing that Joshua were messing with her and not that skanky April May Lester—yeah, stand right there in between Mr. Geller (History II) at his door hither and Mrs. Fletcher (History I) at her door yon, and shout that it's the millennium, for God's sake, that there's got to be something else to do for forty-eight thousand two hundred and sixty-one dollars a year; that he was once young, too, a skinny Virgo with an acceptable jumper from the top of the key, and an expert way with power tools, in addition to a singing voice that didn't pain you too much to hear in St. Paul's version of youth choir. "Hey, look," he wants to holler, "Mr. Masters-degree-himself can burp the entire first verse of 'Silent Night'!" Yeah, Frank Round-Yon-Virgin DeWine, you moles. Frank you-just-would-not-get-it, don't-you-wish-you-did DeWine.

So, okay, it's crowded and noisy, the air thick and institutional, the air smelly and damp and bad for learning, rotten for anything except virulence and nightmares, and right now, while Rammstein and Nine-Inch Nails and Creed and Tupac and Little Fascist Panties and the Holy Modal Rounders are on that Walkman and that CD player and between those ears, and someone—Fishboy, maybe, he's the type, subtle as a circus clown—is bellowing "ho-ho-ho," and while all of the Mountain Time Zone is getting stupid and cranky and old, Whiskey and Tango are unloading their duffels.

Jesus Lord, they are in possession of some seriously impressive ordnance—hand grenades and pipe bombs, all homemade with glass and nails and jacks and BBs—and these guys, breathless and teary-eyed, are practically punch-drunk with glee. The plan, amigo. Everything's proceeding according to plan, approximately a year in the making. Months and months downloading the data from the Net, the only other shit keeping you sane being Buckhorn specialty knives and natural selection and seeing white trash wreck their brand new cars. Nearly a year, man, of putting up with jerks who mispronounce words, plus O. J. Simpson and weathermen and slow people in line in front of you and paying for car insurance. So it's now time for five—and five more, bro—and five on the dark side, too. The time, motherfuckers, is nigh. Oh, sweet Jesus, is it ever.

Which is ten on the dot, and the bell is ringing, the tardy bell, and the doors are closing—boom, boom, boom echoing in the hall—and soon Mr. DeWine, the image of Ms. Petty on all fours fixed like a photograph behind his eyes, takes roll. Surprisingly often of late, he's imagined the room with a Ms. Petty in each of the twenty-six seats. A Ms. Petty in a tiger print corset, growling. A Ms. Petty bound hand and foot, duct tape over the mouth, hands down the naughtiest wench in the area code. A Ms. Petty on her knees, tears dripping from her cheeks, her lower lip trembling, hers the grunts farm animals make. *Ugh. Baw. Eef.* A Ms. Petty laughing, then choking because, hell, if you didn't laugh, really bust a gut, you'd just end up banging your head against the nearest brick wall—the government, for starters, and the freeways, *Friends* and the hopeless porkers at the free weights in Gold's. Oh, man, a Ms. Petty in the back of the room, pulling down the map of the Gadsden Purchase, her fanny shiny and smooth and broad, the ass of a former rodeo queen of Otero County now with unspeakable credit card debt.

But today, no. No frills to fondle. No silk or satin or whatever the dickens it is that brings his blood so quickly to boil and makes his thigh muscles twitch. Today, seat 6A, we find Amanda, too sparkly in the eye, busy as a hamster. And Chelsea, 4F, with earrings and bracelets in industrial quantities—probably couldn't get through an airport with all that hardware. And Todd, his best citizen, A's on everything, including his high-dollar hair. They're all here, it seems. Tarika? Yes, as usual, about as far from Mister Teacher as she can possibly be without leaving the room altogether. Tyson? A simple "here" would do, but, Christ on a crutch, this drama club president and his "present," a response that under his care and feeding seems to have eight—possibly ten—syllables. Bethany? Ah, practically under his feet again, eye shadow like poster paint, but a rack you wouldn't mind warming yourself against during the next ice age.

"Anybody know where Kathi is?" It's the "*i*" that kills him, hanging off the end like a tail, a smiley face above it on all her written work. A letter like a lollipop. "Kathi? Anybody?"

"I saw her in physics." It's Harrison, Todd's foot slave, a junior with the fertile imagination of a dumpster. "That was second period."

"Thanks, Harrison," Mr. DeWine says. "Anybody else?"

They're studying the floor, every blessed one of them. Or the ceiling. Maybe that fascinating crack in the drywall. They don't look at you anymore, these kids. They mumble, they shrug, and they cough. Eye contact? A new social disease.

"She's on the Spirit Committee." That's Suzanne—not Suzy or Sue, if that's all right with you, Mr. DeWine—and she possesses a smile that all but blinds him: more teeth than Jaws, pearly as the path to paradise itself.

The committee, he mutters. A second later, shazam, it hits him. It's Free Cookie Day. The cafeteria. All the chocolate chip and peanut butter and ginger snaps you can eat. Fight, you Wildcats, Fight.

"All right, then," he says. "Turn to page 194."

And so that's the way it goes—"When in the course of human events" blah-blah-blah—time a drip to torture yourself with, time the stick to poke into your eyes, time you wouldn't want to meet alone in an alley. Until it's time—no matter the ifs, ands, and buts—to serve up generous portions of Life, Liberty and the pursuit of ever-loving Happiness, precisely as Master Tom described it. Time, in fact, to turn the page, please.

" . . . Appealing to the Supreme Judge of the world for the rectitude of our intentions," Todd is saying—in*ton*ing is more the hell like it. Good Lord, the kid is a senator already. A justice of the Supreme Court. King Todd is straight out of the Charlton Heston edition of the Old Testament, the words raining down on Room 144B like murrain and flies and frogs, and, while Ben Franklin and John Hancock and the rest of the colonies' ruling class are mutually pledging their lives and fortunes and sacred honor, Mr. Frank DeWine is doing his damndest to concentrate, to keep his eyes open, to hold himself upright and not, weakened by boredom and surprisingly epic fatigue, to lay his impossibly heavy head in Marcy Hightower's fetchingly ample lap.

"Mr. DeWine?"

Our hero finds himself looking straight at Harrison, eyeball to eyeball. The boy has spoken. He has brought Mr. Frank DeWine, our one-time recording secretary for Lambda Chi Alpha and full-time yellow dog Democrat, back to the here and now. Evidently—and this, Mr. DeWine thinks, is truly alarming—he was somewhere else, a there and a then well distant from the rhetoric of revolution, a place and time you most assuredly did not want to visit in the company of humanoids as aggressively disinterested as these.

"Page 208," he says. "Manners, Query XVIII—for man is an imitative animal."

They're good, these children. They appreciate knowing what to do next. They appreciate knowing what's to be done in, say, November—even in a November a decade from now. They're big fans of clean laundry and recreation rooms and pool parties. They like pizza and keggers and Old Navy. Not like Whiskey and Tango—code names, in case of capture behind enemy lines. Whiskey and Tango don't like people who bump into them or country music or freedom of the press. Especially Whiskey, who wants to haul all those who are against the death penalty and who dig commercials and who cut in line and—well, he doesn't know exactly where he'd haul their sorry asses, except that it would be forever, the outer darkness and way beyond here, beyond even time and God and any idea that can't be made plain in four words.

It's the Luvox, Whiskey sometimes thinks. The shit gets in him deep, soaks his bones. It blasts him out there, really out there, where the stars creak and the slop drips off the sun and the angels dress like Baron Frank'N'Furter. But that's no reason, never has been. Instead, the reasons are Fishboy calling you "pussy" and "pansy" and Clinton—the fucking president—blowing his wad on that intern, that Monica. Yeah: Kellogg's and lard-butts and the crap they're spraying on your food. And against that, in opposition to all that stupefies and enrages and disappoints, stand himself—the Whiskey man—and his loyal sidekick, the Tangster. Hi-ho, Silver, you dipshits. Hi the hell ho.

Which is more or less what Mr. DeWine has come to think in the last ten minutes. He thinks to tell them he was in a rock band once, Dr. Filth and the Leather Cup—neat, huh? They specialized in Vanilla Fudge covers, Iron Butterfly. He played drums—the perididdle, the flam, the rim shot—no Ginger Baker, sure, but Ringo enough. Nineteen, freshman year at State, and he's on the stage at El Patio bar in Old Mesilla, pounding out the beat for "Hey, Joe," and urging the unwashed to shake their tail-feathers, joints the size of cigars going back and forth, the singer—man, what was his name?—humping the air, humping the organ, humping the Peavey amp, humping the bass player one time. That's what he wants to say, here, out loud, from atop the desk, having dropped an atlas or two to focus everybody on the present: "Once upon a time," the speech would go, "in a world far, far away, Mr. DeWine, no kidding, had a topless ZTA from Roswell ride him pony-style while he, the selfsame son of a gun huffing and puffing before you, kicked over a cymbal and generally wreaked havoc on the stage décor." Here he would look around, taking stock, with that celebrated pregnant pause. "Ended up on the floor, ladies and germs, a pair of Bermuda shorts between the teeth."

But he won't. Can't. A line, you see, lies between them—a Maginot line, practically. You are the teacher, the incarnation of decrepit, laughingly out of touch with cool, yours the clothes that even Larry, Curly and Moe said "yuck" to. You all but wear your hair in a comb-over, you've gone spongy in the belly, and you gobble goddamn Lipitor and Prinivil because your body—some temple it is, Bunky—has turned on you in outright revolt. And they are the students, the rulers of the wasteland, the tribe yattering in Martian.

And then, thank God, the bell has rung and, only a moment short of a moment that doubtless would have shamed you eternally, you have not told them anything actionable, haven't told them anything at all except that they should know, with the same certainty they know their names, Jefferson's September 25, 1785 letter to Abigail Adams—Yes, Tiffany, this will be on the test—and, instantaneously of a single mind, they rise, legs and arms everywhere, backpacks strapped on, their chatter a noise that becomes a roar, then insensible as static, then nothing for the next few minutes but elbows and ball caps and ponytails, nothing except time diving at you like a missile, you just something else goopy, slow, and warm-blooded that can talk.

The carnage? Still an hour away.

Erika's in orchestra, third flute, trying to catch up, her foot having found a rhythm for some fa-la-la that, duh, there isn't ick to like. Misty's pretending she's not in English, at least not in any English that demands you read such brainless typing as *The Bluest Eye*, not to mention all the footnotes and commas and infinitives they make you use. Todd? He's in the library—study hall—doing math homework and another scholarship essay. The Kiwanis, the Optimists, the Lions—all the do-gooders. They're all looking for heartfelt words and a winning way of saying squat. Harrison, sitting across from Todd, seconds that opinion. Suzanne would as well, but right now she's trying to figure out why Mr. Hart, Latin (fourth period), hates her so much. After all, forty kinds of ablative, ninety noun cases, never mind Horace and Virgil and Cicero—who are these mushmouths anyway? *Mehercle, qui dies!* Which sentiment Alicia would understand were she present, but she's gone to the cafeteria to help Kathi, who's managed to get rid of all the sprinkles and the butterscotch and who's made—Sorry, Ally—a sizeable dent of her own in the gingerbread men. Which leaves April May Lester, who's not really a skank but just wants one of the cool kids—Bethany, for example, or that prep Tyson—to like her, to ask her a question she can say "sure" to.

So back we are to Mr. DeWine. "Francis Michael," his mother used to bark, a genuine drill sergeant. "Francis Michael, you have been a profound frustration today." He can imagine her here, at attention beside his desk, a switch or a flyswatter in her hand. Her plastic hairbrush, more likely. "Francis Michael, I trust we'll have no more of such tomfoolery." Yes, ma'am, no more. No foolery of any kind, Mother. At which promise, she disappears, and Francis Michael finds himself with little to imagine but what, in the first place, his father, not a saint himself, ever saw in her—the former Mary Cobb, of Silver City. Her hair maybe? She had great hair, a thundercloud of it, hair to spare, all of it fine as cotton candy. Plus, she could take shorthand, did so right in front of the TV—one January the pages that were reportedly a faithful transcription of *Gunsmoke* piling up beside her armchair. *Bonanza*, too. She liked the rough-and-tumble, sodbusters blazing at each other with pistols, dust swirling, horses going to panic in the eyes. But other than that—the bang-bang and the frenzy, and, okay, modest expertise in the kitchen arts—what? Oddly, Mr. DeWine can't conjure her now, not a single feature. Just the hair, floating in midair, atop the head of a ghost maybe.

A vision which would scare him if, without warning, he hadn't been distracted by a hard and sharp thing that's settled in him—a bone, he fears. Something small and heavy has tumbled to the flat bottom of him, the thunk like a bolt in a bucket, and right now, before Jason appears to discuss his overdue research paper, Mr. DeWine would like to smoke a cigarette, the first in, oh, ten years. A cigarette. Menthol. Nothing at this instant (and for the several to follow) strikes him as a finer idea. At the very least, business to occupy the hands. An activity to keep them from banging here and here on the desk before him. Another flaw in character, albeit tiny and common, to lie about. And, magically, just when Francis Michael needs him, there he stands, Jason, the most earnest Caucasian youngster since Johnny Appleseed.

"Come in, son," Mr. DeWine says, startled he sounds at all like himself, relieved as well that he speaks any language other than Urdu.

"Something wrong, sir?"

Mr. DeWine, most recently of planet Earth, sneaks a peek at his watch. Eleven on the nose. T minus Tuesday and counting.

"I'm fine, Jason. Why do you ask?"

The boy knows everything, Mr. DeWine has heard. The periodic table, the succession of England's kings and queens. Who kicked hindmost in the Tang Dynasty, how law is made in Kafiristan. So what now?

"It's your face, sir," Jason begins. "It was like you weren't here."

All right, Mr. Frank DeWine thinks. They know he hollers and the comely Ms. Petty from mathematics weeps, and that old Ben Franklin has helped himself to all the tarts in Paris. They gab among themselves, these creatures. They know his dog, the pound-bred Rex, and his weakness for bourbon. They know the sorry state of his socks, his wayward heart. They know the rusting piston in his chest, the sump above his shoulders. They have, indeed, found him out.

"Let's begin, shall we?" Mr. DeWine gestures to a chair and, a minute later, time with shape and density and hue, they have begun.

As have Tango and Whiskey. It's a pop quiz, right there on the hill overlooking the cafeteria. One Stevens pump-action, sawed-off shotgun? Check, Tangster. One Hi-Point 9-mm semiautomatic carbine with the 16-inch barrel? Double-check. One of this, one of that, one of everything they'd started whispering about the summer before. One childhood of *Star Wars*, one of *Doom*. They're wearing their outfits—the flannel shirt, the camo pants, the lace-up boots, the ghoulish smirk. They're about to engage hostile forces, the fitness fuckheads and those geezers who don't use their turn signals. Whiskey has done what he needed to do. He's washed his hands, he touched his ear six times when he got out of the car, prayed to the four corners, touched his other ear six times—the hocus-pocus you do on Tuesday so that on Wednesday you won't find yourself naked in your closet begging the pardon of an audience of Klingons and druids and the Four Horsemen of the Apocalypse. In his room, he identified everything that began with the letter *c*—his carpet, his cat, his cap, his Cap'n Crunch, his cudgel.

And now, goddamn, there's more to inventory. The ammo, the Molotov cocktails in the Piggly Wiggly bag at your feet, the notes that tell the civilians you've morphed, you're about to jump through the only open seam in the universe to join the master race, and so here you are, Attila himself, a BFG 9000 in hand, decay dust in one pocket and in the other a potion from the Wicked Witch of the West, warp speed the means by which you hurtle from A to B, you and your buddy now Knights Jedi and Errant and Black, you and your buddy now the most special of special effects, founding members of the ninth circle, the inner sanctum, the grave, you and your buddy now specters brought into the full light of day by rage and by the heartening prospect of a prodigious volume of gore. Oh, Tango, it is April, the cruelest month. Oh, Tango, it is seventy fucking degrees. Oh, Tango, it is the end of the world as you know it and you feel fine.

"You ready?" Whiskey says. "I am go for liftoff."

To which, for the longest time—a century, it feels like—Tango says nothing, his mouth chewing crazily at the air. His eyes have become narrow and dark, his ski cap down over his ears like a bank robber. He could be thinking about heaven, about saints to goose step with, nectar to sip. He could be thinking about crows that tap dance or storybook Apaches to send on the warpath or a feat impossible to do like carry the ocean across the desert in his hands.

"I'm scared," he says. "Really scared."

Yes, it's springtime, the bell about to ring, a few kids on the lawn, smoking, a few walking in from the lot. Schoolmates, they are called. Peers. Whiskey loves them. No kidding. He must take their lives because he loves them, which fact they will comprehend when he walks among them. This is his lesson. They have been shallow, these Wildcats. They have been arrogant. They have given offense. And now, lo and verily, he will smite them.

"Afterward," Whiskey says, "we'll get nachos."

Tango knows this is not true, can never be true. Afterward is not in the plan. The before has already ended, and nothing will follow but smoke and blood and debris and dreams never to wake from.

"Tango," Whiskey says, a question.

Foot. It is the only word Tango can utter, the only word he remembers from a lifetime of words. Wait, there's another. *Tree.* Which he says and says again until enough minutes have passed for him to say, with nearly incredible relief, *insect.* Then: *wolf.* Then: *night.* Whereupon Whiskey touches his shoulder, and, miraculously, Tango has other words to say, all of them big and new and remarkable as the day itself.

"Pizza, too," he says. "Pepperoni."

The world has already turned red and swirly at the edges, an arctic cold settling at their feet. The world is about to tilt, to wobble out of its groove, about to shrink. The world is cracking, a splintering you can hear in heaven.

"Ready?" Whiskey asks.

This time Tango can answer. His shit is squared away. The epic wind has left his mind. He's copacetic. He salutes, stiff-armed and urgent.

"Heil Hitler," he says.

And now the doors are near, a handle for each to grasp. They have only to pull, which they have done, and they have only to march past several classrooms, Ms. Petty's among them, and toward the library like soldiers, which they are doing, and they have only to arrive at the circulation desk, which they have, and they have only to squeeze off a round, which each does into the ceiling tiles, and at last, the clock ticking toward 11:45, to the dozens of now thoroughly why-faced Wildcats in front of them, those trembling like Todd and those not, those like Harrison wide-eyed with awe and those thinking they ought to be able to claw through their notes for the answer to this unreasonably complicated question, the warriors Tango and Whiskey have only to speak.

"Here we are now," they say. "Entertain us."

He's got a half-hour, Mr. DeWine does.

He could eat. Mystery meat in the cafeteria or the tuna sandwich in the refrigerator in the teachers' lounge. He could pay a bill or two, maybe. He's got his checkbook, a week's worth Pay Up in his briefcase. Instead, he puts his feet on his desk, rocks back in his chair. Why not visit Leanne, a surprise? She's got this period free, too. He could sneak up behind her, grab her at the waist. He's done it before, though only once. The whole time, not more than five minutes, he was overwhelmed by the fear that some-body—a student having forgotten a book, or a teacher searching for the new calcula-tors—would walk in on them. His skin had felt too small, his head too big. He thought he might fall over, his heart like a ferret in his chest, all claws and climbing. Besides, she was herself spooked, slapping at his head like a spaz, hissing—Honest Injun—hiss-ing like a goose or some such. Fucking fowl, for Pete's sake. No, he'll stay put. He takes his deepest breath of the day. He'll do a push-up or two. Work on that spare tire. Tend to the mind and body both, he thinks. Your familiar heart-and-head imbalance. Man, is it quiet. Eerily quiet, only the AC cycling and the clock and the creak of a middle-aged middleweight hauling himself to his feet. It's the quiet from the moon, the quiet where time ends.

Outside, there's nothing, just the school flag, all that Disney-worthy blue. He walks among the desks. "Abandon all hope," someone has scribbled. Dante—what a bozo. Blamed the whole fiasco on Beatrice. At another desk—here is where the lovely Sherry parks her lovely butt—he finds a hair. Blond. Not Sherry's though. No, this is the blond of a practicing protestant. This blond drives an Explorer. Doubtless, this blond aced the ACT. Red would be something else, he guesses. Honest work to be done on a ranch. A career on the stage. He turns on his heel, Mr. DeWine does. And brown, Sue Ellen's color? He doesn't want to think. That's a smart mouth, a wiseacre. Brown's a story with an unhappy ending. Brown is boredom. Brown is a mannequin that drinks vodka gimlets.

Now he's really curious. What have they left behind, these kids? Last fall, he found a spiral notebook with writing in it so peculiar, so detailed and figurative, it could have only come from the hand of an egghead's egghead. Squiggles gave way to squares and those to bouquets of dashes and those to a series of capital L's, the whole of it bizarrely architectural—the castle of a dark-minded wizard, he thought, or a Byzantine metropolis of gnomes and haunts, or a low country in ruin. Yeah, it was a civilization to dig up, you and ten thousand other zombies looking for the reason you can't sleep. He wonders now what happened to the notebook. It might have led to treasure. Jesus H., if only you were fluent in runes and glyphs and smudges and sym-bols, it might have led you out of Deming, New Mexico, and right to the golden threshold of Shangri-La itself.

Gracious, there's so much to know about Mr. DeWine, especially now that else-where the shooting has started. That topless Zeta Tau Alpha for example, at El Patio those many years ago? That was Sue Ellen, his wife. Sue Ellen Bates then. Older by a year. A sophomore business major. But she wasn't really topless. She wore a Moby Grape T-shirt. He likes to embellish—makes the real realer, he thinks. The Bermuda shorts? Those he didn't invent. He didn't invent Roswell either, or the cymbal, or the wreck-age in his wake. Nor, later than night, at his apartment off Solano Street, did he invent the clumsy sex he and Sue Ellen had, or that hour, toward dawn, when he felt that he'd been dropped on the planet for all the wrong reasons. He didn't invent Catherine either, the baby who died six years later. A miscarriage, actually, the first of two. Eons ago, it feels like, when beasts ruled and we were but fish or flesh that crawled.

What else should we consider before he makes up his mind to drop in on Ms. Petty? He was runner-up in the fourth grade spelling bee, *terpsichorean* the word that got between him and the silver trophy Kay Stevenson bragged about. His first girlfriend? Michelle "Mickey" Barker. Went steady the whole summer the Beatles came to America. Behind Timmy Bullard's house, in the onion field, she let him touch her breasts— "For a count of five, Frankie, no more"—the surprising weight of them something he swears he can still feel. Oh, this as well: He wrote a whole book in high school, in Las Cruces. Well, eighty-some pages. But hand-illustrated, lots of forest scenes and a mountain range that looked like eyeteeth. His version of Sir Gawain and the Green Knight. Lots of derring-do in that. Nick-of-time stuff, too. An alluring maiden in distress, of course. He was the Sir, naturally. *Vanquished*—man, he loved that word, that and *dispatched* and *woe betide he who,* all the fancy talk you nowadays don't hear much at Del Cruz's Triangle Drive-In—yes, he vanquished a dragon. Slew the sucker silly. Afterward the Sir found himself bedecked—right, another word stuck-up Kay Stevenson wouldn't know the up from down of—with a sash and more medals than Bayer has aspirin, the king (the maiden's father) the most grateful potentate in all of Pip-pip, Cheerio, and vicinity. Got some serfs out of the deal as well. Mrs. Chew let him read a chapter to his English class, Mickey Barker right under his nose. Made it all the way to the part where Sir Gawain and his friends—the vaunted Sir Fitzroy and the steadfast Sir Palmetto, mainly—lay siege to the manor house of the dastardly Archduke Fussface before the bell rang. Yeah, dastardly. "I think," Mrs. Chew said to everybody, "there's a lesson in this for all of us." It was this event, he still thinks, that made him want to become a teacher—to find lessons everywhere, even in his own needy heart.

Not terrible lessons, though, like those being delivered right now a hundred yards away in the library, where Whiskey, clomping through a tangle of overturned chairs and scattered papers, has announced that he is the Lord Humongous, the Ayatollah of Rock'n'rolla, and Tango has discovered underneath a reading table a girl, Tiffany, to play peek-a-boo with.

"You like me, don't you?" he says, his the grotesque grin you carve on a pumpkin.

What a silly question. Of course, she likes him. He has the gun. Dark and greasy-looking with May Day streamers hanging from it and maybe actual human ribs, gobbledygook like Arabic or graffiti scribbled with Marks-a-Lot on the stock, the gun is pointed at her.

"So," Tango begins, "if I asked you for a kiss, you'd give it to me, right?"

Another asinine question. He can have her purse, her hair, her hands.

But now it appears that all he wants is for that noise—an animal howling in pain, Tiffany thinks—to stop.

"It's a cat," she says, trying to help.

The gun goes off again, another boom wrong for books and study hall and Free Cookie Day, and Tiffany understands that it is she, the only daughter from the house of Hudspeth, who is crying. She is the cat, howling.

"Do her," Whiskey is shouting. "Do the bitch."

But she can't be done, she thinks. After all, she is home, under the covers. She has her pj's on, in her headphones Jack Diesel's greatest hits. A novel lies in her lap, a tearjerker Oprah wanted her to read. She can't be done. No, she certainly can't.

And, mysteriously, she isn't. Instead, the boy—she's seen him before, James or something, from the soccer team—crouching behind a desk chair is done. He has a cute haircut, close at the sides, then he doesn't. Unmoving only a moment before, he is flying—snatched by the collar, it seems, and hurled against a bookshelf, the reference section crashing down to bury him.

"Targets of opportunity," Whiskey is calling them.

He's firing into the floor—*pow, pow, pow*—his shotgun like a pogo stick bouncing him through the room, real astonishment in his eyes. The firepower. The fucking firepower. He's hanging on to the smart end of a contraption that spews out blood and justice, cordite and delicious disorder.

"Dance, tenderfoot," he orders, now Billy the fucking Kid and Triple H and Prince Jericho and Mr. Blue, and immediately one unlucky gomez—gee, Harrison, fancy meeting you here—is dancing, snot smeared across his lips, clearly the loneliest fellow in the hemisphere.

"It's the hucklebuck," Tango says, delighted to be the new host of *MTV World*. "Shake a leg, dude. Trip the light fantastic."

Arms spread as if in ecstasy, Harrison dances, knees higher than a desk, nothing beneath him now that the floor has disappeared, now that Whiskey, giggling, is keeping promises. Now that the present, simple as Simon, is giving way so easily to the even simpler past.

"The hokeypokey," Tango has said. "Turn yourself around."

Events are moving swiftly, many at the same instant. Todd intends to rise, to dash for the door. He's thinking it, yes, but a moment later he's not thinking anything at all, the organ to think with having unexpectedly gone mealy and cold. The world smells sour and sulphuric. A blizzard has roared through here, dust roiling, shreds of paper falling like snowflakes. The floor is pocked and pitted, as if gouged by jackhammers and the picks of giants. Shattered glass lies everywhere—in your hair, down your shirt, in your Nikes. Wood splinters have stabbed you in the arm, the neck, the backs of your thighs. Remarkably, you've heard not a single sound. The muzzle flashes are unmistakable, a spray of wadding and sparks, a window pouring over a desk like a shimmering waterfall, but, huddled behind the body of a girl whose misfortune—thank you, Mr. Hart—was to need the Latin for *Never cut class again, Miss Suzanne Winters*, you can't hear anything. Except your own heart, its fitful thud-thud the rhythm vampires are aroused by. Yes, Tango is speaking—his mouth is working, his awful tongue—but the audio is on MUTE. You want the remote control. But the instant the sound thunders over you like a tidal wave and you have glimpsed Miss Petty at the door, you don't want anything except for time to snap backward so that you'd have a century to warn her, nasty old DeWine's girlfriend, not to come in here, that she can read this week's edition of *Time* tomorrow or the next day. Please, Miss Petty, don't come in here for anything.

But she has. And Tango—his shirt off, his birdlike chest glistening with a war paint of blood and paste and ink—has already, with the formal bow of a Beau Brummel, welcomed her to his intimate get-together.

"You're just in time," he says.

For Whiskey, there's too much to account for. The wall, the floor, the wall again. At this point, he had hoped to be well into Beta phase. The main event. Little Boy and FAT MAN themselves. But his ear has to be checked, and his wrist, followed by his boot and his ankle, before he can move on to his knee and his eye socket. "Say the words," he tells himself. And, soon enough, from his prepared list, he does: "Reason, virtue, plenitude." He glances around. Evidently, he has been shouting. "Being," he hollers, "is not different from nothingness."

"Put that down, James Crawford." Ms. Petty is addressing Tango, stern as a movie actress. "What do you think you're doing?"

What lunacy. Which can't be helped, unfortunately. Ms. Petty is, figuratively speaking, beside herself. She's watching herself stamp her foot—yes, actually stamp her right foot—and put her hands on her hips, a school marm from ancient America. She should shake herself, slap some sense into her pretty head, but she can't because Leanne Petty is not really there. Instead, dumb and foolish and proud, standing not a giant step from the barbarian with the rifle, is a lunatic female using her name and wearing her clothes and saying what would be said if the universe had not so completely melted.

"I said to put that down, Mister Crawford."

He can't, he says. He's committed. Totally.

Committed. It's an expression she's heard before, that fussbudget with the wagging finger and the profound respect for propriety.

"I mean," Tango is saying, "fifteen minutes ago, maybe. But, now? Jesus God, Miss Petty, we're, like, in the second act here."

Against the far wall, still wringing his hands as if scrubbing them in air, Whiskey has almost reached the end of his speech. "Give us this day our daily bread," he is reciting. "The horror, the horror. One if by land, two if by sea. Merry Christmas to all, and to all a good night."

Ms. Petty slowly surveys the room. If only Frank could see this. These kids worship new gods now. They speak a new tongue. They will eat a new food in a new world and grow old in the new way.

"Miss Petty?" It's Tango, his the shrug of youthful impatience. He has work to do now, okay? And little time to do it in.

"What's that on your forehead?"

It's sandpaper, he says. To strike matches on. For the fuses, you know?

"James, you were such a nice boy. I can't believe this."

Another shrug, this one of 18-karat sadness. "I still am nice, Miss Petty. You just don't know me, is all."

She's desperate to return to herself, to step into the person still staring at James Crawford, nice boy. The situation demands organization. She should be telling that girl—Misty or Jewel, something perky anyway—that she can leave now, poor thing. She should be calling the authorities, the principal at the very least. A thousand tasks need attention, if she could only climb back into her own skin. But she can't. Never will. For James Crawford has finished his work, Whiskey having hustled over to observe, and the old self of Ms. Leanne Petty is collapsed on the floor, one leg twisted under her hips, the last of her dribbling out of the shockingly ragged hole in her head.

Whiskey squats down, lifts her limp hand. "Goodnight, air."

The plan. It's Tango's turn to talk. "Goodnight, noises everywhere."

For weeks and weeks afterward, Sue Ellen DeWine will wonder what Frank was doing near the library. She's visited his classroom and it's—what?—a good hundred yards, could be more, from where the murders happened. The papers—*The Headlight*, even *The Journal* from Albuquerque; TV, too, Channel 4 from El Paso, and CBS—have called him a hero, running in to rescue those students that way, but all Sue Ellen will puzzle about, when she goes back to work a week after the funeral, is what Frank was doing there. He should have been on lunch break, the other direction exactly, but he was headed toward the library. In June, admittedly embarrassed to be obsessed with such an inconsequential detail, she will nonetheless phone Dick Spivey, the assistant principal, to ask him, but all he will be able to tell her is that he hasn't the slightest idea. "Maybe he had to return a book," he'll tell her, and, okay, that will be her answer—a book to return, another mystery solved—until the following August when, steering her Camry into the lot of Zia Title for a closing, the merciless logic of curiosity and intuition and suspicion still hard at work in her, she will say "Leanne Petty" aloud, and Sue Ellen DeWine, the widow of a hero, will know. Francis DeWine, the son of a bitch, was on his way to see Leanne Petty.

Which is no more than Frank himself knows as he yanks open the door to the math wing. He's got his tie loose now and he's making good time, bum knee and all, more or less skipping, in his mind a dumber-than-dumb image of gimpy Chester shouting "Mr. Dillon! Mr. Dillon!" in the middle of a Dodge City street. Sir Francis has a personal matter to attend to, a furtive and private concern, so more than several seconds pass before he notices that he's the only person heading toward the weird banging noises. Everybody else, students and grownups alike, is scrambling to get by him. It's an honest-to-goodness fire this time, he thinks. It's not a drill, not a bomb scare like last Halloween. Adjacent to the men's toilet, he spots a kid he recognizes, one of the Goliaths from the lacrosse team, April Lester tugging on his arm.

"What's wrong?" he asks. "Richardson, what's going on?"

The kid's head goes back and forth. It seems to be the only part of him that works. The rest of him is frozen, seized.

"Well?"

Richardson needs a second, clearly. He has the expression of a landlubber crawling out of shark-infested waters.

(*A moment will arrive, soon, when Mr. DeWine will remember this Q-and-A with greatest sorrow. How bone-headed he has been, he will scold himself. What a stone. How could he not have known?*)

"April?"

Mr. DeWine grabs her arm, gets her attention. Good Lord, she's thin, like a ballerina. What, he wonders, is she doing with a behemoth like Richardson. It's like finding Tinkerbell keeping company with The Incredible Hulk.

"The library." She's whispering, as if she has to tell the whole school the dirty word some creep in homeroom yelled at her. "They're in the library."

Somebody is smacking a wall somewhere, Frank thinks. With a bat, sounds like. Really giving it the business.

"Who's in the library?"

She shakes her head, her tiny head. She doesn't know. All she can do is point, another of the species with seemingly only two or three moving parts. (*And this, too, is another instant he will regret when his moment comes.*)

"Go on," Mr. DeWine says. "It's a fire or something. Go outside."

So they go, April practically dragging Richardson, the two of them replaced by five more and three more after that, and here charge a handful more, all of them with crab legs and flying arms, the last kid—Tyson, his orator!—missing a shoe. This is like the end of a period but at fast-forward and without the grab-ass and ha-ha-ha, students appearing from everywhere. One girl he's never seen before—she resembles Marisa Tomei, but chunkier—runs by him screaming "John" over and over. "You can't do this," another girl is saying, "It's just not fair." That's all. Just those two sentences, like a chant, the same sentences he will shortly find himself saying. But right now here are more kids bearing down on him, the short fellow—Fishboy, is it?—with the shiny Penn State jacket tripping and knocking two look alikes down with him, all of them having the devil of a time getting up off the floor. And, shit, here are those goofy noises again, but louder this time.

"You seen Ms. Petty?" He's collared a boy lugging a bass fiddle, the instrument bigger in all dimensions than he is.

"Who?"

Mr. DeWine pulls the kid to the side. Down the hall, the litter is incredible. Books. Purses. Backpacks. Baseball caps. A blouse is there, too. And a pair of coveralls. Christ, what were all the fire drills for? He expects zoo life next. A giraffe would not surprise him one whit.

"Ms. Petty?" he begins. "She teaches junior calculus."

"I don't take that till next year, sir."

So Mr. DeWine asks the next kid—a doofus from student council possibly; he has that squeaky look about him. Another *no.* And another, this one from the dorkier end of the food chain. Nothing but *no, no, no* until, interestingly, there's no one left to ask, the hall having become as still as deepest space. Which means that, despite the jangling of the alarms and sirens woo-wooing in the distance, Mr. DeWine can hear, with phenomenally stunning clarity, what he dares not believe is gunfire.

(*That moment? When he at last apprehends how monstrously dim-witted he is? When he learns how far up his ass his head has been? Friends, it's now. Right now.*)

"No," he says, as much to the brickwork as to himself.

But there it is again. A shot. Like a cannon, he thinks. Shit.

You'd think he would run now, wouldn't you? You'd bet that, knowing what he knows, he'd turn the other way, scram for the doors he came in through. You'd think, because he's read the papers and watched CNN and has heard about those psycho punks in Arkansas and Colorado, and because he possesses the same instinct for self-preservation we all have, that he'd know what to do. At the very least, his body would react independently, right? His muscles, his fist of a heart.

But he does not move. No, Mr. DeWine—get this—sits, leans against the wall. It's a fire—he tells himself, not the last of his wishful thinking. He's no hero, that's not in dispute. And violence? Christ, the only fistfight he had was—when?—maybe in junior high, in the days when they had junior high. Instead, he tells himself again that the smoke in the air, bitter and grainy, is from a fire. Faulty wiring probably. Or some butt-wipe setting off M-80's in the restroom. But, all along, Francis Michael DeWine has known better. It's just like TV, friends. How sad. You go to a movie, a bona fide shoot-'em-up, and it's boom-boom-boom, just like now. Gangsters, terrorists, invaders from another galaxy—God, they're all in the library. It's astounding, really. His lungs have gone slack, the air in here too thin. The knee is seriously hurting now, the throbbing like a tom-tom. Skiing. What a dumb-ass sport. And here it is that he considers his lap, specifically the damp spots on his trousers, and realizes that he, the dumbest of the dumber earthlings, is crying. He's weeping. Silently, without a heave or a tremor, tears are falling from his chin. Tears.

"They didn't work."

Someone—a boy of wicked angles and rattles and marvelous heat—has sat down next to him.

"FAT MAN and Little Boy," the kid is saying. "I must've fucked up the timers."

The kid seems to wobble under a halo of fireflies, blinking lights, and a buzz constant as ocean noise.

"Are you John?" Mr. DeWine says. "A girl was asking after you."

"Whiskey," the boy says, his voice not at all the snarl a villain should have.

The emergency sprinklers have come on now, a fierce shower drenching the hall, the walls slick with running water, the floor shiny like a postcard of a stream from a world where the outside is weirdly in.

"You can't do this," Mr. DeWine says.

Oh, but he can, says the boy.

"It's not fair. Really."

Time has unraveled. Yesterday, Frank DeWine was a Cub Scout stealing LifeSavers from the Stop'N'Go. Only a month ago did his voice change. He was born with a full beard and a three-pack-a-day habit.

"You cold, Mr. DeWine? You're shivering."

Yes. So cold. Between his ears, a glacier has ground through the center of him, the fissures and folds of his brain jammed with ice.

"You want to say anything?"

"Like last words?" Mr. DeWine asks.

Whiskey nods. He takes no particular pleasure in this scene. Business is being conducted, that's all. The "therefore" and "whereunto" pages of the contract. The paragraphs in which the who's who and the what's what become the *ipso facto* and the hey-diddle-diddle.

"I'd like to say something about my father," Mr. DeWine says, though for several breaths he can't think of what exactly he might mean. "He had big hands, like paddles."

Again Whiskey nods. Mr. DeWine is being a good sport. Not like some you could name. Not like, oh, Bethany with her forgive-us-our-trespasses bullshit.

"I don't think he ever struck me in anger," Mr. DeWine is saying.

"My dad, too," Whiskey says. "He just sends me to my room, or takes away the car."

Whiskey has raised the assault pistol and placed it tenderly against the vein pulsing at Mr. DeWine's temple. The boy has an interest, keen but thoroughly professional, in this moment. He wonders what we will make of his own last words, those typed on the page folded in his shirt pocket, after he, at the muzzle velocity of 1,230 feet per second, has transformed himself into liquid and light, meat and whitest bone.

"Anything else?"

Yes, Francis DeWine thinks. Yes, there is.

Abbott on Third-Person Omniscient Point of View

I didn't mean to write a story using the omniscient point of view. Really. So far as I know, youthful experimentation notwithstanding, I'd never used it before. To be sure, I'd employed all the others available to us who will the word: third-person objective, third-person limited, first person, and even (though only once) second person.

So I was thoroughly surprised when what spilled out of my fingers was the opening sentence of the story you've read: *The slaughter hasn't started yet*. My first question did not concern "where" this sentence had come from. As is routinely the case, the first sentences for my stories come to me whole and portentous, the product of the subconscious worrying a problem yours truly didn't know there was to worry about: in them, I find the person I'll persuade you to root for (the hero, the protagonist, the star—whatever critical word you use to talk about the father, the son, the girlfriend, the mother, the heart most imperiled, that mook or bozo or sad sack for whom the stakes are the highest, the consequences the gravest); and the dramatic situation, the moment that occasions what is to happen next and next again. No, my first question this time around was more vexing: Who the dickens is telling this tale? Clearly, the narrator—either in the first or the third person—has foreknowledge, a spooky prescience. Then arrived the second sentence, not *I* but *he*, and the third until—Whoa, Nelly!—I had a whole paragraph and finally a whole page, on which the narrator had "visited" the flawed but all too human sensibilities of at least three different people. I was, on though not off the page, omniscient—God without the burdens that are free will and miracles—and by the time I'd write the last word, my narrator would have set up shop, if only briefly, in the head, heart, and gut of, by quick count, more than ten characters. Whew.

Without question, there are virtues unique to each point of view. In fact, there are many writers, even some high-cotton critics, who argue that POV, the hothouse of heart and head we oblige the reader to reside in, is the only substantive issue to chatter about. Me, I've had my prejudices, usually in favor of the first person. "Immediacy," I've told myself. "Identification. Closeness." And, important to note, first person is almost impossible to violate. Still, when the dust settles—and, believe me, the dust always settles—each choice has its benefits and, yes, its difficulties. With the "limited third," you have but a single character's interior life to explore. With the "second," you get a weird, even discomforting, conflation of the distant and the near, a kind of narrative whiplash (from one perspective, for example, the only proper response to a sentence such as *You were walking down the street* is this: "Heck, no, I'm not. I'm reading a story!"). With "first," you court "unreliability," the notion that ol' Yancy might not know what the dickens he's talking about or, Lordy, maybe he's lying. With "omniscience," you have access to anything on two legs. As always, of course, knowing which two legs to follow is the hard part, for you always run the risk of telling the least interesting story.

Still, my foray into the omniscience was great fun—liberating, in fact—for I found myself exploiting the two oldest (and not unrelated) "moves" in the book of storytelling: *meanwhile, back at the ranch*, and *little did he know*—the most immediate virtues of which are loads and loads of dramatic irony. As a writer, I was able to go anywhere I wanted, at any time. Like me, my reader would know more than any single character; and, like a character, my reader would be similarly helpless to prevent the woe and dread my people were stumbling their way toward. Best of all, without choppiness or abbreviating any single moment, I was able to inhabit different characters in the same scene. Equally satisfying to the aesthetic fuss-budget I can be, I had created suspense—not by concealing important information, but by revealing it first: plainly, even the most casual of readers knew that in the offing was a whopper of a climax—"hair on the walls" as Perry Smith, one of the two killers in Truman Capote's *In Cold Blood*, would say. Conflict of the most rootin' tootin' sort. Had I employed the first person, I would have had to choose among my cast of characters. But I thought them all worthy of a story, never mind the formal peculiarity of a first-person narrator who dies (see Alice Sebold's *The Lovely Bones* for a story—a novel, in this case—told by a dead narrator). Had I chosen the second person, I would have done violence—no pun intended—to the emotional "ooommmppphhh" I meant the story to occasion by keeping the reader at too far a remove from the action.

Of special interest to me even now was that I didn't know, and had no reason to think, that I would write a story based, albeit loosely, on the Columbine school shootings. Such had not been much on my mind. I was not unaware of them, to be sure, but I was not obsessed by them (remember: obsession tops the job description for those of us trying to make life out of language; later paragraphs in that description address grit, self-discipline, empathy, intelligence, a thick skin, sympathy for the devil, and the nettlesome need to know why fools fall in love). Rather, for me the shootings were yet another instance of crosswise behavior to shake my head over, still more evidence of what afflicts our crooked and condemned kind. In the past, my curiosity and imagination have obliged me to write about the Bataan Death March in World War II, and the putative UFO crash landing outside Roswell, New Mexico, in 1947, not to mention the "real" worlds peculiar to football coaches, Vietnam assassins, rock'n'roll stars with the ability to levitate, warrior poets from the future (think Walt Whitman in a mind-meld with Mad Max), and small town bankers. But here, after all, was that sentence about "slaughter" and those people, young and old, at a school. Which meant, gulp, research. (Somewhere Willa Cather, most celebrated for her novel *Death Comes for the Archbishop*, notes that most writers acquire their material by the time they're fourteen, a sentiment I at times agree with. At fourteen, notwithstanding the phenomena unique to teenage years, we already know, even consciously, a great deal about, say, families, those that succeed and those that go "blooey." About institutions, including school. About communities big and small. About the folks, fine and not, who cross our paths. About relationships, including bad love. About celebrity, those minor gods and goddesses we see on TV. About music and food and bodies and history and work and play and politics. About, simply speaking, what one poet calls our "wishes, lies, and dreams." In brief, at fourteen, ours is an examined life and fit, too, for fiction.)

I sometimes encourage—no, educe—my students to ask themselves what the writer had to know—yes, the inviolable if sometimes inconvenient facts of the matter—in order to write any given story. Melville, for example, had to know a boatload about, well, whaling and knots and the high seas and what life was like below decks for a duke's mixture of civilization's less-civilized citizens. Twain had to know The Big Muddy, Faulkner those hardscrabble acres, Hemingway fishing and the exception a bull takes to being poked in the hindmost with a spear—well, you get the picture. Oh, I "knew" rage and alienation and fear and disappointment, the to and fro that animates our ilk, the mess of contrary motives that drive us toward our separate fates—exactly what Ms. Cather said I knew long before I suffered my first pimple. Thankfully, I knew school, having never really left it since kindergarten when Eisenhower was sleeping in the White House. But, as it regards guns and propane gas tanks and contemporary music and video games, I knew nothing. And to make my story credible, to successfully evoke the crossroads of time and character that was this place, I had to know the details peculiar to pop culture in the twilight of the 20th century. What were the murderers wearing? What ticked them off? What are the favorite TV shows of those choosing carnage over calculus? What do "the rulers of the wasteland" think of, say, politicians? What are fashionable given names nowadays? What, pray tell, is the history curriculum for the 11th grade?

Hence, I Googled. Discovered an Internet site called internettrash.com, on which I could read the official police report (I did—essential information) or the autopsy reports (I did not—too gruesome, even for this hard heart). I could watch the films from the various security cameras (I did not—this I would invent, which is the writer's work). I also found the web sites for Klebold and Harris, the killers, which became a crash course introduction to the real world they observed—their opinions, individual and fascinating, on subjects big and small. I also talked to my students, the undergraduates in particular. One even gave me a copy of *Doom* to play. I watched MTV, the Fox network, "Dawson's Creek." I went to a gun shop, hefted the weapons in question, and spent twenty minutes blasting a paper target to smithereens. I called my now-grown sons, made them tell me all they remembered about the gulag that was high school. And I learned a new lingo, the Martian that is necessary when the secrets matter and the game is for keeps.

Mostly, to be honest (remember now: writers are professional liars), I took inventory. I needed to recognize where I made common cause with my characters, even two schoolboys wrought wicked. I needed to understand where in me a stranger would find Mr. DeWine, Ms. Petty, Tiffany from the house of Hudspeth, even April May Lester. To quote a guru from a less harmonious yesteryear, I needed to get in touch with my inner assassin, my inner airhead, my inner jock, my inner footslave, my inner overachiever, my inner realtor—all those inners in my innards who rose up, courtesy of omniscience, and demanded that for two hundred or two thousand words they'd have their words between my margins.

A couple of embarrassing confessions, relative to cobbling the story into its final form, are in order. Through far too many drafts of the story, I understood that I would have to send DeWine to the math wing to put him in harm's way. For the longest time, alas, I had him doing so to apologize to Leanne Petty. Pure bone-headedness (or wishful and sentimental thinking) on my part. DeWine, too full of himself and too craven, never apologizes. But for a riding crop and epaulets, he's a petty tyrant, a tin-pot despot all but breathless for some booty. Fortunately, I recognized that I had, er, mis-motivated him. In the published version, he remains in character, his desires having run roughshod over even his fears of getting caught. Sadly, I also had—and still have—him doing something that only recently struck me as similarly uncharacteristic—not a failure related to the choice of Point of View, but a failure of my own imagination and understanding of character. In the moment before Whiskey sits down with him (the denouement, if it's essential to talk the talk), he weeps. Wrong. He might be shocked, astounded, flummoxed; jeepers, he might be downright appalled. What he's gotten a good look at is his stupidity, his needy nature. But for crying out loud, he's too vain—too proud by half—to cry, so when the story is published in a new collection, I will end that paragraph with these words: *Skiing. What a dumb-ass sport.* And Mr. DeWine can be delivered into white space the same consistently shallow if impermanently chastened man he's always been.

Such mistakes happen sometimes. You hope for the best from our widespread and quarrelsome tribe. The wrong to be made right. The puppy to find a home. The lovers to reunite and the blood-dimmed tide to recede. Off the page, such desires are ennobling, heartening at the very least. But my job isn't to part seas or heal the halt. My job, as John Updike once put it, is to show what it's like to live in the here and now, no matter the "here" and no matter the "now." Which means sometimes finding yourself as a writer keeping company with the unappealing, the unsavory, the morally effete, the truly nasty—with folks, in other words, you wouldn't otherwise let in your door, never mind in your head. Still, if your obligation is to render the world, warts and wens included, then you subordinate what Abraham Lincoln called the "better angels of your nature" to the wants and wishes of those who appear the second you type the magic words "once upon a time."

So what, given all that's a consequence of point of view, is a writer to do? First, as my father used to say, horse around. Yes, change willy-nilly your mind. Take that first-person story you've labored over, and switch the pronouns to third. Ask yourself what you've gained. And what you've lost. Try it in the second person. Try it in the third omniscient. Note the effects unique to each. Second, read, which, if you're reading as a writer, means that you're reading for instruction. Look at, say, "For Esme with Love and Squalor," J. D. Salinger's splendid story. Note that he shifts point of view from first to third about midway through. Why, you'll be obliged to ask yourself. (The answer will break your heart.) Read Joan Didion's artful novel *Book of Common Prayer*. Marvel at how she uses a first-person narrator to report events that the narrator was not around to witness—sleight-of-hand of the most astounding sort. Read *The Great Gatsby*. Why is Nick the narrator? (I mean, folks, he doesn't do a heck of a lot, does he?) Soon enough, and inevitably, you'll teach yourself the possibilities and the risks peculiar to the choice of point of view.

Remember, finally, that nothing cannot be undone. That's why we call what we do a "rough draft."

⌒

Writing Suggestions

1. Many readers make a decision on whether to read a whole story or not on the first line alone. Consider Abbott's first line: "The slaughter hasn't started yet." What a promise it makes to the reader! What sort of promise, what hint of conflict or excitement to come do your first lines make? Write five new first lines, one with action, one that's an assertion, one that's all description, one that's all dialogue, and one that begins with, "I've never admitted this before, but . . . " Take the one(s) that you like most and write a first scene.

2. Write a story set against the backdrop of a contemporary news event—such as the O. J. Simpson trial, the Kerri Strug Olympic victory, the Million Man March, the explosion of Space Shuttle Columbia, the Red Sox winning the World Series, or the death of Princess Diana. How does writing about a well-known event present new challenges for fiction? How will you select a main character for this story? Will your story differ from the actual events—and if so, why?

3. Abbott's short story titles ("One of *Star Wars*, One of *Doom*," "The View of Me from Mars," "Why I Live in Hanoi," and "The Era of Great Numbers," to name just a few) are often real eye-catchers that demand readers read each story. Take one of your own stories and come up with at least two alternate, exciting titles. What makes one story title better than another? What promises do your titles make?

4. Spend a half-hour in a crowded setting that's somewhat foreign to you: an antique store, an art gallery, a museum you've not yet visited, a dorm lobby you've never entered, the first floor of a government or college administration building. Record your observations and thoughts in a notebook. Pay particular attention to how people interact with one another, how they move, how body language comes into play. List background sounds and noises. Notice the movement of light and shadows. Spend another half-hour in a deserted setting, such as a cattle farm, campground area, or cornfield. Record your observations and thoughts again in a notebook. Is it easier to capture details of a scene in a setting with few or no people? Do any of the other senses play a larger role in your experience? Develop a list of words and phrases that realistically describe this location as a possible setting for a story.

> *As an omniscient narrator, you float over the landscape wherever*
> *you want, moving from place to place in the twinkling of an*
> *eye . . . You can show the reader every character's thoughts,*
> *dreams, memories, and desires; you can let the reader see*
> *any moment of the past or future.*
> —Orson Scott Card

Josh Russell

Yellow Jack

From *Epoch* and *New Stories from the South 1998*

Pl. 1—*Louis Jacques Mandé Marchand*, 1845. Half-plate daguerreotype.

It is a mystery why those chronicling the history of photography have chosen to ignore Claude Marchand. This assistant of L. J. M. Daguerre (after whom the subject of this portrait was named) was the first American daguerrian. Marchand opened his

New Orleans studio in the fall of 1838, and in November of the same year he staged the first public display of daguerreotypes. That these dates precede Daguerre's official announcement of 19 August 1839 may be explained by the fact that Claude Marchand, a name so common in the Paris records of the day that a complete biography is impossible, once admitted that he and Daguerre had been working on the invention together, and that he left the city "with one of the earliest cameras and as many of the silvered brass plates as [his] pockets could hold" after a spat with Daguerre. Out of fear of prosecution, or out of an odd respect for the European rights to the miracle that would lead Paul Delaroche to declare on the event of its unveiling, "From today, painting is dead!" Marchand made his way via sail to New Orleans. There he and the marvel he called *soliotype* were warmly received by the French community and the city at large.

Of the hubbub that arose when Daguerre presented his camera obscura and its shimmering trapped moments to the Académies des Sciences et des Beaux-Arts, the New Orleans *Bee* opined, "It is no great surprise that the Europeans are aflutter about a miracle we have had for these many months. Once again America stands at the forefront of Science and Art."

Marchand flourished in the '40s as a photographer of varied stripe but he was best known as a portraitist. It was not purely novelty and the vanity of New Orleanians that led to his success. During the yellow fever epidemics that annually plagued the city it was common for doctors to recommend that the very ill be transported to Marchand's studio so that a last portrait could be made. In the middle four months of 1845, one of the worst summers of yellow fever the city ever saw, Marchand estimated photographing over four hundred terminally ill and recently-deceased fever victims. (For a related example of his landscape work see Pl. 39—*Trees Being Felled Near Lake Pontchartrain to Combat the Yellow Fever*.)

His death the same year was clearly the result of his work in the field. Because of his constant contact with the mercury vapor used to develop daguerreotype images he had lost all of his teeth and was reportedly mad for the final months of his life. A short note in a 13 August 1845 *Daily Tropic* gossip column written by Felix Moissenet describes the day Claude closed his studio: "Marchand flew into a rage and struck a woman when she, made moronic by grief, claimed the infant in a memorial portrait he had made of her child was not hers. He then sent a long line of portrait sitters away after standing on a chair and explaining to them that they were philistines and fools, none of them worthy of his art." His wife died a week later, and Moissenet's column reports that Marchand spent his last weeks wandering the streets "Crazed by grief." On the morning of 28 August 1845, his body was pulled from the turning basin of the Carondelet Canal.

It is assumed that this portrait of his youngest son is the last daguerreotype he made. It holds the only known image of Claude Marchand, his right hand. The hand rests gently on the infant Louis's head, steadying the child before the lens.

Pl. 2—*Nude Female on a Couch*, c. 1838. Sixteenth-plate daguerreotype.

Pl. 3—*"Peter" (Nude Male Standing Before a Shuttered Window)*, c. 1838. Sixteenth-plate daguerreotype.

Pl. 4—*Nude Female Adult Out-of-Doors*, c. 1838. Sixteenth-plate daguerreotype.

Pl. 5—*Nude Female Child Out-of-Doors*, c. 1838. Sixteenth-plate daguerreotype.

The specific dating of these five plates is based on their size and the fact that they appear to have never been cased. A sixteenth-plate daguerreotype barely fills the palm. Marchand may have brought these small 3.5 × 4.2 centimeter plates with him from Paris where the size was popular for miniature oil portraits. He never again uses the sixteenth-plate; the 7 × 8.3 centimeter sixth-plate, also know as the medium plate, was the smallest available in his studio.

In January of 1839 Marchand began placing his daguerreotypes in the same kinds of cases in which miniaturist painters placed their portraits and landscapes. (For a more complete discussion on cases see Pl. 10—*Still Life of Daguerreian's Tools*.) These silver-coated copper plates have aged considerably because they were not protected; all are spotted from dust and moisture and faded by the sun; Pl. 3 bears teeth marks on its upper-righthand edge.

The decision to date these five portraits circa 1838 can also be justified by an examination of their subjects and style. Marchand was yet to experience the rigid confines of expression and prudish morals of commercial art and the unfiltered light and unembarrassed camera angles he utilizes are inspired and free.

In Pl. 2 the slightly plump female reclines on a couch, the plate's deterioration oddly selective. While her face, feet, and the couch have faded to little more than outline, her body from the chin down and ankles up is unflawed. Time has also left a bowl of papayas and grapes unblemished. The fruit looks ripe even in the silvery tones of the daguerreotype. The regal pose and unabashed nudity of the man lit by stripes of sun sneaking in through louvered shutters in Pl. 3 is remarkable, even more remarkable when one considers the extent of the daguerreotype's damage. Aside from the teeth marks, Pl. 3 has incurred many scuffs and scratches. The effect the highly polished surface once gave is lost because of this damage; the man seems slightly out of focus. The name "Peter" is scraped onto the verso of the plate, but a survey of the gossip columns and other social records turns up no Peter in connection with Marchand, leaving the labeling a mystery.

Pl. 4 shows how the elements can destroy a daguerreotype. Sunlight has harshly faded much of the image and humidity has added a patina of tarnish. Only the subject's left breast, left shoulder and head, and a swatch of the flowers upon which she lies retain their original clarity. The adult model's flowing hair, her crown of black-eyed susans, and the carpet of flowers on which she poses hint at what must have been an amazing portrait. Pl. 5 provides the second half of an almost-diptych. The plate has faded to little more than a mirror, but careful scrutiny finds a child similarly posed in the same flower patch, the flower crown of Pl. 4's subject looped around the little girl's right ankle.

The nude disappears from Marchand's work for ten years, a decade marked by brilliant art managed within the narrow bounds of making a living. His wife, ironically, provides the return. (See Pl. 32—*Vivian Marchand Before a Potted Tree*.)

Pl. 6—*Girl on a Rocking Horse*, c.1839–42. Quarter-plate daguerreotype.

Pl. 7—*Man with Sideburns*, c.1839–42. Quarter-plate daguerreotype.

Pl. 8—*Masked Couple*, c.1841–43. Quarter-plate daguerreotype.

Pl. 9—*Butch Billys Dog June 1842*, 1842. Quarter-plate daguerreotype.

The daguerreotype made posing for a likeness more democratic than ever, the price of a portrait even cheaper than that charged by an inept painter. In 1841 a New Orleanian could make an appointment for a Marchand sitting and obtain a cased quarter-plate portrait for as little as two dollars. These inexpensively attained portraits made many happy, but this bargain also put art into the hands of people who did not think of it as such. Oil paintings hang above fireplaces for generations while daguerreotypes are seen as part of the effluvium of a life lived in the 1800s—like stereo card viewers and worm-tunneled croquet mallets—little more than rubbish to be discarded when cleaning out attics. These plates of four unknown human subjects and one identified pet are an excellent example of this egregious tendency. They were found in an antique shop in the French Quarter, a flea market in Arabi, and a junk shop in Grosse Tete.

The dates given Pls. 6, 7 and 8 are based on the backdrops that appear in them. The woodland landscape behind the pig-tailed girl in Pl. 6 and the man with the full sideburns and the top hat in Pl. 7 does not appear in Marchand's work after 1842. Marchand's studio icon, a reversed "R" wreathed in laurels, is embroidered on the backdrop behind the masked sitters in Pl. 8. This backdrop does not appear before 1841 or after 1843. The icon is also visible behind the dog in Pl. 9, and an inked caption barely discernable on the verso of the battered case—*Butch Billys Dog June 1842*—provides an even more specific date.

All four portraits are marvelous examples of Marchand's artistry. Pl. 6's child looks unposed on her hobbyhorse even though she would have had to remain still for the photograph's long exposure. Pl. 7 has the formal stiffness many wanted in their portraits, but Marchand has inserted a unique twist—the man sports a fat magnolia blossom tucked in his top hat's band. Pls. 8 and 9 are lively novelties, even for Marchand. The couple in Pl. 8 wears bawdy masks with long, penis-shaped noses, a sure sign that this portrait was made during Mardi Gras. Now common in snapshots, animals were rarely the subjects of early photographs. When they do appear it is rare that they are as focused as is Pl. 9's Butch.

The most saddening thought occasioned by the lucky discovery of these Marchand masterpieces is that the works which remain may be far inferior to those produced during the genius's lifetime. Who can say that Marchand's greatest art was not stupidly lost or destroyed by those unable to recognize its wonder?

Pl. 10—*Still Life of Daguerreian's Tools*, c.1842–1844. Quarter-plate daguerreotype.

Claude Marchand was the premier daguerretype portraitist in New Orleans from the moment of his arrival in 1838, and despite the leporine proliferation of other studios and daguerreians, he was recognized as the master of photographic arts for many years. He was a zealot with regard to his work, so it is little wonder that he made this still life of his tools: a box camera, a dozen slim-necked bottles, and a trio of shallow dishes.

The daguerreotype is a one-of-a-kind photograph. There is no negative, making it more akin to painting than to modern print photography. The daguerreotype process is arduous and extremely involved. The silvered copper or brass plates are prone to tarnish, especially in humid New Orleans, so Marchand's first step was painstaking polishing, a chore usually done with a spinning buckskin-headed apparatus. Next the shiny plate was suspended over iodine, the vapors uniting with the silver to produce a light-sensitive silver-iodine coating. The prepared plate was transferred to the camera in a plate holder, exposed to catch the image of the subject, removed while still in the holder, and then placed above a dish of heated mercury in a developing box. The mercury vapors reacted with the exposed silver to produce an image in an amalgam of silver-mercury. Finally, the image was fixed by immersion in a solution of salt or hyposulfite of soda.

After it was fixed, the plate was covered with a sheet of glass and the two were sealed together with tape and mounted in a book-like case with a hinged cover. These cases are to be thanked for many of the dates assigned the plates in this study. Marchand's case supplier was W. Lauren Wilson & Co. of Boston, an art and photography supply house still in business and in possession of records over a century old. They provided Marchand with cases of morocco and also with "Union cases" made of thermoplastic (pressed sawdust and resin). All of the cases can be dated by color. Marchand ordered black, oxblood and brown from 1842 to 1844, and replaced brown with red in 1845. Pl. 10's possible dating is based on its chocolate goat leather cover.

The daguerreotype is delicate; New Orleans' climate is perhaps the worst for such photographs. Mildew, palmetto bugs and mice destroy the cases and the sealing tape, exposing the daguerreotype to humidity which pocks faces with tarnish and breaks down the silver-and-mercury images; sunlight makes figures fade as if the past is tugging at them. That the plates in this study have survived is a wonder. Many of the daguerreotypes discussed here were discovered in the attic of Marchand's former residence on Toulouse Street. The plates had been placed in a locked trunk and spent almost a century hidden by discarded furniture. The trunk was watertight, intended to hold papers on ocean voyages, and thus many of these plates are uniquely preserved.

Pl. 11—*Emily Hulbert*, 1844. Mammoth-plate daguerreotype.

It was customary in the social set to have one's portrait made in the Spring and a coming-out of both young person and portrait would often occur if the subject was a prominent bachelor or a marriageable young woman. As Marchand's fame grew his daguerreotypes quickly became part of this ritual.

In her memoir *Life in New Orleans in the Glory Days* (New Orleans: Smith & Herbet, 1870) Emily Moissenet (née Hulbert) offers an amusing note on this unusually large (330 × 432 mm) portrait and the party at which it and she debuted. She says of the daguerreotype "[I]t accentuates each and every imperfection of my countenance. My nose is that of a monster, my chin like a chisel, my eyes like dots. When I complained to Mister Marchand, telling him that my face when rendered in pastel was much kinder, he merely smiled and told me, My dear, the camera does not lie."

The cocktail of art and science the daguerreotype represented was enticing, and even if it did point out strong noses and beady eyes, portrait painters soon found it the preferred medium for the yearly portrait. The loss of revenue was disastrous and many portraitists made slapdash attempts at embracing the new technology. It was obtainable via mail-order and from traveling salesmen who offered their services as portraitists, teachers of the new art, and suppliers of the cameras, plates and other necessities needed to make a living as a daguerreian. An oft-seen newspaper advertisement offered "[a] complete daguerreotype, with plates and appendages, perfect for a man of leisure, or a wise investor in search of a situation." There was money to be made and by 1844 over two dozen daguerreotype studios were listed in the city registry, an impressive number for a small metropolis whose population barely topped 89,000. Many of these studios were operated by artists who had once worked with brush and palette.

Marchand's was the city's most respected photographic studio, yet he was not content to allow inferior daguerreians to go about their business unmolested. He denounced them in farcical newspaper advertisements in which they were given silly nicknames. Exhibitions were held at which their work was paired with Marchand's superior renderings of the same subjects. Rumors circulated that more dastardly forms of sabotage were employed if these means did not drive a competitor out of New Orleans.

Pl. 12—*Canal Street at Noontime*, c. 1844–1845. Full-plate daguerreotype.

What was it about photography that so delighted people in the mid-1800s? Never before had a moment been so perfectly trapped. Painters were encouraged to work from daguerreotypes, not fussy paid models or subjects too busy to sit again and again for a portrait. Architects were promised benefits from images of great buildings with details unattainable from even the best lithographs—every gargoyle's smile visible, the mortar between each brick discernible. Photography advanced armchair travel beyond written accounts and imperfect sketches to accurate views of the Great Pyramids and the Parthenon.

America was in love with technology, but it was most in love with itself. Like Narcissus' still water, the mirror of the daguerreotype was irresistible. Local scenes, like Pl. 12, a busy Canal Street in winter, were more revered than pictures of other cities or distant lands. Marchand's gallery was well known for its wide range of New Orleanian subject matter—persons of distinction, buildings under construction, the bustling port, major thoroughfares at noon. The city had suffered a devastating economic crisis in 1837, and each year of recovered prosperity made its citizens love it more. This image of horses and pedestrians was winner of the First Premium Award at the 1845 Agricultural and Mechanics' Association Fair. For a daguerreotype of moving subjects, the image is remarkable—the dark Xs of workmen's suspenders, the ghostly legs of horses pulling delivery wagons, the domes of gentlemen's bowlers and the cupolas of ladies' parasols.

The *Bee* said of the photograph, "From a rooftop overlooking Canal Street, Claude Marchand has caught in an eye-blink what New Orleans has again become: A Metropolis alive with work and trade, a port where the World brings its goods and leaves with cotton, sugar, and the knowledge that the Crescent City is the Venice of the Americas. We consider Marchand's Soliotype the *ne plus ultra* of excellence in the amazing art which he has brought to us."

Pl. 13—*Francis Marmu, his wife Charlotte, and his daughter Vivian*, 1845. Half-plate daguerreotype.

Perhaps spurred by the warm reception given Emily Hulbert's portrait, dot eyes or no, the Marmus came to Marchand's studio shortly after the New Year. The family was well known; Mr. Marmu was a city councilman as well as a businessman, and his antics were famous. Felix Moissenet relates in his series of pamphlets *Prose Sketches of Notable New Orleanians* that "Francis Marmu was a man of great valor. When a black cat one day found its way into the City Building and then breached the defenses of the Council Room, Councilman Marmu was unafraid. He launched a fusillade of inkstands at the invading feline, chasing and cursing it as it attempted to circle and attack his flank. When other Councilmen were stuck and splattered by the missiles, and thus awoke from dreams of law and commerce, Mr. Marmu was so wise and quick as to be unharmed by the fusillade they launched in revenge. He dispatched the cat and made motions that the session be ended. Motion was seconded quickly and the brave man was carried away to a fine meal in commemoration of his thrilling victory."

At first glance, this portrait is odd due to the positioning of the subjects, Charlotte and Vivian segregated from Francis Marmu by a column with an almost indistinguishable daguerreotype set atop it. A Moissenet pamphlet offers an explanation: The portrait on the pillar is of William Spats, a Newark textile merchant. While visiting the city in October of 1844, Spats met Vivian, proposed, contracted yellow fever, and died. The ribbons both mother and daughter wear pinned to their breasts are in remembrance of the dead fiancé, a fact confirmed by Moissenet—"Vivian wore the grosgrain *in memoriam* of William until she replaced it with one for her father, then replaced that with one for her beloved mother."

Pls. 14, 15 & 16—*Nuptial Triptych, Dr. and Mrs. Victor Benton*, 1845. Quarter-plate daguerreotypes.

The nuptial triptych was a specialty of the Marchand studio, one that his newspaper advertisements claimed he had invented. In fact, his invention was only a modern turn on an old tradition. The triptych's case housed three portraits—the small individual portraits exchanged by courting couples Monday morning after Sunday night proposals as left and right panels (fiancé on the left, fiancée on the right), and a formal wedding portrait as the middle panel. Marchand's triptych was different only in that it utilized three daguerreotypes, not three oil miniatures.

The subjects of Pls. 14 and 15 are posed as was the fashion: young Doctor Benton holds a volume of Horace, his fingers tangled in the pages; Susana, the soon-to-be-Mrs. Benton, chastely clutches the Bible. The props are not unusual. The daguerreotype took from classic portraiture a love and respect for icons: Soldiers held pistols and sabers, mothers their young; schoolteachers leaned against Greek pillars; young lovers clutched flowers and gazed drunkenly. Good daguerreotypists provided trunks of hats, sidearms, musical instruments and great works of literature from which to choose. Marchand's prop shop is rumored to have rivaled the Opera House's.

Pl. 16, the wedding portrait, is oddly unconventional in that the groom's head is turned to gaze upon his bride instead of directly at the camera.

Felix Moissenet reports that Marchand and the doctor, originally from Boston and educated at Harvard College, became fast friends after meeting at a party. Benton, like most learned men of the day, was interested in all technological advances, including the daguerreotype. Marchand was famous for his volatile temper and lack of social graces—he is said to have slapped a woman during a play because she would not stop talking. Despite Marchand's hot blood, their friendship bloomed and Benton even experimented with the art. Sadly, a fire consumed the Benton family home in 1901 and no examples of Victor Benton's work are believed to have escaped the blaze.

Pl. 17—*Greta Dürtmeer*, 1845. Sixth-plate daguerreotype.
Pl. 18—*Memorial Portrait of Georg Dürtmeer*, 1845. Full-plate daguerreotype.

A news item in the *Daily Picayune* tells the story behind these two daguerreotypes. It reports that Mrs. Dürtmeer went to the Marchand studio one June Sunday to keep a portrait appointment. She was served tea and cakes while the camera and plate were readied, then was seated and arranged—neck positioned in the iron rest so that her head would remain still during the exposure, parasol angled against a knee, background adjusted to catch the late morning light. Problems then arose. Mrs. Dürtmeer was, as Pl. 17 proves, a homely woman. Despite the crack Emily Hulbert claims he made about her portrait, Marchand was known by many as a photographer who could manipulate the camera kindly.

Mrs. Dürtmeer's face was full and heavy, but her head small. Marchand knew how to compensate. He raised the camera and adjusted the headrest so that Mrs. Dürtmeer's head projected before her shoulders. She was annoyed and insulted by the adjustments and felt the portrait she was presented with was not good enough to warrant such indignities. She screamed at Marchand that he was incompetent, and she refused to pay. Marchand, the article claims, calmly explained that "The daguerreotype is a mirror, and if the mirror is held before Medusa . . . " Unamused by the reference to her lamentable hairdo, Mrs. Dürtmeer threw her portrait at Marchand and stormed out.

She hurried home and recounted the entire debacle to her husband, adding, one assumes, insults and attacks on her purity. Georg Dürtmeer was furious. He equipped himself with a set of pistols and his wife led the way back to the studio. According to the article, Marchand was suffering through a portrait session with "a brat of Irish origin" when Dürtmeer crashed in, pushed aside an assistant, and challenged Claude to a duel. Marchand accepted. The two men exited onto Canal, crossed to the neutral ground, and prepared.

This is the point at which the article's author, the *Picayune*'s Stanley Roberts, became an active part of the fracas. "I was discussing the season's mildness with a dry-goods shopkeeper when a man I knew as the heliographic artist Claude Marchand and another man, his shirtfront heaving, pulled pistols and began to step off distances." The reporter was pressed into service as Dürtmeer's second; Marchand's studio assistant provided that service for his employer.

Mrs. Dürtmeer and a small crowd watched as the men stood back-to-back, then paced away from each other—"a pickaninny with a fine voice was paid a penny to count aloud"—then turned and fired. Dürtmeer got off his shot first, but it was wide, striking a horse standing before a milk wagon.

Marchand's shot was prefect. Dürtmeer fell dead and his wife "threw herself ulu-lating upon his corpse." The police arrived and arrested Marchand, his assistant, the child paid to call out numbers, and Stanley Roberts. The assistant, Philip Breson, was charged, for some reason, with loitering, Roberts with the same, the number-calling youth for disturbing the peace. Except for Claude, all were released when Victor Ben-ton arrived and paid assorted fines.

Deciding what exactly Marchand's crime was required a day of study. On Monday afternoon he faced the judge to plead guilty to the charge of dueling on a Sunday, an offense surely found in the margin of a document from the century before by a studious clerk. Marchand paid a twenty-dollar penalty and was freed.

He hurried to his studio and gathered a camera and some plates, then made his way to the rooms of Herman Lance, the undertaker to whom Georg Dürtmeer's body had been entrusted. The connections between the physicians who tended to the dying, the photographers who took memorial portraits, and the men who pre-pared bodies for eternal rest is easy to figure. In Pl. 18 Dürtmeer is posed on a plain cooling board much like the ones upon which slain outlaws were posed after Wild West executions.

That evening Marchand rounded up the newspaperman and other witnesses to the duel and paid a visit on the Mrs. Dürtmeer. "He rang the bell and the Widow answered. At the sight of Marchand, she sank into a chair. When he pulled from its wrappings the portrait of her husband, her shrieks were grotesque and the entire party hurried for the relative silence of the street."

Pl. 19—*Memorial Portrait of Francis Marmu*, 1845. Half-plate daguerreotype.

Pl. 20—*Mourning Portrait of Charlotte and Vivian Marmu*, 1845. Half-plate daguerreotype.

Pl. 21—*Spirit Portrait of Charlotte Marmu Standing Behind Her Daughter Vivian*, 1845. Half-plate daguerreotype.

Pl. 22—*Memorial Portrait of Charlotte Marmu*, 1845. Half-plate daguerreotype.

Pl. 23—*Mourning Portrait of Vivian Marmu*, 1845. Half-plate daguerreotype.

Portraits of the dead seem odd and macabre to the contemporary viewer, but dur-ing the mid-nineteenth century they were common and often considered necessary as a means of keeping the deceased in mind. Even the extremely poor scraped and bor-rowed to afford a memorial photograph of a loved one. For many the memorial was the first and only portrait in which they would appear. Careful survey of the obituary sec-tions of New Orleans papers has led to the discovery of hundreds of memorial daguerreotypes affixed to the doors of crypts in the city's many cemeteries. Time and sunlight have turned a large percentage of these to tarnished squares. A very few por-traits hold faint images of the crypts' occupants, but most are dim mirrors that show only the visages of the living.

Francis Marmu was one of the many victims of yellow fever in the summer of 1845, the summer that would host the decade's worst epidemic. In Pl. 19 Mr. Marmu is seated in a chair, a Bible held loosely in his hands. He looks as if he has slipped into a gentle nap. Such "sleep of death" poses are often seen, especially if the subject is very young or very old. Adolescents, teen-agers and young adults are usually posed in bed or in their coffins, a reflection of the fact that their deaths are more startling and sudden. The portrait is in a black morocco memorial case with an engraved silver funerary mat and silvered outlines. Poems, death notices and letters were often pinned to the velvet facing mats of memorial cases; Mr. Marmu's has a small brooch engraved with his initials and those of his wife and daughter pinned to its plum-colored cloth.

In Pl. 20 Charlotte and Vivian stand hand-in-hand, both in second-stage mourning dress, a clue that dates this plate several months later than Pl. 19. It is likely that the two women were absorbed in the details of Francis Marmu's death and unable to take the time for a portrait. Although the cover glass has been cracked and some deterioration has occurred, careful inspection proves that in Pl. 20 Vivian holds Pl. 19, making the daguerreotype an odd diptych.

Pl. 21 demonstrates how a master like Marchand could transform one of the daguerreotype's shortcomings into a wonderful effect. Vivian's pose and both women's dresses are the same as those in Pl. 20; both portraits were undoubtedly made during the same sitting. In Pl. 21 a ghost image of Charlotte Marmu appears to be standing behind her daughter. While spirit photographs became somewhat common in the late 1860s, this is one of the earliest known examples of the technique. The ghost image was managed by having the "spirit" subject move out of the picture before the exposure fully elapsed. Pl. 21's cover glass has also been broken. Pieces of the glass are missing, and the deterioration is much worse than that suffered by Pl. 20, but the ghost effect is still dramatic.

Charlotte Marmu died in the first week of July, and Pl. 22 is a very typical memorial portrait save for the presence of a cat peeking over the coffin's edge.

It was not rare for entire families to be carried away, common for the older members to be the least able to recover. Each summer orphanages swelled with young survivors. Vivian's resilience can be explained by this passage from Felix Moissenet's pamphlets: "The Marmus were originally from Massachusetts, a fact neither Francis nor Charlotte let be forgotten. A trip to the Marmu home in the summer months would invariably set the stage for a sermon on Devil Summer and his Hell Fires and Demon Mosquitoes. Vivian was born in New Orleans, and when young she suffered and recovered from a bout of the Fever. Such good luck made her, as well as so many other natives to this fine City, impervious to Mister Jack. Her parents, alas, were not so lucky—in short order the poor child was left without father or mother."

In Pl. 24 orphaned Vivian is stunningly posed. She holds a lily and gazes at the memorial portraits of her mother and father which stand on a small table at her elbow. Marchand's use of light and shade is a marvel. The drape behind Vivian is a range of peaks and valleys, the folds of valleys dark with shadow, the peaks snow-capped with well-directed light. The table's legs guide the eye upward from the dark pool of the carpet to the pale line of the lily that leads to Vivian.

Pls. 24 & 25—*Wedding Diptych of Vivian Marchand*, 1845. Half-plate daguerreotypes.

Vivian and Claude were wed two weeks after her mother passed away. The *Bee* wedding announcement of 28 July mistakenly states that Marchand hailed from Boston, but does manage to spell *soliotype* correctly, a feat of no small consequence. The couple honeymooned in Natchez, Mississippi. After their return, the Marchands and the Bentons passed many hours together. The omnipresent Felix Moissenet reports in one of his pamphlets that Vivian and Susana spent their time doting on infants—they were both pregnant—while Victor and Claude discussed photography and medicine.

In Pl. 24 Vivian smiles happily, her mourning dress replaced by a light frock pinned with the always-present grosgrain. In Pl. 25 she stands in her wedding dress. The pair of daguerreotypes is in a kidskin-bound case once white that has aged to the color of butter. The mats are engraved with the names of the bride and the groom and the cover is embossed with the wedding date. In both pictures Vivian appears happy—in Pl. 25 her face is contorted with joy.

This groom-less diptych is odd in light of Marchand's special nuptial triptychs. Also odd is the mysterious lack of any photograph of a man who spent nearly every day around cameras. The only known photograph in which even a bit of Marchand appears is Pl. 1, and only his hand and his slim wrist are visible.

Pls. 26–36—*Vivian Marchand*, 1845. Full-, half- and quarter-plate daguerreotypes.

Between July and August of 1845 Marchand made at least these eleven daguerreotypes of Vivian. She appears in an assortment of poses and settings. Most are simple and seem unplanned. The Canal Street studio closed late in July and in August the original Toulouse Street studio reopened. The Marchands lived in a shotgun-style home behind which the small studio was housed in what Felix Moissenet describes as "an outbuilding more suited to horses or slaves than to an artist of Marchand's talents." It is easy to imagine Claude playfully luring his wife back to the studio, or bringing a camera into the house and making the equivalent of a snapshot. In Pl. 26 Vivian holds out a cake as if she's brought it to show her husband. In Pl. 27 Vivian is dressed for the theater, opera glasses dangling from her wrist. In Pl. 28 a servant girl brushes her hair. Pl. 29 is a beautiful study of Vivian looking out a window, her elbow, shoulder and chin forming a triangle through which sunlight gently pours. In Pl. 30 she sits on a blanket with a picnic lunch. The fruits, breads and even the flatware seem carefully placed. The sun is reflected in miniature on the surface of a dish, apples and pears and rolls around it like planets, Vivian in a white dress reclining above the assortment like a constellation. In Pl. 31 she stands in her nightclothes, her eyes bleary with sleep, her mouth a groggy smile.

Vivian appears nude in five of the plates. In four of them her face is in shadow or covered by her hands, but in Pl. 32 she stands before a potted tree smiling happily. Visible is the button of a birthmark on her thigh, a referent proving the woman sprawled on the settee in Pl. 33 and the woman bathing in Pl. 34 and the woman reflected in the mirror in Pl. 35 and the woman supine on the rug in Pl. 36 are all Vivian Marchand.

The *Yellow Jack* Plates:
Pl. 37—*The Howard Association*, 1845. Half-plate daguerreotype.
Pl. 38—*The Charity Hospital Fever Ward*, 1845. Half-plate daguerreotype.
Pl. 39—*Trees Being Felled Near Lake Pontchartrain to Combat the Yellow Fever*, 1845. Half-plate daguerreotype.

Pl. 40—*Jason Meyers, A Stone Cutter*, 1845. Half-plate daguerreotype.

Victor Benton was a member of the Howard Association, a group of doctors and other citizens who cared for the sick during the yearly yellow fever outbreaks. Pl. 37 shows the thirty members of the Association gathered to discuss the epidemic. The City Council annually granted the Howards absurdly small amounts of money to be used to help the city's poor, while at the same time most newspapers ridiculed the selfless men as doomsayers and panics. Both the council and the papers wanted to keep the outbreak as hushed as possible. Even though the summer of 1845 was so filled with fever deaths that newspapers across the nation took to calling New Orleans "The Necropolis of the South," as late as 9 August the *Daily Tropic* was denying the existence of yellow fever in the city. It is easy to understand why—a deserted city holds neither advertisers nor consumers.

In the summer of 1845 Benton and the Howard Association enlisted Marchand to chronicle in daguerreotypes what would turn out to be one of the worst yellow fever epidemics ever to strike the Crescent City. New Orleans' population at the time was 108,699, and that summer the fever carried away almost 3,000 victims, close to one of every thirty inhabitants. These numbers are even more shocking when it's taken into account that as many of the 108,699 who could afford to leave fled the city for the summer. They left to escape not only "Mister Jack," but also the oppressive heat and the annoying clouds of mosquitoes not yet recognized as the means of the fever's transmission. The doctor published a small volume of observations entitled *Yellow Jack* that accompanied a group of Marchand's daguerreotypes displayed late in August of 1845. Few of these photographs remain. Many may have been in Victor Benton's possession—he was the executor of Marchand's will—and were possibly destroyed by the fire that ravaged the Benton home in 1901.

The beds in Charity Hospital's fever ward were filled by middle-May of 1845 and remained filled until the end of October. New immigrants, often the poorest residents of the city, were least immune to yellow fever. Many lived in shanty towns in the swamps north of the city, areas filled with mosquitoes. The large percentage of fever deaths among the poor was constantly offered as proof that they were to blame. Every fall and winter featured numerous calls for bans on immigration—the Irish were a favorite scapegoat.

None of the fifty beds visible in Pl. 38's view of the fever ward is vacant, and most of the narrow cots are shared. Marchand has posed the subjects oddly in comparison to the more impromptu style of the other *Yellow Jack* plates. A dozen nuns stand in a careful line at the end of the aisle separating the double row of beds, several patients prop themselves on elbows to face the camera. Careful scrutiny of the daguerreotype finds at least three beds hold dead men—the first bed of the left row, and the two beds in the middle of the right row.

Pl. 39 is one of the few surviving examples of Marchand's landscape work, and the story that accompanies it is fascinating. In the heat of mid-August, then-Mayor Orion Wagasuc took to heart the advice of an English surgeon, John Redgrave, who in an editorial published in the *Daily Picayune* hypothesized that the fever which attacked the city each summer had its root in "some type of insect or organism or flora that inhabits the trees and foliage near the city." He was close. The fever was being transmitted by mosquitoes, but they were just as prevalent, if not more, in the open sewers of New Orleans than among the trees that stood between the city and Lake Pontchartrain. The mayor agreed with Redgrave's theory and hired work crews and sent them on a mission: Cut down each and every tree. Marchand was hired to record the attempt at salvation of the city's populace. As Pl. 39 shows, the daguerreotype process was far from the stop-action now possible with a brief shutter opening and fast film. The trees fall in arcs across the horizon, thirteen falling at once, the entirety of their descents recorded. The yellow fever went undaunted even after this massive effort, and Wagasuc was not reelected though he ran on a platform that attempted to stress the fact that his family too had fallen victim to the pestilence—his daughter, three year-old Dorcas, died in August of 1845. (Her *Daily Picayune* obituary mentions that Marchand made her memorial portrait.)

Pl. 40 is the last daguerreotype discussed in *Yellow Jack*. The subject's head is obscured in a cloud of marble chips and his arm is a blur of white cloth as he cuts a name into one of 1845's many grave markers. Benton writes, "Mister Meyers tried to laugh when he judged that the Fever was the best thing for the Undertaker, the Priest and the Stone Cutter, but his mirth gave way to tears. His son James and his wife Roberta both died earlier in the summer, victims of Yellow Jack, and Mister Meyers cut their names into stones."

Pl. 41—*Pregnancy Portrait of Vivian Marchand*, August 21st, 1845. Half-plate daguerreotype.

Pl. 42—*Memorial Portrait of Vivian Marchand*, August 29th, 1845. Sixth-plate daguerreotype.

Plate 41 continues Claude's loving record of his wife's short life. The portrait is simple: the entire frame filled with Vivian's bare stomach, a hand-lettered card record-ing the date held just below the navel, the backdrop unpatterned and dark to provide striking definition to her light belly. This is the last plate of what must have been a nine-plate series documenting her pregnancy, and its date makes one interesting fact clear—Vivian was seven months pregnant when she and Claude wed.

While he was documenting the coming of his child, Marchand was also involved in recording the yellow fever epidemic. The many plates of Claude's wife, these two especially, surely had their inspiration in the time he spent away from her. It must have been heartening for Claude to return to vital life after a day photographing death, crush-ing for him to lose Vivian.

She died in childbirth; Victor Benton was unable to save her. Vivian's obituary notice and the engraving on her tomb are the same: "A Loving Mother Who Sacrificed Herself for Her Child." Her son, Louis Jacques Mandé Marchand, died one week later. No memorial portrait of the child is known to exist.

Pl. 42 is out of character for Marchand. He used a sixth-plate, the smallest and cheapest he offered, a size he almost never used for memorials. The lighting is bad, the angle odd. Unlike the usual careful posings in which the dead look as if they are nap-ping, Vivian's face still retains the pain of her passing.

Pl. 43—*Vivian Marchand (?) and a Servant Girl*, n.d. Sixth-plate daguerreotype.

Pl. 43 was found in the sea chest among the many photographs of Vivian Marc-hand, and the servant is the same young woman brushing Vivian's hair in Pl. 28. The face of the woman on the left has been scratched from the plate, but the tiny black loop of ribbon Vivian wore in memory of William Spats and her parents is visible between the scars a knife has inflicted on the daguerreotype's silver plating. The figure on the left must be Vivian. Such damage could only be deliberate. To alter the portrait in this manner someone would have had to have removed it from its case, cut the tape joining cover sheet to daguerreotype, scratched away the image, then retaped and replaced the damaged plate. Even with the brutal erasure, the plate's remaining images are nearly perfect. Both Vivian and the girl hold black kittens, the little cats no more than silhouettes against the women's light laps.

Russell on Third-Person Objective Point of View

The summer after I finished graduate school, I worked packing art in a French Quarter photography gallery. I handled, stared at, and then boxed up and shipped pictures by Walker Evans, Eudora Welty, E. J. Bellocq, Diane Arbus, and Edward Curtis. Inspired by these photographs, I began writing what I called "snapshot stories," one- or two-page riffs or expansions of the scenes in the pictures. It was during that time that I first encountered daguerreotypes, and more than by any other photographs, I was haunted by these ghostly, fading images of formally posed citizens of the nineteenth century. But when I tried to write about those people and the world outside of the gilded edges of their cased portraits, I was stymied. I couldn't figure out how to make into narrative moments as static and beautiful and old as leaves or bugs trapped in amber.

Over the next few months I did some research and learned that many of the worst of New Orleans's yellow fever epidemics occurred around the same time that daguerreotype-process photography arrived in the city. Then I found that the relative cheapness of a daguerreotype allowed people who could not afford to pay a painter the opportunity to obtain a memorial portrait of their loved ones. Raging epidemics in 1840s New Orleans and portraits of the dead provided interesting pieces for a narrative, but I still couldn't figure out how to put together these pieces to tell a story, let alone puzzle out what or who the story was about. Then one day I saw a portrait of an anonymous baby with a disembodied hand palming his or her head. The caption explained that the exposure time for a daguerreotype was long (a fact I knew) and for that reason parents often held the heads of babies still while their portraits were being made (a fact I did not know). For reasons that I still don't understand, reading this snippet of arcane technical information flipped a switch inside my head and I knew at once that the story I had been trying to write was about the man attached to that hand. Now the question was how to tell that story.

There are three types of third-person point of view. In third-person omniscient, the narrator can glean information from anywhere, including the thoughts and feelings of any of the characters, as well as their actions. In third-person limited, the narrative voice can report on only what is in the minds of a select few characters, often only one.

In third-person objective, sometimes called third-person dramatic, the narrator reports only observable details. The objective narrator doesn't have access to the internal thoughts of characters or background information about the setting or situation beyond what can be seen or heard.

In "Yellow Jack" the only information about Claude Marchand and the other characters available to the narrator is that which can be seen in the daguerreotypes and read in newspapers and other published accounts. I chose this point of view because when writing "Yellow Jack" I was limited by my twentieth-century ignorance of the nineteenth century. Like the narrator, I looked at daguerreotypes, read old newspapers, pamphlets, and period medical monographs, and from this information put together a plausible idea of what life might have been like for a photographer in 1840s New Orleans. Then I began to translate that idea into a narrative.

The third-person objective was the right point of view for me to use for several reasons. I was writing about someone very different from me who lived in a time very different from mine, and I worried that having Claude speak in the first person would sound inauthentic. The third-person objective allowed me to imagine the minutiae of life lived one hundred and fifty years ago in a way that seems authentic by using that minutiae, real and imagined, to tell the story: things don't lie. Third-person objective was also the point of view used by the art books that provided the model for the know-it-all tone of the narrator's voice, and that know-it-all voice provided the narrator one more level of authenticity.

Third-person objective is probably the least used of the third-person options, one saved for situations in which an author wants to create distance between the reader and the characters. One goal in fiction (using third-person limited or first-person point of view) is to create closeness between the narrator and the main character—and therefore between the characters, the narrator, and the reader—but in unique stories, third-person objective can be quite effective.

A powerful example is the objective narrator of Shirley Jackson's story "The Lottery," who observes an unnamed American town with the detachment of an anthropologist taking field notes. The narrator describes the townspeople, records their actions, but never enters the minds or hearts of those observed. We never learn the narrator's own thoughts or opinions, which adds to the story's objective quality. You can see this in the opening passage of "The Lottery":

> The morning of June 27th was clear and sunny, with the fresh warmth of a full-summer day; the flowers were blossoming profusely and the grass was richly green. The people of the village began to gather in the square, between the post office and the bank, around ten o'clock; in some towns there were so many people that the lottery took two days and had to be started on June 26th, but in this village, where there were only about three hundred people, the whole lottery took less than two hours, so it could begin at ten o'clock in the morning and still be through in time to allow the villagers to get home for noon dinner.

This matter-of-fact narration is the perfect choice for telling the story Jackson's narrator needs to tell. The narrator's even tone lulls us into a calm that is violently shattered when we learn that the lottery is to pick the citizen who will be ritualistically stoned to death. The cool detachment of the third-person objective point of view both increases the shock of the ending—we never see it coming—and allows this surprise to be more than a trick: the objective narrator neither hid nor foreshadowed anything.

Another well-known example of the third-person objective point of view is Ernest Hemingway's "Hills Like White Elephants," a story of a man and woman having a conversation while waiting for a train. Hemingway's voyeuristic narrator offers a flat transcription stripped of any commentary. The story begins with a simple description and a record of a seemingly unimportant exchange:

> The American and the girl with him sat at a table in the shade, outside the building. It was very hot and the express from Barcelona would come in forty minutes. It stopped at this junction for two minutes and went to Madrid.
> "What should we drink?" the girl asked. She had taken off her hat and put it on the table.
> "It's pretty hot," the man said.
> "Let's drink beer."

Quickly the conversation becomes intense and almost cryptic, and by using a third-person objective narrator, Hemingway lets us listen as if we're sitting at the next table trying to figure out what's going on:

> "You've got to realize," he said, "that I don't want you to do it if you don't want to. I'm perfectly willing to go through with it if it means anything to you."
> "Doesn't it mean anything to you? We could get along."
> "Of course it does. But I don't want anybody but you. I don't want anyone else. And I know it's perfectly simple."
> "Yes, you know it's perfectly simple."

Here the third-person objective allows (or invites or entices) us to make our own interpretations, to enter the story as active participants. We can feel sorry for the woman, the man, for both of them. Because the narrator's investment in manipulating the reader is seemingly nonexistent, the reliability of that narrator is heightened: we believe this is *exactly* what was said.

For "Yellow Jack," I felt third-person objective was the best choice for many of the reasons it works so well in "The Lottery" and in "Hills Like White Elephants." I wanted the calm tone that Jackson's narrator provides so that I too could comment matter-of-factly and with authority on things that I would not have been able to comment on in the same way if I had chosen to use a first-person narrator. I wanted the ability to offer surprises without making the reader feel she or he had been manipulated or short-changed. Hemingway's third-person objective narrator is trustworthy, and I wanted my narrator to be trustworthy, too. Neither "The Lottery" nor "Hills Like White Elephants" is an example of historical fiction, but the benefits they reap by using a detached objective narrator are similar to the benefits I enjoyed by using the same kind of narrator. The objective narrator is able to provide enough specific details to allow the reader the intimacy or immediacy needed to make a story interesting and authentic, while at the same time providing enough distance that a reader must become an active part of the story to maintain that immediacy.

After I figured out that third-person objective point of view was the right way to tell the story, I wrote a two-page description of the portrait of the baby. I decided that the baby was a boy named after the inventor of the daguerreotype, that the man whose hand held his head was the inventor's former apprentice. I threw in some details based on what I had learned about yellow fever and 1840s New Orleans, titled it "Pl. 98" as if it were part of a series, put it in an envelope, and sent it to the literary magazine *Epoch*. Michael Koch, editor of the magazine, called me a few weeks later to tell me he wanted to publish "Pl. 98," which shocked and delighted me, and then asked where the others were.

"The others?" I asked, completely confused.

"This is number ninety-eight," he explained. "Can I see the other ninety-seven?"

"Sure!" I agreed as calmly as I could. "The other ninety-seven! Of course! Give me a month to clean them up and I'll send you the other ninety-seven."

I was at that time working as a helpdesk dispatcher at a software company, and over a month of lunch hours I created a series of imagined daguerreotypes made by the fictional photographer Claude Marchand: "Yellow Jack." The third-person limited objective point of view allowed me the narrative authority I needed to blend a few facts, like the technical details of how daguerreotypes are made, with a lot of fiction.

One final note: When the editors of this book asked me to comment on "Yellow Jack" as an example of the third-person objective point of view, I happily agreed. That's how I intended to write it, and I think that's how most people read it. But let me offer another way to read this story: as a first-person narrative. That know-it-all voice could be the voice of a *specific* art critic and this story could be telling us *his* story based on the way he interprets Claude Marchand's photographs. Think about it: those art history textbooks, just like this textbook, are written by somebody . . .

Writing Suggestions

1. As a general rule of thumb, third-person objective casts the narrator as an observer, preventing the narration from entering the thoughts and interior emotions of the characters. (For models, in addition to "Yellow Jack," read the excerpts from "The Lottery" and "Hills Like White Elephants" above.) In a page or two, describe the discussions you see during your lunch break, keeping in mind that you, yourself, are not a character in this scene. Record the discussions as if you are a video camera mounted on the wall. How does the narration in this scene differ from the narration in a scene told from the perspective of third-person limited, in which the narrative consciousness rests inside the main character? (For an example of third-person limited, refer to Judith Claire Mitchell's "A Man of Few Words," pages 194–210.)

2. Tell a story in third-person objective by simply describing and interpreting photographs found in a photo album—or even images found in an art book or a book of photography. What kind of stories can be told primarily through images? What is the narrator's unstated interest in these photos? How can such a story define characters without having direct access to their thoughts and interior emotions?

3. From a story you've completed, locate a scene you found difficult to write. Recast the experience through the lens of third-person objective narration. Does changing point of view free you, as the author, to explore the scene more honestly? How would casting the entire story into third-person objective change the texture and quality of the writing? If so, how?

4. In his commentary, Josh Russell names two famous examples of third-person objective, "Hills Like White Elephants" by Ernest Hemingway and "The Lottery" by Shirley Jackson. Find these two stories in your library. In your notebook, describe the experience of reading stories cast in third-person objective as opposed to stories told from the perspective of either first person or third-person limited narration. Using materials in the library or on the Internet, can you find advice on how to write in or better understand third-person objective? (Try typing "third person objective" into a search engine.)

> *Writing has laws of perspective, of light and shade just as painting does,*
> *or music. If you are born knowing them, fine. If not, learn them.*
> *Then rearrange the rules to suit yourself.*
> —Truman Capote

Section 7

CONSTRUCTING A SCENE

Introduction
Constructing a Scene

Most films and TV shows are a continuous series of scenes—one scene after another. But most short stories are not a continuous series of such scenes. Rather they are a combination of summary narration and scenes. Summary narration compresses time, moving quickly through many events, while scenes open up into full detail, action, and dialogue. Most stories utilize summary narration for their less dramatic moments and save actual scenes for key sections, allowing readers to experience the drama with authority and power.

In the short story "Of Falling," Aaron Gwyn gracefully moves between summary narration and full scenes. In the following passage, the story recounts the moment George Crider, the main character, witnessed the death of his brother. The story places this moment in summary narration, moving briskly through the potentially sentimental events of his brother's demise, without opening to dialogue or full setting. It compresses time—in this case a great deal of time, two weeks—into a single paragraph. The scene, though important, does not directly explore the story's main themes, such as George Crider's spiritual dilemma. The author is making a decision that other scenes, situated later in the story, are more important and therefore deserve more attention than the scene that follows.

> One day the animal they were riding stepped in a sinkhole and bucked. George caught hold of its mane, but his brother was behind him and fell to the ground. The boy's arm broke the skin, and the bone jutted into dirt. He developed tetanus and in two weeks was dead. George blamed himself for this, as did his parents, and at the funeral, when he climbed into the grave and sought to open the casket, his father lost two teeth trying to retrieve him.

In George Singleton's commentary on fictional time, he investigates the possibilities of full scenes and summary narration so that you will make educated decisions in your own short stories about when to employ one technique over the other. He also explores the way short stories manage and control time through narration, specifically commenting on the use of flashbacks and exposition.

Detail and Setting

In contrast, full scenes are often developed with greater attention to detail and setting. The above example, from "Of Falling," like most good fiction, employs detail and setting. We know, for instance, that the boys were horseback riding on a dangerous terrain with sinkholes, which represents an aspect of setting. We also know that the boy's bone, when broken, poked through his skin and "jutted into dirt," which is a detail that calls forth an exact image. But specificity in this passage is not yet developed to the point where it becomes a full scene. A scene is a single dramatized episode, often uninterrupted by a change of setting, that depicts action with sustained detail and a well-defined location.

Were this a full scene, we might've seen the boy fall from the horse—how his hands let go of the horse's mane, the way his body angled off the animal, the manner that his body crumpled onto the ground. What did it sound like when the bone broke? A snap, a pop, the sound of an oak branch breaking in two? Furthermore, we might've known exactly when this event happened—early morning, in the blistering heat of midday, or as an evening breeze moved off the foothills. We might've seen the entire setting: pine trees rising in the distance, their needles dusted with pollen, or the sun, hovering like a magician's orb, at the edge of the dusty, barren horizon.

Later in the story, when George Crider begins to explore spirituality, the story makes a pointed shift away from summary narration. The scene reprinted below explores more specifically George Crider's experience, paying close attention to details of George's actions and the setting, that of a revival meeting. Within the story, time moves slower here, allowing the language to focus more pointedly on imagery and action, thereby drawing the reader more fully into the scene and suggesting its importance.

> George found much of the service consonant with what he had known from his childhood. There was a low stage and a choir on it, men in folding chairs dressed in ties and slacks and white shirts. There were rows of similar chairs for the audience, stapled pages containing a few hymns, sawdust on the floor, carpets down the aisles. Midway through, paper buckets with crosses stenciled on them were passed for offering.
>
> After Roberts delivered a brief sermon, he asked those in need of healing to form a line to the left of the stage. He told them it did not have to be physical healing.
>
> "There are three kinds of healing," he told them. "There is physical healing and emotional healing and healing of the spirit." He said God could perform all three.
>
> Sadie leaned over, whispered to George. He shook his head. When she went to lean again, he rose from his seat and stepped in line.

Later in this section, Reginald McKnight considers the importance of detail and setting. In particular, McKnight suggests ways to use these elements as a means of further developing facets of a character and even of a story's plot.

Dialogue

Later, in the same scene from "Of Falling," the level of specificity is heightened and the sense of pacing slows, further developing the scene. This section recounts many individual reactions, gestures, and actions as the night at the tent revival continues. The story even opens to full dialogue, recording each spoken line. Consider how much we, as readers, would lose if this exchange were recast in a single paragraph of summary narration.

> The woman began to shiver; then her body became rigid and she fell backward to the ground. A man in a dark suit came and covered her legs with a blanket. Another

member of the audience approached, handed up her card. George watched all this, feeling of a sudden as if someone had hollowed him.

He started to turn, but just then one of Roberts's assistants happened down the line. He noticed George's card was blank and touched him on the elbow, inquiring after his affliction.

George shook his head, tried to step around the man, but found himself blocked by a row of card tables piled with books and pamphlets.

The man looked askance, leaned toward him, and George quickly told the story of his fall. When he finished, the other's face had an amazed look. He took George by the arm, parted the crowd, and led him onto the stage. They stood to the side while Roberts prayed, and then the man went to the evangelist and whispered into his ear.

Roberts turned. He rose, took the microphone from its stand, and walked to George. The crowd quieted. Roberts's voice in the microphone was wet and very loud.

"Tell these people your name."

George shifted from one foot to the other. He brought a hand from behind his back and scratched at his nose. "George Crider," he said.

"And you had an accident?" Roberts asked. "Yes."

"You fell?"

"Yes."

"How far?"

"One hundred sixteen feet."

Many in the crowd gasped; some called to God. "And you were hurt?"

In his commentary on dialogue, Keith Lee Morris examines the way that effective dialogue can contribute to the development of a scene. He offers suggestions for creating realistic dialogue and looks at significant ways that dialogue in fiction differs from real life conversation.

Taken together, the following three stories and their commentaries will help you manage fictional time in your own stories, knowing when to shift between summary narration and full scenes. They will also help you develop your understanding of detail, setting, and dialogue, so that your scenes will ring with authenticity and authority.

George Singleton

Show-and-Tell

From *The Atlantic Monthly* and *The Half-Mammals of Dixie*

I wasn't old enough to know that my father couldn't have obtained a long-lost letter from the famed lovers Héloise and Abelard, and since European history wasn't part of my third-grade curriculum, I felt no remorse at the time for bringing the handwritten document (on lined three-hole Blue Horse filler paper), announcing its value, and reading it to the class at Friday show-and-tell. My classmates—who would all grow up to be idiots, in my opinion, since they feared anything outside of Forty-five, South Carolina, thus making them settle down exactly where they got trained, thus shrinking the gene pool even more—brought the usual: starfishes and conch shells bought in Myrtle Beach gift shops, though claimed to have been found during summer vacation; Indian-head pennies given as birthday gifts by grandfathers; the occasional pet gerbil, corn snake, or tropical fish.

My father instructed me how to read the letter, what words to stress, when to pause. I, of course, protested directly after the first dry run. Some of the words and phrases reached beyond my vocabulary. The general tone of the letter, I knew, would only get me playground-taunted by boys and girls alike. My father told me to pipe down and read louder. He told me to use my hands better, and he got out a metronome.

I didn't know that my father—"a widower" is how he told me to describe him, although everyone knew that Mom had run off to Nashville and hadn't died—had once dated Ms. Suber, my teacher. My parents' pasts never came up in conversation, even after my mother ended up tending bar at a place called the Merchant's Lunch, on Lower Broad, more often than she sang on various honky-tonk stages, waiting for representation by a man who would call her the next Patsy Cline. No, the prom night and homecoming of my father's senior year in high school with Ms. Suber never leaked out in our talks, whether we ate supper in front of the television screaming at Walter Cronkite or played pinball down at the Sunken Gardens Lounge.

I got up in front of the class. I knew that a personal, caring, loving, benevolent God didn't exist, seeing as I had prayed that my classmates would exceed their allotted time, et cetera, et cetera, and then we'd go to recess, lunch, and one of the mandatory filmstrips that South Carolina elementary school students watched weekly, on topics as tragic and diverse as Friendship, Fire Safety, Personal Hygiene, and Bee Stings. "I have a famous letter written from one famous person to another famous person," I said.

Ms. Suber held her mouth in a tiny O. Nowadays I realize that she was a beauty, but at the time she seemed just another seventy-year-old woman in front of an elementary school class, her corkboard filled with exclamation marks. She wasn't but thirty-five, really. Ms. Suber motioned for me to move closer to the music stand she also used on Recorder Day. "And what are these famous people's names, Mendal?"

Ricky Hutton, who'd already shown off a ship in a bottle that he didn't make but said he did, yelled out, "My father has a letter from President Johnson's wife thanking him for picking up litter."

"My grandma sent me a birthday card with a two-dollar bill inside," said Libby Belcher, the dumbest girl in the class, who went on to get a doctorate in education and then became superintendent of the school district.

I stood there with my folded document. Ms. Suber said, "Go on."

"I forget who wrote this letter. I mean, they were French people."

"Might it be Napoleon and Josephine?" Ms. Suber produced a smirk that I would see often in my life, from women who immediately recognized any untruth I chose to tell.

I said, "My father told me, but I forget. It's not signed or anything." Which was true.

Ms. Suber pointed at Bill Gilliland and told him to quit throwing his baseball in the air, a baseball supposedly signed by Shoeless Joe Jackson. None of us believed this, seeing as the signature was printed, at best. We never relented on Gilliland, and in due course he used the ball in pickup games until the cover wore off.

I unfolded the letter and read, "'My dearest.'"

"These are French people writing in English, I suppose," Ms. Suber said.

I nodded. I said, "They were smart, I believe. 'I want to tell you that if I live to be a hundred I won't meet another man like you. If I live to be a hundred there shall be no love to match ours.'"

The entire class began laughing, of course. My face reddened. I looked at Ms. Suber, but she concentrated on her shoe. "'That guy who wrote that "How Do I Love Thee" poem has nothing on us, my sugar-booger-baby.'"

"That's enough," Ms. Suber belted out. "You can sit down, Mendal."

I pointed at the letter. I had another dozen paragraphs to go, some of which contained rhymes. I hadn't gotten to the word "throbbing," which showed up fourteen times. "I'm not making any of this up," I said. I walked two steps toward my third-grade teacher, but she stood up and told everyone to go outside except me.

Glenn Flack walked by and said, "You're in trouble, Mendal Dawes." Carol Anderson, who was my third-grade girlfriend, looked as if she was going to cry.

Ms. Suber said, "You've done nothing wrong, Mendal. Please tell your daddy that I got it. When he asks what happened today, just say 'Ms. Suber got it.' Okay?"

I put the letter in my side pants pocket. I said, "My father's a widower."

My father was waiting for me when I got home. I never really knew what he did for a living, outside of driving within a hundred-mile radius of Forty-five, buying up land, and then reselling it when the time was right. He had a knack. That was his word. For a time I thought it was the make of his car. "I drive around all day and buy land," he said more than once, before and after my mother took off to replace Patsy Cline. "I have a Knack."

I came home wearing a canvas book bag on my back, filled with a math book and an abacus. I said, "Hey, Dad."

He held his arms wide open, as if I were a returning POW. "Did your teacher send back a note to me?"

I reached in my pocket and pulled out the letter from Héloise to Abelard. I handed it to him and said, "She made me quit reading."

"She made you quit reading? How far along did you get?"

I told him that I had only gotten to the part about "sugar-booger-baby." I said, "Is this one of those lessons in life you keep telling me about, like when we went camping?" My father taught me early on how to tell the difference between regular leaves and poison ivy, when we camped out beside the Saluda River, far from any commode, waiting for him to envision which tract would be most salable later.

"Goddamn it to hell. She didn't say anything else after you read the letter?"

My father wore a seersucker suit and a string tie. I said, "She called recess pretty much in the middle of me reading the thing. This is some kind of practical joke, isn't it?"

My father looked at me as if I'd peed on his wingtips. He said, "Now, why would I do something like that to the only human being I love in this world?"

I couldn't imagine why. Why would a man who—as he liked to tell me often—before my birth had played baseball for the Yankees in the summer and football for the Packers in the winter, and had competed in the Olympics, ever revert to playing jokes on his nine-year-old son? "Ms. Suber seemed kind of mad."

"Did she cry? Did she start crying? Did she turn her head away from y'all and blow her nose into a handkerchief? Don't hold back, Mendal. Don't think that you're embarrassing your teacher or anything for telling the truth. Ms. Suber would want you to tell the truth, wouldn't she?"

I said, "Uh-huh. Probably."

"Uh-huh probably she cried, or uh-huh probably she'd want you to tell the truth?" My father walked to the kitchen backward, pulled a bottle of bourbon from a shelf, and drank from it straight. Twenty years later I would do the same thing, but over a dog that needed to be put to sleep.

I said, "Uh-huh. I told her you were a widower and everything. We got to go to recess early."

My father kept walking backward. He took a glass from the cabinet and cracked an ice tray. He put cubes in the glass, poured bourbon into it, and stood staring at me as if I had told secrets to the enemy. "Did she say that she's thinking about getting married?"

I said, "She didn't say anything."

"I've gotten ahold of a genuine Cherokee Indian bracelet and ring," my father said the next Thursday night. "No BS here on this one. Your mother's father—that would be your grandfather—gave them to us a long time ago as a wedding present. He got them when he was traveling through Cherokee country. Your grandfather used to sell cotton, you know. Sometimes the Cherokees needed cotton. Sometimes they didn't have money, and he traded things for cotton. That's the way things go."

I said, "I was thinking about taking some pine cones." I had found some pine cones that were so perfect it wasn't funny. They looked like Christmas trees built to scale. "I was going to take a rock and say it was a meteorite."

"No, no. Take some of my Cherokee Indian jewelry, Mendal. I don't mind. I don't care! Hot damn, I didn't even remember having the things, so it won't matter none if they get broken or stolen. This is the real thing, Bubba."

What could I do? I wasn't but nine years old, and early on I'd been taught to do whatever my elders said, outside of drinking whiskey and smoking cigarettes when they got drunk and made the offer, usually at the Sunken Gardens Lounge. I thought, *Maybe I can take my father's weird jewelry and stick it in my desktop. Maybe I can stick a pine cone inside my lunch box.* "Yessir."

"I won't have it any other way," he said. "Wait here."

My father went back to what used to be my mother's and his bedroom. He opened up a wooden box he had fashioned in high school shop and pulled out a thin silver bracelet plus a one-pearl ring. I didn't know that these trinkets had once adorned the left arm of my third-grade teacher, right before she broke up with my father and went off to college, and long before she graduated, taught in some other school system for ten years, and then came back to her home town.

I took the trinkets in a small cotton sack. My father told me that he'd come get me for lunch if I wanted him to, that I didn't need to pack a bologna sandwich and banana as always. I went to the refrigerator and made my own and then left through the back door.

Glenn Flack started off show-and-tell with an x-ray of his mother's ankle. She'd fallen off the front porch trying to run from bees—something the rest of us knew not to do, seeing as we'd learned how to act in one of the weekly filmstrips. I got called next and said, "I have some priceless Cherokee Indian artifacts to show y'all. The Cherokee Indians had a way with hammering and chiseling." My father had made me memorize this speech.

I showed my classmates what ended up having been bought at Rey's Jewelers. Ms. Suber said, "Let me take a look at that" and got up to take the bracelet from my hand. She peered at it and then held it at arm's length and said, "This looks like it says 'sterling' on the inside, Mendal. I believe you might've picked up the wrong Indian jewelry to bring to school."

"Indian giver, Indian giver, Indian giver!" Melissa Beasley yelled out. It wasn't a taboo term back then. This was a time, understand, before we knew to use terms like "Native American-head penny" instead of "Indian-head penny," like I said before.

I said, "I just know what my dad told me. That's all I know." I took the bracelet from Ms. Suber, pulled out the ring, and stood there as if offering a Milk-Bone to a stray and skittish dog.

Ms. Suber said, "I've had enough of this" and told me to return to my desk. I put the pearl ring on my thumb and stuck the bracelet around the toe of my tennis shoe. Ms. Suber said, "Has your father gone insane lately, Mendal?"

It embarrassed me, certainly, and if she had said it twenty or thirty years later, I could've sued her for harassment, slander, and making me potentially agoraphobic. My desk was in the last row. Every student turned toward me except Shirley Ebo, the only black girl in the entire school, four years after integration. She looked forward, as always, ready to approach the music stand and explain her show-and-tell object, a face jug made by an old, old relative of hers named Dave the Slave.

I said, "My father has a Knack." Maybe I said nothing, really, but I thought about my father's Knack. I waited.

Ms. Suber sat back down. She looked at the ceiling and said, "I'm sorry, Mendal. I didn't mean to yell at you. Everyone go on to recess."

And so it continued for six weeks. I finally told my father that I couldn't undergo any more humiliation, that I would play hooky, that I would show up at school and say I had forgotten to bring my show-and-tell. I said, "I'm only going to take these stupid things you keep telling me stories about if it brings in some money, Dad."

Not that I was ever a capitalist or anything, but I figured early on that show-and-tell would end up somehow hurting my penmanship or spelling grade, and that maybe I needed to start saving money in order to get a head start in life should I not get into college. My father said, "That sounds fair enough. How much will you charge me to take this old, dried Mayan wrist corsage and matching boutonniere?"

I said, "Five bucks each."

My father handed them over. If the goddamn school system had ever shown a worthwhile Friday filmstrip concerning inductive logic, I would've figured out back then that when Ms. Suber and my father had had their horrific and execrable high school breakup, my father had gone over to her house and gathered up everything he'd ever bestowed on her, from birthday to Valentine's Day to special three-month anniversary and so on. He had gifts she'd given him too, I supposed much later, though I doubted they were worthy of monogamy.

But I didn't know logic. I thought only that my father hated the school system, had no trust whatsoever in public education, and wanted to drive my teacher to a nervous breakdown in order to get her to quit. Or, I thought, it was his way of flirting—that since my mother had "died," he wanted to show a prospective second wife some of the more spectacular possessions he could offer a needful woman.

He said, "I can handle ten dollars a show-and-tell session, for two items. Remind me not to give you an hourglass. I don't want you charging me per grain of sand."

This was all by the first of October. By Christmas break I'd brought in cuff links worn by Louis Quatorze, a fountain pen used by the fifty-six signers of the Declaration of Independence (my father tutored me on stressing "Independence" when I announced my cherished object to the class), a locket once owned by Elmer the glue inventor, thus explaining why the thing couldn't be opened, a pack of stale Viceroys that once belonged to the men who raised the American flag on Iwo Jima. I brought in more famous love letters, all on lined Blue Horse paper: from Ginger Rogers to Fred Astaire, from Anne Hathaway to Shakespeare, from all of Henry VIII's wives to him. One letter, according to my dad, was from Plato to Socrates, though he said it wasn't the original, and that he'd gone to the trouble of learning Greek in order to translate the thing.

Ms. Suber became exasperated with each new disclosure. She moved from picking names at random or in alphabetical order to always choosing me last. My classmates voted me Most Popular, Most Likely to Succeed, and Third Grade President, essentially because I got us ten more minutes of recess every Friday.

I walked down to the County Bank every Friday after school and deposited the money my father had forked over in a regular savings account. This was a time before IRAs. It was a time before stock portfolios, mutual funds, and the like. They gave me a toaster for starting the account and a dinner plate every time I walked in with ten dollars or more. After a few months I could've hosted a dinner party for twelve.

On Saturday mornings, more often than not, I drove with my father from place to place, looking over land he had bought or planned to buy. He had acquired a few acres of woodland before my birth, and soon thereafter the Army Corps of Engineers came in, flooded the Savannah River, and made my father's property near lakefront. He sold that parcel, took that money, and bought more land in an area that bordered what would become I-95. He couldn't go wrong. My father was not unlike the fool who threw darts at a map and went with his gut instinct. He would buy useless swampland, and someone else would soon insist on buying that land at twice to ten times his cost in order to build a golf course, a subdivision, or a nuclear-power facility. I had no idea what he did between these ventures, outside of reading and wondering. How else would he know about Abelard and Héloise, or even Socrates and Plato? He hadn't gone to college. He hadn't taken some kind of correspondence course.

We drove, and I stuck my head out the window like the dog I had owned before my mother took him to Nashville. We'd get to some land, pull down a dirt road usually, and my father would stare hard for ten or fifteen minutes. He barely turned his head from side to side, and he never turned off the engine. Sometimes he'd say at the end, "I think I got a fouled spark plug," or "You can tell that that gas additive's working properly."

He never mentioned people from history, or the jewelry of the dead. I took along Hardy Boys mysteries but never opened the covers. Finally, one afternoon, I said, "Ms. Suber wants to know if you're planning on coming to the PTA meeting. I forgot to tell you."

My father turned off the ignition. He reached beneath his seat and pulled out a can of beer and a church key. We sat parked between two gullies, somewhere in Greenwood County. "Hot damn, boy, you need to tell me these things. When is it?"

I said, "I forgot. I got in so much trouble Friday that I forgot." I'd taken a tortoise to show-and-tell and said his name was John the Baptist. At first Ms. Suber seemed delighted. When she asked why I had named him John the Baptist, I said, "Watch this." I screamed, "John the Baptist!" When he retreated into his shell and lost his head, I nodded. She had me sit back down. None of my classmates got the joke.

"The PTA meeting's on Tuesday. It's on Tuesday." I wore a pair of cut-off blue jeans with the bottoms cut into one-inch strips. My mother used to make them for me when I'd grown taller but hadn't gained weight around the middle. I had on my light-blue Little League T-shirt, with SUNKEN GARDENS on the front and 69 for my number on the back. My father had insisted that I get that number, and that I would thank him one day.

"Hell, yes. Do I need to bring anything? I mean, is this one of those meetings where parents need to bring food? I know how to make potato salad. I can make potato salad and cole slaw, you know."

"She just asked me to ask if you'd show up. That's all she said, I swear."

My father looked out at what I understood to be another wasteland. Empty beer cans were scattered in front of us, and the remains of a haphazard bonfire someone had made right in the middle of a path. "Maybe I should call her up and ask if she needs anything."

Although I didn't understand the depth of my father's obsession, I said, "Ms. Suber won't be in town until that night. We have a substitute on Monday, 'cause she has to go to a funeral somewhere."

My father drank from his beer. He handed the can over and told me to take little sips at first. I said, "Mom wouldn't want you to give me beer."

He nodded. "Mom wouldn't want you to do a lot of things, just like she didn't want me to do a lot of things. But she's not here, is she? Your momma's spending all her time praying that she never gets laryngitis, while the rest of us hope she does."

I didn't know that my father had been taking Fridays off in order to see the school secretary, feign needing to leave me a bag lunch, and then stand looking through the vertical window of my classroom door while I expounded the rarity of a letter sweater once worn by General Custer, or whatever. When the PTA meeting came around, I went with my father, though no other students attended. Pretty much it was only parents, teachers, and a couple of the lunch ladies, who had volunteered to serve a punch of ginger ale and grape juice. My father entered Ms. Suber's classroom and approached her as if she were a newspaper boy he'd forgotten to pay. He said, "I thought you'd eventually send a letter home asking for a conference. I thought you'd finally buckle under." He said, "Go look at the goldfish, Mendal," and pointed toward our aquarium.

I looked at the corner of the room. My classmates' parents were sitting at tiny desks, their knees bobbing like the shells of surfaced turtles. My third-grade teacher said, "I know you think this is cute, but it's not. I don't know why you think you can re-court me however many years later after what you did to me back then."

My father pushed me in the direction of the aquarium. Ms. Suber waved and smiled at Glenn Flack's parents, who were walking in. I said, "Can I go sit in the car?"

Ms. Suber said, "You stay right here, Mendal."

"I might not have been able to go to college like you did, Lola, but I've done good for myself," my father said. I thought one thing only: *Lola?*

"I know you have, Lee. I know you've done well. And let me be the first to say how proud I am of you, and how I'm sorry if I hurt you, and that I've seen you looking in the window when Mendal does his bogus show-and-tells." She pointed at the window in the door. Mr. and Mrs. Anderson walked in. "I need to start this thing up."

My father said to me, "If you want to go sit in the car, go ahead." He handed me the keys, leaned down, and said, "There's a beer in the glove compartment, son."

Let me say that this was South Carolina in 1968. Although my memory's not perfect, I think that at the time, neither drinking nor driving was against the law for minors, nor was smoking cigarettes before the age of twelve. Five years later I would drive my mini-bike to the Sunken Gardens, meet one of the black boys twirling trays out in the parking lot, order my eight-pack of Miller ponies, and have it delivered to me without conscience or threat of law.

I pretended to go into the parking lot but circled around to the outside of Ms. Suber's classroom. I stood beneath one of the six jalousies, crouched, and listened. Ms. Suber welcomed the parents and said that it was an exciting year. She said something about how all of us would have to take a national test later on to see how we compared with the rest of the nation. She said something about a school play.

Ms. Suber warned parents of a looming head-lice epidemic. She paced back and forth and asked everyone to introduce himself or herself. Someone asked if the school would ever sponsor another cake-and-pie sale in order to buy new recorders. My father said he'd be glad to have a potato-salad-and-cole-slaw sale. I didn't hear the teacher's answer. From where I crouched I could only look up at the sky and notice how some stars twinkled madly while others shone hard and fast like mica afire.

By the time I reached high school, my mother had moved from Nashville to New Orleans and then from New Orleans to Las Vegas. She never made it as a country singer or a blues singer, but she seemed to thrive as a hostess of sorts. As I crouched there beneath a window jutting out above boxwoods, I thought of my mother and imagined what she might be doing at the moment my father experienced his first PTA meeting. Was she crooning to conventioneers? Was she sitting in a back room worrying over pantyhose? That's what I thought, I swear to God. Everyone in Ms. Suber's classroom seemed to be talking with cookies in their mouths. I heard my father laugh hard twice—once when Ms. Suber said she knew that her students saw her as a witch, and another time when she said she knew that her students went home complaining that she didn't spank exactly the way their parents spanked.

Again, this was in the middle of the Vietnam War. Spanking made good soldiers.

My third-grade teacher said that she didn't have anything else to say, and told her students' parents to feel free to call her up should they have questions concerning grades, expectations, or field trips. She said she appreciated anyone who wanted to help chaperone kids or to work after school in a tutoring capacity. I stood up and watched my friends' parents leave single file, my father last in line.

Fifteen minutes after sitting in the car, five minutes after everyone else had driven out of the parking lot, I climbed out the passenger side and crept back to Ms. Suber's window. I expected my father to have Lola Suber in a headlock, or backed up against the Famous Christians of the World corkboard display. I didn't foresee their having moved desks against the walls in order to make a better dance floor.

My father held my third-grade teacher in a way I'd seen him hold a woman only once before: one Fourth of July he had danced with my mother in the back yard while the neighbors shot bottle rockets straight up. My mother had placed her head on his shoulder and smiled, her eyes raised to the sky. Lola Suber didn't look upward. She didn't smile either. My father seemed to be humming, or talking low. I couldn't hear exactly what went on, but years later he confessed that he had set forth everything he meant to say and do, everything he hoped she taught the other students and me when it came to matters of passion.

I did hear Lola Suber remind him that they had broken up because she had decided to have a serious and exclusive relationship with Jesus Christ.

There amid the boxwoods I hunkered down and thought only about the troubles I might have during future show-and-tells, I swear to God. I stood back up, saw them dancing, and returned to the car. I would let my father open the glove compartment later.

Singleton on Fictional Time

I spent seven years writing bad long novels before I attempted my first short story. I didn't even know how to send anything to an agent or editor, and this might have been because my good professors in both college and graduate school understood rightly that I would get massacred. When I somehow got a job teaching at a college that crammed thirty students into each English 101 course, and the normal load was a heavy four classes a semester, some kind of rare thought finally popped me upside the head. There was no way that I could write more bad novels, teach 120 students a semester, grade the required ten final essays per student, and so on.

I turned to writing short stories, and from 1987 until about the year 2000 I mostly wrote first-person narratives from the male point of view, and for the most part these narrators ranged from twenty-eight to forty years of age, a perspective I knew well. I wasn't daring enough to try out a first-person woman telling a story; likewise, I didn't know enough about life in general to create a sixty- or seventy-year-old male character who might expound on everything from how to make crankcase oil never turn thick, to the secrets of the universe.

And then I really got tired of my own voice, my own characters, myself. I tried to write a couple stories from a woman's point of view, but I couldn't truly figure out if a woman would say, "I'm now going to put on my pajamas," on her honeymoon, or "camisole," or "teddy," or "I'm fixing to get buck-naked, Killer." When I tried the old man narrator, he kind of got stuck complaining way too much. I discovered I needed to write something closer to the life I knew—even if it wasn't specifically about myself.

I began writing a group of what my writer-buddy Dale Ray Phillips calls "dad and lad" stories. "Show-and-Tell" happened to be the first of these, and then I wrote about fifteen more, all from the point-of-view of one Mendal Dawes, a boy from a South Carolina town near where I grew up.

Managing Time

"Show-and-Tell" starts immediately with conflict—Mendal having to naively show off a bogus love letter from Peter Abelard to Heloise. This is also where my work with "fictional time" begins. "Fictional time" is not my phrase, but to other writers, basically it means how I, as the author, handle time within the story. Most stories plunge from Scene A to Scene B to Scene C, right on down to the end. But stories are so much more than that. Though the first scene of "Show-and-Tell" has Mendal Dawes taking a letter to school, the fictional time is not located exclusively on that day. It's mostly focused there, yes. But by managing the time well, I'm able to expand the first scene to encompass much more of Mendal's life.

Managing time in stories means more than using words such as "as," "then," and "before" that connect up scenes. Don't get me wrong—careful use of these words is important. But managing time in a story is so much more.

In film, most scenes are presented in real time. A five-minute fight takes five minutes to watch. But in fiction, the author is able to control the pacing of each scene to greater effect, slowing it down and speeding it up as needed. Fiction allows an author to control how a story releases information to the reader. For example, in my story, I slow down that first scene so that Mendal can explain some things about himself and his father: "I didn't know that my father—'a widower' is how he told me to describe him, although everyone knew that Mom had run off to Nashville and hadn't died— had once dated Ms. Suber, my teacher."

I create backstory by allowing Mendal to explain his life situation: "I wasn't but nine years old, and early on I'd been taught to do whatever my elders said." But in another version of this story, I could stop the forward momentum and offer a flashback (that is, a complete scene) in which readers see Mendal respecting his elders. Both would accomplish the same goal: reveal to readers that Mendal was an obedient boy.

But for the finished story, I felt that a flashback, however quick, would slow down my first scene, so I let Mendal slip in these bits of explanation.

On the one hand, my first scene gives out enough details for a reader to understand the classroom story. It establishes atmosphere, setting, and the beginnings of plot. But on the other hand, it also gives out the details to understand Mendal as a complete character, one who is believably different from his nine-year-old classmates. When I have enough information and emotion packed into that first scene, I just let the rest of the scene roll forward, detail after detail.

Scene and Summary

Here is another aspect of managing time: figuring out which scenes are important enough to render in full detail and which can be related quickly in summary narration.

I know how every English teacher shoves that "Show, don't tell" mantra into conversation whenever possible. Showing means scenes. Telling means summary. The obvious point is that "showing" is generally more effective than "telling." But most stories do a good bit of both. My first scene, because it's so important to the story, delivers a great deal of detail, including dialogue and action, as a full scene. In the common vocabularly of English teachers, I'm "showing." Later on in the story, when Mendal packs his sack for the second show-and-tell experience, I use summary narration because the specifics are not as important. Well, they *are* important. But they aren't important enough to warrant a full scene. I use just a few specific details and quick action. I'm mostly "telling": "I took the trinkets in a small cotton sack. My father told me that he'd come get me for lunch if I wanted him to . . . ."

In the story I suggest tension building and time passing by the comic list of objects Mendal brings to class. There, I'm really "telling." I'm not "showing" at all. I also realized that a reader's patience might be tested if I spent too much time on *telling* the "cuff links worn by Louis Quatorze, a fountain pen used by the fifty-six signers of the Declaration of Independence . . . a locket once owned by Elmer the glue inventor . . ." etcetera. So I lumped them into one giant paragraph and started my race to the end of the story.

Getting to the End

I had a difficult time ending "Show-and-Tell." For me, endings are difficult—so many decisions. When I write a story, I usually have three or four ideas about how to bring it to a close. It's like swimming in a river. I've already treaded water, circled around, and dog-paddled for a few thousand words or thereabouts, taking note as to what drifted by. Now comes the choice.

I can swim upstream and see where I've been—this is what some editors call "kissing the beginning of the story." This type of ending harkens the story back to its beginning to remind readers the ground it's just covered. Or I can go into future tense—swim downstream and see where the character might go in the coming months or years. This type of ending suggests how the events in the story have a significant impact on the main character as he continues through life. Or I can seek the closest shore, get out of the river, and see where the character is at that moment. I save this type of ending for a story where the dramatic impact on the main character is so clear that it seems utterly unnecessary to say any more.

Because I knew that "Show-and-Tell" was going to be part of a longer sequence of Mendal Dawes stories, I didn't need to go way into the future and predict what his life would be like, at least not in a gigantic all-encompassing fashion. In a way I melded all three "river swimming" techniques, unintentionally. I have Mendal hunkered down in the boxwoods as his father and teacher dance post-PTA meeting. There, Mendal learns of the past, or where his father has been (Lola Suber and Mr. Dawes broke up years ago so she could pursue a relationship with Jesus). Also, Mendal looks slightly into the future about "the troubles I might have during future show-and-tells." Finally, back in the car, he opens the glove compartment, sees the stashed beer, and decides in real story time to save it for his father.

I think about my stories long after they are published. In my head, I like to change them around some, still looking for ways to make them better. I do like the way this story ends, but I know, in a world of infinite possibilities, there's probably a better ending for it. The perfect one hasn't hit me yet, but I'll think about it daily, like a fool.

Writing Suggestions

1. Construct two different one-page introductions for the same story. In your first version, introduce the characters and situation using only events and details pertinent to the day on which the story begins. In your second version, introduce the characters and situation using important events and details that occurred long before the actual beginning of the story. Which is the better first page? What does each first page suggest about the story's pacing?

2. Write a story, structured as a letter, about the events that happened to you last summer. Which events will you develop into full scenes? And why? Which events will you render in summary narration—or perhaps exclude entirely? How do the first two pages define the story's internal pacing—the movement between summary and scene, the rate at which time passes in the story? How will you define the qualities of the main character either with exposition or with flashback? As with all stories based on autobiographical experience, feel free to deviate from the actual events of your life to create a more effective story.

3. In George Singleton's "Show-and-Tell," the story develops the personality of Mendal through exposition—short, declarative statements that define his character. Develop a one-page flashback that, in full scene, demonstrates how Mendal learned to be obedient as suggested in the story on page 252: "I wasn't but nine years old, and early on I'd been taught to do whatever my elders said . . . ." What new information about Mendal might be communicated in a flashback that could not be effectively communicated in a brief statement? Reread the first half of "Show-and-Tell" with your own flashback placed into the story. How does your flashback alter the mood and

development of the story? (Variation: After finishing your work on Singleton's story, try this same revision technique with one of your own stories by first locating a section of exposition and then changing it to a flashback rendered in full scene.)

4. Go to your library and find "Hills Like White Elephants" by Ernest Hemingway (in *The Complete Short Stories of Ernest Hemingway*) and "The Jilting of Granny Weatherall" by Katherine Anne Porter (in *The Collected Short Stories of Katherine Anne Porter*). Compare how Hemingway's piece, in which the story is constructed in scene without summary, with Porter's, in which the story is constructed with a series of flashbacks that suggests a lifetime. In a few paragraphs, describe the differences between Hemingway's handling of fictional time with that of Porter. How does each develop emotional intensity? If you were to read three more stories by one of these authors, which would better help you understand the possibilities of fictional time for your own stories?

> *The way in which each novelist, each fiction writer organizes the time structure is what gives his literary work its originality and, again, its sovereignty.*
> —Mario Vargas Llosa

Reginald McKnight

Palm Wine

From *Callaloo* and *White Boys: Stories*

This was fourteen years ago, but it still bothers me as though it happened day before yesterday. I've never talked about this with anyone, and I'm not talking about it now because I expect it to relieve me of painful memory, but because, as they say in Madagascar, the bad is told that the good may appear. So. I was in Senegal on a graduate fellowship. I was there to collect and compile West African proverbs. This was to complete my Ph.D. in anthropology, which, I'm afraid, I failed to do. The things I'm going to talk about now had as much to do with that failure as did my laziness, my emotional narrowness and my intellectual mediocrity. I was a good deal younger then, too, but that's no excuse. Not really.

Anyway, one afternoon, instead of collecting proverbs in Yoff village, which I should have done, I went to Dakar with Omar the tailor—a friend of a friend—to buy palm wine. I'd craved palm wine ever since I read Amos Tutuola's novel *The Palm-Wine Drinkard* in college. Tutuola never attempts to describe the taste, color or smell of palm wine, but because the Drinkard (whose real name is Father of the Gods Who Could Do Anything in This World) can put away 225 kegs of it per day, and because he sojourns through many cruel and horrifying worlds in order to try to retrieve his recently killed palm wine tapster from Deadstown, I figured palm wine had to be pretty good.

As Omar and I boarded the bus, I dreamed palm wine dreams. It must be pale green, I thought, coming from a tree and all. Or milky-blue like coconut water. I had it in mind that it must hit the tongue like a dart, and that it must make one see the same visions Tutuola himself witnessed. A creature big as a bipedal elephant, sporting two-foot fangs thick as cow's horns; a creature with a million eyes and hundreds of breasts that continuously suckle her young, who swarm her body like maggots; a town where everything and everyone is red as plum flesh; a town where they all walk backwards; a town full of ghosts.

I really had no business going that day. I was at least a month behind in my research because of a lengthy bout with malaria. But I excused myself from work by telling myself that since I had no Wolof proverbs on the subject of drinking, I'd likely encounter a couple that day. But I took my pad, pencils and tape recorder along, knowing I wasn't going to use them.

On the ride to town, I could scarcely pay mind to matters that usually fascinate me. For instance, I would often carefully observe the beggars who board the buses and cry for alms. Their Afro-Arab plaints weave through the bus like serpents, slipping between exquisitely coiffed women, and dignified, angular men, wives of the wealthy, daughters of the poor, beardless hustlers, bundled babies, tourists, pickpockets, gendarmes, students. A beautiful plaint could draw coins like salt draws moisture. Some beggars not only sang for indulgences but also sang their thanks. *Jerrejeff, my sister, paradise lies under the feet of mothers. A heart that burns for Allah gives more light than ten thousand suns.* Some of them sang proverbs from the Koran. *Be constant in prayer and give alms. Allah pity him who must beg of a beggar.* Some of them merely cried something very much like "Alms! Alms!" And some of them rasped like reptiles and said little more than, "I got only one arm! Gimme money!" and the proverbs they used were usually stale. They were annoying, but even so I often gave them alms, and I recorded them. I guess it was because I liked being in a culture that had a good deal more respect for the poor than my own. And I guess I tried hard to appreciate art forms that were different from the ones I readily understood. But, honestly, as I say, that day I could think of little more than palm wine. It would be cold as winter rain. It would be sweet like berries, and I would drink till my mind went swimming in deep waters.

We alighted the bus in the arrondisement of Fosse, the place Omar insisted was the only place to find the wine. Preoccupied as I was with my palm wine dreams, they weren't enough to keep me from attending Fosse. It's an urban village, a squatter's camp, a smoke-filled bowl of shanties built of rusty corrugated metal, grey splintery planks, cinder block, cement. It smelled of everything: goatskin, pot, green tobacco, fish, overripe fruit, piss, cheap perfume, Gazelle Beer, warm couscous, scorched rice, the sour sharpness of cooking coals. People talked, laughed, sang, cried, argued—the sounds so plangent I felt them in my teeth, my chest, my knees. A woman dressed in blue flowers scolded her teenaged son, and the sound lay tart on my tongue. Two boys drummed the bottoms of plastic buckets, while a third played a pop bottle with a stick, and I smelled churai incense. Two little girls danced to the boy's rhythms, their feet invisible with dust, and I felt them on my back.

A beautiful young woman in a paisley wraparound pagne smiled at us, and I rubbed Omar's incipient dreadlocks, his wig of thumbs, as I called them and said, "Hey, man, there's a wife for you." Omar grinned at me, his amber eyes were crescents, his teeth big as dominoes. "She too old for me, mahn," he said.

"Oh please, brother, she couldn't be older than eighteen."

"Young is better."

"Whatever. Lech."

I didn't really like Omar. He insisted on speaking English with me even though his English was relatively poor. Even when I spoke to him in French or my shaky Wolof he invariably answered me in English. This happened all the time in Senegal and the other francophone countries I traveled. People all around the globe wanted to speak English, and my personal proverb was, Every English-speaking traveler will be a teacher as much as he'll be a student. I suppose if his English had been better I wouldn't have minded, but there were times it led to trouble—like that day— and times when the only thing that really bothered me about it was that it was Omar speaking it. Omar the tailor man, always stoned, always grinning, his red-and-amber crescents, his domino teeth, his big olive-shaped head, his wolfish face, his hiccuping laugh jangling every last nerve in my skull. He perpetually thrust his long hands at me for cigarettes, money, favors. "Hey, I and I, you letting me borrow you tape deck?" "Hey, I and I, jokma bene cigarette." He was a self-styled Rastafarian, and he had the notion that since the U.S. and Jamaica are geographically close, Jamaicans and Black Americans were interchangeable. I was pretty certain I was of more value to him as a faux Jamaican than as a genuine American.

He was constantly in my face with this "I and I, mahn" stuff, always quoting Peter Tosh couplets, insisting I put them in my book. (I could never get him to understand the nature of my work.) Moreover, it took him six months to sew one lousy pair of pants and one lousy shirt for me, items I was dumb enough to pay him in advance for. From the day he measured me to the day I actually donned the clothes I'd lost twenty-six pounds. (Constant diarrhea and a fish-and-rice diet will do that to you.) But I wasn't about to ask him to take them in, though. I only had a year's worth of fellowship money, after all.

Omar always spoke of his great volume of work, his busyness, the tremendous pressure he was under, but each and every time I made it to his shop to pick up my outfit, I'd find him sitting with four or five friends, twisting his locks, putting the buzz on, yakking it up. "Hey, I and I, come in! I don't see you a long time."

In northern Africa they say, Bear him unlucky, don't bear him lazy. But I bore Omar because he was a friend of my good friend and assistant Idrissa, who, at the time, was visiting his girlfriend in Paris. I went with Omar to get the palm wine because Omar, who knew Fosse a great deal better than Idrissa did, insisted that day was the only time in palm wine season he would be able to make the trip. He told me that Idrissa wouldn't be back till the season was well over. Originally, the three of us were to have made the trip, but Idrissa's girlfriend sent him an erotic letter and a ticket to Paris. And money. We blinked; Idrissa was gone, and since Omar was so "pressed for time," we wasted none of it getting to the city. As I walked the ghetto with Omar I reflected on how Idrissa would often fill things in for me with his extemporaneous discussions of the history, economics and myths about wherever in Senegal we happened to be. Idrissa was self-educated and garrulous. My kind of person. He was also very proud of his Senegalese heritage. He seemed to know everything about the country. As Omar and I walked, I told myself that if Idrissa had been there, I would have been learning things. What did I know?

On our walk, Omar seldom spoke. He seemed unable to answer any of my questions about the place, so after about ten minutes I stopped asking. We walked what seemed to me the entire ghetto, and must have enquired at about eight or nine places without seeing a drop of palm wine. Each inquiry involved the usual African procedure—shake hands all around, ask about each other's friends, families, health, work; ask for the wine, learn they have none, ask them who might, shake hands, leave. It was getting close to dusk now, and our long shadows undulated before us over the packed soil. I was getting a little hungry, and I kept eyeing the street vendors who braised brochettes of mutton along the curb of the main street. The white smoke rose up and plumed into the streets, raining barbecue smells everywhere. I said, "Looks like we're not getting the wine today. Tell you what, why don't we—"

"Is not the season-quoi," Omar said as we rambled into a small, secluded yard. It was surrounded by several tin-roofed houses, some with blanket doors, insides lighted mostly by kerosene or candles. Here and there, though, I could see that some places had electricity. Omar crossed his arms as we drew to a stop. "We stay this place and two more," he said, "then I and I go."

"Aye-aye," I said.

Four young men sat on a dusty porch passing a cigarette among themselves. Several toddlers, each runny-nosed and ashy-kneed, frenetically crisscrossed in front of the men, pretending to grab for the cigarette. Until they saw me. Then they stopped and one of the older ones approached us, reached out a hand and said, "Toubobie, mawney." Omar said, in Wolof, "This man isn't a toubob. This is a black man. An American brother." I answered in Wolof, too. "Give me a proverb and I'll give you money." The boy ran away grinning, and the men laughed. I drew my cigarettes from my shirt pocket, tapped out eight and gave two to each man.

"Where's Doudou?" Omar asked the men.

They told him Doudou, whoever he was, had left a half hour before, but was expected back very soon. One of the men, a short, muscular man in a T-shirt and a pair of those voluminous trousers called chayas, detached himself from his friends, and walked into one of the houses. He returned, carrying a small green liquor bottle. I felt my eyebrows arch. The stuff itself, I was thinking. I imagined myself getting pied with these boys, so drunk I'm hugging them, telling them I love them, and goddamn it where's old Doudou? I miss that bastid. The man in the chayas unscrewed the lid with sacremental delicacy, drank and passed the bottle on. I watched the men's faces go soft when each passed the bottle on to his brother. I took the bottle rather more aggressively than was polite, and I apologized to the man who'd handed it to me. Omar winked at me. "You don't know what bottle is-quoi?" Omar had the irritating habit of using the tag "quoi" after most of his sentences. He did it in English, French, Wolof, and his own language, Bambara. It wasn't an uncommon habit in French West Africa, but Omar wore it down to a nub.

"Paaalm wiiine," I said in a low, throaty voice the way you'd say an old love's name. My God, what was wrong with me? I was behaving as though, like the Drinkard himself, I had fought the beast with the lethal gaze and shovel-sized scales, or had spent the night in the bagful of creatures with ice cold, sandpapery hair, that I'd done some heroic thing, and the stuff in the green bottle was my reward. As I brought the bottle to my lips, Omar said, "It's no palm wine, I and I." I drank before Omar's words even registered, and the liquid burned to my navel. It was very much like a strong tequila. No that's an understatement. If this drink and tequila went to prison, this drink would make tequila its cabin boy. "Is much stronger than palm wine," said Omar.

My throat had closed up and it took me a few seconds before I could speak. All I could manage was to hiss, "Jeeezuz!" And abruptly one of the young men, a Franco-Senegalese with golden hair and green eyes said, "Jeeezuz," but then he continued in rapid Wolof and I lost him. Soon, all five of them were laughing, saying 'Jeeezuz, Jeezuz,' working the joke, extending it, jerking it around like taffy. My blood rose to my skin, and every muscle in my back knotted. I squinted at Omar, who looked back at me with eyes both reassuring and provocative, and he said, "He saying he like Americain noire talk. You know, you say-quoi, 'Jeeezuz,' and 'sheeee,' and 'Maaaaan-quoi.' We like the Americain noire talk." His mouth hovered this close to a smirk.

I was furious, but I had no choice but to grin and play along. I lit a smoke and said Jeezuz and Jeezuz Christ, And Jeezuz H. Christ, "cuttin' the monkey," as my dad would put it. My stomach felt as though it was full of mosquitoes. My hands trembled. I wanted to kick Omar's face in. His hiccupping giggles rose above the sound of everyone else's laughter, and his body jerked about convulsively. Yeah, choke on it, I thought. But I didn't have to endure the humiliation long, for soon an extremely tall, very black, very big-boned man joined us, and Omar said, "Doudou!" and fiercely shook hands with the giant. Doudou nodded my way and said, in Wolof, "What's this thing?" and I froze with astonishment. Thing? I tried to interpret Omar's lengthy explanation, but his back was to me and he was speaking very rapidly. As I say, my Wolof was never very good. Doudou placed his hands on his hips and squinted at the ground as though he'd lost something very small. The big man nodded now and then. Then he looked at me, and said in French, "It's late in the season, but I know where there's lots of palm wine." He immediately wheeled about and began striding away, Omar followed, then I.

The walk was longer than I'd expected, and by the time we got to the place, the deep blue twilight had completely absorbed our shadows. After seven or eight months of living in Senegal, I had become used to following strangers into unfamiliar places in the night. But even so, I felt uneasy. I watched the night as a sentry would, trying to note every movement and sound. There was nothing extraordinary about the things I saw on the way, but even today they remain vivid as if I'd seen them the day before yesterday—a three-year-old girl in a faded pink dress, sitting on a porch; a cat-sized rat sitting atop an overflowing garbage crate; a man in a yellow shirt and blue tie talking to a bald man wearing a maroon khaftan; a half moon made half again by a knot of scaly clouds; Omar's wig of thumbs; Doudou's broad back. I wasn't thinking much about palm wine.

It was an inconspicuous place, built from the same stuff, built in the same way prac-tically every other place in Fosse was. Perhaps a half dozen candles lit the room, but rather than clarify they muddied the darkness. I couldn't tell whether there were six other men in the place or twelve. I couldn't make out the proprietress's face or anything about her, for that matter. The only unchanging features were her eyes, an unnatural olive black and egg white, large, perpetually doleful. But was her expression stern or soft? As the candlelight shifted, heaved, bent, so did her shape and demeanor. At times she seemed big as Doudou, and at other times she seemed only five foot two or so. One moment she looked fifty; a second later, twenty-three. Her dress was sometimes blue, sometimes mauve. I couldn't stop staring at her, and I couldn't stop imagining that the light in the room was incrementally being siphoned away, and that my skull was being squeezed as if in the crook of a great headlocking arm, and that the woman swelled to two, three, four times her size, and split her dress like ripe fruit skin, and glowed naked, eggplant black like a burnished goddess, and that she stared at me with those unchang-ing olive and egg eyes. It's that stuff I drank, I kept saying to myself. It's that stuff they gave me. Then with increasing clarity I heard a hiss as though air were rushing from my very own ears, and the sound grew louder, so loud the air itself seemed to be torn in half like a long curtain, until it abruptly stopped with the sound of a cork being popped from a bottle; then everything was normal again, and I looked around the room half embarrassed as if the ridiculous things in my head had been projected on the wall before me for all to see, and I saw that Doudou was staring at me with a look of bemused dep-recation. I felt myself blush. I smiled rather stupidly at the giant, and he cocked his head just a touch to the left, but made no change in his facial expression. I quickly looked back at the woman.

She told my associates that the wine was still quite fresh, and she swung her arm with a graceful backhand motion before ten plastic gallon jugs apparently full to the neck with the wine. It was very cheap, she said. Then she dipped her hands into a large plastic pan of water on the table that stood between herself and us. She did it the way a surgeon might wash her hands, scooping the water, letting it run to the elbows. In the same water she washed two bottles and laid them aside. Next, she poured a little palm wine into a tumbler, walked to the door, then poured the contents on the ground out-side. I could feel excitement sparking up again in my stomach. "Is ritual," said Omar, but when I asked him what it meant, he ignored me.

The woman returned to the jug, filled the bottom half inch of her tumbler with wine, and took two perfunctory sips. After that she slipped a screened funnel into the first bottle's neck, filled the bottle, then filled the second bottle in the same way. Omar lifted one of the bottles, took a whiff then a sip. I closely watched his face, but his expression told me little. He arched both eyebrows and nodded a bit. The woman handed the second bottle to Doudou, and he did pretty much what Omar had. I don't recall noting his expression. Then Omar handed me his bottle.

It was awful. It was *awful*. It was awful. Though Idrissa had warned me about the taste, I had had the impression that they were trying to prepare me for the fact that it doesn't taste like conventional wines. I was prepared for many things, a musky fla-vor, a fruity flavor, dryness, tartness, even blandness. But for me, the only really pleasant aspect of the liquid was its color, cloudy white like a liquid pine cleaner mixed with water. It had a slightly alcoholic tang and smelled sulfuric. It had a distinctly sour bouquet which reminded me of something I very much hated as a kid. If you could make wine from egg salad and vinegar, palm wine is pretty much what you'd get.

Really, the stuff was impossible to drink, but I did my best. The ordeal might have gone more easily had Omar not been Omar—singing reggae music off-key, slapping my back, philosophizing in a language he didn't understand, toasting a unified Africa, then toasting the mighty Rastafari, toasting me, then Doudou. But the thing that made the ordeal in the bar most unpleasant was that Doudou glared at me for what felt like ten unbroken minutes. He stared at my profile as though my face were his property. I couldn't bring myself to confront him. He was just so fucking huge. He was not merely tall—perhaps six foot eight? or so—but his bones were pillars, his face a broad iron shield. He gave off heat, he bowed the very atmosphere of the room. Wasn't it enough I had to drink that swill? Did I need the additional burden of drinking from under the millstone of this man's glare? Just as I was about to slam my bottle to the table and stalk out, Doudou said, in French, "An American."

"Americano," I said.

"Amerikanski," he said.

"That's right. We've got that pretty much nailed down."

"Hey," Omar said, "you like the palm wine?"

Before I could answer, Doudou said, "He doesn't like the wine, Omar."

"Who says I don't?"

Doudou cocked an eyebrow, and looked at the low-burning candle on our table. He rolled the bottle between his fingers as if it were pencil thin. "I tell you he doesn't like it, Omar." Then he looked at me, and said, "I say you don't." I felt cold everywhere. A small, painful knot hardened between my shoulder blades, as so often happens when I'm angry.

"You know," I said, stretching my back, rolling my shoulders, "I'm not going to argue about something so trivial." Then I turned to Omar, and said in English, "Omar, the wine is very good. Excellent."

Omar shrugged, and said, "Is okay, I think. Little old."

We were silent after that, and Doudou stopped staring, but it got no more comfortable. Two men started to argue politics, something about the increasing prices of rice and millet, something about Islamic law, and when it got to the table-banging stage, Omar suggested we leave. I had suffered through two glasses of this liquid acquired taste, and Omar, much to my regret, bought me two liters of the wine to take home. But I did want to go home, and said so. But Doudou said, "You must stay for tea." Omar said yes before I could say no, and I knew it would be impolite to leave without Omar. We walked back to Doudou's place and I saw that the young men were still quietly getting happy on the Senegalese tequila. Doudou sat in a chair on the porch and sent the young man in chayas into the house and he returned with a boom box and a handful of tapes. He threw in a Crusaders tape, and immediately two of the men began to complain. They wanted Senegalese music, but Doudou calmly raised his hand and pointed to me. The men fell silent, and I said, "I don't have to have American music."

"Sure you do," said the big man. He leaned so far back in his chair that its front legs were ten inches off the porch, and the back of the chair rested against the windowsill. His feet stayed flat on the ground.

"Your French is good," I said.

"Better than yours," he said. He was smiling, and I couldn't see a shred of contempt in his expression, but that burned up the last of my calm. It was full dark, but I could see his broad smooth face clearly, for the house's light illuminated it. It hung before the window like a paper lantern, like a planet. Looking back on it, I can see that I must have offended him. He must have thought I was evincing surprise that, he, a denizen of Fosse could speak as well as he did. Actually I was just trying to make conversation. When the bottle came my way I tipped it and drank a full inch of it. "Thanks for the hospitality," I said. Doudou folded his arms, and tipped his head forward, removing it from the light. "Amerikanski," he said. One of the men chuckled.

Omar sat "Indian" style a foot to my right. He rolled a very large spliff from about a half-ounce of pot and an eight-by-ten-inch square of newspaper. He handed it to the man sitting across from him, the Franco-Senegalese with the golden hair. The comedian. "Where's the tea?" the man asked in Wolof. "Eh?" said Doudou, and then he pointed to the boom box. The man in the chayas turned it down. The golden-haired man repeated his question. Doudou's only reply was, "Ismaila, get the tea," and the young man in the chayas rose once again, and came back quickly with the Primus stove, the glasses, the sugar and the tea.

"Omar tells me that you're an anthropologist," said Doudou.

"That's right," I said.

"The study of primitive cultures." Doudou said this as though he'd read these words off the back of a bottle. A dangerous sort of neutrality, as I saw it. It grew so still for a moment, there, that I jumped when Ismaila lit the stove, the gas had burst into blue flame with a sudden *woof* and I found myself glaring at Ismaila as though he'd betrayed me. I cleared my throat, said, "That's only one aspect of anthropology . . . " I struggled for words. When I'm nervous I can barely speak my own language, let alone another's, but I managed to say, " . . . but I to study the living cultures." There, I thought, that was nice. I went on to explain that the discipline of anthropology was changing all the time, that it had less to do with so-called primitive cultures and more to do with the study of the phenomenon of culture, and the many ways it can be expressed. The light from the stove's flame cast ghost light over the four of us who sat around it. One of the men, a short man with batlike ears, sat behind me and Omar. He was in silhouette as was Doudou, up there on the porch. The man with the strange ears tapped my shoulder and handed me the spliff. I took a perfunctory hit, and handed it to Omar. "Ganjaaaa," said Omar.

"I knew an anthropologist once," said Doudou, "who told me I should be proud to be part of such a noble, ancient and primitive people." He paused long enough for me to actually hear the water begin to boil. Then he said, "What aspect of anthropology do you think he studied?"

"Couldn't tell you," I said.

"Too bad."

"Maybe," I said, "he trying to tell you that primitive . . . I mean, that in this case 'primitive' mean the same thing as 'pure.' "

"Really. 'In this case,' you say."

"I can only—"

"Was I supposed to have been offended by his language? Are you saying we Africans should be offended by words like 'primitive'?" He placed his great hands on his knees, sat up straight. It occurred to me he was trying to look regal. It worked. I could feel myself tremulously unscrewing the top of one of my palm wine bottles, and I took a nip from it. My sinuses filled with its sour bouquet. "Well . . . you sounded offended," I said.

"Who studies your people?"

"What?"

"Do you have anthropologists milling about your neighborhood? Do they write down everything you say?"

"Look, I know how you must—"

Doudou turned away from me. "Ismaila, how's the tea coming?" he said. "No problems," said Ismaila.

"Look here," I said, but before I could continue, the man with the pointed ears said, "I get offended. I get very offended. You write us down. You don't respect us. You come here and steal from us. It's a very bad thing, and you, you should know better."

"What, because I'm black?"

"Black," said Doudou, with a chuckle.

"Is fine, I and I. Is very nice."

"What the fuck's that supposed to mean, Omar?" I said. "Look, I'm trying to help all black people by recovering our forgot things."

"Your 'lost' things," Ismaila said quietly as he dumped two or three handfuls of tea into the boiling water. He removed the pot from the flame and let it steep for a few minutes. One of the men, a bald, chubby man with a single thick eyebrow, rose from the ground and began fiddling with the boom box. He put in a tape by some Senegalese group, and turned it up a bit. The guitar sounded like crystal bells, the base like a springy heartbeat; the singer's nasal voice wound like a tendril around the rhythm. As Ismaila sang with the tape, he split the contents of the pot between two large glasses, filling each about half way, and dumped three heaps of sugar into each glass. While he worked, I kept nipping at the palm wine like a man who can't stop nipping at the pinky nail of his right hand even though he's down to the bloody quick. The more I drank the odder its flavors seemed to me. It was liquid egg, ammonia, spoiled fish, wet leather, piss. The taste wouldn't hold still, and soon enough it wholly faded. The roof of my mouth, my sinuses, my temples began to throb with a mild achiness, and if I'd had food in my belly that evening, I might have chucked it up. Ismaila began tossing the contents of the glasses from one glass to the other. I could see that Omar was following his movements with great intent.

"What's all this about, Omar?" I said in English. "Why are these guys fucking with me?" I hoped he'd understood me, and I hoped that none of his friends would suddenly reveal himself as a fluent speaker of English. I also ended up wishing Idrissa were there when Omar said, "No worry, I and I; the tea is good."

"Things lost?" said Doudou. "That must mean you're not pure-quoi, that you think you can come here and bathe in our primitive dye."

Omar and I exchanged looks, our heads turning simultaneously. I was encouraged by that speck of consanguinity. It emboldened me. "Want some palm wine?" I said to Doudou. "It really tastes like crap."

The giant shifted slightly in his chair. He said nothing for maybe fifteen seconds. "How does it feel," he said, "to be a black toubob?" I felt my face suddenly grow hot. My guts felt as if they were in a slow meltdown. I took a large draft of the wine and disgust made me wince. "By 'toubob'," I asked, "do you mean 'stranger' or 'white'? I understand it can be used both ways."

Doudou leaned forward in the chair and it snapped and popped as if it were on fire. It appeared for a moment he was going to rise from his chair, and everything in me tightened, screwed down, clamped, but he merely leaned and said, "In Wolof, 'toubob' is 'toubob' is 'toubob.'" The blood beat so hard beneath my skin I couldn't hear the music for a few seconds. I tried to breathe deeply, but I couldn't. All I could do was drink that foul wine and quiver with anger. I stared for a long time at some pinprick point in the air between me and Doudou. It was as though the world or I had collapsed into that tiny point of blackness, which, after I don't know how long, opened like a sleepy eye, and I realized that I'd been watching Ismaila hand around small glasses of tea. First to Omar, then to Doudou, then to the golden-haired man, then to the man with the bat ears, then to the chubby bald man with the unibrow. Ismaila didn't even look my way. I sat there with blood beating my temples. Their tea-sipping sounded like sheets tearing.

Then Ismaila brewed a second round of tea, but I received no tea in that round either. When everyone finished Ismaila simply turned off the stove and began gathering the cups, and things. It was the most extraordinary breach of Senegalese etiquette I'd seen in the year I lived there. No one, not even Omar, said a word. Omar, for his part, looked altogether grim. He leaned toward me and whispered, "You got no tea, huh?" I could hear the nervous tremor in his voice.

"It's no big deal, Omar."

"I and I, you tell him for give you the tea-quoi."

"Skip it."

"Quoi?"

"Forget about the tea. I got this." I raised the bottle, and finished it.

"He *must* give you the tea."

"Omar, that big motherfucker don't have to 'must' shit."

Omar relit the spliff and said, "Is bad, mahn, is very bad." He offered me the spliff, but I waved it off and opened up my second bottle. Omar often displayed what one could call displacement behavior when he didn't understand me. He'd swiftly change the subject, or say something noncommittal. You might think that this was one more thing that bothered me about him, but actually I found it rather endearing, for some reason. "Is bad, I and I. He do bad."

"Fuck it."

The other men had moved closer to the big man. Two sat on the ground, two squatted on the porch. They spoke quietly, but every so often they burst forth with laughter. I drank and stared at the bottle. "Listen in you ears, I and I," said Omar. "You must strong Doudou. You must put him and strong him."

"Speak French, Omar."

"No, no. You must. He do this now and every day-quoi. Every day. Only if you strong him he can't do it."

I took this to mean that unless I "stronged" Doudou he would treat me badly every time he saw him, but I wasn't figuring on seeing him again and I whispered as much to

Omar—in French, so there'd be no mistake. "And besides," I said, "as your countrymen say, 'The man who wants to blow out his own brains need not fear their being blown out by others.'" I raised the bottle, but couldn't bring myself to drink from it this once.

"No, mahn, strong him. He do this and then 'nother man, then 'nother, then 'nother man. All the time. All day."

"Sheeit, how on earth could—"

"Believe in me, I and I—"

" . . . anything to do with how other people treat me, man. Let's get out of here. I can't just—"

Omar clutched my knee so firmly I understood—or thought I did—the depth of his conviction. "You make him strong on him now, and it will be fine for you." Then he removed his hand from my knee and touched it to his chest and said, "For me, too." It was then that I realized that the incident with the tea was meant for Omar as much as for me. Omar had brought me as an honored guest, or as a conversation piece, or as his chance to show his friends just how good his English was. But why was it up to me, either as symbol or as a genuine friend, to recover his lustre? I was the guest, right? I told myself to just sit there, and drink, then leave. But suddenly, the men around Doudou burst into laughter again, and I distinctly heard the golden-haired comedian say, "Jeeezuuuz!" and I felt my body rising stiff from the ground in jerky motions. I walked straight up to Doudou, dropped my half-empty bottle at his feet and slugged him so hard I'm certain I broke his nose. I know for certain I broke my finger. Doudou went tumbling from his chair and landed facedown on the porch. He struggled to get up, but fell forward, his head rolling side to side. His blood looked like black coins there on the porch. All the men rushed up to him, excepting the chubby man, who shoved me off the porch. I went down on my ass, but sprung up almost immediately. I was still pugnacious, but in a very small, very stupid way. Omar removed his shirt and pressed it to Doudou's nose.

I said, "Is he okay?"

No one replied.

I said, "We can get him a cab, get him to a doctor. I'll pay for the cab; I'll pay the doctor." And someone told me in Wolof that I could go out and fuck a relative. I stepped closer to the lot of them, out of shame and concern rather than anger, but Omar handed his shirt to Ismaila, stepped toward me with his palm leveled at my chest. "You go now," he said.

"But I thought you said—"

"You are not a good man." He turned back toward Doudou, whom they'd moved to the chair. The man with the strange ears left with a plastic bucket to retrieve fresh water. They all had their backs to me. I stood there a good long while, sick to my stomach from palm wine or shame, or both. After some minutes, Omar turned toward me for the briefest moment, and said, "Don't come again, Bertrand." He said this in French.

I left the little courtyard, and immediately lost my way. I wandered Fosse for what must have been ten years. On my way, I encountered an army of headless men who chased me with machetes. Blood gushed from their necks like geysers. Later, I was eaten and regurgitated by a creature with three thousand sharp fangs in its big red mouth. It had the head of a lion, and its long snaky body bristled with forty-four powerful baboon arms. Months later in this strange new world, I discovered a town where everyone ate glass, rocks, wood, dirt, bugs, etc., but grew sick at the sight and smell of vegetables, rice, couscous, fish. They captured me and tried to make me eat sand, but I brandished a yam I'd had in my pocket and when they all fell ill at the sight of it, I ran away. In another town I met a man who was handsome and elegant in every way, and I followed him to his home simply to jealously gaze at him. But while on the way to his own home, I saw him stop at other people's homes, and at every place he stopped, he'd remove part of his body and return it to the person from whom he'd borrowed it. At each place he'd leave a leg, or an arm, or a hand, and so forth, so by the time he got home, I discovered he was but a skull, who rolled across the ground like a common stone. It made me sad to see his beauty vanish so, and I walked all the way back to my home in Denver with my shoulders rounded and my head bent low. And when my people asked me what I found on my long long journey, I told them, "Palm wine. But it wasn't in season, so I have nothing to give you."

McKnight on Creating Detail and Setting

I have always believed that fiction writers ought to close their eyes and sit very still in order to clearly envision the settings they wish to describe. I know that sounds mystical, which some people may find off-putting, but I want you to suspend your disbelief and perceive my suggestion as a technique no more mystic than squinting one eye before aiming a rifle. After years of reading, years of trial and error, it has become increasingly apparent to me that a writer needs more than direct observation in order to create compelling details and a strong setting.

Both memory and imagination are essential if you're serious about writing vivid descriptive passages. Before I describe so much as a doorknob, I close my eyes and try to picture it clearly. Why, you ask, do I not just get up, walk across the room, eyeball the knob, then write what I see? Well, I do, sometimes, but to do so without variation is to condemn myself to fiction filled with those ugly fake brass knobs that were popular in houses built in the late 1960s. No, I couldn't live without the occasional crystal knob that beams its horseshoe rainbow on the wainscoting. But it's more than variety I'm aiming for. If we are to turn the real world into words we need to first convert it to the currency that will transmit it—strong, precise images. It needs to exist fully in your own mind—not just in the real world—before you will be able to commit it clearly to the page.

My advice isn't new. John Gardner, in *On Becoming a Novelist*, writes, "The writer must summon out of nonexistence some character, some scene, and he must focus that imaginary scene in his mind until he sees it as vividly as the typewriter and cluttered desk in front of him." To put this another way, good fiction provides readers with "a vivid and continuous dream." It allows readers to believe that they're deeply involved in the fictive world, not just cognitively processing words on a page. They're transported to California, or Atlanta, or, in my own story, to Senegal.

Fiction, after all, is not merely an exact reproduction of life. Because you are not writing nonfiction, you must change and adapt real experience to fit the needs of your story. This requires forethought and concentration. You don't write fiction with a palm-pilot while doing your chores, but alone in a room. Imagination and memory are the devices through which you transform the pictures in your head into words that then allow readers to experience your vision. As the novelist Elizabeth Bowen wrote, "Almost anything drawn from real life—house, town, room, park, landscape— will almost certainly be found to require some distortion for the purposes of plot. Remote memories, already distorted by the imagination, are most useful for the purposes of scene."

Establishing a Setting in a Story

When I began working on "Palm Wine," I had no idea that the narrator was going to end up slugging Doudou. I had imagined something so completely different from the printed ending that I'm too embarrassed to tell you what I'd had in mind. Much of what actually occurs does so because the writing process brought me closer to the character and his need to react that way. Only once I had begun writing did I finally understand the narrator and the way he would present Senegal on the page.

I wrote the story fairly quickly, four drafts in two days, a record for me. It felt, at the time, that the story came from nowhere, and by nowhere, I mean the particular details I gathered for my depiction of Fosse. Now, let me say before I go on that I have been to Fosse, and I very likely recorded some of what I saw in the journal I kept while in Senegal. I haven't read those journals in over twenty years. I should also tell you this: I did not refer to them when I wrote "Palm Wine." But I'm quite certain that writing down my observations both solidified and altered my memory of the place.

There's no way a short story can fully describe an entire village, or a house, or even a single man. You need to make choices. You need to select the strongest details. Take, for example, the passage that describes my narrator's first look at Fosse: "It's an urban village, a squatter's camp, a smoke-filled bowl of shanties built of rusty corrugated metal, gray splintery planks, cinderblock cement. It smelled of everything: goat skin, pot, green tobacco, fish, overripe fruit, cheap perfume, Gazelle Beer, warm cous-cous, scorched rice, the sour sharpness of cooking coals." I wanted my details to evoke a larger world for my readers. That's what makes reading a pleasure, allowing readers to construct the larger picture in their heads.

Setting and Character

The idea is not to catalog reality. There's too much reality for that. Rather, the idea is to describe a setting in such a way that it allows readers to understand the character's present state of mind. The fictive world in my story is filtered through the consciousness of Bertrand, my main character. His desires and limitations determined how the setting was rendered in each scene.

In that selection above, I wished for a passage, both rich and spare, that would suggest the narrator is slightly overwhelmed, mildly under assault. It was my aim that the crisscrossing senses reveal him to be incrementally out of his depth. I tried to organize the description by creating a wide-angle view before narrowing down to concrete details. Think of an establishing shot at the start of a movie, slowly zooming in on the main character. Also, description is not merely about the inner eye, but also the inner being—it is about all the senses. I learned this from reading a good many

South American writers, who seem to have a special knack for creating sensually rich but tightly written descriptive passages.

There is one other thing strong fiction has taught me: often there is harmony between the main character and the way the setting is described. In my story, as the setting changes and becomes darker, it suggests the descent of Bertrand into an altered state of mind. "It was getting close to dusk now," I wrote, "and our long shadows undulated before us over the packed soil. I was getting a little hungry, and I kept eyeing the street vendors who braised brochettes of mutton along the curb of the main street." So at this point the reader knows that the narrator is not only slightly disoriented, but likely hungry—not only for food, but also for a meaningful connection to his past.

Later on, when I describe the narrator's walk with Omar and Doudou in the "deep blue twilight" that "completely absorbed our shadows," I am not only trying to show the progression of time, but also setting the stage for the narrator's eventual breakdown. By the time they reach the tavern, he is so disoriented that he can scarcely tell up from down: "Perhaps a half dozen candles lit the room, but rather than clarify they muddied the darkness. I couldn't tell whether there were six other men in the place or twelve."

The passage describes an actual room in an actual place, but I never saw the little tavern at night. Still I imagined it in darkness because it established the best atmosphere to thrust Bertrand into a world both strange and frightening. So the real setting was transformed once through my memory because surely I did not remember it exactly. But more importantly, the real setting was transformed a second time, as I took my memories of the place and adapted them to complement the mood of my story. I made the setting fit the emotional texture of my story and, in doing so, helped drive home the larger point, that the real bush of ghosts are in Senegal; they lie between a person's ears.

Writing Suggestions

1. Think of a moment in your life where something powerful happened and time seemed to stop (the death of a loved one, being dumped, or watching TV as the second plane hit the World Trade Center). Write an entire page on only those few seconds, filling the space with the flood of feelings, impressions, and emotions that you felt at that time. If you can't recall them exactly, use your imagination. Now think of a memorable long period in your life (summer camp, a trip across America, or those weeks spent at a vacation cottage) and see if you can distill that entire stretch of time into one concise paragraph. Which is easier? What particular challenges does each technique entail? How might each be effectively used in short fiction in terms of establishing setting, mood, and atmosphere?

2. Write a story set in a time and place other than those you know well. Do a little research—reread Julianna Baggott's commentary for inspiration (page 53), if necessary, or reread Jarret Keene's "Son of Mogar" (page 91) for a good example of how

this might turn out—and turn your imagination loose. Let setting become a significant presence in your tale. Let your language be dense and lush, or sparse and lean as needed, but make sure that readers feel it and experience it with the same intensity that you do.

3. Using a completed story of yours that you're particularly proud of, rewrite the beginning scene to eliminate nearly all sense of setting (if you have a lot to start with) or add in a heavy dose of details (if you have mostly action and/or dialogue only). How does this radical revision of the first scene of your story affect the pace? The impact of the scene? Is the new draft more effective? How might this sort of tactic change your story overall if you carry the technique through to the end?

4. Locate a story by a writer particularly known for the ability to create evocative settings (William Faulkner's "A Rose for Emily," Edgar Allan Poe's "The Fall of the House of Usher," Tim O'Brien's "The Things They Carried," Eudora Welty's "Why I Live at the P.O.," Ralph Ellison's "A Party Down at the Square," or Shirley Jackson's "The Lottery"). Quickly read through the story once as a regular reader, enjoying it simply as a story. Then, much more carefully, read it a second time and scrutinize how the writer achieves such a vivid sense of place. Is it through a careful use of verbs? Nouns? Characters and physical descriptions? A combination of these techniques? What lessons does this writer have to offer you in terms of place, details, or pacing?

> I'm a Vietnam novelist the way Monet is a lily-pad painter . . . The
> regionalism, the settings, the kind of characters I use are simply
> vehicles into some deeper concerns about the human condition.
> —Robert Olen Butler

Keith Lee Morris

The Children of Dead State Troopers

From *The Gettysburg Review* and *The Best Seat in the House
and Other Stories*

The Amazon frogs were confusing. A hundred-piece puzzle, and it looked simple enough in the picture on the box, but there was little variation in the size or the shape of the pieces, and several of the frogs looked alike, black with green stripes, black with green spots, predominantly yellow with black spots, predominantly black with yellow spots, red legs with yellow stripes on a black body, red back with black legs, and often the legs or the little bulbous toes overlapped, so that when you thought you were looking for a piece with a red leg you really weren't, but would discover the right piece was the black hindquarters of a frog with green stripes or yellow spots. Randall Moon sat cross-legged on the hardwood floor with his three-year-old son Brandon, the puzzle piece of a frog with a blue head in one hand, a coffee mug in the other. It was ten o'clock on a sunny Friday morning in the Moons' new home in South Carolina, and Randall Moon and his son Brandon had already had two Pop Tarts apiece and watched an animated movie with lions in it, though the plot was difficult for Randall to follow because he was thinking about his wife, Connie, who had finally gone to the doctor two hours ago. If nothing was wrong, she should have been home by now.

"And this frog goes here," Brandon said, trying to work the head of a red frog onto the toes of a green one.

"Maybe," said Randall Moon.

Brandon was wearing a T-shirt but no pants. His little wiener dangled on the floor as he shifted back and forth gathering puzzle pieces. Randall thought that he should do something about the dangling wiener situation, and it was the third time he'd thought that since Brandon shed his skivvies to run and take a pee-pee on the pot, and he decided that the third time was a charm and that he *was* going to get around to doing something about it, so he set his coffee mug on the floor far away from Brandon and pointed at it and said, "Don't touch that, Brandon, it's *hot*," the way Connie had taught him to say the word when referring to the stove, with steady but not angry emphasis, and he walked down the hall past the kitchen to his left with all the dirty dishes Connie hadn't had the energy to clean and he himself had not gotten around to, and when he had given up on finding the discarded skivvies, he rummaged through Brandon's top drawer without finding a clean pair there, either, and then the phone rang.

Turning the corner into the living room he saw Brandon holding the receiver. "Who is that?" Brandon said. "Who *is* that?"

Randall Moon grabbed the phone and Brandon did a little stomping dance and furrowed his little eyebrows and opened his mouth wide. Randall reached down and tickled him under his arm to keep him from crying. "Hello?" he said, the receiver slipping down onto his shoulder. He got it back to his ear in time to hear his name. "Randall Moon? Yes. That's me."

"This is Officer Joe Butter Rentals calling on behalf of the State Troopers Association. Mr. Moon you may not know this but in the state of South Carolina three-point-seven state troopers are killed each year in the line of duty."

Joe Butter Rentals wanted money, that much was clear, and although Joe Butter Rentals, despite his strange name and perhaps even because of it, possessed an admirable voice, a commanding voice, pitched low, resonant, precise, with a nearly theatrical tonal gradation, a voice that said very clearly *Listen to me*, Randall Moon wouldn't, because although he was a salesman himself, of pharmaceuticals, he had no patience with phone solicitations. He hung up immediately. He resumed his place on the floor, retrieving his coffee mug with an outstretched arm, forgetting his son's dangling wiener.

He picked up a red rear-end piece and found where it attached over a yellow leg and let Brandon do it. "That's right, turn it this way, that's right, just like that." Brandon giggled and grabbed another puzzle piece, what appeared to be a black knee overlaid with another frog's yellow toes, and Randall had no idea where it might fit in the whole bewildering scheme. A sticky chunk of cherry Pop Tart clung to Brandon's hair, and this reminded Randall Moon somehow about the boy's lack of pants, and he sighed and stared out the front window at the huge beech tree, yellow leaves fluttering from the branches to the ground. Connie should be home by now. Last week she had stood in the bedroom late at night and bent over in her bra and panties, her yellow hair hanging toward the floor, and said, "Here. Right here. Feel." Randall Moon felt the spot on the top of his wife's head and told her that he didn't feel anything, and she asked him to look, and he did, and he said he didn't see anything, either. "When I bend over," she said, bent over, her fingers on her scalp, "it hurts right here."

Within days it hurt all over her head. She wallowed through the household chores, the child-rearing obligations, dizzy, pained, discombobulated, tired, while Randall Moon worked, but when he arrived home in the evening she could do nothing but collapse on the couch, and today he had finally called in sick so she could go to the doctor, and she should be home by now. The pain in his wife's head worried Randall Moon.

"Where does this one go? Where does this one go? Where does this one go? Where does this one go?" Brandon said it four times before Randall Moon heard and said that he guessed right here maybe, guiding his son's hand, but the piece wouldn't fit, a yellow frog with a green head that he thought might fit with a pair of yellow legs, but no, it did not.

The phone rang. It made Randall remember that he had forgotten Brandon's pants. "Mr. Moon, Joe Butter Rentals."

Joe Butter Rentals said no more for the moment, and Randall didn't hang up. He heard a great breath over the line, an insuck that seemed to pull a flurry of leaves from the beech tree. "Three-point-seven state troopers per year, Mr. Moon, so that if one were to do the math, so to say, multiply by thirty, let us say, the number thirty representing the years of a single generation, the number of dead state troopers would total over one hundred, one hundred and eleven to be precise."

Randall heard the great breath over the phone, saw the beech leaves fall in another spasmodic swirl. "And?" he asked.

"Mr. Moon?"

"'And?' I said. I'm here. I said, 'And?'"

The breath again, followed by the low, measured, almost musical tones. "And these three-point-seven troopers, Mr. Moon, annually, one hundred and eleven over a thirty year period if you should choose to do the math, die horrible deaths. They are shot along the roadside, Mr. Moon, bleeding in ditches, they are run over, their bones crushed, or struck by vehicles traveling at—"

Randall Moon hung up. He went to his son's bedroom to get a pair of skivvies and a pair of pants. The phone rang.

"—traveling at indecent rates of speed, killed by speeders, sir, in fact, or held at gunpoint before they could draw their own weapons, sacks over their heads, marched into the bushes and shot execution-style, if you only think of what—"

"What do you want?" Randall Moon said, his hand to his forehead, looking around the room for his coffee cup, which had inexplicably disappeared, Brandon looking up at him now, his rear end grazing the cold floor. "What do you want, exactly," Randall

Moon said. "I'm busy today." As if to prove this point he sat back down at the puzzle, handling a squarish piece with part of a red frog with black spots and part of a black frog with green ones.

"As are the state troopers, Mr. Moon, busy, sir, like you, except that they are busy on the roadways of your state—"

"I'm from Idaho," said Randall Moon.

"—on the roadways of your adopted state, protecting you, Mr. Moon, and your loved ones, and your friends and neighbors and colleagues, subjecting themselves all the time to the whims of an unpredictable populace, a populace primarily populated with good citizens like you, Mr. Moon, but occasionally populated with the kind of person that shoots one, crushes one, drags one into the bushes by the side of the roadway—"

Randall Moon dropped the receiver to its cradle, quickly, as if his arm could not respond rapidly enough to the powerful force of gravity, but he caught a few last words from the baritone voice of Joe Butter Rentals: "—and *think of the children*, Mr. Moon."

Randall Moon thought of his own child, Brandon, and how he didn't have on pants, and how he might forget and have an accident and pee-pee on the floor. Once again, he set off in the direction of his son's bedroom, down the hallway strewn with toys that he hadn't had the energy to transport to their proper places today, and, curiously, he felt as if he were being followed by the voice of Joe Butter Rentals, and he heard for the first time that Joe Butter Rentals had a southern accent, which he somehow hadn't noticed before, not a thick country drawl and not a broad genteel tincture of an accent, but one of the in-between kinds he heard sometimes when he talked to doctors or pharmacists in the small towns or the outskirts of Columbia, one of the kinds he couldn't place in terms of class or education because he didn't understand, didn't know the South, because he and Connie had come from Idaho just three months before because of the job. He was standing with one hand in his son's pajama drawer, and he snapped to, stopped hearing the voice of Joe Butter Rentals, and he rummaged the drawer until his hand found a pair of Tarzan skivvies, but in the pants drawer there were no pants, and so he found an almost clean pair in the laundry hamper, stacked to the top with dirty shirts and dirty pants and dirty bras and dirty towels they hadn't had the time or energy to clean lately, he and Connie, he with his job and she with the pain in her head, and where was Connie now? She should be home already.

The phone rang. Randall Moon picked up the receiver but did not press the answer button until he had seated himself next to Brandon on the floor, Brandon's butt on the cold wood floor and what were they coming to, anyway, the house a wreck and their son partially unclothed half the morning and that distinct smell he smelled each time he walked through the door, sweat and dirt and old food, and Connie not home yet, maybe looking right now at an x-ray of a brain tumor, and where was his coffee cup, maybe behind that towering stack of newspapers and unopened mail on the table, and where did the piece of the red frog with the yellow spots go, did it fit right there next to the back of the black-and-yellow striped one? He laid out the pants and skivvies on the floor and answered the phone.

"Joe Butter Rentals?" Randall Moon said.

"Butter Rentals," Joe Butter Rentals said. "Mr. Moon."

Brandon stood, his wiener dangling. "Who is that?" he said. "Who *is* that?"

Randall moved the receiver from his mouth just slightly. "It's Joe Butter Rentals," he said, and as he said it he realized with some embarrassment that the man's name was *not* Joe Butter Rentals, but that this was just the way he heard it, a product of the accent he didn't understand, its deep bassoonish smoothness, and that the man's name was probably Joe Butler Ennis or Joe Ben Raines or even Allen Cooper for all he knew. So Randall Moon tried very hard, his lips pressed close to the phone, to say the words exactly as he heard them, going over them slowly in his head and letting them come out as they seemed to have been spoken: "Officer Rentals?"

"Rentals," Joe Butter Rentals said.

"Rentals?"

"Rentals."

"Officer Joe," Randall Moon said. "What children?"

"Mr. Moon?"

"*What* children should I think of?"

For a moment there was silence, and then Randall Moon heard the breathing, and he looked out the window at the beech tree to see if the leaves fell, and they did. "I assumed it was clear, Mr. Moon, that we were speaking of the children of dead state troopers."

"Oh," Randall Moon said. Outside the window the beech leaves blew and the South Carolina sun, which seemed to Randall Moon an entirely different sun from the one he had grown up with and felt he knew, a violent sun, this one, in summer like a hot stove coil, and not the one like a pleasant underwater light he used to know during summer in Idaho, and now this one in the fall like a pleasant warm lightbulb when it should have been a rattling space heater trying hard to keep out the chill, *this* sun spun its way to the tops of the swaying pine trees across the road and threw a dancing light in Randall Moon's eyes and on the green and red and yellow and black frog puzzle on the floor. Randall Moon hung up the phone.

He had, apparently, been having a conversation with Joe Butter Rentals about the children of dead state troopers, but he had not been aware of it, and now he tried, as Joe Butter Rentals had suggested, to think of the children of dead state troopers, but he couldn't, only his own child without any pants, back on the floor now trying to fit the wrong piece of a blue frog into a slot that clearly called for a red one with yellow spots, or possibly green. Randall Moon picked up the skivvies and the phone rang.

It was an unusual method of phone solicitation, no two ways about it, this method of Joe Butter Rentals, and effective in a sense, though Randall Moon wondered when the part about money would come around, and as he let the phone ring twice, three times, he compared briefly this temporary job of Officer Joe Butter Rentals—who must surely be out there on the roadways himself most days—to his own job, picking out a suit in the near dark of the bedroom, driving, gliding by the kudzu, the train tracks, the old abandoned railroad depots, the general stores, into the little towns, the main streets lined with once proud homes, dilapidated now, plywood on the windows, rotten porches, peeling paint, and then the doctors' offices, striding in head up, shoulders square, gripping the briefcase tight, then waiting for the doctors, for the breaks between patients, the lunch breaks, and the noises from the rooms in the meantime while he made sure his samples were straight, his tie straight, the coughing, the complaints, the shuffle of feet down a hallway, and then the doctor's handshake and the touting of decongestants, antihistamines, antibiotics, analgesics, pimple creams, none of which would be of much assistance if one were, say, crushed, struck, shot in the head, or if one had a brain tumor like his wife, Connie, thought she had, and she should be home by now, and it occurred to Randall Moon as he prepared to answer on the fifth ring that it might be better if he did not tie up the line, and that if Joe Butter Rentals had something to sell he'd better sell it quick.

"If you only think of what, Mr. Moon, the children of the dead state troopers must abide. Please allow me to tell you that it is not an easy thing. Please imagine a scene, sir, perhaps in the afternoon, and the children of the state troopers have arrived home from school. They are seated in front of the television, let's say, perhaps a cartoon is showing, and maybe there is a bowl of popcorn, maybe the sun shines brightly and colorful leaves fall from the trees, and then comes the phone call . . . are you there, Mr. Moon?"

"Yes."

"The phone call, the communication, the knowledge that one's father, or, in point-two cases annually, one's mother, a state trooper, has been crushed, struck, shot execution-style, or *garroted*, Mr. Moon, if you know the meaning of the word, the children of the dead state troopers are given to understand that the father, the mother, the former state trooper, has been *exploded with dynamite*, Mr. Moon, which did in fact occur once, in Kentucky, in 1973."

Then came a pause, the breathing. Randall Moon looked at the beech tree and said, "What is the *point?*" He ran his thumb over a puzzle piece, a black frog with yellow stripes and tiny black eyes, bulbous, expressionless, and looked at Brandon, who had miraculously found the spot where the left side of a green frog's head fit. "What is the *point* about the children of the dead state troopers?"

There was a heavy breath, a sigh, and a gust of wind outside set the wind chimes on the porch clinking. "Would you allow me, Mr. Moon, to continue, please? A few more moments, and then I promise not to take up any more of your valuable time." The breathing again.

"Okay."

"We come into this world naked, sir," and the voice seemed even more sonorous, resonant, deeper, if that was possible. "We are all naked in the womb, we arrive that way, naked, trusting, unafraid. You have a child of your own, Mr. Moon."

"I do. He's naked now," Randall Moon said, although he couldn't imagine why. "Or almost."

"Mr. Moon?"

"I said he's naked *now*. My son, Brandon. He's sitting right here, and he's not wearing his pants."

Brandon looked at Randall Moon and laughed, looked down at himself and laughed again.

"That's your prerogative, Mr. Moon," Joe Butter Rentals said. "Mine is not to question why. But let me tell you that the children of the dead state troopers are *not* naked, Mr. Moon, the children of the dead state troopers are, indeed, now fully clothed, and they are out there, in the world, and they possess the knowledge that out there also is a man, or on occasion, such cases amounting to the death of less than one tenth of one state trooper annually, a woman, a man or woman who is out there also, if he or she has not already been electrocuted, gassed, lethally injected, shot, hung for the crime he or she has committed, the crushing, striking, shooting, garroting, exploding, in one case *beheading*, in Nevada, in 1984, of a state trooper, this one person is *out* there, whether locked in a correctional facility or still wandering the streets, but in either case sharing the same air, observing the same celestial phenomena, the seasons in their passing. And imagine the effect, Mr. Moon, on the children of the dead state troopers. For even if they are not, have never been, never will be, the victims of such atrocities as were committed against the dead state troopers themselves, they are singularly marked, affected, by those atrocities, and by the perpetrators of the atrocities, as if the perpetrators had, through their acts, left an indelible print upon the foreheads of the children of the dead state troopers. On the one hand innocence, goodness, health, on the other corruption, evil, sickness, like twinning strands, like a bad marriage of opposites. I assume you're married yourself, Mr. Moon?"

"I am," Randall Moon said. "I am. My wife, Connie, she's at the doctor's now. She may have a brain tumor."

"She may," said Joe Butter Rentals. "She very well may. Your wife, Connie, may very well have a brain tumor, Mr. Moon, and if that is in fact the case you can certainly empathize with, understand, grieve for, the children of the dead state troopers and their terrible plight. For in that case, it would be, would it not, Mr. Moon, *as if you had a brain tumor yourself*, and so it is with the children of the dead state troopers, that they feel as if the atrocities have been committed against *them*, the crushings, the strikings, the shootings, garrotings, beheadings, and in some instances, Mr. Moon, when the foulness seeps way down, when the rottenness has its way, the children of the dead state troopers may come to feel that they have in fact *committed the atrocities*, that they are indeed the murderers of their own fathers and mothers, the murderers of the dead state troopers, and in one particular case, in Massachusetts, in 1992, the child of a dead state trooper did in fact *become*—but you don't need to hear that, do you, Mr. Moon? You've already guessed."

Randall Moon wanted to hang up the phone. He had arrived at the conclusion that Joe Butter Rentals was not selling anything, and the house felt cold to him, and the frog puzzle and the cherry Pop Tart in his son's hair and his son's unclothed state and the silent fall of leaves out there in the sunlight weighed on him suddenly, pressed him down, but he held onto the receiver and listened to the low, steady breathing of Joe Butter Rentals.

"Do you see now, Mr. Moon, how it is with the children of the dead state troopers? How it is that they have, in effect, been shot, crushed, struck, exploded, beheaded? How it is true that, in so many, many cases, the children of the dead state troopers may just as well be dead?"

Randall Moon hung up the phone. He had heard enough, heard enough now to understand the terrible plight of the children of the dead state troopers. And for a few moments he did empathize. But his thoughts turned, as they always did, and he wondered at the sinking feeling, the feeling of being pressed down, the feeling, as he watched Brandon attach the very last puzzle piece, the head of a red frog with black spots, to the body of the same red frog with black spots, of being pulled under, as if he saw his half-naked son looming there over the pieces, saw the newspapers and the bills, the toys strewn around the room, the shining sun, the falling leaves, as if he were holding his breath deep down somewhere, beneath the surface of his life, beneath the circumstance, and he wondered why he should smell the dirty laundry, the old food, the sweat and decay so dully, as if his nose were plugged, and he wondered how it was that now, as he seemed to sink beneath the surface, he felt suddenly crushed by the weight of his life, struck blindside by circumstance, blown up to bursting with his own troubles, a hole in the middle of his head, or a tumor, if he did in fact have a head at all, of which he was no longer certain, and he reached his hand slowly, as if it were rising through water or earth, to the top of his head to make sure. The phone rang.

"Have I brought you to an understanding now, Mr. Moon," said the low, smooth voice of Joe Bud Reynolds, because of course that was his name, Randall Moon decided, simple, plain, nothing unusual about it at all, and the voice seemed even lower, smoother, as if it were attempting to soothe a wound, "of the children of the dead state troopers?"

"Yes," Randall Moon said, fingering his scalp. "Yes, you have."

"Then it is time I asked you for a small contribution, Mr. Moon, a small gesture on behalf of the children of the dead state troopers, fifty dollars, say, for which you will receive the official State Troopers Association bumper sticker, the official State Troopers Association copper belt buckle, and the official State Troopers Association ballpoint pen. May I put you down for a fifty dollar contribution, Mr. Moon?"

"Yes," Randall Moon said. "Yes, you may."

"Thank you," said the deep voice of Officer Joe Bud Reynolds. "We will contact you by mail." And Joe Bud Reynolds hung up the phone.

And as Randall Moon hung up the phone himself he felt a lightening, an airy feel, because Joe Bud Reynolds had provided him with an opportunity to relieve the pressing burden associated with the children of the dead state troopers, a chance to unweigh himself, rise back to the surface, where he could see his son's nakedness and the strewn toys and the stack of newspapers and bills and the dirty clothes and dirty dishes for what they were, the circumstances of his life, the moment-by-moment progression, the moments forming a trail like the strewn toys or the dishes expanding away from the sink or the roads he drove down every day, a trail that consisted of the inability to put on Brandon's pants, the frustration, X-rays and brain tumors and violent headaches and the possibility of violent death, guilt, abandonment, headless bodies, blood and brains, the yellow frog with the blue head that didn't seem to fit anywhere no matter how hard one tried, the dirty house leaning so fast toward decrepitude that one couldn't keep up, and all the things one couldn't keep up with and the things one couldn't understand, the chance that one's wife might die and that this would in fact be like one's own death, and Randall Moon wished his wife were home by now, and that her head no longer hurt, and he wished that he could take his fifty dollars and fling it at the sky, a tribute, a testament to the dead and the dying and the ones who felt dead and dying, and looking out at the beech tree, its branches twisting now in an urgent wind, Randall Moon imagined his money and the money of all the other Mr. Moons, as many as Joe Bud Reynolds could contact in a day or a week, or a whole host of Joe Bud Reynoldses, imagined all this money falling from the sky like leaves, and while his son, Brandon, stood there with his weiner dangling, in his trusting nakedness, his eyes and mouth open wide, Randall Moon flung the pieces of the Amazon frog puzzle into the air, returning them to their proper dis- order, the disorder of days and weeks and months and years, and the colors fell with the money too, the greens and reds and yellows and blacks and blues, all the colors of the world, and empathy fell, and grief fell, enough for everyone, enough empathy and grief for every melancholy soul, falling like rain out of a clear blue sky under- neath the strange sun that kept on climbing, unaffected by our gravity, and the chil- dren of the dead state troopers would have their share, as would Randall Moon, who realized, now, that he had been the child of a dead state trooper all this time.

Resp reading to reader *8/4/07*

Morris on Dialogue

To be honest, I never consciously thought of any of the issues I'm about to discuss while writing "The Children of Dead State Troopers." But that's usually how it is. You can discuss technique in a class and ponder over it in private until you're ready to hemor- rhage, but when you sit down to write it all disappears, you hope, and you're immersed in the story you're trying to tell. The story goes where your imagination is capable of taking it, and it's only afterward, looking at what you've written for the umpteenth time, that all those nagging technical questions arise, which is how it should be.

With this story, I was lucky to have things go fairly well from the start. I cranked it out over a Thanksgiving weekend and didn't find it necessary in the subsequent weeks to change it all that much—a rare occurrence, believe you me. The whole thing was based, as you might suspect, on a phone call: I spoke with a guy from The South Car- olina State Troopers Association, and he asked me for money and I said OK (although I never actually sent it), and after I hung up the phone I had the distinct impression that at some point in the conversation he'd actually used the phrase "the children of dead state troopers." The story was simply my attempt to utilize the phrase that stuck with me from this real-life experience. I didn't really know what the story was about until I neared the end, when I began to figure out that it was about Randall Moon's own puzzling sense of victimization, and how he could only feel sorry for other people when he could feel sorry for himself—when he could see everyone, including Randall Moon, suffering from the same rather nebulous plight.

But to get to the point: I've been asked to talk about dialogue in the story, and because dialogue tends either to present *serious* problems or virtually none at all—there really is such a thing as a "knack" for dialogue, and you kind of either have it or you don't, I think, in which case you have to work very hard to overcome the lack of knack, to put it very badly—I'll invite some of you to continue reading and others of you to *skip to the next story right now.*

If you're still reading, if you're one of those folks who has trouble with dialogue— if, to your dismay, you find in re-reading your stories that your characters have said things like, "Wow, Sarah, I certainly do like your new hat" when you don't remember having given them permission to *talk that badly*—then I offer these few general sugges- tions in the hope that they'll help smooth the way.

1. More important than anything else—you've gotta *hear* it. In the same way that you have to visualize the interior of a room in order to describe it in a way that allows the reader to see, you have to actually listen to your characters speak in order to make the reader hear. Put yourself right there in the middle of the scene and listen to what happens. If you're really in there with your characters, really spying on them from behind the coat rack and being careful not to cough, then the dialogue is going to flow. Imagination might be defined as turning the unreal into the real—if it's not real for you, it's not going to be real for anyone else. Think of it as method acting—even your position behind the coat rack might not be enough; you might have to *inhabit* your characters, or, maybe more correctly, your characters might have to inhabit you. They might have to crawl inside you and speak through your fingertips. Now the problem, of course, is how to make that happen, because it's something you can't very well fake. This is where the "knack" thing comes in—for some writers, the process occurs naturally, while for others it requires a good bit of wriggling and stretching to get author and character inside the same skin. Suggestions number 2 and 3 are about how to wriggle and stretch.

2. Know as much about your characters as you possibly can. Know what they eat for breakfast. Know which of the various methods they employee in tying their shoes. Know what fears wake them up at 3 a.m. and what things make them laugh till they can't breathe. Such information might not ever make it into your story, but knowing it will help you to understand what your characters are likely to think and say in the situations you create for them. If you know your characters as well as you know your friends or your family—and that's not as unlikely as it sounds, because you have access to your characters' thoughts in a way that you never do with people in the real world—then they'll begin to talk on their own. They'll tell *you* what they want to say and how they're likely to say it. So, obviously, what I'm suggesting here is a character outline that you should undertake apart from the story itself—it should be done as *preparation* for the story. If you're not willing to go quite that far, at least take the time to jot down several important character traits, a few clear physical details, and a behavioral quirk or two—even this more limited form of character outline will give you a better sense of who you're dealing with when he/she opens his/her mouth to speak.

3. Tap into your own internal dialogue. We invent dialogue all the time. We think in terms of conversation. Example: you've run out of money and you're driving to your parents' house to ask for a loan. What are you thinking on the way? *I'll say this and they'll say this and I'll say but so and so and then they'll say blah blah*, etc. We're constantly improvising these imaginary conversations as a way to work through our problems, and if you can tap into that, if you can hone in on the methods you use all the time, in your own head, to create dialogue, you'll understand better how to do the same thing in your fiction. Part of the battle is simply becoming attuned to your own thought processes; I mentioned before that you need to listen to your characters—you also need to listen to yourself.

4. Now, having said all that—there are differences between the way conversation works in the real world and the way it works in fiction. Thus far, I've been sug-

gesting ways to make your dialogue sound more natural, but that's just the first step. When it comes to fiction, dialogue also has to do some measurable *work*. What is your dialogue accomplishing in the context of the story overall? How is it advancing the narrative, deepening or resolving the conflict? Here's a perfectly believable conversation between a husband and wife at the dinner table:

> "Anything interesting happen at work today?"
> "Interesting?"
> "Yeah."
> "Hmm . . . not really. Amanda invited us over to her house for dinner on Saturday."
> "You're kidding. Again? What time?"
> "I think she said three."
> "Three? I'm playing golf at four."
> "What do you want me to do, then . . . cancel? I told her we'd go."

Etc., etc. It mimics real life, but it doesn't get your story anywhere (unless the husband is having an affair with Amanda and employing the euphemism "playing golf" whenever he sleeps with her, in which case you might be on the right track here). Some writers would probably disagree with this next statement, out of fear that adopting such a strategy might obstruct the natural flow of the story, but I suggest that you outline your scenes beforehand—that you know, when you approach dialogue, what you need to get out of it in order to make it functional within the context of your story. What's the crucial development that has to come out of this particular conversation? What do you want the reader to know about plot, character, theme when he/she reaches the end of this scene? Write *toward* that point, and when your characters have said what they need to say to one another in order to serve your purpose, move on. Don't be afraid to cut away from dialogue, particularly if you've found a sharp line—"Isn't it pretty to think so?" says Brett Ashley to Jake Barnes at the end of *The Sun Also Rises*, but in real life that wouldn't be the end of their conversation. After all, they've still got a cab ride to share, but that doesn't concern the reader, who's heard all that's necessary to hear from these two. Summarize parts of the dialogue, particularly small talk. It's usually enough to know that two characters talked about the weather ("They talked about the recent hot spell") without having to know what they said specifically. It's often a good idea to start a scene in the middle, after the pleasantries are over with:

> "I found out about your 'golf' partner," his wife said at dinner that night.
> "What?" he said.
> "*Amanda*," she said.
> "Oh," he said. A strand of linguine hung from his lower lip. "Damn."

In other words, get in, do what you gotta do, get out and on to the next thing. Dialogue is usually an important element in fiction, but even excellent dialogue is not an end in itself.

5. Remember that dialogue has to work *on the page*. Keep in mind that the written and the spoken word are different forms of communication. You have to listen to your characters speak, but you're not merely taking dictation. You've got other elements

of scene to deal with as well. One of the most important things to keep in mind is that the reader still needs to *see* what's going on. If you concentrate, to the exclusion of all else, on what the characters say, then what you end up with is a series of cartoon balloons with no accompanying cartoon, or a blank movie screen with just the audio. Imagine a conversation in a moving car—the setting is changing every second. There are red lights and buildings and pedestrians and trees and hills and oncoming cars, and it's your job to keep the readers aware of this continued movement. Even inside the car, there are other things going on—someone lights a cigarette, turns on the radio, reaches over to put a hand on someone else's shoulder. And it's not just visual—what about the song on the radio, the wind rushing through the windows, the smell of the poultry farm the car just passed?

Fortunately, keeping your reader oriented to other details of the scene works to your benefit, because one strange characteristic of written conversation is that characters who speak for very long without interruption tend to sound awkward and unconvincing. Often the solution to this problem lies in providing *artificial* interruption—breaking up speech with well-chosen descriptions of the character or the surroundings, for instance. In real life, speech and action can occur simultaneously; *on the page*, they can only happen one at a time, and that fact actually helps you to control the rhythm. And don't forget your ability to enter the world of your characters' thoughts—what people think while they're talking to one another is every bit as important as what they say. Even the lowly dialogue tag (he said, she said) can be your friend when it comes to constructing an effective scene.

Look at this passage from James Joyce's story "Counterparts," in which an employee is about to get fired by his boss because of some misplaced letters:

> "I know nothing about any two letters," he said.
> "You—know—nothing. Of course you know nothing," said Mr. Alleyne. "Tell me," he added . . . "do you take me for a fool? Do you think me an utter fool?"
> . . . Almost before he was aware of it, his tongue had found a felicitous moment: "I don't think, sir," he said, "that that's a fair question to put to me."

Notice how much better the last dialogue line is here just because of the placement of the tag? Its internal positioning heightens the comic effect—*artificially*, as there would be no such pause in actual speech—of the last few words. It's like approaching the punch line to a joke—drum roll, please. Ba da boom.

You've probably noticed by now that I followed very few of my own suggestions in writing the dialogue in "The Children of Dead State Troopers." Nobody actually talks like Officer Reynolds (or not anyone I know), and he goes on for long periods without interruption, and, because he's just a voice on the phone, you never *see* him at all. But dialogue also works according to the reader's expectations, and in writing this story my task was to make the reader expect, or be willing to accept, something out of the ordinary, something that would ordinarily seem ridiculous. The success or failure of dialogue often depends upon the degree to which it works consistently with other elements of the story—particularly *tone*. In "Troopers," the conversation between Randall Moon and Joe Bud Reynolds is essentially absurd; but the tone of the story suggests a level of absurdity from the outset (or at least that was my intention). The second sentence alone would, I hoped, indicate to the reader that Randall Moon was not to be taken entirely seriously (note: it's possible to write a serious story in which the characters are not taken seriously—I refer you to Flannery O'Connor, for starters, or to a contemporary like George Saunders). After all, he's helping to put together a child's puzzle, not performing open-heart surgery, and yet the convoluted sentence structure, the repetition of the frog's colors and body parts, and the emphasis on Randall's growing confusion suggest that he might as well be. Further along in the opening paragraph, you find out that "Randall Moon and his son Brandon had already had two Pop Tarts apiece and watched an animated movie with lions in it, though the plot was difficult for Randall to follow because he was thinking about his wife, Connie . . . " Let's examine this. First, we've got a grown man who not only has seen fit to give two Pop Tarts to a three-year-old, but who has *eaten two Pop Tarts himself*. The "animated movie with lions in it"—we all know this is probably *The Lion King*, and substituting the generic description for the title turns it into a joke. And how hard can it possibly be to follow the plot of an animated movie with lions in it, regardless of what else you might have on your mind? What I'm saying here is that, in a sense, I've already *sold* readers on the absurd nature of the dialogue before they've come to it, simply by making sure that the other elements of the story point in the right direction. I suppose, then, it's true enough to say that any dialogue can be good dialogue—even "Sarah, I certainly do like your new hat"—if the author has prepared me to like it and accept it in the world of a particular story.

As you can see, writing dialogue gets to be fairly complicated at times. But as I said at the outset, don't let it be too complicated *while you're writing your story*. In the middle of the creative act, you've got to go with your impulses. When you've finished a first draft, then it might be time to go back through some of these suggestions and see if they help you shore up the weaker spots. As you continue to write, you'll internalize some of the basic tenets of writing dialogue, and most of it will become second nature. You'll know when to follow the rules and when to break them. Occasionally you'll get lucky, and a story will emerge from your pen or your keyboard as quickly and easily as "The Children of Dead State Troopers" did for me; such unusual and happy occurrences are the payoff, maybe, for all the hard work—everything from entire plot rewrites to the struggle to find just the right word in a particular sentence—that generally goes into producing a good piece of fiction.

Writing Suggestions

1. Write a scene exclusively using dialogue where a young man reluctantly tells his longtime girlfriend that he is dropping out of college to work in his parents' convenience store back in Detroit. Document everything they say to each other during the entire conversation, even small asides or casual chitchat. Now write a new version of the same scene in which you add details. You will also need to pick and

choose which sections of dialogue remain. How can gesture and body language account for part of the information—in addition to the dialogue—that is exchanged between characters? Which scene has more immediacy? More tension?

2. Using your response from Writing Suggestion #1 as the starting point (or using a situation of your own choosing), write a story in which two characters desperately want different things and the conflict emerges primarily through dialogue versus physical action. How can you make verbal conflict as effective as one character slamming a fist into someone else's face? Are there subtle uses of language (dialect, tone, diction) that might help out?

3. Go to a restaurant or other public place and casually listen to conversations around you. Jot down the back-and-forth dialogue between people who interest you. Pay particular attention to their mannerisms in speech, their "umms" and "errs" and other verbal tics. As Morris mentions, this is obviously "real" dialogue, but would it read well on the page? Much of real-life conversation is made up of seemingly empty moments, dialogue without genuine substance. In one of your own stories or scenes, reexamine the dialogue. Rework parts that seem more like "real-life" conversation than dialogue appropriate to fiction (that is, dialogue that reveals character, advances plot, or offers important information that would be unwieldy in exposition).

4. With the sound off, watch a key scene from a movie that won the Academy Award for Best Picture (*Amadeus, American Beauty, As Good as It Gets, The Color Purple, The Silence of the Lambs, The Unforgiven*, etc.). Watch how tension is developed nonverbally through character movement, action, and facial expression. Write a one-page version of that same scene using dialogue as the primary means to create tension. After you're through, watch the scene again with the sound on. What did the scriptwriter do differently than you did to create conflict and tension? Is it easier or harder to create tension through dialogue rather than through other means?

> Sometimes I've read paragraphs a hundred times,
> but I think reading aloud
> allows me to get physical and use my body so I
> can see mistakes more clearly.
> I cut a lot this way. It helps to check dialogue.
> Is this the wrong rhythm? Are these repetitions?
> —Andre Dubus

Section 8

THE SHORT-SHORT STORY

Tom Hazuka

FIVE SHORT-SHORT STORIES

Field Trip

The woman holding court at the Tiki Lounge wore a shocking pink T-shirt, the word MANIAC stretched tight across her chest in black block letters with silver sequins. I was impressed. I was young.

"People take themselves too seriously," she said, tendrils of cancer smoke creeping from her nostrils. "Especially comedians."

People laughed—seriously, they did. They raised cool glasses to their lips, dragged deep on cigarettes, carefully choreographed chance body contact that was anything but. I would have too, but I didn't want to show that I was eavesdropping. I was too cool for that. It was summer and I had just graduated from high school. The names meant nothing to me then, but Woodstock was two months away, Altamont six, the invasion of Cambodia almost a year. As it turned out, I would miss the first two.

The woman squeezed a pale, chubby guy's van-dyked chin as if it belonged to an irresistible infant. Crow's feet of pleasure furrowed around his eyes. She leaned close enough to kiss him.

"I'd be good," she said, "if I wasn't so bad at it."

Everyone shrieked with delight. I was mute. The guy must have smelled her breath, but the crow's feet did not fly away. They acted like they belonged there. The way I belonged there. I'd turned eighteen in April; old enough to vote, or die in Vietnam or any other war my government sent me to, legal in any bar in the land.

I didn't die in Vietnam, just got a Purple Heart and some shrapnel in my spine that still aches in cold weather. It's throbbing right now in the raw December rain, as I crouch surrounded in the land of national monuments: over my shoulder Lincoln's marble Gettysburg Address; through the bare trees Washington stabbing the sky like a bayonet; a grenade toss away three grunts like me frozen in bronze, twenty years old forever.

A stark black ribbon of dead names scrolling downhill at my feet.

It's amazing how the mind works, incomprehensible almost how my first sight of the Vietnam Memorial brings back not the war, but that word MANIAC taut across a T-shirt with a loud woman inside. I never saw her or it again. In the meantime, our leaders saw the light at the end of the tunnel and realized that while eighteen is old enough to get killed for your country, you must be twenty-one to start doing it to yourself.

"Hey, baby," the woman cried as I left the bar. "Lighten up. Rome wasn't burned in a day."

Homeward Bound

Thanksgiving, 1970, changing planes at a midwestern airport. I wasn't feeling thankful, not even for my sky-high draft lottery number. I felt more guilty than good about luck shielding me from decisions I'd never wish on anybody: Canada, prison, Vietnam.

A soldier in a wheelchair was smoking Luckys like his life depended on it. He had a newspaper on his lap but wasn't reading it; I saw ashes on the headlines. After awhile two soldiers sat in front of me, discussing the football game. One hoped the storm would hold off because he hated God-damn turbulence.

A guy and a girl my age—college—came up to the wheelchair. "Vietnam?" he asked.

The soldier nodded.

"Good," she said. "Paralyzed, babyburner? Still got your manhood?"

"Yeah," he said, too quick, so quick it made you wonder.

The bigger soldier jumped up, but the skinny one shoved him aside. He dropped the guy with one punch, then smacked the girl twice in the face.

A black security guard my father's age ran over. "Did you *see* that?" the girl shrieked.

"I saw it." He yanked the guy to his feet. "Now *get* outta here."

His voice was so venomous they fled without speaking. The wheelchair soldier was shaking, pretending to read the paper. The other two sat down again, careful, like they weren't sure the seats fit any more.

"Sorry, man," said the skinny one, his voice full of holes. "I was afraid you couldn't do it."

I remembered going to Niagara Falls as a kid, the disappointment of crossing into Canada and not feeling any different on foreign soil. It was like the world was just all one place.

We took off late in the snowstorm.

Mixture

"Sex and violence don't mix. Why waste good violence on sex?"

I look for a smile; I feel it in his words. But Roger—my best friend as a kid, best man at my wedding six years ago—is concentrating too hard to smile. He's staring down the barrel of his 30.06, waiting for that snapping turtle to stick his head above water again. He doesn't want it eating the game fish in his pond. I've seen him shoot half a dozen since junior high.

"I never hit her," he says evenly. "I never hit her even once."

"Of course you didn't."

"I don't know what makes her say that, Jimmy."

Roger never uses Carla's name since she left. But she's not a "cheating bitch" or "worthless whore" either, like some other friends' ex-wives—or my own, once or twice, when pain won out over pride.

"Come on, don't worry about it. Nobody believes her." The lie feels like dirt on my tongue.

I like Carla. She's smart, and secure enough about it that even in high school she didn't play dumb. One time she told me of a nightmare Roger had, over ten years after he got back from Vietnam. He was writhing on his stomach, she said, whimpering over and over *Burning people smell so bad* without waking up.

"I didn't dare touch him," she said. She put her hand on my arm. "You're the only one I've told this to. Not even him." Carla stared off at nothing, nodding slowly. She shrugged. "Especially not him."

Roger's finger is tight on the trigger. Suddenly he looks away from his target, straight at me.

"Remember when we were kids, and found that dead bullfrog on the other side of the pond? Nailed down on a stump?"

I nod. I can still see that spread-eagle frog, belly-up and leathery black from the sun, its gut a squirming ball of maggots. It gave me nightmares for a week.

Roger takes aim again, out across the water.

"I didn't do that," he says.

Utilitarianism

I return home for the first time as an adult. My parents greet me traditionally, Mom commenting on my long absence and worrying "that woman" isn't feeding me enough, Dad crushing my hand lest I forget which one of us survived Guadalcanal. But an odor of arrested decay has replaced the smells of childhood. The house of my youth is decorated with death.

Stuffed creatures fill the rooms. Local varmints predominate—squirrels, chipmunks, some possums and porcupines, even a bullfrog—but Dad hangs my coat on an eight-point buck, and the TV blares from the belly of a rampant and silently roaring grizzly. We stand entranced, almost touching.

"I bet you could eat a horse," Mom says, and bustles to the kitchen.

"You know Jeremy Bentham, the philosopher?" Dad asks. "*He's* stuffed. Mom and I are going to London to see him."

My father has hardly left the state since World War II.

"Your favorite! Liverwurst on rye."

Mom puts the sandwich and a glass of milk on the dining room table. Then I see that the cat I grew up with, a cat twelve years dead, is the centerpiece.

"You embalmed Kitten!"

"Embalming is for graveyards, son. Mom and I fixed Kitten to be with us forever."

I can't eat with a corpse staring at me. "Where did you get all these, these *dead* things?"

"My God, boy," Mom says. "Open your eyes." A shadow nicks her face. "I thought you loved liverwurst."

"Your mother saw the ad in the magazine," Dad says, the two of them beaming as he puts his arm around her for the first time in my memory.

Vaporware

So I sell vaporware for a living, what's that prove? The money's decent, and maybe the stuff'll work the way the company hopes, the way I guarantee my customers. You can't hang me for giving it a shot. This is America, last I heard.

A woman leaves messages on my machine. She insists she still loves me, uses words like "anodyne" and "inevitable"—but then why'd she move 751 miles away with my brother? I answer the messages. My phone bill is obscene. I wrote a postcard saying this is ridiculous. On the other side were "Greetings from Colorado" and a Jackalope the size of a bull. She gave it to me years ago, during a "cute" period. Cute was *her* word. I trust "cute" about as far as I can spit an eight ball.

So here I sit, naked, taking a day off from peddling vaporware. I drank coffee till noon, beer after that, watched two Steve Martin movies on the VCR and read half an inch of *The Executioner's Song*. I'd bet the farm that postcard arrived today; she'll plan to give herself time to think it over, but won't make it past sundown. I debate whether to put in *The Jerk*. The phone rings. The machine answers.

"You return my present to tell me I'm not worth a few toll calls? I'm not that easy to erase. I love you and don't you forget it. This is the nineties, lover. This is America, last I heard."

Hazuka on Writing the Short-Short Story

Writing fiction, especially literary fiction, should be a process of discovery. I always encourage students to create stories without planning overmuch or expecting to know how a story ends before they begin. If you absolutely must make an outline, go with what works for you, but if you're new to fiction writing, please don't assume that you need one. Most of the writers I know would be hard-pressed to finish anything if they had to know the ending before they started. Having a preordained ending in mind, while sometimes comforting, can also be limiting: the writer might put on literary blinders and rush straight toward that ending, instead of being receptive to fascinating side trips and unforeseen possibilities. Even if you go to Rome to see St. Peter's, it's a mistake not to explore out-of-the-way alleys as well. At the very least, you won't just experience the same things every other tourist does.

Although this advice applies to fiction of any length, it's practically a necessity for writing short-shorts. While coediting *Flash Fiction*, a collection of 72 stories all shorter than 750 words, I read nearly five thousand short-shorts of widely varying quality. Almost all of them had been published, usually in literary magazines. Their authors ranged from the famous to the unknown. I expected that certain patterns would emerge.

They didn't.

The only thing every story had in common was its length, which led me to a conclusion I hadn't foreseen: the shorter the story, the less a writer can rely on (or fall into the trap of) copying predictable patterns. In flash fiction or micro fiction (250 words maximum) it's virtually impossible to write a formulaic story, because there is no set form or structure for fiction this brief. Even if you tried to write a mystery or a romance of, say, five hundred words, readers would take your story as a form of metafiction, a *comment* on the genre rather than a piece of genre fiction itself. And that's what you *would* be doing—trying to create something new, expanding possibilities rather than conforming to the predictable expectations of a genre.

So what am I claiming here, that structure doesn't exist in the short-short? Far from it. What I'm claiming is that any story of this length must discover its own structure with little help from established models—and style is a huge part of that discovery process. This is true of all fiction writing, but the shorter the story the more heightened the effect and the more demanding the writer's job. Shorter might seem easier, but it's tough to write a satisfying story in so few words. You need to do a lot in a small space, and that means making each word count. The best short-short stories display the charged and resonant language of poetry while also managing to tell a story. This is a challenge indeed.

But that challenge needn't be grim or daunting. It's hard to write a great short-short story, so don't worry about trying to. Take the pressure off yourself and focus on having fun instead. No matter what the subject matter, the short-short is a *playful* form. It lends itself to experimentation, to the quirky and the unexpected. It's difficult to be stodgy in only a few hundred words. You have to get in and get out.

Although excellent flash fiction and micro fiction has been written using every conceivable point of view, most of my short-short stories are in first person. That is, there's an "I" character in the story who narrates the action. The shorter the story, the more likely it is that I use first person. Why? Because first person is wonderful for quick, efficient double-duty characterization. By double-duty I mean that anything your narrator says not only provides information to the reader but also characterizes the narrator. What the narrator chooses to tell us, and *how* he or she tells it, shows us a lot about that person. Is that narrative voice sarcastic? Friendly? Snobbish? Clueless? Devious? All of the above?

I hold these truths to be, well, not self-evident but true nonetheless:

1. For a story to feel done, to "work," there has to be movement or change in at least one character, possibly though not necessarily to the extent of an epiphany, a moment of insight. There must be the sense that nothing will ever be quite the same for the character after this.

2. In a first-person story, one of the characters who change has to be the narrator, no matter how large or small the narrator's role in the action. In my story "Homeward Bound" the narrator is an observer, not a participant. But without the narrator's perceptions and presence, the story would just be an anecdote.

The only exception to these rules occurs when the lack of character change is the *point* of the story, such as the heartbreaking example of the butler who narrates Kazuo Ishiguro's *The Remains of the Day*. The reader yearns for him to loosen up and embrace his chance for happiness, but he can't bring himself to do it. Yet the ending is powerful because we vicariously experience the situation through him and realize what he *should* do. In a successful story using either approach, the effect is the same—movement or change in the reader. This is fiction, after all; the characters don't exist. They only matter insofar as they affect real people who read about them.

The shorter your story, the more likely that it will consist of a single scene. To increase the immediacy of that scene I often use present tense, though that's certainly not necessary. What *is* necessary is a context for the scene, a sense that it fits into a larger picture. Without that context the events of the scene, no matter how interesting, will remain inert. There's no resonance in a vacuum.

Context can be created in any number of ways, including voice and language cues, backstory, history, culture (including popular culture), and setting. This list is by no means exhaustive, and the categories overlap big time, but it's a useful place to start. I'll give some brief explanations along with a few examples from my stories.

Narrative voice—through tone, slang, use of languages other than English, or other idiosyncrasies that personalize the voice and make it specific—creates a wider world beyond the events of the story. The first line of "Vaporware" ("So I sell vaporware for a living, what's that prove?") implies a narrator with a chip on his shoulder who is probably insecure about his job. It also evokes the context of a capitalist society, which is soon reinforced by comments about money, customers, and "giving it a shot." In the background is the Horatio Alger ideal of the American Dream waiting for anyone who works hard: "This is America, last I heard."

Backstory provides information about characters and events leading up to the scene. (Don't confuse backstory with flashback, a cut to a scene earlier in time, which the short-short rarely has room for.) "Mixture" gives lots of details about the characters' shared history, without which the story would have little interest for a reader outside of wondering whether or not a turtle is going to get blown away. "Utilitarianism" relies on the conflict between the way things were and the way they are now. When the narrator says, "I return home for the first time as an adult," tension is established between the past and the present. Without that context the piece is just some quirky sight gags about a married couple who become taxidermists. It only becomes a story because of the contrast between the narrator's expectations and the new reality he's forced to deal with instead.

Historical references and dates can be a quick way to establish context. The first line of "Homeward Bound" ("Thanksgiving, 1970, changing planes at a small midwestern airport.") places the story during a volatile period in U.S. history on a national holiday with roots stretching back to the mythical beginning of what it is to be American. I didn't want to be subtle here; I wanted to create context for the scene to follow. The reader needs to know right away that this is a Vietnam-era story. Simultaneously the voice of the narrator starts to emerge and the setting is mentioned. See what I mean about these categories overlapping? Overlap is good—it shows that your language is not inert, but doing double and triple duty. That should be a goal in all your writing, but especially in flash fiction.

Cultural and pop cultural references can serve a variety of functions. They can establish a historical era (overlap again!), such as the mention of Woodstock and a legal drinking age of eighteen in "Field Trip." They can characterize. Someone who listens to Sinatra while riding the subway is different from someone who listens to Kiss while driving a Lexus. Readers get a different impression from a character who reads Shakespeare than one who reads Spiderman comics—and a different impression still if the character reads both Shakespeare *and* Spiderman. It's also fun to play with ironic and/or symbolic titles. In "Vaporware," *The Executioner's Song* and *The Jerk* show that the narrator reads Norman Mailer books and watches Steve Martin movies, but I chose those particular titles for pretty obvious symbolic reasons.

Setting always creates context. The "same" conversation about food in a Siberian gulag and on a Boy Scout camping trip are not the same conversation at all. The context for the characters' dialogue gives those identical words hugely different meanings. In "Mixture" the talk between Roger and Jimmy has an edge because a gun and imminent death are involved, but more importantly because the setting at Roger's pond evokes a chain of memories and shared experiences for both characters. "Field Trip" takes place in a bar to emphasize the absurdity of being old enough at eighteen to kill or be killed in the army, yet not old enough to legally buy a beer. "Utilitarianism" needs to happen at the narrator's childhood home; no other setting is possible to achieve the same effect. "Vaporware" would be a far different story if narrated by someone other than a confused schmo sitting naked in his apartment while playing hooky from work. "Homeward Bound" tries to create a backdrop of isolation ("small midwestern airport," not J.F.K.) and danger (Vietnam, flying in a snowstorm) for the scene with the wheelchair soldier. Once you find the right setting for a story, it should be hard for a reader to imagine it happening anywhere else.

A final word of advice: don't censor yourself during the first draft. Ignore that voice in your head whispering that your stuff stinks and it's hopeless to go on. The main goal of a first draft is not to be good, it's to be *done*. Finish your first draft, flaws and all, then start cutting and polishing your prose into what just might become a gem of a story.

Writing Suggestions

1. In a short-short story, all of the elements of a longer story are condensed into a smaller space. Using only one paragraph—seven sentences at most—develop the entire beginning for a short-short story. Make sure you introduce the characters, establish conflict, and develop an appropriate setting or situation with concrete language and specific details. Remember that effective details often reveal character personalities, build conflict, and set an emotional tone for the story.

2. Tell a story using no more than 25 sentences. The entire story must take place in one scene. Each sentence must have at least one word of concrete description. What individual words or phrases will evoke or suggest the larger personality of the main character? How can you introduce, develop, and resolve a conflict in so short a time?

3. In a full-length story you're already written, have one of your secondary characters retell the events from his or her own perspective, using fewer than half of the words in the original story. Choices will need to be made about what's important, what ought to be paraphrased, what might be left out. Also consider word choices and attitude in your new speaker. Be open to changes in the original story as you write this new draft. How has this new draft informed your understanding of the original?

4. At your local library or bookstore, find a copy of a short-short story anthology (Jerome Stern's *Micro Fiction*, Tom Hazuka's *Flash Fiction*, Irving Howe's *Short Shorts*, or Robert Shepard's *Sudden Fiction*, to name just a few) and read a dozen or so stories. How are Tom Hazuka's short-short stories different from some in these anthologies? Develop a list of rules that separates short-shorts from longer stories. In your opinion, what types of stories might be better accomplished as a short-short as opposed to a full-length story?

> *The short-short story combines the power of poetic language with the power of storytelling. All in under two pages. Blessed be those who work in this challenging genre.*
> —Virgil Suárez

PART
Three

⌒

On Revising

*You have to read and write on a daily basis. You have to be utterly
vulnerable on the page, and utterly ruthless in revision. To write
something good, you have to want it so bad that nothing else matters.*
—Chris Offutt

Introduction

There is no simple way to accurately describe a short story. Edith Wharton defines a
short story as "a shaft driven straight into the heart of experience." Bernard Malamud
believes "a short story is a way of indicating the complexity of life in a few pages."
V. S. Pritchett suggests "a short story is . . . frequently the celebration of character at a
bursting point." Many writers define a successful short story, in part, as fiction that
moves beyond the basics of craft toward clarity of expression and a unique vision, elements that are perhaps best developed through drafting, revision, and reflection.

In the previous section, On Writing, sixteen authors explore those elements of craft
most essential to writing the first draft of a short story, namely character, plot, point of
view, and scene construction. The stories, essays, and exercises in that section are
designed to help you write your first complete draft of a story while understanding the
role each element plays in the construction of fiction.

In this section, On Revising, six writers discuss the process of writing beyond the
initial full draft, paying particular attention to the role of revision and editing, the construction of theme and meaning, a story's relationship to its audience, and the role the

workshop process can play in helping a writer understand his or her own territory. In some ways, these are more subtle and complex elements of craft that, for a writer, are often approached after completing an entire first or even second draft of a story.

Revision Techniques

Melissa Pritchard's and Stephen Graham Jones's commentaries explain the role of revision in the fiction writing process. Pritchard offers techniques that will help revise scenes and story structure, while Jones explains strategies for tightening individual scenes and editing sentences for clarity and precision. Taken together, this pair of commentaries offers the fundamentals for strengthening a story's dramatic unity as well as the language of its individual sentences.

The Story and Its Audience

In his commentary, T. Coraghessan Boyle stresses the importance of controlling tone in order to amplify story meaning. He also discusses strategies to arouse legitimate reader sympathy without resorting to stereotypes, heavy-handed language, or sentimentality. George Saunders explains one of the most underused yet powerful aspects of fiction, humor, and offers ways to effectively develop it within the context of fiction.

Theme, Meaning, and Vision

Mary Gaitskill discusses methods of developing meaning and theme in short fiction, drawing not only on her own experience of writing "A Bestial Noise" but also offering exercises for other writers to develop meaning and theme in their own work. Lastly, Virgil Suárez emphasizes the importance the workshop process plays not only in the role of revision but also in understanding your own territory and vision as a writer as well as the way your own stories might relate and speak to each other.

Identifying Common Revision Concerns: Essay and Writing Suggestions

Writing and editing are two separate tasks requiring vastly different skills. To write a complete draft, an author must fully imagine characters, scenes, and details. But to transform a draft into a finished story, an author must learn to look critically at each aspect of the original story and devise ways to increase its effectiveness and impact. "Remember," E. B. White advises, "it is no sign of weakness or defeat that your manuscript ends up in need of major surgery. This is a common occurrence in all writing, and among the best writers."

Here's the good news: If you find that your story is not perfect after the first draft, you are not alone. Many writers feel that in the first draft they are telling the story to themselves. In each subsequent draft, however, they work towards effectively telling the story to readers—often readers they have not and never will meet. They are revising the story for strangers.

The real challenge of revision is identifying which aspects of a story to revisit and how to go about the process of revision. Unlike the process of writing, when writers intuit their way through a story scene by scene, revision asks you to critically examine your work, paying particular attention to clarity, unity, and effectiveness. Good stories aren't simply written once; they are rewritten and rewritten. "The most essential gift for a good writer," Ernest Hemingway suggests, "is a built-in, shock-proof, bullshit detector."

Some writers revise on the computer, changing the story as they revisit it, while other writers like to make changes on a draft recently printed. To this end, we've developed a list of questions and prompts to help you with the process of revision. The first half of the list focuses on elements of scene and story revision, while the second half offers suggestions for line editing. This is by no means a comprehensive list of revision concerns, but it contains ideas to begin the process.

Suggestions for Scene and Story Revision

- How does this story develop its characters? Are they interesting and engaging throughout?
- Do readers have all the necessary information to understand the characters' motivation?
- Do readers have enough concrete detail to feel grounded as the story progresses from scene to scene?
- How well does the first scene of the story function? Is there a good mix of external change and character explication?
- Does the middle of the story complicate or deepen the tension suggested by the events in the first scene?
- Is the prose style consistent throughout the story?
- Is the point of view firmly established and consistent? Would the story benefit from a change in point of view, or from changing the point-of-view character?
- Do flashbacks interrupt the flow of a story or provide a necessary break from the action?
- Is the dialogue interesting and authentic? Would scenes benefit from more dialogue? When speaking, do your characters sound too similar?
- Does the story establish and maintain the pacing implied in the first few pages? Are some scenes rushed or too slow? Does this story's pace create a satisfying sense of rhythm and momentum?
- Would adding a scene (or scenes) help develop the story? If so, what scene(s) should be added?
- Does the story contain any scenes that can be removed or shortened?
- Does the story contain too many or too few characters?
- Does the ending effectively conclude the dramatic action?

Suggestions for Line Editing

- A reasonable goal for line editing (the process of revising a story sentence-by-sentence, word-by-word for clarity and purpose) is to cut ten percent of a story's length. Reread your story, paying special attention to trimming repeated ideas and unnecessary words, sentences, or even paragraphs.

- Scour your story for the passive voice (using the passive verb construction such as "The book was picked up by John" instead of "John picked up the book"), which often neutralizes immediacy and tension in your story.

- Look for weak adjectives (such as "beautiful" or "good") and adverbs (such as "really" and "very") that don't contribute to specific dramatic development in your scenes.

- If the majority of a story's sentences are clustered around one length, most likely you have a particular sentence rhythm stuck in your head. You want a range of sentence lengths in most stories: shorts sentences, mid-length sentences, long sentences. Find ways to combine or halve existing sentences for variety and effect.

- As they do with sentences, most writers use a variety of paragraph lengths. Short, punchy paragraphs might be only one sentence long. Long, chunky paragraphs often deliver extended sections of description and information.

- In each of your longer paragraphs (four or more sentences), examine the first and last sentence. In general, strong action, details, and noticeable information are found in these sentences, thereby framing each longer paragraph with an introductory hook and solid closure.

- Can you cut any chatty dialogue that doesn't further the story? Is there any dialogue that is actually exposition poorly disguised? Do any dialogue tags (such as "he retorted" or "she said languorously") call undue attention to themselves?

- Lastly, find the weakest detail or description in each of your paragraphs and revise it so that it matches the level of directness and sophistication found in your best passages.

The process of revision can prove as challenging as writing the first draft. Often it can be even more challenging. Some writers prefer to focus on the larger elements of revision, such as scene and story, finalizing the content before polishing the language with line editing, while other writers prefer to attack the story simultaneously from all fronts. Whatever your approach, the process of revision helps clarify, strengthen, and further develop an initial draft, gradually and carefully working it closer to a finished story.

Section 9

REVISION TECHNIQUES

Melissa Pritchard

Salve Regina

From *The Gettysburg Review* and *O. Henry Prize Stories 2000*.

Every angel is terrifying.
—Rainer Maria Rilke

Norah Loft tightened the scarlet strip with its notchings of white numbers around her naked hips. After two weeks of traversing the bedroom floor on her rear end—one hip thrusting out then the other, "walking" back and forth, back and forth—tonight's measurement mocked all her efforts. Stuffing the measuring tape into her ballerina jewelry box, Norah doused a cotton square with Bonnie Bell 1006 and drove it up and down her face as if she were cleaning a rug. She performed the eye widening exercises Lacey had shown her, convinced she was doing them backwards. Lacey liked to describe her own eyes as hopeless, small and too gray, like wet, dead guppies. Dropping on a rosebud-sprigged nightie, Norah skewered empty beer cans on her head, two on top, one on each side, three down the back, so her hair, by tomorrow morning, might almost resemble Lacey's.

Norah snapped off all the lights except the yellow bean-pot lamp on her nightstand. She's hated this room ever since her mother redecorated it in marigold yellows and orange, with the baffling and pointless theme of Spain. Directly over Norah's bed hung a framed travel poster showing a matador in pink balletic shoes, poised to gore a bull, ESPAÑA written in red letters down one side. Her only option was to ignore her surroundings, as if she were stranded in some foreign, second-rate motel. Now, removing her glasses and dropping to her knees, Norah began a fervent series of prayers to the Blessed Virgin Mary as set forth by Reverend Mother Stewart in one of her pocket-sized booklets distributed by Holy Rood Press in Long Island. If Norah's dispute with her flesh

301

had ended in yet another rout, then her will to acquire saintliness seemed, if only by mulish reaction, to be accelerating.

Mo and Mitzi Loft, Norah's parents, went on being pleased with last year's decision to send their only child, in her sophomore year, to a private school. Without appearing prejudiced, they had neatly sidestepped the issue of public school integration. Removing their daughter from a politically volatile climate insured Norah a superior education, at the hands of nuns said to be the female equivalent of Jesuits. The Convent of the Sacred Heart was academically rigorous, the architecture impressive, the grounds parklike and secluded. And though she had never been to Europe, Mitzi exclaimed that the convent looked like something you would surely drive past in France, certainly Paris, where the mother school, Sacre Coeur, was said to still exist. This local convent was attended mainly by the daughters of wealthy capitalists, Catholics naturally, many of whom were boarders. Norah, neither a Catholic nor a boarder, rode her Sears bicycle to and from school each day.

Although there had been the possibility of a second private school in San Francisco, the Lofts deemed it less costly, wiser, to keep Norah home. Mo particularly wanted to supervise his daughter's orthodontia. As a dentist, the alignment of her teeth was of professional and even competitive concern to him. Mitzi felt this a little silly, overinvolved, but didn't think it politic to complain. After all, hadn't she met Morris when he had appeared with a group of dental students at the tooth factory in Scranton? Few people, the tour guide had said, stopping to ogle Mitzi, could appreciate the skill involved, sorting and matching teeth. As if on cue, Mitzi had glanced up from her task of pairing three hundred adult male incisors and paralyzed Mo, or so he would forever claim, by smiling directly, blazingly, at him. People didn't realize, the guide continued, how many thousands of teeth, made here in Scranton, were shipped overseas—even as the demand for false teeth dropped in the United States, other parts of the world, and Europe especially, where people lost as many teeth as ever. In the midst of this, Mo and Mitzi exchanged phone numbers. Eventually they married and moved to California, where Mitzi embarked upon the long and occasionally gratifying process of reinventing herself. The Lofts were Goldwater Republicans, members of the Menlo Country Club, and Mitzi herself kept up with several vaguely prestigious volunteer activities as well as her monthly bridge group, referred to affectionately by its eight members as "Sherry & Therapy."

Mitzi Loft had done well; at the moment, fifteen-year-old Norah was her single vexation. The child was stiff-limbed, morose, socially regressive. Stepping into Norah's room yesterday afternoon to put up the Costa Brava travel poster she'd had reframed in yellow, Mitzi literally stumbled over an untidy heap of religious paraphernalia sticking out from under the orange chenille bedspread. A gloomy-looking black and silver rosary, half a dozen dogeared prayer booklets written in zealous purple prose, three holy cards—one with the image of a crown of thorns wrapped around a heart spurting blood—and of all dreary things, a cheap black face veil. She didn't dare tell Morris.

In the best of times, Mo referred to himself as an agnostic; in the worst, a hardboiled cynic. His moods hinged entirely upon the state of his practice. What no one had warned her about was that dentists, after psychiatrists, had the highest rate of suicide. This terrified Mitzi, so she worked to keep her husband at a constant temperature, like a coddled egg. She had overcome his loudest objection to sending Norah to a convent, saying she would see to it that Norah did not convert, turn into a nun or a missionary in Calcutta; nothing religiously untoward would happen. Now this. Face veils. Rosaries. Thorns poking into hearts.

On a lesser note, Mitzi held out optimism that in a school of girls all wearing the same dull, triangular blue skirts and god-awful cropped boleros (uniforms imported from Cairo, Egypt, for pity's sake), Norah's homeliness would hardly distinguish itself. Behind convent walls, she might outgrow her ugly-ducklingness.

Riding her bicycle to school that first morning after Christmas vacation, Norah wore her new black knit cap and mittens. The brilliant winter air left her cheeks flushed and her eyes watering as she cycled past the gold-lettered sign, Sacre Coeur, past the spiked ironwork gates of the convent, as if she were departing one way of life, even one century, for another. The serpentine road she cycled along, bordered by semicircular beds of sky blue agapanthus and half-wild rose hedges splashed with scarlet, was irregularly shaded by thick stands of oak and feathery palms with regal, supple-seeming gray trunks. Norah rode up to the three-story building made of rose-colored granite with its great columned porte cochere, its crenellated towers and cupolas, feeling, spiritually at least, by way of sanctuary and relief, home. The Sacred Heart religious presided over their domain with the same century-old discipline established by the mother school in Paris. Theirs was a serene, fastidious government, the school and its vast estate sealed as if under a bell jar in an atmosphere rich and seductive, faintly erotic, where school rituals were called by their French names, *prime, gouter, congé*. By contrast, the Lofts' house was a show of modern, one-dimensional conformity. Neighbors commented on how well-kept it was, but to Norah, her home seemed an arid card house imbued with anxiety; indeed, she could scarcely distinguish its square rooms from her father's bland dental suites.

Leaving her bicycle in the small rack by the kitchen, Norah ascended a set of side stairs and went into the building. Passing the library, she went up yet another set of wide, red-carpeted stairs to the second floor, where she slipped into an alcove, knelt on a plain, wooden prie-dieu, and gazed up at the seated life-size figure of the Virgin. On an altar banked by green glass vases of thickly fleshed white lilies, Mary's indigo mantle fell in solemn, anchored folds over her pale rose gown. The twelve stars of the apocalypse encircled her humbly inclined head, and her canted gaze—Norah always felt it personally—was tender, brimming, enigmatic. The Virgin saw nothing, saw without judgment into the heart of everything.

> Remember, O Most Gracious Virgin Mary, that never was it known, that anyone who fled to thy protection, implored thy help or sought thy intercession was left unaided. Inspired by this confidence, I fly to thee O Virgin of virgins, my mother; to thee I come, before thee I stand, sinful and sorrowful. O Mother of the word incarnate, despises not my petitions, but in thy mercy hear and answer me. Amen.

Norah left the alcove and stealthily went downstairs to the chapel. One of her most frequent prayers was to please not be seen in either place. The nuns would surely press for conversion, and the other girls, even Lacey, most of all Lacey, jaded from years of Catholic schooling, might tease her, or worse. The way the two queer girls were shunned was instruction enough. Rose and Deirdre. Norah had never spoken to them. Marooned on an ugly spar of talk, they clung tightly to the wreckage of one another, incurring further derision. No one actually knew if they were queer or not—rumor itself condemned them. On occasion Norah prayed for their souls, but like everyone else she was repulsed by their cowed, doughy faces, their moist, nail-bitten hands, their downcast expressions of shame. Norah had a secret terror of being like them. Not that she was queer, surely not—half the girls in the school had a crush on Mother Fitzgerald, she wasn't alone in that. It was this other, increasing devotion to Mary, to the Virgin (whose image Norah generally mixed up with Mother Fitzgerald's) that caused her to feel generally outcast and mildly disgraced. In the middle of her third academic year, Norah could not help being what she was, a diligent girl. Respected but plain. Never left out, never first to be included. Nun's pet. A model girl, intelligent, obedient, dull as dust.

Shortsighted even with her glasses, Norah, as she walked into the darkened chapel, made out a large, vague object—a table or so she thought—set before the altar. She walked straight up to it. The nun's freckled hands were modestly crossed, a plain black rosary wrapped around them, her black habit and white wimple stiff and pleated, a pair of gold pince-nez placed (as if she would need them!) over her closed eyes. She looked like a small human made of paper or a large doll made of powdered, papery flesh. With her heart flaring, Norah raced from the chapel, bolted up two flights of stairs to the study hall and entered breathless from the back door just as Mother Fitzgerald, mistress of studies for the third and fourth academics, swept in from the front, her black skirts and long, sheer veil pulsing with sensual vitality behind her.

The third floor study hall was a high-ceilinged room, its cream-colored walls trimmed with varnished oak wainscoting. A row of tall, deeply recessed windows along the room's north side overlooked Palm Court, a circular patio area shaded by palm trees, where, during the more clement months of April and May, the girls ate their lunch, and in June, each year's graduating class held a small but elegant commencement ceremony.

Inside the pocket of her habit—designed after a nineteenth-century French mourning costume—Mother Fitzgerald carried a palm-size mahogany clapper, an instrument brought out and clicked in the manner of castanets, not with any rhythm of course, but to command silence, attention, obedience. She now used her clapper, as briskly and confidently as she did everything. As she mounted the platform and stood to one side of her wooden lectern, flanked by the American flag and large color photographs of John F. Kennedy, Jr. and Pope John XXIII, Mother Fitzgerald surveyed the sixty or so blue-uniformed girls seated before her. She was aware that some of them were infatuated with her, though none more so, or more obviously, than Norah Loft. She had been receiving small, delicately folded notes from Norah for weeks now, usually discussing points of theology. Mother Fitzgerald interpreted these as camouflaged love notes. Accustomed to receiving such notes from girls, along with sly, hot glances and small gifts, tokens of affection, she prayed regularly to be forgiven the deep sense of pleasure these aroused in her. She reminded herself that her main task was to take a misguided love and direct it to its true source, God. Still, and she felt some thrilling shame over this, she had saved each letter, each note, sweet evidence of her students' affection for her, in a small pine box with a key.

The girls, she announced, were to proceed down to chapel where they were to attend a funeral mass for Mother Logan, who had been living these past nine years in the nuns' retirement home. The convent's property was quite immense; beyond the main building, the girls were restricted to the tennis courts, hockey field, swimming pool and, on special occasions, the school's religious gardens, a damp, disorienting maze of grottoes where stained marble statues of St. Agnes, St. Joseph, Mater, Our Lady of Lourdes, all with voluptuous yet stern expressions, were enshrined then forgotten. None of the girls had ever been inside the retirement home; none of them knew Mother Logan. They were, said Mother Fitzgerald, her cheeks turning their irresistible rose color, to retrieve their missals and veils from their desks and form ranks. The ordinary school day, she added with a small, reassuring smile, would resume after Mass.

They filed past the closed coffin and, with black veils covering their young faces, knelt to receive communion. Norah sat alone, listening to the elderly nuns in the front two pews sing "*Salve Regina*" in rehearsed, silvery unison. Mantled in black, diminutive and round-shouldered, most wore the same gold pince-nez as Mother Logan and they seemed to have the same parsnip pallor. Except that they were upright, open-eyed, and harmonizing. Norah thought they were no different from their now dead companion. She could never imagine Mother Fitzgerald becoming this, turning into this, could not imagine everything distinctive and vitally exquisite about her stripped away. Perhaps that was the point. Perhaps it was a fact of becoming old. One's personality fell away.

Carrying a batch of essays on martyrdom to Reverend Mother's office as a favor for Mother Fitzgerald, Norah was surprised to see the crèche still in place weeks after Christmas. At the beginning of Advent, each girl's name was typed and glued, a paper girth, around the midsection of a small woolen lamb. The lambs, sixty or so, stood in a solid, snowy bank on the long bottom step of a series of shallow, green-felted stairs leading up to the manger. By Christmas Eve, they were all to have reached the top step, to assemble meekly before the holy family. But throughout the season, infractions of rules, the most minor lapses in conduct, were taken note by the nuns until the flock was broken into punished, straggling ranks. A wild, refractory few lagged four or more steps behind. Norah's lamb, as it had the year before, ascended without incident or interruption to Jesus. Lacey Jenks's was detained five steps down, gazing sideways toward the lavatory, where she had twice been caught smoking. Far from being chastened, Lacey had laughed. She had been obedient for too many years, and where in the world, she asked Norah, had it gotten her?

Norah met Lacey Jenks at the fall tea her first year at Sacred Heart. Lacey had been appointed Norah's "Angel," to watch over and guide her. Despite Norah's resolution never to laugh at the expense of others, she took immediate guilty pleasure in her new friend's humor, a sly, sometimes sniping wit fed by unerring perception. It was Lacey who first pointed out that the backs of Madame Sesiche's legs were unshaven—you could see them when she turned to conjugate active and passive verbs on the blackboard—and that the music appreciation teacher, Miss Trammel, was going bald on the top of her head, a plight she failed to disguise with tortoise barrettes and artful shiftings of her part. And it was Lacey who told her about Mother Fitzgerald, who, it was rumored, the night before her wedding to the son of a Greek prince, took refuge in the convent, where she has been ever since.

Though it was never spoken of, another factor bound these two. Both Norah and Lacey rode bicycles to school, both were reminded in constant, subtle ways by their parents that private school was a privilege, that sacrifices were being made. The boarders, on the other had, accustomed to an unvarying climate of wealth, were oblivious, even careless of its intimidating effect on girls like Norah and Lacey. No one spoke of money, yet friendships fell plainly along economic lines. The wealthier girls kept to themselves, while girls like Lacey and Norah found themselves unexpectedly and sometimes fiercely compatible.

From the very beginning, Mitzi had been unhappy with Norah's Angel. Lacey Jenks was a day student, her mother a city librarian, her father a retired army colonel. They lived in an older, slightly run-down section of Menlo Park. Why couldn't Norah have gotten one of the other girls, one of the Dial soap heiresses, for instance? While she tolerated the friendship between her daughter and this Lacey, she did little to encourage it. Several of the other girls Norah invited home at different times seemed pleasant enough, but these, too, Mitzi ascertained from a few calculated inquiries, were less than sterling liaisons. The task fell to Mitzi to chip out an acceptable social niche for her daughter. Currently, through her connections at the Menlo Country Club, she was lobbying for Norah's invitation to the upcoming cotillion. Were she to attend, her name might well appear in the society column of the *San Francisco Chronicle*, linked with those of local debutantes. She was horrified to see, however, that Norah's complexion was worsening. The crescent-shaped rash of pimples around her chin was migrating up toward her temples. Mo would have to agree to getting her into weekly acne treatments again. Though it gave Norah's skin something of the suggestion of a bad sunburn, the ultraviolet light worked wonders. Besides, Mitzi enjoyed flirting with the dermatologist, Dr. Ferraye. Flirting stabilized a marriage, and Mitzi had long been aware when she "dolled up"—Mo's phrase—to do her errands, men eagerly attended and things got done. She wished Norah could understand the efficiency, the pragmatism of beauty.

DEAR BOOBS,
Merci for your letter. I'm in a poopy mood but you're not ugly. You'd blush if you knew how cute you are. For lunch I had two pieces of white bread, one lamb and gravy, one other peanut butter and jelly. Thing of jello, five round teeny crackers, 500 cal. or more, ergo: no dinner. Ughy Ughy. Helen just asked me if I was writing an encyclopedia. What does life mean— what is love—I want to find out this weekend—Does Mother F. really hate me?—Miss Trammel forgot to put on D.O.—I am a boob—I think I shall take down my girdle and go to pot. I hate you because you're everything I wish I could and should be—I have a hate complex. Am I a boob? Do I look like a boob? Helen is upset cause I won't let her read this and she thinks I am writing nasties about her. Je ne sais quoi.
    I love you with all my toe. Respectful au revoirs, One Little Boob

Such notes to Norah had begun to change. Since the onset of guitar lessons, Lacey's notes were dominated by someone named Arthur Webb. Ever her handwriting grew crimped and stupidly curlicued. For Christmas, her parents had succumbed and given Lacey a Sears guitar along with six months of paid lessons. Classical lessons, not what she'd wanted, but as she told Norah, how else would she ever have met Arthur? Her first lesson was at Kepler's, a small, popular music store in downtown Menlo Park. Arthur, she wrote Norah, had taken her into a tiny, white soundproof cubicle and, sitting inches away, demanded she open her legs wide, no much wider, like so, the guitar had to lie properly across her lap. He made her sing "On Top of Old Smokey" without any accompaniment, in order to get, he said, some idea of her pitch. The whole time she was singing he'd stared at her, his eyes narrowed. Arthur was a graduate student at San Francisco State College, and Lacey thought he was twenty-three or –four, though she'd never asked. She'd brought a news clipping to show Norah, a minuscule announcement of a recital, with his picture. But Norah couldn't tell much; his face was blurred. The impression she got was of two mournful eyes and a great mop of dark shaggy hair. Twice Lacey asked Norah to come to the music shop, but Norah, reticent, embarrassed, said no. Much later, she would wish she had gone, had seen them together, but some part of her dug in, was mad. She missed the old notes, the sly, catty ones, the ones that made her laugh so hard she could only hope to be forgiven.

A second tiresome consequence of Lacey's "romance" was her constant absorption in her appearance. From one day to the next her hair changed, her diet altered, her mood swung. By contrast, Norah's acne had worsened, she'd stopped bottom walking, and her hair, minus Mo's empty beer cans, hipped out on the sides and dwindled like a dying plant on top. Though one day, after flipping through an issue of *Seventeen* (for Christmas—a stocking stuffer—Mitzi had given her a year's subscription) she rubbed her lips with talcum powder, then smeared Vaseline over them, an inexpensive trick, the article promised to get that ethereal English look. Over dinner, Mo har-harred that his daughter looked next in line for Rasputin's Funeral Home. Mitzi tried shushing him, but Norah fled to her room and whammed the door. Alone with Mitzi's wrath, Mo waggled his eyebrows and made an O with his mouth, a ridiculous expression intended to absolve him.

So while Lacey practiced guitar scales, her fingertips turning white with callus and slightly bloodied—for Arthur, she'd sigh—Mitzi got Norah a volunteer job at Stanford Hospital. Now she wore a second uniform, a bibbed, red and white seersucker jumper with white sneakers. She assisted new mothers, helped them into wheelchairs, handed over their newborn infants, rolled them into an elevator, then out to the curb where husbands waited beside the family car like soldiers, like doormen or butlers, like nervous new fathers. Norah held each infant as the mother was helped by her husband into the car, then leaned down to hand over the small bundle. What made these people trust her with an infant? What if she dropped it, what if it rolled under the car? She told Lacey the husbands almost always insisted on a picture of her holding the baby, standing beside the new mother in her wheelchair. Why would they want a picture like that? Norah imagined herself appearing in a photo album of strangers all over the state of California. As a candy striper, she liked the sanitized cheerfulness of the hospital, she liked helping people who invariable expressed curious gratitude for what she found so intolerably awkward, her own youth. Eventually, Norah would receive a red and white enameled pin for working one hundred hours; this would be noted in a small column of the hospital newsletter. Goody Two-shoes, Lacey teased. Norah Brownnoser. Wait until Reverend Mother plops one of her ribbons on you. Lacey was referring to honor ribbons awarded at the school ceremony known as Prime, satin sashes crossing the chest and shoulders, fastened at the hip with a small, bronze medal. Norah did want a pale blue sash across her chest, placed there, in front of the whole school, by Reverend Mother McGwynn, a sign of her exemplary behavior.

How, the Lofts agreed, could you fault a child for taking life seriously? Mo was mainly relieved she had not picked up what he called the God bug. Mitzi tried to be proud of her daughter—she understood she should be. Still, she didn't care for studiousness, for this sort of earnestness in a young girl. Ambition wasn't feminine, it frightened people. And, privately, Mitzi equated religion with moral insurance for the old or dying. Regularly, she checked Norah's room. The gloomy articles were still there. Some nights, unable to sleep, she pictured Norah announcing a vocation. She and Mo would have to drive out to some godforsaken cloister somewhere to visit their former daughter, now Mother Loft, sitting behind bars, prim, humorless, bespectacled. No wedding. No grandchildren. Mitzi would instead bring boxes of unscented soap, rough washcloths, sets of plain homespun underwear. It was her worst nightmare. She had read enough about teenagers to understand you couldn't confront them directly. You couldn't even agree with them. The best strategy was to feign indifference to whatever wrong direction they were headed in, then plop in little facts, like Alka-Seltzers, round innocuous comments, let those sink in, take slow, antidotal effect . . . on average, nuns die a full fifteen years before normal women . . . nuns cannot take vacations . . . have you seen a nun on a roller coaster or riding a horse . . . nuns can't dance or marry or swim in the sea . . . imagine, up at three every morning, grinding away at the same silly prayers, rain or shine, year in, year out. Casually, Mitzi tapped out such little notions of monotony, usually when they were driving somewhere. And though Norah never said a word, never responded, Mitzi never gave up hope.

Norah was responding. She saw what her mother was up to—persecution. Each night, on her knees beneath the picture of the pink-slippered matador, Norah asked for a vision. Sometimes she felt translucent, as though light were pouring through her, as though the air around her were heavy as syrup and she herself were light, porous, all her weight vanishing into her soul and flying upward. She counted these among the happiest sensations she had known.

With the latest note crumpled in her hand (Noser: Music Room, 12:30, News!), she found Lacey sitting on the piano bench, her face ignited by the as yet undisclosed "news." Stealthily, Norah shut the door behind her. No doubt this had to with what's-his-face, Arthur Webb.

"Come over to me, Nose. Close your eyes. Are they closed? Ok."

Norah stood blind in the center of the small practice room, her hands loosely clasped behind her back. First she felt Lacey's hands on her shoulders, smelled her gingery breath, then came the kiss—brief, warm, lovely.

The piano bench dragged on the floor a little. Lacey plinked a bit of "Heart and Soul," softly, on the piano.

"Norah. Open your eyes. Do they look different? My lips? God, I needed to call you, but I didn't want the Colonel eavesdropping, which he would, the big boob. And I didn't dare write anything in case someone else read it. Oh my God. Yesterday, after my lesson, Arthur kissed me. He's been wanting to since the first time he saw me. That's what he said."

Norah thought Lacey's lips looked unchanged, maybe drier. She'd assumed Arthur didn't know what Lacey felt about him, or if he did know, wouldn't care. After all, he was twenty-three or –four and went to college. She and Lacey weren't even sixteen. Now Lacey was pursing her lips and rolling her eyes in the most asinine way.

"You shouldn't do that."

"Why, Norah? He loves me. He's practically said so."

"The man is older than you. Not to mention he's your teacher."

"So? I'm sixteen in two months. We've already decided to wait."

"Wait for what?"

"Honest to God, Norah. Don't be dense. To have sex. Arthur is mature, and he's got this friend who's got a place at the beach we . . . "

"Lacey will you stop? I can't hear this anymore."

"Why? I've been talking to you for months."

Norah was sure their absence from study hall had been noticed, that they were about to be caught, that because of Lacey, she would lose her chance for a ribbon.

"I'm sorry if I'm boring you. There's just no one else I can trust with this. I trust you with my life, Norah. I promise to talk about Arthur less. Not one word. I won't use any word that starts with A. I'll . . . "

"Lacey. We've got to get back to study hall."

"Ok, ok. We're gone. We're there. What about this? If I promise not to say another word about A (she silently mouthed his name) can I still give you a signal that says we've done it? Had sex?"

Norah found herself agreeing just to get out of the music room. And for the next three weeks, Norah did get a respite from his name, did get some part of their old, Arthur-less relationship back, at least until the signal came, a silly double thumbs-up, after which nothing was the same.

On the same night Lacey Jenks was to lose her virginity in, of all places, Kepler's music shop (there was no friend's house, only a ratty old maroon sofa in the back, where Arthur had already seduced two other girls—he was beginning to think he had a knack for this), on that same evening, Mitzi Loft was putting the finishing touches on Norah. Considering the obstacles she'd climbed over, one damned thing after another, she had a right to feel pleased. The biggest obstacle had turned out to be Mo, who was in one of his funks. His practice was down—he had lost three clients in one month—though Mitzi reminded him two of the three had died which could hardly be taken personally, and the third was Sam Widdle, so a high, holy good riddance. But Mo took anything to do with his dentistry to heart, and what Mitzi didn't know was he had also made investments without her and was steadily losing money on them. (In fact, if Mitzi lifted the lid on what a kettle of fish he was in, she would throw a fit, exactly why he hadn't told her. They would have to shag his broken keester down some long, lonesome road, creditors braying all the way, before he'd unload his troubles to her. All he could bring himself to suggest was that Mitzi keep the expenses down to a dull roar.) And Mitzi, ever nervous about his statistical weakness for suicide, accepted a friend's loan of her daughter Helen Marie's cotillion dress from last year. Both girls, it turned out, wore the same size, and the dress, while nondescript, was at least a Lanz original. So she had only to pay for Norah's hair and a pair of white brocade pumps she found at Payless and had dyed emerald green.

So now her daughter—fifteen!—stood before her, wearing a midcalf, white chiffon dirndl skirt with a sleeveless gold lamé top, in emerald heels with a dyed-to-match purse, a wide, emerald velveteen bow perched slightly past the crown of her head, her hair professionally done—to match Mitzi's—in a lacquered, bouffant flip.

"Morris!" This came gaily from Norah's bedroom. "Picture time!"

Helmet head. Freakdoody. With strangely reticent bitterness, Norah regarded her reflection. Her own mother could not see how tacitly ugly she had become, how ready she was to die.

Mo shambled in with the camera, picked his unlit cigar out of his mouth, told his daughter that, orthodontia aside, she was an eyeful. Indeed she did look almost dazzling, reminding him of Mitzi when he'd first seen her—you have got to be the tooth fairy, he'd teased, partly to hide how defenseless he'd suddenly felt. Now he noticed even Norah's acne had been cleverly camouflaged.

"Gorgeous, honey. Let me get some pictures, record this moment for future generations, huh?" A comment which, as soon as he made it, depressed him. A future generation implied his own absence. In the living room, he took the obligatory pictures in front of the fireplace and the picture window. He snapped several of Mitzi and Norah together, pictures that Mitzi would crunch into a ball and plunge into the trash when she saw how, next to her daughter, she looked at least a decade older than she felt.

"Ready for the ball, Cindyfella?" Mo joked, and with that chauffeured Norah to her first and last cotillion, a cramp in her left toe and her mouth aching from having had her braces tightened that morning.

At the expansively lit entrance to the Menlo Country Club, Norah got out of her father's new red Mustang, stood there a moment, leaned down and asked, "Can I come home now?"

Poor kid, Mo thought. I should take her out for a hamburger and a movie, let her mother think she went to this monkey-ass thing. But Mitzi was waiting. She had a surprise, she'd winked almost lewdly from the garage as he backed the Mustang out, and he knew, or hoped he knew, what that meant. The sight of his daughter maturing into a young woman made him remember his own and Mitzi's youth, what was it called, splendor in the grass, and he found himself excited about the how and when and where of her surprise. Would she be hiding stark naked in the laundry room, or wearing some flimsy negligee, waving a bottle of champagne and two glasses—things she had done before—the memories, the possibilities distracted him, and he started to answer his daughter by saying oh, ten, eleven, twelve, when he saw Norah's pleading, myopic expression. He really ought to find a way to finance contact lenses for her.

"Nine-thirty should make your mother happy. You just give your old popster a jingle."

"Ok," her voice sounded small.

He watched his daughter wobble away from him in her cheap, green, obviously painful shoes, so young, the world sweeping her up, the world ahead of her. What if she turned around? Would he be able to resist saving her? Mo forced himself to look away, to drive on home to what was waiting for him, the tooth fairy from Scranton, light of his life.

Norah pinched her glasses off and crammed them in the small green "clutch," as her mother called it, exactly what she was doing, clutching it in her icy hands. Inside its black satin interior were things her mother had tucked in: a monogrammed, lace-edged hankie, a tube of Hot Polka Dot lipstick, a small plastic comb, and change for a phone call. Norah had added her rosary beads, one of Mother Stewart's prayer booklets, and the most recent note Mother Fitzgerald had written to her, on the back of a holy card: *My dearest Norah, Though our paths be different, our goal is still the same.*

Seven o'clock. Two and a half hours. Norah hid behind a feathery broom of potted palms before forcing herself to walk, her feet killing her, into the dimly lit ballroom. Without her glasses, she felt as if she were underwater, a stolid obelisk that whole schools of exotic fish darted around, shot past. She was the only one standing, unasked. And what if she was? Asked? What was she to do with her purse? Her feet were already numb, used to their thick sport socks and old saddle shoes. Norah stood there, grateful for the semidarkness, when she heard or rather felt someone ask her to dance. A tall, gangling, extra-lanky boy, he reminded her of a pinkish, faintly wet looking daddy longlegs, wearing glasses, as she should have been. She hadn't heard him over the noise of the band, so he had poked her in the shoulder to get her attention. Now he clamped her into a wooden-legged box step, and they labored together, he blinking across her shoulder, she staring into his armpit for one whole Frank Sinatra song, then another. Clearly, they were the victims of the same ballroom dance lessons. During a break in the music, her partner towered beside her, his arm soldered to her waist, happy to have zeroed in on his matching half. Norah freed herself, waving in what she hoped was the direction of the powder room.

"I'll be back," she shouted. Not waiting for his reaction, she limped away.

The ladies' lounge was a suite of two huge, expensively furnished rooms, the toilets and sinks like unpleasant, functional afterthoughts. Both lemon-scented rooms glittered feverishly with pale, nervous girls, bobbing and primping in front of long, gold-flecked wall mirrors. Upon coming in, Norah had felt their cold, collectively dismissive glance. The velvet bow on her head condemned her. No one else wore one, and her dress, she saw instantly, was last year's. For some reason, she'd imagined the bathroom would be empty, that she would be able to sit down on one of the dark green club chairs and read. Instead, she walked down to a stall at the far end marked Out of Order, went in, latched the door, nudged her shoes off, and sat sideways on the toilet, her stockinged feet propped on the silver toilet paper dispenser. She planned to say her rosary and read and reread Mother Fitzgerald's notes until, say, nine o'clock.

At six minutes to nine, Norah emerged holding her shoes and purse clipped together and limping since her left leg and buttock had gone completely to sleep. There was a white telephone in the lobby. Her father answered on the fifth ring.

"Sentence served, babydoll?" That made her smile. The dance wouldn't be over until twelve-thirty, yet there he would be, within ten minutes, the door to his Mustang opened for her. Mo took Norah out for a milkshake while Mitzi waited at home in her red silk kimono, pleased at having so easily restored her husband's spirits. Men were simple creatures with primitive needs. She could not yet guess, waiting for Mo and Norah to return—where were they?—how crestfallen she would be by Norah's laconic answers to her inquiries . . . who was there, what were the other girls wearing, whom did she dance with? One would think she hadn't gone at all. The next morning she would search for her daughter's name in the society column (Norah Loft, daughter of Dr. and Mrs. Morris Loft, wearing an all-season gold lamé and white chiffon gown . . .), but there were just the same names that appeared week after week: Leslie Malone, Cindy Rambeault, Betsy Farasyn . . . . She refused to dwell on the hypocrisy of the rich, how doors looked as if they might open but rarely did, how smiles might seem genuine but rarely were. With her usual energy, she launched into her next plan, to have Norah volunteer as a docent at the local art museum. She had heard that a number of girls from the wealthier families over in Atherton had begun doing that.

Lacey Jenks raised the black veil from her face to accept communion from the handsome young seminary priest who had proclaimed in his homily that a girl's sins could be seen in her eyes, that God had so designed it. Coming back down the aisle of the chapel, she paused beside Norah to flash the double thumbs-up—old news, since she and Arthur had already had sex nine times. Still, she had waited so as not to shock Norah, who, if possible, was becoming ever more shockable. Now, Lacey prayed—though it was more like begging—not to be pregnant. Nine times, Arthur had talked her into letting him "pull out." Foolproof, he had whispered. But desperate, with her period three weeks late, Lacey had read in her mom's medical book that it wasn't foolproof at all. Yesterday, Arthur had taken her to a doctor he knew for a test. Today, he would take her back for the results. All morning, during the first day of the school's annual three-day spiritual retreat, instead of contemplating God or reading from the exhausted heap of religious books the nuns trotted out every year, Lacey had written and rewritten her married name, Mrs. Arthur Webb, inked a chain of marguerite daisies, her favorite, around the edges of the letters. She'd designed bride and bridesmaid dresses, imagined a wedding along the lines of the one she had seen in *The Sound of Music*. But unshared happiness was lonely. Arthur didn't talk. He was a musician, he said, not a conversationalist. It still amazed her how easily she'd fooled her parents. At seventy-nine the Colonel could be declared legally senile, and her mother was always at the library, working overtime, or else in the house somewhere, lying down with one of her migraines. Lacey had discovered if she did her chores and her homework without complaint, her parents were so paralyzed by gratitude that they believed whatever she told them. And what she'd been telling them was she had theater rehearsals after school. Arthur waited for her on his motorcycle, took her to his apartment, afterward dropping her off by her bicycle, stashed under some pomegranate bushes near the school grounds. Handsome Father O'Malley was barking out his ass, as the Colonel liked to say. Her eyes, for she had gazed boldly up at him as he placed the dry, white host on her tongue, revealed nothing at all.

> CHER HOLY NOSER,
> I know, I know. I'm not sixteen (seize) yet, so DBM (don't be mad) at me, will explain ALL later. . . .
> If I'm not at school tomorrow, pray for me. I know how much you like to do that (pray) . . . and right now people like me could use that (prayer).
> Toot mon amour,
> Mrs. Arthur Webb
>   (hee)

As she knelt by her bed that night, praying for Lacey, the Virgin Mary appeared like a bit of floating gauze in a corner of the room by Norah's closet, looking somewhat like the pink and blue statue in the alcove, only without any solidity. The apparition, which she later realized also resembled Mother Fitzgerald, lasted perhaps a second, during which Norah received the distant impression she had been asked—or commanded—to befriend the two queer girls, Rose and Deirdre. Feeling foolish yet rarefied, she bowed her head before the hovering, mothlike figure and said, yes, she would obey. When she lifted her head, it was gone.

The next morning, Norah felt as if a thick, satiny light swam around her. She felt calm, slowed with holy purpose. At lunchtime, in the dining hall, she took her tray of food and sat directly across from the two girls, Rose and Deirdre. Because of the retreat's rule of silence, Norah smiled, as beatifically as she could. Suspicious, the girls glowered back, but Norah, undeterred, remained confident in the mission she had been given. And lying across her bed that night, Norah wrote to Mother Fitzgerald (a letter she would later tear up), telling her about the vision. After brushing her teeth—since the cotillion, she had given up any other form of self-improvement—she turned out all the lights except the small yellow lamp beside her bed and waited. She didn't want to appear greedy, but she desperately needed a second vision to prove the validity of the first, which she had begun, ever so slightly, to doubt. She identified with those children who had seen Our Lady of Fatima, with young Bernadette of Lourdes. That led to Norah picturing herself on top of a small hill, her eyes turned heavenward, her arms uplifted, thousands of people gathered below, waiting. Was she crazy? What if this was like *The Screwtape Letters*, that C. S. Lewis book where Wormwood, or whatever the devil's name was, knew your every vanity, his job to corrupt you through diabolical temptations, semblances of virtue? Was spiritual pride tempting her to see herself as famous, chosen, special? As she knelt by her bed, squinting at the corner where she had seen Mary/Mother Fitzgerald the night before, there was a timid rap at her window, then another, then a third, more insistent. Norah got up and went over to see Lacey staring at her, her beautiful long hair flattened with rain, dripping about her face.

"Nose."

Norah could barely hear. She raised the window. "What are you doing here?" The rain became audible, wind blew coolly in. She thought she heard a motorcycle. Arthur's? It was raining hard.

"Norah. This is *trés* serious. I have to go away. But I'll be back in three, maybe four days, by Monday for sure."

"Where are you going?"

"I got in a righteous argument with my parents and left a note on my bed saying I'd walked over to your house. So here's the thing. If they call, can you say I'm here and that I'll be home after school tomorrow . . . "

"If you were here, wouldn't they want to talk to you, not me?"

"Say I'm in the shower or something. Say I'm asleep. Throwing up. The point is, I need to keep them from looking for me right away."

"Why?" Norah felt frightened. "Are you going somewhere with him?"

"We're going to Mexico. Just for a few days."

"Mexico?"

"Arthur knows this clinic in Tijuana where girls from his college go. It's really safe, and he's paying for the whole thing. Jesus, Norah. Now you'll hate me. I wish I was like you, as good as you, but I probably won't ever be. Please. Will you do that? Just tell my parents, if they call, that I'm here, staying with you?" Lacey was crying, her long hair like two shining blades down her shoulders.

"You said his motorcycle was a joke—how will you get all the way to Mexico?"

"He's been working on it all week."

When she heard that, Norah decided to really hate Arthur Webb. His dumb motor-cycle. Dumb everything.

"Ok, I'll tell them. Wait." Norah put her hand out the window, felt cold rain sting her wrist. "Take this?"

Lacey wiped her nose on the hem of her big sweater. "Jesus, Mary, and Joseph. You've gone Catholic on me, Norris. That's ok. I already knew. I was watching you before I knocked, you looked holier than hell. Hey, my mom always says converts make the best saints." Lacey pocketed the rosary in a solemn motion. "I'll hang onto it the entire time."

She looked for Lacey's bicycle on the last day of the retreat, knowing it wouldn't be there, how could it be? Still. After morning Mass, Norah wandered the rain-drenched school grounds until she happened upon the nuns' plain, two-story retire-ment home. Behind it was a neatly kept orchard of apple trees. She sat on a patch of damp, long, yellow grass, struggling to pray, imagining instead what might be hap-pening to her friend. Norah ended up going back to the empty study hall, sitting at Lacey's desk and impulsively writing a letter. In it, she recklessly declared how beau-tiful and perfect she believed Mother Fitzgerald to be. She did not set this letter in the usual place, upon the lectern used by the mistress of studies, but carried it down to the west wing of the second floor, a cloistered area where the nuns lived. The long, low-lit hall looked deserted. She ran down its length before finding the door marked M. Fitzgerald. Amazed by her own audacity, she bent down and slid the let-ter underneath.

At lunch, with somewhat less conviction, she sat across from Rose and Deirdre, who, this time, smiled with a combined, breathtaking trust in her. Norah moved her food around, worrying about the letter, thinking she should write another, retracting what she'd said in the first, when there was a disturbance in the hallway just outside the dining room, a breach of the retreat's heavy silence, the sound of voices conferring. Then Mother Fitzgerald, accompanied by Reverend Mother McGwynn, the mistress general, and the school's Latin teacher, Mother Flaherty, walked in. Mother Fitzgerald looked distraught. At the familiar command of the wooden clapper, the roomful of girls rose, curtsied in the direction of their reverend mother, and received news that during last night's storm, there had been an accident, resulting in the premature death of one of their third academic students. They were to proceed immediately to chapel, to pray for the soul of Lacey Ann Jenks.

> Hail Mary, full of grace, the Lord is with thee, blessed art though amongst women and blessed is the fruit of thy womb, Jesus. Holy Mary, Mother of God, pray for us sinners now and at the hours of our death, amen. Hail Mary . . .

To Mitzi's credit, she did not pray. She calmly held her daughter, then went with her to the funeral at Our Lady of Angels. Mo stayed home. All funerals, he said, espe-cially those of children, depressed him.

At the service, Mitzi thought the parents looked terrible, as though they couldn't live through this, and indeed, Colonel Jenks would die in less than a year's time, in a car accident less than a mile from his home, due, it was said, to his failing eyesight. There was an older brother, who, with other male relatives, bore the casket, which was white and draped in a blanket of pink baby roses. Newspaper details would be scarce, though there would be the most recent yearbook photograph of Lacey. What Mitzi would later hear through friends was that Lacey had been sneaking out of the house to see her guitar instructor. Mo, hearing this from his wife, felt newly protective of Norah, restrictive of her whereabouts. On several heated occasions, Mitzi argued with him, heedless, for once, of his mood. If he didn't want his daughter becoming a nun why in god's name did he suddenly insist on treating her like one, what was the matter with him, couldn't he see the child scarcely left her room anymore? But that would be weeks later, weeks after the death of Lacey Jenks.

At the end of her third year at the Convent of the Sacred Heart, during Prime, an awards ceremony held in the Little Theater, Norah Loft's name was called. Again and again she was made to leave her seat and go up on the stage to be congratulated by Reverend Mother and the other nuns. She accepted medals of merit, academic certificates, even what she had once so dearly wished for, a pale blue honor ribbon. For her scholarship, in particular, for her essay on the benefits of martyrdom, which had won third place in a national Catholic youth essay contest, for her leadership potential and community service, Norah Loft received special commendation. The following year she would be elected valedictorian, and her speech, poetic and slightly scathing—not what anyone expected—would be dedicated to Lacey Jenks. But now, kneeling to receive her ribbon from Reverend Mother, applause rising respectfully behind her, Norah felt nothing she could identify, nothing at all.

Then, at the point when Prime usually ended, Mrs. Jenks, wearing a kelly green suit and matching hat, came forward to announce a small scholarship in her daughter's name, funded by the city's library. She wept as she spoke of the lifelong values instilled in Sacred Heart girls. Then Mrs. Jenks sat down, and the best singer in the school, Kathy Murphy, played her guitar and sang "Today, While the Blossom Still Clings to the Vine," followed by another girl Norah didn't know well, who had composed a villanelle about death, comparing it, in a tedious chain of verses, to a dance whose steps were ever the same. Afterward, all four classes stood to recite a mimeographed prayer in honor of Lacey Jenks, in memory of her innocent, untried soul.

That summer, Mo recouped his losses and was able to pay for Norah's first pair of contact lenses. Her braces had been removed as well, so with straight ivory teeth and wide, impassive eyes, Norah Loft seemed, over that summer, to have traded her ugly-ducklingness for some new, abject radiance. Mitzi noted, with no small relief, the disappearance of her daughter's religious articles. Though Norah now burned purple cones of Bombay incense in her room and wrote poetry, verse after gloomy verse wherein lovers suffered sudden, unjust deaths on the moors, or gypsies rode on horseback down white roads to the sea, disconsolate scenes all set apparently in England. Not a problem, Mo said, when Mitzi waved the poems around, having located them in her daughter's desk while Norah was away at an exclusive girls camp in Lake Tahoe and Mitzi'd begun redecorating her room in a French provincial theme. A phase, he said. No doubt she was copying the stuff out of some book somewhere, it seemed pretty sophisticated, he couldn't make head nor tail of it. Though he did remember writing some pretty sour material when he was trying to get over his first girlfriend's leaving him. Death and heartbreak, he reminded Mitzi, throw you the hardest.

Cecilia Mornay, the daughter of a high government official in Haiti, sat in a yellow damask chair, a cup of tea balanced on her lap, gazing up at the senior girl introduced by Mother Fitzgerald as her Angel. The fall tea, as always, was held in the immaculately appointed front parlor, and up to this point, Norah had successfully avoided looking at Mother Fitzgerald. Her letter, shot under the nun's door, with its reckless avowal of passion, had never been acknowledged. There had been no reply, the long summer had ensued and now, Norah thought to herself, hearing Mother Fitzgerald prattle on about the school's soccer and tennis teams, gesturing with familiar, ruddy, athletic movements, how pathetically jolly, how ignorant. How could she have thought this nun graceful or sensitive, attached hope or perfection to her? The spell was broken, a spell much like that cast by the Blessed Virgin over innocence. What she could not know was how hungrily her letter had been received, how Mother Fitzgerald had, after many written and discarded replies, expressions of love returned in kind, added Norah's cri de coeur to all the others she had saved from various girls, and taken them downstairs to the basement incinerator. With a prayer that she be forever spared wanting to be loved in such deplorable ways, Mother Fitzgerald pitched the letters, bound together, cries of love identical and shallow in each girl's heart, the same in her own, into the incinerator's constant, dirty fire.

After some weeks, Cecilia Mornay found herself content, adjusting to this newest school. She was popular with the other girls and felt some guilt that she no longer relied upon Norah Loft, avoided her anyway, always so serious and, worse, openly critical of the one person she liked best, Mother Fitzgerald. As her soccer team's captain, Cecilia excelled in part to see the nun's face flush with pleasure, to hear her ringing shouts of triumph. Only recently they had begun exchanging small notes handwritten in French, Cecilia's first language. Norah showed no interest in athletics; her attitudes were those of a nihilist, a nonparticipant, an unsmiling intellectual, all of which Cecilia found abhorrent and unappealing. Norah commanded respect, certain cold attributes of leadership and realms of knowledge were hers, but Cecilia felt unsettled in her presence. Back home in Haiti, her mother would explain such a sensation by saying a ghost walked with that one, you could be sure.

Queen of Angels
Of Martyrs
Of Virgins
Of Peace
Of Sinners and Saints
Singular Vessel,
Save us.

Three days after the motorcycle accident, Norah knelt before the Virgin. When at last she stood up, she saw Lacey Jenks sitting beside the statue. Neatly dressed in her school uniform, her hair was darkened, glittering with rain. On her lap was a white index card with blurred red lettering Norah could not decipher. That night, waking up in her bed, Norah thought she saw Lacey, haloed in silver mist, moving toward the window. And for what would prove to be the last time, during Mass the following morning,

Norah would see her dead friend, floating and naked, as if on her stomach, above the handsome and obstinate Father O'Malley, her fingers splayed in a V above his head. She smiled, tenderly and without judgment, before her features were washed over by a fierce, impenetrable gaze, a look Norah Loft began, without awareness, to reflect, drawing to herself all who desired to see what it was that overturned human love, what mystery it was that so crowned the heart with cold braided thorns, one strand glory, the other a blind, perdurable grace.

Pritchard on Drafting and Large-Scale Revision

Origin of "Salve Regina"

In May, 1997, I received a letter from Sister Georgiana Logan, a former classmate at the Convent of the Sacred Heart, a private Catholic school in Menlo Park, California. In this letter, which began "Dear Classmates," I received news that Sister Marnie Dilling, a former teacher, had died of cancer on May 13 at the age of fifty-seven. On countless occasions I had thought to write about this woman who had so profoundly affected my adolescent years at Sacred Heart. Always I balked, feeling I could not do justice to the hidden richness of the time, or to Marnie Dilling herself, a twenty-five-year-old nun whose exuberant beauty could not, it seemed, be weighted or dimmed by the volumes of black cloth she wore. With news of her death, I gave up hope of perfection and wrote, as a kind of passionate, elegiac tribute, what I could. As it turned out, as fiction would have it, the character of Mother Fitzgerald turned out not to be an accurate portrait of Sister Dilling, but rather a splicing together of traits and characteristics drawn from several of the nuns I knew as a student at the Convent of the Sacred Heart.

Setting the Challenge

With "Salve Regina," I set out to write the most boring story possible without, hopefully, being boring. I would, I told myself, attempt a conventionally plotted, slow-paced coming-of-age story that involved seductions and betrayals, both spiritually and sexually. I would draw from the raw material of memory along with the sorrow I felt over Sister Marnie Dilling's death. Private grief combined with a strong desire to pay homage to someone I had loved and admired would be my emotional fuel.

Drafts and Revisions: The Writing Process

With any story, including "Salve Regina," I tend to write a series of drafts and layered revisions. I begin by waiting for the story, which I have only the vaguest hints about, to tell itself to me. I listen patiently, and write down in a notebook any images I might see, any voices of dialogue or monologue I might hear, whole scenes my imagination might present to me. When I see, hear, or imagine something vividly enough, I begin to write, scene by scene, these scenes acting as stepping stones, to take me across the unlit, uncharted terrain of the story. This first "rough" draft is often messy and hastily written, a quick study or sketch for the more fully developed story I envision. I rely almost completely, in this first draft, on intuition, trusting in the images and scenes unfolding on the page, looking to them as clues or a kind of trail to follow deeper into the story in subsequent drafts. The key is to write quickly and without judgment, get the rough sketch, the first draft, down on paper as quickly and uncritically as possible.

The second draft involves interpretation of the "dream" I have written down. Here I work to identify danger, narrative risk, pushing scenes and characters toward deeper emotional peril and dramatic suspense; this requires emotional courage on my part and openness to the entire spectrum of possible actions and outcomes within the story's natural boundaries, its framework. At this point, I begin to reenvision and reorder scenes according to dramatic logic and emotional tension. At this point, I am thinking and intuiting equally, driving images and actions toward greater coherence and dramatic unity. Each subsequent draft forges deeper connections between desire and action, ethical suspense and dramatic resolution. Eventually, the story's shape emerges, and final drafts involve polishing language and tightening sentence structure, achieving cohesive style, consistent rhythm, a detailed pattern of words and sounds and shapes that uphold the emotional energy and ethical tension of the story. Finally, I slowly read the story aloud, testing its musicality, making minor adjustments in phrasing or beats, changing out one word or phrase for another more arresting or memorable one. What began in intuition and heat, ends with a cold focus on craft, an objective assessment of technique. The process of writing a story is one of alchemy and refinement, inspiration and labor, precision and detail shaping a broadly human perspective.

The Art of Contrast

In "Salve Regina" I worked with numerous contrasts in setting, characterization, and imagery to add thematic richness. For example, Norah's home, an arid, atheistic environment, contrasts with the rich, faintly erotic and sensuous atmosphere of the convent. In Norah's bedroom, her mother, Mitzi, puts travel posters on the walls while Norah, on a secret, more interior journey, hides religious "paraphernalia" under her bed. Norah's homeliness contrasts with her friend Lacey's emerging beauty. Norah has a vision of the Virgin Mary; she will later have three visions of her dead friend. Contrast also exists between the "superior education at the hands of nuns said to be the female equivalent of Jesuits," an education her parents intend for Norah, versus the much more dangerous emotional education she receives through events taking place in the story. Norah's infatuation with Mother Fitzgerald, her unrequited, semirepressed longing, contrasts with Lacey's sexual seduction by her music teacher, Arthur Webb. And there is Mother Fitzgerald's guilty pleasure in her students' secret infatuations with her, and the shame and scorn endured by two reputedly lesbian students, Rose and Deirdre. Finally, in considering how females achieve power in a patriarchal society and equally patriarchal religion, Norah's mother, Mitzi, looks to social status for her power, Norah cloaks herself in the heady power of mysticism, while her friend Lacey follows the well-worn path of romance and sexuality. Norah is seduced by Catholicism, Lacey by her music teacher, and Mitzi by an elusive social prestige. Ironically, while Norah seeks visions, yearns for sainthood, and writes a prize-winning essay on martyrdom, it is Lacey who will, by her tragic death, be raised to a martyr's iconic status, glimpsed by Norah in three distinct visions, looking ambivalent, mischievous, and marvelously holy. In "Salve Regina," I created patterns of contrast, deliberately developing connections and parallels between the ethereal and the erotic.

A Terror of Angels

I began this story with an epigraph—"Every angel is terrifying."—a line from Rainer Maria Rilke's *Duino Elegies*. A minor host of angels inhabits and presides over this story. Lacey, of whom Mitzi disapproves, is Norah's assigned "angel" or guide when Norah first arrives at Sacred Heart. By the story's end, Norah will be a reluctant "angel" to a new girl named Cecilia Mornay. Norah has a vision of the "Queen of Angels," the Virgin Mary, and Lacey appears posthumously to Norah as a kind of angel. The unseen angels of Thanatos, death, and Eros, life, preside as etheric, opposing forces over "Salve Regina," and in the end, reveal the twin faces of divinity, creation and destruction, and love both sacred and profane, earthly and ineffable.

Writing Suggestions

1. To warm up for your next writing session, write a one-page sketch about a recent dream. Describe the dream, using all five senses, to make the experience vivid for the reader. Make sure each sentence has at least one significant, specific detail. Whether you're working with imagination, dreams, or reality, readers like to be drawn into the story through the use of evocative, potent language that utilizes the senses.

2. Describe seven things that *truly* mattered to you when you were thirteen. Next, describe seven things that *truly* mattered to you when you were seventeen. Write a coming-of-age story that connects a character suggested by the first list who will become the type of person suggested by the second list. Think of how plot can force characters to mature and come to a better understanding of themselves (of others, of society, etc.).

3. With a story you have not previously read (in this book or elsewhere), examine only the first three pages. Using only this information, write down five things that *truly* matter to the protagonist. What does this character have at stake in this story? What might this character gain or lose? What does this character yearn for? After completing this activity, look at the first three pages of one of your most recent stories and answer the same questions using only the information in those pages. (Variation: Work with a partner. Respond to the first three pages of each other's story. Does your partner's perception match your intentions for this story?)

4. Print up one story from each of the following three magazine websites: *The New Yorker* (www.newyorker.com), *The Atlantic Monthly* (www.theatlantic.com), and *Ploughshares* (www.pshares.org). Read the first three pages of each story aloud. Take note of each writer's prose style—or to use Pritchard's term, the "musicality" of the writing. Of the three, which story exhibits the strongest, most effective, or most pleasing sense of language? In a page, describe the reasons behind your selection, citing specific passages that contribute to this effect.

I feel that fiction—all art, really, any art form, but reading fiction and poetry, especially—ought to have the potential to change your life. It ought to make you a better human in the world. It ought to help you understand other people.
—Antonya Nelson

Stephen Graham Jones

Adultery, A Failing Sestina

From *The Alaska Quarterly Review*

in the absence of grace

Dad brings the angel home from the horse trap. He lets her sit up front, and tells her that the window on her side won't roll down, so don't try it. And she isn't so much pretty as she is fragile. He leaves her in the cab of the truck through dinner, and the dome light which hasn't worked for years extends a halogen filament like a finger across some vacuum, pointing at her as we pretend to eat.

"Another one," Mom says.

Dad nods, looks at her through the window as if for the first time. Chews his grilled cheese and tells us the story of her capture, how he found her dehydrated at the salt lick, nearly transparent. All he had to do was bind her wrists together with baling wire, then lead her to the truck. But still, when she heard the engine idling it took all of his two hundred and twenty pounds to keep her on the ground.

"This is getting out of hand," Mom says.

"I did leave the radio on for her," Dad says back.

"And her . . . the wire?"

"It doesn't hurt them."

"Of course it doesn't."

"Like I said."

"And she believed that about the window?"

"She's an angel."

"What station, then?"

"Church," Dad tell hers, laughing when he says it, and Mom throws back her bourbon in anger.

"That's not what she came for," she says. "You don't know anything, do you?"

"She's different," Dad says back, winking at us, "special," but he said that about the last one too.

After dinner and dishes and shows, the dome light is still a faint reminder in the yard. Dad returns to it again and again, stands at the window, his back to the table, the living room, mumbling about the goddamn battery he's not going to let her run down.

Through the bottom of her glass Mom watches him fill the front door for a moment, then walk away.

"Go to bed," she tells us, her voice flat and hard, and we pretend to do that, too.

In the living room the television set blackens, and Mom sits on her end of couch and doesn't pull the heavy amber drapes which would mute Dad's leaf springs and cab bushings, the dry, awkward sounds of his desire. The dome light is a sheen in his back as he leans over the angel, straining.

He returns breathing hard, with the rearview mirror in hand. It slides across the kitchen counter, nestles against the cutting board.

"Superglue?" he asks Mom.

"It won't work."

"It has before."

"Well then there you are," she says, and his footsteps slouch to the television set, his chin lowers to his chest, and he's asleep for the night. His labored breathing fills the house, and his skin in the glow of the late-night nature shows is pale blue, the color of heaven.

"Go to bed," Mom says to us again, and her hands plunder needle-nose pliers from the pocket of Dad's discarded jacket. The kind with the wire-cutters built into them. She flexes them like a jaw, an inarticulate mouth, and then fills the door herself for a moment in passing.

As she crosses the driveway, moving from the light of alternating current to direct, her layers of nightgown make it hard to tell where she begins and where she doesn't. She gets in the driver side of Dad's truck and the dome light flickers, unsure, the angel rising from the floorboard. One of them nearly transparent, one of them too much there.

The angel offers her wrists because angels by nature are trusting, and Mom bites the wire with the pliers, again and again, and won't begin apologizing for hours yet.

interlude with hyenas

The thing about hyenas is they want to exist at the fringe of the savanna. Ask a talking hyena why all the night footage, the spotlights, the furtive, reflected eyes, and she'll slip off into the darkness without answering. It's not all about shame, though, as the British narrator speculates, mister tongue-in-cheek, his restrained chuckle spooling out over the hushed and expectant grassland, the concave darkness, volplaning down over the hyena, her retreat already footage: long, mismatched forelimbs collect the ground before her in an almost simian manner, pulling enough distance between her and the question that she can locate her own dead by scent, hunch over the carcass, lower her nose into the rough coat. The meat underneath will be dark, bitter, familiar. This is the answer: she doesn't eat her own out of anything so mean as hunger, but a compelling need to leave no evidence for the crepuscular light of morning to reveal. A syllogism: 1) material existence entails displacing mass; 2) displacing mass entails consumption of matter foreign to you; 3) to consume unforeign matter is to deny material existence. The African corollary: through cannibalism, the hyena as a species is accepting an immaterial existence at the night-edge of the savanna—seeking such an existence.

But it's not all about logic, either.

Ask a talking hyena why all the night footage, the spotlights, the furtive, reflected eyes, and she'll slip off into the darkness only to wait just past the headlights, grinning with need, her painted black lips curling in to no easy reduction point.

the legend of the moth man

Dad brings the candy home from the convenience store and fills our mouths with it. Dinner is ruined. Dinner is always ruined. He's already made three runs to the convenience store since work—one for cigarettes, one for baking soda, and the last to fill the tank back up with gas. Our teeth hurt from sugar. He's still got a candy bracelet on his wrist from the gas run, the elastic between the powdery hearts straining.

"That all you have to show?" Mom asks.

Dad smiles at her, a question almost, but then follows her eyes down to his wrist, swallows as if just seeing the bracelet himself. Dinner passes in fits and starts, Dad chewing, chewing, studying the candy hearts. Two swallows later he looks back up and tells us the story of it, how the new cashier at the convenience store has been on-shift for forty-two hours now, is giving the bracelets away just so she won't have to stock them. This draws a smile on Mom's face.

"What else might she be giving away?"

"She has a whole box of them."

"Poor dear."

"Are you wanting one—?"

"Because if I do," Mom says for him, "you can go back . . . "

"It's just down the street."

"Convenient, right?"

"I'm saying I don't mind."

"Of course you don't."

"I did get the baking soda, didn't I?"

"The baking soda, yes. What would we do?"

"Not play twenty questions at dinner, maybe."

"Here's one. Why don't you just bring her home?"

"The cashier?" Dad asks, winking for us, "it's just candy, Mom, geez," but the bracelet when he tosses it over is heavy enough to slide off the table. We feign digestion, and Dad does the opposite, claims indigestion, the sudden need for antacid.

He reaches for his coat and Mom's already cleaning up. "One more for the road," she says to herself.

"The children *are* listening, y'know," Dad says back.

"Is that what it takes? Then they're going with you this time."

And we do, seatbelts and all. To the convenience store. The cashier leans far over the counter in anticipation and there on her finger is a candy wedding ring, her mouth red from it. And she isn't so much pretty as she is pale from working nights. Almost fluorescent. We stand in front of the magazines while they talk on napkins, and instead of antacids Dad buys a kit to glue a rearview mirror on.

"Guess what it is," he says to Mom.

"You don't want me to."

"It's for the car. Always be prepared, y'know."

"My boy scout."

They stand in the hall, facing each other. Mom already has the vacuum cleaner assembled. She directs us upstairs and we don't need to be told twice. Below us the house gets severely clean. Dad counters mops and spray bottles with late-night TV, and the animals, when they die, die at full volume. Just as the bleach and ammonia and laundry detergent reach our room, our nostrils, two separate doors close—the utility (Mom) and the front (Dad). He doesn't turn the headlights on as he backs out.

It only takes him thirty minutes.

By the time he coasts back in, his skin stained pale like the cashier's, we're already packed, or, still packed from four nights ago.

"The clothes are running," Mom says as we pass him in the yard, file into the car, leave him standing under the buglight, token milk in hand. We drive around and around the loop. Mom looks at us once in the rearview mirror, says she's sorry, and soon enough the spin cycle is over and we're at the convenience store pumps with her one more time, pumping gas she isn't going to pay for, and she's staring across the asphalt at the front of the store, the cashier, one of them almost asleep, the other unblinking.

interlude with hyenas, pt. 2

The other thing about hyenas is that when they have to kill for themselves, they select the weakest from the herd. And they can detect the subtlest of infirmities in a passing glance, infirmities even the lioness is blind to, as if such an advantage would take the art out of all the footage devoted to her—the impossibly patient stalk through tall grass, the trademark pounce, the prey suffocating beneath her, the hyena there at the edge of the kill, the outer limit of the spotlight, yawning in anticipation, already in lurk mode. Miss counterpoint for the narrator, his opportunist of the savanna, her radically sloped back speaking to him of generations of skulking away, of lingering, of *mal*-lingering, an inexact usage, he confesses, the cocksure smile audible, but a revealing one nevertheless, an *accurate* one. To malinger in the proper sense is to avoid duty, work, etc., from the French *malingre*, itself a combination of the Latin *malus*—bad, evil—and the North Middle-Eastern *lenger*, used chiefly in relation to immaterial things: to have a hunger or craving; to move about in a secret manner; to hang about a place beyond the proper time; to remain furtively or unobserved in one spot, waiting. In savanna terms, to be a hyena.

But there's more to it than etymology.

The thing about hyenas is that when the lioness chases them off her kill, she does so not with the inexpressive facial features you'd expect her to use outside her own pride, but with the bared teeth and guttural vocalizations typical of intra-specific strife. Features which suggest it's personal. That the hyena is laughing as she runs goes without saying; that she's leading the lioness deeper into the night doesn't.

dr. thomson and his lucretta

Dad brings the painting home from the hospital, leans it casually on the hearth, studies it over salad. Twice he draws our attention to it by almost commenting, his fork raised in thought, but each time withdraws. And it is well-executed, give her that: a night-study of fecal matter in short grass, days of it, rendered in white so as to evoke the counter-intuitive reversals involved with photographic negatives. The effect is one of incompleteness, of continuation. At the table, Mom already has her back to it.

"So are we officially her patron now?" she asks.

"Tax write-off," Dad says, winking to us, but then when we're too old for his humor, too young yet to pity him, he launches into the painting, how it's from her *Latrine* series—"$Ca_3(PO_4)_2A1.5\ Ca(OH_2)$," the chemical composition of digested bone. The spoor is the spoor of nocturnal scavengers, is the obverse of the long night they inhabit; the painter is Mom's old art student, in the hospital now with an ulna that cracked too easily for her fifty-one years.

"Scavengers?" Mom asks, her voice incredulous.

"For obvious reasons," Dad says, "she's interested in bones."

"Of course she is."

"It'll be worth something, someday . . . "

" . . . to someone."

"She was admitted M—. I was on call. There's nothing I can do about that."

"I should ring her up, I suppose."

"Yes. She'd like that."

"After all these years."

"That was a long time ago."

"Yes. It was."

"She talks about you, y'know."

"Yes. I noticed you were late."

"It's a good painting," Dad says, studying it again.

Mom smiles, for us, together at the table once more, and says that as far as feces goes, but then trails off into the obvious. We stab the salad in unison, with resolve, avoiding eye contact. It could be fifteen years ago, and for a few moments it is—it really is—but Dad's beeper pulls us violently forward.

"She has your pager number," Mom says. It's not a question.

Dad excuses himself, opts for the phone in the kitchen over the remote behind him.

In his absence Mom studies the painting with narrow eyes. Like the rest, it's a finger painting. In the lower corner, too, instead of a signature, is the imprint of an armband from the hospital, an ID, a name rolled in backwards. Mom laughs.

Dad returns with a medical journal in hand, one of the ones he subscribes to in order to keep up with 'popular' medicine. On the cover is an over-the-shoulder shot of a recently retired gentleman, the road opening up before his RV. Looming in the rearview mirror, though, are a host of maladies—arthritis, osteoporosis, Parkinson's, etc.

"So is she better now?" Mom asks.

Dad holds up the magazine in disgust. "She thinks her bones are becoming *lighter*, for Chrissake."

"She's a fragile woman."

"M—."

"She needs special attention, I mean. I understand."

"Well, you know her," Dad says.

"Yes," Mom says, "I do."

Not long afterwards they fall into their apologetic routine about having to go to bed, and in the silence they leave all the television has to offer in the way of distraction is the Serengeti. We mute it without forethought, can just make out Dad fumbling the straps of Mom's nightgown off her shoulder.

"Who am I?" Mom asks in the darkness of their bedroom.

The bedsprings are motionless, suspended. "I'm home," Dad says, "isn't that enough? M—?"

Mom pulls him into her, her forearm surely pressing against the back of his head, and when the beeper screams on the dining room table we simply turn our heads on it, wait for it to cease.

Hours later Mom descends, thinking we're asleep, and pads into her studio, emerges minutes later with the pint can of halogen white paint from the top shelf, the one with lead deposits in it. The one we were never supposed to touch. Mom is humming to herself as she passes, oblivious of us, the fecal matter on her hearth. She turns the television off out of habit, stands in its afterglow, and then becomes the shape of our mother silhouetted against the dining room window, placing two things next to the beeper for Dad to take to work, as gifts from a former teacher: the paint with the lead in it, and her own calcium supplement pills. Because of the latter, the former won't be questioned.

We feign sleep and feign it well.

all the beautiful sinners

In the morning the smell from the horse trap drives us from our beds, and we make our way through the front door, across the drive, to Dad's truck, his angel, her wrists turned inside out from Mom removing the baling wire again and again. And she's not so much dead as she is beautiful, draped across the bench seat, her eyes still open. Trusting. We don't talk about her, though; we don't talk about anything. In the long hours before lunch we'll hang Dad's floor mats on the line to dry, we'll bring Mom water to drink, but now, before they wake, before they can remember, we take the angel to the barn, remove her bones—already dry, brittle—and with the refashioned meat grinder with the battery-driven mortar and pestle with the apparatus

with desire

we reduce her bones to chalk, and to the chalk we add salt, weak glue, geometry: in this manner it slowly becomes another cube, a lick to be placed in the bed of Dad's truck for delivery, and the horses in the trap when they apply their tongues will apply their tongues with care, because they need it too.

Jones on Revising at the Sentence Level

Every now and then, I don't even mess with revising—at least on the sentence level. If a piece turns out broken, I might just throw it away. Sometimes starting over is the best way for me to "revise" a story. For me, writing is a learning process. I take what I've learned from writing the first flawed draft and give it another go from the start.

In situations where I talk to my students about revision, I usually start with the example of Raymond Carver, who would never leave a story until he was done changing all the commas. I also mention that many other well-known short story authors, whose work we study in textbooks and major anthologies, tinker with their short stories for years before they are done.[1] For some of these writers, revision is the actual act of rewriting—developing a complete first draft into a second draft and then into a more polished third and so on. I imagine these writers reworking their stories endlessly. But too, there are those beautiful little accidents, those stories scribbled on napkins and receipts, those stories that come whole and complete, of their own accord, little Kubla Khans you'd trade teeth for if you could.

And then there's another way to think about revision, something I call "revise-as-you-go": take your time writing the piece, but never leave a scene, sentence, or word until it's as good as you're ever going to get it. In practice this means much more than spending a few hours on each scene; it means spending days, perhaps weeks, actively working on each scene. Maybe this is what William Faulkner meant in a sidelong way, when, according to his brother, he said, simply, "Never revise. You're wasting your time."

I know working writers who develop whole drafts and then work with the sentences. I also know working writers who spend days agonizing over each scene—every grammatical move—before moving forward. For these writers, it's like building a house: you have to get the foundation good and strong before building the frame atop it.

All beginning writers should know this as well: revision is up to you. There are no editors out there who will take a poorly (or even averagely) developed story and polish it into a gem. The days of Maxwell Perkins, that hands-on New York editor who helped Fitzgerald and Hemingway, are long gone.

Personally, how do I revise? I write drafts and then throw them away. I learn about my stories by writing them. For each story that finally finds its way into print, there are three or four complete drafts, thrown away. (Some stories I abandon altogether because, after that first draft or two, I realize my vision for the story was flawed from the start.) This is how I've always rewritten. If something's wrong with a draft, instead of trying to rehabilitate it scene by scene, I just tear it down to nothing, save maybe the title, a string of words, a character or two, then tell it all over again. I need to capture each scene perfectly before I'm able to move on to the next. This means I throw away many drafts until I'm able to get the story just right.

I revise in that traditional sense as well. Not stories, so much, but novels. I mean, just looking at the numbers, with me they fall about the same: for each novel I've pub-

---

[1] Keeping it to, say, five, it goes something like Updike's "A&P," Mona Simpson's "Lawns," Arthur C. Clarke's "The Nine Billion Names of God," Tobias Wolff's "Liar," and Thom Jones's "The Pugilist at Rest"—stories that *end* well, which is the hardest thing to pull off. This is the reason we have so many novels, I suspect.

lished, there are two or three I slammed into my keyboard over eight months or a year, just to get them out of my system. But the ones that *have* been published, yes, I've rewritten them. Over and over.

Really, the reason I grew to value sentence-level revision in the first place was because of my novels: I realized that, whereas I can throw away a ten-page story and start over, it really hurts to do that with a four-hundred-page novel. So, I gave them a second chance. A painful process at first, but, finally a rewarding one: it actually *worked*, this type of traditional revision.

Going back into a piece after the requisite, say, two-week waiting period—so you have some objectivity—puts you in that Raymond Carver mode,[2] excising all the filler, the trash, the fluff, both from the narrative and from the prose. It forces you to attack the dangling clause or poorly worded phrase with the same knife that you would use on the unnecessary scene. Nothing feels so good, I think, as to cut fifty pages out of a novel and have it still do what it was initially doing.[3] I'd rather have a tightly muscled three-hundred-page novel than a baggy one that weighs in at four-hundred pages.

I have come to realize it's the same with stories.[4]

But, of course, what we need here is some method of revision, some angle to take back into your own work that will, each time, improve it. Essentially, some way to internalize that old-style editor who says the hard thing about your work that finally makes it better.

One method—the most obvious, it seems—is to define for yourself the ideal of a successful story, then simply use that ideal as a stencil: lay it over your own draft, see where your story falls short. Here're a few questions I find useful when examining my own first drafts.

- On the first two pages, does this story establish fresh, believable characters and place them in an engaging situation?
- Does this story attempt to cover too much ground? (My own early drafts often cover too much ground.) What scenes can fall away?
- What additions might help this story? Does this story need an additional scene (or scenes)? Does this story need summary narration to better connect the existing scenes?

A corollary method here, I suspect, is to pretend the story's already in print, and you're reading it five years later. What sentence or scene or development is going to be most embarrassing to you? Which are you going to regret? What looks like narrative economy now might actually be dramatic convenience, to a later you. And, no matter how we slick them up, slip them past, as writers we're still always ashamed of the contrivances we allow ourselves sometimes, to get from sentence to sentence, scene to scene. With time, they only grow more obvious.

---

[2]Or, I guess Poe kind of said it first—allow nothing that doesn't contribute to the end—but then Hemingway's in there too, saying pretty much the same thing. But I didn't cut my teeth on them, either.

[3]I'm guessing the logical extension of this has to be that paring a novel down to a sonnet would be blindingly powerful, that first double-shot of espresso, after which all prose might look trite.

[4]To get you to trust me, buy that I'm a reliable narrator, the story I'm including along with this is the only one I've ever worked on for a marathon six months.

Personally I have internalized many aspects of revision. They have become simply something I do. But after the editors of this textbook asked me to write on revision, I paid more attention to what I was doing each time I went back into my novel to revise. I have a tendency to overuse transitional phrases—specifically, additive (*too*), contrasting (*though*, *but*, etc.), and logical (*then*)—and I knew it, had actually done some embarrassing word counts on my *thoughs*; what I was doing in revision was simply going back into my prose, culling each transitional phrase I could, rebalancing the sentences so they could roll into each all on their lonesome. Essentially, trying more and more to have my stuff read like Walker Percy's, which is so clean it kind of terrifies me.[5]

Other things I looked for, which you've probably noticed here: overuse of colons; relying on *italics* for emphasis; letting my sentences just spool out into paragraphs; opening sentences too often with conjunctions, as if the reader is for sure riding that same slender narrative thread I'm on. That kind of stuff and more, the little weaknesses you only become aware of after there's thousands and thousands of copies of them out in the world. Ideally, of course, I'd just learn my lesson, not write them in the first time. Unideally, though—where I live—I tend to write on little enough sleep and enough coffee that I can't hear anything but the CD I have in at the moment, which is of course turned up loud enough to cancel out any thinking I might get involved in, which never, on the first draft, helps.

Granted, this method of revision is specific to my own prose. These are the problems found in *my* early drafts. Part of revision—or of learning how to effectively revise your own stories—is to understand your own weaknesses. Revision is an individual act, decidedly different for every writer—different perhaps for every short story.

In the end, it's all about economy, about stuffing the most possible meaning and entertainment into as small a space as possible. Never indulging yourself at the expense of your readers. Ideally, we should be able to turn to any page of your story, pick any sentence out of context, and recognize that it's been sculpted, shaped for effect.

With my students, I suggest the following list is a good way to begin to understand their own process of revision.

- Avoid passive voice.
- Cut unneeded words and sentences.
- Shy away from adverbs and cheap modifiers.
- Remove clichés and overused expressions.
- Rework details to be specific and significant.
- Don't get caught showing off—with language, punctuation, or information.
- Vary your sentence structures—some short sentences, some long ones.
- Vary your paragraph structures.

Read your words aloud (really *aloud*) so you can hear the rhythm, the music.

I strive to make each sentence clean, the type of language that Walker Percy would appreciate. When I read Percy's fiction, I'm constantly aware how little his sentences rely on coordinating conjunctions ("though," "but," all those). But I notice these things

---

[5]Seriously.

because I'm aware how often I use coordinating conjunctions in my own early drafts. I believe that's what line editing is, in general: it's identifying the consistent problems in your own early drafts, and then consciously revising so that each sentence rolls into the next, building momentum as the paragraph continues to gain speed.

For me, at least for now, it's coordinating conjunctions. For you, it could be overused adverbs or unrealistic dialogue. Effective line editing pushes your fiction up to the next level, sentence by sentence, until it resembles the fiction of Walker Percy or Raymond Carver or the author who made you want to write in the first place.

Writing Suggestions

1. Here's the opening scene to a hypothetical story, in which Joe needs to ask his aunt for another loan. Read through it carefully, and create your own version that eliminates the many first-draft mistakes that are identified in Jones's commentary. Scrutinize each adjective, adverb, and specific noun. Rework sentences to make them smoother and more efficient. Cut unnecessary words. Add details where necessary. Rework the entire scene as needed to further define the emotionally complex relationship between Joe and his aunt.

> It was raining cats and dogs that Tuesday when it all happened. Joe Stewart came home from work and was absently playing with Cubbie, his bull terrier that recently had to be dewormed after a weekender at Aunt Mildred's, who was visiting him for dinner. She simply didn't understand dogs, nor did she care for them much. Joe loved his aunt, yet he needed her as well. She was the most well-off member of his entire family. Joe, sad and dejected since he didn't receive his raise, went into the kitchen like a beaten mule because, once again, he would need to ask Aunt Mildred for a loan. He was reaching for the fridge handle, stretching for it, when he saw out the kitchen window, his aunt's car pull up to the curb. The car was a chocolate brown Mercedes, recently washed and waxed. Yet, she wasn't driving; she was the passenger. There was a man with her—a man twenty years younger. The man, probably in his mid-thirties, wore a button-down Oxford, yet had Brad Pitt hair. Joe had seen other such young guys use his aunt for money before. He suspected the worst.

   In class, compare your rewrite of the above passage with one completed by another student. Where do you differ in your rewrites? Which changes are most effective?

2. Try this strategy for story development as you begin your next story. At the moment that you feel this new piece is starting to fall apart, do what Jones does: throw it away (or if you prefer, save it under a file named "story version one"), then start over. Do not look at your old draft while writing the next one. Use new language to describe the characters and the scenes. Perhaps start the story at a different point in time. Use a different point of view. Add or subtract a minor character. You should find that by continually retelling your story you begin to discover new aspects of

your characters and their situations. Repeat this process until you have an entire draft—until you're able to work through the story from start to finish without feeling as though you've lost your way. Does throwing away a draft or partial draft free you to try a different angle at the same story? Does it force you to better understand your characters? Is the throwing away method one that you can live with?

3. Sometimes revision seems overwhelming because effective fiction needs to control many elements at once. You might indeed have characters, scenes, dialogue, conflict, and details, but your story can still seem a mess. Where to start? Pick one fiction element—such as developing a believable character or using realistic dialogue—then with vigilance, work through your entire story line by line and challenge each word, each sentence that relates to this idea. Ignore all other problems for now. When you get to the end, reread the entire story. Has it improved in this one area? Has strengthening this one element helped the entire story? Often you'll find that fixing one problem—or strengthening one element of a story—helps solve other fiction problems along the way. If the story still needs more work, select another element to guide your revision. Do this until your story is the best version that it can be.

4. One writer best known for his lean, tight sentences is Raymond Carver. He got this reputation deservedly, but his writing received a lot of help from an editor, Gordon Lish, who mercilessly chopped away at drafts until sometimes less than one-third remained. For Carver, this external editing proved helpful. Find your own "perfect reader." Find someone who is the ideal audience for you—whether a writer, whether a fan of short stories, it doesn't matter. You don't even need this person to take a red pen and mark up your drafts—just give you open, honest feedback that you respect. Don't go to your mother, spouse, or best friend who will simply love everything you produce. Find someone whose critical eye is attuned to the problems you're currently unable to see in your own work. Keep this person close —he or she is an invaluable resource even if you already have a writer's workshop group or you're in a creative writing program. Whether you end up with Gordon Lish, a coworker, a dorm-mate, or a friend from high school who now works on Wall Street, locate your perfect reader and let that person help you make better fiction through astute comments and honest observations.

> *I have an affection for a layered sentence and a sentence that has*
> *a logical track in it that has some dialectic . . . It will propose a*
> *thesis and then there'll be the antithesis to it, then there'll be a*
> *synthesis, all in one little—or, not little—but all in one*
> *grammatical package.*
> —Bob Shacochis

Section 10

THE STORY AND ITS AUDIENCE

T. Coraghessan Boyle

Greasy Lake

From *The Paris Review* and *T. C. Boyle Stories*

It's about a mile down on the dark side of Route 88.
—Bruce Springsteen

There was a time when courtesy and winning ways went out of style, when it was good to be bad, when you cultivated decadence like a taste. We were all dangerous characters then. We wore torn-up leather jackets, slouched around with toothpicks in our mouths, sniffed glue and ether and what somebody claimed was cocaine. When we wheeled our parents' whining station wagons out into the street we left a patch of rubber half a block long. We drank gin and grape juice, Tango, Thunderbird, and Bali Hai. We were nineteen. We were bad. We read André Gide and struck elaborate poses to show we didn't give a shit about anything. At night, we went up to Greasy Lake.

Through the center of town, up the strip, past the housing developments and shopping malls, street lights giving way to the thin streaming illumination of the headlights, trees crowding the asphalt in a black unbroken wall: that was the way out to Greasy Lake. The Indians had called it Wakan, a reference to the clarity of its waters. Now it was fetid and murky, the mud banks glittering with broken glass and strewn with beer cans and charred remains of bonfires. There was a single ravaged island a hundred yards from shore, so stripped of vegetation it looked as if the air force had strafed it. We went up to the lake because everyone went there, because we wanted to snuff the rich scent of possibility on the breeze, watch a girl take off her clothes and plunge into the festering murk, drink beer, smoke pot, howl at the stars, savor the incongruous full-throated roar of rock and roll against the primeval susurrus of frogs and crickets. This was nature.

I was there one night, late, in the company of two dangerous characters. Digby wore a gold star in his right ear and allowed his father to pay his tuition to Cornell; Jeff was thinking of quitting school to become a painter/musician/head-shop proprietor.

They were both expert in the social graces, quick with a sneer, able to manage a Ford with lousy shocks over a rutted and gutted blacktop road at eighty-five while rolling a joint as compact as a Tootsie Roll Pop stick. They could lounge against a bank of booming speakers and trade "man"s with the best of them or roll out across the dance floor as if their joints worked on bearings. They were slick and quick and they wore their mirror shades at breakfast and dinner, in the shower, in closets and caves. In short, they were bad.

I drove. Digby pounded the dashboard and shouted along with Toots & the Maytals while Jeff hung his head out the window and streaked the side of my mother's Bel Air with vomit. It was early June, the air soft as a hand on your cheek, the third night of summer vacation. The first two nights we'd been out till dawn, looking for something we never found. On this the third night, we'd cruised the strip sixty-seven times, been in and out of every bar and club we could think of in a twenty-mile radius, stopped twice for bucket chicken and forty-cent hamburgers, debated going to a party at the house of a girl Jeff's sister knew, and chucked two dozen raw eggs at mailboxes and hitchhikers. It was 2:00 A.M.; the bars were closing. There was nothing to do but take a bottle of lemon-flavored gin up to Greasy Lake.

The taillights of a single car winked at us as we swung into the dirt lot with its tufts of weed and washboard corrugations; '57 Chevy, mint, metallic blue. On the far side of the lot, like the exoskeleton of some gaunt chrome insect, a chopper leaned against its kickstand. And that was it for excitement: some junkie half-wit biker and a car freak pumping his girlfriend. Whatever it was we were looking for, we weren't about to find it at Greasy Lake. Not that night.

But then all of a sudden Digby was fighting for the wheel. "Hey, that's Tony Lovett's car! Hey!" he shouted, while I stabbed at the brake pedal and the Bel Air nosed up to the gleaming bumper of the parked Chevy. Digby leaned on the horn, laughing, and instructed me to put my brights on. I flicked on the brights. This was hilarious. A joke. Tony would experience premature withdrawal and expect to be confronted by grim-looking state troopers with flashlights. We hit the horn, strobed the lights, and then jumped out of the car to press our witty faces to Tony's windows; for all we knew we might even catch a glimpse of some little fox's tit, and then we could slap backs with red-faced Tony, roughhouse a little, and go on to new heights of adventure and daring.

The first mistake, the one that opened the whole floodgate, was losing my grip on the keys. In the excitement, leaping from the car with the gin in one hand and a roach clip in the other, I spilled them in the grass—in the dark, rank, mysterious nighttime grass of Greasy Lake. This was a tactical error, as damaging and irreversible in its way as Westmoreland's decision to dig in at Khe Sanh. I felt it like a jab of intuition, and I stopped there by the open door, peering vaguely into the night that puddled up round my feet.

The second mistake—and this was inextricably bound up with the first—was identifying the car as Tony Lovett's. Even before the very bad character in greasy jeans and engineer boots ripped out of the driver's door, I began to realize that this chrome blue was much lighter than the robin's-egg of Tony's car, and that Tony's car didn't have rear-mounted speakers. Judging from their expressions, Digby and Jeff were privately groping toward the same inevitable and unsettling conclusion as I was.

In any case, there was no reasoning with this bad greasy character—clearly he was a man of action. The first lusty Rockette kick of his steel-toes boot caught me under the chin, chipped my favorite tooth, and left me sprawled in the dirt. Like a fool, I'd gone down on one knee to comb the stiff hacked grass for the keys, my mind making connections in the most dragged-out, testudineous way, knowing that things had gone wrong, that I was in a lot of trouble, and that the lost ignition key was my grail and my salvation. The three or four succeeding blows were mainly absorbed by my right buttock and the tough piece of bone at the base of my spine.

Meanwhile, Digby vaulted the kissing bumpers and delivered a savage kung-fu blow to the greasy character's collarbone. Digby had just finished a course in martial arts for phys-ed credit and had spent the better part of the past two nights telling us apocryphal tales of Bruce Lee types and of the raw power invested in lighting blows shot from coiled wrists, ankles, and elbows. The greasy character was unimpressed. He merely backed off a step, his face like a Toltec mask, and laid Digby out with a single whistling round-house blow . . . but now Jeff had got into the act, and I was beginning to extricate myself from the dirt, a tinny compound of shock, rage, and impotence wadded in my throat.

Jeff was on the guy's back, biting at his ear. Digby was on the ground, cursing. I went for the tire iron I kept under the driver's seat. I kept it there because bad characters always keep tire irons under the driver's seat, for just such an occasion as this. Never mind that I hadn't been involved in a fight since sixth grade, when a kid with a sleepy eye and two streams of mucus depending from his nostrils hit me in the knee with a Louisville slugger; never mind that I'd touched the tire iron exactly twice before, to change tires: it was there. And I went for it.

I was terrified. Blood was beating in my ears, my hands were shaking, my heart turning over like a dirtbike in the wrong gear. My antagonist was shirtless, and a single cord of muscle flashed across his chest as he bent forward to peel Jeff from his back like a wet overcoat. "Motherfucker," he spat over, and over, and I was aware in that instant that all four of us—Digby, Jeff, and myself included—were chanting "motherfucker, motherfucker," as if it were a battle cry. (What happened next? The detective asks the murderer from beneath the turned-down brim of his porkpie hat. I don't know, the murderer says something came over me. Exactly.)

Digby poked the flat of his hand in the bad character's face and I came at him like a kamikaze, mindless, raging, stung with humiliation—the while thing, from the initial boot in the chin to this murderous primal instant involving no more than sixty hyperventilating, gland-flooding seconds—I came at him and brought the tire iron down across his ear. The effect was instantaneous, astonishing. He was a stunt man and this was Hollywood, he was a big grimacing toothy balloon and I was a man with a straight pin. He collapsed. Wet his pants. Went loose in his boots.

A single second, big as a zeppelin, floated by. We were standing over him in a circle, gritting our teeth, jerking our necks, our limbs and hands and feet twitching with glandular discharges. No one said anything. We just stared down at the guy, the car freak, the lover, the bad greasy character laid low. Digby looked at me; so did Jeff. I was till holding the tire iron, a tuft of hair clinging to the crook like dandelion fluff, like down. Rattled, I dropped it in the dirt, already envisioning the headlines, the pitted faces of the police inquisitors, the gleam of handcuffs, clank of bars, the big black shadows rising from the back of the cell . . . when suddenly a raw torn shriek cut through me like all the juice in all the electric chairs in the country.

It was the fox. She was short, barefoot, dressed in panties and a man's shirt. "Animals!" she screamed, running at us with her fists clenched and wisps of blow-dried hair in her face. There was a silver chain round her ankle, and her toenails flashed in the glare of the headlights. I think it was the toenails that did it. Sure, the gin and the cannabis and even the Kentucky Fried may have had a hand in it, but it was the sight of those flaming toes that set us off—the toad emerging from the loaf in *Virgin Spring*, lipstick smeared on a child: she was already tainted. We were on her like Bergman's deranged brothers—see no evil, hear none, speak none—panting, wheezing, tearing at her clothes, grabbing for flesh. We were bad characters, and we were scared and hot and three steps over the line—anything could have happened.

It didn't.

Before we could pin her to the hood of the car, our eyes masked with lust and greed and purest primal badness, a pair of headlights swung into the lot. There we were, dirty, bloody, guilty, disassociated from humanity and civilization, the first of the Ur-crimes behind us, the second in progress, shreds of nylon panty and spandex brassiere dangling from our fingers, our flies open, lips licked—there we were, caught in the spotlight. Nailed.

We bolted. First for the car, and then, realizing we had no way of starting it, for the woods. I thought nothing. I thought escape. The headlights came at me like accusing fingers. I was gone.

Ram-bam-bam, across the parking lot, past the chopper and into the feculent undergrowth at the lake's edge, insects flying up in my face, weeds whipping, frogs and snakes and red-eyed turtles splashing off into the night: I was already ankle-deep in muck and tepid water and still going strong. Behind me, the girl's screams rose in intensity, disconsolate, incriminating, the screams of the Sabine women, the Christian martyrs, Anne Frank dragged from the garret. I kept going, pursued by those cries, imagining cops and bloodhounds. The water was up to my knees when I realized what I was doing: I was going to swim for it. Swim the breadth of Greasy Lake and hide myself in the thick clot of woods on the far side. They'd never find me there.

I was breathing in sobs, in gasps. The water lapped at my waist as I looked out over the moon-burnished ripples, the mats of algae that clung to the surface like scabs. Digby and Jeff vanished. I paused. Listened. The girl was quieter now, screams tapering to sobs, but there were male voices, angry, excited, and the high-pitched ticking of the second car's engine. I waded deeper, stealthy, hunted, the ooze sucking at my sneakers. As I was about to take the plunge—at the very instant I dropped my shoulder for the first slashing stroke—I blundered into something. Something unspeakable, obscene, something soft, wet, moss-grown. A patch of weed? A log? When I reached out to touch it, it gave like a rubber duck, it gave like flesh.

In one of those nasty little epiphanies for which we are prepared by films and TV and childhood visits to the funeral home to ponder the shrunken painted forms of dead grandparents, I understood what it was that bobbed there so inadmissably in the dark. Understood, and stumbled back in horror and revulsion, my mind yanked in six different directions (I was nineteen, a mere child, an infant, and here in the space of five minutes I'd struck down one greasy character and blundered into the waterlogged carcass of a second), thinking The keys, the keys, why did I have to go and lose the keys? I stumbled back, but the muck took hold of my feet—a sneaker snagged, balance lost— and suddenly I was pitching face forward into the buoyant black mass, throwing out my hands in desperation while simultaneously conjuring the image of reeking frogs and muskrats revolving in slicks of their own deliquescing juices. AAAAArrrgh! I shot from the water like a torpedo, the dead man rotating to expose a mossy beard and eyes cold as the moon. I must have shouted out, thrashing around in the weeds, because the voices behind me suddenly because animated.

"What was that?"

"It's them, it's them: they tried to, tried to . . . *rape* me!" Sobs.

A man's voice, flat Midwestern accent. "You sons of a bitches, we'll kill you!"

Frogs, crickets.

Then another voice, harsh, *r*-less, Lower East Side: "Motherfucker!" I recognized the verbal virtuosity of the bad greasy character in the engineer boots. Tooth chipped, sneakers gone, coated in mud and slime and worse, crouching breathless in the weeds waiting to have my ass thoroughly and definitively kicked and fresh from the hideous stinking embrace of a three-days-dead-corpse, I suddenly felt a rush of joy and vindication: the son of a bitch was alive! Just as quickly, my bowels turned to ice. "Come on out there, you pansy motherfuckers!" the bad greasy character was screaming. He shouted curses till he was out of breath.

The crickets started up again, then the frogs. I held my breath. All at once there was sound in the reeds, a swishing, a splash: thunk-a-thunk. They were throwing rocks. The frogs fell silent. I cradled my head. Swish, swish, thunk-a-thunk. A wedge of feldspar the size of a cue ball glanced off my knee. I bit my finger.

It was then that they turned to the car. I heard a door slam, a curse, and then the sound of the headlights shattering—almost a good-natured sound, celebratory, like corks popping from the neck of bottles. This was succeeded by the dull booming of the fenders, metal on metal, and then the icy crash of the windshield. I inched forward, elbows and knees, my belly pressed to the muck, thinking of guerillas and commandos and *The Naked and the Dead*. I parted the weeds and squinted the length of the parking lot.

The second car—it was a Trans-Am—was still running, its high beams washing the scene in a lurid stagy light. Tire iron flailing, the greasy bad character was laying into the side of my mother's Bel Air like an avenging demon, his shadow riding up the trunks of the tress. Whomp. Whomp. Whomp-whomp. The other two guys—blond types, in fraternity jackets—were helping out with tree branches and skull-sized boulders. One of them was gathering up bottles, rocks, muck, candy wrappers, used condoms, pop-tops, and other refuse and pitching it through the window on the driver's side. I could see the fox, a white bulb behind the windshield of the '57 Chevy. "Bobbie," she whined over the thumping, "come *on*." The greasy character paused a moment, took one good swipe at the left taillight, and then heaved the tire iron halfway across the lake. Then he fired up the '57 and was gone.

Blond head nodded at blond head. One said something to the other, too low for me to catch. They were no doubt thinking that in helping to annihilate my mother's car they'd committed a fairly rash act, and thinking too that there were three bad characters connected with that very car watching them from the woods. Perhaps other possibilities occurred to them as well—police, jail cells, justices of the peace, reparations, lawyers, irate parents, fraternal censure. Whatever they were thinking, they suddenly dropped branches, bottles, and rocks and sprang for their car in unison, as if they'd choreographed it. Five seconds. That's all it took. The engine shrieked, the tires squealed, a cloud of dust rose from the rutted lot and then settled back on darkness.

I don't know how long I lay there, the bad breath of decay all around me, my jacket heavy as a bear, the primordial ooze subtly reconstituting itself to accommodate my upper thighs and testicles. My jaws ached, my knee throbbed, my coccyx was on fire. I contemplated suicide, wondered if I'd need bridgework, scraped the recesses of my brain for some sort of excuse to give my parents—a tree had fallen on the car, I was blindsided by a bread truck, hit and run, vandals had got to it while we were playing chess at Digby's. Then I thought of the dead man. He was probably the one person on the planet worse off than I was. I thought about him, fog on the lake, insects chirring eerily, and felt the tug of fear, felt the darkness opening up inside me like a set of jaws. Who was he, I wondered, this victim of time and circumstance bobbing sorrowfully in the lake at my back. The owner of the chopper, no doubt, a bad older character come to this. Shot during a murky drug deal, drowned while drunkenly frolicking in the lake. Another headline. My car wrecked; he was dead.

When the eastern half of the sky went from black to cobalt and the trees began to separate themselves from the shadows, I pushed myself up from the mud and stepped out into the open. By now the birds had begun to take over for the crickets, and dew lay slick on the leaves. There was a smell in the air, raw and sweet at the same time, the smell of the sun firing buds and opening blossoms. I contemplated the car. It lay there like a wreck along the highway, like a steel sculpture left over from a vanished civilization. Everything was still. This was nature.

I was circling the car, as dazed and bedraggled as the sole survivor of an air blitz, when Digby and Jeff emerged from the trees behind me. Digby's face was crosshatched with smears of dirt; Jeff's jacket was gone and his shirt was torn across the shoulder. They slouched across the lot, looking sheepish, and silently came up beside me to gape at the ravaged automobile. No one said a word. After a while Jeff swung open the driver's door and began to scoop the broken glass and garbage off the seat. I looked at Digby. He shrugged. "At least they didn't slash the tires," he said.

It was true: the tires were intact. There was no windshield, the headlights were staved in, and the body looked as if it had been sledge-hammered for a quarter a shot at the county fair, but the tires were inflated to regulation pressure. The car was drivable. In silence, all three of us bent to scrape the mud and shattered glass from the interior. I said nothing about the biker. When we were finished, I reached in my pocket for the keys, experienced a nasty stab of recollection, cursed myself, and turned to search the grass. I spotted them almost immediately, no more than five feet from the open door, glinting like jewels in the first tapering shaft of sunlight. There was no reason to get philosophical about it: I eased into the seat and turned the engine over.

It was at that precise moment that the silver Mustang with the flame decals rumbled into the lot. All three of us froze; then Digby and Jeff slid into the car and slammed the door. We watched as the Mustang rocked and bobbed across the ruts and finally jerked to a halt beside the forlorn chopper at the far end of the lot. "Let's go," Digby said. I hesitated, the Bel Air wheezing beneath me.

Two girls emerged from the mustang. Tight jeans, stiletto heels, hair frozen like fur. They bent over the motorcycle, paced back and forth aimlessly, glanced once or twice at us, and then ambled over to where the reeds sprang up in a green fence round the perimeter of the lake. One of them cupped her hands to her mouth. "Al," she called. "Hey, Al!"

"Come on, " Digby hissed. "Let's get out of here."

But it was too late. The second girl was picking her way across the lot, unsteady on her heels, looking up at us and then away. She was older—twenty-five or -six—and as she came closer we could see there was something wrong with her: she was stoned or drunk, lurching now and waving her arms for balance. I gripped the steering wheel as if it were the ejection lever of a flaming jet, and Digby spat out my name, twice, terse and impatient.

"Hi," the girl said.

We looked at her like zombies, like war veterans, like deaf-and-dumb pencil peddlers.

She smiled, her lips cracked and dry. "Listen," she said, bending from the waist to look in the window, "you guys seen Al?" Her pupils were pinpoints, her eyes glass. She jerked her neck. "That's his bike over there—Al's. You seen him?"

Al. I didn't know what to say. I wanted to get out of the car and retch. I wanted to go home to my parents' house and crawl into bed. Digby poked me in the ribs. "We haven't seen anybody," I said.

The girl seemed to consider this, reaching out a slim veiny arm to brace herself against the car. "No matter," she said, slurring the t's, "he'll turn up." And then, as if she'd just taken stock of the whole scene—the ravaged car and our battered faces, the desolation of the place—she said: "Hey, you guys look like some pretty bad characters—been fightin', huh?" We stared straight ahead, rigid as catatonics. She was fumbling in her pocket and muttering something. Finally she held out a handful of tablets in glassine wrappers: "Hey, you want to party, you want to do some of these with me and Sarah?"

I just looked at her. I thought I was going to cry. Digby broke the silence. "No, thanks," he said, leaning over me. "Some other time."

I put the car in gear and it inched forward with a groan, shaking off pellets of glass like an old dog shedding water after a bath, heaving over the ruts on its worn springs, creeping toward the highway. There was a sheen of sun on the lake. I looked back. The girl was still standing there, watching us, her shoulder slumped, hand outstretched.

Boyle on Managing Tone and Controlling Reader Sympathy

I'd been contemplating a story about the heady teenage mix of triumph and vulnerability for a long while before I sat down to write "Greasy Lake." The initial inspiration came from my fascination with Bruce Springsteen's early albums and the way in which he was able to capture the experience in a number of his songs, particularly "Spirit in the Night," from which derive both the title and epigraph of this story. There *is* a spirit of rock and roll, and that spirit speaks to our most joyful and ecstatic moments, as well as to our most brooding and uncertain. The song gave me a point of departure—but not a structure, simply a scenario: teens at a lake at night—and once I had that, the first line came to me ("There was a time when courtesy and winning ways went out of style, when it was good to be bad, when you cultivated decadence like a taste") and I followed it.

To say that the line "came to me" and that "I followed it" may not be particularly helpful to a neophyte writer, but it suggests the essential truth of artistic composition: you do not plan out a story/painting/song beforehand, but rather open yourself up to the possibilities of discovering it. Nearly all the writers I know work in this way (see Raymond Carver's essay "On Writing," for instance), allowing the unconscious mind to establish conflict, create scenes, and build structure—the process is far too abstract to allow for anything else. No story or novel I've ever written has begun in any other way—that is, all my work starts with only the vaguest idea of what might come to transpire or what the story will mean on a thematic level.

Which is not to say that the writer just throws the words on the screen in the way of automatic writing (or gibberish, if you will), but that he or she controls the process with the input of the conscious mind. Think of it this way: the process of writing is an analogue for the process of reading. Just as when you are absorbed in a book with the writer when he is creating the story, or rather, allowing it to unfold in an organic way.

Of course, I can analyze this process and speak to the subjects—Managing Tone and Reader Sympathy, for example—the editors have asked me to address, but only after the fact. I cannot stress this enough: all the elements of creating a story are instinctive, and they proceed from an assimilation of everything the writer has read, spoken, and experienced. That said, I'd like to look at the finished product—in this case, "Greasy Lake"—and see how the artistic choices have been made through the process of its composition.

First of all, we have the tone of the piece, and this tone is colored by the fact that the protagonist is speaking in retrospect and in the first person. The story could have been narrated in the moment, perhaps even in present tense and in the young narrator's vernacular, but if that were the case, the piece would lose a great deal of its authority and beauty. Because the speaker has been to Greasy Lake at some time in the past, he is viewing his young self and his friends from an ironic distance ("We were all dangerous characters then"). This allows him to comment on the action in a way that would be less effective if he were narrating in the moment. It also allows his reflections and allusions to expand far beyond the consciousness of a nineteen-year-old.

As for reader sympathy: this is an element of composition that has little place in discerning how a story will unfold. Some of the most unsympathetic characters can be among the most appealing, like, for instance, Shakespeare's Iago, Dostoevsky's Underground Man, or Ronnie Sommers from my own *Drop City*. Whether your characters are likable or heroic or even faintly despicable is inconsequential—all that matters is that they live not as clichés but as credible simulacra of real people. In the case of "Greasy Lake," the reader does establish sympathy for the narrator and his hapless companions for a number of reasons. Even though they were "scared and hot and three steps over the line" and "anything could have happened," the self-mocking, reflective tone lets the reader know that the worst will not happen and that these characters, despite their boastful (and hopeful) self-anointing as "bad characters," are really no different from any other teenagers out roaming in search of something they can't define. That they do not commit the "Ur crimes," that they in turn become victims and discover something about badness—true badness—that they could never have imagined or admitted, puts them firmly in the arena of the human and the vulnerable. Readers recognize in these characters something of themselves, even if it is distasteful. And so: we do have sympathy for the unnamed narrator and his two companions, and that sympathy serves to leaven their actions and create a kind of rooting interest in the outcome.

I've spoken of the organic process of composition, and I would like to add that while the writer must trust his/her instincts and let the story flow on its own, there is nonetheless the element of conscious shaping that each draft refines. Whether you work spontaneously, writing through each discovery to the end in a kind of fever (see Jack Kerouac) or revise through draft after draft, you must exert control over the material at some point. My method is to work slowly, paragraph by paragraph, day by day, revising constantly as I go. A story like "Greasy Lake" will typically take two to three weeks to compose, and the slow process of rewriting what is already on the page, of recasting lines and finding the caesuras that become scene breaks, frees the unconscious mind to leap ahead and resolve problems of structure and closure without my being aware of it. Of course, I don't want to sound too mysterious here—at some point, the writer becomes consciously aware of what the story means and how it will end, but sometimes that doesn't happen until he actually gets there.

For me, all stories are an exercise of the imagination and all are essentially mysterious—they are puzzles, all of them—until I find the key to unlock them. Yet still, stories are usually built in scenes, and I find myself working each day toward the end of a scene, knowing that the scene blooming on the page will give rise to the next, in the way of building blocks, until the story is complete. I like to cut scenes at a dramatic or ironic moment, so that the space between them can be filled by the images flowering in the reader's mind. In the case of "Greasy Lake," the narrative is continuous, without clearly demarcated scenes, and yet there are breathing spaces—or moments of rising and falling action—throughout. An example is when the narrator steps away from the scene with regard to mistaking this particular Chevy for his friend's in order to list his mistakes. This not only supplies ironic distance, but it also allows the scene to break so that when we return to it ("In any case, there was no reasoning with this bad greasy character"), both the drama and dark comedy are intensified.

Let me emphasize, however, that each story is radically different in its meaning, outlook, and unfolding from any other story, and though I've published some 150 of them, when I sit down to the next I know that whatever has worked previously may have no bearing at all on the current scenario. That is how it should be. Otherwise, I would be writing the same story over and over again. So here's my advice again: read deeply, study the models here, incorporate all the experience, emotion, and technique that you can, and then—just let fly. Your story will come from some deep place you can't name and it will unfold in a way you can hardly begin to imagine.

Writing Suggestions

1. Part One: In no more than three substantial paragraphs, begin a story in which a first-person narrator—let's say a twenty-one-year-old woman—describes a scene in which she met a man the previous week. Part Two: In no more than three substantial paragraphs, begin a story in which the same woman, now forty-six, describes meeting the same man twenty-five years earlier. How does the insertion of time—in this case, a quarter of a century—between the narrator and the event she describes change the way the scene is rendered? What details, important to the twenty-one year old, are no longer important to the forty-six-year-old? In your opinion, what story possibilities are present in the version told by the twenty-one-year-old narrator in contrast to those suggested by the version told by the forty-six-year-old narrator? How did changing only the narrative distance—that is, the temporal space between the narrator and the event—in effect, change the entire story? Or did it? Consider ways to more effectively use the narrative distance in your own stories.

2. Boyle claims, "Some of the most unsympathetic characters can be among the most appealing." Develop a character who, from a distance, appears unsympathetic: a pickpocket, an arsonist, an adulterer, a deadbeat dad, et cetera. Then, as in Boyle's story, develop this character to the point where he or she is fully believable, has a complex mixture of generosity and selfishness, and compels us, as readers, to feel sympathy despite his or her obvious flaws.

3. Reread a story you've recently completed, identifying those areas where—using Boyle's term—you are most "absorbed" with the story. Where do you lose yourself, again, into the world created by the writing? After identifying one or two such paragraphs or scenes, make a list of reasons why, in your opinion, those one or two sections are more absorbing or satisfying than other sections of your story. Did you feel differently while writing those sections than while writing other parts of the story? Many fiction writers have noted that writers, more or less, teach themselves how to write effectively. With this in mind, can you think of ways to elevate other sections of your story so that they are as accomplished as those scenes or paragraphs you've identified?

4. Boyle claims that his story was inspired by a Bruce Springsteen song: "The song gave me a point of departure, but not a structure, simply a scenario: teens at a lake at night." Sort through your music collection, locating a few songs that speak most

clearly to you. Consider ways that you can translate the emotion, suggested by the song, into a scene, a situation, or a first line for a story.

You have to be ready, willing, and able to cut things as soon as
you sense that they're going in a bad direction. You have an inner
critic that knows when something's off.
—Alice Sebold

George Saunders

Jon

From The New Yorker

Back in the time of which I am speaking, due to what our Coördinators had mandated us, we had all seen that educational video of "It's Yours to Do With What You Like!" in which teens like ourselves speak on the healthy benefits of getting off by oneself and doing what one feels like in terms of self-touching, which what we learned from that video was, there is nothing wrong with self-touching, because love is a mystery but the mechanics of love need not be, so go off alone, see what is up, with you and your relation to your own gonads, and the main thing is, just have fun, feeling no shame!

And then nightfall would fall and our facility would fill with the sounds of quiet fast breathing from inside our Privacy Tarps as we all experimented per the techniques taught us in "It's Yours to Do With What You Like!" and what do you suspect, you had better make sure that that little gap between the main wall and the sliding wall that slides out to make your Gender Areas is like really really small. Which guess what, it wasn't.

That is all what I am saying.

Also all what I am saying is, who could blame Josh for noting that gap and squeezing through it snakelike in just his Old Navy boxers that Old Navy gave us to wear for gratis, plus who could blame Ruthie for leaving her Velcro knowingly un-Velcroed? Which soon all the rest of us heard them doing what the rest of us so badly wanted to be doing, only we, being more mindful of the rules than them, just laid there doing the self-stuff from the video, listening to Ruth and Josh really doing it for real, which believe me, even that was pretty fun.

And when Josh came back next morning so happy he was crying, that was a further blow to our morality, because why did our Coördinators not catch him on their supposedly nighttime monitors? In all of our hearts was the thought of, O.K., we thought you said no boy-and-girl stuff, and yet here is Josh, with his Old Navy boxers and a hickey on his waist, and none of you guys is even saying boo?

Because I for one wanted to do right, I did not want to sneak through that gap, I wanted to wed someone when old enough (I will soon tell who) and relocate to the appropriate facility in terms of demographics, namely Young Marrieds, such as Scranton, PA, or Mobile, AL, and then along comes Josh doing Ruthie with imperity, and no one is punished, and soon the miracle of birth results and all our Coordinators, even Mr. Delacourt, are bringing Baby Amber stuffed animals? At which point every cell or chromosome or whatever it was in my gonads that had been holding their breaths was suddenly like, Dude, slide through that gap no matter how bad it hurts, squat outside Carolyn's Privacy Tarp whispering, Carolyn, it's me, please un-Velcro your Privacy opening!

Then came the final straw that broke the back of my saying no to my gonads, which was I dreamed I was that black dude on MTV's "Hot and Spicy Christmas" (around like Location Indicator 34412, if you want to check it out) and Carolyn was the oiled-up white chick, and we were trying to earn the Island Vacation by miming through the ten Hot 'n' Nasty Positions before the end of "We Three Kings," only then, sadly, during Her on Top, Thumb in Mouth, her Elf Cap fell off, and as the Loser Buzzer sounded she bent low to me, saying, Oh, Jon, I wish we did not have to do this for fake in front of hundreds of kids on Spring Break doing the wave but instead could do it for real with just each other in private.

And then she kissed me with a kiss I can only describe as melting.

So imagine that is you, you are a healthy young dude who has been self-practicing all those months, and you wake from that dream of a hot chick giving you a melting kiss, and that same hot chick is laying or lying just on the other side of the sliding wall, and meanwhile in the very next Privacy Tarp is that sleeping dude Josh, who a few weeks before a baby was born to the girl he had recently did it with, and nothing bad happened to them, except now Mr. Slippen sometimes let them sleep in.

What would you do?

Well, you would do what I did, you would slip through, and when Carolyn un-Velcroed that Velcro wearing her blue Guess kimono, whispering, Oh my God, I thought you'd never ask, that would be the most romantic thing you had ever underwent.

And though I had many times seen LI 34321 for Honey Grahams, where the stream of milk and the stream of honey enjoin to make that river of sweet-tasting goodness, I did not know that, upon making love, one person may become like the milk and the other like the honey, and soon they cannot even remember who started out the milk and who the honey, they just become one fluid, this like honey/milk combo.

Well, that is what happened to us.

Which is why soon I had to go to Mr. Slippen hat in hand and say, Sir, Baby Amber will be having a little playmate if that is O.K. with you, to which he just rolled his eyes and crushed the plastic cup in his hand and threw it at my chest, saying, What are we running in here, Randy, a freaking play school?

Then he said, Well, Christ, what am I supposed to do, lose two valuable team members because of this silliness? All right all right, how soon will Baby Amber be out of that crib or do I have to order your kid a whole new one?

Which I was so happy, because soon I would be a father and would not even lose my job.

A few days later, like how it was with Ruthie and Josh, Mr. Delacourt's brother the minister came in and married us, and afterward barbecue beef was catered, and we danced at our window while outside pink and purple balloons were released, and all the other kids were like, Rock on, you guys, have a nice baby and all!

It was the best day of our lives thus far for sure.

But I guess it is true what they say at LI 11006 about life throwing us not only curves and sliders but sometimes even worse, as Dodger pitcher Hector Jones throws from behind his back a grand piano for Allstate, because soon here came that incident with Baby Amber, which made everybody just loony.

Which that incident was, Baby Amber died.

Sometimes it was just nice and gave one a fresh springtime feeling to sit in the much coveted window seat, finalizing one's Summary while gazing out at our foliage strip, which sometimes slinking through it would be a cat from Rustic Village Apartments, looking so cute that one wished to pet or even smell it, with wishful petting being the feeling I was undergoing on the sad day of which I am telling, such as even giving the cat a tuna chunk and a sip of my Diet Coke! If cats even like soda. That I do not know.

And then Baby Amber toddled by, making this funny noise in her throat of not being very happy, and upon reaching the Snack Cart she like seized up and tumped over, giving off this sort of shriek.

At first we all just looked at her, like going, Baby Amber, if that is some sort of new game, we do not exactly get it, plus come on, we have a lot of Assessments to get through this morning, such as a First-Taste Session for Diet GingerCoke, plus a very critical First View of Dean Witter's Preliminary Clip Reel for their campaign of "Whose Ass Are You Kicking Today?"

But then she did not get up.

We dropped our Summaries and raced to the Observation Window and began pounding, due to we loved her so much, her being the first baby we had ever witnessed living day after day, and soon the paramedics came and took her away, with one of them saying, Jesus, how stupid are you kids, anyway, this baby is burning up, she is like 107 with meningitis.

So next morning there was Carolyn all freaked out with her little baby belly, watching Amber's crib being dismantled by Physical Plant, who wiped all facility surfaces with Handi Wipes in case the meningitis was viral, and there was the rest of us, just like thrashing around the place kicking things down, going like, This sucks, this is totally fucked up!

Looking back, I commend Mr. Slippen for what he did next, which was he said, Christ, folks, all our hearts are broken, it is not just yours, do you or do you not think I have Observed this baby from the time she was born, do you or do you not think that I, too, feel like kicking things down while shouting, This sucks, this is totally fucked up? Only what would that accomplish, would that bring Baby Amber back? I am at a loss, in terms of how can we best support Ruth and Josh in this sad tragic time, is it via feeling blue and cranky, or via feeling refreshed and hopeful and thus better able to respond to their needs?

So that was a non-brainer, and we all voted to accept Mr. Slippen's Facility Morale Initiative, and soon were getting our Aurabon® twice a day instead of once, plus it seemed like better stuff, and I for one had never felt so glad or stress-free, and my Assessments became very nuanced, and I spent many hours doing and enjoying them and then redoing and reenjoying them, and it was during this period that we won the McDorland Prize for Excellence in Assessing in the Midwest Region in our demographic category of White Teens.

The only one who failed to become gladder was Carolyn, who due to her condition of pregnant could not join us at the place in the wall where we hooked in for our Aurabon®. And now whenever the rest of us hooked in she would come over and say such negative things as, Wake up and smell the coffee, you feel bad because a baby died, how about honoring that by continuing to feel bad, which is only natural, because a goddam baby died, you guys?

At night in our shared double Privacy Tarp in Conference Room 11, which our Coördinators had gave us so we would feel more married, I would be like, Honey, look, your attitude only sucks because you can't hook in, once baby comes all will be fine, due to you'll be able to hook in again, right? But she always blew me off, like she would say she was thinking of never hooking in again and why was I always pushing her to hook in and she just didn't know who to trust anymore, and one night when the baby kicked she said to her abdomen, Don't worry, angel, Mommy is going to get you Out.

Which my feeling was: Out? Hello? My feeling was: Hold on, I like what I have achieved, and when I thought of descending Out to somewhere with no hope of meeting luminaries such as actress Lily Farrell-Garesh or Mark Belay, chairperson of Thatscool.com, descending Out to, say, some lumberyard like at LI 77656 for Midol, merely piling lumber as cars rushed past, cars with no luminaries inside, only plain regular people who did not know me from Adam, who, upon seeing me, saw just some mere guy stacking lumber having such humdrum thoughts as thinking, Hey, I wonder what's for lunch, duh—I got a cold flat feeling in my gut, because I did not want to undergo it.

Plus furthermore (and I said this to Carolyn) what will it be like for us when all has been taken from us? Of what will we speak of? I do not want to only speak of my love in grunts! If I wish to compare my love to a love I have previous knowledge of, I do not want to stand there in the wind casting about for my metaphor! If I want to say like, Carolyn, remember that RE/MAX one where as the redhead kid falls asleep holding that Teddy bear rescued from the trash, the bear comes alive and winks, and the announcer goes, Home is the place where you find yourself suddenly no longer longing for home (LI 34451)—if I want to say to Carolyn, Carolyn, LI 34451, check it out, that is how I feel about you—well, then, I want to say it! I want to possess all the articulate I can, because otherwise there we will be, in non-designer clothes, no longer even on TrendSetters & TasteMakers gum cards with our photos on them, and I will turn to her and say, Honey, uh, honey, there is a certain feeling but I cannot name it and cannot cite a precedent-type feeling, but trust me, dearest, wow, do I ever feel it for you, right now. And what will that be like, that stupid standing there, just a man and a woman and the wind, and nobody knowing what nobody is meaning?

Just then the baby kicked my hand, which at that time was on Carolyn's stomach. And Carolyn was like, You are either with me or agin me.

Which was so funny, because she was proving my point! Because you are either with me or agin me is what the Lysol bottle at LI 12009 says to the scrubbing sponge as they approach the grease stain together, which is making at them a threatening fist while wearing a sort of Mexican bandolera!

When I pointed this out, she removed my hand from her belly.

I love you, I said.

Prove it, she said.

So next day Carolyn and I came up to Mr. Slippen and said, Please, Mr. Slippen, we hereby Request that you supply us with the appropriate Exit Paperwork.

To which Mr. Slippen said, Guys, folks, tell me this is a joke by you on me.

And Carolyn said softly, because she had always liked Mr. Slippen, who had taught her to ride a bike when small in the Fitness Area, It's no joke.

And Slippen said, Holy smokes, you guys are possessed of the fruits of the labors of hundreds of thousands of talented passionate men and women, some of whom are now gone from us, they poured forth these visions in the prime of their lives, reacting spontaneously to the beauty and energy of the world around them, which is why these stories and images are such an unforgettable testimony to who we are as a nation! And you have it all within you! I can only imagine how thrilling that must be. And now, to give it all up? For what? Carolyn, for what?

And Carolyn said, Mr. Slippen, I did not see you raising your babies in such a confined environment.

And Slippen said, Carolyn, that is so, but also please note that neither I nor my kids have ever been on TrendSetters & TasteMakers gum cards and believe me, I have heard a few earfuls vis-à-vis that, as in: Dad, you could've got us In but no, and now, Dad, I am merely another ophthalmologist among millions of ophthalmologists. And please do not think that is not something that a father sometimes struggles with. In terms of coulda shoulda woulda.

And Carolyn said, Jon, you know what, he is not even really listening to us.

And Slippen said, Randy, since when is your name Jon?

Because by the way my name is really Jon. Randy is just what my mother put on the form the day I was Accepted, although tell the truth I do not know why.

It is one thing to see all this stuff in your head, Carolyn said. But altogether different to be out in it, I would expect.

And I could see that she was softening into a like daughter role, as if wanting him to tell her what to do, and up came LI 27493 (Prudential Life), where, with Dad enstroked in the hospital bed, Daughter asks should she marry the guy who though poor has a good heart, and we see the guy working with inner-city kids via spray-painting a swing set, and Dad says, Sweetie, the heart must lead you. And then later here is Dad all better in a tux, and Daughter hugging the poor but good dude while sneaking a wink at Dad, who raises his glass and points at the groom's shoe, where there is this little smudge of swing-set paint.

I cannot comment as to that, Slippen said. Everyone is different. Nobody can know someone else's experiences.

Larry, no offense but you are talking shit, Carolyn said. We deserve better than that from you.

And Slippen looked to be softening, and I remembered when he would sneak all of us kids in doughnuts, doughnuts we did not even need to Assess but could simply eat with joy with jelly on our face before returning to our Focussed Purposeful Play with toys we would Assess by coloring in on a sheet of paper either a smiling duck if the toy was fun or a scowling duck if the toy bit.

And Slippen said, Look, Carolyn, you are two very fortunate people, even chosen people. A huge investment was made in you, which I would argue you have a certain responsibility to repay, not to mention, with a baby on the way, there is the question of security, security for your future that I—

Uncle, please, Carolyn said, which was her trumpet cart, because when she was small he had let her call him that and now she sometimes still did when the moment was right, such as at Christmas Eve when all of our feelings was high.

Jesus, Slippen said. Look, you two can do what you want, clearly. I cannot stop you kids, but, golly, I wish I could. All that is required is the required pre-Exit visit to the Lerner Center, which as you know you must take before I can give you the necessary Exit Paperwork. When would you like to take or make that visit?

Now, Carolyn said.

Gosh, Carolyn, when did you become such a pistol? Mr. Slippen said, and called for the minivan.

The Lerner Center, even when reached via a blackened-window minivan, is a trip that will really blow one's mind, due to all the new sights and sounds one experiences, such as carpet on floor is different from carpet on facility floor, such as smoke smell from the minivan ashtrays, whereas we are a No Smoking facility, not to mention, wow, when we were led in blindfolded for our own protection, so many new smells shot forth from these like sidewalkside blooms or whatever that Carolyn and I were literally bumping into each other like swooning.

Inside they took our blindfolds off, and, yes, it looked and smelled exactly like our facility, and like every facility across the land, via the PervaScent® system, except in other facilities across the land a lady in blue scrubs does not come up to you with crossed eyes, sloshing around a cup of lemonade, saying in this drunk voice like, A barn is more than a barn it is a memory of a time when you were cared for by a national chain of caregivers who bring you the best of life with a selfless evening in Monterey when the stars are low you can be thankful to your Amorino Co broker!

And then she burst into tears and held her lemonade so crooked it was like spilling on the Foosball table. I had no idea what Location Indicator or Indicators she was even at, and when I asked, she didn't seem to even know what I meant by Location Indicator, and was like, Oh, I just don't know anymore what is going on with me or why I would expose that tenderest part of my baby to the roughest part of the forest where the going gets rough, which is not the accomplishment of any one man but an entire team of dreamers who dream the same dreams you dream in the best interests of that most important system of all, your family!

Then this Lerner Center dude came over and led her away, and she slammed her hand down so hard on the Foosball table that the little goalie cracked and his head flew over by us, and someone said, Good one, Doreen. Now there's no Foosball.

At which time luckily it was time for our Individual Consultation.

Who we got was this Mid-Ager from Akron, OH, who, when I asked my first question off of my Question Card they gave us, which was, What is it like in terms of pain, he said, There is no pain except once I poked myself in my hole with a coffee stirrer and, Jesus, that smarted, but otherwise you can't really even feel it.

So I was glad to hear it, although not so glad when he showed us where he had poked his hole with the stirrer, because I am famous as a wimp among my peers in terms of gore, and he had opted not to use any DermaFill®, and you could see right in. And, wow, there is something about observing up close a raw bloody hole at the base of somebody's hair that really gets one thinking. And though he said, in Question No. 2, that his hole did not present him any special challenges in terms of daily maintenance, looking into that hole, I was like, Dude, how does that give you no challenges, it is like somebody blew off a firecracker inside your freaking neck!

And when Carolyn said Question No. 3, which was, How do you now find your thought processes, his brow darkened and he said, Well, to be frank, though quite advanced, having been here three years, there are, if you will, places where things used to be when I went looking for them, brainwise, but now, when I go there, nothing is there, it is like I have the shelving but not the cans of corn, if you get my drift. For example, looking at you, young lady, I know enough to say you are pretty, but when I direct my brain to a certain place, to find there a more vivid way of saying you are pretty, watch this, some words will come out, which I, please excuse me, oh dammit

Then his voice changed to this announcer voice and he was like, These women know that for many generations entrenched deep in this ancient forest is a secret known by coffeegrowers since the dawn of time man has wanted one thing which is to watch golf in peace will surely follow once knowledge is dispersed and the World Book is a super bridge across the many miles the phone card can close the gap!

And his eyes were crossing and he was sputtering, which would have been funny if we did not know that soon our eyes would be the crossing eyes and out of our mouths would the sputter be flying.

Then he got up and fled from the room, hitting himself hard in the face.

And I said to Carolyn, Well, that about does it for me.

And I waited for her to say that about did it for her, but she only sat there looking conflicted with her hand on her belly.

Out in the Common Room, I took her in my arms and said, Honey, I do not really think we have it all that bad, why not just go home and love each other and our baby when he or she comes, and make the best of all the blessings what we have been given?

And her head was tilted down in this way that seemed to be saying, Yes, sweetie, my God, you were right all along.

But then a bad decisive thing happened, which was this old lady came hobbling over and said, Dear, you must wait until Year Two to truly know, some do not thrive but others do, I am Year Two, and do you know what? When I see a bug now, I truly see a bug, when I see a paint chip I am truly seeing that paint chip, there is no distraction and it is so sweet, nothing in one's field of vision but what one opts to put there via moving one's eyes, and also do you hear how well I am speaking?

Out in the minivan I said, Well I am decided, and Carolyn said, Well I am too. And then there was this long dead silence, because I knew and she knew that what we had both decided was not the same decision, not at all, that old crony had somehow rung her bell!

And I said, How do you know what she said is even true?

And she said, I just know.

That night in our double Privacy Tarp, Carolyn nudged me awake and said, Jon, doesn't it make sense to make our mistakes in the direction of giving our kid the best possible chance at a beautiful life?

And I was like, Chick, please take a look in the Fridge, where there is every type of food that must be kept cold, take a look on top of the Fridge, where there is every type of snack, take a look in our Group Closet, which is packed with gratis designer-wear such as Baby Gap and even Baby Ann Taylor, whereas what kind of beautiful life are you proposing with a Fridge that is empty both inside and on top, and the three of us going around all sloppenly, because I don't know about you but my skill set is pretty limited in terms of what do I know how to do, and if you go into the Fashion Module for Baby Ann Taylor and click with your blinking eyes on Pricing Info you will find that they are not just giving that shit away.

And she said, Oh, Jon, you break my heart, that night when you came to my Tarp you were like a lion taking what he wanted but now you are like some bunny wiffling his nose in fright.

Well, that wasn't nice, and I told her that wasn't nice, and she said, Jesus, don't whine, you are whining like a bunny, and I said I would rather be a bunny than a rag, and she said maybe I better go sleep somewhere else.

So I went out to Boys and slept on the floor, it being too late to check out a Privacy Tarp.

And I was pissed and sad, because no dude likes to think of himself as a rabbit, because once your girl thinks of you as a rabbit, how will she ever again think of you as a lion? And all of the sudden I felt very much like starting over with someone who would always think of me as a lion and never as a rabbit, and who really got it about how lucky we were.

Laying there in Boys, I did what I always did when confused, which was call up my Memory Loop of my mom, where she is baking a pie with her red hair up in a bun, and as always she paused in her rolling and said, Oh, my little man, I love you so much, which is why I did the most difficult thing of all, which was part with you, my darling, so that you could use your exceptional intelligence to do that most holy of things, help other people. Stay where you are, do not get distracted, have a content and productive life, and I will be happy too.

Blinking on End, I was like, Thanks, Mom, you have always been there for me, I really wish I could have met you in person before you died.

In the morning Slippen woke me by giving me the light shock on the foot bottom which was sometimes useful to help us arise if we had to arise early and were in need of assistance, and said to please accompany him, as we had a bit of a sticky wicket in our purview.

Waiting in Conference Room 6 were Mr. Dove and Mr. Andrews and Mr. Delacourt himself, and at the end of the table Carolyn, looking small, with both hands on her pile of Exit Paperwork and her hair in braids, which I had always found cute, her being like that milkmaid for Swiss Rain Chocolate (LI 10003), who suddenly throws away her pail and grows sexy via taking out her braids, and as some fat farm ladies line up by a silo and also take out their braids to look sexy, their thin husbands look dubious and run for the forest.

Randy, Mr. Dove said, Carolyn here has evinced a desire to Exit. What we would like to know is, being married, do you have that same desire?

And I looked at Carolyn like, You are jumping to some conclusion because of one little fight, when it was you who called me the rabbit first, which is the only reason I called you rag?

It's not because of last night, Jon, Carolyn said.

Randy, I sense some doubt? Mr. Dove said.

And I had to admit that some doubt was being felt by me, because it seemed more than ever like she was some sort of malcontentish girl who would never be happy, no matter how good things were.

Maybe you kids would like some additional time, Mr. Andrews said. Some time to talk it over and be really sure.

I don't need any additional time, Carolyn said.

And I said, You're going no matter what? No matter what I do?

And she said, Jon, I want you to come with me so bad, but, yes, I'm going.

And Mr. Dove said, Wait a minute, who is Jon?

And Mr. Andrews said, Randy is Jon, it is apparently some sort of pet name between them.

And Slippen said to us, Look, guys, I have been married for nearly thirty years and it has been my experience that, when in doubt, take a breath. Err on the side of being together. Maybe, Carolyn, the thing to do is, I mean, your Paperwork is complete, we will hold on to it, and maybe Randy, as a concession to Carolyn, you could complete your Paperwork, and we'll hold on to it for you, and when you both decide the time is right, all you have to do is say the word and we will—

I'm going today, Carolyn said. As soon as possible.

And Mr. Dove looked at me and said, Jon, Randy, whoever, are you prepared to go today?

And I said no. Because what is her rush, I was feeling, why is she looking so frantic with furrowed anxious brow like that Claymation chicken at LI 98473, who says the sky is falling the sky is falling and turns out it is only a Dodge Ramcharger, which crushes her from on high and one arm of hers or wing sticks out with a sign that says March Madness Daze?

And Slippen said, Guys, guys, I find this a great pity. You are terrific together. A real love match.

Carolyn was crying now and said, I am so sorry, but if I wait I might change my mind, which I know in my heart would be wrong.

And she thrust her Exit Paperwork across at Mr. Slippen.

Then Dove and Andrews and Delacourt began moving with great speed, as if working directly from some sort of corporate manual, which actually they were, Mr. Dove had some photocopied sheets, and, reading from the sheets, he asked was there anyone with whom she wished to have a fond last private conversation, and she said, Well, duh, and we were both left briefly alone.

She took a deep breath while looking at me all tender and said, Oh Gadzooks. Which that broke my heart, Gadzooks being what we sometimes said at nice privacy moments in our Privacy Tarp when overwhelmed by our good luck in terms of our respective bodies looking so hot and appropriate, Gadzooks being from LI 38492 for Zookers Gum, where the guy blows a bubble so Zookified that it ingests a whole city and the city goes floating up to Mars.

At this point her tears were streaming down and mine also, because up until then I thought we had been so happy.

Jon, please, she said.

I just can't, I said.

And that was true.

So we sat there quiet with her hands against my hands like Colonel Sanders and wife at LI 87345, where he is in jail for refusing to give up the recipe for KFC Haitian MiniBreasts, and then Carolyn said, I didn't mean that thing about the rabbit, and I scrinkled up my nose rabbitlike to make her laugh.

But apparently in the corporate manual there is a time limit on fond last private conversations, because in came Kyle and Blake from Security, and Carolyn kissed me hard, like trying to memorize my mouth, and whispered, Someday come find us.

Then they took her away, or she took them away rather, because she was so far in front they had to like run to keep up as she clomped loudly away in her Kenneth Cole boots, which by the way they did not let her keep those, because that night, selecting my pajamas, I found them back in the Group Closet.

Night after night after that I would lay or lie alone in our Privacy Tarp, which now held only her nail clippers and her former stuffed dog Lefty, and during the days Slippen let me spend many unbillable hours in the much coveted window seat, just scanning some images or multiscanning some images, and around me would be the other facility Boys and Girls, all Assessing, all smiling, because we were still on the twice-a-day Aurabon®, and thinking of Carolyn in those blue scrubs, alone in the Lerner Center, I would apply for some additional Aurabon® via filling out a Work-Affecting Mood-Problem Notification, which Slippen would always approve, because he felt so bad for me.

And the Aurabon® would make things better, as Aurabon® always makes things better, although soon what I found was, when you are hooking in like eight or nine times a day, you are always so happy, and yet it is a kind of happy like chewing on tinfoil, and once you are living for that sort of happy, you soon cannot be happy enough, even when you are very very happy and are even near tears due to the beauty of the round metal hooks used to hang your facility curtains, you feel this intense wish to be even happier, so you tear yourself away from the beautiful curtain hooks, and with shaking happy hands fill out another Work-Affecting Mood-Problem Notification, and then, because nothing in your facility is beautiful enough to look at with your new level of happiness, you sit in the much coveted window seat and start lendelling in this crazy uncontrolled way, calling up, say, the Nike one with the Hanging Gardens of Babylon (LI 89736), and though it is beautiful, it is not beautiful enough, so you scatter around some Delicate Secrets lingerie models from LI 22314, and hang fat Dole oranges and bananas in the trees (LI 76765), and add like a sky full of bright stars from LI 74638 for Crest, and from the Smell Palate supplied by the anti-allergen Capaviv® you fill the air with jasmine and myrrh, but still that is not beautiful enough, so you blink on End and fill out another Work-Affecting Mood-Problem Notification, until finally one day Mr. Dove comes over and says, Randy, Jon, whatever you are calling yourself these days—a couple of items. First, it seems to us that you are in some private space not helpful to you, and so we are cutting back your Aurabon® to twice a day like the other folks, and please do not sit in that window seat anymore, it is hereby forbidden to you, and plus we are going to put you on some additional Project Teams, since it is our view that idle hands are the devil's work area. Also, since you are only one person, it is not fair, we feel, for you to have a whole double Privacy Tarp to yourself, you must, it seems to us, rejoin your fellow Boys in Boys.

So that night I went back with Rudy and Lance and Jason and the others, and they were nice, as they are always nice, and via No. 10 cable Jason shared with me some Still Photos from last year's Christmas party, of Carolyn hugging me from behind with her cute face appearing beneath my armpit, which made me remember how after the party in our Privacy Tarp we played a certain game, which it is none of your beeswax who I was in that game and who she was, only, believe me, that was a memorable night, with us watching the snow fall from the much coveted window seat, in which we sat snuggling around midnight, when we had left our Tarp to take a break for air, and also we were both sort of sore.

Which made it all that much more messed up and sad to be sleeping once again alone in Boys.

When the sliding wall came out to make our Gender Areas, I noticed that they had fixed it so nobody could slide through anymore, via five metal rods. All we could do was, by putting our mouths to the former gap, say good night to the Girls, who all said good night back from their respective Privacy Tarps in this sort of muffled way.

But I did not do that, as I had nobody over there I wished to say good night to, they all being like merely sisters to me, and that was all.

So that was the saddest time of my life thus far for sure.

Then one day we were all laying or lying on our stomachs playing Hungarian Headchopper for GameBoy, a new proposed one where you are this dude with a scythe in your mother's garden, only what your mother grows is heads, when suddenly a shadow was cast over my game by Mr. Slippen, which freaked up my display, and I harvested three unripe heads, but the reason Mr. Slippen was casting his shadow was, he had got a letter for me from Carolyn!

And I was so nervous opening it, and even more nervous after opening it, because inside were these weird like marks I could not read, like someone had hooked a pen to the back leg of a bird and said, Run, little bird, run around this page and I will mail it for you. And the parts I could read were bumming me out even worse, such as she had wrote all sloppenly, Jon a abbot is a cove, a glen, it is something with prayerful guys all the livelong day in silence as they move around they are sure of one thing which is the long-term stability of a product we not only stand behind we run behind since what is wrong with taking a chance even if that chance has horns and hoofs and it is just you and your worst fear in front of ten thousand screaming supporters of your last chance to be the very best you can be?

And then thank God it started again looking like the pen on the foot of the running bird.

I thought of how hot and smart she had looked when doing a crossword with sunglasses on her head in Hilfiger cutoffs, I thought of her that first night in her Privacy Tarp, naked except for her La Perla panties in the light that came from the Exit sign through the thin blue Privacy Tarp, so her flat tummy and not-flat breasts and flirty smile were all blue, and then all of the sudden I felt like the biggest jerk in the world, because why had I let her go? It was like I was all of the sudden waking up! She was mine and I was hers, she was so thin and cute, and now she was at the Lerner Center all alone? Shaking and scared with a bloody hole in her neck and our baby in her belly, hanging out with all those other scared shaking people with bloody holes in their necks, only none of them knew her and loved her like I did? I had done such a dumb-shit thing to her, all the time thinking it was sound reasoning, because isn't that how it is with our heads, when we are in them it always makes sense, but then later, when you look back, we sometimes are like, I am acting like a total dumb-ass!

Then Brad came up and was like, Dude, time to hook in.

And I was like, Please, Brad, do not bother me with that shit at this time.

And I went to get Slippen, only he was at lunch, so I went to get Dove and said, Sir, I hereby Request my appropriate Exit Paperwork.

And he said, Randy, please, you're scaring me, don't act rash, have a look out the window.

I had a look, and tell the truth it did not look that good, such as the Rustic Village Apartments, out of which every morning these bummed-out-looking guys in the plainest non-designer clothes ever would trudge out and get in their junky cars. And was someone joyfully kissing them goodbye, like saying when you come home tonight you will get a big treat, which is me? No, the person who should have been kissing them with joy was yelling, or smoking, or yelling while smoking, and when the dudes came home they would sit on their stoops with heads in hand, as if all day long at work someone had been pounding them with clubs on their heads, saying they were jerks.

Then Dove said, Randy, Randy, why would a talented young person like yourself wish to surrender his influence in the world and become just another lowing cattle in the crowd, don't you know how much people out there look up to you and depend on you?

And that was true. Because sometimes kids from Rustic Village would come over and stand in our lava rocks with our Tastemakers & Trendsetters gum cards upheld, pressing them to our window, and when we would wave to them or strike the pose we were posing on our gum cards, they would race back all happy to their crappy apartments, probably to tell their moms that they had seen the real actual us, which was probably like the high point of their weeks.

But still, when I thought of those birdlike markings of Carolyn's letter, I don't know, something just popped, I felt I was at a distinct tilt, and I blurted out, No, no, just please bring me the freaking Paperwork, I am Requesting, and I thought when I Requested you had to do it!

And Dove said sadly, We do, Randy, when you Request, we have to do it.

Dove called the other Coördinators over and said, Larry, your little pal has just Requested his Paperwork.

And Slippen said, I'll be damned.

What a waste, Delacourt said. This is one super kid.

One of our best, Andrews said.

Which was true, with me five times winning the Coöperative Spirit Award and once even the Denny O'Malley Prize, Denny O'Malley being this Assessor in Chicago, IL, struck down at age ten, who died with a smile on his face of leukemia.

Say what you will, it takes courage, Slippen said. Going after one's wife and all.

Yes and no, Delacourt said. If you, Larry, fall off a roof, does it help me to go tumbling after you?

But I am not your wife, Slippen said. Your pregnant wife.

Wife or no, pregnant or no, Delacourt said. What we then have are two folks not feeling so good in terms of that pavement rushing up. No one is helped. Two are crushed. In effect three are crushed.

Baby makes three, Andrews said.

Although anything is possible, Slippen said. You know, the two of them together, the three of them, maybe they could make a go of it—

Larry, whose side are you on? Dove said.

I am on all sides, Slippen said.

You see this thing from various perspectives, Andrews said.

Anyway, this is academic, Delacourt said. He has Requested his Paperwork and we must provide it.

His poor mother, Dove said. The sacrifices she made, and now this.

Oh, please, Slippen said. His mother.

Larry, sorry, did you say something? Dove said.

Which mother did he get? Slippen said.

Larry, please go to that Taste-and-Rate in Conference Room 6, Delacourt said. See how they are doing with those CheezWands.

Which mother did we give him? Slippen said. The redhead baking the pie? The blonde in the garden?

Larry, honestly, Dove said. Are you freaking out?

The brunette at prayer? Slippen said. Who, putting down her prayer book, says, Stay where you are, do not get distracted, have a content and productive life, and I will be happy too?

Larry has been working too hard, Andrews said.

Plus taking prescription pills not prescribed to him, Delacourt said.

I have just had it with all of this, Slippen said, and stomped off to the Observation Room.

Ha ha, that Larry! Dove said. He did not even know your mom, Randy.

Only we did, Andrews said.

Very nice lady, Delacourt said.

Made terrific pies, Dove said.

And I was like, Do you guys think I am that stupid, I know something is up, because how did Slippen know my mom was a redhead making a pie and how did he know her exact words she said to me on my private Memory Loop?

Then there was this long silence.

And Delacourt said, Randy, when you were a child, you thought as a child. Do you know that one?

And I did know that one, it being LI 88643 for Trojan Ribbed.

Well, you are not a child anymore, he said. You are a man. A man in the middle of making a huge mistake.

We had hoped it would not come to this, Dove said.

Please accompany us to the Facility Cinema, Delacourt said.

So I accompanied them to the Facility Cinema, which was a room off of Dining, with big-screen plasma TV and Pottery Barn leather couch and de-luxe Orville Redenbacher Corn Magician.

Up on the big-screen came this old-fashioned-looking film of a plain young girl with stringy hair, smoking a cigarette in a house that looked pretty bad.

And this guy unseen on the video said, O.K., tell us precisely why, in your own words.

And the girl said, Oh, I dunno, due to my relation with the dad, I got less than great baby interest?

O.K., the unseen voice said. And the money is not part?

Well, sure, yeah, I can always use money, she said.

But it is not the prime reason? the voice said. It being required that it not be the prime reason, but rather the prime reason might be, for example, your desire for a better life for your child?

O.K., she said.

Then they pulled back and you could see bashed-out windows with cardboard in them and the counters covered with dirty dishes and in the yard a car up on blocks.

And you have no objections to the terms and conditions? the voice said. Which you have read in their entirety?

It's all fine, the girl said.

Have you read it? the voice said.

I read in it, she said. O.K., O.K., I read it cover to freaking cover.

And the name change you have no objection to? the voice said.

O.K., she said. Although why Randy?

And the No-Visit Clause you also have no objection to? the voice said.

Fine, she said, and took a big drag.

Then Dove tapped on the wall twice and the movie Paused.

Do you know who that lady is, Randy? he said.

No, I said.

Do you know that lady is your mom? he said.

No, I said.

Well, that lady is your mom, Randy, he said. We are sorry you had to learn it in this manner.

And I was like, Very funny, that is not my mom, my mom is pretty, with red hair in a bun.

Randy, we admit it, Delacourt said. We gave some of you stylized mothers, in your Memory Loops, for your own good, not wanting you to feel bad about who your real mothers were. But in this time of crisis we must give you the straight skinny. That is your real mother, Randy, that is your real former house, that is where you would have been raised had your mother not answered our ad all those years ago, that is who you are. So much in us is hardwired! You cannot fight fate without some significant help from an intervening entity, such as us, such as our resources, which we have poured into you in good faith all these years. You are a prince, we have made you a prince. Please do not descend back into the mud.

Reconsider, Randy, Dove said. Sleep on it.

Will you? Delacourt said. Will you at least sleep on it?

And I said I would.

Because tell the truth that thing with my mom had freaked me out, it was like my foundation had fallen away, like at LI 83743 for Advil, where the guy's foundation of his house falls away and he thunks his head on the floor of Hell and thus needs a Advil, which the Devil has some but won't give him any.

As he left, Dove unhit Pause, and I had time to note many things on that video, such as that lady's teeth were not good, such as my chin and hers were similar, such as she referred to our dog as Shit Machine, which what kind of name was that for a dog, such as at one point they zoomed in on this little baby sitting on the floor in just a diaper, all dirty and looking sort of dumb, and I could see very plain it was me.

Just before Dinner, Dove came back in.

Randy, your Paperwork, per your Request, he said. Do you still want it?

I don't know, I said. I'm not sure.

You are making me very happy, Dove said.

And he sent in Tony from Catering with this intense Dinner of steak au poivre and our usual cheese tray with Alsatian olives, and a milkshake in my monogrammed cup, and while I watched "Sunset Terror Home" on the big-screen, always a favorite, Bedtime passed and nobody came and got me, them letting me stay up as late as I wanted.

Later that night in my Privacy Tarp I was wakened by someone crawling in, and, hitting my Abercrombie & Fitch night-light, I saw it was Slippen.

Randy, I am so sorry for my part in all of this, he whispered. I just want to say you are a great kid and always have been since Day One and in truth I at times have felt you were more of a son than my own personal sons, and likewise with Carolyn, who was the daughter I never had.

I did not know what to say to that, it being so personal and all, plus he was like laying or lying practically right on top of me and I could smell wine on his breath. We had always learned in Religion that if something is making you uncomfortable you should just say it, so I just said it, I said, Sir, this is making me uncomfortable.

You know what is making me uncomfortable? he said. You lying here while poor Carolyn sits in the Lerner Center all alone, big as a house, scared to death. Randy, one only has one heart, and when that heart is breaking via thinking of what is in store for poor Carolyn, one can hardly be blamed for stepping in, can one? Can one? Randy, do you trust me?

He had always been good to me, having taught me so much, like how to hit a Wiffle and how to do a pushup, and once had even brought in this trough and taught me and Ed and Josh to fish, and how fun was that, all of us laughing and feeling around on the floor for the fish we kept dropping during those moments of involuntary blindness that would occur as various fish-related LIs flashed in our heads, like the talking whale for Stouffer's FishMeals (LI 38322), like the fish and loafs Jesus makes at LI 83722 and then that one dude goes, Lord, this bread is dry, can you not summon up some Butter-Sub?

I trust you, I said.

Then come on, he said, and crawled out of my Privacy Tarp.

We crossed the Common Area and went past Catering, which I had never been that far before, and soon were standing in front of this door labelled Caution Do Not Open Without Facility Personnel Accompaniment.

Randy, do you know what is behind this door? Slippen said.

No, I said.

Take a look, he said.

And smiling a smile like that mother on Christmas morning at LI 98732 for Madpets.com, who throws off the tablecloth to reveal a real horse in their living room chewing on the rug, Slippen threw open that door.

Looking out, I saw no walls and no rug and no ceiling, only lawn and flowers, and above that a wide black sky with stars, which all of that made me a little dizzy, there being no glass between me and it.

Then Slippen very gently pushed me out.

And I don't know, it is one thing to look out a window, but when you are Out, actually Out, that is something very powerful, and how embarrassing was that, because I could not help it, I went down flat on my gut, checking out those flowers, and the feeling of the one I chose was like the silk on that Hermès jacket I could never seem to get Reserved because Vance was always hogging it, except the flower was even better, it being very smooth and built in like layers? With the outside layer being yellow, and inside that a white thing like a bell, and inside the white bell-like thing were fifteen (I counted) smaller bell-like red things, and inside each red thing was an even smaller orange two-dingly-thing combo.

Which I was like, Dude, who thought this shit up? And though I knew very well from Religion it was God, still I had never thought so high of God as I did just then, seeing the kind of stuff He could do when He put His or Her mind to it.

Also amazing was, laying there on my gut, I was able to observe very slowly some grass, on a blade basis! And what I found was, each blade is its total own blade, they are not all exact copies as I had always thought when looking at the Rustic Village Apartment lawn from the much coveted window seat, no, each blade had a special design of up-and-down lines on it, plus some blades were wider than others, and some were yellow, with some even having little holes that I guessed had been put there via bugs chewing them?

By now as you know I am sometimes a kidder, with Humor always ranked by my peers as one of my Principal Positives on my Yearly Evaluation, but being totally serious? If I live one million years I will never forget all the beautiful things I saw and experienced in that kickass outside yard.

Isn't it something? Slippen said. But look, stand up, here is something even better.

And I stood up, and here came this bland person in blue scrubs, which my first thought was, Ouch, why not accentuate that killer bone structure with some makeup, and also what is up with that dull flat hair, did you never hear of Bumble & Bumble Plasma Volumizer?

And then she said my name.

Not my name of Randy but my real name of Jon.

Which is how I first got the shock of going, Oh my God, this poor washed-out gal is my Carolyn.

And wow was her belly bigger!

Then she touched my face very tender and said, The suspense of waiting is over and this year's Taurus far exceeds expectations already high in this humble farming community.

And I was like, Carolyn?

And she was like, The beauty of a reunion by the sea of this mother and son will not soon again be parted and all one can say is amen and open another bag of chips, which by spreading on a thin cream on the face strips away the harsh effect of the destructive years.

Then she hugged me, which is when I saw the gaping hole in her neck where her gargadisk had formerly been.

But tell the truth, even with DermaFilled® neckhole and nada makeup and huge baby belly, still she looked so pretty, it was like someone had put a light inside her and switched it on.

But I guess it is true what they say at LI 23005, life is full of ironic surprises, where that lady in a bikini puts on sunscreen and then there is this nuclear war and she takes a sip of her drink only she has been like burned to a crisp, because all that time Out not one LI had come up, as if my mind was stymied or holding its breath, but now all of the sudden here came all these LIs of Flowers, due to I had seen those real-life flowers, such as talking daisies for Polaroid (LI 101119), such as that kid who drops a jar of applesauce but his anal mom totally melts when he hands her a sunflower (LI 22365), such as the big word PFIZER that as you pan closer is made of roses (LI 88753), such as LI 73486, where as you fly over wildflowers to a Acura Legend on a cliff the announcer goes, Everyone is entitled to their own individual promised land.

And I blinked on Pause but it did not Pause, and blinked on End but it did not End.

Then up came LIs of Grass, due to I had seen that lawn, such as an old guy sprinkling grass seed while repetitively checking out his neighbor girl who is sunbathing, and then in spring he only has grass in that one spot (LI 11121), such as LI 76567, with a sweeping lawn leading up to a mansion for Grey Poupon, such as (LI 00391) these grass blades screaming in terror as this lawnmower approaches but then when they see it is a Toro they put on little party hats.

Randy, can you hear me? Slippen said. Do you see Carolyn? She has been waiting out here an hour. During that hour she has been going where she wants, looking at whatever she likes. See what she is doing now? Simply enjoying the night.

And that was true. Between flinches and blinks on End I could dimly persee her sitting cross-legged near me, not flinching, not blinking, just looking pretty in the moonlight with a look on her face of deep concern for me.

Randy, this could all be yours, Slippen was saying. This world, this girl!

And then I must have passed out.

Because when I came to I was sitting inside that door marked Caution Do Not Open Without Facility Personnel Accompaniment, with my Paperwork in my lap and all my Coördinators standing around me.

Randy, Dove said. Larry Slippen here claims that you wish to Exit. Is this the case? Did you in fact Request your Paperwork, then thrust it at him?

O.K., I said. Yes.

So they rushed me to Removals, where this nurse Vivian was like, Welcome, please step behind that screen and strip off, then put these on.

Which I did, I dropped my Calvin Klein khakis and socks and removed my Country Road shirt as well as my Old Navy boxers, and put on the dreaded blue scrubs.

Best of luck, Randy, Slippen said, leaning in the door. You'll be fine.

Out out out, Vivian said.

Then she gave me this Patient Permission Form, which the first question was, Is patient aware of risk of significantly reduced postoperative brain function?

And I wrote, Yes.

And then it said, Does patient authorize Dr. Edward Kenton to perform all procedures associated with a complete gargadisk removal, including but not limited to e-wire severance, scar-tissue removal, forceful Kinney Maneuver (if necessary to fully disengage gargadisk), suturing, and postoperative cleansing using the Foreman Vacuum Device, should adequate cleaning not be achievable via traditional methods?

And I wrote, Yes.

I have been here since Wednesday, due to Dr. Kenton is at a wedding.

I want to thank Vivian for all this paper, and Mr. Slippen for being the father I never had, and Carolyn for not giving up on me, and Dr. Kenton, assuming he does not screw it up.

(Ha ha, you know, Dr. Kenton, I am just messing with you, even if you do screw it up, I know you tried your best. Only please do not screw it up, ha ha ha!)

Last night they let Carolyn send me a fax from the Lerner Center, and it said, I may not look my best or be the smartest apple on the applecart but, believe me, in time I will again bake those ninety-two pies.

And I faxed back, However you are is fine with me, I will see you soon, look for me, I will be the one with the ripped-up neck, smacking himself in the head!

No matter what, she faxed, at least we will now have a life, that life dreamed of by so many, living in freedom with all joys and all fears, bring it on, I say, the balloon of our excitement will go up up up, to that land which is the land of true living, we will not be denied!

I love you, I wrote.

I love you too, she wrote.

Which I thought that was pretty good, it being so simple and all, and it gave me hope.

Because maybe we can do it.

Maybe we can come to be normal, and sit on our porch at night, the porch of our own house, like at LI 87326, where the mom knits and the dad plays guitar and the little kid works very industrious with his Speak & Spell, and when we talk, it will make total sense, and when we look at the stars and moon, if choosing to do that, we will not think of LI 44387, where the moon frowns down at this dude due to he is hiding in his barn eating Rebel CornBells instead of proclaiming his SnackLove aloud, we will not think of LI 09383, where this stork flies through some crying stars who are crying due to the baby who is getting born is the future Mountain Dew Guy, we will not think of that alien at LI 33081 descending from the sky going, Just what is this thing called a Cinnabon?

In terms of what we will think of, I do not know. When I think of what we will think of, I draw this like total blank and get scared, so scared my Peripheral Area flares up green, like when I have drank too much soda, but tell the truth I am curious, I think I am ready to try.

Saunders on Humor and Audience Concerns

While writing a story, I don't think much about plot, theme, conflict, audience, setting, et cetera. Those things make me too nervous. Instead, I simply try not to be dull. I've found that if I can do this—avoid dullness—all other concerns are addressed.

How to avoid dullness? One approach is to make sure you don't know what's going on. Take all of your ideas about What My Story Means, and Why I'm Writing This, and The Secret Thing About Humanity I Am Wisely Demonstrating Here—and lose them. Go down to the sentence level and ask yourself: If I was not the Writer, but the Reader, would I keep going? The thing that drives me through a story, generally, is language: Trying to come up with sentences that don't sound workmanlike or average. This is not everyone's approach—but it is mine. It's really the only way I know how to do it.

For me, it's also important to be entertaining: to be surprising, and funny if possible, to make the reader sort of light up inside.

In this way, writing is, perhaps, not far from simple personal charm. If you were trying hard to make someone like you, and you liked them very much, what would you say and do, how would you behave? In a sense, literary style has to do with bringing your best self forward, albeit in a formal and polished way.

To me, that is what editing and revision are all about. Taking the story from early-draft form (which sounds like other people, and has dull corners, and is somehow predictable) to late-draft form (which, hopefully, sounds more like you, and has gone in directions you couldn't have imagined when you first started) involves making and remaking hundreds of choices. I have sometimes heard this approach called "lapidary," which means either "having to do with polishing a rock" or "the feeling of having a camel in your lap." I think and sincerely hope it means the first.

At any rate, revision is basically the process of having strong opinions and imposing these on your story, on a line-by-line basis. It's important, I think, to let go of what you did yesterday. Yesterday, a paragraph may have seemed perfect and undeniable—but the great writers I know are able to forget yesterday and see how they feel about the paragraph today. They are not, in other words, attached to what they've already done. They are only interested in making the story the best it can be.

Rewriting involves an almost psychotic level of obsessiveness and repetitiousness, at least in my experience: Going through the story over and over again, even hundreds of times, to see if there might be any last shred of power to be had.

In this way, the best bits (the least dull bits, the most compelling bits) stick around, while the lesser bits—the bits that aren't you—tend to get cut.

Over time, your piece will come to sound more and more like you, and your story will get deeper and deeper. The level of Writerly Manipulation (i.e., cheap tricks) drops. The story becomes more natural, more believable, and seems to be churning up richer, more ambiguous, ground.

Also—strangely, maybe—the story's vision of humanity becomes, if not happier, then at least more generous, more fair: story Evil becomes more like real Evil, story-Good becomes more like real Good.

The best stories come, I think, not from the precise execution of some preconceived intent, but from prolonged goofing around with some basic material the writer initially found interesting, sometimes for the most trivial, personal reasons. In my case, I'll write down a few lines that interest me—a certain way of talking, maybe, a description of some odd setting, just a nicely compressed sentence—and then this sort of seed-crystal phenomenon occurs: other paragraphs appear before and after the "seed," things start getting moved around for logic—and soon, something we might call "plot" appears. That is, something starts to matter. Someone is in trouble, or is wanting something. The story suddenly has momentum. Its level of randomness has dropped.

My approach also often involves letting several unrelated elements come freely into the story, for no other reason than that they present themselves to me at the time. In the case of "Jon," which you have either just read, or are about to read, or have decided to skip altogether because of this long-winded discussion, some of these disparate elements were:

A Student Paper

I was grading some student papers about Kafka's "The Metamorphosis," which one particular student didn't like a bit. In his paper was the line, "Upon the reading of this fiction, suddenly I felt at a distinct tilt." I thought: Well, that's vivid. And I was struck by this idea: that even the oddest diction can be overflowed. A working-class diction, a Valley Girl diction, corporate diction—as long as there is a thinking, feeling, human being on the speaking side of it, a diction can be overflowed. That is, it can be made to express genuine emotion.

So, having discovered a little fragment of this new language (which I heard as part advertising, part demagogue, part surfer, part I-typed-this-paper-the-night-before-and-didn't-bother-to-read-it-afterwards), I tried to tell a whole story using it, and in this way, find out why the person speaking it (Jon) was speaking that way.

A Literary Reading

I had just done a reading of one of my stories at *The New Yorker* Fest, and something about the extreme panic I felt while reading that story (which was in a sort of restrained and clipped voice) made me want to write something over-the-top and reckless, so that, the next time I did a reading, I would have something crazed and flamboyant to read, and wouldn't feel at all nervous, and would sort of float above the crowd, intoning this wild language, being admired and loved by all.

Funny thing was, I read "Jon" at *The New Yorker* Fest last year, and felt equally panicked, this time because the language was so crazed and spastic. I did not float above the room, after all, but only stood on the floor as usual, sweaty and red-faced, feeling unadmired and unloved.

Guinea Pigs

My daughter had a guinea pig, which we acquired as a pup, or a calf, whatever—a baby. We were assured this was a very new baby. Maybe it was, but it was also, turns out, a pregnant baby, who soon was a tiny little mother giving birth as we all watched, making faces and sounds I can't even describe to you. So then we had four guinea pigs. We really hadn't even wanted the first one that much, so we were troubled. We grew even more troubled when we learned that guinea pigs—even true baby guinea pigs, who had just been born, like two days before—are almost instantly romantic, and in every direction at once, even towards their own mothers. In addition to troubled, this made us a little nauseous. So I separated them by gender, two pigs in one cage, two in the other. Every day, as I fed them and gave them fresh water, I would find the boys and girls looking over at one another with longing. Often they were desperately sniffing one another's snouts through the bars, like a pathetic form of kissing. This made me feel sad but also, perversely, kind of powerful and God-like. They would never have sex, I knew, unless I really messed up.

Which I have not done, so far, by the way.

They are still down there, in the basement, filled with longing, settling for the occasional carrot.

So all this found its way into the story too, in the form of the Gender Areas, and the stern cruelty of Facility Management.

Something I Saw on TV

I saw a show on TV that explained how MTV does its market research: They go into the house of an "average teen"—and this means he/she should be neither too hot, nor too smart, nor too cool, nor too popular—and inventory every mediocre thing he/she owns, while the poor shmuck stands there pathetically watching, smiling all brace-mouthed, hoping MTV will approve of something. MTV also convenes "peer retreats," during which they quiz other "average teens" on how much they like or dislike certain products, bands, et cetera. This struck me as sinister. Why not do it the old-fashioned way, where somebody makes something (a song, a dress, a movie) and sends it out to the world, and the world hates it or loves it, and the creator either moves to Malibu or begs for his old job at the car wash?

So this found its way into the story in the form of the place where Jon works.

My Own Marriage

My wife is smarter than I am and sees things way before I do. She understands what life is about long before I do and has the vision to do what she thinks is right. So when Jon suddenly had a girlfriend, and then suddenly had a wife, and was in need of a particular wife, my wife made her way into the story, in Carolyn's superior intelligence and the way Jon is insanely in love with her.

My wife, by the way, likes this story very much.

But I would like to reiterate: None of this was thought-out, or planned in advance. I didn't "decide" on these elements. They just pushed their way in, a little at a time, as I was writing. While writing, I was just trying to avoid being dull, while staying in that voice. It was a long, slow process, over about three years. What decisions were made were, mostly, visceral, on-the-spot, based on how the story was reading line-to-line. At one point the story was a little novel, 130 pages or so. But I found that, at what was then about page 34, I was always either 1) nodding off, 2) getting up for coffee, or 3) going on an errand (such as drifting downstairs to watch the guinea pigs stare at one another in horny awe). Then, one day, I woke up to find myself literally drooling on page 34, and that was it: I cut the story back to its present length.

The wonderful thing is that this process of going over and over a piece, making those hundreds (thousands?) of decisions, in time leads to a story that is a deeply personal one. For example, my wife and I are Buddhists, and one of the Buddhist ideas I find most interesting is: We are not our thoughts. Our thoughts, in fact, can be a form of slavery. This found its way into the story, and I was very surprised to see it there.

Also, this is the story I was in the middle of on September 11. In the months that followed, like many writers, I was at a loss as to what possible use literature could be in the face of such grief and sadness. But I kept working, out of habit maybe, or faith. And I think the horror of that event, and the resulting dark political time our country experienced—a short-sighted time, of fear and aggression, in my view—made its way into the story, too. In the end, what I concluded, in my life, is what Jon concluded in his: Our first responsibility is to make ourselves free. Free from fear, but also free from the need to harm others. Free from propaganda, free from agenda-laden thoughts imposed on us by others. There is something pure and luminous at the core of us human beings, but we can only get there by thinking freely, using our intuitive wisdom to explore and celebrate that most precious thing: our own mind.

I very much enjoyed writing "Jon," I and hope you get some pleasure from it, too.

Writing Suggestions

1. In one long paragraph describe an activity that you've done repeatedly (riding a bike, making a club sandwich), focusing only on the physical details of this experience. In a second long paragraph, describe an activity that you've never done but have often wanted to do (skydiving, hunting for lions), again focusing on the physical details of this experience. Through imagination or research, how can you create details in the second paragraph that are as convincing and authoritative as those in the first? Read the two paragraphs aloud to friends or classmates. Can they tell which paragraph is imagined and which is based on personal experience? (Variation: Describe an activity that doesn't actually exist—such as those the characters from "Jon" engage in—and develop the details to a point where they appear authentic.)

2. Develop a story that in some way explains your generation's attitude toward life. Like George Saunders, gather ideas from various sources. Consider: reality TV, *Cosmopolitan*, *Esquire*, MTV, Top 40 music, summer blockbuster movies, news stories, advertisements, clothes, body image, etc. Look at people your age and notice conflicts and tensions that might help shape this story. How can you develop a piece of fiction that—in addition to being compelling and engaging—also translates your generation's experience for others?

3. Recall a story you've written (perhaps didn't even finish) that never quite came to life on the page. Without looking back at the story, rewrite the first page from memory. What specifically do you remember from that original first page? What details shimmer and make themselves memorable? After finishing this one-page memory rewrite, locate the original and compare the two drafts. In both versions, look for "dull" or uninteresting details around those that shimmer. How can you make some of the "dull" details more specific, more interesting, or more compelling? In your story, what will keep readers wanting to read from one sentence to the next? (Variation:

Try this technique with story endings or the climax of a story. See which parts of those scenes remain most memorable. Perhaps after a new draft, a third—better—draft will emerge.)

4. In your local library or bookstore, find a collection of stories by George Saunders. Read any story that catches your eye. How does Saunders use fiction to provide social commentary on contemporary culture? What does "Jon" say about western culture, life in America, and the relationships between individuals and corporations? Which of these topics would you like to address in your own fiction?

> *A character has to want something to be worth writing about.*
> *I think the relationship between what they want and what they*
> *get is pretty complicated. [Milan] Kundera talks about this—*
> *the complicated nature of action. You're trying for something and*
> *you reach for it, and in the course of reaching for it, you get*
> *something entirely different.*
> —Kevin Canty

Section 11

⌒

THEME, MEANING, AND VISION

Mary Gaitskill

A Bestial Noise

From *Tin House*

Elizabeth woke too early again on Saturday morning. She sat up, opened the curtains and looked out. It was a bright day in early spring. The branches of the maple tree in the front yard were shocking against the white house across the street. Beyond the white house were fir trees and soft blue sky. Each thing—tree, house, fir trees, sky—was defined and distinct according to the elegant and beautiful character of this planet. But to Elizabeth they seemed undifferentiated: a single vast organism breathing slowly and deeply outside her window, as dense as her own body, full of tissue, blood, bones, all the tiny things you can't see that keep everything going. She felt like a space traveler staring out of her capsule, an invader blind to her own world. She closed the curtain.

Elizabeth was pregnant. She was only six weeks pregnant but still she felt it powerfully. She felt like an hourglass being crazily tipped back and forth, except instead of sand the glass was filled with homunculi, all screaming and clawing and holding each other for balance—some bravely trying to assist the others—as the glass swung top to bottom. She was 42 years old and she had not expected to get pregnant. For most of her life she hadn't wanted it, not one bit. There were certain terrible moments when she wasn't even sure she wanted it now, and this morning was turning into one of those moments.

It was as if there was a tiny, faceted sensor in her brain that stored terrible information where she wouldn't have to think about it—except that her unstable system had triggered an alarm and the sensor had gone crazy, sending an unbroken shriek of warning in the form of grotesque images, each surging into each other with the sickening truth of dreams:

A starving polar bear collapsed on its side, so emaciated it looked more like a dog than a bear. The sun had gotten too hot too fast and melted the ice it hunted on. It lifted its head and let it fall again. Five-year-old girls grew breasts and pubic hair because of pesticides that mimicked estrogen. Parents gave them drugs that produced symptoms of menopause and then had to take them to therapy in order to cope with their emotions.

Millions of Africans died of AIDS, leaving millions of orphaned children. A magazine printed a photograph of a dying African woman. She lay in an empty room on a cot covered by a piece of cloth. Her skeletal body was exhausted by its slow descent through layers of suffering, and her eyes stared up from the pit. But her spirit came up through her eyes in full force. Her spirit was soft and it was powerful, and it could hold her suffering, and it would stay with her until she fell into darkness.

Thousands of Americans died of AIDS too. They also died of diet drugs, liposuction and anorexia. Their pictures were in a magazine too. They were smiling from wedding photos, school yearbooks, family albums. Their eyes were bright with happiness and want, one woman looked nearly out of her mind with happiness and wanting of more of it, and terror of being without it. "I'd rather die than be fat!" cried a nineteen-year-old anorexic. And then she died.

Elizabeth's heart pounded. She groped over her night table for the packet of crackers she kept there to calm her stomach. The salty biscuit was dry in her mouth, and she had drunk the water she had put on the table the night before. Muttering irritably, she rolled from bed and went to the bathroom to drink from the tap. She bent over the sink and slurped the cold, faintly metallic water running sideways into her mouth, visually tinged with the tiny toothpaste flecks on the faucet.

She remembered the first time he had said it: "I want to make you pregnant." They were fucking, and the words opened a scalding pit in her imagination. He wanted to see her breasts swell with milk, he wanted to feel her giant belly from behind. She pictured herself swelling, straining until her body showed its fleshy seam, slowly bursting, screaming as she broke open. Her mind abject before her body, her words dissolved, her personality irrelevant. They had made it a fantasy of abjection, sometimes his, sometimes hers. They made sounds of pretend abjection, grunts and bestial moans, making fun and playing. Except that something earnest and yearning started creeping into the sounds, then something fierce, like a roar—and then it had happened for real.

She stood and wiped her mouth. She imagined an ice plant growing over the ground with impossible speed, its fleshy leaves glistening with vesicles, growing hungrily and busily, devouring the earth and feeding it too. It was a signal from another part of her brain, saying, "But wait! Look at this!" She pictured Matt pointing at the ice plant and giving a roar of triumph and solidarity. "It grow!" he would roar. "Life good!" She would roar back, they would crouch down with their legs apart, raise up their fists and jump around roaring. They did this when they were happy and excited; they did it a lot. If they were in public, and couldn't roar, they instead made faces of bestial satiety and uttered quiet grunts of affirmation.

She grunted to herself as she turned off the water and left the room. She thought of going to Matt's room to get under the covers with him and decided she wanted a snack first. She put on her thick socks and went downstairs. The curtains were still drawn so the house was dim and a little cold. She put on the tea kettle and looked into the refrigerator. She had been thinking bread and cheese, but when she saw the tin-foiled remains of the Chinese food they'd had the night before—crispy Peking duck!—she began to salivate. She took out the container and peeled back the tin-foil; the crisp, fatty meat was irresistible. She got herself a glass of cranberry juice for sweetness, poured salt on the meat and sat at the kitchen table eating crispy duck with her fingers in a trance of pleasure. She felt like she had when she was eight years old and had for some reason come home from school a few hours early and found that her mother wasn't home. Because she was alone, she got a chicken drumstick from the fridge, salted it and ate it while watching cartoons on TV. It was a wonderful sensation of independence and solitude and salt.

Then came her family, crashing in. Her father a boiling tumbleweed, her mother a wet amoebae of love, her sister a geyser of pain squeezed off with a tourniquet of madness and will. When people asked her to describe her family she said, "They're like people who've been sent on a camping trip with a tent and no stakes." What she meant was, there wasn't anything wrong with them; she always thought that if they could be placed in a more congenial environment—say, in another solar system where they would not be bound by the personality requirements and bodily structure of human beings, they would do extraordinarily well. Somewhere, for example, where you didn't need a tent.

She especially thought this of her sister Angela: a beauty at nine, with a tender mouth and huge gray eyes full of gravity and joy, she was obese by age fifteen, with the affect-less face of a wood totem. The story Elizabeth always told: When Angela was in high school, a psychologist came to visit her science class in order to demonstrate psychology to them. He gave each student a deck of cards and told them to arrange them in a pattern, so that he could explain what the patterns meant at the end of the exercise. He went around the class, analyzing everyone according to their card pattern. When he came to Angela, he stood and frowned. "What did you do?" he asked her. She could not tell him. He re-shuffled her cards and told her to do it again. She did, repeating the pattern. He shook his head. "I have never seen anything like that before," he said, and then went on to the next student. The teacher made a face. "It figures," she said.

The physical flavor of crispy duck ran together with the emotional flavor of her sister and her handful of unwanted cards; pain with sweetness. Memories came to her like several different tastes all at once, hard to sort. She remembered lying on the thin maize carpet of her childhood home, feeling the furnace make the floor hum slightly as the warmth came up through it. It was like feeling her mother's body through her sweater. One Thousand and One Strings was playing on the stereo. Listening to One Thousand and One Strings felt like flying through a peaceful sky filled with light, limitless yet absolutely safe. It made you picture everything moving outwards in an endless, revelatory triumph. She put her face down eye-level with the floor; the small house grew vast, and the thin maize carpet became a happy traveler, live as a rippling field in a Technicolor movie, rambling through the bedrooms, the living room, Daddy's private room. The music was all smooth, like pudding in the mouth, and the carpet was rough and nubbly, with bare patches and lumps under the legs of Grandmother's table.

She got up on the couch and lay against Mama. Mama was rough and nubbly too, with tiny watery noises in her stomach, and secret voices all trying to talk to Elizabeth while Mama listened to music and read her magazine. Her mother didn't know about the voices, even though they were hers. They said things without words, and because we live in a world of words, nobody listened and because nobody listened Mama forgot about them herself. But Elizabeth was new in the world of words; she had recently come out of her mother's body, and she couldn't help but listen. The voices saw this, and they reached for her.

Some of the voices were sad and scared. Others were gentle and intrepid as the sky in One Thousand and One Strings. Some were all rage, like a flailing ax, rage at everything, including Elizabeth. Others were delighted and loving, like children themselves, wanting to play. Some were a hole of need, a hole made of sucking, tactile voices that clutched at Elizabeth and tried and pull her in. Elizabeth was afraid of the voices; they were a tangled knot she did not want to get lost in. So she went past them, whistling and looking straight ahead like a traveler in a haunted place. She sent her attention further down, searching for the solid thing underneath them all; her mother's furnace, running deep inside her, sending warmth and power and blind, muscular love.

Elizabeth sat in her cold kitchen, six weeks pregnant with a faint acrid nausea in her mouth. She heard another voice, a voice inside her now, the sound of her sister screaming. Angela had screamed at night and was told to shut up, to stop being a baby. They did not realize that she had spinal meningitis. When they finally did realize it, they took Angela to the hospital, where she screamed for Mama not to leave while Mama waved good-bye.

Now Angela was thirty-eight, and her voice sounded like a scream had gotten stuck in it. It was jagged and too bright except when it sounded half-dead. She'd been on welfare since she'd gotten fired from a chain pharmacy for stealing drugs, moving from one SRO hotel to the next. She came in and out of their lives like a figure in a dream, calling from pay phones to ask for money. Except for the previous year, when she had been hospitalized after a stroke bashed in one side of her face and made her walk with a limp. Then they knew where she was, and went to visit her. Their mother tried to get Angela to come live with her but Angela said she preferred her freedom.

Angela had been overjoyed to hear that Elizabeth was pregnant. "I think it's really going to ground you," she said. Then she paused and Elizabeth heard her through the pay phone, working for breath after the long sentence.

"She didn't feel the furnace," thought Elizabeth. "That was the problem. She got lost."

She put away the food and headed up the stairs to Matt's room.

Probably their friends wondered about their having separate bedrooms; possibly some of the married ones envied the arrangement. It had been a condition of their moving in together, and Elizabeth was grateful to Matt for understanding, even sharing her special need to not have his corporeal reality pressed upon her at all times. Of course, this special need would be literally pissed on by the approaching infant, who would soon—again, literally—be pressed upon her at all times *starting from the inside*. Her first feeling about this was one of soft, blind opening, like a viscous plant efflorescing in a nature show. Then the hourglass tipped. She felt lost in the middle of her mother's voices, except they were her voices now, a winding knot that she could not sort, yelling one thing, then another.

She opened Matt's door; he was still asleep, she could tell even though he was faced away from her towards the wall. She crouched on the floor with her hands planted in front of her and made a monster face. They liked to do that: sneak up, crouch, make a face and wait for the other person to see. She waited. He stirred but he didn't turn. She uttered a soft guttural sigh. You could deliver a baby squatting on the floor. You could fuck that way too, and once they had, him behind her. He'd said, "Do you want a baby? Do you want a baby?" and there was the scalding pit. She made a noise like a cow with a hot ass. She was joking, but she was liking it too. She pictured a woman kneeling with her butt in the air, her face dissolved in want, bellowing, "just give me a baby!" All the middle-aged, Pilates-trained, surgically-enhanced, middle-aged women progressing in their therapy and loaded with fertility drugs, finally letting it all out. The queen throwing her fit. She bellowed like a cow with a crown on its head, charging through the forest.

She emitted a sultry little noise at Matt's sleeping form. He lifted his head and turned, an affable dog with rumpled skin and sleepy eyes, answering her with his own noise, a doggish question mark on the end of it. She came off the floor and into the bed, under the covers with their chests touching. Even half asleep, his body was busy with the sniffing, scratching, licking, proudly trotting energy of a loyal pack animal.

"Matt," she asked, "do you remember Elsie the cow?"

"Sort of. What was she?"

"The cow on the cartons of milk. She had big soft eyes and she wore a crown." Mama took the milk in from the chute in the kitchen where the milk man delivered it for breakfast. A slur of Mama in her flannel robe, moving in the kitchen.

"She didn't have a crown," said Matt. "I remember. She wore a garland of flowers." He paused. "Her husband was Murgatroid the bull."

He ran his hand down her body, slipping it into her pajama bottoms to feel the rough hair on her crotch.

"I'm in a horrible mood," she said.

He hesitated, then withdrew his hand.

"I feel like we're living in an enemy world," she said. "Or I am anyway."

"Enemy world how?"

"I'm thinking about Angela. How she was destroyed by the world."

"She isn't destroyed. We just talked to her."

"She's destroyed."

"She's homeless. She's not destroyed."

"Oh come on!."

"Anyway, you aren't Angela."

"But I'm like her."

"No, you're not. You have friends and you're able to—"

"I don't really have friends. I'm able to perform socially better than Angela. I understand the codes better. I know the ways you're supposed to arrange the cards." Matt of course had heard the story.

"What about Liane?"

"Liane? Are you kidding?"

"Well, she was your friend for awhile."

"But she turned on me." She was vomiting self-pity, and she couldn't stop it; the hourglass had turned into a carnival ride where they spin you upside-down and then make you hang there. Besides, it was true! "People are always turning on me. I've never had a real friend except Doreen, and she's in Texas. And anyway, she's crazy."

"People turn on each other," said Matt. "I've turned on people, so have you."

"I know," she said. "That's what I mean. The world is so ugly. I feel like I'm another species, like my whole family is another species and now I'm creating another one. Why? They killed my father and they're killing my sister, and those fuckers at the office would kill me if they could. In a primitive society, they'd stone me. Why would a baby want to be here?"

The ride flipped around again and everyone screamed. Matt was sitting up looking like a concerned middle-aged man who'd never made a bestial noise in his life.

"Beth," he said. "Your dad died of cancer and Angela, well, if she wants to kill herself, that's her choice. And what are you talking about, the people in the office? You were really liking them last week."

How to explain? She did like them, even Liane who had last month joined forces with the bitch who'd tried to get her fired. Just last week she had sat in a meeting looking at them all in wonderment; it seemed as if their discontented, ironic personalities were flimsy costumes they could barely keep in place, and that she could see beneath the absurd make-up and false noses just enough to intuit the innocence and strangeness flashing, deer-like, beneath. Even the sweet personalities seemed a garish imitation of the real, the hidden sweetness she could sense the way she had sensed her mother's purring furnace.

But now they just seemed like pigs. Even worse, it seemed like they were deliberately choosing to turn themselves into pigs made of complex masking, with entire layers made of barbed-wire and booby traps, anything to hide and pervert the tender thing beneath.

"Your co-workers are not going to stone you. You're too tough and besides, you're pregnant—once they know that, they'll cut you a lot of slack."

"Yeah, you're probably right. It'll all get better when they can ID me as one more stupid cow." She stood up. "Just a minute."

Quickly, she went back down the hall to the bathroom. A light sweat broke on her forehead as she knelt before the toilet. She lifted the lid, leaned forward and puked. When she and Angela were little and they got sick, Mama would sit with them and stroke their backs while they puked into a yellow bucket. There were no crazy voices, just her strong, warm hand. Elizabeth's mind followed the example of her mother's hand, and was gentle with her puking body.

When she was finished she felt calm, dense and heavy. She rinsed her mouth and sat on the edge of the tub. She pictured a dense, heavy demon, a creature of flesh and stone, sitting with its chin in its hand. She imagined herself inside it, the whole room inside it. Matt was there too, in another room. Somewhere in it was the office and everybody that worked there, somewhere else was her mother, making tea and watching television. They might be in the liver section, where they were saturated with bitterness and bile, or they might be near the heart, saturated with the tremendous, singing energy of blood. Wherever they lived, they went about their lives, amid the inner organs of the demon. Outside, something else was happening, but that's not where they were.

"Earth," she thought. "Physical life."

She pictured her child, the size of a fingernail, deep in her own demon body. She pictured him questing through it, as if through a living mountain, guided by a strand of gossamer, finding his way out.

She went back to the bedroom and sat on the bed.

"I'm sorry," she said. "I know I'm being weird."

"Well," he said, "I was sort of wondering. Do you want to kill them?"

"Who?"

"Like the people at work. Anybody, everybody."

"No," she said. "I don't want to kill them. But I'd like to replace them."

"With what?"

"I don't know." She considered a moment. "Maybe cartoons?"

He threw back his head and laughed, and she loved him laughing, as if her self-pity were a cartoon with a wonderful character that you liked no matter what. Now she was only half in the mucky rich inside of the demon and half in a place of light and shimmering particles. She shifted back and forth between the two places, enjoying both of them. She pictured their child, age two or three, sitting in a sunny room, rubbing both hands in finger paints, palms down, smearing the heavy paper with wonderful purple and red mud. He would like the mucky richness too. Or maybe not. He might be finicky and ethereal, all light and surface. He might think she was gross! She smiled and got under the blankets with Matt. They put their arms around each other, and each sensitive hair of her personality extended to feel each sensitive hair of his.

"What kind of cartoons?" he asked.

"I don't know. Something nice for him to play with."

"Maybe Pokemon?"

"Yeah. Maybe those."

Matt put his hand on her belly. She put her hand on his; they made soft lowing noises of herd animal recognition. She tried to recall the ice plant, but instead she got pictures of the people who'd died of diet drugs or liposuction, their eyes wanting more and starving to get it. They were made to want like the plants were made to grow. Their want was as persistent as roots through concrete, twisting and turning, finding every way to want and every way to satisfy and then wanting again. It suddenly seemed to her that if you untwisted the want, you would see a different version of the growing. If one was terrible, so was the other. Her father used to say "I hate nature. Nature is trying to kill us, and if we didn't fight it twenty-four hours a day, it would kill us. I wish they could just pave the whole damn thing over so all you'd have to do would be hose it down every once in awhile." She smiled; her father had been funny.

"You know," said Matt. "I wouldn't blame you if you did want to kill people. I think it's pretty normal. I was thinking of killing Ted Agrew just last night."

"Who's he?"

Matt produced plays in a small theater, and the people he worked with came and went.

"The director of that company, Blue Bug. You met him, he wears ridiculous glasses and he tells horrible sex stories, like dogs ejaculating on women's faces and stuff."

"Oh, yeah."

"I imagined coming up behind him and stabbing him in the back of the neck with an ice pick."

"You couldn't do that, Matt, you're too short."

"I could too!" He sat up and made the face of a retarded psychopath, one hand clutching an imaginary ice pick. "Like this!"

They laughed and pressed against each other. But this time the closeness agitated instead of comforting her, and she pulled away.

"The thing about Angela." She frowned and lay on her back. "My parents always said she was a cry-baby, and she was. But it was like, it was like she wasn't wired like everybody else and so they couldn't help her grow up. Because she couldn't receive their signals."

"Ummm!"

"That's what I mean about enemy world. Not that people are actively trying to kill her. Just that they can't recognize what she has and so it's rotting. Like Africa. It's so beautiful and it's spirit is so big. And it doesn't do any good. It's dying anyway. Because the world doesn't know that spirit anymore."

They were quiet a moment. The heat came on and the vent behind Matt's bed began to ping and tick. Elizabeth considered all the things that worked without thinking; machines, plants, bacteria, bugs, the hearts of mammals. She pictured a vending machine: a waxed paper cup rattling into place and thin, sugary hot chocolate streaming into it.

"I feel it too sometimes," said Matt, "the enemy world thing. In a different way. I feel like a small tugboat chugging through hostile waters. I cast my search light up on the hill—and there's Ted Agrew's smirking face, illuminated and staring down."

"But people aren't your enemy," said Elizabeth. "People like you. You don't have these alien feelers coming out of your forehead. You have this earthy thing that makes them feel safe. They don't realize you want to stab them in the neck with an ice pick."

"Then the baby will have it too. He'll have that and the feelers. He'll have everything. And as soon as he's old enough, we'll send him to African dance class so he'll find out about African spirit."

"But it won't help if *he* knows about it, that's not the point. The world is killing Africa. It doesn't care about the dances."

Matt sighed. "You're just being self-indulgent now. The world is not killing Africa."

"But it is! That's what I'm saying. The climate that has been created by other cultures is antithetical to the spirit of Africa. Africa is being spiritually suffocated. That's why they're getting AIDS and having those wars."

"Okay," said Matt. "Okay. We'll arm the house like the Swiss Family Robinson and stay in."

"Then they'd just get us for being crazy."

Matt was silent for so long that she thought he might be fed up. She considered apologizing, but she was suddenly too tired. A cloud covered the sun; the room became soft and dim. Matt put his hand on her stomach. He sang: "Roses love sunshine/Violets love dew/Angels in heaven/Know I love you." He kept singing, except instead of words he sang soft little syllables: "ma ma ma MA ma—"

Tenderness opened inside her with erotic force. It was impossible to close herself to it. Strangely, she thought of her co-worker and former friend, the treacherous Liane. She thought of her asleep, her ovaries cycling through, making blood and eggs while her head dreamed, innocent of treachery. She thought of her own body building flesh and bone, tiny nails and teeth and an unknowable, electrical brain. She pictured Angela, holding her arms up like she was calling something down from the sky. The hair on Elizabeth's arm stood up. The eye on the collapsed side of her sister's face looked out as if from a secret, exalted place. She was calling all her hidden power from the world beyond the stroke to bless her sister's baby.

The cloud moved off the sun and a pool of light spilled across the floor, full of trembling shadows: nervous little branches, a preening bird, a flying bird, water dripping off the roof. The rippling shadows of heat and air. She imagined herself and Angela and Matt as motes of light. She imagined Christopher—because suddenly she knew his name—working his way through the warm density of her body to the light, following the cord that guided him to her. Because she wanted him. She wanted him.

Gaitskill on Building Story Meaning
On Understanding Meaning

When I published my first book I was interviewed and, for the first time, asked what my stories were about. One of these interviews took place live on the radio and when it was over I was given a taped copy of it. On playing this tape I heard the host, Michael Silverblatt, asking me one intelligent, lively question after another. To each question my answer was more or less the same: a long, tense silence punctuated by "um" or "uh" noises and finally broken with an "I don't know." Mr. Silverblatt began to come up with answers disguised as further questions, to which I could reply, "Yeah. Yeah, that's why. That's what I meant, uh-huh." As I listened I was sympathetic to him for shouldering the bulk of the thing, and grateful too. I was also very embarrassed. I had let someone else define my work for me, and I had sounded like an idiot.

Two years later, when my second book came out, I did an interview on the same show. This time I talked nonstop. I talked like I was driving an armored car with anti-idiot guns mounted at both windows, and in it I almost ran Mr. Silverblatt over as I careened around shooting at questions he hadn't even asked yet.

I had in two years time learned how to think and speak analytically, in a sophisticated manner, about my own work. I went on to teach university courses that required I analyze and talk at length about other people's work. Understandably, I was proud of myself, and when I played the first tape for a boyfriend, it was for laughs. By the time my third book came out, analyzing and public speaking came so naturally I didn't need an armored car anymore.

Now I am working on my fourth book, and I find I have no desire to talk or think analytically about it at all. I don't know if I still have tapes of either radio show, but I think if I played them back to back, the first would seem the wiser. If the question is "What is this story about?" or "Why did you write this story?" or "How?" I can give a very interesting and/or pleasing answer, which might actually be relevant. But the truest answer is "I don't know;" the more intelligent answer might even be silence.

This may seem a strange start to an essay on meaning, but for me it's an apt one. What we call craft in writing is performed with invisible tools on live, changeable materials. It is mysterious. Its rules are like nature's rules—complex, various, and endlessly adaptable. What will work in one instance will not in another; the worst idea may become wonderful in the right context and vice versa.

On Writing and Revising Toward Meaning

So how and why did I write "A Bestial Noise"?

What is available to me is this: I woke up one morning, looked out the window, and saw the world outside as "a single vast organism" that I or anyone might stare at forever without seeing it for what it is. This sight came with a sudden-descending sense of the weight and mass of physical life. Some time later it was followed by the thought that human beings are like tiny containers for too much feeling, thought, and experience, and that while we are usually only aware of our contents one layer at a time, sometimes an extreme physical or emotional state will for an instant cause us to see several at once, each overlapping the other. During this time a friend of mine had unexpectedly become pregnant in her forties, and I was trying to imagine what that would be like. I was also involved in a new relationship and was thinking a lot about the private language of couples—including weird faces and noises and the eccentric mixture of subjects and emotions—and how that intimate life form exists in this vast organism that is both inside and outside us, this unknowable weight and mass.

I wasn't exactly excited by these thoughts, but I was fascinated and to some extent oppressed by them. I found them beautiful in a way but also frightening. Perhaps I wanted to put a story around them to contain them. The first draft was a bare seven pages, most of which was taken up by dialogue. It was written quickly in a state of chaotic anger and a feeling that too much of the world was beyond my understanding or my words, which is probably why my character finds herself in a like state. I may have chosen to tell the story through a domestic conversation in order to dramatize the fragile inadequacy of human communication in the face of life's harsh and unknowable complexity, which Elizabeth rails at with petty anger and fear. Perhaps I also wanted to show how accommodating, loving, and healing that communication can be regardless of its inadequacy.

When I said I do not want to think analytically about my writing I meant I don't want to think globally or thematically; the act of revision is innately analytical. One has to judge and evaluate constantly which word, which phrases, which arrangement of words and phrases best gives form to the as-yet formless qualities, feelings, and events that make up the world you want to create. This is a kind of analysis, albeit not of a strictly rational sort.

When trying to describe it to my students, I sometimes tell them that the classroom we are sharing is a scene and in this scene are thousands of elements: speech, thought, feeling, perceptions, physical objects, light, shadow, the peeling paint, the cinder block wall, the wastebasket, the sun shining through the fingerprints on a half-empty bottle of water. What I'm saying to them and what I'm not saying, but what they are sensing; what I am sensing about them. What this scene is about depends on which of these elements they choose to bring forward, and how they do that is going to be a matter of intuitive, analytical decisions that can only be made line-by-line, word-by-word.

I also tell my students, "I want to hear, see, and feel this as only your character can hear, see, and feel this—as only you could describe it. Ask yourself, what would this feel like, look like, sound like? Then try to find the most exact words you possibly can for it." I rewrote "A Bestial Noise" by constantly asking myself those questions, and I found myself resenting my own advice. The story blurs emotion, physicality, and abstraction so that one continuously bleeds through the other, and I was tearing my hair out trying to describe how that felt, looked, and sounded.

On Communicating a Story's Meaning to Readers

There was an unusual step between the first draft and revision of this story, which might be of interest of students; I workshopped it. This is something I haven't done since I was a college sophomore. I did it because I had been teaching workshops for some years at that point, and I was teaching a particularly intelligent class of people I respected. As an experiment, I gave them a very rough draft of this story.

It was like having twelve people stick their heads into your dream. Your dream makes total sense to you, but for other people, your dream may seem weird and perhaps boring. It was a strange and jarring thing to understand my story through my students' responses. But it challenged me to articulate my world more fully. It forced me to go deeper into each scene, and I began to follow my own advice: What does it look like? What does it feel like? What does it sound like to this woman who is a container for boiling water and also the container for a human life?

It's too early for me to tell if I answered those questions successfully, if I articulated my meaning. But I answered these questions as best I could, as only I could answer them.

Writing Suggestions

1. In her commentary, Gaitskill explains the initial story idea that inspired "A Bestial Noise": "I woke up one morning, looked out the window and saw the world outside as 'a single vast organism.'" Following her example, literally look outside your own window. In a single page, try to capture whatever elements of what you see that interest you. Don't analyze or ponder or try to plan how it might play later into a story scene—just write it down as carefully and imagistically as you can. Try this exercise for five days in a row. After five days, examine your work and see if certain elements continue to appeal to you. What are they? What is their appeal? Which elements of the scene did you ignore?

2. Use one of the following characters as the protagonist for a new story: a young girl whose father is sent to prison for selling drugs, a driver of a hit-and-run accident, a CEO who wears NASCAR t-shirts and drives a jacked-up Chevy S-10 pickup, a mother of four children under ten who returns to college to finish a degree in biology. What complications exist in your character's life? What does your character want? How might the exploration of this character suggest a type of dramatic tension within the story? In literary fiction, the development of character rarely is subordinate to plot.

3. Gaitskill's "A Bestial Noise" effectively mixes action, gesture, and observation into scenes focused on dialogue. Select two scenes from her story and examine all of the

dialogue, paying close attention to how it is combined with other elements of scene construction. Now look at one of your own stories or long scenes and, using a highlighter, mark all the dialogue. How does your fiction handle the mixture of dialogue with action, gesture, and observation? Is dialogue placed by itself? Would the addition—or removal—of action, gesture, or observation help develop the meaning, the flow, the way readers would understand the dialogue? Revise your scene or story accordingly.

4. At your local bookstore or library, locate a short story collection published within the last five years. Carefully select and read one short story, then go home and rewrite the first scene from memory, using language in as faithful an imitation of the writer as possible. Compare your scene to the original. Stylistically, how close is it? Is the rhythm similar? Sentence lengths? Word choices? Is it easy to imitate an author's writing after reading only a few pages? In class—or with other writers—discuss the specific skills necessary to successfully imitate another author's style.

> *Writing a story or novel is like finding your way around a strange*
> *room in the dark. When you get through the first draft, you think*
> *the light will go on. But it often doesn't.*
> —John Casey

Virgil Suárez

Lalo's Skin

From *Glimmer Train*

My father and his friend, Lalo, worked together as window washers at the Colgate Building in Madrid, Spain. Lalo arrived in Los Angeles a year after we did, and never worked another day in his life. This is what my parents, many years later, before my father died, said about a man I remembered more for his skin condition than for his chronic lies.

In 1974 he mingled with other Cuban exiles at Alvaro's Garage on Gage Street in Los Angeles, where men talked about going home, a thick longing in their voices, spitting out their words. Alvaro, the garage's owner, liked having these guys around because they brought him business, and it was the only place at that time in Los Angeles where Cuban men could go and relax, shoot the breeze, discuss cockfights in Las Villas, killing pigs for Christmas, dancing the night away when they had been young— *jovénes. Qué buenos días.*

They met Saturday mornings to wash their cars and fix odds and ends. Those were the days when my mother and father bickered about spending too much money on insignificant repairs. Broken door handles, noisy mufflers, loose trim.

My mother wanted our 1965 Dodge Dart to run just well enough for my father to take her to and from work, but nothing more. She didn't care if the paint lasted, or if the tires were shiny black doughnuts.

My father, though, took pride in knowing his car looked and ran clean. *Suavecito,* he liked to say.

I always accompanied him to the garage and in the afternoon he took me to bat around some balls at the park. He'd bat and I'd catch flies in deep left field where the grass was tall and the gopher holes tripped me up. Bugs stuck to my socks and bit my legs.

I liked the garage because I could always drink Coca Colas and eat those Mrs. See's apple pies in the vending machine. Music blared in an eight-track player: Pérez Prado mambos or Orchestra Aragon's "Cachita" or "*El Bodegero.*" Or Alvarez Guedes' taped jokes. The men laughing at jokes about Gallegos and Puerto Ricans.

When they were not washing their cars, the men gathered in the shade and talked about Cuba. Havana right before the revolution, the sharp clothes everybody was wearing. The Tropicana Night Club, then the beaches on Sundays. Most of my father's friends had done voluntary work back in the fields of Cuba. They despised having done it on their precious Saturdays and Sundays, picking potatoes or tomatoes, cutting sugar cane. A few showed their scars. I remember Lalo's right leg, the one with the half-crescent scar from the knee to his upper thigh, thick like a rope, pink and winding. He claimed he got that scar cutting sugar cane.

It was the first time Lalo showed everybody his skin, the blotches of purple and red, bad veins, bad skin. "*La circulación,*" he'd say to the men. "*Mala.*" Bad circulation. His skin was flaking off in parts. Everybody knew that Lalo drank, the tip of his nose reddened into the classic gin blossom.

Some of the men called it *culebrilla,* a form of shingles closely related to nerve disorders, not simple skin rashes and allergies.

"That, *compay*—what you have—is *sarna,*" one man said, and then laughed. *Sarna* was a skin disease only mangy dogs got, before scratching themselves raw. Lalo's skin, on the other hand, was simply flaking off, slivers of dead skin around his eyebrows and mouth.

"*Tu madre.*" Lalo would then curse.

Sometimes the men got in a few games of dominos, or they played poker. For money. They sat on folding chairs. Like Lalo, most of the men smoked. He kept a couple of cigarette packs in the pockets of his cotton *guayaberas.*

Lalo's clothes were always stained; even his undershirt, which I could see through the linen of his shirts. Wrinkled khakis with dirt around the pocket lip. Some of the men smoked cigars, and I gagged when the smoke reached me back by the red tool cases, next to the workbench where Alvaro kept oily pieces of car engines. I kept myself busy with ratchets and bolts.

Then one fine Saturday, Lalo, my father's best friend, didn't show up. The men asked my father what was up, but my father didn't know.

Later that afternoon we drove to Lalo's house, a stucco Spanish-style house on a palm lined street. There was little difference between this neighborhood in South Gate and ours in Bell, California. Same dirty, grassless sidewalks. When the grass lawns died, people replaced them with rock and cacti gardens. Prickly pears everywhere. *Nopalitos*, the Mexicans called it. Working class neighborhoods, that's where we lived.

My father knocked on the door but there was nobody home. Nilda, Lalo's wife, kept empty cement flower pots on the two stairs of the front porch. No flowers. I looked inside one and saw cigarette butts, twisted, coiled like dead grubs in the dusty bottom.

The windows were drawn, the lights out, and my father knocked a few times, then went around the back and tapped on the kitchen window with his car keys. No answer, so we left.

The next week when Saturday came, still no Lalo. Again the men asked, and again my father didn't know either. None of the men worked in the same factories, so that was yet another reason they liked to gather at Alvaro's on the weekends.

Alvaro said to call Lalo at home, see if he was there. Maybe something came up with Nilda's sister in Miami. Or maybe Teresita, Lalo's daughter, had gotten sick. Teresita was my age and, though my parents said we met in Madrid once, I don't remember. My parents didn't spend much time with Lalo and Nilda in Spain.

Here in Los Angeles it was a different story. The isolation and distance from Miami's Cubans made people bond with others from whom they normally would shy away. Teresita was an only child, like me. But she was a girl, and I didn't enjoy playing with her.

I remember her greasy hair, her bony legs, and the way she blinked when she was nervous. We went to different schools. Her parents placed her at St. Mathias, a school for girls. I went to public school, with the ruffians and the *gangeros*, as my father's friends called *pachucos* or gang members.

We'd visit on Sundays a few times and then I'd mostly watch television, the football games. Or baseball, depending on the season. Teresita kept to herself in her room. My parents didn't like me going in her room because they said it wasn't appropriate. I didn't care.

I visited her room once and nothing about it impressed me except for a shelf stacked with books. Nancy Drew mysteries, like those in the school library, except hers were new. She liked to read, that much we shared in common. She didn't have toys, not even a radio. Her bed was pushed to one corner of the room, away from the curtained window. The window sill was dusty, a fly and a dead moth pressed between the screen and the glass.

"What's wrong with your father's skin?" I asked her.

She turned away from me and shrugged. Her dress hung over her shoulders, wrinkled and scraggly. I couldn't help but feel sorry for her.

Dandruff formed a crust around his receding hair line. His epidermis couldn't resist soap, that's what I'd heard my mother say of Lalo's condition.

"Maybe it's the shampoo," I said.

"My father doesn't use shampoo," she said.

She walked over to her desk, opened the drawer and pulled out a picture of a dog. She showed it to me.

"That's the kind of dog I'd like to have," she said. "But—"

She put the picture back and slid the drawer shut.

"Allergies," she said.

My father walked into Alvaro's grungy office and dialed Lalo's number. He stood by the entrance where Alvaro kept his women-in-bikinis auto parts calendars. My father leaned into the door frame, the phone in the crook of his shoulder and neck.

Nobody answered at first, then my father got through to Nilda. I could see his face as he turned it first toward the men, and then away toward the traffic on the street.

He said, "*Está bien*, Nilda. *Está bien*," meaning fine, everything's okay.

Then he hung up and told the men that Nilda was crying. She didn't want to say what was the matter.

Next Sunday we visited and Lalo, Nilda, and their daughter were home. Lalo was sitting in the living room in his undershirt and a pair of cut-off pants. Part of his face was bandaged so he couldn't wear those black, thick-framed glasses he wore, the ones cloudy with smudges and dirt.

His face was shiny around his cheeks, and we could see that parts of his skin under the bandage were dark, a little purple.

My parents and I sat with them in the living room and talked about Cuba. About how much work life was here in the United States. I watched television when Nilda turned it on, low volume, because she always knew how much I liked it. Either that or she read the boredom in my eyes.

"What happened?" my father asked Lalo.

Lalo's gold chain, the one with the big San Lazaro medallion, hung around the wrinkled flesh of his neck. His eyes were watery, swollen.

"The doctor'll know soon."

"*Cancer de la piel*," said Nilda. Skin cancer.

"Ah," said my mother, "that has a cure, *mi amiga*."

"Melanoma," said Lalo and turned to me.

Silence filled the room, laying between us like thick air, like the humidity of a rainy California Sunday.

I had a hard time watching television and keeping track of all those words in Spanish they rifled at each other. Their Spanish was becoming harder to decipher, especially when Nilda and my mother talked. They spoke rat-tat-tat fast. Lots of tongue-clicking and "r"s.

Teresita came out of her room once and walked back with a glass of milk.

Nilda asked me if I wanted a glass too and some Cuban crackers with guava jelly on them.

"No, *gracías*," I told her.

Between the Rams losing to the Redskins and Lalo's naked feet, I thought about Teresita reading in her room.

The veins around Lalo's ankles looked like the bloodworms the science teacher fed the guppies at school. Budding flowers of them around his instep, and around the sides toward his soles. His toes were long and crooked.

Lalo was telling my parents how sick he felt. Tired. Worn out. It'd been a terrible mistake for them to have left Madrid where they were all right. He didn't mind the cold. He liked the people, and the food. It was a different thing here altogether. All the work in the lamp factory, such long hours.

This was always the conversation and prelude to Lalo's asking my father for a couple of hundred dollars to pay the rent. To pay for groceries. Usually Lalo asked when my mother and Nilda went to talk in the kitchen. I guess he thought I was too wrapped up in the game to pay attention to his voice growing soft, breaking up.

"*Coño, mi socio, está de madre la cosa,*" he would say and turn toward my father. Things were really bad.

Lalo told my father he didn't know how much longer he could stand it, being sick and all.

My father sat there, leaning back against the beat-up sofa, his hands weighed down on his knees.

"I'm dying," Lalo would finally say.

My father would tell him he'd lend him the money, and I never knew if he did so to cheer up his friend, to help Nilda and Teresita out, or both. He knew what in later years I came to know, that Lalo was a bum with no intention of ever working.

Once I asked my father out of the blue if Lalo ever worked in Madrid. My father looked up at me in the rear-view mirror and he said yes, Lalo had worked as hard as the next man.

"It's this country," my father said. "It takes it out of you."

I had never realized the difference between this country and Spain, or the next. I was too young to know better then, I guess, but I remember that Lalo hit up my father for money several times, each time more embarrassing for both men.

I remember my mother bringing up the fact that Lalo owed my father money for years, and it looked like he, Lalo, had no intention of ever paying it back.

My father always told my mother the same thing, to forget it. "*Deja eso.*"

Later, when I was in high school already, I once walked in on my father shaving. I needed to blow-dry my hair because I was going out to a school dance, and I saw my father's lathered-up face in the mirror, a little askew, work-worn, and I thought of Lalo's skin. All that flaking off. The veins. The clusters of them branching into dark rivers.

"Haven't you ever seen a man shave?" my father asked.

I smiled. I could hardly hear him over the noise of the blow-drier. His chest looked soft, pudgy around his pecs, with the tan-lines of the short-sleeved shirts he wore to work. Little red moles between patches of chest hairs.

It'd been years since we'd visited Lalo and his family. I hadn't accompanied my father to Alvaro's garage after it burned down. Rumor had it Alvaro's son burned it down so they could collect on the insurance. But that was only a rumor. Or that he blow torched it out of hatred for his father leaving his mother.

And I stood there thinking about Lalo's skin falling off his body in layers, like leaves, settling all around his feet. My mother came to call Lalo the biggest charlatan she ever knew. My father refused to ever talk about it.

For all I knew Lalo was still sitting in the same dim and grungy living room of that old house in South Gate, California, going to pieces. Moving through rooms like an unfriendly, luminous ghost.

Suárez on Staking Out Your Own Territory

For me, the choice was clear.

When I was in high school in Long Beach, California, I wanted to write fiction and poetry that told the story of my people—Cubans who had moved to the United States to escape Castro's regime. In English class, we read beautiful books (*The Great Gatsby*, *The Adventures of Huckleberry Finn*, *A Tale of Two Cities*, and the stories of Edgar Allan Poe), but nowhere in any of these books did I see my own experience represented. The characters in these books did not remind me of my father, or my mother—who to this day has not learned English—or my American cousins. And so the "vision" for my fiction and poetry was given to me by my circumstances. I wanted to write about being a Cuban exile because, in the early 1980s, there was no fiction that captured this story. Or if there was, I couldn't find it.

I knew I was on the right track with my writing when I ran across books by Toni Morrison, Amy Tan, N. Scott Momaday, and Louise Erdrich when I attended Long Beach State University. These writers blew me away because the protagonists of their stories were nothing like Jay Gatsby or Huck Finn. These new characters worked against assimilation: these characters didn't want to lose their heritage and cultural identity to become "Americans." In "Lalo's Skin," the father knows this pain. He longs for his past, his people, his lands, all of which form the basis for the conversations he has with his *compadres* at Alvaro's garage.

In part, my vision was a gift. At the time I was in college, American literature developed a growing hunger to understand the experiences of its people—all its people, not just the Jay Gatsbys. And so, though I originally saw myself as a writer who spoke about the Cuban-American experience, I soon realized that I was working within one of the contemporary currents of creative writing. I remember thinking how fortunate I was to be writing at such a time. My writing professors were encouraging me to write about my passion; editors allowed me to write what I knew.

On a very basic level, I understood that I wrote about the Cuban-American experience much in the same way that Amy Tan wrote about the post–World War II Chinese-American experience, and how Toni Morrison absorbed the pain and conflict of the African-American experience. These were our visions, our literary territories. Only years later did I understand that most writers stake out their territory, their own fictional space. Quite simply, they write about what matters to them. My own concerns were obvious: I wrote about my blood.

When I talk to students, I tell them to take each story in-and-of-itself and make it the best story it can be. That's always the #1 rule with fiction. Don't let any preconceptions about what a story should be get in the way of what a story *is trying* to be. I tell them to look inside their own past—particularly within strong memories of trials, hardship, or pain—and pull from these experiences. This is very furtive ground for fiction. To stake out one's territory is not a conscious effort. Rather, it happens because writers by nature are often obsessive creatures. They burn with a handful of experiences that, quite naturally, influence many stories.

Unlike the other essays in this textbook, my essay is not primarily about the practical side of writing a story so much as it is about a writer's territory. By territory, I mean those topics or themes that truly resonate within a writer's work. I wish I could say, "Do X, then Y, then Z, and I guarantee that you'll find your own territory." It's just not that easy. Sometimes students find their territory through the workshop process, which means writing a lot of stories and *really* listening carefully to peer responses. Just this past spring, one of my students, "Sally," workshopped her third story of the semester, which was about a young girl's strained relationship with her mother. Much to Sally's surprise, the class responded much more positively to this story, though it was not necessarily better crafted than the first two. Sally didn't realize this in class, but during the workshop, she was beginning to find her territory. What was going on was that she was learning *how* to tell this type of story, meaning that she was connected to this story in a way that didn't happen with the first two.

I keep a journal. Actually I keep three or four journals: one by my bed, one in the car, one in the office. And I love to journal out my ideas. I fill these journals with poems and memories. I fill them with the raw experience of my life. I'm surprised how often I come back to the same experiences—preparing to leave Cuba, spending time with my father at his job, the violent childhood games we used to play, and of course my father's death. I approach these feelings in different stories, with different characters. Sometimes these stories don't seem autobiographical (at least not in their details and situations), but to me, the emotional connection is still apparent.

In my own writing classes, I often see students who, after writing a loosely autobiographical story, decide to move on from it, to write about something entirely outside of their own experience. It's no surprise that this second story—the one that has no autobiography, no emotional truth from the author's life—is often a lesser story. It simply doesn't have the gut punch of honesty.

I think some writers, early on, feel obligated to try to master many different stories, many different characters. And yes, there's something to be learned from experimenting with new characters, new stories. But what I often say to these students is this: "What is your relationship to your story? If this particular story doesn't somehow burn inside of you, it will never burn on the page for a reader." By that, I mean a good story comes from the soul, from the accumulation of the author's experiences. The events may be changed, the characters disguised, but there must be some piece of fire, some truth, that links a story back to its writer.

This is why so many authors return to the same topics repeatedly. Tim O'Brien, a wonderful novelist and short story writer, repeatedly dips back into the well of his Vietnam memories. In 1973, he published a fine memoir, *If I Die in a Combat Zone, Box Me Up and Ship Me Home*, about his tours of duty in Vietnam. Two years later, he published a novel, *Northern Lights*, about two brothers, one of whom has recently returned home wounded from Vietnam. O'Brien's next novel, *Going After Cacciato*, tells the story of a soldier who runs away from duty in Vietnam. His next book, a superb collection of stories, *The Things They Carried*, follows a single platoon through Vietnam and chronicles the ways wartime changed their lives.

My point is this: O'Brien did not feel he needed to write about everyman's experience. He wrote about an experience of which he was an expert and that mattered to him more than growing up in the suburbs of Minnesota or falling in love in high school. For other writers, these might prove fruitful fiction topics, but not for O'Brien. Though his Vietnam experiences (two tours of duty) clearly affected him profoundly, he didn't repeat the same story, but he explored the experience as he approached it from many different angles.

Ever since I recognized this about O'Brien's work, I've noticed how so many other writers have staked out their territory, too. John Updike crafts his novels and stories from the New England suburbs, particularly their trials with love and infidelity. In her novels and stories, Lorrie Moore returns to the twin themes of maturation and attempting to fall in love. George Saunders's short fiction probes the absurdity of corporate America. David Leavitt explores contemporary gay identities in many of his works.

I am right there with them, returning to core experiences.

"What are the three defining moments in your life?" I ask students. I tell them to write about these key moments in journals and, hopefully, later in stories. I tell them, if they don't feel a twinge of reluctance while writing a story, if the story doesn't expose a meaningful part of their life, even if that meaning is robed deep inside a costume, I doubt whether it would be successful.

Becoming a writer is part of the long process of self-exploration. It's about knowing one's heart. It's about placing those emotions into dramatic situations and seeing what unfolds.

If I buy a book by Saul Bellow, I know it will be a wonderful narrative of Jewish-American identities. Or if I buy a book by Don DeLillo, I am most likely buying a book that will investigate America's national identity. These writers embrace their obsessions. I tell my students to do the same.

Writing Suggestions

1. Following Suárez's recommendation that a good story often "comes from the soul, from the accumulation of the author's experiences," recall a moment from your high school or middle school years when you discovered something important about yourself, your friends, or your family. In one to two pages, describe the events leading up to that discovery, using full scenes, vivid description, and emotional detail. Focus on finding the exact right words to communicate the feeling of that day and how the discovery changed you.

2. Toward the end of the semester, look over the work you've completed for your writing class. Identify at least two major themes recurring in your work and that might suggest, as Suárez puts it, "your territory." Write a new story that consciously explores these themes from another perspective or with different characters.

3. Working with a partner, exchange stories you've recently written. On each page of the story, identify the three weakest descriptions and suggest stronger, more specific replacements. In particular, look for ways that stronger descriptions can better define character, action, and setting.

4. Like many of the contributors in this book, Suárez is a prolific writer in multiple genres. Locate one of his poetry collections in your local bookstore or library and examine a few of the poems whose titles leap out at you. If you are more Internet savvy, see if you can find a few poems by searching for "Virgil Suárez" online. Do you see any of the issues that appear in "Lalo's Skin" also explored in the poems? List three recuring concerns, themes, or ideas in his work. Consider doing this with any other contributor from this book, as well. Are they similarly staking out their literary territory, too? Where are the boundaries of your own writing? What matters to you?

> Productivity is a relative matter. And it's really insignificant: what is ultimately important is a writer's strongest books. It may be the case that we all must write many books in order to achieve a few lasting ones—just as a young writer or poet might have to write hundreds of poems before writing his first significant one.
> —Joyce Carol Oates

Appendix A

⌒

BIOGRAPHIES

Lee K. Abbott is the author of six collections of stories, among them *Living After Midnight*, *Love is the Crooked Thing*, and, most recently, *Wet Places at Noon*. A new collection, *Space, Time and Massy Earth: New & Selected Stories*, is forthcoming. His fiction has appeared in nearly one hundred literary magazines and journals, including *The Atlantic Monthly*, *The Georgia Review*, *Harper's*, *The Kenyon Review*, *Ploughshares*, and *The Southern Review*. Twice his stories have been reprinted in *The Best American Short Stories*, and twice they've been reprinted in *The Prize Stories: The O. Henry Awards*. He has won two National Endowment for the Arts Fellowships in Fiction, the Major Artist Fellowship in Fiction from the Ohio Arts Council, the St. Lawrence Award for Fiction, and the National Magazine Award for Fiction. He has taught at Case Western Reserve University and as a visiting professor at Colorado College, Washington University in St. Louis, Rice University, and the University of Michigan. Since 1989 he has taught in the M.F.A. Program in Creative Writing at The Ohio State University in Columbus.

Julianna Baggott is the best-selling author of five novels, including *Girl Talk* and *The Madam*, and one collection of poems. The recipient of fellowships from the Delaware Division of Arts, Virginia Center for the Creative Arts, Ragdale Foundation, and Bread Loaf Writers' Conference, she lives in Tallahassee, Florida, with her husband and three children. She teaches in the graduate creative writing program at Florida State University.

Amy Bloom is the author of a novel, *Love Invents Us*, and two collections of stories: *Come to Me*, nominated for a National Book Award, and *A Blind Man Can See How Much I Love You*, nominated for the National Book Critics Circle Award. Her stories have frequently appeared in *Prize Stories: The O. Henry Awards*, *Best American Short Stories*, and numerous anthologies. She has written for *The Atlantic*, *The New Yorker*, *The New York Times Magazine*, and *Vogue*, among many other publications, and has won a National Magazine Award. A practicing psychotherapist, she lives in Connecticut and teaches at Yale University.

T. Coraghessan Boyle writes, "I didn't come to writing until I'd switched majors three times as an undergrad at SUNY-Potsdam, where I'd originally gone to study music. In my junior year, I blundered into a creative writing workshop and began to think seriously of myself as a writer and to read widely. In the next few years, while teaching high school English in New York, I wrote a number of short stories, sent them out to various magazines, and had the great good fortune of seeing two of them accepted by *The*

North American Review. On the strength of this, I applied to the University of Iowa Writers' Workshop, where I earned both my M.F.A. and Ph.D. degrees. Over the years I've published seventeen books of fiction and seen my work appear in all of the major magazines and win many distinctions—the PEN/Faulkner and PEN/Malamud Prize and France's Prix Médicis Étranger and Prix Passion among them—and since leaving Iowa I have taught in the English Department at the University of Southern California. My work has been translated into some twenty-five languages. All this is very rewarding. But most rewarding of all is that I get to dream over the page every day of my life and wake each morning to discover what the next story will be."

Janice Eidus has twice won the O. Henry Prize for her short stories, as well as a Redbook Prize, a Pushcart Prize, and a National Writers Voice Residency Award. She is the author of the story collections *The Celibacy Club* and *Vito Loves Geraldine*, and the novels *Urban Bliss* and *Faithful Rebecca*. She is coeditor of *It's Only Rock And Roll: An Anthology of Rock and Roll Short Stories*, and her short fiction and essays have appeared in *Arts & Letters*, *Fourth Genre*, *The North American Review*, *Southwest Review*, *The Village Voice*, and many other literary journals, as well as in such anthologies as *The Oxford Book of Jewish Stories* and *Neurotica: Jewish Writers on Sex*.

Tom Franklin, recipient of a 2001 Guggenheim Fellowship, is the author of *Poachers*, a book of stories, and *Hell at the Breach*, a novel. His stories have been included in anthologies such as *New Stories from the South*, *Best American Mystery Stories*, and *Best Mystery Stories of the Century*. He is a writer-in-residence at the University of Mississippi, where he lives with his wife, the poet Beth Ann Fennelly, and his daughter.

Mary Gaitskill is the author of the novel *Two Girls, Fat and Thin*, as well as the story collections *Bad Behavior* and *Because They Wanted To*, which was nominated for the PEN/Faulkner in 1998. Her story "Secretary" was the basis for the feature film of the same name. She has taught creative writing at the University of California, the University of Houston, New York University, and Brown University; she is currently an associate professor at Syracuse University. Her stories and essays have appeared in *The New Yorker*, *Harper's*, *Esquire*, *Best American Short Stories* (1993), and *Prize Stories: The O. Henry Awards* (1998). In 2002 she was awarded a Guggenheim Fellowship for fiction.

Elizabeth Graver is the author of three novels, *Unravelling*, *The Honey Thief*, and *Awake*. Her short story collection, *Have You Seen Me?*, was awarded the 1991 Drue Heinz Literature Prize. Her stories and essays have been anthologized in *Best American Short Stories*, *Prize Stories: The O. Henry Awards*, *Best American Essays*, and *Pushcart Prize: Best of the Small Presses*. "The Mourning Door" was awarded the Cohen Award for Fiction from *Ploughshares* and was included in three annual prize story anthologies. The recipient of fellowships from the National Endowment for the Arts and the Guggenheim Foundation, Elizabeth Graver teaches creative writing and English at Boston College and is the mother of two young daughters.

Aaron Gwyn is the author of *Dog on the Cross*, a collection of stories, and the forthcoming novel, *Ink*. His work has appeared in numerous journals and anthologies, including *American Literary Review*, *Louisiana Literature*, and *New Stories from the South*. He holds a Ph.D. from the University of Denver, and he teaches creative writing at the University of North Carolina at Charlotte.

Tom Hazuka graduated from Fairfield University, and spent 1978–80 with the Peace Corps in Chile. He received an M.A. in English/creative writing from the University of California at Davis and a Ph.D. from the University of Utah; he is currently a professor of English at Central Connecticut State University. He is the author of three novels: *The Road to the Island*, *In the City of the Disappeared*, and *Last Chance for First*. He has received the Bruce P. Rossley Award for New England Writers and has been a Bread Loaf Scholar at the Bread Loaf Writers' Conference. He has also coedited two short story anthologies: *A Celestial Omnibus: Short Fiction on Faith* and *Flash Fiction*. His new book, *A Method to March Madness: An Insider's Look at the NCAA Final Four*, is forthcoming in 2006.

Adam Johnson is the author of *Emporium*, a collection of short stories, and a novel, *Parasites Like Us*. His work has appeared in *Esquire* and *Harper's Monthly*, in addition to many other magazines and literary journals. He holds a Ph.D. from Florida State University and presently teaches creative writing at Stanford University.

Stephen Graham Jones is the author of five novels, including *The Fast Red Road—A Plainsong* and *All the Beautiful Sinners*. His work appears in numerous magazines and literary journals, including *Alaska Quarterly Review*, *Black Warrior Review*, *Meridian*, and *Open City*. The recipient of a National Endowment for the Arts Creative Writing Fellowship, he teaches at Texas Tech University and lives in West Texas with his wife and two children. He is a member of the Blackfeet Nation.

Jarret Keene's fiction has appeared in *Clackamas Literary Review*, *Louisiana Literature*, and *New England Review*. He is the author of the poetry collection *Monster Fashion* and editor of *The Underground Guide to Las Vegas*. Keene teaches creative writing and literature at the University of Nevada, Las Vegas, and serves as the A&E editor for *Las Vegas CityLife*.

Michael Knight has published fiction in *Esquire*, *GQ*, *The New Yorker*, *The Paris Review*, and *Virginia Quarterly Review*. He is the author of two collections of short stories, *Dogfight & Other Stories* and *Goodnight, Nobody*, and a novel, *Diving Rod*. His work has been anthologized in *Best American Mystery Stories*, *Stories from the Blue Moon Café*, and *New Stories from the South*. He teaches creative writing at the University of Tennessee.

Reginald McKnight is the author of two novels, *He Sleeps* and *I Get on the Bus*, three short story collections, including *The Kind of Light that Shines on Texas*, and two collections of nonfiction. His honors include the Drue Heinz Prize, a Whiting Writers Award, a Pushcart Prize, and a special citation from the PEN/Hemingway Foundation. His stories appear in *New Stories from the South* and *Prize Stories: The O. Henry Awards*. He is currently the Hamilton Holmes Professor of English at the University of Georgia.

John McNally is the author of two works of fiction, *The Book of Ralph* and *Troublemakers*, and the editor of four anthologies of short stories. He's the recipient of the Chesterfield Film Writer's Project Fellowship (Paramount Pictures), the Jenny McKean Moore Fellowship, the Carl Djerassi Fellowship, and the James Michener Fellowship. A native of Chicago, he teaches fiction writing at Wake Forest University in North Carolina.

Alice Mattison is the author of four novels, most recently *The Wedding of the Two-Headed Woman* and *The Book Borrower*, which was a *New York Times* Notable Book. Her collection of intersecting stories, *Men Giving Money, Women Yelling*, was also a *New York Times* Notable Book. She is the author of two earlier collections of stories, *Great Wits* and *The Flight of Andy Burns*, and a collection of poems, *Animals*. She is coeditor of *As I Sat On the Green: Living Without a Home in New Haven*. She lives in New Haven, Connecticut, and teaches fiction in the graduate writing program at Bennington College in Vermont. She is at work on a collection of connected stories, *Brooklyn Sestina*.

Peter Meinke is the author of thirteen books, including *Zinc Fingers*, which received the 2001 Southeast Booksellers Association award as the Best Poetry Book of the Year, and *The Piano Tuner*, which received the 1986 Flannery O'Connor Award. His work has appeared in many venues, such as *The Atlantic*, *The New Yorker*, and *The New Republic*. He directed the Writing Workshop at Eckerd College for twenty-seven years and now lives in St. Petersburg, Florida.

Judith Claire Mitchell is the author of *The Last Day of the War*, a novel. Her work has appeared in *The Colorado Review*, *The Iowa Review*, *StoryQuarterly*, and *Scribner's The Best of the Fiction Workshops*. A graduate of the Iowa Writers' Workshop, she has also been the recipient of a James Michener/Copernicus Society of America Prize and a James C. McCreight Fiction Fellowship. She teaches creative writing at the University of Wisconsin-Madison.

Lorrie Moore is currently the Delmore Schwartz Professor of Humanities at the University of Wisconsin-Madison. Her work has appeared in *The New Yorker*, *The Paris Review*, *Harper's*, *Best American Short Stories*, *The Yale Review*, *The New York Review of Books*, *The New York Times*, and other places. She is the author of two novels and three short story collections, the most recent of which, *Birds of America*, was a National Book Critics Circle Award finalist and the winner of *The Irish Times* International Prize for Literature.

Keith Lee Morris is the author of a novel, *The Greyhound God*, and a short story collection, *The Best Seats in the House and Other Stories*. His work has appeared in numerous literary journals, such as *The Georgia Review*, *New England Review*, and *The Southern Review*. Among other honors, he was awarded the South Carolina Fellowship in Fiction in 1999. He is assistant professor of English at Clemson University, where he also serves as associate editor of *The South Carolina Review*.

Melissa Pritchard received a B.A. in comparative religions from the University of California and an M.F.A. from the University of Vermont. Her first short story collection,

Spirit Seizures, received the Flannery O'Connor Award, the Carl Sandburg Award, and the James Phelan Award. She published two additional story collections, *The Instinct for Bliss*, which received the Janet Heidinger Kafka Prize, and *Disappearing Ingenue*, which contains stories reprinted in *Prize Stories: The O. Henry Awards* and the Pushcart Prize anthologies. Pritchard is also the author of three novels, *Phoenix, Selene of the Spirits*, and *Late Bloomer*, and has received fellowships from the National Endowment for the Arts, The YMCA Writer's Voice, and Brown University's Howard Foundation. As a professor of English and women's studies, she teaches in the M.F.A. Program in Creative Writing at Arizona State University.

Josh Russell's novel *Yellow Jack*, which grew from the story of the same title, earned him a fellowship from the Bread Loaf Writers' Conference and was a finalist for the Barnes & Noble Discover Award. His stories have appeared in the *Antioch Review, Epoch, French Quarter Fiction, New Stories from the South*, and *The Southwest Review*. An Illinois native—born in Carbondale and raised in Normal—he lives in Newnan, Georgia, and teaches in the English department and creative writing program at Georgia State University.

George Saunders is the author of two short story collections, *Pastoralia* and *CivilWarLand in Bad Decline*, both of which were *New York Times* Notable Books. In addition, *CivilWarLand in Bad Decline* was a finalist for the 1996 PEN/Hemingway Award and was chosen by *Esquire* as one of the top ten books of the 1990s. He is also the author of the *New York Times* best-selling children's book, *The Very Persistent Gappers of Frip*, with art by Lane Smith, which has received major children's literature awards in Italy and the Netherlands.

Saunders's work, which has been widely anthologized and published in fifteen foreign countries, has received three National Magazine Awards and has four times been included in O. Henry Awards collections. In 1999 he was chosen by *The New Yorker* as one of the twenty best American fiction writers forty years old and younger. A recipient of a Lannan Fellowship, he has recently written the introductory essay for the Modern Library's paperback edition of *The Adventures of Huckleberry Finn*. Saunders teaches in the creative writing program at Syracuse University.

George Singleton is the author of three collections of stories, including *The Half-Mammals of Dixie* and *Why Dogs Chase Cars*, and a novel called *Novel*. His work has been repeatedly anthologized in *New Stories from the South*. He teaches at the Governor's School for the Arts and Humanities in Greenville, South Carolina. He lives with the artist Glenda Guion, as well as their eleven dogs and lone cat.

Virgil Suárez, born in Havana, Cuba, in 1962, moved to the United States in 1974. He received his M.F.A. in creative writing in 1987 from Louisiana State University. He is the author of fourteen books, including the novels *Latin Jazz* and *The Cutter*. Suárez has achieved such distinctions as the Florida State Individual Artist Grant and a National Endowment for the Arts Creative Writing Fellowship. He lives in Florida and teaches creative writing at Bennington College.

Appendix B

FURTHER READINGS

Books on the Theory and Craft of Fiction:

Gardner, John. *The Art of Fiction: Notes on Craft for Young Writers*. New York: Vintage, 1991.

Gardner, John. *On Becoming A Novelist*. New York: W. W. Norton & Company, 1999.

Lamott, Anne. *Bird by Bird: Some Instructions on Writing and Life*. Landover Hills, MD: Anchor, 1995.

Reference Books Designed to Aid Fiction Writers:

Browne, Renni, and Dave King. *Self-Editing for Fiction Writers*. New York: Harper-Collins, 1993.

Henry, Laurie. *The Fiction Dictionary*. Cincinnati, OH: Writer's Digest Books, 1995.

Schecter, Steven, and Lloyd Jassin. *The Copyright Permission and Libel Handbook: A Step-by-Step Guide for Writers, Editors, and Publishers*. New York: Wiley, 1998.

Magazines on Writing:

Poets & Writers (PO Box 543, Mt. Morris, IL 61054). A bimonthly publication that contains interviews, reviews, articles, and essays, as well as contest and publishing information. This is a professional publication, so it may be of more use to the intermediate and advanced writer than to the novice.

The Writer (Kalmach Publishing Co., 21027 Crossroads Circle, PO Box 1612, Waukesha, WI 53187-1612). Website: http://www.writermag.com/wrt/default.asp. *The Writer*, founded in 1887, is a monthly magazine about writing for writers. It features how-to and inspirational articles focusing on the writing of fiction, nonfiction, poetry, and children's and young adult literature. It also offers limited market and contest information.

Writer's Digest (1507 Dana Avenue, Cincinnati, OH 45207). Website: http://www. writersdigest.com. *WD* is a monthly magazine that includes how-to articles, market reports, technique discussions, and contest information. The editorial mission is to be a monthly handbook for writers who want to get more out of their writing. Because their subscription base is so large (200,000), many of the articles and information are geared to the intermediate and beginning writer.

Organizations:

Associated Writing Programs (Tallwood House, Mail Stop 1E3, George Mason University, Fairfax, VA 22030). Website: http://www.awpwriter.org. AWP is a nonprofit organization of writers and (mostly graduate) creative writing programs. It publishes bimonthly *The AWP Chronicle*, which includes interviews, articles, essays, reviews, and useful information on conferences, publishing opportunities, contests, and writing colonies.

PEN American Center (568 Broadway, New York, NY 10012-3225). Website: http://www.pen.org. Among the activities, programs, and services sponsored by the headquarters and the five branches are public literary events, literary awards, outreach projects to encourage reading, assistance to writers in financial need, and international and domestic human rights campaigns on behalf of the many writers, editors, and journalists censored, persecuted, or imprisoned because of their writing. All PEN members receive the quarterly PEN Newsletter and the literary journal *PEN America* and qualify for medical insurance at group rates.

SPAWN (Small Publishers, Artists, & Writers Network) (PO Box 2653, Ventura, CA 93002-2653). Website: http://www.spawn.org. SPAWN is a web resource that contains information relevant to writers, publishers, editors, illustrators, artists, booksellers, and photographers at all points in their career. SPAWN also has local chapters that focus on career success, professional seminars, and networking.

Market Guides:

CLMP Directory of Literary Magazines (Council of Literary Magazines and Press, 154 Christopher Street, Suite 3C, New York, NY 10014-2839). This listing of literary journals nationwide contains brief descriptions and a useful state-by-state breakdown. This publication is less comprehensive than *Poet's Market* or *The International Directory of Little Magazines and Small Presses*, but because it focuses exclusively on literary journals, it might be more useful to the student writer.

The International Directory of Little Magazines and Small Presses (published annually by Dustbooks, PO Box 100, Paradise, CA 95967). Although this annual guide contains thousands of publishing opportunities, many are for poetry, nonfiction, or reviews. Entries are listed alphabetically and contain specific information about the publishing format, submission guidelines, and editorial interests of each.

Novel & Short Story Market and *Writer's Market* (published annually by Writer's Digest Books, 1507 Dana Avenue, Cincinnati, OH 45207). These readily available books contain a wealth of information on commercial markets and writing contests, though both also have sections on small presses, university presses, and literary markets. Both also contain How-I-Made-My-First-Big-Sale success stories.

Appendix C

~~~~~~~~~~

ALTERNATE TABLE OF CONTENTS

These categories are by no means exhaustive, nor are they intended to make the claim that the entire body of a writer's work vividly exhibits these particular areas. The stories listed in each category are quite strong in this particular aspect of fiction craft and offer prime examples for enjoyment, study, and discussion.

The commentary by the writers included in this book can be used as a leaping-off point to engage other writers of like (and unlike) strengths.

Point of View
First Person
Steve Almond, "The Soul Molecule"
Julianna Baggott, "Dr. Ishida Explains his Case"
Amy Bloom, "By-and-By"
T. Coraghessan Boyle, "Greasy Lake"
Jarret Keene, "Son of Mogar"
Michael Knight, "Gerald's Monkey"
Reginald McKnight, "Palm Wine"
George Saunders, "Jon"
George Singleton, "Show-and-Tell"
Virgil Suárez, "Lalo's Skin"

Second Person
Adam Johnson, "The Death-Dealing Cassini Satellite"

Third-Person Limited
Janice Eidus, "Vito Loves Geraldine"
Tom Franklin, "Nap Time"
Mary Gaitskill, "A Bestial Noise"
Elizabeth Graver, "The Mourning Door"
Aaron Gwyn, "Of Falling"
Tom Hazuka, "Field Trip," "Homeward Bound," "Mixture," "Utilitarianism," "Vaporware"

Stories Prominently Featuring Various Elements or Techniques:

Dialogue

Amy Bloom, "By-and-By"
Peter Meinke, "Unheard Music"
Lorrie Moore, "Debarking"
Keith Lee Morris, "The Children of Dead State Troopers"

Epiphany

Amy Bloom, "By-and-By"
Aaron Gwyn, "Of Falling"
Alice Mattison, "In Case We're Separated"
Melissa Pritchard, "Salve Regina"

Experimental Writing

Elizabeth Graver, "The Mourning Door"
Stephen Graham Jones, "Adultery, A Failing Sestina"
Josh Russell, "Yellow Jack"

Flashback

Mary Gaitskill, "A Bestial Noise"
Jarret Keene, "Son of Mogar"

Humor

Lorrie Moore, "Debarking"
Melissa Pritchard, "Salve Regina"
George Saunders, "Jon"
George Singleton, "Show-and-Tell"

Interior Monologue

Julianna Baggott, "Dr. Ishida Explains his Case"
Tom Hazuka, "Vaporware"

Popular Culture

Lee K. Abbott, "One of *Star Wars*, One of *Doom*"
Steve Almond, "The Soul Molecule"
T. Coraghessan Boyle, "Greasy Lake"
Jarret Keene, "Son of Mogar"
Lorrie Moore, "Debarking"
George Saunders, "Jon"

Research

Suspense

Symbolism

Appendix D

GLOSSARY

Abstract Words   words that denote things we understand the meaning of, but cannot feel or see or apprehend by any of the five senses. Examples: love, beauty, justice, soul.

Allegory   narrative with two levels of significance, one being the literal happenings of the story and the other being a symbolic level where abstract ideas clearly unfold. While a **symbol** usually has multiple meanings, an allegory suggests only one interpretation. Two of the most famous allegorical short stories are Nathaniel Hawthorne's "Young Goodman Brown" and Franz Kafka's "The Metamorphosis."

Allusion   reference in a literary work to a historical event, cultural artifact, or another literary work. See also **symbol**.

Antagonist   most significant force or **character** opposing the **protagonist** and his or her goal(s). See also **hero**.

Antihero   modern variation on the traditional **protagonist** who is lacking the moral qualities of the classic hero. Holden Caulfield from J. D. Salinger's *The Catcher in the Rye* and Huckleberry Finn from Mark Twain's *The Adventures of Huckleberry Finn* are two well-known examples of antiheroes.

Atmosphere   dominant mood of a work, usually established through setting and emotional landscape. See also **tone**.

Backstory   useful history that situates or helps establish the main plot of the story; significant events that happen before the story begins. See also **flashback**, which is one method of dramatically including this information in full scene.

Character   imagined person who appears in fiction. See also **antagonist** and **protagonist**.

Cliché   expressions that were once effective uses of figurative language, but through overuse, have become ineffective ways of conveying meaning. Some examples: "Hotter than hell," "It takes two to tango," and "I have a bone to pick with you." See also **sentimentality** and **stereotype**.

Climax   moment of greatest intensity or the moment providing the greatest potential for change in a **protagonist**. Contemporary writers often place the climax—usually a decisive confrontation between the protagonist and the **antagonist**—near the end of the story. See also **structure**.

Conflict   struggle between two (or more) opposing forces or **characters** in a literary work. Conflict is often the direct result of a **protagonist** wanting to achieve a specific goal and finding difficulty in doing so. See also **suspense** and **tension**.

Description   careful use of specific details to depict **characters**, situations, and **settings**. See also **imagery**.

Dialect   distinctive speech patterns or verbal idiosyncrasies particular to a region, class, or ethnic group. See also **dialogue, diction**, and **monologue**.

Dialogue   representation of actual conversation between two or more **characters** in a story. See also **dialect, diction**, and **monologue**.

Diction   choice and use of words in speech or writing. See also **dialect, dialogue**, and **monologue**.

Epiphany   term coined by James Joyce, meaning a moment of discovery or revelation in a story, usually occurring at the **climax.** The term comes from the Greek 'epifánia, meaning "to show forth."

Exposition   part of a literary work, most often located near the beginning, that provides the background information needed to understand **characters** and their actions.

Flashback   episode or **scene** in which an earlier event is substituted into the normal chronological order of a story. See also **backstory**.

Foreshadowing   clue or suggestion of later events of importance in a literary work, achieved through careful use of words, details, or actions. Foreshadowing helps unify a plot and ultimately can make a story more satisfying. See also **plot** and **structure**.

Freytag's Pyramid   visual diagram created by Gustav Freytag, a nineteenth-century German critic, to help understand Greek dramatic works and the plays of Shakespeare. Though it proves somewhat less adequate in terms of the analysis of contemporary fiction, it does offer a number of ways to better understand and talk about narrative **structure**.

Genre   category of literature marked by a distinctive **style**, form, or content. Genre can be used to denote broad divisions, such as poetry, drama, or fiction, but it is also commonly used (often derogatorily) to refer to the following subcategories of narratives: romance, fantasy, horror, science fiction, mystery, and thriller.

Hero   central **character** of a literary work, who typically embodies one or more of the classic heroic traits: bravery, honesty, intelligence, and trustworthiness. Modern critics often now call female **protagonists** heroes versus heroines. See also **antagonist**.

Imagery   use of vivid, specific language to represent actions, ideas, or objects. Imagery is represented by words that express not only sight but also sound, touch, taste, or smell. See also **description**.

Immediacy   quality of making fiction seem to be happening right in front of the reader. It is achieved through careful pacing, proper **settings**, and well-described **scenes** using crisp, tight language. See also **verisimilitude**.

Irony   utterance marked by a purposeful contrast (usually the exact opposite) between what is said and what is meant; also, a literary **style** that uses contrasts for rhetorical or humorous effect.

Metafiction   primarily associated with postmodern literature, metafiction self-consciously explores the conventions of writing and its own nature as a literary text. Metafiction was popularized through the work of Donald Barthelme, Jose Luis

Borges, Italo Calvino, Robert Coover, William Gass, and Jeanette Winterson, among others.

Metaphor   figure of speech where a phrase or word that ordinarily designates one thing is used to mean another; a nonliteral comparison, or more generally, one thing conceived as representing another. Examples: "My father is an ogre" or "All the world's a stage" (Shakespeare).

Mimesis   originally used by Plato, the imitation and realistic representation of aspects of the sensible world in art and literature. See also **verisimilitude**.

Monologue   dramatic or literary form of discourse in which a **character** speaks aloud to himself or the audience, thereby revealing thoughts. A monologue also is a long speech made by a single person. See also **dialect, diction,** and **dialogue**.

Motif   recurrent element of a literary work that suggests a **thematic** meaning.

Narrative   relation of events; storytelling; a continuous account of the particulars of an event or series of events. See also **short story.**

Narrator   **character** or voice that conveys a story to a reader.

Novel   prose **narrative** longer than a **novella,** often 50,000 words or more. Compare to **short story** and **short-short story.**

Novella   prose **narrative** longer than a **short story** but shorter than a **novel**. Novellas are often 20,000 to 50,000 words—long enough to be published as a single work. Examples: Franz Kafka's *The Metamorphosis*, Joseph Conrad's *Heart of Darkness*, and Alessandro Baricco's *Silk*.

Plot   logical pattern of events that comprise a drama or **narrative.** Plots often follow a cause-effect relationship between **scenes**. See also **foreshadowing** and **structure**.

Point of View   position or viewpoint from which a **narrator** relates the happenings in a story. The usual choices are first person ("I"), second person ("you"), and third person ("he" "she" "they"), though further subdivisions exist.

Protagonist   principal or central **character** in a literary work. The protagonist's desires and goals are often in direct **conflict** with those of the story's **antagonist**, which creates story **tension**. See also **hero**.

Resolution   part of a literary work that satisfyingly ends the dramatic situation by ending the **conflict** or providing a logical solution.

Revision   act of improving early (and later) drafts of fiction into better **narratives** through careful attention to language, **structure**, and **character**. Revision includes both minor grammatical changes and large-scale reworking of **scene** and story.

Scene   single dramatized episode, often uninterrupted by a change of **setting**. Some scenes, such as John Updike's "A & P," last the entire story, though most **short stories** are composed of several scenes.

Sentimentality   purposeful manipulation of a reader's emotions, usually sadness or pity, by a writer without proper justification. See also **stereotype** and **cliché**.

Setting   physical location and time that a **narrative** occurs. **Character** is often greatly influenced by a writer's choice of setting in a literary work.

Short Story   prose **narrative** shorter than a **novel**, usually focusing on a single **character** in a causally linked series of **scenes**. See also **novella** and **short-short story**.

Short-Short Story   contemporary type of prose **narrative** that became particularly popular in the 1990s with such books as *Micro-Fiction* and *Sudden Fiction*. Short-short stories often compress the elements of a traditional story into an abbreviated form, often limited to a few pages or, in some cases, a few hundred words. See **novel**, **novella**, and **short story**.

Show, Don't Tell   popular maxim for fiction writers, which advises the use of specific, significant details to allow readers to participate more fully in a story. A writer who "tells" writes, "The beautiful woman walked angrily past me into the room." A writer who "shows" instead writes, "The leggy blonde stormed into the kitchen without glancing at me or anyone else."

Simile   figure of speech in which two essentially unlike things are compared using "like" or "as." Example: "You are acting like an ogre today!" or "Her name was like a summons to all my foolish blood" (James Joyce, "Araby").

Stereotype   conventional opinion or perception; an often oversimplified or biased mental picture held to characterize the typical individual of a group. See also **cliché** and **sentimentality**.

Stream of Consciousness   modern **narrative** technique that seeks to capture the likeness of actual thought—ungrammatical and disjointed as it may be—in language. Stream of consciousness stories often incorporate **interior monologues** and are highly **imagistic**. One of the most famous examples of this type of story is the Molly Brown section of James Joyce's *Ulysses*. Katherine Anne Porter's "The Jilting of Granny Weatherall" and Virginia Woolf's *Mrs. Dalloway* also exhibit the qualities of stream of consciousness fiction.

Structure   general plan or pattern in a literary work; the **narrative** framework resulting from **plot** and the sequencing of **scenes** in a fictional piece. See also **foreshadowing** and **climax**.

Style   collective distinctive ways in which an author uses language to create a literary work. Some of the key components in style are **diction**, figurative language, **imagery**, and **tone**.

Suspense   reader apprehension or anxiety stemming from an uncertain or mysterious **narrative** situation. Suspense helps maintain a reader's psychological interest in a literary work and is often a function of **structure** and **plot**. See also **conflict** and **tension**.

Suspension of Disbelief   willingness of a reader to accept the **characters** and events of a **narrative** as if they were true.

Symbol   something specific that suggests meanings beyond the literal sense. While an **allegory** has a single meaning beyond the literal story, a symbol can suggest multiple meanings. The green light at the end of Daisy Buchanan's dock in F. Scott Fitzgerald's *The Great Gatsby* is literally a light, but it is also a symbol to Jay Gatsby of many things: money, power, hope, and greed. See also **allusion**.

Tension   excitement created in readers by the struggle between opposing forces in **narratives**, often the **protagonist** and **antagonist**. Tension also can occur between literal and **symbolic** levels of meaning to a story. See also **conflict** and **suspense**.

Texture   a distinguishing quality given to a literary work most often suggested by a unique prose style. For example, *The Catcher in the Rye* is textured by the distinctive juvenile voice of its **narrator,** the conversational Holden Caulfield.

Theme   central idea of a literary work, suggested by **character** interaction, **plot**, and use of language. Well-written fiction, especially **novel**-length works, often supports two or more broad themes that can prove hard to paraphrase abstractly.

Tone   apparent attitude of an author toward the literary work. Tone is one of the ways in which writers create distance between readers and the **characters** in a **narrative**. For example, the tone of most of Edgar Allan Poe's stories is eerie and gloomy. See also **atmosphere**.

Verisimilitude   quality of a literary work that appears particularly realistic, usually achieved through precise choices in **dialogue, character**, and evocative **imagery**. See also **immediacy** and **mimesis**.

Workshops   common method for writers to receive feedback. In university creative writing programs or in private groups, writers typically distribute copies of their story to all members, who then respond with critical feedback through written notes and group discussion.

CREDITS

Abbott, Lee K. "One of *Star Wars*, One of *Doom*" appears by permission of the author.

Almond, Steve. "The Soul Molecule," first published in *Tin House*. Reprinted here by permission of the author.

Baggott, Julianna. "Dr. Ishida Explains his Case" appears by permission of the author.

Bloom, Amy. "By-and-By," first published in *Ms. Magazine*. Reprinted here by permission of the author.

Boyle, T. C. "Greasy Lake" from *Greasy Lake* (Penguin Books, 1990). The story appears by permission of the author and Penguin Books.

Eidus, Janice. "Vito Loves Geraldine" from *Vito Loves Geraldine* (City Lights Books, 1997). The story appears here by permission of the author and City Lights Books.

Franklin, Tom. "Nap Time" first published in *The Georgia Review*. Reprinted here by permission of the author.

Gaitskill, Mary. "A Bestial Noise" first published in *Tin House*. Reprinted here by permission of the author.

Graver, Elizabeth. "The Mourning Door" first published in *Ploughshares*. Reprinted here by permission of the author.

Gwyn, Aaron. "Of Falling" from *Dog on the Cross* (Algonquin Books, 2003). The story appears by permission of the author and Algonquin Books.

Hazuka, Tom. "Field Trip," "Homeward Bound," "Mixture," "Utilitarianism," and "Vaporware" appear by permission of the author.

Johnson, Adam. "The Death-Dealing Cassini Satellite" from *Emporium: Stories* (Viking, 2002). The story appears by permission of the author and Viking Books.

Jones, Stephen Graham. "Adultery, A Failing Sestina" first published in *The Alaska Quarterly Review*. Reprinted here by permission of the author.

Keene, Jarret. "Son of Mogar" first published in *New England Review*. Reprinted here by permission of the author.

Knight, Michael. "Gerald's Monkey" from *Dogfight, and Other Stories* (Plume, 1998). Reprinted here by permission of the author.

McKnight, Reginald. "Palm Wine" from *White Boys: Stories* by *Reginald McKnight*, © 1998 by Reginald McKnight. Reprinted by permission of Henry Holt and Company, LLC.

Mattison, Alice. "In Case We're Separated" first published in *Ploughshares*. Reprinted here by permission of the author.

INDEX

403